WHERE DESTINY COMMANDS

1939-1945 A Time of Love & War

Leila Sen

To the Gods who rule us all, and
To my beloved Parents – the cornerstone of my life.
With everlasting love and gratitude.

Santi Pada Dutt:

14th September 1914 - 19th January 2001

Hoda Khayat Dutt:

6th April 1908 - 5th October 2001

WHERE DESTINY COMMANDS
1939 - 1945 A Time of Love & War

First editon published in the USA by Leila Sen, 2018
Second, revised edition © Leila Sen, 2022.
Hob Hollow Publishing, San Francisco.

Print ISBN: 979-8-9874263-0-2

Ebook ISBN: 979-8-9874263-1-9

Library of Congress Cataloguing-in-Publication Data is on file.

AUTHOR'S NOTE

This book is part memoir, and part historical fiction. Based on first-hand accounts, both verbal and written, on found letters and diaries, as well as historical data from official documents and books, it is a story born in truth. The military ordeals and those of the Armenian genocide experienced by Santi and Hedeya have been recorded here as accurately as was possible. Any errors are unintended.

That said, the better to weave diverse elements and events into a narrative whole, some licence has been taken with certain personal time-lines, with some dialogue, and a few secondary characters and names that either could not be perfectly re-called, or otherwise would have fallen beyond the scope of this story. These have been drawn from the author's imagination and should not be construed as real.

Cover Design by LeppanenStudio & Jacqueline Gilman
Interior design by Gilman Design, Larkspur, CA

PHOTO CREDITS

P. 281: Sgts. Chetwyn & Fox, No.1 Section, Army Film & Photographic Unit

P. 299: G.J. Keating & Sgt. S. Morris, No.1 Section, Army Film & Photographic Unit

Pages 308, 322, 353, 370, 385: Sgt. L.Chetwyn, No.1 Section, Army Film & Photographic Unit

P. 318: Lt. W.G. Vanderson, Sgts. R.H. Morris, G. Morris, No.1 Section, Army Film & Photographic Unit

P. 379: Sgt. James, No.1 Section, Army Film & Photographic Unit

P. 400: Sgt. Smales, No.1 Section, Army Film & Photographic Unit

P. 528: Capt. Cash, No.1 Section, Army Film & Photographic Unit

P. 373, 575: Gurkha Museum, Winchester, UK

All other photos from the Sen family archives.

In my soul, beloved, I can feel that you and I
Have traversed many worlds together, hand in hand;
For we are one, you and I, and like a song,
Some whispered echo on the breath of eternity,
Together, we shall traverse many more.

Contents

viii

PREFACE

Come, fill the cup, and in the fire of spring
The winter garment of repentance fling:
The Bird of Time has but a little way
To fly…and lo! The Bird is on the wing.

– Omar Khayyam, *Rubaiyat of Omar Khayyam*

AFTER CONSULTING THE OLD astrologer at the temple of *Kali* in Calcutta, it was decided – following cremation, the auspicious time for both departed souls to free themselves of their earthly bondage would be 6:31am, precisely, on the first day of the new year. That same day of January 1, 2002, in far away Cairo it would be exactly 3:01am. And, on the other side of the world, the old year not quite departed from San Francisco, would be lingering still at 5:01pm on December 31, 2001. Three places across the world, one precise moment in time…

Amid an offering of prayers, the ashes would be scattered in all three places simultaneously, completing the journey of two souls upon this earth – a journey that began like the new year's first sunrise slowly kindling the old, heartworn city of Calcutta, turning its crumbling buildings into palaces of gold; a journey that came to its crossroads and burgeoned forth like the full moon presently gilding the ancient mosques and minarets of medieval Cairo; a journey that finally drew to its close, like the old year's last sunset slipping silently into the shroud of mists and night-shadows over San Francisco.

———•◦•———

JANUARY 1, 2002, 6AM. Dakshineshwar, a little north of Calcutta: The temple bell tolled through the chill pre-dawn air, mingling with the soft chant of ancient prayers; *Om Bhur, Bhubah, Swaha, Tat Savitur Varainyam*…Great Lord of the Earth, the Ether and the Heavens, Divine Creator through the Sun…

The Nabaratna Temple of Kali stood, glittering, on the eastern bank of the Ganges, its nine spires silhouetted against the still dark morning skies. Guarded by the twelve shrines of *Shiva,* it kept vigil over the night laden waters of the old river on its silent journey to the Bay of Bengal. Within the temple a family knelt before the Goddess *Kali,* rising from a thousand-petalled silver lotus; heads bowed, they prayed for the souls of the departed. The inner sanctum of the temple echoed with the sounds of reverence spiraling towards the heavens, fragrant with incense of sandalwood and camphor.

As night's shadows dissolved slowly into the wintry west, the sun rose like a great ship, golden sails billowing across the eastern sky. It cast its blessings of warmth and light upon the throng of half-clad bathers who stood, shivering, in the dawn waters, their invocations to *Kali* and *Shiva* melding with the murmured chant of the *Surya Mantra* that rose like a mist floating up to the heavens: *Jobakushumo Shankashng Kashyopeyam Mohaduthyim Tamorim*: Oh Son of Kasshyop, brilliant as the scarlet hibiscus flower, Thou Great Radiance who washes away darkness and sin…

6:31a.m. It was time. Emerging from the temple, the bereaved made their way down the steps to the river's edge. A conch shell blew its plaintive farewell. An earthenware vessel carrying ashes and fragrant white tuberose was surrendered to the river to thread a path through the sun-dappled flotilla of scarlet hibiscus – the sacred *joba* offered to *Kali* by her faithful. A *prasad* of blest sweetmeats and marigold flowers was strewn after the small vessel as it disappeared down river into waters woven with the dawn's first colours. One journey's end and another's beginning…

January 1, 2002, 3:01a.m. Maadi on the Nile, near Cairo: A full moon hung in the sky like a large luminous lantern. Beyond the banks of the river, the desert stretched endlessly, steeped in a haunting moonlit silence. Far away in the distance the pyramids stood under the stars, like ghosts guarding the gateway to heaven. At their feet the lights of Cairo and Giza glittered, like Pharaoh's jewels scattered in the darkness. A boat rode the moonwashed waters of the Nile. On board, a close group of figures moved, through the shadows, to the deck rail. Carefully, they lowered a clay urn of ashes, plunging the heart of the moon's reflection, splintering that gleaming orb into a thousand shimmering fragments. Nestled amid aromatic garlands of sweet-scented jasmine, the casket floated away, mingling its memories with those of the river.

December 31, 2001, 5:01p.m. The Pacific Ocean, San Francisco: Though darkness had flung its mantle over the city, a memory lingered still of the late sunset's final farewell to both day and year. Beyond the Golden Gate Bridge, its embers had melted into a sea of molten gold, setting the western sky ablaze with rose-hued fire. But twilight's panorama was short lived, brushed away by the fingers of night as they closed a dark fist on a small clay pot bobbing and bouncing in the ocean waters. The air was redolent with the heady perfume of strewn gardenias. From a small boat a family watched the tiny object make its last, intrepid journey through the darkness of this world into the bright infinity of the heavens beyond.

———•◦•———

SOME THREE MONTHS LATER.

My thoughts of you aspire heavenward
Like the sweet-scented wood smoke of an autumn fire.
My mind is strewn with many-hued memories
That rustle, like the restless, whispering leaves of Fall,
Filling my soul with a remembered love.

– Author

April, 2002: Their house in San Francisco had remained closed, undisturbed by time or the passing world outside. Over three months had passed since she scattered her parents' ashes, three long months before she could bring herself to enter the place. Now, she unlocked the door and stood, hesitating, in the doorway. It would be all right, she told herself, she could do this. Slowly, she stepped into the still-ness; onto the dark wood floor, the familiar creak of each old plank speaking to her…the drawing room…the kitchen…daylight softly spilling in through the overhead skylight, warming the emptiness as it tiptoed across the floor on quiet feet…the bedrooms, first one, then the other. She stopped and closed her eyes, trying to shut out the pain, but not the ghosts. After a moment she opened them again. Yes, they were there, her ghosts. She could not see them, yet she could feel them, holding out their arms to her as she walked into their embrace.

The late afternoon sun streamed in through the window, light-fingered, probing the memories in the room. Memories, lingering in the shadows, crouching in the corners, floating like dust moats in the sunlight…memories bestirred, nudging each other as they reached out to touch her from all the old well-known objects that sat, sad and silent, as though they'd already become a part of the past.

An intense wave of desolation swept over her. The loss of her parents had devastated her far more than she would have believed possible. Sorting through their possessions would be difficult, she knew, but that intimacy could not be allowed to any but herself. After all, she had shared her entire life with them. Through childhood, their guidance had led her to womanhood, the ins, the outs, the ups, the downs. They knew each other so well, there were no secrets – and if there were, they would be safe with her.

She was surprised, therefore, when she came upon the old box labelled Memories; and, sifting through its various documents, letters and mementos, to find she had stumbled upon incidents in their lives unfamiliar to her: military recruiting orders that had set a determined young man on the adventure of a lifetime; a small, battered diary hastily written amid the heat and horror of battle; a telegram from GHQ officially informing his family he was missing in action; a letter from a dutiful son reaching out across the miles, "Respected Mother, to whose feet I bow…I have met someone very special…." Then, there were the letters between two lovers, Santi to…Hedeya. Hedeya? Her mother's name was Hoda! Who, then, was this person! Had there been someone else in her father's life? And if so, what part had she played in the story of her parents?

Instinctively she reached for the two wedding rings nestled at her throat. During that final farewell, she had removed her parents' wedding bands and hung them on the gold-bead chain around her neck. Now, she held the two gold circlets in the palm of her hand and, as she ran her fingers gently over their polished surface, she spied an inscription on the inside of her father's ring: H.Khayat 16May1943. Her mother's name. But, that date…therein lay yet another mystery! Intrigued, she examined her mother's ring and, sure enough, there it was again: S.Dutt 16May1943. No mistake.

She was puzzled. She'd always believed her parents were married in April 1944! There were wedding pictures, right here, in the well-thumbed family album. A year later, together, they had brought her into the world, a living manifestation of their love for each other. And here she was, looking up from a photograph that had slipped from the album: eight months old, held in her father's arms, his face beaming joy and laughter as he lovingly fastened the gold-bead chain she still wore about her neck – the keeper of her memories.

But now…this new information…how did it all fit? Where had it really begun? Curious, she continued her search through the lives of these two young strangers she was meeting for the first time, searching for the mother and father who were such an integral part of her…and slowly, piece by piece, an amazing story began to unfold.

PROLOGUE

A glance at history, the peoples, places & times of this story.
To be read – or not – as each reader may desire…

The Stage Is Set

The Moving Finger writes; and having writ,
Moves on: nor all thy piety nor wit
Shall lure it back to cancel half a line,
Nor all thy tears wash out a word of it.

– Omar Khayyam, *Rubaiyat of Omar Khayyam*

THE SECOND WORLD WAR has been the greatest catastrophe perpetrated by man on his fellow man. The enormity of such a conflict, and the extent of its cataclysmic destruction, had never before, nor has it since, been witnessed in the history of humankind. For, in some way, it touched nearly every living being on this earth – and, subsequently, those who were to come.

As though in some deadly game, the world divided itself into two teams – the Allies and the Axis. They faced each other across continents, and their battles raged on land, on the seas and in the heavens. Their battle-fields knew no boundaries – military, civilian or humanitarian. Almost every country, in every hemisphere, became engulfed in the turmoil, and over a period of six terrible years impoverished nations were decimated, and the world was set on fire. This fearful inferno was set alight by incidents which seemed, at first, to be far removed from one another, both in time and place. In actuality, the flames of WWII began in the smoldering ashes of WWI, that Great War of 1914-1918. The intervening years were merely an uneasy hiatus while momentum was building…

WWI spilt the life-blood of those nations who had fought it. At its end, Germany lay defeated, and her ally, the Ottoman Empire as Turkey was then known, found herself in a crumbling state of demise. Within Turkey, an ethnic cleansing had all but annihilated millions of Armenians who had been an active and productive part of that country's populace for centuries. Many official records bore witness to the atrocities committed on men, women and children who were slaughtered mercilessly, or sent on tortuous death marches. Despite warnings from American and German diplomats and missionaries, then present in Turkey, this massacre, now recognised as the first genocide of the twentieth century, went unheeded as the rest of the world tended to its own.

Spoils of war usually go to the victors. And those exhausted nations, having suffered four years of bloody sacrifice with a monumental and hitherto unimagined loss of life and property, were not inclined towards magnanimity for the vanquished. Consequently, the Treaty of Versailles took apart both Germany and Turkey, apportioning their various territories to the powers that had prevailed.

The misery of deprivation and hunger was rampant in Europe, making countries like Germany and Italy ripe for the picking by anyone who promised to alleviate the suffering and restore national pride. Other countries, like Russia, had fallen to bloody revolution. Minorities and subjugated colonies that had given of themselves in the service of their occupiers during the war now rose up and, with a newfound voice, demanded their rights to freedom and justice. Such a one was India. So too were certain Arab countries, including Egypt.

On this stage, out of the mists of turmoil, stepped two men who in their madness were to co-author the most violent period of history the world has ever known. The first, Adolph Hitler, was a man from Vienna, Austria. The second was Benito Mussolini, born to a blacksmith in Predappio, Italy.

Vienna 1914 saw Hitler, a lone drifter, with the failed aspirations of a painter. With WWI came the opportunity to improve his means. The Austrian army, however, refused him on grounds of physical deficiency. Thus it was that fate, in the guise of failure and rejection, led Adolph Hitler to a Germany looking to build its army as quickly as possible. Having found acceptance at last, from that moment his allegiance to his adoptive country was absolute.

Hitler would pull through WWI, albeit with some narrow escapes favoured by an uncanny streak of luck that would serve him to the bitter end. The first was a gas attack in the trenches of France. He survived, despite the impediment of his whiskers to the proper fit of his gas mask. But the devil looks to his own, and Hitler would crop his whiskers to what would become his signature 'Hitler Moustache'. The second escape was far more dramatic. 28 September 1918, injured outside a French village, Hitler found himself in the sights of a British soldier's rifle. Private Henry Tandey, a highly decorated veteran of the Green Howards Regiment, realising his enemy was wounded, lowered his rifle. This act of mercy allowed the German soldier to nod his thanks and walk away.

If this event were indeed factual, it would make for one of those fateful moments that so terrifyingly alter world history, for that inconsequential German corporal would go on to unleash a most diabolic evil upon mankind. By ruse of thunderous pledges, pageantry and propaganda he would place himself at the helm of a mesmerized Germany, and beneath the billowing Nazi swastika (a terrible corruption of the Aryan symbol sacred to Hindus), he would set a juggernaut course of destruction and death across Europe.

Benito Mussolini too would survive the Great War. He would go on to organize the Fascist Party, and while his Black Shirts spread terror, he would posture, strut and scheme his way into the leadership of a demoralized Italy. With dreams of becoming a modern-day Caesar, he poised for a Fascist takeover of Africa. In the early dawn of 3 October 1935, with much flamboyance and fanfare, Mussolini marched his armies into Abyssinia (Ethiopia).

If Europe was to be Hitler's chess board, then Africa, it seemed, would do well to start Mussolini's new Roman Empire!

A few months later, in March 1936, Hitler thumbed his nose at the Treaty of Versailles, and goose-stepped into the Rhineland confiscated from Germany post WWI. The Fuhrer did not face much opposition. Rather than risk a confrontation, it was easier to believe – maybe even understand – how he would want to undo the ignominy of Versailles. Hopefully, that was all there was to it.

Not so, for in March 1938, Hitler manipulated the annexation of Austria. The rest of Europe looked on with growing unease, but involvement came with a price tag too high to pay, and it was hoped that reason would prevail. It did not.

Encouraged by the ease of success, Hitler set his sights on Czechoslovakia. First, he demanded the return of the Sudetenland. Britain's Prime Minister, Neville Chamberlain, tried to broker a deal – the Sudetenland in exchange for 'peace with honour'. The deal was short-lived. When the Czech government sent out a call for help, other countries, still suffering the ravages of the last war, balked at further interference.

In late August, 1939, a cryptic order was sent down the chain of command from Adolf Hitler, Fuhrer of Germany, to his SS Chief Heinrich Himmler who, in turn, relayed it to his second-in-command, Reinhard Heydrich: there was an immediate requirement for a number of Polish army uniforms. Even more bizarre was the additional demand for thirteen German convicts to accompany the uniforms.

When these unusual demands were met, twelve of those convicts were ordered into those uniforms and transported by select members of the SS Einsatzgruppen – Special Task Forces – to a forest near the German/Polish border. Here, they waited. Finally, a coded message, "Grandmother Has Died," prompted a furtive journey to a custom's post in Hochlinden and a forestry station in Pitschen, where the disguised convicts were drugged, then shot. The bodies were arranged to convey the impression that Polish soldiers, apprehended in an aggression on German territory, had, in all good conscience, been shot.

For good measure, further chicanery played out in the small German town of Gleiwitz. A similar band of SS officers, together with the thirteenth convict, disguised themselves as Poles and staged a dramatic takeover of the town's radio station. A fictitious announcement over the air declared Poland had attacked Germany, and all Poles were being called to arms. In a sham tussle, as for control, the last disguised convict was shot, and left as 'evidence' of Polish incursion and aggression.

Hitler's stew was cooked and ready for serving. The stage was set, and the skies over Europe were dark with the presage of the storm to come. World War II was about to begin, and a terrible tragedy impended the world. In the cold, dark shadows that preceded the dawn of 1 September 1939, Hitler invaded Poland – and finally, reluctantly, Britain and France girded their loins for war.

In Britain, Chamberlain's government was unceremoniously ousted, and on 4 June, 1940, the new Tory Prime Minister, Winston Churchill's famous words rang the rafters in the House of Commons: *"We shall fight on the seas and oceans, we shall fight with growing confidence and strength in the air, we shall defend our island whatever the cost maybe, we shall fight on the beaches, we shall fight on the landing grounds... we shall never surrender..."* And with that resounding cry, Britain and her allies went to war.

Incidents were apace in the Far-East as well where the dogs of war had been let loose, and were steadily on the run. Japan, on the winning side in WWI, nonetheless believed itself rebuffed and slighted by the Treaty of Versailles. Now, it decided to carve out its own portion of the world. Having previously occupied Korea and Taiwan, it proceeded in a violent take-over of China, then Malaya, Singapore, the Philippines.... Finally, it invaded Burma, its sights set firmly on British-controlled India.

Over the centuries, Britannia's rule had spread across the waves to many lands worldwide, including those of the Middle East, the Near East and the Far East. And that small island nation, with the heft to build an empire on which it proudly claimed the sun never set, came to believe in its right to dominion. This belief, naturally, was not shared by the peoples she had colonised.

Above all her dominions and colonies, the jewel in Britain's crown was India. So much so, the British sovereign's title proclaimed him, not only King of England, but Emperor of India as well. It was the wont of the English to believe, in all earnestness, that India – the British Raj – was a legacy bequeathed them by their forefathers as an integral part of the British Empire; an inheritance, the safekeeping of which was their destiny. Predictably, India believed otherwise.

Howbeit, the tendrils of over two hundred – nay, more three hundred – years of intertwined history, in some ways evolved both cultures, bringing long-lasting changes to both nations. The result was a shared ambivalence, further complicated by the fact that India was a land of diverse people, and a true understanding of her many cultures was not easily to be grasped.

India, in fact, had been fighting for independence for years, and of her vast multitude of sons a select few made it their life's work to champion this cause. Among them, an intensely patriotic young nationalist, Subhas Chandra Bose, founded a faction that proudly declared itself the Indian National Army.

The scion of a well-to-do Bengali family, Bose received, like so many of India's affluent sons, an English education at home and abroad. He passed from Presidency College and Scottish Church College in Calcutta to Fitzwilliam College, Cambridge, in England. Despite this, Bose was, first and foremost, an Indian passionately determined to rid his country of the British – and among his following were many who hailed from the oldest and best families of Bengal. Making it abundantly clear India would no longer tolerate a foreign master, that all was fair in time of war, they now advocated joining hands with Britain's enemy. In an attempt to discourage him and his followers, Subhas Chandra Bose was incarcerated by the British.

Not everyone was of the same ilk. Mahatma Gandhi, India's spiritual and political leader, was equally determined India should be rid of her British yoke; but he rejected violence. As the means to his end of self-rule or *swaraj* for India, the preferred choice in his arsenal was *satyagraha*, a peaceful civil disobedience based on the precept of non-violence.

Mohandas Karamchand Gandhi had not been born the Mahatma.

As a young man, and indeed throughout his life, he spent years fighting his own demons as well as the British. Quite often his journey had been a veritable trial by fire. But, eventually, the young Indian lawyer from the Inns of Court in London, emerged as a man whose precepts were to be revered far and wide. So much so, the world would come to know him as the Mahatma, the Great Soul.

Bose and the Mahatma – two men of diverse beliefs tending towards a common goal – each in his own time, and in his own way, eventually would have to deal with Winston Churchill, Prime Minister of Britain. With his unshakeable belief in the greatness of his country, and his own destiny in upholding it, Churchill, staunch advocate and knight exemplar of the British Empire, had made it his life's career to thwart any and all ambitions that might lead to its demise. It was little wonder, therefore, on the subject of India's independence, Churchill was at his most uncompromising. Imbued with his father's belief that history itself was well served while Britain was in its rightful place presiding over India, he refused to so much as contemplate Indian independence.

Time, perforce, brings change, and in this terrible time of war Britain needed allies. Consequently, following several occasions of having clapped both Bose and Gandhi in jail, Churchill was ultimately forced to concede, albeit most unwillingly, to post-war Dominium Status and eventual independence for India. Upon being presented with the message, Mahatma Gandhi remarked quizzically, *"They are offering us a post-dated cheque on a crashing bank."*

Be that as it may, India ultimately made a judgment call and, for reasons both practical and moral, decided on the lesser of two evils. Putting aside their differences, she aligned herself alongside Britain in this war against the greater evil. The decision was not an easy one as the burning desire for freedom pitted patriotism against morality, causing friction and creating factions among good men. Nevertheless, for a second time, and with mixed feelings, as she had done once before in World War I, India sent her soldiers of diverse cultures, creeds and religions to fight in special brigades, regiments and battalions in what was then known as the British Indian Army. Field Marshal Claude Auchinleck, Commander-in-Chief of the British Indian Army, reportedly stated that the British "couldn't have come through both wars (World War I and II) if they hadn't had the British Indian Army".

There gathered, from the four corners of Mother India, the largest volunteer force ever known, as 49 states fielded two and a half million men, ranging from platoon to divisional strength, and each fought gallantly with an honour that upheld both name and heritage. Among the many that proudly bore their banners and badges to war were...Queen Victoria's Own Madras Sappers, 3rd Madras Regiment...4th Bombay Grenadiers...6th Rajputana Rifles...1st Coorg Battalion...11th Sikh Regiment...18th Royal Garhwal Rifles...10th Baluch Regiment...King George V's own Bengal Sappers...17th Dogra Regiment...and, among too many more to mention, the legendary 4th Prince of Wales's Own Gurkha Rifles, 2nd Battalion.

In these battalions and regiments, enlisted soldiers were all Indian. The officers were mainly British with, recently initiated, a smattering of Indians here and there. And of this army of courageous men who answered the call of their country, almost 87,000 were never to return to their homeland again.

INDIA

Lalit Mohan Rai m. Kushum Kumari

Nripendra Kumar (Boro Mama)	Surendra Kumar (Dhan Mama)	Hemendra Kumar (Mejo Mama)	Kiron Kumar (Phool Mama)	Bimal Kumar (Kuti Mama)	Usha Moyee m. Jagadish Pada Dutt	Sorojoni Bala	Chhaya Rani

Santi Pada Dutt m. Hoda (Hedeya) Khayat	Bela Dutt (Bulu - Didi)	Kanti Pada Dutt (Mezda)	Bina Dutt (Mezdi)	Sudha Dutt (Kuti)	Kamala Dutt (Matu)	Shobha Dutt (Lebu)

Leila Dutt Sen

EGYPT

Samuél Khayat (Baba Taht) m. Saidé Kiriakos (Bajo)

(Hoda) Hedeya Khayat

1st Marriage Mahran Merzian	2nd Marriage Santi Pada Dutt
Victor Merzian (Armand) Louis Merzian (Loza) Violette Merzian-Dutt (Bebe)	Leila Dutt Sen

CHAPTER ONE

Following The Yellow Brick Road

"Let me light my lamp," says the star,
"And never debate if it will help to remove the darkness."
– Rabindranath Tagore, "Firefly"'

I T WAS THE AUTUMN of 1940, and a searing chapter of world history was being written. Resolved to play his part in the unfolding drama that was to become World War II, a young East Bengali house surgeon from Calcutta Medical College applied for a commission in the Indian Medical Service (IMS). He did so against the wishes of his father who had himself been a doctor in the British Indian army during World War I, serving in a country then known as Mesopotamia, and known to us today as Iraq. Experience, however, cannot usually be taught second hand, more so to an eager 26-year-old, and so, Santi Pada Dutt, unable to withstand the pull of history, finally obtained his father's blessing and resolutely prepared to follow where life would lead.

His father, Dr. Jagadish Pada Dutt, Head of Obstetrics & Gynaecology at Campbell Medical Hospital and Professor of Midwifery and Gynaecology in Campbell School, had given him the best education he could afford. With two boys and five girls to educate and launch into the world, it went to his credit that his efforts culminated in the successful careers of three doctors, two headmistresses and a daughter espoused to a diplomat. Nonetheless, when the call went out to all Indians for a return to their grass roots and a boycott of English education (so India's heritage might not be diluted by undue influence from the West), Jagadish Pada Dutt, being a patriot, insisted his children do their stint at a vernacular medium school – what had been good enough for him, after all, was quite good enough for them. But this hiccup in their education was short lived, for he was, as well, a man of sound common sense with an understanding of the ways of the world. He soon realised the impracticality of an education that lacked the requisite means to deal with the British – and, indeed, with the world – on equal terms.

And so it followed that Santi passed through the hallowed halls of Hare School, an establishment counted among the foremost in Bengal. He then crossed its playing fields to enter the hostel of Presidency College, that oldest and most august of institutions that had bred such venerables as Poet Laureate Sir Rabindranath Tagore, and Sukumar Ray another much loved poet and author in the vein of Lewis Carroll and Edward Lear (and father of a later alumnus, world renowned filmmaker and Oscar recipient, Satyajit Ray.)

Over the next few years Santi tread the corridors that once had resounded with their eminent footsteps, ever under the watchful eyes of other equally acclaimed alumni whose portraits peered from those walls – Narendra Nath Datta, famed as the philosopher Swami Vivekananda; Satyendranath Bose, collaborator with Albert Einstein; and Jagadish Chandra Bose, inventor of wireless communications. With these esteemed figures as role models, Santi matured into manhood. He grew by leaps and bounds, both in stature and character, and when he had successfully completed his medical studies he went on to train as house surgeon at Calcutta Medical College. Finally, the young doctor was ready to be of service to the world.

Being the firstborn of their seven children did not make his departure an easy one, and it filled his parents' hearts with trepidation to offer up their oldest child into the monstrous mouth of so greedy a war. Each morning as she lit her *diya*, the little oil lamp shaped like a cupped hand, and burnt incense at the small altar in her bedroom, his mother invoked the blessings of both *Durga* and *Kali*, with the fervent promise that she would, in return for her son's safekeeping, fast twice weekly and abstain from all meat for the duration of his absence. His father, having given his reluctant consent, did not speak of the matter again. He retreated into silence and quietly prayed that, somehow, the life of his firstborn would be sanctified by his name, Santi, which meant "peace".

Such qualms had no place in the mind of a young man preparing to thrust himself into the arena of life; a young man who, much like a determined Odysseus in his prime, was lured by adventure and the prospect of mastering his fate. Nevertheless, as a true son of his country and his culture, Santi too, before his departure, sought the favour of the Almighty; and much to his good fortune the time for this was most propitious.

Hindus pay obeisance to the one Great Spirit of *Brahma* whose many attributes are symbolised in the form of various chimeric gods and goddesses and their protean avatars. The autumn seasons of *Ashwin* and *Kartik* are sacred and dedicated, with much celebration, to the goddesses of India. Except for a scant few, it is at this time of year, in accordance with the lunar calendar, when most of their holy festivals are observed. In Bengal the season is collectively known as *the pujos*, a time of joyous devotion when doors are thrown open and families converge in neighbourly communion. In the suburb of Kumartuli, just outside Calcutta, *murtis* are sculpted from clay in depiction of each goddess as her time approaches. Hundreds of these images can be seen, standing row upon row, in various stages of completion, their artisans assiduously plying their craft, passed down from generation to generation.

Durga pujo is Bengal's first and most elaborate festival. It continues over a period of ten days and heralds the start of *the pujos*. Believed to be the occasion of goddess *Durga's* visit to her parental home, numerous canopied pandals are set up throughout the city to honour this Mother of the Universe, and to provide temporary lodgings for the many gorgeously attired and bejewelled *murtis* skillfully fashioned to represent her.

The celebrations begin with *Mahaloya*, first of the seven days of welcome which usher in *Durga pujo*. In the still dark, predawn hours of a late autumn morning, the entire city of Calcutta is awakened to the *Vedic slokas* of *Chandi Kabya, Durga's Song: Jago, thumi jago…*Awake, thou, awake!

Wrapped in their shawls, blankets and quilts, the people of Bengal avidly gather around their radios – and, at precisely 4am, over the air waves of All India Radio, Birendra Krishna Bhadra's exquisite rendition of *Mahaloya*, the invocation of *Durga*, the Mother Goddess, would stir the hearts of young and old alike. The story of her victorious battle with the Demon is chanted and sung to a rapt audience. It is brought to a close with *anjali*, an offering of flowers with prayers, and finished with *arti*, a graceful worship performed with dance and lighted oil lamps.

Their spiritual sustenance having been cared for, the devotees now turn to nurturing their mortal needs. Servants are hastily dispatched to favourite, local sweetmeat shops to purchase freshly made sweets and savouries, still-hot *jalebi, amriti, kochuri*, and more, for the celebratory consumption by their exuberant households.

Thus, the worship, feasting and gaiety continue in earnest until *Bijoya Doshami*, the tenth and final day of *Durga pujo*. It is a day tinged with sadness, for the time has come to bid farewell to the goddess who must now return to her husband's home. Symbolic of her departure, her *murtis* are carried, in loud and vivid procession, to be immersed in the Hooghly – that part of the Ganges which runs through Calcutta, and has been appropriated by name as the city's own. Despite their nostalgia however, and true to form, Bengalis sweeten the occasion with an exchange of their famous sweetmeats and much neighbourly goodwill.

During *Purnima*, the night of the autumnal full moon, the golden goddess *Lokkhi* is worshipped. Held aloft on a lotus blossom, this goddess of prosperity occupies a special place in the prayer room of almost every household in Bengal. By contrast, it is during *Amabashya*, the pitch-black night of the winter new moon, when veneration of the dark goddess *Kali* takes place. An incarnation of goddess *Durga*, this Divine Mother and fearsome warrior was created by the combined powers of all the gods to battle that most evil of evils the gods themselves were unable to vanquish. Her four arms, signifying her multiple powers, and her necklace of skulls, a symbol of retribution, provide ample proof of her victories over the wicked who would attempt to flourish in this world.

Kali might well be considered the patron goddess of Calcutta, or *Kalikata*, which, it is widely believed, was named after her. Fierce yet protective, she has had both good and evil attributed to her. She has – like every other god of any religion one cares to mention – unwittingly been made responsible for the whims and vagaries of mankind which have, in some lurid cases, gone so far as to include the *Tantric* rituals of human sacrifice in her worship.

It was the month of November in the late autumn season of *Kartik*, and Calcutta was caught in the throes of the *pujos*. Throughout the city young boys from each locality went door to door collecting *chanda*, festival money, so neighbourhood might vie with neighbourhood, in the grandeur of its canopied *pandal*, in the richness of its jewel-laden, silk-swathed *murti*, and in the blaring capacity of its multitudinous loudspeakers. Sounds of gaiety and laughter were everywhere, among young and old, rich and poor alike. The wail of the conch shell could be heard, and the air, filled with the perfume of incense and flowers, throbbed with the excited sound of drums and bells being rung in worship. Festivities came fast and furious as each deity had its day.

When the goddess *Kali's* turn came around, Santi visited her temple at Kalighat to pay his obeisance, and to beseech the goddess for her protection. After all, goddess *Kali* was herself a warrior, patron of all warriors against evil, and in Bengal she is venerated with a festival of lights. Every house, every doorway is filled with the flickering flames of tiny, clay, oil lamps. It is hoped that the myriad lights would drive out the darkness of evil, and fill each home with the radiance of the goddess's blessings.

Finally, *Bhai Phota* is celebrated to reaffirm the bond between brother and sister. With Santi's departure imminent, this year held special meaning. Prayers for his safety, well-being and good fortune were offered, and then the five sisters and two brothers anointed one another with sacred symbols of abundance, healing and comfort as they exchanged blessings, both spiritual and material. This year, Santi was especially grateful for the ceremony. To have foregone these shared prayers and blessings with his siblings would have been regrettable indeed.

Then, when it was time, as was the custom Santi paid his respects to both his parents. He did *pranam*, first to his father, and then to his mother, touching their feet with reverence that he might receive their blessing as he bid them farewell.

Thus, adequately armed with the well wishes of his family and the blessings of his god, Lt. S.P. Dutt prepared to carry out the orders he had received on 8 November from Army Headquarters, the Adjutant General's Branch, Medical Directorate, New Delhi. On the morning of 13 November, after insisting that all farewells be said at home, he departed in a taxi with a minimum of personal belongings, and all the requisite articles recently acquired pertaining to his new life.

OUTSIDE THE GREAT RED edifice that was Howrah station, he was met by a rush of red-shirted *coolies* proffering their services. Distinguishable from each other only by their black-numbered armbands, Santi selected *coolie* Number 37 who was not the sturdiest of the lot, but looked to be most in need of the work. Immediately chasing away all other contenders, the *coolie* quickly laid claim to the new Army & Navy Stores luggage, hoisting first the tin trunk onto the coiled cloth pad on his head, then heaving the bedroll to balance atop the trunk. Watching him, Santi wondered a touch guiltily if he had, perhaps, made something of an unwise choice. However, his suggestion of calling for help was met with loud protest; and, by way of proving his point, the *coolie*, with a few expert shrugs to his precarious burden, scurried off at a speed that belied his scrawny legs. Santi hurried in his footsteps and, together, they proceeded through the press of bodies to locate his train.

The Imperial Indian Mail train had pulled up at Platform Number 9. It was so crowded, it seemed about to burst at the seams and spill its human guts into the already seething masses on the platform.

The military had reserved a number of first-class compartments for its armed forces. Being six-foot-one in height gave Santi something of an advantage above most of the turbans, fez and Gandhi caps, sola topees and uniform hats as he fought his way through the milling crowds behind his *coolie*. He managed to locate the car with his name printed on a reservation card posted outside the right-hand side of the door.

Prior to embarking, he and the *coolie* found and stowed his trunk in the baggage compartment in the bogie at the rear of the train; then, returning to his four-berth carriage, the *coolie* stacked Santi's bedroll on the unoccupied upper berth assigned to him. The upper berth opposite had someone already fast asleep in it. Santi paid the coolie four *annas* – two *annas* being the going rate for each piece of luggage carried – and prepared for the usual bargaining. This, he knew, would begin with a well-rehearsed display of shocked disbelief, replaced by a show of righteous indignation, and culminating in a guilt evoking plea for mercy. Both parties understood, no matter what one started out giving, no transaction could be satisfactorily completed without this last exchange. It was just the way of things, and that was all there was to it. Finally, Santi paid the *coolie* an additional two *annas*, fully aware but not grudging the overpayment, and sent him on his way. He then laid out his bedding, flipped up his berth, and fastened it back in order to make more headroom. Lastly, he tucked his hand luggage securely into the luggage rack and settled down to make the acquaintance of his fellow passengers.

Lt. P. K. Mazumdar had just been inducted and, like himself, was on his way to Poona while 2nd Lt. B.S. Ghoshal was headed back to Bombay after emergency family leave. The incumbent figure asleep above them was, by dint of deduction, a Mr. S.N. Bose who was some sort of civilian contracted to the army. Santi sat down on the hard, coir-stuffed seat, its leather worn and shiny from contact with many a derriere. He stretched out his legs, crossing right over left, settled back comfortably and pulled a packet of Capstan from his left side breast pocket. After offering it around to his companions, he tapped one out, lit it, and drew a long, satisfied breath. A couple of puffs later, he leaned down and peered out the window.

It had been a while since last he'd left from Howrah Station. Usually, it was Sealdah Station the family used when they took their holiday trips to Dhaka, Mymensingh and Darjeeling – local trips by train and river ferry to Dhaka and Mymensingh, while Darjeeling was reached after changing from the everyday broadgauge railway to the picturesque narrow-gauge mountain railway, the little "toy train" as it was commonly known.

Howrah, the larger of Calcutta's two stations, was her gateway to the rest of India; and today, as always, it was a hub of squirming humanity. Outside the train window hawkers touted their wares, mendicants pleaded for the charity of a few *paise*, and passengers, both native and foreign, vied with each other as they elbowed and pushed their way to and from the trains, threading their way between groups of travellers – some sitting on their luggage, others spread out on the platform, all of them waiting to make their next connection with a patience born of the Indian nation's resignation to fate.

Beneath loudly coloured posters advertising the latest consumer goods and cinema releases, a mother squatting on her haunches was fanning the heat and flies off the small child that lay fast asleep beside her. They had been waiting on the platform for thirty-six hours, Santi heard her complain to her older companion. Their train had been requisitioned by the army for transportation of military personnel and supplies. Which was all very well, but what

"Toy Train" to Darjeeling, 1932.

was to become of them, stranded here like this? The older woman nodded agreement. It was worse than usual, she sighed, as she took a small *paan* from the cloth pouch at her waist. She popped the tightly folded betel leaf stuffed with condiments into her already red-stained mouth, tucking it securely inside her cheek, and began chewing slowly. It's the big war in the foreign lands, she explained, that's what this mess was all about, and all these soldiers coming and going only added to the *gol-mal* and made things worse. She shook her head in disgust and spat a stream of bright red liquid in the direction of the rail lines.

A bearer from the dining car dodged the offensive missile and shouted at the woman to mind what she was doing. She retaliated disdainfully that she *was* minding what she was doing and, to prove her point, she squirted another stream of *paan* juice with perfect precision, just missing the man's dusty shoes. He jumped back and she laughed at his discomfiture, adding to his fury which he vented by flinging a few choice invectives at her. Then, composing himself with as much dignity as he could muster under the circumstances, he made his way into the nearby compartment.

In his uniform of starched white cotton trousers and tunic belted with a red cummerbund, his head crowned with a pleated, long-tailed turban, the bearer saluted the passengers and offered the menu for both that day's meal and the following day's breakfast. Santi retrieved his spectacles from his jacket and, after a quick perusal, gave his order for dinner: chicken curry and rice, a side order of minced-mutton potato chops and, for his pudding, a slice of jam roly-poly. The bearer confirmed his order in vocabulary not quite within the realms of English, but somewhere thereabouts. With some random pickings from the King's own language, which he moulded to suit his tongue and his purpose, he held forth: *"Ji sahib. Chickain curry-rice, mutton champ, jomrullypully."* A brief pause, followed by a respectful enquiry, *"Aar breakphast, sahib? Phried egg, mamlet na rumble tumble? Sasit na becon?"*

Ah, breakfast! Santi was decidedly against fried eggs, which often tended to be hard and leathery. Between omelette and scrambled eggs, his preference was omelette, and he chose sausages over bacon. Having done the rounds of the compartment – except for S.N. Bose, who was still asleep – the bearer *salaamed* and left. Santi settled back with his cigarette and proceeded to watch the world outside through the bars of his window.

"Paan-bidi, paan-bidi." The vendor's offer of betelnut and cigarettes was declined.

"Chai-eeee garam." A young boy sang in the inimitable way only a station teaboy can, as he proffered small earthenware cups of hot tea to tempt both travellers and their well-wishers alike. *"Chai-eeee garam"*, the singsong cry rang up and down the platform as the *chai-walla* strolled the length of the train, swinging his large aluminium tea kettle. Santi bought himself a *khuri* of the steaming, sweet, milky liquid and then succumbed to the wail of the peanut vendor.

"Chiiiiiina-badam." The cry was a plea and a complaint at the same time…for the plight of his three hungry children at home, for his

fourth-time pregnant wife, for his own unfortunate lot in this wretch-ed life. He took his woven cane stand from under his arm and set it on the ground. On it he balanced his basket of freshly roasted pea-nuts in their shells. In the centre, a small earthenware vessel filled with burning coal kept everything piping hot. The vendor deftly shovelled some of the nuts into a small funnel-shaped packet fash-ioned from old newspaper and handed it to Santi, just as the engine whistle blew a warning of imminent departure. There was no better way to pass the time than to sip one's tea while shelling and eating hot peanuts as the changing scenery whipped by. And, as the train would proceed on its journey westward, rattling its way through the varied and colourful states of middle India, its progress would be reflected in the peanut vendor's cry, which would change with the local lingo of each successive station they passed through: *"Chiiiiii-na-badam…Moooom-phali…Time-pass, Time-pass…"*

The Station Master's whistle rent the air, creating a flurry of last-minute excitement and activity. With a sudden lurch and a steamy, sibilant hiss, the wheels of the train ground into motion, slowly at first, and then faster. The platform with its motley crowd began to slip away. They left the hustle and bustle of the city and its outskirts as the train picked up speed and then settled into a comfortable, swaying rhythm. They swept through the lush, green countryside of Bengal, with its fields and villages, its coconut palms leaning over *pukurs* thick with water weeds of lotus blossom, water lily and water hyacinth – the *poddo, shapla* and *kochuri-pana* a dense, veiled invitation to both man and beast to step into their hidden, wa-tery embrace. As Santi watched the old familiar sights disappear to-gether with the world as he knew it, the train bore him out of Bengal towards the more arid middle regions and, further still, across the breadth of India. It was the first leg of a relentless journey that was to take him from Calcutta to Poona, from civilian to soldier, from a man of peace to a man of war.

CHAPTER TWO

A Time For Miracles

*Then to the rolling Heav'n itself I cried,
Asking, "What Lamp had Destiny to guide
Her little children, stumbling in the dark?"
And – "A blind understanding!" Heav'n replied.*

– Omar Khayyam, *Rubaiyat of Omar Khayyam*

CAIRO WAS AN EXOTIC tapestry of contrasts, its weft and warp woven through with a melee of East and West, culture and chaos, the ancient and the modern. Sophisticated and commonplace at the same time, she was a city of magic, mystery and mayhem. More so now than ever before, with armies from all over the world converging upon her, filling her already noisy streets with their babble in strange tongues, her crowded bazaars with their bargainings, her thoroughfares with the sound of their marching boots, and her nightclubs with their dancing and merrymaking. Turbans, tarbooshes, fezzes, caps and hats jostled one another. Spiffy gentleman officers, rough and ready other ranks, gold-braided, red-tabbed General Staff, and short-on-time war-weary frontline troops rubbed shoulders with each other. And mingling silently amidst them all were the spies from both sides. Diverse as they were, these denizens of daybright and shadow all had one thing in common: today was for living; tomorrow could not be counted upon.

In the midst of all this, the ordinary Cairenes carried on with everyday life as best they could. They were the life blood that ran through the arteries of this throbbing metropolis. It was in their midst, be it the backstreets and alleyways of the old districts, or the palatial mansions and well-laid out gardens of the new, that the real heartbeat of this age-old capital could be felt. The rest was transient, like the *khamsin*. Throughout history, armies had come and gone, blowing over the city like a desert storm, and the city had hunkered down until the storm had passed, leaving behind a few faint footprints in the sand which soon were assimilated. Persians, Greeks, Romans were succeeded by the Byzantines, the Turks, the French who all came and went; and the city remained behind its many-gated walls with its soul stronger than ever before.

The final foreign dominance was that of the British, and although Egypt by this time had been declared a sovereign state, their presence and "protection" were still very much in evidence in the country. It was no surprise therefore that Egypt, like India, had various factions of ardently patriotic nationalists who were adamant on getting rid of the British at all costs. Egypt's ruler King Farouk, however, found it to his advantage to tread a line somewhere down the middle. Plagued by some would-be contenders for his throne, that beautiful but weak young prince who had turned into a sadly profligate king, sought to retain a handle on his crown by running with the fox as well as the hounds. He maintained tenuous relations with the British, while often, quite openly, leaning towards their enemy in order to appease the nationalists.

Now, with the Italian threat of invasion, and Mussolini's bombastic promise of a victory ride into Cairo astride his favourite steed, there were those in the country who believed that here was the very opportunity they had long been seeking. Of special interest were two fervent young army officers – Gamal Abdel Nasser and Anwar Sadat – who belonged to a secret officers' association. In years to come, and unbeknownst to any at the time, both would become presidents of the country they now believed the Axis would help to free of its foreign presence.

That November of 1940, it was business as usual in the playgrounds of Cairo – the nightclubs and country clubs, the hotels and bars spilling over with power, politics and intrigue, going head-to-head with a feverish lust for life, love and laughter. And now, reaching deep within the great city, its steady heartbeat was touched by these unsettling ripples of the incoming war.

The afternoon tram from Bab el Louk to Cairo squealed to a halt at the Choubra stop on Tir'a el Bulaqiya. Among the passengers who disembarked was a striking young woman wearing a dark-blue suit crisply trimmed in white. It followed the lines of her figure in a perfect fit. Her handbag and high heels were fashionably matched to her suit, and her dark-auburn hair, cut short in the mode of the day, wisped in soft waves around her face and the nape of her neck.

Two Tommies, red-faced young soldiers just out from England, leaned eagerly out a rear window of the tram and whistled after her. She ignored the intrusion, her head held high, her chin thrust slightly forward as though she dared the world to deal her what it would. About five foot six inches tall, she had a trim figure with strong shapely legs that flashed beneath her skirt as she crossed the street with long, purposeful strides. Reaching the local pharmacy, she disappeared inside only to reappear ten minutes later, armed with an address and a small medical box of supplies for an injection. She walked down briskly to the corner of Sharah yal Bogha and, before proceeding to No.312, the two-storied brick building where she lived, she stopped at Bhamun's Chapellerie.

Hedeya with her children, Victor, Violette and Louis, Cairo, 1933.

"Mr. Bhamun?"

"Ah, Madam Khayat," the Indian shopkeeper put down the hat he had been fixing. "Please, come in, come in. How are you?"

"I am good, thank you, Mr. Bhamun. But tell me, how is Louis doing?"

"Your son is a good worker, Madam, a good boy all-round. He carries a sensible head for business on those small twelve-year-old shoulders. In India he would make a good *banya*, a good money merchant. I have already given him the sound Indian name of Harish, and I must tell you that he can even recite in the vernacular of my country now," Mr. Bhamun rolled both his head and his eyes from side to side as he spouted *"thora cheenee thora cha, Bombay bibi bahut accha!* A little sugar, a little tea, the ladies of Bombay are very pretty! You see, he makes an apt pupil, and I will teach him well. Or maybe," he chuckled, "yes, yes, maybe he will teach *me* a thing or two!"

The lady gave a small smile which immediately softened the anxiety in her eyes. "Well, let us hope no one will be able to cheat him in life then." Behind the casual tone, a brittle hint of bitterness edged her voice. She opened her handbag and took out a shilling which she handed to Mr. Bhamun. "Here is Louis's salary for next week. Remember, this is between us. I want him to believe he is 'earning' his own pocket money so he will understand the importance of responsible work and independence."

Mr. Bhamun nodded sympathetically. Hedeya Khayat was an upstanding lady who taught her children well. Capable and hardworking, she spoke five languages; yet things had not been easy for her. She had gone through some hard times, he knew, but she was proud, so not many people realised just how difficult her life had been. He had a fair inkling as he'd watched her, through the years, trying to raise three children on her own while taking care of her old mother; all on her meagre teacher's salary of four and a half *geinehs* a month, supplemented with what she earned from the embroidery and sewing she did for private customers. She had an arrangement as well with Dikran, the pharmacist, whereby she earned three *piastres* out of every five that he charged for the occasional in-home injections she gave his patients. Today would be one of those days.

Each weekday he saw her catch the morning tram to Bab el Louk, from where she took the train to Helwan and the school where she taught cutting, stitching and embroidery. Gamaya il Khariya el Islamiya lil Banat was a charitable organisation for Muslim girls, about 15 miles (25 kilometres) away. Bhamun knew that, sometimes, to save a few *malleem* of the fare, Hedeya Khayat would walk a good part of the way from the Bab el Louk train station instead of taking the tram all the way home.

According to Mr. Hassaram, a fellow Indian and the cloth merchant who sold Madam the material for her work, she had been six months pregnant with her third child when she walked out on her husband, Mahran Merzian. It had happened in 1932, fuelled, among other things, by his persistent belief in his right to her share of the substantial wealth Merzian believed her father had managed to smuggle out of Turkey.

Her parents had brought Hedeya to Egypt as a young girl, after escaping the genocide of the Armenians in Turkey. But nothing could persuade her husband that Samuél Khayat, known by some as Baba Taht, and his wife, Bajo Saidé, had fled with only their lives, their one remaining child, and little else to sustain life other than a small bag of gold guineas that had been hidden, tied around the child's waist to dangle between her legs. Risking grave danger, Samuél Khayat had managed to save one other very important item – his eleventh-century family bible with its gold scyphate Byzantine coin on the cover. Beggared of all her belongings, Bajo Saidé too could not be parted from her personal gold cross with its single small ruby in the centre, the pair of blue enamelled and rose-cut diamond earrings from her first marriage, and her first gift to her daughter, the tiny gold heart pendant she had inscribed with Hedeya's name. Everything else – their house in the city, and the one in the village with all its land and livestock, the tins of gold coins and other valuables buried beneath flagstones in the courtyard, in windowsills and fireplaces – all that had remained behind. They were lucky to have come away with what little they had. Ah yes, there were the two carpets as well, one large and one small, that had played an especially interesting part in the story of their survival.

Sadly, Mahran was unconvinced that nothing remained of the gold guineas after Samuél Khayat's investment in a friend's trucking business and his own small shoe shop. And so, despite an attempt at reconciliation, the friction continued to grow. Eventually, for Hedeya, it reached the point of no return. Ruefully recalling a wise old saying, one from a vast collection her mother often brought to bear when she had a point to stress – 'be careful of the hand that grabs your beard; once caught, it can be jerked whichever way that hand may please' – she finally decided to put her marriage behind her, with a vow that, henceforth, no one ever again would compromise her dignity.

Samuél Khayat died of pneumonia in 1936, four years after Hedeya Khayat Merzian walked away from her marriage and returned with her children to her parents' home. His death was a grievous loss to his only daughter, who suddenly felt rudderless in the world of responsibilities he had left her. Additionally, in spite of the long separation, Mahran Merzian refused to give her a divorce. Hedeya had gone to her church and pleaded with Asis Habib, the priest, to reason with her husband; but to no avail. Mahran remained adamant, there would be no divorce. It was rumoured that, eventually, out of sheer desperation, Hedeya Merzian sought a way out of her predicament by taking the advice of two teachers in the Muslim school where she taught.

"Go to the *Miglis Millie*, the religious court, and become a Muslim," Nafisa Ali had advised her. "Then you don't need his permission for a divorce."

Jamila Hussein had nodded agreement. "All you will have to do is swear, *'La ila il Allah, Mahammad Rasul Allah*...There is no God except Allah, Mahammad is the messenger of God'. Then you will be given a Muslim name of your choice, and when you pay the *Miglis Millie* the required fee in *geinehs* and say *talaq* three times, you will be divorced in accordance to Muslim law. *Khalas*. There is nothing he will be able to do about it. Don't you see, it is the only way."

Hedeya Merzian had thought long and hard about it. How amazingly simple it seemed to be; she would be free at last! And yet, she held back. Seeking refuge in such a ruse was, actually, not quite that simple; not after having endured those terrible years at the hands of the Muslim Turks and Kurds. Those memories made even the pretense of such an act hard to contemplate! But then again, consider, what other choice did she have? Besides, merely going through the outward motions wouldn't in actual fact change her inwardly, now would it? She knew in her own heart, in her soul, what she really was; and, with all due respect, would any God, Christian or Muslim, honestly hold her feet to the fire for using this as her key to freedom? Who was she harming, anyway?

When a decision had to be made, Hedeya Merzian was not one to skirt the issue. Rumour had it that she had, indeed, discreetly gone through the motions of converting to the Muslim religion. However, all that was known for sure was that she got her divorce, she reverted from her married name of Merzian back to her maiden name of Khayat, and she still attended Asis Habib's church just the same as she had before. The only clue, if anyone had bothered to probe further, was in the required change of her first name – Hedeya, a name common to both Christians and Muslims, was changed to the more notably Muslim name of Hoda. The new name, as similar in sound to the old as could be managed, was chosen as well for its fortuitous meaning of "guidance". It was stamped on all her official papers, and would follow her thereafter through the rest of her life. Of course, not many people saw these official papers and so, for all intents and purposes, she remained Hedeya to all in her day-to-day life.

"Let me bring you a cup of *ahwa*, Madam, hot but not too sweet. I know just the way you like your coffee. You will be tired after teaching all day, and the trams are crowded at this time – now more than ever, with these foreign sailors and Tommies everywhere in the city." As a long-time Cairene seeing his city overrun by outsiders, Mr. Bhamun could not keep a hint of indignation from his voice.

"*Shukran* Mr. Bhamun, you are very kind, but I must go home to see if my mother needs anything before I go to old Mr. Zaglul's house. Today is the day for his injection." She placed a hand on the hatmaker's arm. "But, please, make sure Louis does not know this money is coming from me. He must learn to work for the things he wants in life, otherwise he will not know their value."

Hedeya climbed the flight of stairs to her first-floor flat. Bajo looked up as her daughter entered the kitchen, noting the weariness with which she lowered herself into the chair. Only thirty-two years old, she thought sadly, and already the lines of worry are beginning to show on her face; and I have to add to it by telling her we have nothing for dinner.

"What is it, Bajo?" Hedeya asked, catching something of the shadow that flit across her mother's face.

Hedeya Khayat in Cairo, 1937.

"I was just thinking about dinner. Maybe we can eat light today – *gibna uw aish*. I feel like having feta cheese and bread tonight. The children have enough food left over from yesterday…"

Hedeya sighed softly. She knew her mother wanted her to believe the suggested menu was one of choice, not necessity. Fortunately, the three *piastres* she was about to earn that evening, together with the money she had in her purse, would be sufficient to buy *fool medemes* on her way back, and that would do for tonight's dinner. Bajo could prepare the *fool* with olive oil, *lemoon and thom* since the children liked their fava beans best with lemon and garlic – and there would still be enough for tomorrow with hard boiled eggs. She remembered, ruefully, the plenitude of her early childhood in Turkey.

A memory flashed through her mind, a memory of the night she had woken to the sound of soft voices; she had followed that sound to her parents' room where a small table had been set up. Her mother had been rolling out sheets of warm wax in which her father was stacking gold coins, front to back, rolling them into long sausage shapes that they then packed tightly into large tins. They had seen her peeking in through the door, and they had told her that it was a secret she must never ever talk about, not to anyone. It was very late at night, in the dark silence while the household slept, they buried those tins of gold under the flagstones in the courtyard.

She shivered. What wouldn't she give for just one of those shiny gold coins right now! Or for a single necklace of Bajo's, made of those gold guineas, laid flat one on top of the other, so close they looked like quarter moons stitched to a leather strip, so long it had to be lifted into her lap when she sat down. If only...

Quickly, she pulled herself back to the present. Reminiscing about what they had lost didn't help any. It invariably opened the floodgate of memories, cruel, painful memories that were best left buried deep in the past.

"Don't worry, Bajo, you know God will provide," she said, soothingly, trying in the same vein as her mother to make light of the situation and, at the same time, drawing on the old lady's deeply religious faith. "He always has, hasn't he?"

She rose and went into the bathroom to freshen up, then popped her head into her bedroom. Her youngest, eight-year-old Violette, was lying on the big brass bed playing with her one and only doll.

"So that's where you are." Hedeya smoothed down the beautiful bedcover she had embroidered all over with roses, as she sat on the bed beside the little girl. She kissed her forehead and ran her fingers through the dark, tousled curls. "I'm going to Mr. Zaglul, but I won't be long. When Victor and Louis come home, tell them I want them to finish their schoolwork..." She broke off as a sudden ruckus at the front door heralded the arrival of the two boys. A moment later they rushed into the bedroom.

"Mama, Mama, we saw the army today." The words tumbled from Louis's lips. "Soldiers and tanks and great big guns, many, many of them, all marching to fight in the desert just like the hymn we sing in school." He stomped around the room in imitation of the marching soldiers as he sang, "Onward Christian soldiers marching as to war, with the cross of Jesus..."

"Loza! *Istanna*, stop! Haven't I told you to stay away from all that? Where have you been? Victor-Armand, as the oldest you should know better. Why did you..."

"I did nothing," Victor defended himself, indignantly. "Baba took us in his taxi. He came to school, and on the way home we drove by Malika Nazli. Every afternoon they close the whole road for two hours, just for the army. You should see them, Mama, all sorts of soldiers from all over the world, English and Australian and French, and we saw Indian soldiers too – some of them wore funny tarbooshes with long tails – and there were South Africans… I would make a good soldier. I'm almost as tall as Baba, you know. I think I should join the army now. Soon I will be fourteen."

"I think you are still thirteen and should put your mind to your studies, that's what I think. Now, go and have your milk. You can have some of the *balah agwa* I brought yesterday, your favourite dates. But first, I want you both to put your jackets and your shoes by the door, so you don't have to go looking for them in the dark if there is an air raid tonight – and wash your hands."

A movement in the doorway caught her eye. She turned slightly and saw Bajo standing there, holding a live chicken under her arm and wearing a look of quiet triumph on her face. The bird cocked its head, curiously, and looked around the room.

Hedeya stared incredulously at her mother. "Bajo," she asked in amazement when she found her voice, "wherever did that thing come from?"

"You said God would provide, and He did", Bajo replied matter-of-factly. "I went into the dining room to draw the curtains, and when I returned to the kitchen, I found this sitting on the chair where you had been sitting. A nice, fat one too," she said happily, looking up towards heaven and making the sign of the cross. "You see," she nodded to the children, "have I not always said? Believe, and it will carry the prayer from your lips to God's ear. He listens, no need to tear at His clothes. Look at this!" she crooned, holding the bird out to be examined. "When He gives, He gives with a full heart."

"Nonsense," Hedeya exclaimed, exasperated. "Chickens don't suddenly fly down from heaven. This bird must belong to someone." She saw the look of determination on Bajo's face, a look that said, you think what you will, but I know an answer to a prayer when I see one.

"Bajo," Hedeya warned, wagging a finger at her, "you cannot even think of cooking that bird. It has not been sent to you by God. He is busy with more important things going on in this world right now than sending you a chicken. This *farkha* has lost its way, and someone will be looking for it at this very minute. You cannot eat someone else's property!"

"Maybe God has a big farm in heaven where he keeps all the animals, and the angels look after them." Louis pondered the thought for a moment, then tucked his hands into his armpits, and flapping his folded arms like wings, he jumped onto the bed next to his little sister, clucking like a chicken. Violette giggled.

"You see what you do with your stories!" Hedeya admonished her mother. "I try to teach them to work hard and depend on themselves because nothing comes for free, and you will have them grow up expecting manna to fall from heaven. Louis, stop that noise."

"The trouble with you, Hedeya," Bajo announced sternly, "is that you don't believe in miracles."

As it happened, in spite of sending the three children from door

Hedeya with her growing family in Cairo, 1937.

to door, the owner of that chicken was not found. None of the neighbours, it seemed, knew anything about a lost bird, and it was a mystery that remained unsolved. Triumphantly, Bajo went to work in the kitchen. She laboured with love and exaltation over the preparation of the meal, filling the house with an aroma that proved irresistible. That night, the family sat down to dinner, baffled but grateful, and feasted on the best roast chicken they had ever tasted; and when grace was said, it was offered with genuine fervour, "Thank You God for all Your gifts…"

CHAPTER THREE

Brave New Ventures

The untold want by life nor land e'er granted,
Now voyager sail thou forth to seek and find

– Walt Whitman, "The Untold Want"

ON THE FORENOON OF 15 November, 1940, Santi Dutt reported to the Indian Hospital Corp Depot in Poona. He went through fourteen days of rapid initiation at the IHC Depot and upon completion, on 28 November, HQ Southern Command Poona transferred Lt. Santi Dutt as GDMO (General Duties Medical Officer) to the Indian Military Hospital, IMH Poona.

The Collecting Camp at Poona was a large, sprawling place through which assorted units passed on their way to various theatres of war. Here the men were examined, inoculated and treated as necessary, and the medical documents of each outfit were updated as required. At the hospital, Lt. Dutt was kept busy from morning to night with the process of readying hundreds of men on their way into battle. There were times he felt as though he stood sentry at the gates of destiny; that each man he deemed fit to step through those gates, he was, in effect, permitting rite of passage into that unknown realm of the Moirae – many of them never to return again. It was a sobering thought indeed. However, filled with the eagerness and bravado of youth, he thought mostly of the great adventure unfolding out there that he was not yet a part of. It was practically the end of January, and at this rate surely the war would pass him by!

Consequently, after a couple of months chafing at the bit, Lt. Dutt put in a request to join one of the outgoing units. He was ready to contribute more actively towards the war effort.

At first Lt. Col. Phelan attempted dissuasion, but he soon realised he was making no inroads whatsoever. Finally, he sighed and gave it one last, half-hearted try. "Look here Dutt, are you quite sure it's what you want?"

"I am, sir. Very sure," replied Santi Dutt, firmly.

The Colonel regarded the determined young lieutenant standing to attention before him, the unflinching gaze, the set jaw, the ramrod straight back, and he reluctantly gave in. "Well, in that case, we'll have to see what we can do to accommodate you. Mind you, I'd like to keep you on…if you should change your mind…"

With that the die was cast and Santi bided his time to see the hand that fate would deal him.

Later that week he received a letter from his sister Bela, affectionately called Bulu by their parents, and Didi – elder sister – by the younger siblings. A house surgeon in Calcutta Medical College, and eighteen months his junior, she was now, in his absence, the oldest among the remaining siblings in the family.

Bulu wrote they were all doing well. But they missed him, especially Mother, who bore the brunt of his absence in silence since it was she who had persuaded Father, eventually, to let him go. Moreover, as there now seemed a good chance their only other son might soon follow suit, poor Mother had to contend with even more of Father's exasperated grumblings. Kanti, born eighteen months on Bela's heels and known as Mezda or Middle Brother, was sounding off about joining the Navy. Father was unimpressed. Knowing his second son only too well, he could be heard muttering in disgust, "Bah! That one! It is only because he fancies the uniform. He'll be strutting like a peacock in full plumage, fanning his feathers for every woman he sees!"

J.P. Dutt had hoped for a third son, but when the fourth child arrived, two years eight months after Kanti, it was not a boy. Clinging still to hope, the little girl named Bina became known also as Mezdi or Middle Sister. Bela now reported that Bina had decided to finish her Master's, followed with a BT degree, in order to achieve her ambition of becoming a teacher.

Three years and two months later, when the family had been blessed with yet another daughter, J.P. Dutt began to falter. He pondered the wisdom of continuing in his efforts for another son. After all, he did have five children – and two sons and three daughters made for a large enough family by any standards. So it was that Sudha, the newest addition, became familiarly known as Kuti, Little One, since it was the intent that she should be the last of their progeny. Bulu wrote now that Sudha had joined Bethune College, but was undecided still as to what her goal in life would be.

Santi smiled, remembering how anxious Sudha had been before her Senior Cambridge hygiene exam. He had sat up all night coaching her, and when she'd passed with flying colours, to celebrate he bought her five pounds of the best chocolate from Firpo's – without doubt one of her great weaknesses. Since Father had him on a very strict stipend (to teach him the value of things) and he had no money to spare after his College and boarding expenses, he earned the money for her gift by giving blood.

The going rate for Indian blood was a paltry Rs.30 compared to Anglo-Indian blood valued at the tidier sum of Rs.50 per bloodletting. But Santi had been fortunate; upon learning what the money was for, the attending nurse, sympathetic to his cause, informed him that as an athlete, he would receive Rs.50 instead of the usual Rs.30. Sudha had been more than pleased with her gift.

With the passing of time, J.P. Dutt began to reconsider his decision of curtailing his efforts for a third son. Thus, two years and two months after Sudha, a sixth child was added to the fold. When this newborn, Kamala, his fourth daughter, was placed in his arms, J.P. Dutt's initial disappointment was replaced with an inexplicable tenderness. Holding the infant who was to become his favourite child, J.P. Dutt deemed it was now, most definitely, time to quit! He took it as a sign that he should count his blessings, accept his lot gratefully, and get on with the job of providing for his more than substantial family.

His family planning had not worked out quite as intended, however, and both he and his wife were surprised with yet another little girl who refused to be denied her rightful place in their family. A year and six months later Shobha, or Lebu as the family came to call her, finally closed ranks on J.P. Dutt and Usha Moyee's family of five daughters and two sons; and, much to everyone's surprise, in spite of his thwarted hopes, as strict a father as he was to his two sons, it was his five daughters who softened and filled J.P. Dutt's craggy heart with gentleness and mellowed his somewhat taciturn demeanour.

The two youngest sisters became very close despite their diverse characters. Kamala, lovingly called Matu, or little mother, by a father she had completely won over after his initial reaction to her arrival, was the more diffident by nature. Shobha, on the other hand, had a mind unlike most girls of her time. She differed from her older sisters with their elegant sense of dress, and their darkly flowing tresses that reached well below their waists, or worn sometimes decorously pinned up in buns as the culture of the times dictated. Not so Lebu whose harum-scarum attire and short riotous curls were an exclamation that perfectly expressed her exuberant nature. The last part of Bela's letter ended with the latest truancy of these two youngest members of the family; it had been prompted by a recent incident that was the talk of all Calcutta.

Had Santi heard the news of how Subhash Chandra Bose had slipped the bonds of house arrest following his illness in jail? The escape had taken place in the early morning hours of 17 January. It was widely rumoured that he had fled the country and made it to Germany by way of the Middle East; but those in the know whispered that in truth he had slipped the net to Berlin through Afghanistan. (Years later declassified documents would prove the latter to be true. In fact, while British Special Operations in Cairo were on alert to locate and, if necessary, assassinate him, Subhash Bose passed himself off as a deaf mute in the native garb of an Afghani *pathan* – baggy trousers, headdress and all. Thus disguised, and with the combined help of his nephew, and Admiral Wilhelm Canaris of the Abwehr, the German Intelligence Service, he managed his escape to Kabul, and through Moscow on to Berlin.)

Being the impetuous firebrand that she was, Lebu had hardly been able to contain her delight at the news of Netaji's escape and had promptly advocated joining a protest march in his support. As usual, she had managed to override Kamala's protests and, despite her sister's timid nature, embroil her as a partner in crime.

"Listen to me, you," Lebu had commanded, wagging a finger in Kamala's face, "this is for a great cause. You might be Father's favourite, little Miss Goody Two Shoes," she had grimaced impudently at her older sister from a wisely safe distance in case of any sudden reprisal, "but just you remember, I'm much smarter than you when it comes to these things."

The two girls had been in the thick of it when the police arrived to disperse the crowd. Fortunately, Bela was there with the ambulances from Medical College. She managed to extricate them from the impending riot, packing them off with a stern promise they would find themselves facing Father's wrath if they failed to heed her advice to go straight home.

Subhas Bose – called Netaji, Respected Leader, by his faithful followers – was a national hero, and Bengalis in particular were fiercely proud of their native-born freedom fighter. Santi was no exception, but he believed too that India would need soldiers to defend her after she won her independence. Like so many Indians, he had wrestled with a situation fraught with the demons of contradiction. It had not been easy threshing through one's loyalties in an effort to achieve the right perspective. Eventually, however, the priority of fighting for the freedom of the world had to take precedence over that of fighting for the freedom of one nation, even if that nation happened to be your own. Besides, one did not consort with evil like the Nazis without being vitiated by it, and though the British might be resented in India as rulers, they were, nevertheless, respected as a nation. In fact, Gandhi had declared quite clearly, "We do not seek our independence out of Britain's ruin."

———— · ◆ · ————

THE COLLECTING CAMP HUMMED with the preparations for war. Arriving units had a few scant weeks, before being shipped out, to ready themselves for desert or jungle warfare, depending on where they were bound. From the bugle's call of reveille which tumbled them out of bed every morning at 0530 hours till the evening's welcome sound of retreat or last post, officers and soldiers were kept on the go. They were initiated into the mysteries of Morse code, compass and map reading, signalling, tactics, target and bayonet practice, and whatever else could be crammed into this short but intense training period of how to kill and how to avoid being killed. For Santi, enjoying sports as he did, a particular favourite was the riding course with Queen Victoria's Own 17th Poona Horse Cavalry Regiment. When time permitted, recreational games of wrestling, boxing and football were encouraged as well. They built discipline, team spirit and morale which were, as everyone knew, an integral part of the all-round training that was the cornerstone of any good army.

Medical College Days – 1938.

Santi Dutt had, at one time, aspired to be one of India's foremost athletes. His father, however, did not share his dream. Being a practical man well experienced in life's hardships and the commitments required by a large family (his extended beyond his immediate own), he felt there was more security in the age-old, respectable profession of medicine. And so, the son had tried to accommodate both his father's dream and his own. He attended Medical College where he achieved outstanding success in several athletic fields, making a name for himself as a long-distance runner and an avid football player. He even captained the Bengal basketball team which won the 1938 All India Olympics. Consequently, now, when the opportunity presented itself and he could be spared from his duties, Santi found a good way to relax both mind and body was to join the lads in a stimulating game of football. It was to lead to a chance meeting of a lifetime.

Sometime in the first week of March 1941, the camp saw the arrival of 21 Brigade. It arrived amid a flurry of bag and baggage after having endured a prolonged stint in the rough and rugged terrain of the North West Frontier of India. This brigade was to be seconded to the newly formed 10th Indian Infantry Division which, rumour had it, was bound for Malaya.

21 Brigade comprised three battalions: the 4th Battalion of the 13th Frontier Force Rifles, the 2nd Battalion of the 10th Gurkha Rifles and, finally, the 2nd Battalion of the 4th Prince of Wales's Own Gurkha Rifles.

Officer Training, Indian Military Hospital, Poona 1940,
2nd Lt. S.P. Dutt, second row from front, eighth from left.

The Gurkhas are short, sturdy tribesmen from the hills and Terai of Nepal, a country perched amicably on the north-east shoulder of India. Hidden among the Himalayan Mountains, it nudges up with comfortable amity against India's hill stations of Darjeeling, Kalimpong and Gangtok in the east, and Pithoragarh, Askot and Nainital in the west. This is the stairway to the roof of the world, a land of perpetual ice and snow. Its very name, Himalaya, derived from Sanskrit, is a paean to its regal splendour: *hima* meaning snow and *alaya* meaning abode, The Abode of Snow. Reared to best the rigours of this rugged, isolated region, the mountain tribes are hardy and muscular in physique while being simple and steadfast by nature. The men, renowned for their fierce courage and loyalty as soldiers, thunder into battle with a warning cry of *Aayo Gorkhali!* Being staunch Hindus, this battle cry of their impending charge is rendered even more chilling by its dedication to the dark goddess of war: *Jai MahaKali! Aayo Gorkhali!* Hail, Great Kali! The Gorkhas are here! It is a war cry that has curdled the blood of many a worthy opponent.

Queen Victoria's Own 17th Poona Horse Cavalry
Regiment 1940, 2nd Lt. S.P. Dutt, centre.

From the bygone days of the East India Company, Gurkhas have been recruited into the army as ideal soldiers – tough, faithful, uncomplicated and, as such, easily led. In the summer of 1857, the need arose for a new regiment of Gurkhas. Raised at Pithoragarh, it saw the light of day simply as 33 Extra Gurkha Regiment. Some time later, inducted into the Bengal Native Army as the 19th Infantry Regiment, it remained such for a few short months before finally becoming the 4th Gurkha Rifles. The Regimental home-base at Bakloh, near Dalhousie, was where the 2nd Battalion was formed and added in 1886. The honourific title of Prince of Wales's Own was bestowed on the Regiment in 1924. Its commissioned officers were all British, its noncommissioned officers and soldiers were Gurkhas, and its chosen motto was proud and to the point: *Kaphar hunnu bhanda mornu ramro. Better to die than live a coward.* It was this 2nd Battalion of the 4th Prince of Wales's own Gurkha Rifles that had arrived at Poona as part of 21 Brigade – and it was about to play an important part in Santi's life.

One evening, Lt. Alistair Temple of the 2/4 happened to be in the Military Infirmary Room. Lt. Temple (inescapably nicknamed 'Shirley' by his cohorts) was perched on the corner of the MI Room desk, gloomily having his sore throat swabbed with Mendel's Throat Paint. He was still recovering from the eye-watering discomfort caused by the invasion to his throat when a tall, young Indian walked in. His muddy white shorts and football jersey proclaimed he had come directly from the playing field. He had an athletic body with long, lean limbs and an easy gait. Lt. Temple noted his well-proportioned features – high brow, straight nose and full, sensitive mouth. His dark, wavy hair was dishevelled and, despite the blood he was trying to stem from a nasty gash that had split open his left eyebrow, his countenance remained gently relaxed. His broad shoulders, squarely set, he held himself very straight as he approached the British medical orderly with a request: he would like his wound tended to and stitched.

The orderly looked at him askance. "I don't have the facility to do that, sir."

"Why not?" queried the young man, peering at the contents of the medicine cabinet. "You have all that's required right here – needle, gut, iodine."

"But…I…the anaesthetic, sir…surely…I can't…," the orderly stammered, aghast.

The young Indian pursed his lips, and an exasperated frown creased his otherwise smooth forehead. His steady gaze rested on the orderly for a long moment. Then, apparently having reached a decision, he walked over to the wash basin and began to wash his hands. "Do you have a mirror?" he asked over his shoulder. The question was short and to the point.

"Yes, sir."

Temple, who had been looking on with interest, cocked an eyebrow in disbelief as the young man's intentions began to dawn on him. *Bloody hell! Would he…actually…?*

Sure enough, the nervous orderly was instructed to hold the mirror he'd produced while the 'patient' donned a pair of spectacles. He then doused the gash with iodine, passed the needle through a flame to sterilise it and, with matter-of-fact determination, proceeded to stitch his own brow.

Temple observed the medical orderly's face grow pale. It was interesting how his colour drained away completely, leaving him a deathly shade of pasty white. His hand began to shake quite visibly while his eyes slowly started to roll up into his head. As he crumpled to his feet in a dead faint, bringing an annoyed curse to the injured man's lips, Temple darted forward, grabbing the mirror before it fell. In the aftermath of trying to revive the orderly, he neglected to ascertain the Indian officer's name. However, since there were not that many Indian officers around sporting evidence of facial surgery, a rudimentary inquiry soon produced results: Lt. Santi Pada Dutt was a doctor at the camp and had requested active duty.

In the Officers' Mess that night, Temple recounted the story for the benefit of his fellow officers. "Damned if I didn't see it with m'own eyes. Steady hands, good nerves." He turned to the company adjutant, Acting Captain, Lt. John Masters – Jack to his friends. "I say, Jack, this chap might be just the ticket. Regimental MO, I mean. Haven't been assigned a medical officer yet, have we?"

When the story reached their Battalion Commanding Officer, Lt. Col. W.R.W. Weallens, it took 'Willie' a single afternoon to pull all the right strings so that two days later, on 16 April, Jack Masters looked up from his desk in response to a firm knock at his office door.

"Come in," he ordered. The door opened and a long-limbed, young, Indian officer strode in to snap crisply to attention three feet away from his desk. He was clean-shaven, his dark hair neat under his brand-new Service Dress Hat, the unseasoned leather of his Sam Browne across shoulder and waist still stiff from lack of use, his starched uniform unfamiliar and loose on his lean form. His resolute demeanour and set jawline belied any unease he might have felt in his unaccustomed surroundings. He saluted, his clear, serious brown eyes fixed in a level gaze at some point just above and behind the seated adjutant's head.

"Well?" Masters prompted.

"Good morning sir," the newcomer replied, politely

"Morning. What's your name?"

"Dutt, sir."

"Rank?" barked the adjutant.

"Lieutenant IMS, sir."

"Christian name?"

There was a slight pause and a flicker of irritation in the brown eyes. "None, sir."

Masters looked up, annoyed. "Look here, what in the blazes..." he sputtered.

"I'm not Christian, sir." Lt. Dutt cut in, stiffly. "I'm Hindu. I don't have a Christian name." For a split second he glanced down into the adjutant's astonished eyes. What he saw there allowed him to relax somewhat; the surprise was genuine, untainted by arrogance or prejudice of any sort. A hint of a smile twitched the corners of Lt. Dutt's mouth. He lifted his gaze respectfully. "I do have a first name," he offered, with quiet satisfaction. "Santi. Middle name, Pada. Santi Pada Dutt – sir."

Upon his retirement years later, John Masters would author several books with a couple of films to his credit. In his autobiography, *The Road Past Mandalay*, he would wryly recall this first encounter with Lt. Dutt. It offered a revealing glimpse into a culture he believed he knew well. After all, his ancestral ties with India went as far back as 1804, with a muted whisper that somewhere in the dim and distant past there might have been a 'mingling' of sorts. As for Santi, he remained unaware that this incident would be told and retold to generations of Indian Officers who would follow in his footsteps, thereby taking its place in the annals of the 2/4 Gurkha Rifles.

IT DIDN'T TAKE LONG for the Battalion to get the measure of their new Regimental Medical Officer, and vice versa. On occasion, Lt. S.P. Dutt's forthright manner might very well have given rise to offence if not for the fact that it was tempered by a deep sense of respect and consideration for his fellow man. All he expected in return was some of the same. And if his candor at times bordered on the verge of bluntness, well, what of it? Once ascertained that a chap played with fairness and honour, his fellow officers willingly accommodated the odd quirk or quiddity. Dash it all, there could be no argument! Where an eccentricity of sorts was acceptable, verily, dullness was not. Without a doubt, a plain speaker was preferable to a crashing bore, was he not!

Of course, all would not be smooth sailing along the way; the occasional squall could hardly be avoided. It must be understood that for most of those concerned, this direct encounter with an Indian officer thrust into their midst was an uncharted experience. Without circumspect navigation it would be treacherously easy to flounder! Already one could feel the winds of reform blowing through the British Raj that would sweep away the shadows of its spent past to let in the light of a new era. Obviously, the shifting kaleidoscope would require some adjustment for changing patterns to fall into place; but the time was here for both Indian and Briton to come to terms with one another as peers and comrades-in-arms.

One episode might illustrate just how both sides were taking their measure of the other; it happened one evening in the Officers' Mess. With the recent talk of independence, the uncertainty of their future was being discussed. What would it mean for the Battalion? Indeed, what would it mean for those who had been civilians in India before the war? Were their days in the country numbered?

"What a devilish business that would be!" 2nd Lt. Roger L.H. Werner, an ex-planter from Hathikera Tea Estate in Assam, looked crestfallen. "I daresay," he groaned, "we shall all have to up sticks and push off home."

"Rotten luck, eh Roger?" the Battalion's red-headed Second in Command, Major 'Ginger' A. Fullerton called out in banter. "No more bearers or *bawarchis* to carry and cook. And", he added wickedly, "you'll miss those nubile young tea pickers, I'll warrant."

With a look somewhere between injured innocence and shocked sensibilities Werner managed to sidestep the jibe and, with elaborate politeness, toss it right back at the 2/IC. "I say, steady on sir! Haven't the foggiest what you mean, I'm sure. Although," he grinned cheekily, "by the sound of it, might one gather that you'd be referring to a favourite pastime of yours, sir?"

Amid general laughter there was a free-for-all.

"He has the cut of your jib, eh, Ging old man? Hoisted by your own petard, what!"

"A well-spun googly! You left yourself wide for that one Fullerton!"

"Nice one! That's the ticket, Roger me buck, that's telling him!"

Levity aside, there was an element of truth to Fullerton's quip which referenced a not uncommon custom among expatriate *Bara Sahibs* and *Chhota Sahibs* of the tea estates. These British Managers and Assistant Managers came from all walks of life.

The adventure of life in India was a beacon that shone brightly for many in Britain. Among those who followed the promise of its light came representatives of all classes, from the highest echelons to the ragtag and bobtail of society. For many, the luxury of servant-filled bungalows, exclusive clubs and gymkhanas, and the privileges of a 'ruling-class' was a novelty not heretofore enjoyed; and for those unaccustomed to this rise in circumstance, it quite often produced a sense of entitlement.

On the tea estates, for example, it would be arranged for young tribal women who worked on the tea plantations to be brought up to the Managers' and Assistant Managers' bungalows to provide a certain kind of 'comfort.' And, if an assignation were to have an 'unfortunate outcome,' there were always places like Kalimpong Homes in Kalimpong and the Birkmyre Hostel in Calcutta to deal efficiently, and discreetly, with the problem. These institutions had been set up by Dr. 'Daddy' Graham, a Scottish Church missionary. His wife had organised Kalimpong Home Industries. Here fine hand-crocheted, embroidered and woven goods were produced and purveyed in Good Companions in Calcutta, in Liberty's of London and Jenners in Edinburgh. But, no matter how discreetly or efficiently dealt with, after a certain age, in the outside world, these illegitimate children of mixed blood often faced life in an uncomfortable limbo, somewhere between the two cultures that had bred them.

There is always, of course, the exception to the rule, and on occasion one did happen across a man of principle, willing to stand up to social prejudice and stigma. But even then, the consequences could quite often be tragic.

A case in point involved the *Bara Sahib* of a tea garden in the Dooars, a swath of plantations that lies below Darjeeling. Having sired a child with a local Nepalese woman, he followed through with the honour of a true gentleman. Both mother and child lived with him in his bungalow where he saw to their welfare as well as to the child's education. But his actions caused much indignant furore in his social circle; so much so that in his absence on the customary two-month home leave to England, allowed every three years, both mother and child were banished. He was charged with behaviour unbecoming to his social standing; the London Office was persuaded to terminate his services forthwith and to dispatch someone much his junior as a replacement. From abroad, all his efforts to locate the whereabouts of his woman and child were unsuccessful. The result was tragic. Having lost his family and been tarred a pariah by his peers, his anguish was so great that it ended with the suicide of the good man. This was not the British at their best!

Santi had walked into the Mess at the tail end of the repartee between Fullerton and Werner without paying much mind to it. He'd had a busy day and was looking forward to a relaxing drink. Having given his order of Scotch with water to the Mess Orderly, he sat himself down to light a cigarette when Ginger turned to him.

"By the way, Doc, what's *your* opinion on the subject? One hears about the push to get us out of India but, really, what would you do if you did bring about independence?"

The question fell like a dead weight between the two men. The room, suddenly emptied of voices, grew heavy with an awkward silence. Taken by surprise, for a split-second Santi stood stock still. Through a jumble of emotions, he felt affront well up inside him, a rising heat reaching up into his head. His ears burned and his chest felt constricted. Impulse prompted him to snap back, to tell this arrogant young Englishman to go to hell. With an effort he had quelled the furious retort. Taking a long drag of his cigarette he allowed a stream of smoke out through his nostrils as he struggled to contain his anger. When he spoke he forced himself to sound normal.

"It is surprising you should find it necessary to ask," he'd kept his voice deceptively even. "Any man with pride of nationality would know the answer to that one, don't you think – sir." There was no mistaking that his words, though measured, were clipped with an edge of anger.

"Oh, give over, Ginger you chump." Unexpectedly, it was Masters who chipped in, trying to make light of the matter. Casually, in an attempt to further diffuse the situation, he turned to Santi. "Don't mind us, Doc. We've been away from it all far too long, you know. What with the last couple of years spent in the wilds of the North West Frontier, some of us have come away rather unsophisticated in the matter of politics, I'm afraid."

Santi had acknowledged the adjutant with a short nod. It was decent of Masters to try to mitigate the strained atmosphere. But then, unlike Santi, he was at ease in his surroundings, wasn't he! There was a shared camaradarie among these men with their common history and way of life, whereas the part thereof that they shared with him – a two-hundred-year presence in his country that they took so *bloody* much for granted – was the very barrier between him and them.

(In actuality, it would have surprised Santi to know that John Masters' intervention had been prompted by a certain empathy for his situation. Having spent his own formative childhood years in India, Masters long remembered his unease as a young boy being packed off to boarding school in England. He had found himself very much an outsider in unfamiliar surroundings.)

Santi was aware it had been the flippancy, the nonchalant manner with which Fullerton had lobbed his question that rankled above all else. Though, he had to confess, he was equally annoyed with himself for having risen to the bait, for allowing the remark to rile him. Unaccustomed as they were to each other, it was quite possible Fullerton had spoken without forethought; and the abrupt question, so brashly posed, had resulted in an awkward moment that he, Santi, had compounded by permitting the tone of his response to betray his feelings. He would need to do better!

Of course, that was easier said than done! It was all too easy to stumble or, worse still, come a cropper as had Father's elder brother who had attended Edinburgh University for further studies. Having excelled in his final DSc. Exam, Uncle had been summoned to the study of the School Head to be congratulated on standing first. However, when the results were formally announced, he found he had been relegated to second place with an Englishman placing first. Distraught beyond measure, he departed the University, forsaking his belongings, taking his leave of no one, and boarded a ship back to India. His travails dogged him, however, for when he arrived in Calcutta, he discovered the job promised him had been given instead to the same Britisher for whom he had been passed over in Edinburgh. The shock and humiliation of the double insult, abroad and again in his own country, was too much to bear. Santi had been young at the time, but he remembered Uncle had taken a stick to the offender after suffering an emotional breakdown from which he never quite recovered.

An even more intolerable example of this discrimination was practised by some of the most elite clubs in Calcutta such as Saturday Club, the Tollygunge Club and Bengal Club – this last a misnomer if ever there was one, for no Indian, Bengali or otherwise, was allowed to cross the threshold of those 'white-only' establishments. It was no wonder, therefore, that the subsequent position of being made to feel like a second-class citizen in his own country was so irksome to any self-respecting Indian. The feeling was not one of inferiority but rather one of inequality – inequality of choice, freedom and respect.

Be that as it may, this was not something to be acknowledged in the presence of these young Englishmen who were, by their own account, insulated in their beliefs of his people and removed from the politics of his country. How could they possibly step into his skin as an Indian and understand his feelings with regard to their presence as rulers in his country! Anyway, he was damned if he was going to allow himself to be dragged there, and he was irritated that his tetchy reaction might have betrayed his sensitivity on the subject. He considered it a weakness he would not allow.

It was only a matter of time, he told himself; the world was changing irrevocably about them all, and there was nothing for it but that they would have to adjust to that fact. No matter that he was Indian and they were British, he was here on equal terms, and the only yardstick should be one of honour and courage. And someday, when their countries stood side by side on equal terms, they would come to respect a free Indian nation. It was going to be a long learning experience, Santi thought wryly; he hoped it would not be too painful, for him or for them.

———•◆•———

Towards the end of April, rumours began to abound once more. Malaya, it seemed, was out. Instead, things had been escalating for a while in the Middle East, where broken promises after WWI had left the Arabs feeling betrayed and the political division of their land had bred bitterness against the British. Now, the situation there had tipped out of kilter and the 2/4 Gurkhas, along with the rest of 10th Indian Infantry Division, was to be thrown into the breach.

In September of 1940, Mussolini's Italians had invaded Egypt from Libya, a country they had colonised along with Eritrea and Somalia, since WWI. Here the Italians came face-to-face with Britain's Army of the Nile under command of General Sir Archibald Wavell, Commander-in-Chief Middle East Forces (C-in-C, MEF). This Army comprised the Anzacs (Australians and New Zealanders), the Indians (the 4th Indian Division which would lead the assault), and a contingent of British troops which included some rather colourful Yeomanry regiments.

That December, and the following January of 1941, the Army of the Nile retaliated, and with less effort than anticipated pushed the Italians right back to where they had started. The Allies were surprised and almost overwhelmed to find themselves landed with almost 40,000 Italian POWs. It was like netting great shoals of fish with no place to put the haul. It was fortunate, therefore, that most of those taken prisoner seemed to have lost faith in their leadership and were, by and large, only too glad to be done with fighting. Large groups of compliant POWs filed into captivity escorted by a single guard, their conduct so orderly and well-behaved, they were termed 'gentleman prisoners.'

Among those bagged were a few high-ranking officers, probably the most pontifical being Lieutenant General Annibale Bergonzoli. Dubbed 'Electric Whiskers' by his troops on account of the magnificent moustachios he flew proudly like a pennant, the redoubtable General, determined to prove that his present circumstances had put him out not one whit, marched into captivity belting out his favourite opera with true Italian showmanship.

But this was not to be the end by a long shot. The Italian Army might have toppled off its perch and taken a Humpty-Dumptian fall, but unlike that erstwhile hero, its set-back in the Western Desert was to be a temporary one. Mussolini, much put out by the bloody nose he'd suffered, looked to his ally, Hitler, for support; and Hitler did not fail him. The Fuhrer dispatched General Erwin Johannes Eugen Rommel to North Africa to wipe up his mess. The General's orders were to stem the damage and, somehow, to piece together what remained of the shattered Italian Army.

Romell's tanks and crack panzer troops landed on the shores of Tripoli on 12 February 1941. He paraded his Afrika Korps through the streets of that town with a veritable rattling of sabres and a pageantry befitting 'all the king's horses and all the king's men.' In what was to be the first deception in a long line of deceptions in the North African campaign, he had his tanks covertly circle back to drive repeatedly past the gathered crowds in order to give the impression of strength in numbers. This ruse was expressly for the benefit of any spies who happened to be present. He had begun, immediately, to weave the myth of invincibility that was to become a part of his desert legend.

Thus began a tango that would, over the next three years, sweep the two opposing armies back and forth across the desert. Locked together, first with the one partner and then with the other in the lead, they would advance and retreat and advance again in what the weary participants would come to call 'The Benghazi Handicap.'

Rommel's first front against Britain's victorious Army of the Nile – now gaining renown as the British Eighth Army – opened on 24 March in Libya. Churchill insisted on immediate retaliation, but Wavell was opposed to the idea – and with good reason. It was an inconvenient time for British forces, weakened by the departure of a large contingent of its most experienced troops bound for Greece. They were to stave off a simultaneous Axis invasion of that country. What remained of the Eighth Army was not prepared for a full-scale attack.

Churchill, however, would have none of it. And eventually, against his better judgement, Wavell gave in to his persistence. The result was disaster. Rommel pushed the Allies swiftly back towards the Egyptian border and, with the exception of Tobruk where the Australians dug in and hunkered down with their backs to the sea, most of Eighth Army was swept eastward in a pell-mell retreat, barely one step ahead of the enemy. The British ruefully acknowledged this desperate race across the desert as 'A Dash for the Wire.' But then, when all seemed lost, the gods smiled: Rommel outran his supply lines and was forced to stop, just short of the Egyptian frontier. The desperate Allies were given just enough time to catch their breath and turn their fortunes around.

Meanwhile, elsewhere, the worm was turning as well. To add to prevailing consternation, Iraq, seething with discontent, had decided to boot the British out; to this end, it was preparing to jump into bed with Germany. It fell to General Sir Claude Auchinlek, C-in-C India, to assemble and dispatch a force from that country to the troubled area, to prevent this undesirable tryst and forestall disaster. The 2/4 Gurkha Rifles was to be part of this upcoming force. It would be sent to Iraq, ostensibly, to protect that country against a German 'attack.' In reality it was to protect Britain's vital supply routes to India and South East Asia, and to prevent the oil fields, the lifeline of the Allied troops, from being handed over to the enemy. So much for their training in jungle warfare! They were now headed for the desert and Santi hadn't the faintest inkling what to expect!

"Get used to it, Doc," Major John Strickland offered by way of solace, "it's the usual way when one's 'taken the king's shilling,' don't you know. You receive orders to march east which means, more than likely, you'll end up heading west." He laughed. "But, not to worry, you'll soon get to be an old hand along with the rest of us. Besides, the desert ain't so bad. We've had a taste of it up at the North West Frontier and, from what I hear tell, our lot could be worse, I suppose."

Of course, the North West Frontier of India, rough and unpredictable as it was, held little similarity to the Libyan Desert where they eventually would be blooded in battle. They would learn then that no prior experience could have prepared them for that grim reality, or for the final outcome.

The evening of 24 April 1941, a few officers were enjoying after-dinner drinks in the Officers' Mess. Roger Werner strolled in with a 78 rpm record his sister had sent from England. He made a beeline for the bar.

"*Koi hai?* Anyone there?" The customary summons was promptly answered by the bearer in attendance, and Werner gave his order for a brandy.

Koi hai. The call for service employed in British Officers' Messes and in Clubs throughout India. Years later, back in England, officers who'd spent time in India would use humorous nostalgia to identify themselves as 'The Koi Hais.' The name was worn as a badge of honour by officers who had learnt and passed the tests of language and customs before being allowed entry into a Gurkha unit.

With drink in hand, Roger made for the phonograph in the corner of the room. He placed his new record on it, carefully set the needle in its groove, and the evening mellowed to the silken voice of Vera Lynn caressing one of the latest wartime melodies.

> *"The moon that lingered over London town,*
> *Poor puzzled moon, he wore a frown…*
> *The whole darn world seemed upside down…*

At the time, London was suffering horribly at the height of the blitz. But plucky Londoners, in defiance of anything the Germans might throw at them, woke up each day glad to be alive, and determined to live to the fullest. They buoyed their spirits however they could, with music and song playing no small part. *"A Nightingale Sang in Berkeley Square"* had become all the rage recently – a battle cry of the harrowed city and its undaunted citizenry, it could be heard in nightclubs everywhere.

> *"How strange it was, how sweet and strange,*
> *There was never a dream to compare,*

In the Officers' Mess the music, mingled with cigarette smoke and chatter, filled the air…

> *"With those hazy, crazy nights we met…*
> *When a nightingale sang in Berkeley Square…"*

The wistful words were rudely interrupted by Jack Masters who burst in with news – mobilization orders had just come through! But hold on, hold on, he attempted to calm the stir of excitement, there was still no confirmation as to their exact destination. All they knew for sure was, they had three days to pack up and move out. The rest would come later.

This was it. For over five months, Santi had watched as other men had stepped into the pages of history and now, at last, it was his turn. About time too! The news brought no sense of consternation, nor any fear of what dangers might lie ahead; rather, the tightness that lay at the pit of Santi's stomach was the thrill of anticipation. Nothing he could bring to mind could be greater than the adventure he was about to embark on.

Back in his quarters he checked his gear, mostly army issue now. His revolver, a Webley Scott .38 calibre, looked strangely at odds lying next to his stethoscope. The first time he had held the weapon in his hand, felt its deadly cold weight and hefted it at arm's length, it had commanded a sense of deep respect within him; there was no mistaking it was an instrument of lethal capability and power. He was, as yet, innocent of the full horror and destruction of such power. At that moment he felt only elation and a sense of the invincible. He was young, he was strong, and he was imbued with hope. He had not yet attained the wisdom to be cautioned by fear.

April 25 saw the regiment in Khadakwasla for a last feverish bout of Combined Operations training. There, on the lake, they practised as best they could the embarkation and landing of troops, guns, tanks and trucks against enemy opposition, and they were given training in communications between the various factions involved. It was hoped, rather optimistically, that somehow this halcyon training ground would prepare them sufficiently for the real thing to come. And, indeed, by the end of it all, they believed themselves to be in pretty decent trim. Of course, the truth of it was such rudimentary training was woefully inadequate; and before too long, the excitement of preparation, the fever pitch of anticipation would be replaced by the awful reality and carnage they were about to face.

During a river-crossing exercise, Santi's brown boots, tooled of the finest leather Calcutta's Chinese cobblers could supply, came apart at the seams. Obviously, they were meant for parade grounds rather than battlefields. Santi went in search of a replacement. Simpson, the regular Quartermaster, had suffered a broken leg from a motorcycle accident and his replacement, Madge, proved himself an astute businessman. He was sorry, there were no brown officers' boots available, but Santi could have a pair of black infantry boots in exchange for a certain four-celled flashlight the acting Q.M. had observed in the doctor's possession. Since Santi could hardly go barefoot into battle, there was nothing for it but to agree to the wily Quartermaster's terms.

On the 27th night they entrained for the short journey to Bombay. Upon arrival at Victoria Terminus Station, they were taken by truck to the Bombay docks, now writhing with the activity of inbound and outgoing troops. Here they were met by moist-eyed ladies from the Women's Volunteer Service who served them tea, cake and encouragement. Then, to the wail of regimental pipers playing "Kenmure's On And Awa'" – the traditional band and bagpipes being an essential part of any British army's arsenal – they embarked on His Majesty's Troopships, *HMT Neuralia* and *Devonshire*. It was the forenoon of 28 April, 1941.

The ships sat anchored midstream and waited two days for the formation of a convoy – and for the various quartermasters to complete, as hurriedly as they could, the loading of ammunition, equipment and medical supplies. There was a feeding frenzy caused by insufficient materiel: a shortage of mortars, no helmets, and not a single Red Cross badge to be had. On the other hand, there was an over abundance of gas masks available.

Not in the least put out, Madge set to work, and his well-honed talents stood the Battalion in very good stead indeed. Undeterred by the lack of vouchers, and unperturbed by having to resort to what could only be termed as out and out pilferage, the Quartermaster outdid himself. Colonel Weallens would declare later with unabashed satisfaction, "I'll give the blighter this: we got away, I'll warrant, better equipped than any other unit in the force."

Finally, on 30 April, the sealed orders disclosing their destination were opened, and Convoy BP.1A set sail. Past the Gateway of India, on board the *Neuralia*, Santi watched the dwindling shores of home gradually melt into memory. Under the aegis of the armed merchant cruiser *AMC Kanimbla* and the *Sloop Falmouth*, the convoy with the 2/4 Gurkhas headed for Basra, the Middle East and the fortunes of war.

SS Neuralia, built in Glasgow in 1912 for the British India Line, was a passenger liner converted to wartime service in WWI & WWII. Ferrying school children in the interim, WWII saw her return as a troopship between Bombay-Basrah & Calcutta-Madras-Rangoon. She assisted as well in the retreat from Burma, the evacuation of Singapore, & the Normandy Landings on D-Day, 6 June '44 when she would carry 27,055 American & British soldiers on fourteen roundtrips from London to the beaches of Omaha, Utah, & Gold. Surviving several U Boat attacks, she hit a mine and sank just one week shy of VE Day. A postage stamp issued by the Govt. of HM Queen Elizabeth II commemorates HMT Neuralia's lifetime of loyal service.

CHAPTER FOUR

Over The Waves And Far Away

One moment in Annihilation's waste,
One moment of the Well of Life to taste....
The stars are setting and the caravan
Starts for the Dawn of Nothing...oh, make haste!

– Omar Khayyam, *Rubaiyat of Omar Khayyam*

Lt. S.P. Dutt
c/o Middle East Forces
Letter No.1   *2nd May 1941*

Shree-Charaneshu, Revered Father and Mother,

We are finally on our way and I am writing to you from my cabin on board ship. I shall number my letters so you may keep track of them and know should one go astray. This, my first letter to you after leaving the shores of my motherland, I am addressing to Father and Mother, but it is in fact to all of you – my family.

This sea voyage is a new experience for me – the first of many no doubt – and more so for the Gurkhas, most of whom have never seen the ocean before. The ships are crammed to capacity with troops, all of us living in very close quarters, sweltering in the May heat, breathing the smell of engine oil which is all pervasive as the convoy zigzags its way across the open ocean. We are always on the look out for the enemy, above and below. No sign so far, thank goodness, just the flying fish and porpoises that follow us from time to time, and are a pure delight to behold.

My medical abilities have not yet been called upon other than to treat rampant seasickness caused by the incessant yawing and rolling of the ship. Since none of us have acquired our sea legs yet, this can vary between mild to severely disabling, and I have been dispensing bromide quite regularly, depending upon the ocean's whim. Although the Gurkhas are by nature a forbearing lot, this new malady with its uncontrollable heaving and up-chucking is quite disconcerting for the sturdy mountain men.

There have been a couple of other wrinkles that needed to be ironed out. As you know, the Gurkhas do not eat beef for the same religious reasons that most Hindus do not, but the ship's all-British crew is unacquainted with their customs. The kitchen staff knows little of chapattis and rice, or how the Gurkhas prepare their vegetables and meat which is, of course, quite different to the fare offered up by the ship's uninitiated food preparers. It has taken a fair amount of persuasion on the part of our C.O. – more akin to arm twisting, I should say, by way of a threatened hunger strike – before our boys were given their own area for cooking. But now that an understanding has been reached, much to everyone's relief, things are settling into a routine of sorts.

I wish I could describe to you how mighty and endless this mesmerising waterscape is. Our ships plough through the dark blue ocean in obedient, military formation, and I must say it is an impressive sight; yet, this convoy of steel giants, these man-made gargantuan intruders churning the ocean into foamy phosphor-tipped wakes, are dwarfed by the immense expanse of water and sky. What a strange and awesome world it is out there, its power and mystery beyond the scope of man – like the barest glimpse into infinity. In a short while the sun will begin to set. It will light the heavens with its flames and turn the ocean to gold. One is truly standing in the presence of God! Yet, here too, our insatiable greed and fear have begun to mar the magnificence of this grand masterpiece, for that is what this journey is about, is it not?

Well, I shall not dwell upon that. Better men than I have wrestled with the morality of war and tried to fathom its reason. But I do believe it is a necessary battle that we are about to fight and, in spite of the contrariness of my being an Indian in the British Army, I am convinced that in this instance I am on the right side, otherwise I should not be here. I shall end now and take a stroll up on deck so that I may catch the evening's last light as day changes to night. Maybe the immutable ways of nature will enable me to reaffirm my own convictions as we sail into the unfamiliar world of change that lies ahead.

I will write again after we land. Please give my love to everyone at home and be assured that I am well in body, mind and spirit. My pranams to you both.

Affectionately, your son,

Santi

—————•◆•—————

SHERJANG DILBAHADUR RANA, Lt. Dutt's batman, saw to it that his uniform was faultlessly pressed and his boots perfectly polished at all times, his belongings kept in order and his daily needs attended to with unfailing routine. He began, as well, to teach him Khaskura which was his dialect of the Nepali language. The orderly was a soft-spoken man with a childlike soul that belied the ferocity with which he faced an enemy. Indeed, his very name, Sherjang Dilbahadur Rana, was meant to imbue its bearer's heart with the strength and courage of a lion. During battle simulation, Santi had seen this gentle person transform into a powerful warrior to be reckoned with.

Slowly, a relationship began to develop between the two men. Initially, the groundwork was laid on mutually guarded respect which, through time and experiences shared, would grow into a bond surmounting the barriers of rank, class and circumstance. Having taken stock of Santi, and deciding he liked what he saw, the old veteran took the fledgling officer under his wing, much as a mother hen would its chick. It would seem he viewed Santi's solitary plight among his British counterparts much the same as that of childhood's fabled 'ugly duckling' – an outlander, separate from its companions until, lo and behold, it turned into a swan! Here, Dilbahadur discerned astutely, was that same potential.

Realising quite early that food from the men's *langar* would probably make a welcome change from that in the Officers' Mess, Dilbahadur regularly brought Santi offerings from the soldiers' kitchen – whole wheat *chapattis* or rice, with well spiced *dal,* and the curry of the day – all comforting reminders of home. Santi was touched by this small gesture of concern which, in months to come, would benefit him tenfold when his officers' drab rations of tinned meat and vegetables, M&V, was his only sustenance – tinned bully beef, tinned carrots, tinned peas and tinned peaches was not the sort of fare to appeal to an Indian palate. And even now, on board, where meals were none too shabby, he had reason to be silently grateful for Dilbahadur's consideration as he rarely ate in the dining room; the outcome of an incident during training in Khadakwasla.

It had happened at the fag end of a full day's hard exercise. They had returned to camp and were seated for the evening repast in the makeshift Officers' Mess. A vindaloo curry of sorts was served up, and Santi was fortunate to land himself a marrow bone to which he was most partial. However, there appeared to be no marrow spoon, or similar utensil, to extricate marrow from bone. But Santi was not to be deterred. Where he came from, anyone with a modicum of sense knew this most desirable part of the bone, chock full of heartiness and flavour, was not a delicacy to be passed up. Pondering his choices, he concluded, some improvisation was called for; he would tackle the problem with whatever tools were available. After all, needs must when the devil drives.

In India, food was customarily eaten with one's fingers. Not only was this considered wholesome, it was a fact that the enjoyment of food through the usual senses of taste and smell, was heightened by the additional sense of touch. Unarguably, it was the best way to manage anything on the bone, and the only sensible way to deal with certain foods such as fish curry; particularly Bengal's famous *hilsa*, when in season, one of the tastiest fishes despite its bones.

This traditional manner of eating was an art perfected through practice, wherein only the fingertips made contact with the food, leaving the palm of the hand pristine. Back home, faced with the challenge of a marrow bone, Santi would simply pick up the bone with his fingers and, using his teeth, break through to the goodness within. Now, however, allowing for present place and company, he abstained. Setting aside his spoon, he took his fork in his right hand. Then, holding the bone steady on his plate with the first three fingers of his left hand, he tried, with what finesse the procedure would allow, to insert the tines of his fork into the bone. This met with little success, and before he could think further on the problem, he was pulled up short by a brusque voice from further down the table.

"I say, Doc, do you mind? The use of fingers at table in the Officers' Mess is not actually done you know."

Santi looked up to catch Fullerton's disapproving eye. Once again, he seemed to have run afoul of the 2IC. Once again, he could feel the searing heat of mortification begin to suffuse his face. Anger at being pulled up for the impropriety of what was custom in his country stung deep. He clenched his jaw hard to prevent spilling the furious words that pounded through his head: *It is 'actually done' in my country which, damn it all, is where you happen to be!*

He bit back the words. Frowning with the effort to control his feelings, Santi regarded the 2IC through slightly narrowed eyes while he sorted through his options. This Mess, he reminded himself, makeshift though it may be, was their home ground, not his; as such he was obliged to abide by their social mores. But this was *his country* wasn't it, he fumed, why must he relinquish his custom in favour of theirs! Sitting at their table may give them the right to demand he conform to their ways, but he had the choice to walk away from it, didn't he? To hell with them! Swallowing the offence that felt like a knot stuck in his throat, he pushed back his chair and rose from the table. He did so unhurriedly. Keeping his face as expressionless as he could, he chose the words for his reply carefully. His voice was brittle but level when he spoke.

"In which case it would seem expedient I be excused from this table so I may take my meal elsewhere, unbound by etiquette foreign to my country." Suppressing the urge to storm out, he mustered what dignity he could and left the dining room, still smarting at having been rebuked like some ill-behaved child.

What an intolerable position, to be embarrassed on account of his traditions when, in actual fact, it was *they* who had come here with their foreign falderal. And even now, after two hundred years here, they believed they could change and improve his culture!

Confound them! What arrogance! What sublime arrogance this heartfelt conviction in their superiority as a nation, and the consequent belief in their capacity as rulers to bring 'civilisation to the backward natives!' Did it not occur to them that this would manifest itself as insolence in the eyes of his people, and others like them elsewhere, who felt deeply insulted by the uninvited relationship thrust upon them and their ancient civilisations? Which, in some cases, were hundreds of years older than that of the British, thank you very much!

But, somewhere inside his head, a small voice pulled him up short: *Now, hold on there. Even if two hundred years of association has taught them nothing of your culture, it very well ought to be sufficient to put you in mind of theirs; their ways might be foreign, but by no means are they unfamiliar, now are they?* Santi had to concede the point. After all, he had spent years at David Hare School where the education was based largely on the British school system.

But his ire was not to be stilled: *True enough,* came the stubborn retort, *but even there it had been perfectly acceptable to pick up a marrow bone or a mango stone in one's fingers since commonsense dictated it was the most practical way to deal with the darn things. And on occasion, even the British made use of the utensil known to them as the finger bowl, did they not? And why the marrow spoon if not to manually tackle marrow from bone? Well, then! When would they come to terms with the fact that India was not to be made over in the image of England and never would be!*

Over a hundred years ago, Lord Macauley's earnest advocacy – well-intentioned and intellectually, if rather unfortunately, rendered – for "a class of persons, Indian in blood and colour, but English in taste, in opinions, in morals, and in intellect" had set the course for India's education. Admittedly, one could not refute the advantages of being thus prepared to meet and deal with the British on their own terms; no doubt, as well, after independence it would stand his nation in some good stead in its forthcoming international dealings. Still, the situation was a complex one, for even if one could not fault the sincerity of Macauley's beliefs, the lack of all understanding and respect for India's identity, its languages, religions and cultures, made the price in national pride a high one indeed. As an outcome, anyone who emulated British ways too closely was scoffingly referred to as a *'brown sahib'* or labelled with the derogatory epithet of *'Brindian.'*

But did any of that apply to their present situation? Here they were, in the middle of training for the ruddy war, surely the small niceties of etiquette and table manners were of little consequence?

Not so, apparently, the small voice in Santi's head persisted: *Come now, since protocol is after all protocol, you've been called out on a faux pas. And, you must admit, you are in this man's army of your own choosing, are you not?*

Santi sighed. Sometimes it was confoundedly difficult trying to straddle two cultures whose boundaries had begun to blur. He found, these days, that he tended to think increasingly more in English and less in his own mother tongue. The realisation took him by surprise, and he determined that from now on he would write home in Bengali – that is, of course, if censorship would allow it. Ah well, since it was obvious that neither party at present could disengage from the other, they would just have to learn to live with one another as best they could. What made it so irksome was the domination of the one over the other! If he and his countrymen had foisted themselves on the English in like fashion, what then? How would such an incursion of their homeland have sat with them? He deliberated the idea. Ah, sweet revenge! The thought had a certain delicious smack of justice that afforded him a mild comfort merely in the thinking of it.

If anyone had told him then that history would, in his lifetime, bring about a reckoning of sorts, that England's Empire would turn Commonwealth and its subjects migrate in droves to roost in that tiny island, that the cuisine of his country and its manner of consumption – the very subject of their present quibble – would become as English as Roast Beef and Yorkshire Pudding, well, the absurdity of it would have been met with complete and utter disbelief!

THE SECOND AND FOURTH days at sea delivered two events that shattered the peace and stirred the ships into action. The first occurred on one of those extremely hot afternoons so common to the Persian Gulf at that time of year. It was mid-afternoon, and the air lay heavy, weighed down by the sweltering heat so that nothing, animate or inanimate, seemed able to move. Suddenly, commotion broke out on the HMS Devonshire, sending men running to peer over the ship's side. Man overboard!

The story, when related later, went thus: Master's had been reclining in a deck chair in the shade, trying to catch any small breath of a breeze that might stir over the water and bring a degree or two of cool relief. Half asleep over his book, he had been jolted rudely from his stupor by a most frightful sound that almost made him leap out of his skin. It sounded like the mad shrieking of a wild banshee in pain. His eyes flew open in shock to meet the impossible vision of a near naked apparition ripping off its last clothes, flinging them frantically about as it hurtled past. For one awful moment, Masters feared heat stroke had caused this appalling hallucination or, heaven help him, he had taken sudden and complete leave of his senses! It took a split second to realise it was neither.

The streaking figure was that of a boiler room fireman. Unable any longer to stand the rampant heat multiplied ten-fold in the engine room, the poor demented *laskar* had fled from his pit of purgatory and burst forth onto the open deck. Screaming like a bat out of hell, he had shot past Masters and flung himself naked over the edge, plunging headlong into the blazing ocean in a desperate attempt to cool his boiling brains. Galvanising himself to action, Masters tried to raise the alarm as he hotfooted it to where the man had exited. The initial manifestation of this endeavour was a sound produced by his vocal cords much like the croak of a startled frog. When he did manage to recover both voice and wit, he made up for this lack with a shout loud enough to reach Neptune's own kingdom. There ensued a great deal of pandemonium as rescuers fished the unfortunate man out of the water – sadly, too late. He was too far gone to be revived. (John Masters: *The Road Past Mandalay*)

The second break in routine occurred when a signal arrived for Lt. Col. Weallens. It seemed, consequent to a recent military coup having taken place in Iraq, the Iraqis spurred on by the Germans, had revolted against the British presence in their country. In view of the spreading hostilities and imminent dust-up, preparations were to be made for an assault landing at Basra. It fell upon Masters to ready the Battalion, which threw him into a proper stew and a feverish bustle of adjutant-like activity.

Signals went back and forth sending a flurry of anticipation running through both ships. Rifles and bayonets were oiled and readied, anti-aircraft light machine gun manoeuvres were practised on the boat deck, landing drills were rehearsed, and the air hummed with activity. Masters, when he appeared from behind his mountain of paperwork, stomped around looking like thunder, cursing under his breath as was his wont when some crisis was afoot and time was short. Dash it all! They were not ready by a long shot!

Lt. Col. Weallens, on the other hand, looked to be in high spirits. Now that they were given the chance to prove their mettle, he puffed up like a proud father, willing to wager his men would outshine the whole bloody British army and then some! As far as he was concerned, they were in fine fettle and no one was a patch on his Gurkhas.

Twenty-four-hours later, a final signal ordered them to stand down. The rebels had been pushed back and all was under control. Col. Weallens looked cheated, but Masters' scowl vanished, and one could approach him once more without danger of having one's head bitten off.

And so the long days passed, sandwiched between sun and sea. Each day was a learning experience for these men who had lived alongside each other for so long and yet been separated by their stations in history. Santi was Indian, and India was his country, his birthright. Nevertheless, all his life he had been conscious of the fact that in his country an Englishman enjoyed a greater sense of entitlement and privilege by dint of having been born and reared in that great, all powerful entity, the British Raj. Foreigners they might be, but it was given to them to set the rules by which his country and countrymen were governed. For Indians it was a hard pill to swallow! But times, perforce, were changing and with it, no doubt, the privileges of Empire. Both Englishman and Indian would have to reach for new footholds on more level ground than that upon which they had, till now, been standing. That was becoming apparent.

Moreover, Santi was soon to discover that all was not equal, even among the British officers, given that they hailed from sundry walks of life. Some claimed the heritage of a long line of army officers who had served in India; many among them had been born in his country where they spent their childhood before being sent to Sandhurst or some other boarding school in England. Others were career officers but comparative newcomers to the East. In the case of the subalterns, i.e., 2nd Lieutenants, most were emergency commissioned officers, a number having been tea planters recruited from the gardens of Darjeeling, Assam and Ceylon. And then there were the FOBs, those fresh off the boats, new recruits sent out from England for the very first time and considered by the well-seasoned veterans of India to be greenhorns, miserably wet behind the ears.

But no matter these diversities, they shared a common bond – they were British; and their sceptred presence in his country, forged over two hundred years, reinforced their bond. It dawned on Santi, with somewhat of a shock, that in the bedrock of that bond many of these young men felt deeply rooted in India, sincerely regarding it almost as much a part of their heritage as he did! And, if one were capable of looking past the irksome inequities and social disparities foisted on the Indian nation, one would have to concede, in spite of themselves, his people had imbibed, through some variation of osmosis, enough western culture to have changed their own forever. Like two sides of a coin, the affinity and the adversity of their two nations, bound together by circumstance, could not be denied.

And here they were at present, Indian and Briton, both standing for once on the same side and, more unusual still, with a view to a common goal; an oddly conflicted situation. It would take some getting used to, and hopefully that would come in time for, by and large, they seemed like a decent lot of chaps. Put it down to luck perhaps, but so far it had been fairly smooth sailing if one discounted the couple of minor run-ins sparked more probably by their inexperience of each other in close quarters rather than any deliberate malice aforethought. Here, they were no longer the invader and the invaded. They stood now alongside each other, in this British Indian Army, foreigners both, about to invade someone else's land. The irony of the situation could hardly be missed. Politics, as they say, really did make for strange bedfellows!

As for the politics pertaining to that part of the world towards which they were headed, this was a good time to gen up on information regarding their destination.

Through the ages, Iraq had been conquered and re-conquered and had undergone many a metamorphosis. Before World War I, as part of the Ottoman Empire, it had been known by the ancient Greek name of Mesopotamia – The Land between the Rivers – and it was well named, lying as it did between the great rivers Tigris and Euphrates.

During World War I, the Ottoman Turks allied with Germany against Britain. In June 1916, Faisal ibn-Hussain was declared King of the Arabs. With the carrot of independence dangled under his nose by the ever enterprising British, and under the auspices of Colonel T.E. Lawrence, better known as Lawrence of Arabia, he led his people in a successful revolt against their Turkish rulers. It is noteworthy that as far back as that time the Gurkhas had history in the region. Riding their camels across the desert against the Turks, a detachment from a brother battalion, the 3/4th Gurkha Rifles, served under Lawrence of Arabia.

At the culmination of World War I, Iraq had been carved out from the rump of the defeated Ottoman Empire. It was bordered by Iran to its east and by Syria and the Arabian Desert to its west. It shared the mountains of Turkey in the north and north-east and slipped into the Persian Gulf in the south and south-east.

When time came to make good her promise, Britain was loath to give up her foothold in this area which was the air and land link between India and British-controlled Palestine and the Suez Canal. Consequently, it was negotiated that Iraq remain a British Mandate ruled by King Faisal ibn Hussain until, finally, in 1930, under a 25-year treaty, it would gain sovereignty – with, of course, the continued agreement that Britain would be allowed to transport troops through Iraq when necessary, and retain the use of all railways, rivers, ports and airfields. She would, as well, maintain two air bases, one at Shaibah, and the second at Habbaniyah, a town approximately three hundred miles due north of Basra. Additionally, Iraq would provide protection for those vital pipelines running from the oilfields of Mosul and Kirkuk to Haifa on the Mediterranean coast. That was the deal forged.

By the onset of World War II, however, Arab nationalism had grown, stemming from a sense of betrayal with the Balfour Declaration of 1917, whereby Britain had promised to support the establishment of a Jewish homeland in Palestine. This division of Palestine, followed by more broken promises, inflicted deep wounds and a festering anti-British sentiment.

Through the ensuing years, the Arab perception of British double-dealing was deeply exacerbated by the ongoing Jewish immigration and settlement policy which resulted in the displacement of large numbers of Palestinians. They lost their homes, their lands and their country. This dispersal of a people would create a desperation that would rift the area and, eventually, spawn a breed of terrorists who would inflict mayhem on the world and plague generations to come.

The Iraqi government, now under the Premiership of General Nuri-as-Said, had been pro-British. But, on 3 April 1941, Arab nationalism had culminated in a military coup by a group of Iraqi generals calling itself the 'Golden Square.' They were led by the Prime

Minister, Rashid Ali al-Ghaylani who was leaning towards Germany on the desperate premise that it would help him rid his country of the English. Since Iraq was strategic to Allied war efforts, it was essential to put a stop to this mutual backscratching with the enemy and, hence, the sudden rush of British troops to preserve His Majesty's interests in the area.

Unfortunately, too many wrongs had been done to be righted, and time would prove this to be a mere stopgap rather than a solution to the growing problem. In years to come history would, sadly, not only repeat itself in this part of the world, it would, eventually, engulf the rest of humanity in painful violence and mistrust.

CHAPTER FIVE

Childhood's Footsteps

And when the summer heat is great and every hour intense,
The Katthal Champa's subtle flowers intoxicate the sense.
Ah, see the marble temple wall, long white reflections make;
The echoes of its silvery bells are blown across the lake.
The evening air is very sweet and from small secret bowers
Come scents of Moghra trees in bloom and Oleander flowers.

– Violet Nicolson, *The Garden of Kama*, "Story of Udaipore"

THE CONVOY SAILED WEST, dwarfed by the mighty ocean. The deep solitude of that immense surround of empty water was in sharp contrast to the situation aboard ship. There, one could hardly find elbow room to move. Despite the overcrowding, however, there were times one could steal brief intervals of near peace.

In the quiescent hours of an upcoming dawn, when the world was still blushed and dewy, barely touched by the first brush-strokes of light, and the melee of day was yet stilled in sleep, one could catch a breath of fresh, salt-spangled air while enjoying a first ciga-rette up on deck. Then too, at day's end, Santi found the hours of deep night lent themselves to quiet reflection as well. A stroll on the empty deck, with starlit skies overhead and only silent shadows for company, was a good time for contemplation and communion with one's thoughts. But, day or night, always present, were nudging reminders of the impending war as the ships zigzagged, constantly on the lookout for danger.

Santi had seen nothing that compared to the nightsky out at sea. The ships maintained a complete blackout; so much so, even the glow of a cigarette on deck during hours of darkness, small as it was, could spell disaster, and was strictly prohibited. Overhead, however, a million stars glittered in a jewelled canopy stretched across the heavens. A few hung so low and bright, one imagined an ethereal lamplighter had passed by and only just reached up to light them. Cradled on those dark waters one felt strangely suspended between the heavens and the earth – fathomless, silent, except for the throb of the ship's engine, running like an insistent heartbeat through the infinite stillness.

Santi wondered if an unborn child felt the same: floating, suspended in its dark amniotic fluid, the maternal heartbeat permeating its surroundings, reverberating through its entire being, just as he could feel the soft pounding of the ship's heart pulsing through his body. In a way, it might be said that both were on a journey into the unknown embrace of the fates...

He thought of the last time he had felt the waters move beneath him. It had felt quite different then. School holidays had brought a much looked-for journey from Calcutta to his Grandfather's house in Dhaka, made by train and river steamer. He remembered the mounting anticipation as he neared Dhaka and Dadu's house. The ferry had carried him across the broad waters of the Padma, or Podda as the mighty river Ganges comes to be known once it leaves West Bengal to enter East Bengal. What memories he cherished of those childhood years! There was a timeless quality about them. Even now, so far removed in time and place, he could smell the fragrant spices of the chicken curry, taste the mutton curry served with steaming hot rice on the boat. The recollection made his mouth water! As for the *bakorkhani*! Ah, those rolled-out rounds of buttery soft flatbread beggared description! The light, flaky layers, so delicate they simply melted in one's mouth...

All at once, this unbidden memory from his childhood brought an intense sense of isolation, of being unmoored, out of place. Santi remembered, with a rush of nostalgia, the warm feeling of homecoming as the steamer chugged down the Podda after pulling out of Goalando – a place famous for its *pathkhir*, a delightful confection of thickened sweet cream wrapped in banana leaves, the perfect round-off to a perfect meal.

Now, he was sailing away from all that was known to him, leaving behind the comfort of familiar surroundings. He found himself among those who were alien to his background, with neither understanding nor appreciation for his culture or his customs. A momentary stab of self doubt gripped him as to the wisdom of his actions. What would Dadu have thought of his precipitous decision? The remembrance stirred, once more, his grief over the loss of his Grandfather, a patriot and freedom fighter who had passed away barely a year and a half ago, at the outbreak of this war.

His maternal grandfather was a man who stood very tall in Santi's memory. Lalit Mohan Rai had been a barrister in Dhaka in East Bengal. His main residence and office had been at 67 Lokkhi Bazaar, auspiciously named after the goddess of wealth. He had been a *zamindar* as well, owning lands in the village of Shati Para which he rented to the *projas*, the tenant farmers who cultivated the local crops of jute and paddy. The proceeds were shared fair and square between landlord and tenant, after almost two-thirds had been taken first in land taxes, compliant with the unpopular Sunset Law imposed by the British Government.

Since Shati Para was down river from Dhaka, the commute to Dadu's *zamindar bari*, country-squire's house, was made on one of Grandfather's two small steamers that plied the Buri Ganga, a small residual tributary of the main river Ganges. The journey was usually undertaken by the family during the *pujo* holidays, the season of festivals that celebrated the various Hindu goddesses.

Grandfather's country house was in the district known as Naroshinghadwip or, colloquially, simply as Norshingdi. Literally translated, it meant the island of the lion-man deity. Santi could picture Grandfather's home as clearly as if it were yesterday. Four long, unpretentious brick buildings that bordered the four sides of a central courtyard; two of the four buildings were single-storied and two were double-storied, home to all manner of aunts, uncles, siblings and cousins who lived together in the tradition of the joint family system. The property stood by the river and, not far from it, on the riverbank, stood a house of worship open to all. On the other side of the house lay a lake covered, for the most part, with *podho, kochuri pana* and *shapla*, that dense growth of lotus blossom, water hyacinth and water lily that flourished so verdantly throughout the countryside of Bengal.

A tall, straight man with white hair, Lalit Mohan Rai refused the use of a car if he could help it. He had eschewed western dress as well. He would be seen striding along, his black umbrella employed as a walking stick, always attired in a *dhuti-panjabi*, that male attire of a long, loose shirt for the upper body, with the lower body wrapped in five yards of fine, white, hand-woven *tap* cotton, or a ruder variety of mill-spun cloth. This latter garment, often edged with a slim black border – or gold if a special occasion called for it – was worn neatly hand-pleated in front, the remainder passed between the legs, front to rear, where it was pulled up and tucked into the waist at back to form a loose pant of sorts, leaving the *kocha* or pleats to swing elegantly in front. Dadu's garments were always made from local cloth, and his *panjabi* or *kurta* was made of *khadi*, a coarse hand-spun cotton.

During the *Pujos*, a *khadi dhuti panjabi*, or a *khadi sari* was given to each male or female member of his household, without distinction or preference for family members, domestic help or guests. A staunch advocate of widow remarriage, a heretofore unthinkable concept in India, he set an example by promoting the marriage of his second son to a young widow from Chittagong.

As was customary, Lalit Mohan Rai and his wife, Kushum Kumari Rai, had an ample family of five sons and three daughters. One day, on a postprandial walk with Santi, he had pointed to the gnarled, old banyan tree at the far end of his property. He had explained to his first-born grandson that a family was much like that great, stalwart *bot gach* spreading its ancient branches, reaching wide to let down aerial roots, each root growing to form a sturdy trunk of its own, to branch out, to let down more aerial shoots, on and on, carefully building a canopy of passages, arches and hallways. Similarly, he proclaimed, a family grew into a mighty living edifice, independent yet connected, each part giving and drawing sustenance, wisdom and strength from the next.

Lalit Mohan Rai's own family was a prime example. His first-born son, Nripendra Kumar, was closely followed by Surendra Kumar and then by Hemendra Kumar. Not long after, Kiron Kumar swelled the ranks of the growing family and, last of all, bringing up the rear, was the youngest son, Bimal Kumar. He was blessed with three daughters as well, Usha Moyee, Sorojoni Bala and Chhaya Rani, who were born at varying intervals between the boys. The family name of Rai would evolve later into Roy.

Besides these names endowed at birth, with each successive generation, the children of a large family bestowed their elders with certain honourific titles. As a mark of respect, these were earned simply by way of family rank, and, oftentimes, embellished by some child's playful whim or mispronunciation. The whys and wherefores were unimportant.

Accordingly, the next generation that made its way into the Rai family did not refer to the aunts and uncles by their proper names. Instead, Usha Moyee became Boro Mashi or Senior Aunt, Sorojoni Bala was known as Mejo Mashi or Middle Aunt, and Chhaya Rani, being the youngest, was appropriately called Chhoto Mashi or Small Aunt.

Likewise, Nripen Kumar, henceforth, became Boro Mama or Elder Uncle; Suren Kumar (was he especially generous with gifts or sweets?) earned the title Dhan Mama, Bountiful Uncle; Hemen Kumar became Mejo Mama or Middle Uncle; and Kiron Kumar, by some long-forgotten prompt of whimsy, would venture forth as Phool Mama, Flower Uncle. Finally, Bimal Kumar was ascribed his place in the ranks as Kutti Mama, Little Uncle.

There was nothing little about any of Lalit Mohan Rai's children. Like him, they were tall and well-built. The girls were well above average at a height of five foot six inches to five foot nine inches, while the boys were all above six feet tall. In fact, it was later considered that 'Kutti' Mama might have been somewhat of a misnomer for Bimal Kumar, who made for the strangest sight as he zipped down the road at full throttle in his tiny Fiat car, his long legs scrunched behind the steering wheel, his head protruding out of the sunroof, much like that of a giraffe's.

Lalit Mohan Rai was proud of his country and his heritage. One day soon, India would achieve her independence and, when that day came, she would have to be prepared for the responsibility. Consequently, Lalit Mohan Rai decided it would be expedient to send some of his sons abroad. The usual choice would have been England but, in protest of British Rule, he decided otherwise.

Of his five sons, Boro Mama was needed in Shati Para to run the estate and care for the paddy and jute fields, while Kutti Mama was too young to be sent out into the world quite yet. Ergo, the remaining three sons were dispatched abroad – Dhan Mama and Phool Mama to America, the former to Harvard, the latter to MIT, and Mejo Mama forthwith to Germany. All three earned engineering degrees.

Upon their return, Dhan Mama and Phool Mama established Jadavpur Engineering College which would expand to become Jadavpur University, just outside Calcutta. When Mejo Mama returned, all five brothers joined in a venture to establish Bengal Lamps Ltd. and Belrex – manufacturing light bulbs and electric fans, respectively. The first exclusively Indian company, it would provide employment for the flood of displaced refugee families who would later pour over the border from East Bengal into West Bengal during India's bloody partition.

Santi's childhood memories of Grandfather's house were fond, crisp and clear. Upstairs, in the two-storied building that had housed him, were numerous family bedrooms, the *pujo* or *thakur ghor,* i.e. the prayer room, and the *atur ghor* or child-bearing room. Both the *pujo ghor* and the *atur ghor* were much used by the women in the family. Morning and evening the call of the conch shell would be heard accompanied by the sound of bells and the aromas of *dhoop* (incense) that pervaded the *pujo ghor* during, and after, worship. As for the *atur ghor,* that room was surprisingly busy, what with all the comings and goings of a considerably large joint family where someone or the other always seemed in the throes of adding to it.

On the ground floor, Dadu's office occupied one end of the building. The other end was Dida's, Grandmother's, domain. Here were the eating and cooking areas. Nearby, in the courtyard, stood a cement tank from where water was collected, and where the men and servants could wash and bathe al fresco any time they pleased. The women's ablutions, naturally, always took place in the privacy of an enclosed bathroom.

The eating area was a semi-enclosed porch, unencumbered by furniture so the floor could be washed spotlessly clean following every meal. In one corner was kept a stack of *pirhis*, used for seating – small, square wooden stools that sat an inch or so off the floor. At mealtimes the *pirhis* were set out appropriate to the count of people who happened to be staying in the house at the time.

Seated cross-legged on a *pirhi*, each person received a large brass *thala* or platter with a heaped mound of rice. Several small *batis*, brass bowls, were arranged as well on the *thala* for the various dishes that were to be served. Individual brass tumblers were provided for water.

Food was simple yet substantial: hot rice with a dollop of *ghee* was the basis on which the meal was built. One might start with a slice of *baygun* or *kumro phool bhaja*, delicately fried brinjal or pumpkin flower, or perhaps some crisply fried bitter melon to stimulate the appetite; some *dal*, lentils cooked, day to day, in a variety of ways; a *torkari* of vegetables; sweet chutney made of tomatoes and dates or raisins; and a fish curry – usually the local *ileesh* (hilsa), *bhetki* or *rui* (grass carp) – prepared in a simple, light gravy, or more elaborately with yogurt, or coconut milk or, at times, a ground paste of mustard seeds. On rare occasions a meat curry would be served, and chicken curry was an infrequent and much anticipated delicacy indeed. To refresh the palate, one ended the meal with *mishti doi*, a yogurt made with *gur* prepared from the sweet dark sap of the date palm, or one of the delectable sweetmeats for which Bengal is so rightly famous. The widows in the family cooked and ate separately since widows were, traditionally, strict vegetarians – and for some reason no one could quite fathom, Santi insisted the food prepared in their kitchen, somehow, tasted better.

The optimum time for hilsa was during the rainy season when the fish was at its most tasty. After the gusty thunderstorms of *Kal Boishaki* (April) had blown in and out with their dark drama and dire warnings of impending summer, the blistering heat would begin in earnest, heralding the month of *Joishttho* (May). Through the long summer days, *Joishttho* roams in search of her sibling, *Ashaar* (June), and as they journey, one following the other, their feet scorch the earth leaving man and beast gasping for reprieve. But they are not without bounty; by way of recompense, they bring with them that king among fruit – a wealth of mangoes, abundant in variety, flavour and sweetness.

And so the sisters of summer hold court till, finally, at the very pinnacle of their reign, when the sweltering days seem never ending, and the long afternoons quiver with heat, a subtle change is felt in the air; a strange expectancy stirs earth and sky as dark clouds gather as for the staging of a play. All at once the opening notes of a thunderstorm roll and crash, like the cymbals of the gods overhead. And, as arterial lightning rips across the sky, in a sudden flash *Borsha*, the monsoon, arrives, bringing with her the season of misty, undulating rains. With her first footsteps come raindrops like a tinkling of anklet bells, with her first cool kiss the sun-baked earth brings forth the sweet, steamy scent of newborn life. Slowly, she begins her seductive dance. Like a temptress she lets fall her muslin sari of rain, winding it around the parched countryside, baring her sinuous curves to the fingers of the wind. Faster and harder she dances, till the gentle maiden turns into a whirling dervish, sweeping all before her in a torrent that deluges road, river and field into a seeming sea of water. This is the season of *Shrabon* (July), when the monsoon is at its most tumultuous and the heavens are split asunder with gigantic storms of thunder and lightning that make the earth burst forth with the birthing of new life.

It is during the dance of the monsoon that the fish begin to spawn, and their tiny eggs are considered a great delicacy. Children sing a little ditty composed by Poet Laureate Rabindranath Tagore, eulogizing this special time of year: *"Ilshaguri, Ilshaguri, ileesh maccher deem...*myriad dancing raindrops like the hilsa fish's eggs..."

The room that Santi and his sisters were most partial to was, without a doubt, the storeroom. Here, in addition to everyday kitchen essentials, *boyems* held delectable treasures – these large pottery jars were filled with mango *aachars* and lime pickles; chutneys of *kul* and tamarind; as well as *moa,* the sweet, sticky balls of crisp puffed-rice rolled in *gur* syrup; *aam shotto,* sheets of sun-dried mango juice; sesame and coconut *laddoos* the size of large marbles, and other seasonal delicacies. The keys to this heaven of delights were always kept tightly tied to the end of Lokhi's sari, the maidservant who ruled the household with an iron fist. They dangled tantalisingly over her left shoulder, just out of reach of tiny mischievous fingers…except, that is, when she fell asleep!

In between the office at one end and the food areas at the other, were the rooms where the guests slept. Usually, the guests were those clients of Dadu's who had neither the means to pay him nor the wherewithal to afford their accommodation. Their sojourn usually lasted the period it took to solve their problems; although, in one such case, the guests remained to become permanent members of the family.

These were two married sisters, Jhoompa and Janoki. Left on their own in the village while their husbands were away in town pursuing work, they had attracted the unwelcome attentions of a local lout who would harass them when they went to draw water from the well, or wash clothes in the river. Finally, when the sisters could endure his behaviour no longer, they decided to teach him a lesson. The next time the man accosted them, the sisters beat him; and when he fled like the coward he was, he hit his head against a low-hanging branch and keeled over dead.

Gossip of the incident spread, leading to unsavoury rumours; the husbands, believing their wives to be compromised, abandoned them without any means of support or defence. This was exactly the kind of ignorance and prejudice Lalit Mohan Rai fought so hard against. Brought to his attention, both sisters were given shelter in his home in Norshingdi where they stayed in an upstairs room with the rest of the family. He fought their case successfully on the grounds of self-defence and paid for their education thereafter. The children called them *pishi*, which denoted an aunt from the father's side, and Grandfather fondly gave them the *daak nam* or pet names of Hashi and Khushi – with the blessing that their lives be filled with just that, Laughter and Joy. And the blessing must indeed have worked, for, years later, Hashi Pishi became a highly regarded teacher at Kamanissa School and College, while Khushi Pishi immigrated to America where she married again and lived a full and contented life. Their younger brother's story had no less of a happy ending – educated by Dadu as well, he rose to become an eminent judge in Calcutta. Thus it was that Lalit Mohan Rai's family grew exponentially, not only with the help of his wife, but through his many altruistic deeds as well.

Being the first-born grandchild, Santi was his grandfather's favourite, though the old man would never admit it. To the boy, his grandfather was his idol. That, however, did not mean Dadu could be disobeyed, or his words taken lightly. Santi recalled an incident in the city house in Dacca. He had been about eight years old and had gone up to the roof to play. Hearing his grandmother call, he had run, helter skelter, down the spiral stairway behind the house, lost his footing and tumbled to the ground. Fortunately, he did not fall far; unfortunately, he landed mere inches from where Misri the cook was slicing vegetables on his dangerously sharp *boti*, an instrument with a wickedly curved sickle-blade set erect in a wood board.

The shock of seeing his master's young grandson land practically on top of the deadly blade sent Misri into what could only be described as an acute apoplectic fit. With an enormous yell he had jumped up, almost falling over backward in a tangle of feet. When he stopped spluttering, and recovered his breath, he shook his fists and, bellowing at the top of his voice, he had called upon all the gods in heaven to bear witness to his anguish and suffering at the mischief he was made to endure. Finding a *khonti* near to hand, the irate cook snatched up the metal spatula and, brandishing it above his head, he chased after Santi hurling hideously violent threats of dismemberment at the *shoitan chelé*, the devil child, for having frightened him almost out of his wits. His quarry very wisely fled and stayed hidden till things quieted down somewhat.

Meanwhile, brought out by the commotion, Dadu was apprised of his grandson's near miss by the still shaken cook. After that it was expressly forbidden for the children to go up to the roof alone. Dadu promised, should anyone dare disobey his orders, he would take his cane to the offender's backside and make sure he rendered it a painful shade of bright red that would linger for at least a week.

Not too long after, while playing outside, Santi happened to spot a kite fight taking place in the sky, high above some nearby rooftops. Caught up in the thrill of battle, he forgot his grandfather's warning and dashed up to the roof for a better view. Kite fighting was a skilled sport, and kites were carefully chosen and prepared. Each flyer mixed his own bonding concoction of ground glass and raw egg to reinforce his kite string, turning it into a razor sharp *manja* that would, hopefully, annihilate any opponent foolhardy enough to come within striking distance.

That day the kites fought well, with many close calls; first one kite and then the other, dodging, dipping, attacking, escaping in the very nick of time. Running up and down the terrace, Santi followed the aerial fight, his eyes glued to the two contenders, oblivious of all else.

All at once, one kite swooped in and slashed the *manja* of the other. It was done! With a victorious shout of *bhokatta* from the winner, the defeated kite swirled and spiralled uncontrollably on the breeze, making a beeline for Grandfather's roof.

With all caution thrown to the winds, Santi chased the dancing kite across the roof. His hands stretched upward, his eyes focussed only on the prize, he leapt off his two-storied terrace onto the neighbour's roof just as he had done dozens of times before – except this time he misjudged the distance – and he fell between the two buildings, his grandfather's warning coming too late to mind.

Fortunately, the space between the houses was narrow, so he bounced as he fell, first off the wall of one building and then off the wall of the other, all the way down to the ground. This broke his fall, and although it broke his left arm as well, all things considered, he got away otherwise unscathed. The errant boy was rushed into the house by a panic-stricken Phool Mama. As he was carried in, with the consequences of his misdeed looming large on his mind, he pleaded with his uncle, "Please, Phool Mama, *please*, don't tell Dadu…"

Lalit Mohan Rai had not only been a man of principle, he had been a fervent patriot and nationalist as well. He had defended many a freedom fighter, those who could afford his services and those who could not. Eventually, the British jailed him for "aiding and abetting in subversive acts against the British Raj." While he languished in jail, speculation grew from a rumour that he had depleted a large part of his resources helping those in need. He had built a local school, and it was common knowledge even his life insurance money had gone towards aiding the victims of a riot-stricken village, a result of the burgeoning mistrust between Hindus and Muslims; a mistrust that was being fanned into a conflagration by political elements on both sides while the canny British, seeing the division as a distraction from the fight for independence, quietly let them have at it.

The majority of Lalit Mohan Rai's tenant farmers were Muslim; yet, despite his being a Hindu, they were devoted to their *zaminder*. When the rumour got around that his past generosity had left him without adequate means to pay the high bail required for his release, they started a collection; each contributed what little he could afford, no matter the pittance. Eventually, a colleague came to his aid. Chittaranjan Das, a famous Bengali barrister who had been dubbed *Deshbandhu*, Friend of the Country, stood in his defence. And so, it was through the intercession of friends and well wishers Lalit Mohan Rai was finally released.

The day Dadu was due to return, the *projas* waited on the *ghat* for the steamer to bring him home. The riverbank was a sea of white Muslim caps as far as the eye could see. It was that special time of evening, just before twilight, known in Bengal as *go dhooli* – the hour of cow dust – when a golden haze of dust is stirred and raised, shimmering, into the dwindling sunlight by village cows returning home from the fields. And that day, as dusk began to settle over the world, and the hot air began to cool beneath the soft touch of evening breezes, they brought with them the mingled perfumes of flowers from both land and water; and the river boatmen's song came wafting across, haunting and beautiful in its melody.

> *Waters glisten and sunbeams quiver,*
> *The wind blows fresh and free.*
> *Take my boat on your breast, O River,*
> *Carry me out to sea.*

When Dadu set foot on the *ghat*, a great welcoming cry of "*Raja Babu ki joi*" swelled into a crescendo, "Long life to our venerable master!" Dadu had come home to his people and it was plain to see, regardless of caste or creed, he was revered and loved by them all.

CHAPTER SIX

The Adventure Begins

"It seems a shame," the Walrus said,
"To play them such a trick,
After we've brought them out so far,
And made them trot so quick!"

– Lewis Carroll, *Alice Through the Looking Glass*

MAY 5, 1941: THAT night the convoy reached the mouth of the Shat-al-Arab, the confluence of those two ancient rivers, the Tigris and the Euphrates, which runs from their meeting point one hundred and forty miles before emptying itself into the Persian Gulf.

Dilbahadur had already packed Santi's effects, and his tin trunk stood by the door, ready for disembarkation the following morning. Earlier in the day, Santi had checked his list of supplies in the ship's dispensary; now, with the ship swaying gently at rest, he was seeing to his personal belongings before turning in for the night when there was a knock on his cabin door.

He opened it to find Jack, who had come over from the *Devonshire*. He was leafing through a thick sheaf of papers. "Here you go, Doc," he said briefly, drawing out a short stack which he handed to Santi.

Santi thanked him, glancing quickly through the last-minute orders and checklist of inventory.

"All set are you?" the Adjutant enquired. "Tonight's our last aboard these old tubs, and I'd like to make sure all is in order when we disembark at Basra tomorrow. First impressions and all that, you know." He grimaced. "Won't do to make a bad start, now, would it."

"Not to worry, sir, I'll have my end sorted," Santi promised.

"Right you are then. Tomorrow we make our acquaintance with the land of 'A Thousand and One Nights'; we shall soon see what sort of magic it has to offer." He didn't seem too optimistic, however, for as he walked away Santi heard him mutter, "But *I* shan't be holding my breath."

The following morning, they weighed anchor once again and steamed eighty miles upstream, past sandy shores lined with date palms. It was late afternoon when they arrived at Basra's port of Margil with its large wharves and railway station, but near dusk before they finally disembarked amid the usual commotion of an army with all its wartime paraphernalia. After standing around for hours in the crowded quarters of the sweltering ship, loaded down with kit and caboodle, everyone was eager to get ashore. But relief was short-lived, for no sooner had they done so than they suffered their first attack – concerted and vicious – by swarms of flying insects. Some magic! Santi thought, wryly.

As a precautionary measure they had made their way into cover provided by a thicket of palm trees in the Port Trust gardens. So far, however, they had met with no opposition except for the combined onslaught of heat and insects. This was the height of summer and temperatures ran approximately 43 to 49 degrees Centigrade (110 to 120 degrees Fahrenheit), with humidity at a hundred percent. The rivers were flooded, as was usual this time of year, turning the surrounding lowlands into marshy lakes wherein human habitations seemed to float, like Noah's Arks, in the flood waters.

They bivouacked in tents and tried to get some rest, but sleep was impossible. When the flies abated at night, mosquitoes abounded; and then there were those devilish little sand flies, and the dust, which no mosquito net – had they had any – could keep out. After that wretched first night on land, they made their way, in the early hours of the morning, to the Jubaila barracks and prepared to settle in. But it was not to be.

Basra was as ancient as history itself and its heart was the old city of Ashar. It sat five miles downstream, held by the 2/7 Gurkhas of 20th Brigade; but now it seemed the rebels were hammering at its gates and urgent assistance was required to hold them back. And so, a return to the Port of Margil it was. They hurried to embark once again and proceed downstream to where Ashar lay in distress. Arriving at the old city, however, it was discovered that order had, once more, been restored; the rebels had been beaten back, and there was little to do other than help secure the area and, for the curious, perhaps take a look around the city.

Indeed, it was akin to taking a step back in time. Here, amid a profusion of oleander flowers, could be seen the old Arab architecture known as *shansheel* or *mashrabiya*. The buildings, with their wood-lattice facades and balconies, peered down into narrow, winding streets and covered bazaars, where the aroma of spices and coffee mingled with the stench of rotting garbage.

It soon became apparent, however, that Basra was no Arabian Nights city – not by a long shot! The magical *Basorah*, as once it was known, seemed a fairytale place of mysterious canals, creeks and palaces. Now, these waterways choked with contents, much mercifully unrecognisable, threaded the city doing little to enhance it. Basra could only be described as parched, pungent and putrid. The fact that it had, of late, suffered from an epidemic of cholera, merely added to its pitiful state and air of decay.

This land they stood upon was heralded as the cradle of civilization. What had become of all that learning, that beauty and greatness? Sadly, one wondered what catastrophe could have destroyed it so completely. Was it the ravaging hordes of Gengiz Khan? Or Timur Lang? Or both? Whatever it was, it was glaring proof of man's unending stupidity. And here they were again, Santi thought wryly as he made his way back to camp, about to unleash more of the same.

Three days later the Battalion retraced its steps to Margil to safeguard that vital port's railway station and nearby airport. A few scant miles north lay the Island of Sinbad. In name only, alas, for gone was the enchanted haunt of that fabled adventurer where, so legend had it, once stood the Tower of Sinbad. Today, it took a powerful leap of imagination to see that little island, cowering close to the riverbank, as anything but a few ruins, a sorry heap of rubble.

Further north, approximately sixty miles from Margil, where the Tigris and Euphrates merged into the Shatt al Arab, at the very tip of their delta, lay Al Qurna. It was thought by some to be the actual Garden of Eden where, according to the bible, all creation began. A twisted, gnarled stump that purported to be the tree of Adam and Eve was all that remained of that supposed birthplace of mankind. It was impossible to glean truth from fable; but, if true, here was a moral if ever there was one!

Though some things had surrendered to time, others seemed to have held it at bay. The delta's vast six thousand square miles of marshland cloistered a people who had survived, practically unchanged, since biblical times.

The fair-skinned Marsh Arabs, or *Ma'dans*, said to be descendants of the Sumerians, lived in this watery world of rushes and reeds, in floating villages held together by cane fences built into the bottom of the swamp. This prevented parts of the village from being washed away. The homes were built with a local reed called *berdi*; each house, together with a stable for livestock, rested on a floating island made up of countless layers of rushes and buffalo dung which had to be replenished every year.

The tall, long-robed Marsh Arabs and their veiled womenfolk manoeuvred the narrow waterways and canals in flat-bottomed boats. Lush with fish and fowl, ducks and geese, and water buffalo, the *Ma'dan* were completely insulated and self-sufficient in the everglades and water meadows of their delta. It was a strange world, indeed, where the past almost tripped on the heels of the present.

Returning to the present, the 2/4 was to be deployed along the north-western bank of the Shatt-al-Arab. The immediate task was to secure the Girder Creek Bridge and, a mile and a half north of that, the Habib Shawi Creek Bridge which, unfortunately, had been destroyed by Rashid Ali's rebel forces. Consequently, the next few days were spent reconnoitering the area by boat and by land. Since the enemy, however, was far better acquainted with the lay of their own land, they proved, for the most part, to be as elusive as phantoms.

The only incident of some interest took place on an expedition led by Masters. When his patrol boat finally sighted a suspicious-looking Arab vessel, it set out in hot pursuit of the prey. Through the winding waterways they gave chase until, eventually, closing in, they opened fire. Although they missed the intended target they managed, with admirable accuracy, to nail the Airport Hotel – and, more specifically, the room which housed their own Divisional Headquarters. The suspicious vessel got away, unscathed. The Big Brass at Div. HQ, understandably indignant and jumpy as the dickens, sent out immediate inquiries, "Which damn scoundrel…"

When Masters returned with his report, Col. Weallens asked him for the precise location of his little adventure and his direction of fire.

"Somewhere about…here, I should say, sir," Masters offered, taking a stab at the approximate vicinity on Willy's map. "Firing about southeast."

The strange look on Willy's face prompted Masters to enquire further and, when apprised of the complaint, he was most contrite. "I say sir, it was quite unintentional! Any casualties?"

There was the slightest of pauses. "Unfortunately, no," came the Colonel's rueful reply.

Later, for sake of appearance, a note of commiseration was delivered to Div.HQ. It read "Sorry to hear about the incident, gentlemen. Awfully glad there was no loss of life or limb." And it ended with this innocent query, "Any ideas yet as to the perpetrators?"

Men began succumbing to malaria, sandfly fever and heat stroke, all of which proved more debilitating than anything the rebels had so far thrown at them. Dysentery was another devil that plagued all and sundry; they had to be extremely careful with regard to what they ate and drank. Santi was kept busy doling out tablets: quinine for malaria, sulphaguanidine for dysentery, and salt to prevent heat stroke. Later in the war, he would begin to see the first signs of venereal disease, a consequence of lonely men away from home succumbing to the rather dubious pleasures provided by the mostly overblown crones in the local brothels.

Basra was surrounded with date palms and the fruit they bore was plentiful and delicious. There were any number of varieties available and the men feasted on the fruit – that is until they were made aware of just how the harvested dates were being processed. The method, most likely, had changed not one jot since the days of Abraham.

Date pitting was a 'cottage industry,' so to speak, carried on by generations of local women ranging from the ages of nine to ninety. The women squatted, each with a pile of dates before her, and with the speed and dexterity that can come only with years of practice, they ripped the stones from the fruit using their front teeth. Revolted by this unsavoury procedure and its abysmal disregard for sanitation and hygiene, the men foreswore the fruit altogether – and who could blame them? Nevertheless, it was a pity since dates were a good, cheap and nutritious source of energy; so much so that Santi made a half-hearted stab at explaining that the fruit actually contained too much sugar to harbour much bacteria. It was hard to be convincing, however, in light of the fact he himself was never seen to partake of the fruit from that day forward.

On 12 May, wild rumours circulated that Rudolph Hess, Hitler's right-hand man, had embarked on a secret flight from Germany to England with the fantastic idea of brokering a peace treaty between the two feuding countries. He was supposed to have crash-landed in Scotland some two days earlier, where he was immediately captured by a pitchfork-wielding farmer and clapped into prison by the astonished authorities. Could such a bizarre tale possibly be true? Nobody believed it. More than one put it down to a practical joke started by someone out of sheer boredom and passed down the pike – until, that is, a few days later when, against all odds and to everyone's utter amazement, the confounding story turned out to be fact!

On 17 May, a platoon under command of Lt. C.W. Marten was sent out to capture the still intact Girder Creek Bridge and, beyond that, the damaged Habib Shawi Bridge. In the unsuccessful skirmish that followed, Marten had the dubious honour of becoming the regiment's first battle casualty. He was brought in and handed over to the tender ministrations of Lt. Dutt and his medical orderlies.

Lt. Marten was jocularly known as 'Slogger' – he mightn't be quickest off the mark, but come hell or high water, he was sure to get stuck in and get there in the end! Now, he hobbled in and sat himself down with a sheepish grin.

"Bit slow off the mark, Doc," declared Slogger, "'fraid some blighter pipped m'left foot. Big toe, actually." He peered down at his foot, adding wryly, "Bright side though, shan't need to worry about my dratted bunion any longer…"

Neither did he have to worry about the war for a while. With only nine toes, Slogger Marten had to be replaced temporarily by someone with all the requisite parts in all the requisite places. His replacement turned out to be 2nd Lt. Peter McDowall. One glance at the young, fresh-faced tea planter from Ceylon brought a crease of worry to Col. Weallens brow – this ingenious newcomer looked to be dismayingly unversed in the ways of the world, certainly this off-kilter world they now found themselves in. Pondering the subject, the CO decided it might be wiser than not to keep something of an eye on the young pup.

CHAPTER SEVEN

A People That God Forsook

Oh Thou, who man of baser earth didst make,
And ev'n with Paradise devise the snake:
For all the sin wherewith the face of man
Is blacken'd…Man's forgiveness give…and take!

– Omar Khayyam, *Rubaiyat of Omar Khayyam*

THEIR ENCAMPMENT STOOD IN an open area alongside a canal. In a near-by spot, Santi pitched a couple of tents to accommodate the infirm. On the other side of the canal, however, he had noticed a building, shuttered and deserted. Upon some investigation, this turned out to be a school, temporarily abandoned by its students due to the hostilities.

It was here that destiny dealt Santi a card which was to change his life forever.

The caretaker of the school, he discovered, was one of its teachers; an amenable Armenian lady who, when approached, allowed that the indisposed should be housed ad interim within the school building. With further generosity, she offered assistance in tending the sick, and it was during these vigils of mercy that she introduced Santi to a potent beverage which, she informed him, was imbibed routinely throughout the entire Middle East.

Ahwa was a sweet, dark, thickly sedimented coffee – Arabic or Turkish, depending on where it was served – a concoction that shot through one's veins like a lethal electric shock, and could jolt the weariest of minds wide awake in a jiffy. Santi considered it a pity the army hadn't discovered this invaluable libation and made it a compulsory brew for all soldiers on sentry duty.

Gradually, in the days that followed, he and Samira got talking. As they worked side by side, a polite word exchanged here and there extended into courteous interest. Haltingly, words grew into sentences and sentences blossomed into conversations that built a bridge between their two cultures. And, as the acquaintance strengthened, from her side of that bridge a terrible story began to unfold which drew him across, step by painful step, into the dark world of her childhood and a way of life that was at times idyllic and at times terrifying.

"We are of Armenian-Greek descent. Our home was in southeast Anatolia, in Turkey. I was born in the old stone town of Midyat where

I lived with my father, Emanuél Kiriakos Anawis, a priest, and my mother, Susanne. I also had three brothers – Habib and Zachary who were older to me, and little Anîs, the baby of the family."

In addition to the immediate family, Samira explained, they had a large extended family and, as was the custom of their culture, it was a close-knit one.

"My father, Emanuél, had two sisters and two brothers. They were five, but the youngest brother was killed when Turks attacked their village in 1895. That left just my father, Emanuél, his brother Shamun, and two sisters, Saidé and Farida."

Aunt Saidé, known to the children as Bajo, was the eldest and lived in the ancient walled city of Diyarbekir. She was married to Samuél Khayat from Siirt; he was her second husband, and their only child was a daughter named Hedeya.

"Of all the cousins," Samira said, "Hedeya and I were closest in age and in our fondness for one another."

Santi was told that Bajo Saidé, in actual fact, had been considered past the normal age of childbearing when she married Samuél Khayat. In her first marriage she had borne six children, and she had lost them all, husband and children, killed in the intermittent Hamidian massacres of 1894-96.

In the first year of that dreadful time, four of her children were killed. A year later her husband met the same fate as he fled with their ten-year-old son from a Turkish soldier giving chase on horseback. The soldier had caught up with them, his drawn sword glinting in the sunlight as it arced through the air. Suddenly, the boy felt something warm and liquid hit his face and hands, and he glanced down to see a strange red fluid splattered all over his clothes. Frightened and confused he looked to his father, and saw, instead, a headless body running beside him, the legs still pumping away with a volition all their own, as though unaware they were lifeless with no need, any longer, to carry on.

For five days the boy had been unable to speak. Eventually, when he did, they found the body of Bajo Saidé's husband, and his head a fair distance from it, and they buried them together.

The next time the soldiers came they killed the boy in front of Bajo Saidé. And as she hunched protectively over the babe in her arms, they cut her with their swords, again and again, cursing and laughing at the sport.

She had managed, in the nick of time, to hide the family bible in the bucket used to draw water from the well, lowering it out of sight just before they came. She saved it thus, but she paid dearly. With fourteen slashes to the back of the head, neck and shoulders, she collapsed and was left for dead beside the village well. It was deemed a miracle when she was revived, but the baby, her last child, had suffocated at her breast. She had lost them all and, God have pity on her, she alone had survived to bear witness to the murder of innocents.

Bajo Saidé had survived through divine intervention, but the back of her neck had been so severely lacerated, the wounds defied stitching. The American missionary doctor declared, unequivocally, that the flesh simply would not hold any stitches. So Bajo Saidé went away and she treated herself with a poultice of her own special healing herbs till the flesh repaired sufficiently for the doctor to stitch the wounds a week later. After which, to help continue the healing process, she applied a poultice of *chekum*, a sticky paste of crushed seeds, very like peppercorns, used to draw out any infection that might occur.

Those wounds healed, but other scars remained and spread within her. Bajo Saidé had declined all ministration and sunk into a deep depression. She had withdrawn from the world for almost seven years; till, one day, through her brother Emanuél, she met Samuél Khayat. His gentle nature and kind temperament gradually drew her out so that she began to consider, once again, how sharing her life might be preferable to growing old alone. Eventually his patience won her affection and she agreed to marry him.

Under the auspices of Brother Emanuél, the couple were married in Mardin. After two years, Bajo Saidé's heart had healed sufficiently to allow just enough space for thought of another child to enter and find its place beside the six children who, till then, had filled it so completely. Slowly, the seventh child stirred and blossomed within her heart and, at last, Bajo Saidé decided it was time to try and give the little creature life.

"My aunt, Bajo Saidé, knew much about herbal remedies, and so she went looking for a special plant, a plant of the nightshade family that grows along our ancient volcanic slopes of Karaça Dagh. The root, you see, is shaped like…almost like…the form of a man. This is used for many things, and also for fertility purposes. But care must be taken, as too much can cause hallucinations, even death. And they say, when the plant is pulled from the earth, it makes a sound like the cry of a baby. It is believed that misfortune will befall anyone who hears the cry."

But Bajo Saidé knew this, of course, so when she found what she was looking for, she attached one end of a long rope to the plant, while the other end she tied to a mule. The animal was then taken safely out of earshot, till the rope was stretched tight enough that the plant could be pulled from the ground.

Bajo Saidé's efforts proved fruitful for, one day not long after, she felt something shift within her, and she knew the child that had been growing within her heart was now growing within her belly as well. Nine months later she gave birth to a girl child, a precious child she believed was both a reprieve from the guilt of her own survival, as well as restitution from God for the unbearable loss of her previous six children.

Her husband, Samuél, who had not dared believe he would be blessed thus at his age, lifted his daughter into his arms, and he was overjoyed. He swore he would protect her, come what may; and he raised her to heaven and gave thanks for this late gift from God. He vowed that this little girl would be a survivor, and so he called her Hedeya, a name with the sound of liquid music, a name both soft and strong. Hedeya, a name which meant 'warrior'.

Bajo Saidé's first husband had come from a wealthy family. Those good people had welcomed her into their fold with a fondness that continued even after she had been widowed. When she remarried, and the family came to know Samuél, they grew to like him too, and they gave Bajo that share of land which would have been hers had her first husband, their son, remained alive.

So it was that Bajo Saidé inherited large fields, a variety of orchards and vineyards, and several pigeon houses in the Christian village of Karabash, approximately three hours' journey from Diyarbekir. The fields were tended by tenant farmers, and all was overseen by Bajo's second brother Shamun and her sister Farida, both of whom lived with their families in the village itself. And so, the families shared and prospered together.

"As young children, we enjoyed our large family of many aunts, uncles and cousins, at home and at school. In the summer, our families would go down to the *Diçle*, the Tigris, where we spent a few days camping by the river. Each family had its own *houlé*, a wooden shack built on stilts, and we children loved sleeping on the roof of the *houlé* under the stars, listening to the soft darkness filled with strange little night sounds."

There were watermelon, sweet melon and cucumber fields by the river. In the silent dark, as small drowsy heads began to nod off, they would hear the watermelons grow and stretch – 'tchik', 'tchik' – expanding, till they grew so large (sometimes to 40 kgs), small children could sit on them and dangle their feet without touching the ground. These enormous melons were crisp and sugar-sweet, right down to the white rind. And after the fruit was eaten, children would hollow out the skins to place lighted candles inside. As twilight descended on the river, bringing the first cool breath of night, dozens of watermelon 'boats' would be seen floating downstream. Bobbing along in the dusk under a growing starlit night sky, they turned a fragile, uncertain world into a child's fleeting paradise.

Those soft-summered evenings by the riverside lived on like clear snapshots in the mind's eye; the children playing carefree and, when the river ebbed, digging in the sand for *juju ayis*, a stringy, black plant with a minty flavour. As the seasons changed, so too did the river. When the dry months arrived, it could be forded on foot, but when the waters were in full spate, men, mules, donkeys and horses had to be rowed across by boat.

Then there were picnics by the *fiskeya*. Samira told of the waterfall, tumbling out of the mountain, its spray caught by the sunlight and spun into fine veils of shimmering mist that sparkled with a million dancing rainbows. In winter, the waters froze into glistening icicles that hung like fine crochet lace along the edges of rocks that stood like the ramparts of some radiant, glittering ice palace in a fairytale.

Karabash stood to the east of Diyarbekir. The three-hour journey crossed the river to the small village of Q'iterbal where the boat would unload its passengers and cargo, and from there one proceeded on foot to Karabash. The name translated to 'black heads' and may have had something to do with the Karabash sheepdogs specific to the area. However, legend has it that it derived from an order of black-hatted monks who once resided in the vicinity, some time long ago.

The remainder of the summer vacation would be spent here. Long, lazy afternoons in the fruit and nut orchards where one could pick fresh plump apricots warmed by the sun, ripe figs bursting with sweetness, and such a variety of nuts – walnuts, almonds, hazelnuts; and *buttam,* small clusters of nuts that could be eaten, shell and all, until they matured when only the kernel was edible.

The vineyards abounded with seven types of grapes, the boughs heavy with their clustered fruit in various shapes, sizes, and colours. The pigeon houses on the outskirts of the village were full. Hundreds of baskets hanging along the inside walls allowed pigeons to hatch every three months. The pigeons earned their keep; while their droppings were used for manure and the curing of leather in tannng, pigeon kebabs were a delicacy to be enjoyed almost every day during the sojourn in the village.

Paradise! Short-lived though it was, in those tender childish minds it forged memories that endured through pain and terror and lasted a lifetime.

"Hedeya and I, and also our cousins Anisa and Sayïda, all went to boarding school, the American High School of Mardin. Anisa was one of Uncle Shamun's daughters, and Sayïda one of Khalé Farida's – Aunt Farida's – daughters. Our school, it was run by American missionaries. Our principal, Miss Fandanga called Mardin 'a citadel city', Roman built. Because it is on the side of a rocky hill, the gardens of the upper houses become the roofs of the lower houses, like terraces, all the way down. When it was time to return to boarding school, I travelled about forty-five miles west from my hometown of Midyat to Mardin. Hedeya, Anisa and Sayïda, their journey was a much greater distance from Diyarbekir."

At the end of the holidays, Anisa and Sayïda would bid goodbye to their families in Karabash and set out for Hedeya's house in Diyarbekir. This medieval city, hunkering atop a basalt plateau high above the right bank of the *Diçle* River, lies along the old Silk Route to China – the very route once travelled by Alexander the Great on his way to India. The city was famous for its distinctive silver and copper artefacts, as well as its carpets, intricately woven with sumptuous motifs of animals, birds, trees and flowers. These symbols of heaven and earth, fertility and fortune, life and eternity derived their vibrant hues from nature's bounty – tobacco, madder root, oak apple and walnut, and from pomegranate, indigo and chamomile. Known in its early history as Amida, the city changed hands several times; Assyrians, Macedonians, Romans, Persians, Arabs, Seljuks, and more came and went till, finally, in 1515, the city fell under Ottoman rule.

Black basalt walls, built during the Byzantine era, still encircle the city like a grim girdle five and a half kilometres long, with ramparts wide enough for a carriage to be driven along. It holds sixteen keeps and five gates, with a fortified citadel to the northeast. The four main gates were Yenni Kapu or the New Gate that faced the river to the east; Dagh Kapu, the mountain gate that led to the city of Harput in the north; Urfa Kapu led to the western road and the city of Urfa; and, lastly, Mardin Kapu took a traveller to Mardin in the south. All gates stood heavily fortified between two semi-circular pillars, guarded by day and securely locked down for the night.

Just outside the Mardin Gate stood the *Deliller Hani,* the black basalt and white limestone inn where guides would stop their caravans to unload, reload, replenish and refresh before continuing their journey. The road from here was steep, and in order to prevent horses and mules from slipping, it was built to zigzag down the mountain, the cobbled pathway slithering down like an uncoiling, scaly snake. Here, too, outside the Mardin Gate, a short way from the city was the *Khisla,* the army academy and opposite it, on the other side of the road, stood the military hospital, the *hastanesi.*

Before their departure for school, the girls would spend their last night in Hedeya's large three-storied house on Kuçuk Kewaz Serit in Diyarbekir. Hedeya's father, Samuél Khayat, was known to the children as Baba Taht. It meant 'Father from Below' – a name given by Hedeya when she was little because he spent so much time at work on the lower floor of the house. Both Samuél and Bajo would fuss over the girls as they prepared them for their journey.

Each girl carried her own bedding and bundle of clothes; and packed along with her belongings there would always be a plentiful supply of nuts, dried fruits and plaited *kileecha* biscuits sufficient for the journey and, later, for school as well. This pack of essentials would be thrown onto the backs of the mules the girls would ride.

Rendered thus into the safekeeping of God and *Burak katirçi,* the caravan headman, they would set off through the Mardin Gate and down the rough and rocky road on the three-day trek to the American Missionary School in Mardin. (Years later the same journey undertaken by car was a matter of a few scant hours.)

The caravan travelled in a long line; two children to a mule, all except the *peshang* or lead mule which carried no load at all other than a large, sonorous bell that bade the others follow where it led. Through daylight or darkness, through halcyon weather or inclement, that diligent little animal would need no guidance. With each sure-footed stride, the deep tolling of its bell echoed from the front of the caravan, a pleasant sound as they travelled through the day. And even more so at night, when the travellers lay on the moonlit mountainside or under the desert stars with the distant clang of some passing caravan's *peshang* resounding through the stillness of the night; a beautiful, albeit, melancholy sound, the music of solitude that was at the same time reassuring, a sound both comforting and forlorn at once.

Those were the good times. The times of decency and humanity.

The times when things were as they should be. But then, it would come. Like some demented devil-storm that twisted and distorted and ravaged everything in its path. When decency was lost in savagery, and humanity was contorted into mindless butchery, till the human soul was deformed and degraded beyond all recognition and was certainly not the gift that God had given to man.

"It was the summer of 1915," Samira said. "We lost everything. Our homes, our loved ones, our way of life. My oldest brother, the Turks shot him in front of us. My father was dragged by his beard from his church, and as they stabbed him to death, they mocked him: *pray to your God, priest – ask him to save you now.* My mother ran to help him. She threw herself on him, begging them to stop. *He's a priest,* she said, *a good man who has harmed no one.* I don't think they even heard her. They stabbed her, again and again, as she tried to protect him with her body."

"And our little blonde, blue-eyed Anîs was with my mother when they did this. They dragged him away, screaming. My father always said he was God's child, marked at birth with a star just like the star of Bethlehem, on his left temple. But the Kurds have him now. Some months later, he was seen in the marketplace, riding a donkey. He was with a Kurdish woman. At least we knew he was alive."

"My brother, Habib, and I managed to escape and make our way to my school in Mardin where the American missionaries kept us safe. Eventually, when we got news that our Uncle Shamun and his family had escaped from Karabash to Qamishli, in Syria, the missionaries managed to send us to them. That's where we met cousin Anisa again and we heard that her sister, cousin Nahmeya, had been killed. Khalé Farida's husband had been killed as well – a Kurd cut off his hands because he was holding some bread. Then they cut his throat. After that Khalé Farida and cousin Sayïda were dragged off but, somehow, they escaped the death march from Karabash to Deir ez Zor and managed to reach Baghdad.

"Sayïda's older sister, Februnia, and younger brother, Edward, had not survived. Poor Februnia, beautiful girl that she was, what bestiality she endured! It doesn't bear speaking of! Their oldest sister, Rahel, and brother, Hanna, had become separated from the rest and were left behind. Later, they were rescued by the missionaries who managed to send them both to Beirut. Such loss, such suffering! Half the family gone, the rest scattered like leaves in the wind."

She paused for a moment before she spoke again. "I suppose," her voice was barely audible, "we were luckier than many, since some of us survived. And it was good to be with family again. We stayed with Uncle Shamun and his family for a year. But all that time the pain of our loss remained with us – and my nightmares! Those terrible nightmares that would not stop! Finally, Uncle Shamun felt that perhaps Qamishli was too near the old places with all their bad memories, so he sent Habib and me to visit Khalé Farida and cousin Sayïda in Baghdad.

"It was there we learned that Rahel and Hanna had been taken by a family who had managed to get passage from Beirut to Cuba. Khalé Farida gave us news, as well, of my cousin Hedeya. She and her parents had travelled to Mardin where they were caught and became separated. But somehow, God knows how, they found each other again in the terrible refugee camp in Tel Abiad." Samira shook her head as though she would clear it of the thoughts and images that crowded in there. "Deir ez Zor and Tel Abiad – cursed names of cursed places. How can anyone live in a place filled with so much suffering!

"We were told by some who survived that in Tel Abiad thousands of people had been crammed into a courtyard, no food, water or shelter, vermin-infested, most of them naked because even the clothes they were wearing had been stolen. Exhausted, starved, sick, children holding onto dead mothers, mothers clutching their dead infants. They lay, waiting for the end, a few yards away from the mass graves that were dug, each day, for the dead and, may God forgive them, the nearly dead.

In all that, it was a miracle that Baba Taht found Bajo Saidé and cousin Hedeya. He owed his life to the compassion of a Bedouin sheikh from the Anese tribe – a Muslim, a true Muslim, a man of God. We were so thankful to receive news, at last, that all three had reached Cairo safely."

Samira fell silent. In the silence, the depth of her pain was palpable. Santi could sense it, and it touched him in a troubling way; it was a pain he could find neither words nor means to assuage.

Eventually, Samira spoke again. "Habib and I moved here, to Basra. This is probably the furthest place in Iraq from Turkey. But even here the memories are with us. No matter how far we run, we will never escape that cruel past when we witnessed a whole people murdered without mercy, families destroyed, scattered like dust to the four corners of the earth. Why? What was our crime?

"Two years ago, we got news of a young man living in Istanbul. A young Kurdish man, married, with two children. He had a star on his left temple, just like the star of Bethlehem. We had found Anîs. But his name was Jemal. He had been raised a Muslim, and he was raising his children in the same faith. He remembered nothing of us. When we met him, the small memory we stirred was like a bad dream. He had become a stranger to us, our beautiful little Anîs. He had become one of them."

Samira's voice was very soft. "They heaped humiliation and destruction on our nation but, in the end, one wonders which humiliation was the greater, that of the butcher or the butchered. We have been taught that man was created in the image of God." She shook her head. "There is something wrong with that. How could this possibly be the image of God?"

CHAPTER EIGHT

The Lands Of Araby

Tweedledum and Tweedledee
Agreed to have a battle,
For Tweedledum said Tweedledee
Had spoilt his nice new rattle!

– Lewis Carroll, *Alice Through the Looking Glass*

THE IRAQIS WERE NOT quite the pushover everyone had assumed they would be. The expectation that they were a mere ragtag bunch of raw recruits who would take to their heels upon first sight of the impending British army proved to be a false one. Somehow, it seemed forgotten that this 'enemy' had but lately enjoyed the status of ally; an ally who insisted, in order to repulse any kind of attack or aggression by the enemy – then, ostensibly, the German enemy – it would require in-depth details of all relevant British manoeuvres and tactics pertaining to the defence of the very areas and installations now being fought over. The problem was, of course, that the 'ally' had now gone over to the enemy and was using the information so readily imparted to them by the British, not to defend British interests but, rather, to attack them. Moreover, with an astonishing lack of discernment for which way the wind was blowing, the British had armed Iraqi forces with the latest and best in equipment and ammunition, ironically leaving their own troops in sad short supply.

Admittedly, as a nation, the achievements of the British were in many ways much to be admired. That said, Santi often wondered at their inability to perceive themselves as anything but welcome in the eyes of an occupied country. In this case, whether their misjudgement had stemmed from arrogance or naiveté – or possibly a little of both – such a short-sighted decision made their present situation a rather unpleasant one. And it fell to one disgusted British officer, when informed his request for supplies was denied due to unavailability, to raise his glass in a succinctly caustic toast to the whole politically wrought mess – "Damn, if this isn't the bloody best of British bugger all! Perhaps we should ask the Iraquis if they could spare us some of our own supplies!"

Whatever else might be thought of the British, there is something to be said for their ability, on the odd occasion, to look themselves squarely in the eye and tell it like it is.

All that aside, at the end of the day, despite mistakes made by the powers that be, and the superior numbers of Iraqi forces, the outcome here was British victory and Iraqi defeat.

As for this army of Gurkhas, they had taken short measure of the enemy and their land and were not in the least impressed with either. From the fighting men's point of view the war so far had been no more than a few sporadic kerfuffles, a dawdle they considered a total waste of time. This became abundantly clear during a visit from Major General William J. Slim, General Officer Commanding 10th Indian Infantry Division in Iraq.

William J. Slim was a highly respected officer and leader, deeply devoted to the well-being of men under his command. True to form, while inspecting his troops on this occasion, the GOC tarried here and there to enquire into the concerns of his soldiers. One such was a JCO, a *risaldar major* from the armoured car regiment.

A *risaldar major* was a senior Indian soldier who, having risen through the ranks, held his commission from the Viceroy of India rather than the King, and was therefore known as a Junior Commissioned Officer. Now, this JCO was questioned if everything was satisfactory, and what his thoughts were, so far, on the situation in Iraq.

Not one to quibble ('rather a blood-for-breakfast sort of chap, sir', his commanding officer ruefully explained later to the General) the JCO replied, politely yet firmly, with a perfectly dead-pan face, "Bad country, *sahib*. Bad country, bad people and bad war – no fighting!"

Caught short in the moment, Major General Slim recovered sufficiently to promise the disappointed warrior a good fight in the not-too-distant future. Whereupon the *risalda major* is said to have answered – respectfully enough, albeit without much confidence either in the General's ability to remedy the situation or the Almighty's interest in doing so – "If it is the will of God."

It seemed quite clear to the old soldier that the General, being a general, might feel he had an official line of communication to the All Powerful; however, from where *he* stood, he very much doubted a resolution would be forthcoming from either party any time soon. (Cassel & Co: *Unofficial History: Field Marshal Sir William Slim*)

The heat and the plague of flies fed off each other and were an indescribable pestilence. Salt tablets were part of the daily ration and Santi reminded everyone to take their tablets regularly to replenish salt-loss due to perspiration. Despite this, men suffered heat stroke, their faces suffused and swollen, their eyes bulging, and their brains fried.

The Brigade prepared to have another go at Habib Shawi Bridge. The operation was optimistically called *Scoop*. With the help of the Australian sloop HMAS *Yarra* and its guns, it was hoped that this venture would meet with more success than had their last. In the dead of night, a recce was undertaken, and it was quite a remarkable cloak and dagger affair.

The Commander of the *Yarra* and a member of his crew, both disguised as Arabs, stole up the creek to take soundings and measure the lay of the land. Meanwhile, a large rather ramshackle house that stood by the river was selected as the most convenient spot for the placement of their back-up Vickers machine guns, its roof providing a decent all-round view of the city's immediate vicinity. Upon completion, Willie drove over for a final inspection. When he emerged from the building, he wore a worried expression and made a beeline for his Adjutant.

"I say, Jack," he hesitated, momentarily. "I do believe that place is not quite the thing. Do you realise it seems to be a…well…a house of…ahem…ill-repute?"

"A brothel, sir."

Willie nodded, anxiously. "Quite. My point exactly. Do you think it safe, or even advisable, for us to…er…you know…have the men traipsing in and out of such a place? And what about the youngsters? That cub, McDowall! You'd best keep a close eye on the lad."

"Sound idea, sir." Masters gravely promised to bear his Colonel's orders in mind. Privately, he was willing to lay a wager, neither young Peter McDowall nor anyone, unless he be suffering from a complete loss of his faculties, could possibly be in jeopardy from this particular devil of lust. Perish the thought! These were certainly no Birds of Paradise! And if ever they had been, then they had shed their plumage long since, in some forlorn, forgotten past. All in all, for the present at least, Masters was fairly confident the moral integrity and physical well-being of the men would remain uncompromised and offer no distraction to the pressing matters at hand. (John Masters, *The Road Past Mandalay*)

The clandestine operation took place under cover of darkness. Ostensibly, the assault was to proceed forward on land with 'B' Company and the Pioneer Platoon, together with a section of Sappers and Miners. Under command of Ginger Fullerton, this contingent made a bold show of marching forth with every intention of fully engaging the enemy. Behind this smoke screen, meanwhile, the *Yarra*, manned by the rest of the Battalion, crept stealthily up the creek to land just north of Habib Shawi Bridge. This group was to constitute the main attack.

Just before dawn, the barrage started up. The sound of machine guns, howitzers and mortars was impressive. The land party put up a great show of confusion, which turned real when it ran afoul of a well-hidden enemy machine gun. To add to the sorry mess, the protection from the armoured cars was lost when those vehicles became firmly stuck behind the lead car which had ditched in the dark.

Fortunately, under cloak of the chaos playing out on land, the *Yarra* took the enemy quite by surprise, turned the tide of battle and, none too soon for the harried land party, had the rebels on the run. They fled up the road in whatever they managed to find, and up the river in their *feluccas,* the small local boats made of wicker – their escape due largely to Colonel Weallens' orders that no women and children who might be among them should be put in danger. Ultimately, however, the outcome was a good one; though the Iraqis knew the lay of the land far better and had, at first, far outnumbered them, it wasn't long before British troops reached their objective and Basra was secured.

Afterwards, the victors gathered their wounded and their dead; the enemy was left to tend to its own. This was Santi's first actual encounter with the results of war.

In medical school he had worked with corpses, and later, as a doctor, he had seen his share of the injured and bleeding. But that had been different. The bodies lying here were a far cry from the unknown cadavers he had worked with then. These deaths were all the more awful in that they were not strangers. They were companions in arms, and this connection could not but touch him personally.

In the textbook world of a classroom, and during his internship, he had been preparing himself to help humanity. On the training field he believed he was preparing himself to protect and defend it. But this was no impersonal classroom or dispassionate training field; and here, in the real world, this first ugly experience of war left him queerly at odds with his previous, neatly devised conceptions. Sensitive to being considered an unwelcome invading force, and the instigators to boot – much the same as the British were seen in his country – he did not feel much like a saviour or protector. Who was on the side of right and who on the wrong? It was dismaying to realise that this time he might be wearing the shoe on the other foot.

So far, the Main Dressing Station had housed primarily the sick; now, the war-wounded began filling the MDS. Some of the wounds were minor enough to be patched up right there, while others had to be evacuated to the base hospital at the rear. And then there were those casualties who were beyond help – seven Gurkhas and six Madras Sappers. It was time to say farewell to some old friends – among them *Jamedar* Sakasbahadur Gurung – and give them as decent a burial as was possible in this hostile desert land so far from home; alone, without the comfort of their own religious rituals or ceremonies, with no personal epitaph to memorialize their deeds or praise their courage and loyalty. Nevertheless, memories require neither stone nor wood, they are etched in the hearts of those who remember. These men would be remembered, with honour and the deep gratitude of their brothers-in-arms. Santi prayed silently to his God and theirs that their passage be a peaceful one, unfaltering in its direction and rewarding in its destination.

———•◆•———

JUST A LITTLE OVER THREE hundred miles north of Basra, where the road turns left towards Damascus in Syria, there lies the town of Habbaniya. Here, on the banks of the Euphrates, the RAF had built a station in 1934. Known as RAF Habbaniya, originally it had been used mainly for training purposes. It was strategic as well to the gathering and dispersing of vital military and diplomatic information.

Now, called upon to make up for the shortage of regular planes and crews, the instructor pilots and pupils of RAF Habbaniya stepped up to the plate. Not only did they ferry troops and equipment across the desert skies, some of their planes were outfitted for bomb runs, and they were only too glad to pitch in and lend a hand where they could to give the enemy a proper what for.

The RAF personnel and their families were housed within the station itself, unlike the civilian workers and their kin who lived in town. When the coup took place, large numbers of civilian women and children were evacuated from Baghdad to RAF Habbaniya, pending an airlift to safety. The insurgents promptly besieged the overcrowded station, effectively thwarting plans for an airlift, and though the garrison managed to hold the enemy at bay, it soon became clear that assistance was needed.

In Cairo, responding to orders from Churchill, General Wavell, C-in-C, Middle East Forces, manoeuvred two troop formations into Iraq, one from Transjordan and the other from Palestine. Together, they formed a fast-mobile unit code-named Habforce. The objective

was the relief of the beleaguered forces in Habbaniya; and the 2/4 Gurkhas, having secured Basra, were to assist in that RAF base's defence.

On 15 May 1941, A Company, under Major J.W. Strickland, was
flown to Habbaniya as an advance party. Five Vickers Valentias and
three Douglas DC2s flew them out at dawn. The rest of the Battalion was to follow by 25 May; all except D Company – and, of course,
the ground transport – which would remain behind to hold Basra a
while longer.

Santi packed up the MDS and prepared for departure. He thanked
Samira warmly for her help and her friendship; and, as they bid each
other good luck and goodbye, she handed him a piece of paper with
a name and address on it. He was not to know at that moment, the
hand of Fate had just set the course for his life to come.

"Remember my cousin, Hedeya? Hedeya Khayat, in Cairo? We
have had no news of her in over a year and…and…all we hear are
the rumours…there have been bombings there. Who knows what
has happened with this war." She held out an old, rather faded photograph showing four young girls of varying ages. "Our last year at
school, when it all began…after that…. See, there is Anisa, and that
is Sayïda, I am in the middle. And this," she pointed to the girl on
the right, "this is Hedeya."

The girls all wore loose-fitting pinafores, their hair braided into
plaits that hung on either side of their serious young faces. Santi
looked to where Samira had pointed. The face that looked back at
him was that of a child's, but the expression in the eyes was much
older; something haunting, inscrutable about those eyes seemed to
pull one into the depths of that little girl's soul. It left him with a
sensation that was profoundly strange.

"Please," Samira's voice brought him back to the present, "if any-
time you go to Cairo, if you can, will you go and see her and Bajo
Saidé? Baba Taht is gone, but they live in Choubra still. I have written
the address. See, the street is Tir'a el Bulaqiya. Oh also, she got married, but not anymore. Now she is divorced. She is still Khayat. Just
ask her to write, to let us know all is well, yes?"

Santi was not at all sure where the war would eventually take him,
but he promised Samira he would not forget; if he reached Cairo, he
would do his best to find her cousin. It was the least he could do in
return for her help and her friendship.

Packed and ready at last, he accompanied 2nd Lt. Ronald J. Smith
and 'B' Company as they were herded into the back of a Vickers
Valentia transport biplane. Twenty-two men with all their luggage

and equipment were a snug fit that left little place for comfort. Right then, however, it was concern of a different nature that hung heavy in the air.

Though no one spoke of it, there was but one thought on every man's mind. This new business of leaving terra firma in a noisy, closed, coffin-like metal container to climb high up, suspended in the heavens, with nothing substantial between them and the ground below, was dismayingly unnatural to say the least. In truth, the very idea of it was alarming, an unnerving experience no one was looking forward to.

They boarded in silence, the doors closed, and inexorably the plane taxied, its engines revving. Then, with a sudden jerk, they thrust forward and leapt off the runway. As they made their slow, lumbering way up and across the skies, bumping and lurching through space with the earth so very, very far below, the taut expressions on those twenty-two faces grew exceedingly more anxious. Santi thanked God the journey was no longer than two hours!

To the relief of all, the first half of the flight went smoothly enough. Then, just as everyone had begun to relax somewhat, Santi heard Ronnie call out.

"I say, would you look at that!"

"What is it?" Santi shouted back.

"Well…it looks like…rather bad news, I'm afraid, Doc. I think it's… damn me, it *is* the flaming Luftwaffe!"

Luftwaffe! Heads craned in his direction as the same thought bolted through every mind: Now what! They were on a transport plane without any means of defending themselves, a prime target, plump and ripe for the picking! And all they could do was…hope? Pray? They waited glumly, the silence tense and heavy in the cabin.

After a moment, Ronnie Smith leaned back. When he spoke again, he made an admirable stab at nonchalance. "By the look of it, we could be in for a spot of bother. I must say, it's confounded bad luck being caught with our jacksies hanging in midair like this – but the pilot's probably a dab hand at this stuff, wouldn't you say?"

Dab hand or not, it was confounded bad luck indeed! Santi thought as they all braced for the coming attack. Out loud he called, "You think he might manage to outrun the blasted thing?" He already knew the answer, of course.

"Only with divine intervention, Doc," Ronnie snorted, drawn back helplessly for another quick look out the window. A moment later, he gave a jubilant yell. "What the…? Jesus!"

"What is it? What's going on?"

One minute the Heinkel had been approaching them, the next it was gone, falling back, trailing a long plume of black smoke. Smith shook his head, amazed. "I say, if that don't beat all!" He pressed an eager nose to the window. "Oh, ruddy good show!"

"If what don't beat…er…I mean…doesn't beat…what's *happening*? Smith, what the heck are you burbling on about?"

"I'll be jiggered! Wouldn't have believed it if I hadn't seen it with m'own eyes. All I can say, Doc, is one of us must have a direct line to the Almighty, because someone's prayers just got answered – sent the chappie off with a flea in his ear. Shot down, by Jove! You should have seen him nosedive – prettiest sight I ever did see!" Smith paused as a thought struck him. "I say, there must be something to this biblical land after all – I believe I've just witnessed my first miracle!"

The miracle was explained when they reached Habbaniya: a Luftwaffe Commander had been killed by 'friendly' fire when Iraqi soldiers mistakenly fired on his aircraft. Who said God wasn't listening to the good guys!

The danger was not entirely over, however, as they were soon to find out on their approach to landing at the airfield.

Habbaniya was built on low ground on the west bank of the Euphrates River. To the south rose a plateau, now an effective vantage point for the rebel forces. Behind the plateau Lake Habbaniya provided a stop-over landing area for Imperial Airways' Short Empire flying boats, enroute from England to India. These had been temporarily discontinued, of course, due to the hostilities. The main RAF airfield, as well, lay outside the fence that protected the garrison, rendering it useless under present conditions.

As a temporary solution, the Polo pitch and golf course within the fence had been turned into makeshift airstrips. It was here the Valentia carrying Santi, Ronnie and 'B' Company landed – as luck would have it, smack dab in the middle of a bombing raid. The Germans were using Mosul and Baghdad as bases to launch their bombing runs. The Valentia managed to land, and scurried down the improvised airstrip, chased by a Heinkel. Two bombs hit the runway close upon its tail. The minute the plane stopped, the door was flung open and everyone piled out as fast as they could, making a mad dash for the slit trenches. None too soon as it happened. The German Heinkel came back for one more vicious swoop and caught the Valentia like a sitting duck, wiping out the left wing and setting it on fire. Luckily, no life was lost.

———•◆•———

WHEN THE GURKHAS MET up with Habforce in Habbaniya, it created quite a stir. Habforce included 350 Bedouin tribesmen of the Arab Legion who were commanded by Lt. General Sir John Bagot Glubb, known to all and sundry as Glubb Pasha. His Bedouins were irreverently known as Glubb's Girls, attired as they were in flowing robes, sporting long hair and gaily debonair head scarves. The Gurkhas accustomed though they were to the Scottish kilt had, nonetheless, seen nothing quite so exotic before in the army, and they found this new mode of uniform-dress highly entertaining.

Adding even more colour to Habforce were the Household Cavalry Regiment, the Royal Wiltshire Yeomanry, and the Warwickshire Yeomanry. The officers of these Yeomanry regiments hailed from the landed gentry of England. Accustomed to a squire's way of life – which they felt absolutely no need to abandon merely because circumstance required they leave England – their exploits, past and present, made for some unusually flamboyant stories.

There is the one told of a certain officer who travelled abroad accompanied by his faithful valet. The good man was charged, among his other wonted duties, with the acquisition and service of a large stash of the finest champagne; a stash substantial to the needs of an exceedingly thirsty company of gentlemen about to be banished to a backwater sadly devoid of life's such essentials. Another recounted story was that of an officer who saw fit to take along his favourite horse – not for purposes of war, as past custom would have dictated, but purely for those of personal pleasure. And, for any willing to believe it, a further tale filtered down the pike came from the Sherwood Rangers. Upon being informed they were bound for Palestine, these fine gentlemen made a valiant attempt to take along a pack of foxhounds in hope that sometime, somewhere there might come the call to hunt.

Well, anything might be possible, might it not? After all, it *was* the British way of things!

Lending lustre to their legend, these dashing gentlemen had once cut quite a figure in the scarlet, green and gold of their various company regalia, their brilliant black boots, shiny breastplates, and magnificently plumed headgear. It was quizzically said that a mere show of their sartorial splendour was sufficient to so confound an enemy as to have it on the run.

Previously, Santi had merely heard the adage, "Only Mad Dogs and Englishmen…" Now, regaled with the stories of these sons of England, he found no reason to doubt its veracity.

Be that as it may, and legends aside, it wasn't long before a concerted effort of all forces saw the enemy pushed back. With the bombardment of enemy supply lines, and the resultant fuel shortage, the Germans were forced to withdraw their aircraft. As a result, Iraqi resistance became weakened, and eventually collapsed on 30 May.

Rashid Ali escaped, and there are conflicting versions as to how and where he fled. Some maintain it was Iran, where he supposedly lived in a luxurious hill-garden setting till such time he was forced to safer pastures in Germany. There he helped broadcast Nazi propaganda. Others have it on good authority that he slipped into neutral Turkey, where he came under close surveillance of the Turkish, British and German secret services. And yet, he is said to have nipped out from under their noses with the help of Johann Eppler, a German spy who would reappear on the scene almost one year later, smuggled into Cairo to aid Rommel's North Africa campaign. To the present, many accounts had Eppler visiting Rashid Ali at his residence where, being of similar build and stature, they switched identities. Disguised as Eppler, Rashid Ali took a plane to Germany where he remained a guest of the Fuhrer till the war's end.

However it actually played out, Rashid Ali was now out of the way. His lieutenant, Yunis el-Sabawi, was captured and hanged; but a third staunch follower known as Khairallah Talfah fled capture. He would, in years to follow, mentor his four-year-old nephew to whom, eventually, would pass the baton of power in Iraq. That nephew was Saddam Hussein and the world would be called to reckon with him some sixty years down the line.

For the time being, however, Iraq had capitulated to the Allies, and on 31 May an Armistice was signed by both sides in Baghdad.

ELSEWHERE, THOUGH, THE NEWS was disturbing. Greece had fallen and King George of Greece had fled to Egypt. Thousands of stranded Allied soldiers had been evacuated, thousands more were taken prisoner. It was shades of Dunkirk all over again, and refugees were crossing borders all across Europe in a desperate bid for safety.

It was at this point in time that Lt. Nigel Quentin Browne flew in from Malaya to join the Battalion. His feet had barely touched the ground before he was felled by the dreaded dysentery bug. Looking pale and peakish, he managed to drag himself to Santi's MDS, where he was met by the medical orderly on duty that day.

Hirasing Limbu was a simple man, eminently proud of his ability – albeit imperfect – to read and write the English vernacular. After all, most young men from his walk of life were fortunate for the competence of signing their name in their own language, let alone in English! He was prouder still of the rudimentary training befitting a medical orderly that he had received under Santi's tutelage.

In the process of acquiring the new patient's particulars, Hirasing gave careful consideration to his name. 'Nigel Sahib' was not something he could easily wrap his tongue around; as for 'Brown Sahib', well, a short time ago, while serving as batman to another officer, he had gathered that such a title might carry a somewhat uncomplimentary connotation. Fortunately, this officer's middle name was one that rang familiar, since he dealt with a substance of similar name almost on a daily basis.

"*Daktar Sahib,*" Hirasing addressed Santi. "*Yo Lt. Quinine Sahib chha.*"

"*Quinine Sahib?*" Santi was puzzled.

"*Hunchha, Sahib,*" the medical orderly reiterated firmly. "*Quinine Sahib.*"

Santi made his way over to 'Quinine Sahib'. He leaned over the patient whose face was pinched in pain. "I'm Lt. Santi Dutt. Let's see...I believe you are...um..."

"N.Q. Browne. Nigel Quentin Browne."

"Ah!" Enlightened, a hint of a smile flickered across Santi's lips. That explained Hirasing Limbu's mix up! It was easy to see how the Gurkha might confuse the two names – Quentin and quinine; for him they would be remarkably similar. "Of course! It's...Quentin... Nigel...Quentin."

"Right you are, Doc, on both counts. Better known as Ben, however. That's what they call..." All at once he grabbed his stomach. "Ohhh...damn and blast! Doc...which way, for Christ sake?" he pleaded, doubling up in agony.

Santi quickly pointed him towards the 'thunder boxes'. Those makeshift wooden thrones with their removable pans, when clean, were a luxury compared to the latrine trenches the troops invariably had to dig for use out in the field. A little later, the patient returned looking unmistakably wan and wobbly-kneed.

"Not doing so good, eh Browne?" Santi sympathised while administering the usual dose of sulphaguanidine. "That should settle your stomach in a bit. Make sure you drink plenty of fluids, and with twenty-four hours' bedrest you should soon feel much better. How's the head?"

"Perfectly filthy, thank you. Feels like I'm dying, Doc. Just my luck, wouldn't you know!" he muttered, gloomily. "Bloody awful place to end one's days!"

Santi laughed. "Oh, you're not dying. I know it feels that way right now but, not to worry, we'll have you back on your feet in no time at all."

"Hope you're right because, at present, they insist on slipping out from under me." Light-headed from exhaustion and dehydration, Nigel Quentin Browne peered up at the Indian doctor leaning over him. He'd had little close experience of Indian officers till now. "I say…"

"Yes?"

Ben grimaced. "This really is some hell hole, isn't it! Well, I daresay it's for King and Country and all that good stuff…but you…what about you, Doc? What the devil are you doing here?"

"Much the same as you, Browne," Santi replied, straight faced. "I'm here fighting for my country as well. You see, I'm making damn sure we don't exchange British rule for a German, or Japanese one. After all, a known devil, you know…" He smiled sweetly at the newcomer.

And thus, thanks to Hirasingh Limbu, Nigel Quentin Browne, better known as Ben, earned a private moniker that day. So it was, from that time on, and in all the years to follow, when memory recaptured the young officer in Santi's mind, he forever would be remembered, not as a simple 'Nigel' or 'Quentin' or 'Ben', but rather by Hirasingh's perfectly reasonable solecism – 'Quinine' Browne.

In spite of the Iraqi armistice, nothing was to be left to chance. Mosul – like Basra and Habbaniya – had to be properly secured against any recalcitrance which might be encouraged by the Germans. This was strategically imperative since Mosul was, both, the crossways through which passed the road and railway to Syria and Turkey as well as the link to the oil fields of Kirkuk, which supplied both Syria and Palestine. Hence, on 3 June 1941, the 2/4 Gurkha Rifles were flown to the northern city of Mosul to occupy and preserve its airfield for RAF use.

The landing at Mosul was a tense one to say the least. No one knew quite what to expect so soon after the armistice. The airport bristled with Iraqi guns levelled at the runways from the long, low ridge that flanked its western edge. Apprehensive men behind the guns were still uncertain who was friend and who foe. A single nervous trigger finger could ignite a nightmare. Fortunately, no one lost his head or his life. The 2/4 disembarked without mishap and their stay in Mosul proved equally uneventful; but then, certainly, no one was complaining.

They were kept busy forming piquets and defences to guard the airfield and patrol the surrounding area. Off duty, it was good to sleep, write letters home, eat without being shot at, sleep some more, bathe, relax with a drink, and sleep even more. Sleeping and bathing were luxuries of which one could not get enough. And Santi had the time, and the facilities, to give proper care to the sick and the wounded. It was a well-deserved respite; for despite being outnumbered three to one, and in spite of superior German air power, the British had outmanoeuvred the enemy and managed to conquer Iraq in four weeks. It was, all in all, a job well-done.

CHAPTER NINE

Oh, What A Lovely War!

For in and out, above, about, below,
'Tis nothing but a Magic Shadow-show
Play'd in a Box whose Candle is the Sun,
Round which we Phantom Figures come and go.

– Omar Khayyam, *Rubaiyat of Omar Khayyam*

IN THE MIDDLE EAST, former allies, Britain and France, found themselves on opposite sides in the war.

In September 1939, both France and Britain had finally made their stand against Germany. The ensuing months – dubbed the Phony War – had been relatively quiet, but tense with unease as all Europe held its breath in the face of an imminent German invasion. It came in May 1940, when Hitler invaded France. Marching through the Ardennes, he broke through French lines and pushed the British Expeditionary Force north to the sea, at Dunkirk. With shocking speed, France, Norway, the Netherlands, Belgium and Luxembourg fell to Hitler's *blitzkrieg*.

The Allies, with their back to the sea, suffered a terrible debacle on the beaches of Dunkirk. But when news reached England that thousands of their soldiers were stranded across the Channel, an amazing volunteer flotilla set out to the rescue. Operation Dynamo was made up of every military, civilian and private ship, boat and yacht that could be pressed into service. Many were not to return. Regardless, they braved the heavy gunfire pounding the beaches and waters where crowds of wounded, exhausted soldiers queued silently, as they waited to be evacuated. Between 26 May and 4 June, 338,226 British, French, Belgian and Dutch troops were rescued off those blood-soaked sands. Sadly, thousands more remained behind to become prisoners of war or to die. It was a small victory managed in the face of defeat; a costly triumph snatched from the jaws of tragedy. It tested the fibre of Britain as a nation. It sharpened her resolve – and it upheld her morale.

It was this redoubtable spirit of the English, often exhibited in their most desperate hour that had made so small a nation so great a one. There were those who recognised the indomitable nature that lay at the heart of Britain and, then again, there were those who did not.

In the aftermath of Dunkirk, Luftwaffe General Hoffman von Waldau stood gazing across the twenty odd miles of choppy Channel waters to the white cliffs of Dover. After a moment, bringing his gaze back to bear on the destruction that littered the beach around him, he made the mistake of unseasonably dismissing his enemy.

"Here is the grave of British hopes in this war, and these" referring contemptuously to some empty wine bottles strewn in the sand, "are the gravestones."

His companion, Inspector General Erhard Milch, with rather more foresight, shook his head and warned, "They are not buried yet." And, indeed, in time this prophecy would prove true. (Samuél W. Mitcham, Jr., *Eagles of the Third Reich*)

France, however, had lost faith and in June of that year, when German troops entered Paris, Verdun and Loire, the French Premier Paul Reynaud was deposed by Marshal Henri-Philippe Petain. The new Premier switched allegiance and signed an armistice with Hitler. Petain, an octogenarian, believed it was the only way to save France and should not, therefore, be conceived as a sell-out, but rather as survival. Indeed, later that same month, when Germany went on to invade the British Channel Islands, he felt himself vindicated and bound to agree with his counterpart, General Weygand, when that old man woefully declared, "In three weeks England will have her neck wrung, like a chicken!"

When this remark was repeated to Churchill, it elicited an indignant snort; appropriately so, for the invasion of Britain never did come about, and the only part of her ever to come under Nazi occupation was the Channel Islands. Hence, after England, standing alone, had survived the Battle of Britain, the French General received his reply from the English bulldog who growled back, "Some chicken, some neck!"

Petain set up his government of collaboration in Vichy, a famous spa town, and consequently, his troops became known as the Vichy French. General De Gaulle, on the other hand, exiled in Britain, continued to exhort his countrymen to keep up their fight against the Germans: *"To all Frenchmen. France has lost a battle, but France has not lost the war!"* Many French units answered his call, and his troops became known as the Free French. As a consequence, some French colonies opted on the side of the Vichy French, while others remained loyal to De Gaulle's Free French forces. In the ensuing chaos, Frenchmen fought each other on both sides in the war.

Syria witnessed this sorry conflict. That country, under French control before the war, came down on the side of the Vichy who battled the Free French forces fighting alongside the Allies. The Germans had used Syria as a launching pad for their bombers and fighters into Iraq. It was strategic as well to the Mediterranean, and there was a very real threat that Germany would use Vichy-held Syria as a stepping-stone to influence Turkey, perched precariously on an unstable wall of neutrality. Since it was always wiser to be safe rather than sorry, a decision was made to pre-empt this.

From his post in Cairo as C-in-C, General Wavell hammered out an invasion force. Pincer-fashion, the Australians and Free French were to move in from the south, while the British would push through from the east. The 10th Indian Infantry Division was preparing for this eastern push, when the 2/4 Gurkhas were ordered to join it at Taji, about six miles north of Baghdad. This time, instead of flying, they would stage across the country by road. In readiness for this, the Battalion was re-joined by its ground transport and 'D' Coy, which had remained behind in Basra when the rest had flown from there to Habbaniya. Now, once again, the Battalion had recombined and was complete.

On 21 June, a brother battalion, the 2/8 Gurkha Rifles, arrived in Mosul to take over as the relief force; it would be their job to keep a stringent eye on the Turkish border to the north. The 2/4 Gurkhas were transported out in their trucks. John Masters, however, was not in their company. He had contracted a severe case of athlete's foot, which Santi had treated as best he could with gentian violet. Since the trek through the desert would have undone whatever good this treatment had achieved, it was decided he required a few more days of bed rest before being flown to join his outfit later. Confined to hospital under dire threat that failing to heed his doctor's orders might very well result in parting company with one or more appendages of the afflicted limb, the adjutant, sporting one foot painted a violent shade of purple, and a face set in glum resignation, was left behind to recuperate while his Battalion followed the drums of war.

The 21st Indian Infantry Brigade began gathering in Taji and were reinforced under Brigadier Weld. It comprised the Prince of Wales's Own 2/4 Gurkha Rifles, the 2/10 Gurkha Rifles, 21st Brigade Signal Section, 4/13 Frontier Force Rifles, RAF 127th Fighter Squadron, 13th Duke of Connaught's Own Lancers, 157th Royal Artillery Field Regiment, 9th Field Company (engineers), 29th Field Ambulance Detachment, 7th Motor Ambulance Section and 16th (Mobile) Workshop Company. Lastly, in addition to its own Transport Company, 21st Brigade had those belonging to 17th and 25th Indian Infantry Brigades, as well as the 35th General Purpose Transport Company to complement its numbers.

The Brigade was informed by General Slim, GOC 10th Indian Infantry Division, that the job of this strike-force into Syria was: first, to secure Abu Kemal and Deir ez Zor; second, to put down, once and for all, the likes of the Palestinian guerrilla leader, Fawzi Qawukchi, who was aiding and abetting the enemy; and, finally, to oust General Dentz and his Vichy Forces from that area. Moreover, good relations were to be encouraged with the locals in preparation for the Allied advance into Aleppo.

This last was easier said than done. The loss of Palestinian lands due to the ongoing settlement of Jewish refugees had bred bitter discontent among the Arab countries. It spawned just such malcontents as Qawukchi, sowing the seeds of a deep hatred that was to span decades and spread consequences across the globe which would prove terrible in their scope.

As they sat listening to General Slim's exhortation, Santi heard a soft exclamation to his right.

"I'll be dashed!" He turned to see Shirley nod, indicating Colonel Williams. "Take a gander at our Willie, would you! He couldn't be more chuffed – like the cat that got the cream!"

Santi glanced over. "I see what you mean. What gives? Is he actually grinning…?"

"I'll say! The old boy's been pawing the ground to get stuck in. Rather browned off we weren't the first Gurkha unit to make it into combat." Shirley chuckled, softly. "Well, now he has a chance to have his bash at the enemy, it's quite made his day. Pleased as Punch is good ol' Willie!"

22 June brought further news, astounding news – Germany, despite its previous pact with Russia, had launched a surprise attack on that country. The general feeling, following incredulity, was one of relief, since it meant the Allies now had the power of the Great Bear on their side. After that bit of excitement and the initial bustle of preparation had subsided, the camp settled back, restlessly awaiting final moving orders. How soon would that be? Soon, pretty soon, probably as soon as…

On 23 June the men had all been given permission to bathe and wash their clothes. They went about their chores, using the time to advantage. Jack Masters had just flown in to rejoin the Battalion. In the nick of time, as it turned out, for wouldn't you know it, orders arrived that very day – they were to move out immediately. Tents were brought down, official and personal belongings were packed, and the restive air of a camp on pause was replaced by the urgency of an army going to war.

———◆———

THEY BEGAN THE TREK northwest towards Syria. As far as the eye could see, the terrain that stretched around them was nothing but vast distances of desert plains with little more than the odd scrub or boulder to break the monotony. And the monotony could be almost hypnotic, described by the Tommies most aptly as *"miles and miles, and bloody miles of damn all."* The unending expanse of sand and glaring heat sometimes took on a peculiar characteristic, a sort of life of its own; it seemed to move in shimmering waves, undulating around one's feet and head, creating watery mirages that would float somewhere between the blurred world of reality and the imagination it melted into. It was 140 degrees in that merciless sun.

There was no escape from the sand. The dust churned up by the convoy itself, added to their hell. The drivers couldn't do much to avoid the sand kicked up and swirled into the air by the wheels of the vehicle in front. It was everywhere, and it reached into everything, socks and shoes, clothes, skin and hair, eyes, nose, mouth, and food. When they were on the move, the vehicles were covered in it, inside and out. When they camped, despite sand parapets built around the tents to prevent the desert seeping in from beneath, the winds blew it in anyway. You lived, slept, breathed, and ate the bloody sand!

Sandstorms were the worst. *Ghiblis* – hot sirocco-like winds that blew fine, burning grit into the eyes and nose, choking the throat and lungs. As tongues thickened and eyes were swollen shut, the brain would begin to sizzle and distend, till it felt as though one's skull would surely burst. Helmets were eschewed as they added to their misery, the metal burning skin wherever it touched head or hands. For the moment, the heat was far more deadly than the enemy, and heat stroke took its toll. Masters sent an urgent message to Santi: could he please come at the double – Paramdas Gurung, a veteran of thirteen years had been found behaving most strangely.

"I tell you, Doc," Masters announced, looking on anxiously while Santi examined the Gurkha, "it fair gave me the willies to see his eyes roll back and his body jerk in spasms. At first, I thought he was having a fit, dash it all, till I noticed him clutch at his fly. And he seemed to be mumbling something, so I put my ear close to his lips and bare-ly made out the word '*peshab*'. That's when it suddenly came to me! I remembered you telling us heat stroke made urination difficult."

He broke off, rubbing his chin nervously as he watched Santi. "Good thing I recalled that. We quickly undid the poor blighter's trou-sers and loin cloth, and I dribbled water over his winkle. There was I, bending over his privates, coaxing him to perform with little shush-ing sounds, just like my *ayah* used to do when I was a nipper – and I look up to see a circle of dumbfounded faces staring at me. I believe they thought I'd taken sudden and complete leave of my senses!"

Santi couldn't help grinning at the interesting picture Masters' words conjured up in his mind's eye.

Masters grimaced. "No, really Doc, you know what a private lot the Gurkhas are! Taking a gander at someone's tackle is considered an unpardonable intrusion. How in the world was I supposed to ex-plain myself! Felt a right royal chump, I'll have you know. Fortunate-ly, I was vindicated when it blasted well actually worked! Did poor Paramdas a power of good, once we'd got him to relieve himself. Astounding how quickly it eased his discomfort – but, by George, did it knock the stuffing out of him!" Masters stopped to draw breath. "What say you, Doc, will he be o.k.?"

Doing his best to keep a straight face as he listened to Masters' turbulent account of his discomfiture, Santi tried to comfort the dis-traught officer. "You did well, sir. He must have been delirious, but he should be fine after he's had some rest. What you did probably saved his life, you know."

Masters looked gratified. "One does what one can," he said, dep-recatingly, though obviously pleased at having his heroics duly rec-ognised. Even more obvious was his overriding relief to be shot of the episode, now in more capable hands.

Besides heat stroke, there were other strange dangers that lurked in wait for them. Though they were following the course of the Eu-phrates, they had been warned off the temptation to drink or bathe in the river for fear of diseases the water carried.

The area was known for bilharzia – a disease transmitted to un-suspecting humans by river snails, through parasites that bored into the skin, and thence to the lungs and the liver. Also rampant was the guinea worm – a most disgusting infestation caused by ingesting water fleas that carried the larvae of the worm. Over the period of a year, the worm would develop and grow (sometimes to as much as three feet), burrowing its way out of the stomach and through the tissues, to lie just beneath the skin's surface, where it caused a blister. The only way to rid oneself of the pest was to wait for the blister to burst. Then, as the worm's head pushed its way out, to wind its body, very patiently, around a matchstick or toothpick, being careful not to rip the worm before it was completely extracted. This was a long-drawn-out, most unpleasant procedure, and a situation to be avoided at all costs. Though moving waters were relatively safer than stagnant waters – which were the actual breeding ground of the worm – Santi cautioned it was wise to forego the lure of the river as much as possible.

Their convoy reached Haditha in the evening of 24 June. Haditha, also known as K3, was an oil refinery and pumping station where the Kirkuk pipeline bifurcated to carry its precious cargo to, both, the French at Tripoli in Syria, and to the British at Haifa in Palestine. Upon arrival at this destination, they discovered it had been vandalised by the infamous Fawzi Qawukchi. Fortunately, both refinery and pumping station had been spared. It seemed, whatever their differences, and however heated the battle, all sides had the good sense to realise oil was too important a commodity to destroy, and to do so might very well prove to be much like shooting oneself in the foot.

They enjoyed a two-day respite in the shade of the surrounding orchards, eating cool, juicy-sweet watermelons that the Arabs sold them; and then the 2/4 was sent ahead as vanguard on the hundred-mile journey to the Syrian border. Once more, they faced the desert head on. By now they had learnt that layering clothing, like the Arabs did, helped to keep the body cool during the day. At night, they would lay out all garments, down to socks and banyans (vests), to absorb the dew fall. This condensation was later squeezed out and collected as water; every last, precious drop, notwithstanding the mingled sweat, would be put to multiple good uses during the day.

At last, on 28 June, the 2/4 crossed into Syria and arrived at Abu Kemal. Here, they caught up with the 4/11 Sikhs. who had preceded them into the town to guard the pipeline. The small, stocky, Mongolian-featured hill men were dwarfed even further by comparison to the burly, bearded, turbaned Sikhs. Yet, as different from each other in appearance and culture as can possibly be imagined, there remained in that foreign, faraway land a longstanding bond of brotherhood between these geographical neighbours who here hailed one another, each in his own language.

"*Oi prhaji! Ki hal hai?*" from the Sikhs. "Hey there, brothers! How are you?"

And the Gurkhas' reply, "*Ramro chha, bhai sab, ramro chha!*" "We're fine, respected brothers, we're fine!"

Their arrival was soon acknowledged by the Vichy French. They had started to dig their slit trenches, and none too soon, when enemy aircraft came overhead and bombed them. The attacks continued sporadically throughout the day. The Battalion suffered five casualties, and that day they lost Jamedar Sarbdhan Bura. He was brought to the Main Dressing Station by Subedar Major Sahabir Gurung and Narbahadur Rana, one of Santi's medical orderlies. Santi kept a special look out for Narbahadur, who happened to be his batman Dilbahadur's younger brother. Gently setting down his injured comrade so Santi could examine him, the old Subedar Major remained beside him, while the younger Narbahadur withdrew to a respectful distance by the tent entrance.

As soon as he heard the news, Jack rushed over; Sarbdhan Bura had watched him grow, as Jack himself put it, from a callow cub to an experienced officer. Santi examined the small hole in Sarbdhan's side. The grizzled old warrior did not look good and, no matter they all assured him he would be just fine, his eyes told them he knew his time had come. Santi operated on him and stayed by his side through the night, till he died. With the help of two medical orderlies, Basantbir Thapa and Tularam Bura, Santi and Jack buried him that morning, knowing, with regret, that they had to move on. They would leave him, another one of their number, laid to rest beneath the unending sands of this vast, inhospitable desert land.

On 29 June, the Battalion headed for Deir ez Zor, eighty miles to the north. They had opted to move by night in order to avoid the Vichy bombers by day. However, the terrain thwarted all plans of slipping through in the dark. Twenty-five miles out, as they passed through Wadi Es Sawab, their lorries got bogged down in the dry riverbed, and it wasn't till dawn that they got clear of the soft sand. It was bad luck, really, for now they would be sitting ducks in broad daylight when the bombers came.

But as it happened, the new day brought with it a problem of a different ilk. A blinding sandstorm wrapped the world in an opaque grey sheet and swallowed the convoy whole. The drivers, incapable of seeing two feet ahead, became so disoriented that C Company found itself heading for Tripoli. Santi and his medical orderlies, together with the cooks' lorries, were ensconced in B Company. Unable to make out a single vehicle through the swirling dust and fearing it had been left behind, B Coy made a mad dash forward and ended up way ahead of the column, almost running headlong into the arms of the enemy.

Fortunately, here the sandstorm worked in their favour; the enemy, rendered as blind by it as everyone else, was completely unaware that the British army had been blown, willy-nilly, almost onto their doorstep.

The following day, 1 July, when everyone had been safely herded back into the fold and the remainder of the Brigade had arrived, they proceeded on to the outskirts of Deir ez Zor, where they set up camp. Although the town seemed quite unremarkable, with nothing to distinguish it from any they had passed through thus far, Santi remembered only too well Samira's recollections of the hell it had once been. The memory put a stain on the place, its foul past a blight that tainted the air, as once again, he recalled the depth of her pain. The Battalion had arrived at the first of those terrible border towns tainted by the infamy of the 1915-1917 Armenian refugee camps.

CHAPTER TEN

The Forgotten Holocaust

I am the Way into the City of Woe,
I am the Way to a Forsaken People,
I am the Way into Eternal Sorrow....
Abandon all Hope Ye who enter Here.

– Dante Alighieri, *Inferno, "Canto III"*

HEDEYA WAS IN THE midst of a mediation and a meting out of equity. It had all begun propitiously enough when Dikran, the pharmacist, had sent some extra work her way. After essential finances had been seen to, she had decided it was high time the children were given a treat.

"The Adventures of Robin Hood," starring Errol Flynn and Olivia de Havilland, was playing at the Cinema Dolly, and Louis had been clamouring to see it. Hedeya had given them permission, with strict instructions they were to come straight home after the show; they didn't know it, but she had planned a surprise for their tea with some of Groppi's famous profiteroles. It had been such a long time since she had splurged like this. Of course, it wasn't very practical, she realised with a small stab of guilt, but really, they were children after all, and it wasn't often she had a little extra to indulge them in this manner – and they did deserve it!

All three children had had haircuts the previous day. Hedeya had shorn each one in turn, as short as she could go without having a rebellion on her hands. Even Violette's curls bubbled on her head almost the same length as the boys. In fact, attired as she was in her checkered blouse and blue shorts, the little girl could almost be taken for the youngest of three brothers. Victor was given charge of the money for the picture tickets and, after being reminded once again not to be late, the trio set off as happy as you please. When they returned, however, their mood was not what one would have expected; much to Hedeya and Bajo'surprise, instead of being eager to share the afternoon's experience, the boys looked suspiciously sheepish while Violette was sullen and teary-eyed.

"What's the matter, Bebe? Didn't you enjoy the movie?" Bajo's solicitous query brought a slight tremble to her granddaughter's lower lip. Slowly, her eyes filled with tears that brimmed over and rolled down her cheeks in large, splotchy drops. She gave a small hiccupping sob.

"Well, Victor?" Hedeya turned to her oldest son for an explanation. Her voice was soft, but it had a certain edge to it that was unmistakable. The boy had no trouble recognising the underlying note that warned him, *be careful, for I will brook no nonsense.* And when his mother gave him that particular look and crossed her arms in just that manner, he knew for sure that he had better pick his way warily through the situation confronting him.

"Na, Mama, it was a good picture, but we ran into a small problem." Victor gave his mother a disarming smile he hoped would soften her heart and remind her that, no matter what, she loved him. "You see, Bebe wanted an ice-cream..." he began rather lamely, but his voice trailed off in mid-sentence. He was a truthful boy and a quick look at his little sister's face brought the truth tumbling from his lips.

"We thought we could share an ice-cream, but after we bought it, we found that we didn't have quite enough money for three tickets. We tried to make the icecream man take it back, but he was quite rude and told us just because we were idiots didn't mean he had to be one as well. So then, we...well, we had to...think of something and...I...so I..."

At this point Bajo, observing her grandson's bright red face, took pity on his plight and decided it would be expedient to step in. Acting with the wisdom of her years, she deflected attention away from Victor by turning to Violette. "Come, Bebe, sit here beside me at the table and tell us all about it. But first, see what your mother has brought for you – Groppi's profiteroles – for all of you!" She added the last quickly in case Hedeya was contemplating abstinence for the boys as punishment. "Come *indi*; first eat and then tell us your story."

The profiteroles did much to coax Violette out of the sulks, and in between mouthfuls and hiccups, she confided her woes to her grandmother. The story unfolded thus: The three children had arrived at the cinema house, and just as they were about to buy their tickets they had, it seems, been swerved from their purpose by the ice-cream man. Putting their heads together, they had calculated that if they bought just one cup of neapolitan ice-cream to share between the three of them, they would have just about enough money left for their tickets. Having thus given in to temptation, they then made their way to the ticket window, clutching their purchase, only to find that they had miscalculated and were a mere fraction short of the funds required for a third ticket. The stony-hearted man behind the ticket window would not be swayed; and the icecream man, well, he had been quite horrid, hadn't he, telling them to get lost even when they had been ready to return the icecream for half price, although, really, it had barely been licked and was almost as good as new!

Eventually, it was Victor, bright boy that he was, who had come up with the perfect solution. Rather than all three of them missing the picture – which would be a really silly thing to do – he and Loza would buy two tickets for themselves and the rest of the money, although insufficient for a third ticket, would be more than enough to buy a second ice-cream, and maybe a small bar of chocolate, or even some candy floss, which Bebe could have all to herself if she promised faithfully to wait right there in the lobby where they left her, till the picture gave over. It was explained to her that she would actually come out the winner since she would not only get to enjoy all the goodies, she would later get to hear the story as well; and they promised to describe it to her, scene by scene, down to the very last detail.

It hadn't been hard to convince the little girl. For almost an hour she had munched through her goodies and busied herself studying the large, coloured posters advertising both current and future attractions, while the glossy portraits of famous film stars smiled down at her. They were all so beautiful! But soon enough this pastime began to pall; her treats were all gone and, after she had walked the length and breadth of the lobby twice, it hadn't taken long for her to realise she had been handed the short end of the stick. She had waited fitfully for a while longer, and then the sniffles had started. She couldn't help it.

At first, they were so soft they were almost inaudible. But then, with each passing minute they seemed to gather momentum and, try as she would to stop them – first by wiping her right sleeve across her eyes, then by using her left sleeve likewise for her nose – they grew louder, and louder still, all of their own accord, till the man standing at the door to the cinema heard her.

"*Walad?*" The usher had approached, mistaking her for a boy. "What is the matter? Are you lost?"

Shaking her head, Violette had hiccupped, tearfully.

"Well, why are you crying then? Where is your mother?"

"A..at home."

"If she is at home, what are you doing here all by yourself? How did you get here? Come now, *walad*, speak. Are you alone?"

Again, Violette shook her head. "My b...b...brothers are in th.. there," she pointed to the closed doors of the cinema hall, adding a touch indignantly, "and I am n..not a boy. I am a g..g..gi..girl," she ended in a wail.

Astonished, the man stared at her for a moment. "You could be a girl, I suppose," he conceded, a trifle doubtfully. "You were crying like one just now." Violette gave a loud sniff with the hint of a sob attached to it, and he added hurriedly. "There, there, no more of that. Let us go and find those brothers of yours and see what they have to say for themselves."

Inside the hall, it took a few minutes and caused a fair amount of annoyance as the man shone his torch down each row before, finally, two startled young faces were caught in the beam of its light.

"There they are!" Violette tugged urgently on the man's sleeve. "Those are my brothers."

In a sibilant whisper that carried through the darkness and earned the two miscreants a good number of reproving looks from people nearby, the man had then made it abundantly clear what he thought of irresponsible "louts" who would leave their little sister alone outside while they enjoyed themselves at the cinema. Shame!

A certain amount of musical chairs had been necessary as people rearranged themselves to accommodate the small girl with a seat beside her brothers; and all should have gone well from then on except, unfortunately, not more than ten minutes after everyone had shuffled around and finally settled down, the film came to an end, and Violette realised she had missed practically the whole thing. She pouted all the way home, and the boys had been unable to persuade her to forgive and forget. But now, having unburdened her grievances, having been comforted and cosseted, and her belly replete with treats, forgiving and forgetting was a much easier proposition.

"Always remember," Bajo said to the children after things had been put to right once more, "you must take care of each other. If you do not, who will? Family is very important. You must never forget that. Always love one another; it is through our love of family that we touch the souls of our ancestors.

"Tell us about our ancestors, Bajo," Louis said. "Are they still in Turkey?"

"Our ancestors are all dead, silly." Victor slapped the top of his brother's head playfully. "They are people who lived a long time ago, that's why they are called ancestors. But Bajo," he turned to his grandmother, questioningly. "Why don't you ever talk about your family in Turkey?"

"Yes, yes, yes," Violette chanted. "Bajo, tell us about them. Tell us a story."

"Tell you a story? *Lao, lao,* I have become a story!"

"Tell, tell, tell," the little girl tugged at her grandmother's sleeve. "I want to hear about Baba Taht's house, and the gold coins hidden in the secret place."

"Bajo!" Hedeya's low voice held a warning. She laid a gentle hand on her mother's shoulder as she turned to the children and deftly steered their attention away from the painful past. "Enough! Now leave your grandmother in peace. If you promise to wash up quickly and get ready for bed, she will tell you a story about Goha."

Without giving the boys a chance to demur, she ushered them towards their room while Bajo took Violette to undress. When she returned, she sat down at the kitchen table and tried to push away the black memories that threatened to crowd in on her. At all costs, the children should be kept safe from them. There was no place here for those awful...no, no need to rake up the fear, the grief. She could hear their young voices getting ready for bed; in a little while they would quiet down. And she would hear her mother's voice and the words of a long familiar story from her childhood...

Now you know that Goha was a simple soul. And because he had a simple mind, and a simple heart, he believed anything and everything anyone told him. Often this got him and the people around him into trouble, which sometimes made them angry and sometimes made them laugh; but no matter what, in the end they all said, "oh, that Goha! He is just the village fool!" So, as you can imagine, there are many stories about Goha, and today I will tell you about the day his mother sent him out for some firewood.

It was a good day to be out, bright and sunny, so he set out with his donkey and his axe, and after searching for a while he came upon just the kind of tree he had been looking for. Pleased with his find, he told his donkey to wait for him under the tree while he climbed up into it. When he found a good sturdy branch that would do well for firewood, he climbed onto it. Yes, this would do just fine; he would get as much of it as he could. Facing the tree trunk, he slowly crawled backward, along the length of the branch till he reached the middle. There, he sat himself firmly, and began cutting the branch right where it joined the trunk. As he was doing so, he heard someone singing and, looking down, he saw Hadadian Bey, the village blacksmith, on his mule, passing below.

"Hello, Efendi! I see you are enjoying this beautiful day," Goha called out.

The blacksmith looked up, and when he saw Goha he gave a startled cry. "Goha, what are you doing? Stop! Stop what you are doing and come down at once. You are going to die!"

Taken aback, Goha stopped and stared at the man, amazed. "Really? How do you know this? You must be able to see the future! And if so," he began to climb down as fast as he could, "then, please Efendi, you must tell me when I am going to die."

Hadadian Bey made an impatient sound. "Tsk! Don't be a fool, young Goha. Of course I cannot tell the future." He rapped his knuckles on the forehead of the wide-eyed man now standing before him. "Any idiot would tell you that sitting on the outer end of a branch while cutting it where it joins the tree would cause you to fall along with the branch. Even you must understand what that means – you will most certainly die."

"There, you said it again! Now I am sure you know when I am going to die. Please, you must tell me so that I can prepare…"

And after that, no matter what the unfortunate blacksmith said, no matter how hard he tried to explain, or plead – hairan kurban – Goha refused to let him go. At last, exasperated beyond endurance, Hadadian Bey blurted the first thing that came to mind.

"All right Goha, listen to me carefully. When…er…your donkey brays… hmm…three times, you will die." Satisfied, Goha nodded, and the relieved blacksmith, without any further ado, made quick his escape.

There was a pause, a small giggle from Violette, then Bajo's voice continued.

Goha packed his things and, with his donkey, he began walking home. He was deep in thought when, suddenly, his donkey brayed. "I hear you, old friend," he said, patting the animal's head.

They had gone but a short distance further when the donkey brayed a second time. "Is it so soon?" he asked the gentle beast.

For a while they continued to walk in silence. Finally, the donkey brayed for the third time. Goha stroked its head. "You have always been a faithful companion, and I thank you. Now, go home and give them the news – tell them 'Goha is dead,' and they will take care of you."

The good little creature obediently trotted off. Then, right there, in the middle of the road, Goha began digging; and when he had dug a hole large enough, he sat in it and waited…and waited…and waited…

It was well past the noon hour when Topalian, the cripple, came hobbling down the road carrying his bundle of ribbons and buttons to sell in the souk. Now, although Topalian had one lame leg, he never forgot to thank God for his other good one. In fact, he told himself, it was only because he was special that he had been chosen thus, and so he kept in good spirits with constant praise for his blessings.

Unaware of what lay ahead, he limped along as he sang out loud – "Sheelee ya erd ma' aleki illa ana. Carry me, oh earth, for there is none other such as I" – when, all at once, with a frightened yell, he found himself tumbling, bundle and all, into Goha's hole, falling right on top of the crouched figure.

When at last he picked himself up and looked around, he became very angry. "Goha," he shouted, "did you not see me coming? Isn't it enough that I have one crippled leg, do you want me to break my neck as well? What are you doing in this hole in the middle of the road?"

"I am waiting to die," Goha replied to the astonished man.

"Waiting to die?" Topalian spluttered, "What are you talking about? People don't dig holes in the middle of a road and sit in them waiting to die. You lump of a fool, it will more than likely be some unsuspecting passers-by who will fall in and meet their death." With that, he gave Goha two slaps and added, "Now, help me out, then fill this hole and go straight home; and let us have no more nonsense." He shook Goha by the shoulders. "Straight home, mind you."

Goha promised faithfully to do exactly as he was told. He filled the hole and then started down the road towards home. All went well till the road came to the house of Najarian Bey, the carpenter, where it made a sharp bend – and it stopped Goha in his tracks. Remembering that he had given Topalian his solemn word to go 'straight' home, Goha scratched his head, puzzled. Simple though they might call him, no one had ever accused him of being untruthful, and they were certainly not going to start now! His word was his word, and straight meant straight, therefore, there was only one way around the problem that faced him.

Inside his house the good carpenter had just finished lunch and was having his afternoon siesta when, suddenly, he heard a loud banging on the outside that made the whole house shake. Frightened out of his wits, he ran out to find Goha breaking down the front wall of his home. Shouting and yelling at the top of his voice, he started beating Goha till passers-by pulled them apart and asked what was going on.

"Going on? Ask this dolt, this mad fool! Ask him why he is destroying this house that I have just finished building..."

Hedeya smiled to herself as she listened to her mother's voice and her daughter's giggles carrying from the bedroom. She remembered that voice so well from her own childhood, recounting the stories of Goha's exploits and misadventures. Most of the time she shut out all childhood memories; except for a very few, they were fraught with too much pain, so she kept that part of her life tightly shut away. And, yes, at all costs it was to be kept hidden from the children. This was her personal Pandora's Box of nightmares. There was no need to share those nightmares – bad enough that every so often some unbidden reminder would pry open the lid, and the merest chink would bring them rushing out to haunt her, making her relive the terror over and over again.

Her memories of those last days in Turkey – the killings and the death-marches out of that country – were ragged, with entire stretches missing in places. But what remained was still more than enough to torment her, to fill her, now and then, with the fear, bewilderment and shame that had defiled her childhood. It had all started with the greatest of deceptions, one that led to the betrayal of an entire nation of people and to their ethnic cleansing.

At first, with the change of government had come great hope. Under the Young Turks, a proclamation was made throughout the land – *Adalat, Masawat, Akhawat!* There was to be Justice, Equality and Brotherhood for all! For Armenians, after years of prejudice as second-class citizens, labouring under the burden of additional taxes, restriction of religion, and freedom of movement, after the frequent violence and killings that had plagued them, at long last there was to be justice, equality and brotherhood for all! Subsequently, the government decreed all Armenian men were to hand in any weapons they might possess as they would have no further need of them.

In the ensuing euphoria, an invitation had been issued for all grown Armenian males to attend a town meeting to discuss the coming changes. It was eagerly attended, with very few exceptions, one of whom was Samuél Khayat. He had a mistrust of the proceedings; his unerring instinct told him something did not seem right. Then, rumours began, there were disappearances; at which time Samuél Khayat decided to take his family and leave the city with as much haste as possible.

Although their village, Karabash, was not the safest refuge, it would have to do as a temporary one. As to the house on Kuçuk Kawaz, in view of the uncertain future, the length of their absence and the possibility of their return being unknown, it was hurriedly given into the care of the priest, Father Daniél Nahoum Savçi. And what about Hedeya's beloved cow, Ankara, and her horse, Zaino? Dear Ankara who gave her a glass of sweet, fresh milk every morning; and Zaino who would nuzzle sugar from her hand and neigh with pleasure. What of them? Father Daniél promised they would be well looked after until her return. Hedeya ran down to the stables and tearfully bade her two friends goodbye. Then it was time to leave. To avoid drawing any undue attention, they took next to nothing when they slipped out of the city, as though merely for a day's outing.

As it turned out, Samuél Khayat's suspicions were justified; none of the men who had gone to the meeting returned home. A period of anxious enquiry followed, until, finally, the families received letters that purported to be from their missing kinsfolk. They bore the men's *muhurs*, private seals, and enjoined their womenfolk to pack all their valuables, and whatever personal belongings they could manage, for a temporary relocation to Mosul where their menfolk awaited them.

Although there were great misgivings at this turn of events, the gendarmerie stood by as escort, so there was no choice but to obey and hope for the best. In actual fact, the men had already been butchered, and their families were about to face much the same fate. It was the beginning of a terrible slaughter that would later come to be known by the term "genocide." This, the first genocide of the twentieth century would set an example for Nazi Germany to follow some thirty years later.

Soon, the forced deportations and mass killings were in full spate. Long columns of bedraggled, sick and starving men, women, and children were driven down from the north through miles of desert. These unfortunates were mercilessly robbed, raped and abused by groups of armed Kurds, as well as by the Turkish soldiers who purported to guard the helpless refugees. The large numbers of dead left in their wake portended that this was not just one of those intermittent uprisings against the Armenians. What was taking place was on a far larger and far more organised scale.

When Bajo, Hedeya and Samuél arrived in Karabash, they were met by Farida, Bajo's sister. She had remained in the village with her family; brother Shamun and his family, however, had left for Mardin some time ago, and there had been no news of them since. In fact, their news, so anxiously awaited, would be a long time coming.

Samuél Khayat and his family slipped quietly into the routine of life in the village, and it was hoped that here they would escape the notice of the authorities. However, Samuél was known to be a man of considerable property, and it wasn't long before the soldiers came looking for him.

In the village, floors of the houses were polished to a smooth shine with a mixture of hollyhocks soaked in water. In Samuél Khayat's house a space had been hewn into the floor of the front room, before the fireplace. Long and narrow, it was just large enough for a man to lie in, but not somewhere he could remain for any length of time.

At first warning, Samuél Khayat went into hiding here. But when the old *kezir*, the town crier, brought news that Siko Bakerçi, Siko the cowherd, had seen soldiers surrounding the village, it was considered too dangerous for him to remain in his own house. He was moved by the loyal villagers to the house of the elderly *mukhtar*, the village headman. Here he was hidden in a hollow space beneath a windowsill, between the double walls of the house. A peep hole in the outer wall let in air and light, and allowed for a restricted view onto the outside world.

Samuél Khayat remained thus for two days. On the third day the soldiers rounded up some of the villagers and tried to beat the information of his whereabouts out of them. When it was not forthcoming, they promised that every house would be searched, and when their quarry was found, the few remaining men in the village would be taken away regardless of the fact that here, like elsewhere, only the very young and very old remained. No man in between, no matter his circumstance, was exempt other than those few considered to be absolutely necessary for services essential to the Turkish government or to society.

When told of this, Samuél Khayat insisted on giving himself up. The villagers did their best to dissuade him. Experience had taught them that even if he did surrender, harsh punishment would inevitably be visited upon the village for having hidden him, and for the inconvenience it had caused the soldiers. Giving himself up, therefore, was not the answer; some other solution had to be found. What that was remained to be seen – and time was crucial.

FOR ALMOST FOUR MONTHS the soldiers had been looking for Hagop Saydjian, the shoemaker from Karabash. When he got wind of this, he prudently did not wait to find out why; he disappeared overnight and, thus far, the soldiers had been unable to find him. What they didn't know was that he, along with his wife Derouhi, and son Diran, had gone into hiding in Diyarbekir, in Mustafa the Muslim's house. That good man, being a practical individual, had devised a plan that proved lucrative for him and suitable for everyone concerned – in return for refuge, Hagop and his son plied their trade of making shoes which Mustafa sold. This arrangement more than adequately repaid their host for their upkeep; the risk he was taking on their behalf, however, could not be calculated or repaid in coin.

One day the leather seller from Karabash brought news to Mustafa that Turkish soldiers, on the hunt for Samuél Khayat, had surrounded the village and begun attacking the villagers. Rather than allow that to continue, Samuél Khayat had decided to give himself up in the hope that it would mitigate the consequences. Yet, everyone knew, whether he was found, or he surrendered, it would most certainly bode ill for all who lived in the village.

Always an astute businessman, when Mustafa came to hear of the situation, and learned of Samuél Khayat's standing in Karabash, he contrived a possible answer to the problem at hand. Among other things, there was a shortage of food in the city, much of it a result of the disruption and chaos caused by the upheaval and displacement of so many Armenian tradesmen and farmers. Bread was scarce and could only be transported under guard. It was common to see Kurdish refugees from the mountain areas roaming the streets, bundled under quilts for protection against blows rained from bread sellers' staves when they tried to steal their bread. It was even said that people had eaten tortoise eggs with dire consequences. Mustafa's proposal was simple: if Samuél Khayat would keep him and his family supplied with wheat and bulgur from his secret stores in the village, then he in return would provide Samuél Khayat and family the shelter they so desperately required.

In the village, essential stores of grain had been well hidden to prevent pillaging by constantly roving Kurds and Turks. After the autumn harvest, the bulgur and wheat were prepared for storage for the harsh winter months ahead, and beyond.

Long troughs were dug into the earth, then set alight with fire; the broken bulgur – *burghul* – was filled into massive metal vessels and parboiled in water over the fired trenches. The grain was then cooled and laid out on sheets to dry. When the *burghul* was ready, some portion of it would be stored, along with the *sheeshay*, the uncooked cracked wheat, in *quwaras*. (These mud and straw jars dispensed the grain through an opening at the bottom, operated by a wooden slat that pulled up to open, and down to close.) The remaining grain was then filled into large pits, dug in the fields under cover of darkness, and lined with straw. When completely filled, they were covered over with more straw and, finally, a natural camouflage of sod. Along with the winter stores of dried fruits, nuts and *bastarma* (sun dried meat cured with spices), the very livelihood of the village depended on the secrecy and safety of these hidden grains.

So, it was decided. Since the imminent danger was his, Samuél Khayat would be secreted out of the village first, under the merchandise in the leather seller's cart; his wife and daughter would follow after a safe interval. And the village would share its lot of grain with Mustafa and his family.

All went as planned, and Samuél Khayat's escape was made under the noses of the soldiers, so to speak. When the village was searched, the soldiers came up empty-handed. To vent their frustration, they summarily handed out a few random beatings, then they looted the livestock and, ignoring the pleading and wailing of the distraught villagers, picked out four of the oldest boys and four girls and carried them away. Among the latter were Samuél Khayat's protégées, Shamuné and Baizar, two girls whose education and board he had made provision for in return for their attendance on his daughter at boarding school.

Bajo and Hedeya, who were unknown by sight, had remained in Farida's house purporting to be part of her family. Now, unsure how much information the soldiers would pry from their captives, it was decided, for their own safety, and that of the village, that they too should leave as soon as possible.

They said goodbye to Farida and her family, and undertook the journey on foot the following night. They were careful all the while to avoid the rampaging Kurds as well as the columns of deportees being driven through the desert by soldiers who did more to abuse than to guard them. Every so often a light would be seen in the distance, and from the strength of its glow could be discerned its origin – a campfire lit to warm the guards transporting a group of miserable refugees, or a pyre to burn the bodies of those killed, so the ashes could later be sifted through for valuables their desperate owners might have ingested.

The dangers were many and the going was slow, and when dawn broke Bajo and Hedeya were still some short distance from the city. The gates, secured for the night, would soon be unlocked. Meanwhile, the two weary travellers sought shelter beneath a solitary tree not far from the city walls.

It so happened, earlier, that a Turk seemed to have broken journey there as well. He had, apparently, climbed into the tree to wait for morning, and admittance to the city. What prompted his next move will forever be beyond the reckonings of a normal mind; but then, these were not normal times, and these degenerate people were far from normal. He knew nothing of Bajo or Hedeya, he knew neither who they were nor why they were there; and whether it was for amusement, or to degrade the old woman, or merely because the fancy took him at that moment to do so, from his perch in the tree the man defecated on her. Covered in his faeces, Bajo looked up at him and asked him the simple question – *why?* Then, without another word, she went down to the river to wash off his filth and as much of the insult as she could.

Before setting off once more for the city, Hedeya needed to quench her thirst. Bajo, busy squeezing the water from her wet clothes and hair, bade her go a few feet upstream from where she had washed. Finding a convenient spot, Hedeya lay flat on her belly and, reaching over the bank, she put her mouth to the water. It ran cold and clear, and she immersed both hands the better to cup the water to her face. She took large gulps, feeling their cool passage down her throat, and through her chest, before they vanished into her stomach.

She was hit by both object and smell simultaneously, and she crinkled her nose in distaste as she looked up to find the source. What she found herself staring at forced a strangled cry from her throat that brought Bajo running to her daughter's side. Bobbing gently beside her head was the small, disfigured form of a near-birth sized foetus still attached by its umbilical cord to the mutilated, swollen body of a young woman caught in the undergrowth of the riverbank. Her belly had been sliced open, and much of her insides trailed in the water so that she looked like some grotesque, tentacled, half-human half-water creature floating in the weeds.

The violence done to the two bodies, and the stage of their decomposition, associated with the sickening knowledge of having drunk the very water they were decomposing in, was a horror that turned Hedeya's stomach and mind. It made her so ill that she retched violently, again and again, and by the time they reached Mustafa's house she had become highly feverish, her face flushed, her body burning up. Over the next few days her condition worsened; her body was wracked by fevers and chills, her nose became congested, her throat swollen and painful so that she found it increasingly difficult to breath. Feyruz, the old maidservant of the house, took one look at her and shook her head gloomily. This was not good.

"Open your mouth," she ordered. There, at the back of the throat, was a large, grey balloon-like mass almost entirely blocking the air passage. Diphtheria! A childhood malaise that was fatal in most cases.

"Open wider," Feyruz demanded, peering in as Hedeya choked and tried to wriggle free. "No, no, open wide and let me take a good look at what you are hiding in there."

With lightning speed, before anyone could stop her, the old woman reached a hand in, grabbed the distended grey membrane and squeezed hard till it burst. Hedeya screamed, but the only sound she produced was a hoarse raspy one. Tears streaming down her face, her body shook with ague. But a fortnight later, the fever was gone, and she could swallow and breathe with ease once again. It was obvious she was on the road to recovery, and a few weeks' further rest and care would restore her to health. It would take much longer, however, for the nightmares of her experience to stop haunting her.

———————

At Mustafa's house, Bajo joined Derouhi, the shoemaker's wife, in cooking for the family. For two months, all went well; the men lived and worked in the room that had been turned into their workshop, Samuél Khayat helping the shoemaker, while the women and children stayed together in a separate room. From time to time, as needed, Bajo and Derouhi would go to the village and bring back grain enough for the household, being very careful not to get caught.

Then, one day, the lady of the house, known to all as *ana* (mother), was visited by her brother. It was an inauspicious visit. He was an iniquitous man with a dark soul ridden by the devil. Noticing his disquiet, his sister enquired as to its cause; she was ill prepared when her brother unleashed the demons that had been tormenting him.

"These past few nights my sleep has been strangely disturbed," he began. "You see, I had an encounter the other day..."

He told how he had happened upon a young boy with a bloodied head wandering outside the city walls, crying. Somehow the boy had escaped and returned from the desert where he had witnessed his father and a group of other men, young and old, being killed. "I want to go home," the child had sobbed.

"Do not be afraid. Tell me where you live and I will take you home," the brother had offered, whereupon the boy had explained as best he could, and so they set off.

After walking for a while, however, the boy stopped and said, "*Ammu*, uncle, this is not the way home."

"It is a shortcut I know that will get us there quicker. Don't worry, just follow me, I am taking you where you belong," he was told.

A little further on, passing through some rocky terrain, they came to a heap of stones piled haphazardly, under which could be glimpsed, just barely, a tangle of human limbs. Quick as a flash the man lifted the child by his feet, swung him up into the air, and brought him down hard, smashing his head with a sickening sound against a large boulder. Without waiting, he repeated this once more, blood from the small head arcing, splattering him and the surrounding area as it swung through the air and hit the rock a second time. It burst open like a melon, spilling its contents. He then left the small, broken body in that unhallowed place of death and ran away.

Hearing this, his sister cried out in horror. "In God's name, who are you? Surely you cannot be my brother! I swear before *Allah*, it is *haram* that we have drunk milk from the same mother's breast. Go, and take your sin with you! It is an abomination that defiles my house."

Angered by his sister's words, the brother promptly went and informed the captain of the local gendarmerie that he suspected her of hiding some Armenians.

When the Turkish soldiers came that evening, they took everyone by surprise. Bajo and Derouhi were caught immediately while washing down the grey slabbed area of the front courtyard, a routine job at the end of each day. Hagop and his son, however, had gone down the road just prior to the soldiers' arrival, and thus escaped being apprehended. As for Samuél Khayat, he had been leaning out of a rear window just moments before with a slice of watermelon for Hedeya, who was in the courtyard outside. She had stood on tiptoe to reach it, and her father, laughing and patting her head, had handed it down to her, then disappeared back into the shadowy room; and that was where Hedeya had remained, sitting below the window, enjoying her melon when the soldiers came.

When *ana* realised what was happening, she grabbed Hedeya and pushed her into the coal cellar.

"Quickly, hide in here," she had whispered urgently, "and don't make a sound."

Hedeya stayed as quiet as a mouse while the soldiers stomped about looking for the *giaour* (unbelievers). "Where are the others?" the gendarme captain shouted at the terrified women. "You'd better tell us, or it will be the worse for them – and for you – when we find where they are hiding."

Unsure if her husband had been caught, and afraid to leave her daughter alone if he had, Bajo called out to Hedeya with an urgency that eventually persuaded her to come out of hiding. Angered at the delay she had caused, the captain grabbed her by the shoulders and shook her with a force that snapped her head back and forth so that it seemed her neck would break.

It was obvious he had been told about Samuél Khayat, for he kept yelling, "Where is your father?"

When she didn't answer, he swung his *kirbaç* so the length of hippopotamus hide snaked out and caught her legs in a stinging whip-lash that made her scream in pain.

Unable to intervene physically, Bajo tried to console her daughter with words. "Never mind," she said in Arabic, "*tabbakh el-simyi-dawa'uh.* One who cooks poison will taste it. God will punish him, you'll see."

Unfortunately, the soldier understood Arabic, and her words increased his fury so that he whipped Hedeya even harder, the leather of his *kirbaç* cutting into her flesh, until her pitiful screams made Mustafa intervene to say the young girl truly knew nothing.

"No one here knows where her father is. But I did see him going down the road just a short while before you and your soldiers arrived. Believe me when I tell you this. I too have two sons in the army."

Declaring it was the only reason he did not arrest Mustafa – and his family as well – the captain made him swear on pain of *talak* (divorcing his wife) that he was speaking the truth; and the good man, having honestly mistaken Hagop the shoemaker for Samuél Khayat, made the oath in all good faith. It was only later, when Hagop and his son returned mere minutes after the soldiers had taken Bajo, Hedeya and Derouhi, that Samuél Khayat was discovered in the *hamam* (washroom), and Mustafa realised what he had done. He shuddered at the enormity of his sin.

It so happened that Samuél Khayat, after handing his daughter the melon, had visited the *hamam* and thus been completely oblivious of all that was taking place outside. When he was told, he became so distraught there was no consoling him, and he was all for rushing out right then to find them. It was with much difficulty that Mustafa persuaded him no good could possibly come from so foolish an action; especially in light of the unwitting sin he had just committed to save him.

"There is much penance I will have to do. Please, let it not be in vain! You will be committing suicide if you go after them now, then where will your family be? All is not lost yet. There is so much confusion out there, something might still happen to save them. Diran can follow them to where they are taken and, meanwhile, let me see if one of my two sons in the army can intercede on their behalf. Now go, you and Hagop hide in the stables. And be patient. Above all, have faith."

And so, while Hagop and Samuél Khayat hid in Mustafa's stables, Diran went out to see what news was to be had. It was dusk before he discovered where the detainees were, that they had been taken to a holding compound in the southern part of the city. Travelling across the rooftops, making sure to keep well out of sight, he went from building to building, till he located them. From the rooftops, he watched as they were moved into a holding area, and into a building with small barred windows, crowded with faces piteously peering out. He then settled down to wait out what was left of the night.

Early the following morning Diran was woken to the sound of orders being shouted, and he witnessed a large crowd of people being driven out of the compound. Many of them were near naked, a large number seemed too weak to walk, their wounds and injuries clearly visible. Some hobbled along on feet badly swollen and contused from vicious beatings they had endured on their soles. Again, Diran followed from rooftop to rooftop till, finally, the detainees reached the Mardin Gate where they joined an even larger crowd of refugees herded together like so much cattle.

Columns of deportees had been brought from Bitlis, Wan, Erzurum and Siwas. Clothed in rags, starving and sick, they were in a most pitiful, wretched state; and as the soldiers counted them and recorded their names, they laughed, calling them *hynsyrlar* (pigs) being rounded up for the march into the desert and a fate worse than death. By the end of their torment, most of this wreckage of humanity would not survive.

In the midst of this swirling pool of misery Diran spotted his mother, Bajo and Hedeya just as they reached the gate. Although he could not hear what was said, he saw the gendarme captain address Bajo. He watched, helpless and filled with despair. And then, something unbelievable happened.

"What is your name?" the captain barked in Armenian.

Bajo stared at him blankly. She shook her head, feigning ignorance.

"Your name! What is your name?" the captain shouted at her, this time in Turkish.

Again, Bajo shook her head, her face a picture of nervous bewilderment.

"Stupid woman! Are you deaf or dumb? What is your name?" the captain yelled, trying Kurdish, and quite angry by now.

"*Araby?*" Bajo pleaded with her interrogator, affecting utter confusion. "*Ana bet kellem Araby.* I speak Arabic. Please, can you tell me... where I am to go...I don't know why I..."

"*Iscuti!* Silence! I speak Arabic," the captain cut her off impatiently, but he sounded relieved as well. "Now, who are you and what is your name?"

As though he had released a floodgate, the words poured from

Bajo in a frightened, jumbled stream. "Who am I? I am an Arab woman, a poor washerwoman, sir. I was doing my washing...as I usually do this time of day...going about my business, when these soldiers came by with this group of people...and I had done nothing, nothing at all, as *Allah* is my witness, but they pulled me away from my work, without any reason...it is a meagre living that I earn...oh, what will become of me and my child now...washing is left...lost..." Bajo wailed, wringing her hands in despair.

"Oh, be silent woman!" the captain said in disgust, giving Bajo a sharp slap across the head. "You have wasted enough of my time, you and your stupid washing. I should send you with the rest just for annoying me. Ignorant creature! Get out of my sight before I change my mind."

He turned to one of the soldiers and shouted, angrily. "You! Come here at once. Which imbecile brought this babbling idiot? Have you people no sense at all? Get her out of here at once, and make sure it doesn't happen again or I will have your hide."

Holding Hedeya's hand tightly in her own, and with Derouhi silently tagging behind, Bajo quickly followed the soldier back to the gate and into the city.

From his rooftop perch, Diran watched in utter amazement, unable to comprehend what his eyes had just seen. Somehow, they seemed to have talked their way out of almost certain death! He saw them disappear, quickly, into the crowds below. He lost sight of them, but his heart was light, and his feet had wings.

He scrambled over the rooftops, carrying the good news back. But when he got there and told of what he had witnessed, Samuél Khayat refused to believe him. Such things do not just happen, it would take a miracle – and if one had taken place, where then was his daughter? And so, all that first day he prayed, and as the first day passed into the second, he continued to pray, but when the third day came and they still could not be found, he began to mourn.

Meanwhile, Bajo, Hedeya and Derouhi were cautiously making their way back, mingling inconspicuously with the crowds, dodging and hiding when they spotted any soldiers or marauding Kurds. The bazaar was a good place to lose oneself and, as they wandered through the ins and outs, Hedeya suddenly caught sight of a cow in one of the stalls. She stopped, pulling on Bajo's hand. There was no mistaking those eyes.

With a sudden cry, she ran towards the animal calling out, "Mankara! Mankara!"

Afraid the girl would attract attention, that someone would recognise who they were, Bajo tried to stop her, but Hedeya had already reached the animal and thrown her arms about it.

"Mankara," the girl whispered, "I've found you. I knew at once it was you."

The cow nuzzled her face, its velvet nose wet against her skin as it lowed softly, answering her; and what seemed like a tear rolled from its large, sad eyes mingling with those on the girl's cheeks. Bajo quickly pulled Hedeya away, apologising to the stall owner who was observing them suspiciously. And as they left, they could hear Mankara calling after them as she strained against her tether. No matter that Hedeya cried for hours after that, all her tears could not wash away the pain that filled her heart and made her feel as though it would break.

They eventually took sanctuary in the grounds of the Syrian church of *Meryem Ana Kilisesi*. Hedeya, still inconsolable, was able to rest some, and she began to recuperate, albeit slowly. It was here that Mustafa's two sons finally found them.

When the two men in army uniform first came looking for them, Bajo and Derouhi quickly lost themselves in the churchyard crowd. The other refugee women hid Hedeya beneath their *cherchefs*, the voluminous skirts providing ample camouflage for a small girl. When questioned, the women disclaimed all knowledge of anyone. However, the men returned on a second, and a third quest. Ultimately, realising that Hedeya, still unwell, would do better were she properly sheltered and fed, Bajo decided to trust the veracity of these two who claimed they were Mustafa's sons, charged with a message from her husband.

When Samuél Khayat finally saw his daughter, he was convinced he was dreaming; and then he believed his imagination must have run amok. He touched her face, hesitating, almost afraid she would disappear right before his eyes; he whispered her name, again and again till, at last, the little girl put her arms around his neck – and then he folded her in his arms, and wept tears of gratitude as he praised God for the return of his most precious gift.

———•◆•———

THE TIME EVENTUALLY CAME when things quieted somewhat, and Samuél Khayat tentatively ventured back to his own house on Kuçuk Kawaz. He found the top half of the house had been turned over to Dr. Liddel of the American Near East Relief. With Father Daniél

Nahoum Savçi's blessing, it was being used as a makeshift hospital and halfway house for the hundreds of destitute Armenian girls and abandoned orphan children being sent out of Turkey. Everyone knew time was short, and the lull in the killings was temporary only because there had been such a glut of violence in the area; the brief pause merely meant the butchers were catching their breath. No matter the reason, for a hounded and hunted people, the reprieve allowed a chance to brace for the coming bloodbath – or, if somehow possible, to escape it.

Dr. Liddel was grieved to give them news of Mankara and Zaino. Both animals had been taken away by some Kurds not long after Samuél and family had left, and he had been unable to prevent it. It was the last he had seen of Mankara. But, one day, there had been a rough pounding at the door, and when it had been opened, they discovered Zaino – she had found her way home and was waiting patiently to be let in. She was rubbed down, fed and watered, but the Kurds came again, demanding her return. Dr. Liddel tried to dissuade them, but they became aggressive, and as he had no legal standing regarding the horse, or indeed the house, he could not risk trouble with the law. And so, they took her away. Weeks later that pounding at the door was heard again, and when they opened it, they found Zaino had come home once more. Her heart knew where she belonged, and her will proved stronger than those who would have taken her; so this time, she laid her head at the door of her home and she died – she had come home, finally, to stay.

Although their living quarters were now below stairs, so to speak, Hedeya had never enjoyed her home as much as she did now. After what they had been through those past months, the accommodation downstairs was more than adequate, and there was no need to disrupt the essential work the Near East Relief was doing upstairs.

At first, she hardly left sight of her parents. Bajo and Baba Taht went about the big house doing what they could to help Dr. Liddel and the other Americans, and like a shadow she followed, watching, listening, always keeping close to one or the other. After a while she began to be less afraid. The resilience and curiosity of childhood sent her roaming on her own, observing and talking to those who came and went. One day she met an old friend.

Orphaned Armenian children and girls, fortunate to be rescued, were brought from all over and, whenever possible, groups would be sent out of the country to stop-gap places like Aleppo and Beirut. The Americans were working as fast as they could, taking advantage of the short lull to get as many as possible to comparative safety. One day, a small group was brought in by Father Daniél, and among the older girls Hedeya recognised Shamuné, one of Baba Taht's two protégées who had been kidnapped from Karabash by Turkish soldiers. Where was Baizar, then, Hedeya wanted to know? She had been taken as well. What had become of her?

Shamuné gave her the news: After the soldiers had done with them, they had both been put to work in Turkish households not far from each other. Shamuné had managed to run away and she had gone straight to the priest's house, but poor Baizar was still there in the house of a Turk named Osman Oztürk.

"It is not far from where we are. Come, I will take you; not all the way mind, in case they see me, but I will show you where it is. And since they don't know you, maybe you will be able to get close enough to see Baizar."

As a precaution, Shamuné covered her head and the lower half of her face with a scarf and made Hedeya do the same. After that, she led Hedeya down several cobbled streets, turned right and left a few times, and then she stopped and pointed to the end of the road. "Turn left at the end there, go all the way down to the second last house on the right, that's where she is."

Hedeya followed the instructions, and the closer she came to the house, the harder she could feel her heart thump inside her chest – like some small, frightened animal trying to escape. Instinctively, she began to walk on tiptoe as though that might prevent her being discovered. As luck would have it, she saw Baizar at once, sweeping the entrance. Removing her scarf, she called softly to her. Baizar looked up, her eyes widening when she saw Hedeya. Looking around quickly to see if anyone was watching, she continued to sweep as she approached closer to the street.

"Hedeya, what are you doing here? I was afraid you had all been killed!"

"Baizar, listen! The Americans have brought one of those big trucks, and it is leaving for Aleppo today. Shamuné is going, and if you come to our house, Baba Taht will tell the Americans to put you on it."

"How will I go?" Baizar said tearfully. "The neighbours know me, and someone is sure to see me if I try to run away." She thought for a quick moment. "I don't care, I will go! Give me your scarf," she said, urgently. "I will use it to hide my face. Wait for me at the corner. Give me five minutes to make sure the way is clear, and I will meet you there. Go quickly, I think someone is coming."

Hedeya did not wait to see if Baizar was right. She ran back to Shamuné as fast as she could and told her what had transpired. Then they waited. Five minutes. Ten. They grew more nervous with every passing minute now. Shamuné must not get caught! If one of the neighbours walked by and recognised her.... Fifteen minutes had now passed, and still there was no sign of Baizar. Something must have happened. They would have to leave without her!

"Just two minutes more," Hedeya pleaded, desperate not to give up on her friend. She crossed her fingers, hopping impatiently from foot to foot as the seconds slipped by. Nothing. At last, they could wait no longer. Reluctantly, they turned to leave when, suddenly, they heard running footsteps. Half afraid of who might be approaching, they were ready to run when Baizar, nearly slipping in her haste, rounded the corner.

"Quick! I was seen talking to you and it made them suspicious," she gasped, breathless, as shouts could be heard behind her. Needing no further encouragement, all three girls took to their heels and fled as fast as their legs could carry them, stopping only when they reached the house and passed through its gates to safety. Two hours later Shamuné and Baizar were on their way to Aleppo.

Baizar finally settled in Beirut, where Hedeya would visit her forty years later and reminisce about old times; but Shamuné captained her ship to much further shores. When she left Diyarbekir, the priest gave a letter into her safekeeping. It was from Samuél Khayat's brother, Ohan Khayat, who had immigrated to America some years before, and had written the priest requesting a hometown bride.

In Diyarbekir by now, the pickings were few. Of those who had survived, most had fled to cities like Aleppo and Beirut. As such, the priest believed – and rightly so – that Ohan Khayat's search would fare far better in those cities where there would be any number of contenders for a proposal such as his. And so, the letter was to be handed over to Ohan Khayat's cousin in Aleppo in the belief that she would best broker his wishes.

As it happened, Shamuné took matters into her own hands. Having opened the letter and read it, she asked herself the question: surely, she was as good as any? Concluding that she was, she determined to avail herself of the opportunity fate had handed her, which meant that she would do exactly what had been asked of her, with one small deviation – she told Ohan's cousin in Aleppo that she had been chosen as his bride. Her ingenuity and resolve got her on a ship to New York, where she met and married Ohan Khayat, and went on to live a long, fruitful and safe life, trying to forget the strife of her girlhood.

With the departure of the two girls, that should have been the end of that story; but, as it happened, it did not quite finish there.

In better times a visit to the *Hamam*, the Turkish bath, was a regular affair, not merely for the purposes of ablution, but for social pleasure as well. It was segregated, for the men in the morning, with the women visiting towards the latter part of the day. Time slots were reserved, and one dressed in much finery, almost as though one were attending a party of sorts.

An accompanying *natora* (maid) carried the essential items to be used: a brass box with compartments to contain a paraphernalia of combs, soaps, and two kinds of sponges – a soft *loofah* and a rough *keese* glove. Other essentials were a couple of *takhtayas* (short wooden stools) for seating, and the *kazan*, a large three-to-four foot high vessel for hot water with a second metal bowl, the *tasset el hamam*, that fit in its mouth and was used for pouring. And, of course, some small eats for the bathers' enjoyment.

Large and steamy, the *Hamam* had an enormous cold-water pool in the centre; and for the more affluent customers who could pay for the comfort, there were cubicles where hot water was available. The Turkish bath was a place for social chit chat, gossip, and the sharing of nuts, dried fruits, *lokum* (Turkish delight), and sometimes even an orange, expensive and rare as they were, as well as any other such delicacies one might procure.

For the first time since their return, Bajo decided to venture a visit with Hedeya to the local *Hamam*. No longer one of the privileged, she was bathing in the general area and catching up with the latest news while Hedeya was roaming the hall. Suddenly, there was a piercing scream.

A large Turkish woman, her face purple with anger, ran towards Hedeya screaming, "That's her! I saw her! That's the little devil who took Baizar from my house!" and she hit the girl with her *tassset el hamam* chasing her around the room, flailing the metal bowl like a lethal weapon. Hedeya, small and quick, outran the lumbering woman, and eventually managed to hide behind Bajo, who tried to calm her pursuer, saying she must be mistaken. But the woman would have none of it. Quivering with rage, she wagged an accusing finger at the cowering girl.

"I know what I know, and I saw what I saw. Just wait till I get my hands on her!" she screeched. "I'll teach her to steal from me!"

Judging the woman was beyond reason, that the situation was beyond amelioration and verging on the dangerous, Bajo astutely determined it was time to beat a hasty retreat. Fortunately for all concerned, no more came of it, and that day ended the story of Baizar's escape.

Then there was Arè Valous, a big, beautiful girl endowed with a strapping body, lovely doe-like eyes and long, thick hair like the tail of a horse. She had been taken from her mother's house, and for a year no one knew where she was – until one day she was spotted in the house of Berevan Chelki, the Kurd.

When her mother heard the news, she found *Burak katirçi*, the caravan headman in whose charge the girls would travel to school, and she bribed him to bring her back. As proof that he had, indeed, been sent by her mother, he was given a piece of embroidery that Arè Valous had once made as a gift for her.

When Arè Valous was given this, she cried; the situation, it turned out, was not as simple as anticipated. Over time the Kurd had grown fond of her and shown her kindness; and she, eventually, had borne him a child. In fact, while she was pregnant, his favour had extended to the consideration of taking upon himself the chore of drawing water from the well to save her the trouble. Of course, it was not something he would be caught dead doing! And so, to maintain his reputation, he would perform this task by night rather than by day, as was usual with the women.

Now Arè Valous was torn between her child and her real family, between motherhood and her own identity. If she left, she would have to leave without her child, for she was never allowed out alone unless it was to draw water from the well. She knew too that her son would be reared as a Muslim, just as she had been forced to convert. Whether she stayed or left, there was nothing she could do about that fact. Her heritage was lost to him. But now, she was being given the chance to return to it, to her own people. Either way, it was a painful decision, and she wept many tears over it. In the end, Arè Valous held her son in her arms, she crooned to him, and kissed him goodbye. Then, she went to draw water from the well where the *katirçi* had said he would wait for her, and she never returned.

One day a badly disfigured woman came to the Americans. She was an elderly woman whose nose had been partially cut off, and she was accompanied by a young girl. "My son is dead," she said, "so is my daughter-in-law. This is my granddaughter. She is all the family I have left. Take her. She is just eleven years old. Save her, please."

She told them how it had happened. Her daughter-in-law had

been pregnant. The soldiers had bet on the gender of the child. Then they slit open her belly with a sword, and everything inside had fallen out. The girl had started to scream; a horrible sound, a terrible gurgling in her throat like she was being strangled, inhuman almost, unbearable to hear. She sank to the ground, tried desperately to reach for the child to stuff it back into her belly, her hands slipping through her entrails; and then, one of the men cut off her head. It was to stop the "damnable noise" she was making, he said.

"They wouldn't allow me to help her; when I tried, the soldier cut off my nose with his sword. I saw it lying there on the ground and as I bent to retrieve it, he hit me on the back of my head with the wooden end of his rifle. Here." She showed them a deep, ugly wound just behind her right ear where the skull had split open. The small girl, her face expressionless as stone, had not uttered a sound. The woman pushed her forward. "There is no one left to protect her. She is the last of our family. Please, see that she lives."

And so it went, day after day. Brutalised, violated, tortured and killed – the helpless looking for help, and the time and ability to give it running short. As months passed, and seasons changed, and the deportations still continued, it was hoped that the snows of winter, oftentimes severe enough to barricade people in their homes, would bring a halt to the forced marches; that maybe time would scab over some of the wounds of that dreadful summer. For those few who remained of a once proud and ancient people now hounded to near extinction, it was all they could hope for – a chance to crawl out of the dark pit of annihilation and despair they had been thrown into, a chance for faith to repair and re-affirm itself.

All felt the threat of persecution hanging over them like the sharp-edged sword of Damocles; yet, such is the perseverance of the human spirit, each day of respite that followed the one before, somewhat blunted the urgency of the moment. So much so that when the gendarmes finally did come once more, looking for Samuél Khayat, the shock sent a renewed tidal wave of panic that swept all else before it.

Dr. Liddel told them that Samuél Khayat had not been living there for months; that the house had been given into the keeping of Father Daniél Nahoum Savçi who had allowed the use of it to him for the American Near East Relief. No, no one knew the whereabouts of the man they were looking for or, indeed, of his family. Dr. Liddel's prevarication bought a short reprieve; the soldiers departed, but there was no doubt whatsoever that they would be back before long. The time had come for Samuél Khayat and his family to leave the country.

The departure had to be immediate. This time their absence would be an extended one; however, it was still hoped that it would be temporary. Once again, the care of the city house on Kuçuk Kawaz and the holdings in the village of Karabash were left to the care of Father Daniél. Everything else, including the hidden valuables and gold coins, was left undisturbed and undisclosed. The hiding places were well chosen, and all had remained safe through times of peace and war. Why make change where no change was required? After all, God willing, it would be only a few months till their return. The question was, however, where should they go?

"My brother, Ohan, has been asking that I join him in New York," Samuél Khayat pondered the thought. "But what a world away that is! Too far a journey, too distant a shore. Someday, maybe...maybe... For now, however, I think we should visit my relatives in Egypt."

That night they put together what little they had at hand and made ready their departure. Since it was more than likely the Near East Relief truck would be watched, they travelled instead with an Arab caravan carrying carpets to Lebanon. Samuél Khayat used this to advantage.

He selected two of his best carpets from the house, richly woven works of art. In one, he placed a small box containing Bajo's gold flower-shaped earrings with blue enamel and small rose cut diamonds, her little ruby cross, Hedeya's gold heart pendant, and the small bag of gold coins Hedeya had carried previously, tied at her waist to dangle between her legs. Beside these he laid Bajo's gift to him, the carefully wrapped eleventh-century family bible written in the old script, its capital letters scrolled and festooned with brilliantly hued birds and flowers, its cover adorned with the ancient gold coin of the Byzantine Empire. All these he rolled securely inside the one carpet, after which he rolled the other and placed both alongside those belonging to a Bedouin carpet merchant. As an added precaution, to further reduce the chance of recognition, Bajo and Hedeya were to travel as part of a separate Arab family.

Getting past the soldiers at the city gates was harrowing, but the search was a cursory one, and they made it through without mishap. It was after reaching Mardin, when Baba Taht had gone to find the whereabouts of an old friend, that word got out about them. A servant from that household sold them out. His price – a mere pittance! But it was enough. After all, what could one expect in exchange for Armenian swine! It was the age-old betrayal for thirty pieces of silver!

Baba Taht had not returned when the gendarmes came and

took Bajo and Hedeya away. The servant had pointed them out and, thereafter, the soldiers would brook no interference. Mother and daughter were made to join a ragtag group of deportees on its way to Tel Abiad in Syria. For Hedeya, the rest was a jumble of broken memories and very dark places filled with terror and shame. They had been forced to travel a circuitous route, mile after unnecessary mile. They had dragged themselves across the desert on blistered, bleeding feet, they had suffered hunger and thirst, eating grass when they could find it and sucking their own perspiration and the morning dew from their clothes to bring some relief to parched lips and swollen tongues. Hedeya's young eyes witnessed atrocities and cruelties she would never speak of because her mind, unable to comprehend, unable to cope with the degradation and fear, finally closed down on itself and she became delirious with a high fever.

Bajo carried her, comforted her, foraged for scraps of food and clothing, and prayed that the good Lord would spare her. Had He not, in His mercy, given her this last child as restitution, as recompense for all that was lost? Surely, He would not abandon them now!

She had been unaware that Baba Taht had escaped capture with the help of the Bedouin sheikh. When the soldiers had tried to arrest him, the sheikh told them they were mistaken. "He is one of us. Do you not hear he speaks Arabic like I do? Look, here are some of his carpets. He can describe them to you, and you can open them and see for yourself." They did – luckily, the one they opened did not have anything hidden inside it! After that, the sheik denounced them as anti-Muslim sinners for the evils they had perpetrated on helpless women and children.

She had not known that Baba Taht had hurried desperately after them; and when the caravan arrived in Tel Abiad, with the help of the same Bedouin sheikh, he had, somehow, against all possible odds, found them in that terrible camp. He had sunk to his knees beside them, holding them within the circle of his arms, and he had thanked God, once again, for the miracle of bringing them together.

A few days later they managed to get on a train to Aleppo, and thence on to Beirut in Lebanon, where they bid a grateful goodbye to their Arab benefactor. They spent almost a week there before obtaining passage on a small Egyptian passenger ship bound for Alexandria, Egypt. The train, the ship, the sea, a blur of strange unreal images that slipped by barely touching Hedeya's fevered brain. At Alexandria they boarded a train for Cairo; when they arrived, she was still quite ill and hardly recalled the journey at all.

Slowly, with care and nourishment and rest, she recovered her health – and then life in the big city proved to be remarkable! There was so much to see and do that was new. Cairo, known as the Paris of the East, threw itself open to the cosmopolitan world of fashion and glamour; the people, the languages, the buildings, vibrant and varied, fast, frenzied and fascinating – and free from fear and treachery. The modern metropolis of Cairo was vastly different from the old-town, village atmosphere of Diyarbekir and Karabash. And slowly Hedeya began to settle in, to make friends and enjoy her new surroundings.

Months went by, and news that filtered out of Turkey was unsettling. To set an example, and to affirm his rule, Mustapha Kemal Ataturk, new leader of Turkey, had ordered some public hangings of certain key individuals known to have propagated the recent mass killings, and who had, even more recently, tried to assassinate him. It seemed it would be a while before the time would be propitious for a return home. And yet, knowing that the small amount of gold coins they had brought with them would eventually run out, Samuél Khayat considered returning to Diyarbekir alone. But Bajo would have none of it; it was still too risky. When the time came to return, they would do so together, but that time was not quite yet. They should wait a while longer.

The months passed into a year, and beyond; and still they waited. Then they heard that Mustapha Kemal Ataturk had sent out a proclamation to the effect that all who owned property were required to put in their claims, along with proper proof of ownership. It concluded with a deadline that had to be met.

Bajo Saidé discovered her husband sitting alone with his head in his hands. "What is the matter, Samuél?" she enquired, anxiously.

Her husband lifted his head slowly, his pale face wet with tears. "We are too late, Saidé. We have lost all." His voice broke. "The news arrived too late; the deadline is past. When he did not hear from us, Father Daniél claimed the property for the church to prevent the government taking it." He shook his head in disbelief. "There is nothing now for us to return to in Diyarbekir. Nothing! What are we to do?"

Gone! With the world spinning around her, Bajo Saidé gripped the back of her husband's chair and closed her eyes. She must not faint. After all they had been through, now this! What were they to do? Travel to America was out of the question, since their remaining funds would be inadequate to buy their passage as well as provide sustenance at the other end. She took a deep breath and summoned all her faith. There was only one thing to do.

"We will stay here." She was surprised how steady her voice sounded. "We will do God's will. He has brought us to a good land; it is a land unmarked by blood. He has saved our lives, and if He has led us this far, then it is for a reason. Let us find out what it is. See Samuél, this now will be our new home."

Samuél Khayat's 11th Century Family Bible.

Byzantine gold coin (front/back) from cover of 11th Century Bible. 1071-1078 AD Michael VII El Histamenon Nomisma.

CHAPTER ELEVEN

The Shadow Of Kali

As then the Tulip for her morning sup
Of Heav'nly Vintage from the soil looks up,
Do you devoutly do the like, till Heav'n
To Earth invert you…like an empty Cup.

– Omar Khayyam, *Rubaiyat of Omar Khayyam*

THE DAY STARTED AT 5am. As usual, Dilbahadur made Santi's morning tea and brought it, steaming hot, in his mess-kit tin mug to the trench where he had spent the night. Under combat conditions, the trench became home; it was here one ate, slept and washed. As for a soldier's white-enamelled tin mug, it was a much-valued, multi-purpose vessel from which one drank, washed and shaved. After having put it to just such good use, Santi made his way to the large tent emblazoned with a red cross that housed the field ambulance's Main Dressing Station.

There, among the wounded, lay Basantbir Thapa and Gunprasad Thapa, their last names indicative not so much of family as that they hailed from the same locale back home. Basantbir had been shot in the chest a little above and to the left of his heart when, as a medical orderly, he had gone to Gunprasad's aid. Gunprasad, a rifleman, had suffered a leg wound which wasn't too serious. He would recover and live, Basantbir was not expected to.

Santi was checking a head wound when Roger Werner arrived with orders that the 2/10 Gurkhas, with a squadron from the 13th Lancers, were to spearhead the attack on Deir ez Zor. The rest of the 13th Lancers, together with the 4/13 Frontier Force Rifles, were to go around to the rear of the town, to lock down the backdoor, so to speak. Since petrol was in extremely short supply, Werner, as Motor Transport Officer, had been given strict orders that the vehicles of all other units were to be emptied, and their petrol held ready to facilitate the flanking column's backdoor sally.

"Not my ambulance, surely!" Santi protested. "Damn it Werner! What about the wounded? What if they have to be moved in a hurry?"

Werner shook his head. "If it comes to that, we'll all be in the same leaky boat – and up the proverbial creek, don't you know." He grimaced. "Sorry Doc, I'm afraid it can't be helped."

Glumly resigned to hoping for the best, Santi headed to the Officers' Mess. Maybe he could grab a bite before the action started.

The "Officers' Mess," such as it was, comprised two parallel trenches established in a small area to one side of the camp. Still anxious about his commandeered fuel, he was approximately thirty yards away from it when the attack came.

Santi heard the aircraft before he saw them. It took a fleeting moment for the sound to register. When he looked up, he saw them coming in, like avenging arrows shot from some goliath's bow – one, two, three formations swept out of the sky and honed in on their targets. As they drew nearer, they peeled off and closed in. One of the Martins actually seemed to be heading straight towards him. He got ready to sprint to the Mess trench when he realized, with sudden horror, there was no way he could make it – and there was nothing nearby that might adequately shield him from the bomb he knew was about to be dropped on him!

My God! He thought, suddenly frantic. NO! Not like this...

For an instant that seemed an eternity, he stood rooted to the spot as his fate rushed towards him with a power and surety that was paralyzing. His body seemed weighed down by an outside force sweeping over him so that, incredibly, for the very life of him, he couldn't get his limbs to move!

Through the din of the approaching aircraft's engine, he thought he heard a voice call out behind him. Unclear, but oddly familiar, it made him turn around, which was how he came to notice the partially dug slit trench roughly twenty-five feet away. It was hardly more than a hole in the ground, and his thoughts registered in snatches... won't do...too small...inadequate protection...

He stood six feet one inch tall! No way would that ditch accommodate his entire torso! Well, even so, surely something was better than nothing. He couldn't just stand there like a lightning rod, waiting for disaster! And he had better make his decision damn quick. Question was, if he did make it, should he dive in headfirst, or feet first.

Hell's bells! What was he thinking! He was wasting precious seconds weighing the merits of preserving head over backside when he knew full well if his head were exposed and he lost it, he was bloody well done for anyway.

Unbidden, a wayward thought nudged aside that voice of sense, flashing an illogical picture in his mind's eye: head down, arse exposed to the unreliable humour of the gods – the indignity of a peppered derriere and the consequent discomfort of those long hours in convoy! Oh, horror!

Quite suddenly, the absurdity of his thoughts hit him, and he almost laughed out loud. For goodness sake! This was no time for his wits to go awandering. Not with that damn aircraft tearing straight down towards him!

Reality finally took hold and galvanized him into action. Quickly, he pulled himself together, muttering through gritted teeth, "Oh no, you French bastard! You don't get me that easily, you don't!"

He turned, and sprinted. And now his training as a runner and long jumper stood him in good stead. From the approaching roar of the Martin's engines, he sensed it gaining on him. He heard the shrill scream of the bomb behind him, nearer and nearer, chasing him, and he leapt the final distance into the slit trench. He landed in the dugout and clapped his hands over his ears.

There was a strange silence; then, a tremendous burst of sound and a violent upheaval of sand where he had been standing a few moments ago. The impact of the explosion flung him with painful force against the side of the trench. It felt as though his head had been ripped off his shoulders, the air knocked out of his body like so much stuffing. His chest felt crushed, as if some solid, heavy weight had slammed into it. For a few seconds, he was unable to suck the air back into his lungs which felt as though they had collapsed.

I'm hit! he thought, pressing his hands hard against his chest. Oh damn, I'm hit!

At least it didn't hurt the way he'd imagined it would. He opened his eyes. There was a strange ringing in his ears, and showers of sand were falling silently all around him. His faculties were probably slipping away, he thought, almost matter of factly. If this is what it felt like…to die…

His lips parted and, with a sudden gush, air rushed into his lungs. For a few moments he lay there, his lungs filling with air, his breath quietening. Slowly, he moved his hands over his chest. There didn't seem to be much wrong there – nothing broken, nothing bleeding. No, everything was as it should be. He felt a profound relief as sensation began to return to his body. He was all in one piece.

Strangely, though, the world around him seemed to be enveloped in complete silence. He couldn't hear a thing. His body was trembling, and he realised with something of a shock, it was the delayed reaction to both fear and exhilaration. Fear over his hair's-breadth brush with death, and exhilaration that he had actually scraped through with his life. When the shaking eventually subsided, he took a moment to make doubly sure all his various parts were in their right place. He shook himself free of sand like a dog coming out of water, picked up his hat-felt Gurkha which had blown off his head, and looked around for the person who had called out to him.

There was no one there. He was quite alone. He could have sworn he hadn't imagined the voice, but as far as he could see, there wasn't another soul in sight. He was still puzzling over what had just taken place, when an even stranger thought struck him – from what he recalled, the voice he'd heard was female! And certainly, there were no women anywhere in the area! He shook his head, bewildered.

His bewilderment would have been manifold had he but known that, far away, almost at that precise moment, an uncanny incident had occurred in Calcutta.

At his home, his Mother had collapsed on the kitchen floor. Sudha, about to leave for college, was at the front door when she heard the strangled cry. Already running late for her History of English Language class, she dropped her books in the open doorway and rushed to the kitchen. She found her Mother sitting in a heap on the floor. *What happened, Ma?*

Usha Moyee saw the concern in her daughter's eyes as she allowed herself to be helped up. Still shaken, she sat down on the small kitchen stool. She had just taken the fish out to prepare for dinner when a terrible noise started in her head. She saw Santi and a gigantic, shiny bird swooping down towards him as though to carry him away. She tried to call out, to warn him, but her voice stuck in her throat, almost suffocating her. Clutching at her breast, when at last she found her voice, her instinctive cry, "Oh, Ma!" had been to the Mother Goddess for help in protecting her son.

Whether the two episodes – far removed from each other, in two separate countries – were merely coincidental, or whether the desperate plea of one mother to another touched and softened the fierce heart of the Goddess Kali, will never be known. But some mysteries are best left that way, and the mercy of a blessing should be accepted with simple gratitude and without question.

No matter the case, Santi was aware it had been a close call, and he was grateful to have come through alive. The relief, however, was short-lived. In spite of the combined efforts of the Bren guns and machine guns, the Martins returned, braving the tracers that arced through the sky. Once more Santi saw them bearing down, choosing their targets...towards him...over him... unwavering...straight for the MDS. He leapt to his feet, shouting, all thought of personal safety gone. He sprinted towards the MDS as if, somehow, he would shout down or outrun the aircraft.

Two bombs fell on the hospital tent. An ugly haze built up around the area. Santi tried to peer through it while he continued to run as though his life depended on it. His breathing was ragged. A painful, choking sensation gripped the base of his throat, and there was a terrible pounding in his head near his temples – and, the thing of it was, oddly enough, it wasn't his legs that hurt with running, but the rigid muscles in his jaw and his neck.

When he arrived on the scene, it was one of utter devastation. Many of the wounded and sick now lay dead, as did some of the nursing staff. Santi realised the strange haze he had tried to peer through was not just the dust-up from the explosion, it was a rush of futile anger that had welled up from his throat and misted his eyes. It made him clench his fists so hard, his nails, short as they were, had cut into his palms. His jaws, clamped tight as a vice, made the muscles in his neck and face stiff. Surveying the damage, he found it difficult to speak. In any case, there were no words to describe the tragedy. Both Basantbir Thapa and Gunprasad Thapa were among the dead. It was almost as though Fate, having been thwarted once, refused to be cheated of them in the end.

The bombing continued all that day and into the next. Allied air cover was sadly inadequate – four Hurricanes and four Gladiators – and all four Hurricanes were shot down. The attack on Deir ez Zor lasted two days, until finally, on 3 July, the city was captured, its suspension bridge intact. Next day, new orders sent the 2/4 Gurkhas on to Raqqa, while the rest of their Brigade remained to hold the town.

RAQQA LAY SOME ONE hundred miles up-river, due west. A squadron of the 13th Lancers, an 18-pounder battery from 157 Field Regiment, a section of 9th Field Company Sappers and Miners and a detachment of 29 Field Ambulance under charge of the 2/4 Gurkhas set out for the town.

The convoy left under skies still dark in order to avoid the attentions of the Vichy bombers. It crossed the river and headed into a desert quite unlike any they had experienced so far. The *Jazirah* was the steppe land of Syria. During the melting of the snows in the mountains of Turkey, the area became marshy wetlands thick with riverine vegetation and reed beds. Now it was a rippling desert of dry, brown grass through which men and machines had to trek.

The going was hampered by a one-inch-to-sixteen-mile map not worth the weight of the paper it was drawn on. Often what it depicted as a mere dip turned out to be an impasse, and what might appear to be an unfordable gorge proved to be a *nullah*, a deep drain.

"Damn and blast!" Colonel Weallens exploded, finally. "Which bloody idiot produced this…this…good for nothing piece of rubbish! A more confounding and useless implement I have yet to come across. I daresay it would do much better as a red herring to misdirect the enemy, rather than a guide of any reliability to lead one's way."

There were no visible roads through the swaying sea of brown grass. After a few false stops and starts, Jack Masters drew attention to some litter that lay scattered about.

"Look here, sir. I believe we might follow this trail of discards. It appears recently made, quite probably by the fleeing French. It's certainly headed in the right direction and worth a try, wouldn't you say?"

For lack of a better option, Col. Weallens agreed – and indeed, it turned out a fortuitous decision that served their purpose well. They began making good time. Santi had taken permission to march up front with Masters and the vanguard of Lancers. They halted every so often to get their bearings and relay those back to Col. Weallens. He noticed each time they did so, back would come the cryptic reply, HOA, following which the column would move on.

Try as he would, Santi could not call to mind any reference or code that might throw light on this particular form of communication. Ultimately, he bit the bullet and turned for enlightenment to Jack, who was happy to acquaint him with the traditional niceties of cavalry lingo: HOA, it would appear, was the abbreviation for "Hack on, Algernon!" That might be all well and good…but…who in the world was Algernon? Everyone and no one, perhaps starting with someone, somewhere in time, Jack endeavoured to explain. Whatever its origin, translated into layman's parlance, it meant, simply "Carry on, old chap!"

Was he serious! Or was he…? Santi sighed, and gave in – despite being educated in English, it seemed apparent he never would completely understand the idiosyncrasies of the Englishman's vernacular.

They finally arrived at Raqqa, a town so old one could supposedly trace it back, so they were informed, to the time of the Arabian Nights Stories. Surrounded by a huge mud-brick wall, it had a tower in the centre inscribed by the ancient Medes or Persians. To the west was an old-style 'Beau Geste' fort, encircled by trenches and barbed wire. A new town had sprung up next to the old one which sat, hunched and brooding over its dark past. And though, here too, there were no longer any obvious traces of the Armenian refugee camp of a few years ago, Samira's stories still lingered in Santi's mind, and hung like a veil of horror and misery over the place and its surroundings.

It turned out the Vichy French and their friends had abandoned the town, leaving it a complete shambles – the perpetrator, it would seem, was no other than their elusive quarry, Fawzi Qawukchi. That slippery customer had managed, once more, to keep one step ahead of them. Speaking to the good, however, they were able to take Raqqa on 5 July without so much as a skirmish.

Howbeit, before they could rest on their laurels, the sound of low-flying aircraft approached the town. The first evening they caught a lucky break – a dust storm spared them a visitation from the bombs. Not so the following day. The French came back, and they came in force, with six Morane multi-gun fighters, all barrels blazing. Each fighter carried six to eight guns and each gun fired 1,300 rounds a minute, raining shot and shell as the planes lunged at their enemy on the ground. They swooped in, and up, and out, and around again, glinting in the sunlight, looking, for a few fleeting moments like a gracefully choreographed ballet, beautiful, yet deadly.

Major J.W.A. Lowis – "Beetle" to his cronies – entertained no such appreciation. Bristling with indignation at enduring pot shot after pot shot, he decided to return the favour personally. Manning the nearest machine gun, he went for the nearest plane – and got it. With an enormous shout of victory, he watched as the wounded aircraft wobbled and sputtered away into the distance. Take that, you French flea! Ah, the sweet taste of revenge!

Meanwhile, Shirley Temple was enjoying a leisurely bathe in the river. Heedful of Santi's cautions, he was careful to wade in where the current of free-flowing waters minimised the danger of worm infestation. It was here the enemy found him.

Having shed his clothes on the bank, he was stark naked when he noticed the Moranes making an apparent beeline for him. He glared up at them. Then, undeterred by modesty, he leapt from the water in the altogether, grabbed his revolver, and emptied it defiantly at the intruders. To make sure his message was received and understood, as clear as it had been loud, he waited till they were directly overhead to give them a two-finger salute, followed, for good measure, by bending over and very deliberately wiggling his bare arse skyward.

For those who knew him – and, indeed, even for many who did

not – this peerless gesture left no doubt the two-finger salutation was not an imitation of Churchill's famous victory sign. Certainly not! His compeers would lay their money on a far more robust, far ruder message, which prompted delighted whoops and encouraging cries from all fortunate enough to witness it.

"Oh, nice one, Shirley!"

"Atta boy Shirl! Show 'em your assets."

And, by far the best – "Bums awayyyy!"

Notwithstanding this appreciation of his eloquent display, Shirley decided against any further derring-do and scampered off to take cover. All said and done, better men than he had conceded wisdom to be the greater part of valour – a sound motto, suggesting a man not push his luck too far!

The Moranes came back again that day, and the next. Jack limped into the ADS tent for some first aid. Just a small patch-up job. The oddness of his injury, however, caused much speculation. At first he was glumly reticent, but when pressed, he grudgingly admitted that sheer bad luck had caught him in the wrong position, in the wrong place, at the wrong time. As bullets showered down from the aircraft, they very nearly got him. It was such a close call, in fact, that one actually zipped through the seat of his trousers, scorching a neat hole, and administering on the way, a small yet painful graze to his behind. The hilarious response he received was fully what he had anticipated! And, as if that were not bad enough, Shirley insisted on adding greatly to his annoyance when he took to humming "Pennies from Heaven" every time Jack was within earshot.

After the Moranes' morning visit on the second day, no one was surprised to hear them return for a repeat performance in the afternoon. They were ready for them. The Bren guns and the machine guns opened fire together, chasing the aircraft as they whipped by, strafing the camp. Only when they were overhead did Col. Weallens and Jack, simultaneously, notice the RAF markings on the planes. Bloody hell! They were being shot at by their own side!

"Dash it all! What the devil do they think they're playing at!" spluttered the CO, rushing off to fire a broadside of his own, via field telephone, at whoever was responsible. "Don't the blighters have any idea what they are about? It's bad enough being done in by the bloody enemy, but when your own side lends a hand…" As he strode purposefully towards the office and the telephone to give some poor sod at the other end what for, he could still be heard, grumbling…"Flaming great idiots, don't know arse from elbow…"

Such were the fortunes of war.

IT WAS UNDERSTOOD THE Vichy had been pushed north, up against
the Turkish border. At any rate, other than the forays of its aircraft,
the enemy on the ground was nowhere to be seen. The night of
6 July, quiet reigned over the camp at Raqqa. All except the sentries
were at rest, and the dark desert night was soft with starlight. It was
sometime deep into the night when a sudden commotion splintered
the silence and roused the camp from its sleep.

Catching sight of a movement in the shadows, one of the sentries
issued a challenge. "Halt! Who goes there?"

Instead of the usual answer of "Friend," the Gurkha sentry was
met with, what sounded to him, a spate of unintelligible gibberish.

"Advance and be Recognised!" the sentry shouted a second warning. His bayonet at the ready, he peered into the night.

Instead of a verbal reply, he was surprised to glimpse the dim outline of an approaching rider hoisting a white flag. He immediately
sounded the alarm. The night erupted in pandemonium, setting
the whole camp about its ears with much conjecturing as to what
was afoot. Finally, when order was once more restored, much to everyone's amazement, it was discovered that a squadron of French
Spahis had ridden in to surrender themselves. From these voluntary prisoners it was learnt that the small French garrisons all along
the Turkish border were being vacated, and the enemy was escaping
west, across the Euphrates to Djerablous.

Hearing this, Col. Weallens immediately leapt to the occasion. He
sent a request for permission to pursue the enemy as far as Tel Abiad,
the old border town approximately sixty miles north of Raqqa. After
some consideration, permission was granted, and on the night of 8
July, leaving a small contingent to hold Raqqa, the rest of the battalion left for Tel Abiad.

They drove through the moonlit desert, and since there are no
landmarks of any sort in those vast expanses, it was very like navigating one's way on the open sea. However, Masters had done such a
slap-up job of navigating their way to Raqqa, it had drawn Col. Weallens' approbation – "You seem to know your onions, Jack."

So, once again, Jack and Amarsingh Gurung hung on the running board of the lead truck, armed with a compass, a torch and
a map – which, true to form, didn't impart much of anything.

Peering into the light beam thrown by their torch, they attempted, as much by guesswork as anything, to pick their way through the desert night.

A serene stillness had settled on the desert, and in that world of silver shadows it was hard to imagine there was a war going on. Their progress was slow, travelling eight miles per hour. At one point, Jack called a halt to the convoy to check the direction of some tracks in the sand. Once the throaty rumble of the engines subsided, the sudden silence of the night was startling. The quiet of the desert enveloped them like a velvet blanket. The stars in the sky were legion; a profusion of brilliant, icy pinpoints, like a myriad glittering diamonds thickly scattered into the ink-black canopy of the heavens. Most of the men were asleep. Except for the occasional rustle or clink of equipment, as someone eased a cramped muscle or shifted a numb limb, there was not a sound to be heard.

A single rifle shot barked through the air. The sudden, violent sound exploded, shattering the night and startling everyone awake. Then, somewhere out in the darkness, a deuce of a ruckus ensued. Shouts and shots rang out simultaneously as bullets, stones, sticks, a burning torch, and a slew of pots, pans and other unrecognisable objects came hurtling through the air.

Everyone, wide awake now, hastily prepared for action. Santi jumped down from the lorry just as a lethal looking missile sailed past his head, missing it by a hairsbreadth. Propelled by its handle, like a long-tailed comet, it whistled past his ear and met its demise against the side of his truck. Santi peered at the absurd object in astonished disbelief – the felled trajectile was a *kanaka*, for goodness sake! A vessel to brew Arabic coffee! He remembered it from his coffee drinking days with Samira in Basra, and it was the darndest thing to be staring at in the middle of the night, out here in this God-forsaken desert! Then, as suddenly as it had begun, the commotion ceased. Soft, hesitant voices could be heard in the shadows beyond.

"Don't shoot," yelled Jack. "For Christ's sake, hold your fire. Don't shoot."

The voices grew louder and, one by one, figures began to emerge from the shadows. It turned out the convoy had arrived at the Arab village of Ain Arous. The villagers, mistaking them for Qawukchi's bandits, and determined not to give in without a fight, had thrown everything at them that they could lay hands on, including, it would seem, the proverbial kitchen sink!

"What's all this, then?" Weallens demanded, roaring up to the front of the convoy in his truck. "What in heaven's name is going on here, Jack?"

"Bit of a cock-up in a tin hat, sir. We were taken for that scoundrel, Qawukchi, and his scurvy lot. Not too popular with the local citizenry I gather. But, not to worry, sir. I'll admit, it was a tad ropey there for a while – however, we're all sorted out now."

To make up for their inadvertent lack of hospitality, the villagers were eager to offer whatever help they could. Yes, the French had already been by that way. No, they had not stopped, except to draw water from the nearby spring. Yes, they were headed due west, in the direction of Tel Abiad, which was only four miles away.

Thanking the villagers, the convoy set off once again. Before long, just as dawn was breaking, they saw it. Tel Abiad. A walled fortress straddled a hill, with the town spread out about it like the ruffled fringe of a skirt. And the border between Syria and Turkey was simply a railway line that ran behind the town.

Tel Abiad, quaint and innocuous, basking in a serenity that belied its part in the Armenian genocide, those shameful, blood-soaked days of the declining Ottoman Empire. A once-great regime that descended into a depravity so barbaric as to have been condemned by the world, friend and foe, alike; disowned by its brethren Muslim countries who declared that those who commit such *'haram nedjin'*, dreadful sin, against women and children, forfeit all religion.

As the Ottoman Empire sank to its knees, its burden of sin and shame was buried and hidden away in its mountains and valleys, its deserts and rivers, its cities, towns and villages. It has remained unacknowledged. The inhumane cruelty that governed its final days should have served as a warning to the human race of its capability for evil. Instead, it was touted by Hitler as the precedent for his crimes: *"After all, who remembers the Armenians?"*

Once again Santi remembered Samira's words, recalling the horrors of the camp. This, then, was where they had come. He imagined the huddling crowds, within the courtyard and without. Mostly women and children, starved, naked and abused, without the protection of their men. The very young and the very old had not survived. And everywhere, the foul stench of human fear and degradation.

He remembered the face in the photograph Samira had shown him. Hedeya. In his mind's eye he saw that young girl here, small and emaciated, as she lay very still, almost lifeless, her head in her mother's lap. He remembered her eyes, he had been inexplicably drawn to them. Eyes that would witness what could never be spoken of. He could imagine those eyes filled with an unfathomable fear and mistrust of the world. Eyes that held a deep inscrutable pain, a haunting sadness; world-weary eyes, not the eyes of a child. In the photo they'd had an indefinable quality. Had there been some premonition of what was to come?

Samira's words had moved him in a way he couldn't explain. *"We have been taught man was created in the image of God. There is something wrong with that. How could this possibly be the image of God?"* He had been touched by her emotions beyond his understanding. And now, with the town bleached white against the hillside, he saw those ghosts, haunted and haunting, mute in their pleas for mercy, unheard, abandoned, pitiful in their anguish and despair.

Church bells began to ring, and the townspeople flocked to welcome them, ordinary people like anywhere else in the world. Here, too, they were informed that the French had already departed. The order to bivouac was given, and the dawn came alive with the sounds of setting up camp. Close to noon, like bees to a honey pot, the enemy aircraft found them once more. Col. Weallens and Santi were standing in the open, discussing the placement of the Advanced Dressing Station, when they came roaring in.

"Damn and blast!" Weallens swore, angrily, as they dove into the nearest slit trench, just missing the machine gun fire marching along in deadly lines above their heads. But after a minute or two, the frustration of sitting impotent while the Martins made merry, swooping in time and time again, was intolerable.

"Bhagwan Singh," Santi turned to the stretcher bearer beside him in the trench, *"ma lai timi raifal dinu."*

Borrowing two rifles from his stretcher bearers, he and the CO took potshots at the aircraft. It was to no avail, of course, they might as well have been throwing stones at a passing gaggle of geese – but doing something was better than doing nothing at all, and it did serve to take one's mind off the imminent danger.

All was not for naught, however. Anti-aircraft gunners Ganbahadur and Deba Gurung, manning a machine gun post close by, managed to take a toll of the enemy. Not a whit deterred by exposure, the two intrepid young Gurkhas held their ground in the direct line of fire as they trained their sights on the fast-approaching aircraft. Machine gun bullets spat all around them, but they did not flinch. Once, twice, thrice the planes honed in on them – and missed. Finally, one of the fighters got its comeuppance and, belching black smoke, sputtered down inside the Turkish border. Satisfied they had thumbed their noses at the enemy, that the *dushman* had been served his just desserts, then, and only then did the two young Gurkhas pack up, calm as you please, and move on. Col. Weallens, chock full of pride at their undaunted nerve, delivered them a hearty *shabash*, and made sure the commendation was followed later with the Indian Distinguished Service Medal.

It was soon observed that other than their regular air attacks every morning, the enemy on the ground was nowhere to be seen. "Done and dusted by all accounts," Temple scoffed, "I dare say the bastards are making for the hills."

Santi nodded. "So it would seem. From the odds and ends left behind, they must have pushed off in rather a tearing hurry – likely knew we were pretty close on their trail."

The Vichy, it seemed, had indeed given up the fight. Sadly, though, the Battalion had paid with the loss of a few more men. With every victory came a price. And now, this situation being well in hand, it wasn't long before fresh orders arrived. The only problem was, when they arrived, no one could make head or tail of them. After a fair deal of back and forth, it was discovered, someone had changed the code and no one had thought to give them the new one! When the confusion ultimately was sorted, and the omission put right, they found they were returning to Raqqa and Dier ez Zor once more.

They reached Raqqa on 11 July, and thence on to Dier ez Zor, arriving just in time for Vichy capitulation and the Syrian armistice which was signed on 12 July.

The next three weeks were spent between training and relaxing. They practised desert patrolling, and driving, and the use of their newly acquired mortars, after which the diversion of swimming in the bathing pool at Ain Arous and shooting sand grouse made for a much welcome break and hearty meals to boot.

In early August, when all was certain that Syria had been secured, they were relieved by the 4/6 Rajput Rifles of 17 Brigade, 4th Indian Infantry Division – and then it was time to backtrack to Iraq and their old stomping ground, Habbaniya.

Meanwhile, at GHQ in Cairo, there had been a change in command. Churchill had reassessed his game and repositioned his chessmen. General Sir Archibald Wavell, C-in-C Middle East Forces, was transferred as C-in-C to India. He switched places with General Sir Claude Auchinlek (the Auck), who went from India to Egypt as C-in-C MidEast Forces. With this changing of the guard, the Prime Minister was once more getting his ducks in a row.

CHAPTER TWELVE

A Short Respite

The desert is parched in the burning sun
And the grass is scorched and white.
But the sand is passed, and the march is done,
We are camping here tonight.

– Violet Nicolson, *The Garden of Kama*, "The Tamarind Tank"

HABBANIYA MEANS "OF THE oleander." After their trek through miles of barren, parched desert, the city's eucalyptus-lined avenues and flower gardens were a healing sight for sore eyes – despite the continuing heat, tremendous as ever, and the constant irritant of sand flies and ants.

The Division, camped around Lake Habbaniya, enjoyed two weeks of relative quiet. Life took on a normalcy of sorts. They slept in comparative comfort in the privacy of their own tents, rather than burrowing nightly, like animals, in slit trenches. Meals were taken – officers in their Mess tent, men in their langar – with immense gratitude for the abundance of fresh meat and vegetables. It was a happy break from their M&V rations of tinned bully beef, carrots, potatoes, peaches, dried egg powder, pre-digested milk powder, and the almost inedible hardtack biscuits.

And later, when dinner was done and the sun was setting, they relaxed, admiring the gloaming as it deepened into velvet shadows, the stars like diamonds scattering through a clear moonlit sky. With the world on the edge of slumber, a faint, quavering melody would strum the air. Softly, very softly, the undulating chorus of tiny night creatures would meld and mingle with the raucous serenade of bull-frogs answering from irrigation ditches, their song rising and falling like the sound of vespers in the desert night.

Capt. S.P.Dutt
c/o Middle East Forces
Letter No.6   *14 August 1941*

My dear Bela,

We are enjoying a few days respite from our meanderings across this land of limitless deserts, and it gives me the opportunity to write to you. My last letter (No.5, written on 28 July) was not much – just a couple of hurried lines to wish Sudha for her birthday, and to let you know that all is well with me.

How is Medical College treating you, and how do you like living in quarters? It is a sound idea to have Bina staying with you while she does her Masters. I am sure you both are glad of the company. How is your internship coming along? It must be difficult remaining focused in this time of turmoil. Tidbits of news from India filter through to us – not much – so please write and fill me in, as and when you can.

I received Lebu's letter. It seems our youngest has already determined she, too, is for the medical field. Good for her! The fourth doctor to swell the ranks of our immediate family. Father must be well pleased. I know he was disappointed we – I – did not opt for a family-run hospital. Perhaps later, when the world returns to its senses, you three might still make it possible, while I soldier on. I believe there can never be too many healers and places of healing; however, there is the need for those who guard the peace as well.

Lebu gave me news of Kanti joining the Navy! Has he left for training on the Dufferin yet or not? How are Father and Mother taking it? I know they can count on you to help keep things together till we both get back. I'm afraid we've shunted our responsibilities onto your capable shoulders!

As you know, we are not allowed to be specific regarding the details of our position, or time and place of manoeuvres, so I must be careful what I write. There is so much I want to say, and yet, somehow, it is difficult to talk about life here. War is such a terrible waste! I have come to realise the rules that govern our lives in wartime are very different to one's normal beliefs of right and wrong. Can anything normal survive in this terrible world hellbound for destruction? It is hard to imagine that little more than three months has passed since our arrival here! And yet, this seems to have become our reality, usurping the past, shifting everything else out of focus, into a hazy memory of some dim, distant lifetime.

I understand now Father's objections to my going to war and can only thank him for trying to protect me. I am sure much that I write here will be quite familiar to him and will stir memories of his own experiences in this region during the last War. How monstrous must human aggression be that it can overshadow such pain, sorrow and loss, for a repeat performance such as this!

Summer here is different to back home – blisteringly hot and dry by day and surprisingly cold by night. The red woollen blanket Mother gave me comes in very handy. (Although, I must say, the colour has drawn a few cheeky remarks, as expected!)

The desert is an uncanny place, stony and scrubby in most places and fluid hills of molten gold in others. When the wind blows, the sand dunes are set in motion and the desert seems to be on the move. Sometimes the dunes drift from place to place, creating floating frontiers and a curious sense of disorientation. After a while, a person's senses are deadened by the neverending sameness of the landscape, and it causes a kind of stupor we have come to call "Desert Weariness." It helps when we spend a few days in a town or city, but that brings with it a different set of problems – typhoid, cholera, and an increasing number of cases of venereal disease.

Our lives are a strange combination of the ordinary and the extraordinary: days filled with sweltering fatigue from endless riding in convoy; blistered feet, and the aches and pains from marching for miles through the awful heat. Then, the welcome respite of rest periods, when one tries to catch up on the body's need for sleep, food, bathing and, when possible, other necessary functions of life such as laundry, mending, and all those mundane, ordinary tasks I am grateful my orderly seems to manage so well. He does a splendid job of looking after me under such rudimentary circumstances, but even he cannot disguise the taste of chlorine and alum in our tea, starting with that first cup he brings in the morning. You know, I have almost forgotten what the real thing tastes like!

Of course, on the march, even that concoction is a luxury as each man is allowed just one pint of drinking water per day. Water for washing is non-existent out in the desert, but necessity makes for innovation, and we consider ourselves lucky when we get the chance to use water from a vehicle's cooling system for our most basic ablutions. Afterwards, the water is strained and dutifully returned to its vehicle.

Yes, I am sure you are aghast at the lack of hygiene, but it is a matter of survival, believe me. So much so that, on occasion, I have managed to bury the reservations of my medical training and been most grateful to my orderly for procuring me the means for such a wash – a true blessing, however rudimentary. I am informed, on the best authority, that in even harder times the same water has been put to such use by two, sometimes three men, after being allowed to stand between uses so the soap scum can be skimmed off the top! God forbid! I sincerely hope it never comes to that!

For much of the time nothing dramatic or exciting happens. We are a foreign army of soldiers, cobbled together from the four corners of the earth, different from one another, each with his own thoughts and dreams carefully hidden away in some private place within. We carry on, doing the everyday things it takes to sustain life in this arena of sun and sand. But all this can change in a heartbeat, for the war is never far away. Like a gathering storm, lowering on the horizon, it descends with a violent swiftness that turns an ordinary day into mayhem and madness. And then, one wonders, how many of these men will live to fulfill those private dreams...

Although I was given sixteen men to train as stretcher bearers and medical orderlies (usually they are the pipers of the regiment), I had no time before departure to impart to them much more than the most elementary instructions on first aid. We were not even issued Red Cross badges before we left. But the Gurkhas are good men, and my medical orderlies, such as they are, having been thrown in at the deep end are learning quickly through experience. I am getting to be quite fluent in Khaskura, the Gurkha's native tongue, and that helps of course.

I have just been informed by our 2/IC (2nd in command) that medical supplies have arrived which need my attention. Please tell Mother and Father I shall write soon, and I hope all is well with them. Everyone must be enjoying the mango season, in full spate by now with all the best varieties out – langra, himsagar, alphonso, daseri. I am torturing myself with the thought! Although, it also brings to mind an incident from our schooldays – Sudha and I and a bucketful of phojlis. Being juice mangoes, we were, as usual, enjoying them by cutting a hole in the top to suck out the juices. She will, I am sure, never forget how we had worked half-way through those sweet ripe mangoes before the churning in our stomachs warned us something was amiss. So, we sliced one open to find the worms had beaten us to the fruit! Those mangoes were literally alive! We were both violently ill, as you can imagine. And Bina, far from showing any sisterly concern, declared we were – if I remember correctly – a pair of greedy gluts and, ha ha, it served us jolly well right for starting without her!!

Now, I really must end and get back to my duties. My love to you and all our sisters, and to Kanti. Please convey my pranams to Mother and Father. Take care of yourself and the family.

Affly, Dada

AROUND THE SAME TIME in mid-August, far away in the Atlantic Ocean, a meeting shrouded in great secrecy (code name, 'Riviera') was taking place. Its intent was to change the ways of the world. Unknown to friend and foe alike, British Prime Minister Winston Churchill left England aboard the battlecruiser *HMS Prince of Wales*. He set sail across treacherous, enemy-patrolled waters to a pre-ordained meeting place off the coast of Newfoundland. There, aboard the heavy cruiser *USS Augusta*, he met his American counterpart, President Franklin Delano Roosevelt. These two heads of state reached an agreement, and signed their names to the Atlantic Charter which, later, would form the basis for the United Nations Charter.

Among the policies set forth and ratified that day were those that addressed non-aggrandizement, territorial or other; disarmament with a view to peace, and freedom from fear and want; collaboration between all nations, great or small, victor or vanquished, with respect to equal rights of economic and social advancement and security; and, finally, the right of all peoples to sovereignty and self-government of their choice. This last Roosevelt insisted upon, no matter it opposed Churchill's imperialistic policies and was much like pulling teeth. (*I have not become the King's First Minister in order to preside over the liquidation of the British Empire.* Despite these avowed sentiments, he was soon to witness the de-colonisation of both the Middle East and India, England's coveted "Jewel in the Crown.")

THE BOAC EMPIRE FLYING boats had resumed their scheduled landings and take-offs on Lake Habbaniya, en route to the Far East. The residents in the cantonment, and at the RAF base, had returned to a more or less daily routine. And things in general were slowly drifting towards the norm. But the scars of past battle remained. Although the bombed-out airstrips had been repaired, and the golf course and Polo pitch had been restored to their original use, the outer walls of the RAF club were still pockmarked, in some places resembling Swiss cheese. During bad dust storms, the sand whirled in through cracks and holes in glass and wood, and danced with the abandon of a dervish, egged on by the overhead fans into spreading a fine, brown mist that settled layers of dust, smothering everything.

Not that it deterred anyone from enjoying the facilities the club had to offer. Many an evening the sounds of raucous laughter, song and merriment would pour forth from the building to bestir the evening air. It was obvious to any passer-by that the occupants therein believed the good moments of life, no matter how fleeting, were too precious to waste. Jack, Shirley and Ben instructed their new RAF cronies in a rather irreverent song set to the tune of the German national anthem. Once mastered, it became immensely popular, and was bawled out with cheerful gusto. According to Jack, the song went something like this:

> *Ours is not a happy household, no one laughs or ever smiles,*
> *Mine's a dismal occupation, crushing ice for father's piles.*
> *Jane the under housemaid barfs each morning just at eight,*
> *To the horror of the butler, who's the author of her fate.*
> *Sister Sue has just aborted for the forty second time.*
> *Uncle James has been deported for a most unusual crime...*

And it didn't end there. Not to be outdone, a budding minstrel from another unit informed the musical trio of the 2/4 that the German national anthem, versatile as it was, had been put to further good use:

Deutscher, Deutscher, uber alles,
In the sands outside Tobruk,
Saw a Jerry acting wary,
Thought I'd go and take a look.
He was sitting, pants down, shitting,
Down a little shady pass.
Put a trifle up my rifle,
Aimed, and shot him up the arse!

There were softer moments, of course. There were those nostalgic love songs for times when someone or the other was feeling senti-mental about news he had, or hadn't, received from home…

We'll meet again, don't know where, don't know when,
But I know we'll meet again some sunny day.
Keep smilin' through, just like you always do
Till the blue skies drive the dark clouds far away…

CHAPTER THIRTEEN

On The Road To Persia

Into my heart an air that kills from yon far country blows:
What are those blue remembered hills,
What spires, what farms are those?
That is the land of lost content, I see it shining plain,
That happy highway where I went and cannot come again.

– A.E. Houseman, "A Shropshire Lad," 1896

SINCE ALL THINGS, MERRY and maudlin, good and bad, must perforce come to an end, 24 August dawned and brought with it their marching orders. 21st Brigade – less the 4/13 Frontier Force Rifles who remained in Haditha to patrol the pipeline – pulled down its tents, packed up its bags and moved out in Division strength. They had been ordered eastward into Iran to help the British and Russian troops, already present in that country, prevent a German takeover. To avoid any confusion between the similar sounding names, Iraq and Iran, the British had reverted, for military purposes, to calling Iran by its ancient name – Persia.

The contingent drove the short distance to Baghdad over harsh, dusty plains. As usual, the heat was substantial, and as the morning wore on it increased in intensity. They passed some Marsh Arabs on the way. Heralded by fresh camel dung along the road, the great beasts, those 'ships of the desert', soon hove into sight, lumbering towards the city single file, with their human cargo swaying high up on their backs.

It wasn't long before the city itself loomed into view. A flat, drab city fringed with palm trees, Baghdad was the country's capital. It was built on both banks of the Tigris River, 220 miles north of the Persian Gulf. The eastern and western sections of the city were linked by the famous Bridge of Boats. Once known as *Madinat-as-Salam,* the City of Peace, it had boasted four roads radiating outward from the *khalif's* palace in the town centre, to four gates in the wall that encircled it. In those days it was a bustling centre for trade routes between east and west, famous for the beauty and magnificence of its gardens and architecture. Caravans passed through its gates carrying riches beyond belief. They travelled from far off places like Damascus in the west to Persepolis in the east, and on their return, from

Isfahan in the east once more through Baghdad, southward to the grand cities of Babylon and, further still, to Basra or Basorah as it was then known. Those days of glory were long lost, dulled by time and dimmed by history.

Now, as the convoy entered the city from the west and made its way north, the full impact of its sights, sounds and smells hit them. Although they stuck to the main thoroughfares, they caught glimpses of narrow, dusty streets that led off into the bowels of the city. Shaded from the intense sunlight by painted, overhanging balconies were marketplaces and residential quarters, crowding in, one on top of the other, choked with traffic – human, animal and mechanised – that jostled out into the main streets.

The human element was a motley mix of natives and foreigners: long-robed donkey drivers with their little beasts of burden trotting beside hefty Kurds transporting massive, weighty objects on their backs – sofas, cupboards, and even a refrigerator or two; Arabs in their 'abbas and galabiyas mingling with suited gentlemen; and in the midst of it all were soldiers from various countries.

Threading their way through all this were buses packed to the brim and spilling their human cargo, vying for right of way with taxis darting in and out of the crowds, horns screaming a warning to all and sundry that not a jot would be given, no matter who or what stood in the way. This great cacophony of incessant horns, blaring Arabic music, and diverse people in loud, competitive communication blended perfectly with the stench of sewage and the smells of food cooking in open stalls and cafes. This was the essence of Baghdad, and it pervaded the city.

The convoy was called to a halt. "How in heck do we make it through this mess, Jack?" Col. Weallens barked in irritation. For a full Division, with all its military paraphernalia, to cleave its way through this throbbing heart of Baghdad seemed an insurmountable task. "It's like swimming en masse against high tide!"

After some consideration, Masters came up with an idea. "Rather than trying to circumvent the situation, might it not be better to muck in, sir? Fight fire with fire, so to speak."

Willie listened with interest. A couple of minutes later, orders duly went out, and the regimental pipers struck up a march. The wail of bagpipes swelled and swirled over the chaos which, after a single, stunned moment, miraculously parted like the Red Sea had for Moses, and the convoy drove through, unimpeded. Past the Kadhimain mosque with its four minarets and elaborate blue and pink mosaic work; across the long-travelled Tigris river, its waters dark with hidden, violent memories in stark contrast to the painted boats tied along its banks, lined with the city's washing laid out in colourful array; and, finally, out through the North Gate onto the clear, hot desert road that led to Baquba.

Approximately half a mile outside the Gate, on the right side of the road, they came upon the North Gate War Cemetery. It was built on low, level ground, circumscribed by a high earthen bund to protect it from the floods which often chastised the area. To further preserve the sanctity of the place, an iron fence had been erected within the bund and a domed metal gatehouse gave entrance to the graves with their rows of silent headstones. Here lay the dead of World War One. Some in single graves which proclaimed their names, hundreds more in multiple graves – sad in their obscurity, unknown and lost to history. The convoy once more was called to a halt, and in silence, the soldiers of the present paid their respect to the soldiers of the past.

It was a moment of reckoning. The cemetery was neglected, overrun with scrub and bracken. Against the vast, unforgiving landscape of the desert, the graves looked lonely and forlorn. An avenue cut a swath through the middle, splitting the cemetery in two, separating the British graves on the left from the Hindu and Muslim ones on the right. Santi thought it ironic that even in death, which was supposed to be the great leveller, this distinction had been maintained. Did anyone truly believe that a man took his religion or nationality with him beyond the grave? What of these men in this anonymous grave, of whom all that could be said was *"A soldier of the Great War, known only unto God?"* Which God? Hindu, Muslim or Christian? Did anyone really know? And, in the end, did it matter?

Santi walked over to the centre. There stood the tomb of Lt. General Sir Stanley Maude, inscribed with the epitaph, *"He fought a good fight, He kept the faith."* In the southwest corner was a memorial to the 13th Division he had commanded. It was surrounded by the graves of the Division's officers and men: *"At the going down of the sun, And in the morning, We will remember them."*

A little further on, Sergeant Reginald Pickford, 29 years old, of the 1st Battalion, Connaught Rangers had left a last message as he departed this earth on Monday, 6 August, 1917, *"My beloved Violet, Somewhere, sometime, we shall meet again."* Were they together now, Violet and Reginald? Or had she wept for him and then, eventually, found solace in someone else's arms?

A short, dusty step to the right lay the disintegrating grave of Major Andrew Bellamy, 32 years old, of the 1st Division, 4 Hampshire Regiment who, with his dying breath, that Tuesday of 26 March, 1918, promised a loved one, *"I shall wait, forever..."* Was she still waiting as well, or had she too buried her pain and grown old with someone else?

On Thursday, 21 March, 1918, the final thought of Private D. Bruchard, aged 20, from the Infantry Machine Gun Corps was for his parents, *"Dear Mum and Dad, When in heaven we meet again, God will link the broken chain."* What had his parents been doing that morning when they got the news that they had made the ultimate sacrifice of their only son for the preservation of their country? Had they just sat themselves down to a breakfast table laid for three, as they had done each day since his departure, in the hope that this small act of faith would bring him safely back to them so their lives might go on as before?

A little further along, the broken headstone of Private P. O'Maly, 22 years of age, from the 2nd Battalion, Royal Irish Rifles read, *"To those who have outlived me, To those I leave behind..."*, the rest of his message had disappeared into the dust, an unfinished story, the lost, discarded shards of a broken life. Who were his loved ones? How long after he died, that day of 23 June 1916, had his memory lingered among his friends who continued to meet down at the local pub where he had always been the life of the party?

A few of the multiple Hindu and Muslim graves of the 3rd Indian Army Corps, the Hariana Lancers, and the 6th Indian (Poona) Division read merely, *"Buried near this spot...."* How inadequate an epitaph for the courage and sacrifice, the pain and loss interred there. Many of these men should have been cremated according to their custom, and to allow their souls to rest in peace their ashes would have been scattered in the holy Ganges. That was the Hindu's staunch belief. But there they lay, unsanctified by their religious rites, their bones intermingling, Hindu with Muslim, in graves of foreign sand. Had these brave exiles found the peace they deserved? Santi had to believe they did. No God could be that merciless.

And then, they discovered the grave marked with the inscription for the Gurkha Rifles. *"They shall be remembered for having given unto us."* Here were their brothers in whose footsteps they now trod. Silently, the Gurkhas gathered round and said a special prayer. What a travesty of human life was war!

As they made their way out of that forgotten place, they passed

beneath the saddest words of all:
"When you go home, tell them of us, and say,
For their tomorrow, these gave their today"
And they carried those words with them as they left; words they held in sacred trust, to commemorate their own dead later, in a memorial chapel of the old Hastings Church at Stoke Poges, a small hamlet nestled in the Buckinghamshire countryside in England.

Many of these men had been very young, Santi thought. Young men like us, strong in body and will, vibrant of mind, hopeful of heart, who had laughed and talked, endured and shared as they marched to a war where they had ended up killing and being killed. Men, who had once lived, and loved, and been loved. A son or a brother who had been held dear to someone's heart; a husband or a father whose departure forever changed the lives of those he left behind; and the families, whose pain was interred in the passing years which slowly, mercifully, dimmed their sorrow into bruised memory, as they gradually bleached the bones of these once flesh and blood heroes, incarcerated here beneath this unrelenting ground.

Most of these men were from the Indian Expeditionary Force 'D', and had probably fought alongside his father. J.P. Dutt had survived to live out his dreams, while they had not. When he found out, Col. Weallens reminisced about that time with Santi. He too had been there, twenty-four long years ago, during World War One. They had used motor transport to carry them into battle for the very first time, and their 2nd Battalion's Brigade had been the vanguard, the first to enter Baghdad.

They stood there, the old warrior and the new. Both could feel the lingering anguish of these souls cut down in their prime, the tenuous tragedy of their unfulfilled dreams, the intangible longing for the love they had foregone. These poor, fragile ghosts, Santi thought ruefully, lying here in the bright sunlight, watching helplessly as history repeats itself. It seemed a sad truth that the pain of the past can rarely save the future from its folly.

Leaving that place of stilled timelessness to the sanctity of its fragmented memories once more, the living pressed on. Approximately one hundred and four miles north of Baghdad, the Division passed through the city of Baquba. It then continued north-eastward, past Shahraban, towards Khanikin on the mountainous Iranian border. The journey was especially fraught with memories for Col. Weallens who had marched along this very same road with the Battalion in April of 1917. Only two soldiers remained from the old 2/4 of that bygone era, Bhisti Hira Singh and himself, and together the two old veterans wandered down memory lane…

By Jove! Look, Hira Singh, there is the old outpost line…! H.St.G. Scott had been wounded…and…

Sahib, see, still the broken picket. Wire all twisted now, all rusting.

Yes, yes…and there, right there, the trench where Bruno Brunless…ah, remember? Over here…where we finally drove the Turks back into the Jebel Hamrin Mountains. What a day that was!

Yes Sahib, I am remembering…

And, as they walked the pilgrim's path, sadly, it brought to mind old faces and old friends, long gone, but never, never forgotten.

CHAPTER FOURTEEN
The Wages Of Sin

From the solemn gloom of the temple
Children run out to sit in the dust,
God watches them play
And forgets the priest.

– Rabindranath Tagore, Quotes

A*LALLA YA GABIR.*" THE vendor selling *lahmat raas* sang out from the street below. From their first-floor balcony Bajo and Violette watched him pass beneath, carrying his large bowl and stand, seeking customers for his beef-head and onion soup. Not to-day, Bajo shook her head when he looked up, enquiringly. Today there was just enough money to buy vegetables.

She turned her attention back to the vegetable seller, watching hawk-eyed as he carefully filled the basket she had lowered down to him; ten *rattl* of vegetables, roughly equivalent to ten pounds, for one *piastre*. Bajo hauled the basket up, examined the produce and nodded. It was all good, fresh. The peas were full and firm, and so were the tomatoes. They would make a good dish of *bisella* for today, and there would still be enough tomatoes to cook *fasoulya* with the green beans tomorrow.

Bajo gave Violette some money and sent her off to the neighbour-hood baker to buy fresh *aish baladi*. "Two for the house and one for you. Be careful, now."

Past experience had taught Bajo to make provision for her grand-daughter's love of freshly baked bread, and to compensate for her inevitable consumption of at least half of one flatbread on the way home. "Mind now, bébé, straight there and back. Then you can help me shell the *bisella*."

The bread shop was down the block and around the corner. Even before one saw it, the aroma of bread being baked, hot and fresh, wafted down the street and assailed the nostrils like the magic spell of a genie. It lured passers-by, whether they intended it or not, to the realm of Mustaffa Moussa, master baker, so that at all times there was a small crowd gathered outside his shop.

Mustaffa spotted the little girl, no more than waist high from the ground, squirming her way between the legs of his faithful clientele, and he called out for room to be made. Courteously, a path cleared, and Violette found herself being pushed into the presence of the baker, her nose at a tantalising level with the mounds of bread displayed in their baskets. Moustaffa knew the routine. He wrapped two hot, oven fresh *aish baladi* in paper and put the packet into the girl's shopping bag. Then, he chose one that was not too hot, but still nice and warm. He wrapped it carefully, leaving one end open, and handed it to the child "with a blessing on each *gezza* you eat."

Happily munching, Violette had just turned the corner when she came upon Louis. He was holding a big bag filled with grapes, and he seemed to be giving away the *ai'neb* to everyone and anyone he could waylay in the street! She stopped and watched him, puzzled. Why, whatever was he doing?

"Here, take some," she heard him plead, as he ran beside a man on a cycle who was trying his best to get away. "See, they're free!"

"Nothing in life is free," said the man, peddling away.

"What are you doing, Loza?" Violette called him by his pet name. "Why are you giving all your *ai'neb* away? Are they bad?"

"Of course they're not bad," Louis replied indignantly. "Why would I give anyone bad grapes? Here take some, see for yourself how sweet they are."

"Why are you giving them away, then? I thought you liked *ai'neb binyati*. Mmmmm…" She munched a few of the small, sweet grapes Loza had given her. *Ai'neb binyati* was a favourite of theirs, and the name, roughly translated, meant 'daughter's grapes'.

"*Iskooti!* Don't ask so many questions, just put the *aish* away and eat these. Here," Louis piled her small hands high with more fruit than they could hold, so that some spilt into the street, and when she opened her mouth to protest, he quickly stuffed another handful of grapes into it.

"Eat!" he ordered, effectively quashing any further questions she might have been about to ask.

A young lady was walking past. "Mademoiselle, have some, please." Louis thrust a bunch of grapes into the hands of the young lady. He tucked a few more into Violette's already full mouth. Amused, the lady accepted his gift and thanked him. "No, no, *it fadil,* you are welcome, it is I who thank you," said the boy, gratefully, urging another bunch on her.

Approaching them at a fast pace was a man dressed in a suit. *"Efendi, Efendi,"* Louis accosted him. "Wouldn't you like some *ai'neb?"*

The startled passer-by stopped and stared at the young boy with the large bag of grapes who was blocking his path. Louis quickly reached out and pushed a bunch into the man's hand, hanging by his side.

Overcoming his surprise, the man laughed. "You are most generous," he said. "But, you know, one does not accept gifts from strangers, so maybe you will tell me your name? That way you will no longer be a stranger, then I can accept your gift, and you will be my benefactor instead."

"My name is Louis, sir. But please, try my *ai'neb binyati?* You will be amazed at the sweetness."

The man chuckled. "So young and already you speak of 'your daughter's grapes?" the accosted stranger teased, playing on the meaning of the word. "And such a pretty little girl, too." He smiled at Violette who tried to smile back through the grapes still bulging her cheeks. Her mouth was filled to capacity, notwithstanding which, Louis kept stoking it from time to time.

"*Efendi,* I am not that young, I am twelve years old; and this is not a joking matter," Louis reproached him, stepping in front of his sister to shield her from this frivolous stranger. "Here, take these," he shoved some more grapes at the man. "Come bébé," he grabbed Violette by the hand, and dragging her behind him, hurriedly walked her away to safety.

Violette watched as, willingly or not, every person who happened down the street was either cajoled or stupefied into accepting some grapes. And each time she herself managed to swallow a mouthful, Louis would shovel more into her mouth, ignoring her grunts of protest till, at last, the little girl stamped her foot and pulled away from him. She sat down on the step of a nearby doorway, her eyes filling with angry tears.

Louis glared at her, impatiently. Then, after a moment he sat down beside his sister. "I can't take the *ai'neb* home," he explained, at last, with a heavy sigh. "I took the money from Mama's dressing table."

He saw the look of horror on Violette's face. "I did ask her," he added hastily, trying to defend his actions, "but she said she was in a hurry. And since she didn't say no, and I knew she had left some money on her dressing table, I didn't think she'd mind if I took *nusu franc,* just two *piastres,* no more."

His sister gulped down her last mouthful. "You stole the money!" she accused him, when at last she was able to speak.

"I did not!" Louis shot back, heatedly, his ears beginning to burn with a confused sense of indignation and shame. "I knew she would have given me the money if she hadn't been rushing out of the house. So...I..." he gulped "...that's only why I took it," he finished, lamely.

"Stole it," Violette said stubbornly, shaking her head.

Louis didn't reply, but his whole face had turned bright red by now. Violette shuddered to think of the trouble he was in. Oh, she was glad she was not in his shoes! She took a quick sideways peek at her brother. His woeful expression made her feel sorry for him, so she put a small, comforting arm around his shoulders. "The *shaitan* made you do it. But don't worry, Loza, I won't tell."

Louis hugged her, gratefully. He sat silent for a moment, his eyes downcast, feeling deeply ashamed and close to tears. When he looked up, his eyes fell on a donkey-cart parked by the roadside. After a moment, he got up and went to it. The scrawny little animal stood, patiently awaiting the return of its master. Louis patted its head, and then slowly began feeding it the grapes.

"Maybe God will forgive me if I give them all away," he said, hopefully, but he sounded as though he himself rather doubted that the penance would suffice to mitigate the crime. He had not considered its effect on the donkey, however.

The small, dumb animal, unable to voice its gratitude, nibbled away gratefully. And when Violette came up to it, and gently stroked its head and neck, unknown to the two children, they earned the blessings of that weary creature which, for those few short moments, was transported by their kindness to animal heaven.

About to turn a corner down the street, the man who had teased Louis looked back over his shoulder and saw the children with their newfound friend. The sight made him smile, and he was still smiling when he rounded the corner and bumped into someone.

"Ah, Yussef, s*adeeki-l-'azeez*, my dear friend!" said the newcomer. "You do not see where you are going, eh? *Izzayyak?* But why do I ask? I can see that you seem to be in such good spirits." Spotting the grapes, he continued. "Tell me, is it the enjoyment of what you eat that has put a smile on your lips? And if so, will you not share some of your pleasure with me? They do say that sorrows shared are sorrows halved, whereas happiness that is shared is doubled."

"*Ahlan wu sahlan,* Sallah!" Yussef laughed, offering him the fruit. "You are right, these grapes have, indeed, been the source of much delight. Not only in the eating, mind you, more in the manner in which I obtained them. I was just held up by the purveyor of these goods; a very generous young man with an enchanting little girl in tow. Come, poke your head around the corner and you might see them still, at the end of the street. There, you see? It seems they have abandoned people for the little donkey they are feeding now."

A look of surprise came over Sallah's face. "Those two? I know them!" he exclaimed. "Louis and Violette, they are the children of a friend." He contemplated the little pantomime for a while, then shook his head, perplexed. "I wonder what those two little *shaitan* have been up to."

"Surely not devils! Only angels share their good fortune with complete strangers."

"It depends on how they came about their fortune, does it not?" Sallah laughed. "Actually, they are good children; but there is something of a mystery here, and somehow my nose tells me there is more to this than the eye can see."

Before he went home, Sallah dropped in at Hedeya's. She lived a few blocks away from his house, and on his way back from the office he would stop by, usually on Wednesdays and Saturdays, to make sure all was well with the family. It was a Saturday, and being somewhat a creature of habit, he stuck to his routine.

Sallah Farag had met Hedeya Khayat through his two sisters. When his older sister was getting married, Hedeya had prepared her a trousseau of beautifully embroidered bed sets, tablecloths with serviettes, monogrammed towels, and exquisitely delicate lingerie. The day before the marriage, Sallah was bidden to collect the trousseau on his way home from work, so it might be properly arranged for display during the ceremony. He had gone over to the seamstress's house, and immediately been smitten the minute he'd laid eyes on her.

Over the following year, he surprised his sisters by selflessly volunteering himself, at every opportunity, to run their errands of fetching and delivering the garments Hedeya made for them. It took time and a great deal of patience, and slowly, almost painfully so, a relationship of sorts developed – an acceptance of friendship on Hedeya's part, the hope of a little more on Sallah's – till one day, recently, he had declared his feelings for her, and asked her to marry him.

He had not done so lightly. The difference in their religions was bound to be an obstacle that would not be easy to surmount, especially with the older generation. If it came to it, would she agree to become a Muslim? He had heard rumours as to how Hedeya got her divorce – and, if they were true, it was obvious to him it had been a ruse, merely the means to an end, nothing more. He was not sure how she felt about actually converting and accepting the Muslim faith; knowing her circumstances, however, he had an inkling it would not be a viable proposition for her.

For a while his declaration put a strain on their relationship. She distanced herself from him, and he immediately assured her, very sensibly, that she should take as much time as was needed to think on it; the decision was much too important to be hurried, and they both understood the complications it entailed.

After that, things went on much the same as before, with only the merest acknowledgement that a new inflection had been added to the relationship. Very occasionally, Sallah would cautiously test the waters, drop a hint, a passing reminder, and almost six months passed before he decided to push the envelope, to reaffirm his position ever so gently. That day he arrived with a ring and, before she had a chance to demur, he placed the ring on her mantelpiece in the drawing room and walked over to where she sat on the sofa.

"Keep it there till you decide," he said. "When you do, and if your answer is what I hope it will be, then I will see it on your finger. That is all I ask." And that was how the matter was left.

Now, as he climbed the stairs to her flat, Sallah wondered where he really stood with Hedeya. After all this time, she was still an enigma to him. He knew how he felt about her, but her feelings for him were another matter altogether. So far, he had been unable to get close enough to find out much. She seemed to hold all of life, including him, at arm's length, as though wary of her emotions being touched in any way. He wondered if he would ever be allowed into the inner sanctum of her mind and heart.

At the top of the stairs his knock was answered by Bajo. He greeted her and, still munching on the grapes his friend had given him, he followed her into the kitchen where Hedeya was pouring thick, dark Turkish coffee from the *kanaka* in which she had made it into two small demitasse cups.

"Have some *ahwa*, Sallah?" Hedeya asked him. "I've just made it, and there's more than enough." He inclined his head in acceptance, and she added a third cup for him. "You'll need a little more sugar, I know you like it sweeter than I make it." She pushed the sugar pot towards him.

"More so now, after the *ai'nab* I've eaten, thanks to Louis. I must say, they are excellent. Here, try some." He offered her the grapes as he took the cup she handed him, and sat down opposite her at the kitchen table.

"What do you mean? Thanks to Louis?"

"Yes. Actually, I was hoping you would enlighten me as to why your son is sweetening the mouth of everyone in the neighbourhood. Are you celebrating some auspicious occasion I don't yet know about? Is it possible that I should be celebrating too?"

Ignoring the innuendo, Hedeya frowned. "Are you telling me Louis is distributing *ai'nab* to people in the street?"

"You did not know? Well, you hold the proof in your hands," Sallah pointed to the grape Hedeya was thoughtfully rolling between her thumb and forefinger. The look on her face made him realise he might have said more than was good for young Louis and so, when she continued to remain silent, he attempted to make light of the matter. "Anyway, there is probably a simple explanation to the mystery, and you might want to go easy on the boy when you consider how many people went home the happier for his generosity." He paused before adding, "Whatever the motive."

It didn't take long for Hedeya to work out what must have happened. That morning, when she'd told him she hadn't time to attend him, Louis must have decided on a little self-help and taken some of the money lying on her dressing table. Knowing her son, she believed he had not meant to steal. Having convinced himself she would have given him the money when she returned, all he was doing, in his mind, was expediting matters a little. Nevertheless, a small part of him must have known he was doing wrong, why else would he be striving so hard to rid himself of the evidence of his actions.

Hedeya sighed. However innocent his action, he was guilty of wrongdoing. Even if it was the minor error of thoughtless misjudgement, if left uncorrected that sort of thing could hurt him in later life. And although she understood he had acted on impulse, the problem was, when he came to realise his misdeed, he had tried to hide it instead of facing up and rectifying it.

The childlike artlessness of his actions made her rue the punishment she must visit upon him. She could afford to give him so little! Her primal instinct was to let the whole matter slide, to gather him up into her arms and shield him from the world. But she knew that was not the way to prepare him for the painful realities of life. If she really were to protect him, then regardless of the heartache it brought her, she must guide him to make the right choices by teaching him the cause and effect of his actions.

That night Hedeya borrowed a small piece of the belladonna plaster Bajo applied to her joints; the soothing heat it created on contact with the skin, greatly relieved the old lady's rheumatic aches and pains. Hedeya had used it once on Victor when he had sprained his ankle, as the curative heat was known to help with many ailments, including sore throat and whooping cough in children. Conversely, it could produce a temporary blister as well, like a rash on the skin, if the plaster was left too long. However, this usually disappeared fairly quickly with no ill effect.

While her son lay asleep, Hedeya applied the plaster to the back of his right hand, making sure she removed it in good time before he awoke. All that remained was a small red welt – exactly the result she had hoped for.

"What is that on your hand, Loza?" she queried him while he was brushing his teeth.

The boy looked at his hand and shook his head, puzzled. He rinsed his mouth out and examined the red welt closely before turning to his mother. "I don't know. It wasn't there yesterday. It must have happened at night, while I was asleep."

"Are you sure? Think carefully, Louis. This looks very much like the mark of an angel. Have you done anything at all that could have made God angry with you? It seems to me…" Hedeya stopped as sudden understanding dawned on her son's face, followed quickly by a look of acute guilt. "Well! It seems to me that you do remember something! Do you feel you would like to tell me about it?"

The story of the grapes came tumbling out. In fits and starts at first, and then in a rush, Louis's words came, falling over one another in his desperate need to unburden himself. At the end, overcome with shame and remorse, he burst into tears. His mother kissed his hand and promised him that all would be well. He would see, now that he had acknowledged what he had done, and shown remorse for it, the angel's mark would be gone in no time.

By the time he got to Sunday School assembly at Madressa Rasullayah, the School of the Apostle, Louis had begun to wear the mark as a badge of honour. He had been marked by God, he told his schoolmates, just like in the bible!

Hearing about it, Asis Habib took him aside and asked him to explain himself. The mark was already beginning to fade, but Louis eagerly showed him his hand: See? He had committed a sin and, heinous crime that it was, an angel had been sent to warn him.

Asis Habib raised his eyebrows. Really? And had Louis seen this angel?

Of course not, replied the boy, he had been asleep! But the mark was proof of the visit. Moreover, he assured Asis Habib, now that he had been washed clean by remorse and saved, he had learnt a lesson never to be forgotten, and clearly, it was his duty to pass that lesson on.

The priest sighed. Louis had an abundantly active imagination, but he was no liar. And though Asis Habib couldn't make head or tail of the story the boy had just told him, somewhere in there lay the truth, he was sure – but this was not the time to tangle with it. So, he patted the boy on the head and said, "Beware the sin of pride, my son," and he let it go at that.

CHAPTER FIFTEEN

Land of Milk and Honey

And hear ye the beat of the ages' feet
In strides of thousands of years;
A muffled note that low doth float
On history's breath to the ears

– E. LLoyd Pease, "Time"

KHANIKIN WAS THE FINAL halt in Iraq. The Battalion rested for three hours, and after being joined by a light armoured brigade and two more Gurkha battalions, it crossed the border at Khosrovi into Persia. Afternoon was well past now, and since it was deemed that the Zagros Mountains were better tackled by day, a decision was made to set up camp around Sar-e-Pol-Zahab and settle in for the night.

The heat of the desert they had suffered so long had vanished with the setting sun. Now the air whispered of mountain breezes and snow, somewhere far above them, sending chills to turn the night cold. As Jack remarked, it was a new taste on their tongues, a new smell in their nostrils, and it brought out blankets, jumpers and great coats. Bundled up well, both men and machines wearily dug in for the night.

Very early, the morning of 25 August, they started their climb through the imposing heights known as The Gates of Zagros. Past sudden, gushing waterfalls they edged their way upward, through the Paitak Pass. This narrow gorge was threaded by a mountainous road thirty kilometres long that wound and looped its way up to almost four thousand feet at the very top. It was much like climbing a spiral staircase, and the going was slow.

The 4th Gurkhas were the vanguard. They led the way, and the convoy followed, past two picturesque towns, snaking single file up the mountainside. There were many stops and starts as the three-ton lorries and the gun and howitzer carriers precariously rumbled around sharp bends that fell steeply away.

As they journeyed upward, they seemed to travel back in time, passing ancient carvings and sculptures that had been hewn into the massive mountain cliffs thousands of years before the birth of Christ. Adjoining the path was the Taq-e-Gara grotto. Within it, could still be seen the remains of enormous statues of the Ashkanian and Sasanian kings, their warriors and their gods – ancient mythology that told of bygone civilisations. It was an impressive doorway to the past!

The present, alas, could not be kept at bay for long. It broke through with a sudden, sporadic attack of enemy fire which was promptly returned with interest. It would seem the Persian army might be readying itself for a fight! Whatever their plan, perforce, it would have to wait, as once again night intervened and called a halt to further proceedings.

At first light the following morning, they prepared to do battle. However, when the area was reached where they had thought to engage the enemy, to everyone's surprise, they found no one there. Sometime during the night, the Persian army seemed to have had a change of heart. Abandoning its post, it had melted away into the countryside, leaving the way clear for them to proceed into the valley of Chashmeh Shah.

They spent the next thirty-six hours verily chasing the shadow of the White Rabbit as they tried in vain to make contact with the enemy. And no wonder! It turned out the Persians had already surrendered and signed an armistice to that effect. Well, would someone kindly pass on the news!

It was 27 August, their Persian campaign was over before it had even begun and, since this had been an adventure without mishap, it was time to celebrate. Would that all their battles were as speedy and bloodless as this one!

They spent the ensuing seven weeks enjoying their new surroundings. The glittering magnificence of snow-clad peaks encircling the valley was a benediction for eyes, quite literally, burnt in their sockets by unending miles of flat, brown sand.

Chashmeh Shah was a verdant green chalice, lush with flowers and orchards, and tiny villages tucked away into its folds. The villagers were not so much apprehensive as curious, and the curiosity turned to hospitable friendliness, once they were assured the foreign soldiers posed no threat.

Best of all, cold mountain streams afforded a plentiful supply of fresh, clear water for drinking and washing. And, oh heaven, what luxury it was to bathe without scrimping on water – water that was clean and not obtained from the bowels of some dusty, grease-laden engine or, worse still, salvaged after use by another!

The weather too was dramatically different. The bracing mountain air was as heady as perfume after the hot, arid desert. The days were breezy and cool, the nights were sparkling and chilly. The desert uniform of light-khaki cotton shirt and shorts was replaced by the darker olive-green short jacket and wool pant of the winter barathea battledress. Sweaters and scarves were the order of the day, balaclavas and great coats were required at night.

At first, the camp with its guns, vehicles and soldiers stuck out like a sore thumb against the halcyon mountain landscape. But gradually, it seemed to blend in, absorbed and tamed in some inscrutable way by its sylvan surroundings – and, before long, it too nestled comfortably into the valley, almost as though, given half a chance, the nomadic intruder had gladly put down roots.

Close to the campsite, a small mountain rill splashed crystal-cold water that gurgled invitingly over a pebbled bed. It hinted of the snows whence it came, and the Gurkhas, mountain men undeterred by its chilly origins, joyously commandeered a spot for their ablutions. The sight and sound of their frequent comings and goings spoke to the nostalgic pleasures they enjoyed in those freezing waters.

Soon, a trade agreement was reached with the villagers. In return for medical attention and army rations of 'foreign' canned foods, the camp was provided with an abundance of fruit from surrounding orchards, fresh goat's milk and cheese, partridge, quail, and chicken, loaves of home-baked *nan-e-barbari* and, on occasion, even some locally made red wine.

In nearby towns, the restaurants offered simple yet sumptuous local fare – *khoresh*, an aromatic Persian stew, *chelow* the fragrant long-grain saffron rice served with succulent kebabs prepared with a variety of meats. All in all, life took on a leisurely pace, and it was deemed that Fate had not been too unkind a mistress after all. With the drab and dreary desert behind them, surely they had found Arcadia!

Early one evening, as twilight's dusky veils began to lower soft purple shadows over the mountains and valleys, Santi sat writing a letter inside his tent. Strains of Beethoven wafted through the camp from the direction of Jack's tent where the adjutant was poring over orders for the week's training. Ben 'Quinine' Browne drove up in a vehicle snagged from Motor Transport with the help of Roger Werner. The two of them, together with Shirley Temple, were off to reconnoitre the lay of the land, and Ben recollected that Santi had expressed a desire to visit the nearby town of Shahabad, some ten kilometres away.

"There's a nice little restaurant, the Sheherazad, where they serve top-notch kebabs, so we've heard. Thought we'd give it a try. Did you still want that lift into town, Doc?"

"Thank you, I certainly do." Santi was surprised the young Englishman remembered, and more so that he had thought to ask. Their relationship had evolved into one of guarded respect. "How long do I have?"

"Half an hour be ok?" Ben peered sideways at Santi, and after a moment's hesitation, he added, "I say, Doc, would you mind if I threw you a rather personal question?"

"Oh? Such as?"

"Noticed you seldom eat with us in the Officers' Mess. Does it have anything to do with your caste system?"

Taken aback, for a split-second Santi was dumbfounded – and then, as the full purport of the question hit him, he couldn't help laughing out loud. The irony of it! He caught himself when he realised the young British officer was staring at him, nonplussed.

"Nothing at all to do with caste, Browne, I assure you," he said, still grinning widely. "Whatever gave you that idea? Actually, if truth be told, I'm not too comfortable with the formalities that are de rigueur at the Officers' Mess. Besides, the food from the men's langar is more what I'm accustomed to, and Dilbahadur does make sure I'm well provided for."

"Well then, if that's all it is, and if you have nothing on, why don't you join us, Doc? They say Persian kebabs are quite something to write home about – beat the heck out of bangers and mash, so they tell me."

Santi was touched by the invitation. "I believe I will. Thank you. And maybe," he smiled slowly, remembering the incident with Fullerton in the Officers' Mess, "this is my chance to initiate you chaps into the pleasures of eating eastern style." His grin widened as he considered how far removed from the truth Ben's surmise had been. What a priceless joke, he thought; but a joke he decided to keep to himself. These past months they certainly had come far together – still, there remained a fair distance to go yet.

Later that evening, when they arrived at the restaurant, the owner welcomed them effusively and insisted they treat his establishment as their own. Nothing, he assured them, was too much trouble. Should they require help with the menu, he would be glad to assist. His suggestions? Ah! Most certainly the kebabs! Finely spiced, perfectly prepared, fit for an emperor – *kubideh kebab* made with ground lamb, *jujeh kebab* with chicken, and the *shishlik* or lamb chops. Best of all, he closed his eyes and kissed the tips of his fingers, was the king of kebabs – *kebab-e-donbalan*; no one had lived till he had tried this very special dish. Roger Werner succumbed. Completely won over by such ecstatic persuasion, he decided to live a little – *kebab-e-donbalan* it was.

When the food arrived, everyone agreed that Werner's dish more than promised to live up to expectations. His first mouthful proved he had not been led astray! The aromatic flavour, he announced to his companions, far surpassed anything words could express. Pleased with his choice, he signalled the waiter to thank the proprietor, and gestured an enquiry into the contents of his dish.

Delighted to have such a highly satisfied customer, and with the prospect of a large tip in the offing, the waiter bowed and smiled, and offered an explanation – in Farsi. Catching the look of bewilderment on Werner's face, the man tried again. He paused and pondered for a moment. Finally, he pointed to Werner's plate with one hand, grabbed his crotch, bag and basket, with the other, and embellished his gestures with a loud bleating sound.

"Testicles!! Oh crikey!" yelped Werner, horrified, amid shouts of laughter from the rest of the table.

———••——

IT HAS BEEN TOLD that wine was first discovered by the Persian King, Jamshid, who received the seeds from a grateful bird he had saved. When grown, the fruit was presented to the king who ate his fill and, much pleased, he stored the remaining grapes in vats. As will happen, fermentation took place, whereupon everyone believed the fruit had turned to poison. Now, the king's favourite slave girl suffered terrible headaches and, finally, in a desperate attempt to end her misery she drank the "poison." To everyone's astonishment the wine cured her instead, and the king, overjoyed, made it freely available to all his subjects as *daru shah*, the king's medicine.

Whether that tale be true or not some of the most beautiful poetry ever written about wine has come out of Persia. The ancient poet, Omar Khayyam, lauded the pleasures of wine and the beauty of his country's gardens with such ecstasy, his exquisite verse was, itself, enough to inebriate the reader. Santi's acquaintance with the Persian poet had, till now, been brief. That was about to change.

About fifty kilometres distant from the camp lay the picturesque town of Kermanshah with just such perfumed gardens and orchards as those eulogised by the poet. The officers and soldiers were given permission to sample the delights of this frontier fortress town. One day, while browsing through the shops selling engraved copper, goat-skin jackets, Persian rugs and other local goods, Santi came across a tiny bric-a-brac store, hidden away among the twists and turns of a little crooked street. It was fitting that it would be in just such a place as this that Santi should discover a small, rather worn, but elaborately wrought copy of the Rubaiyat of Omar Khayyam.

Hailing from Bengal, Santi's favourite poet and literary hero was, naturally, the Bard of Bengal – Rabindranath Tagore. Awarded the Nobel Prize for literature in 1913, he was knighted by the British in 1915. Formerly Bengal's pride and joy, he became India's hero when he renounced his knighthood in protest of the massacre in Amritsar's Jallianwala Bagh Square, where hundreds of unarmed Indians protesting incarcerations by the British were surrounded and, without avenue of escape, mercilessly mowed down.

Back home Santi possessed a treasured copy of Tagore's Gitanjali. Now, he decided to send home the Rubaiyat. This newly acquired gem would serve as a perfect dual birthday gift for two of his sisters – and it would ensure the book's safety as well.

Lt. S.P. Dutt
c/o Middle East Forces
Letter No. 7   *27 August 1941*

My dear Sudha,

I trust letter No. 6 has been received. How did you spend 9 August? A good day, I hope. Letter No. 5 had a 'card' I attempted to draw for you (not too well, I'm afraid), and though sent in good time, I do not know if it arrived for your birthday. Since Kamala's birthday is coming up as well in October, I will be sending a gift for you to share – a first edition copy of the Rubaiyat of Omar Khayyam, published in 1859. I found it in an old shop, hidden away in a dark and dusty corner of a bookshelf. It is all I have at present, I'm afraid, but I think you might enjoy the poet's ruminations.

I haven't had news of the family in a while. I trust all is well? Please keep me informed. In these uncertain times silence is cause for anxiety. Isolated here from all things familiar and normal, one really looks forward to mail from those who are near and dear.

I must admit, however, at this precise moment I have no reason to complain. We consider ourselves to be doing very well, indeed. Against the backdrop of our past meanderings, the place where we are now billeted seems akin to paradise. We are eating like lords…fresh fruit and vegetables, with plenty of game to be had. I know, in writing about it, I will be unable to send this letter until we are well away from here, but so be it, because the beauty of this region is worth sharing.

The countryside here is full of legend, and there is much to see. Last week we were lucky enough to find a local guide who took us to Tagh-e-Bostan. The grottoes and caves there are filled with history. The Sasanian emperors' coronations, their royal ceremonies and court scenes are recorded on the mountainside for all posterity to witness. The majesty of it is quite awe inspiring!

One panel of rock carvings depicts the Persian King Ardeshir, flanked on the one hand by Ahoura Mazda, their god of truth, life and goodness, and on the other by Mithra, guardian against drought and famine. Beneath their feet lay Ahriman, god of darkness and evil, and out of the mountain a sacred spring gushed, emptying itself into a reflecting pool. The ancient Persians seem to have had a pantheon of gods, similar to ours and to the Greeks it would seem.

There are little villages all through these valleys. We visited the village of Bisotun, which sits along an old caravan route that runs beneath the smooth, umber cliff-face of the Behistun Mountain. On one side of the road a large pool of water, very probably, provided a resting place for travellers of yore. Standing on that spot, surrounded by the stillness of the mountains, one could imagine the caravans stopping on their weary journey, the travellers with their donkeys and camels gratefully gathering around to slake their thirst.

On the opposite side of the road, looking down from a towering three hundred feet above the village, we could see the Tablet of Darius, erected by him around 519 BC, ostensibly in his own honour. Remember, Darius was the Persian king who invaded India with the grandiose dream of expanding his kingdom. That dream, luckily, was short-lived. But there it was, inscribed in Ancient Persian, Babylonian and Elamite, the story of his ascension, his reign and his battles. The gigantic panel stood some forty by sixty feet, tawny in the early morning light. With the aid of my binoculars, I could see the king, his enemies sprawled at his feet bound in chains – and the inscription: 'I am Darius the Great King…By the favour of Ahura Mazda I am King of Kings'…

Ah, the ego of man who would be immortal! It couldn't fail but bring to mind Shelley's Ozymandias: 'My name is Ozymandias, king of kings: Look on my works, ye Mighty, and despair!' Different time, different place, the one far removed from the other – and yet the same reach for glory…

On another occasion, while out on one of our training route-marches, we came upon a small town called Kangavar. It lay in the valley of Asad-abad, its gardens abundant with flowers, its vineyards with fruit, and all around, fields of watermelon, pumpkin and cucumber. There, we came across the remains of some marble steps and columns of a now ruined temple, once dedicated, so we were informed, to the water goddess Anahita. She is purported to be protector of the earth and mother of fertility and birth. A rather strange and appealing circumstance committed the name to memory as we were passing through a small village thereabouts.

The locals were engagingly friendly, and some brought us tea which, over here, is drunk black. First, a piece of rock sugar is placed in the mouth, then hot tea is sipped over it. Many of their old folk can be seen, sitting outside their dwellings, using metal cutters to break cone shaped blocks of solidified sugar-cane juice into pieces for this purpose.

Well, while we were enjoying our tea, a little girl came up to me and offered me some biscuits. She called them 'nan-e-berenji' and 'kak'. On her tiny feet she wore a pair of coarse cloth and leather 'givehs', shoes that are made and worn locally. She was the most beautiful child I have ever seen with her long golden-brown hair and angelic blue-grey eyes! I asked her name, and although she didn't speak any English, she seemed to understand me. Her name, she said, was Anahida.

Together, we shared the biscuits, which I hand-signed to her were very good indeed, and she made me put the remaining few in my pocket. I gave her one Iranian Toman so she could buy herself something nice, but all the while she kept eyeing the Gurkha regimental badge on my cap. I removed my cap so she might take a closer look. The shiny silver pin seemed to fascinate her as she ran a small finger over the two crossed kukris, tracing the three feathers that crown them. And although I knew I would have some explaining to do before the Quartermaster would be persuaded to issue me a replacement, I could not help but remove the badge from my cap and pin it to her blouse. Her smile, and the wonderful way her eyes lit up, made the inevitable wrangle with my QM completely worthwhile.

I am secretly convinced, though nobody else might believe it, the little girl I met that day was none other than the water goddess, Anahita.... Here, in these valleys amidst the mountains might not anything be possible? One need only listen in the still of a moment to hear the quiet whisperings of previous lives, reincarnations through time. And so it is, each soul is a thousand echoes of the past, the beauty and the bestiality, two sides of the same coin. Even here, one wonders, how many battles had once been fought in these peaceful valleys, how many warriors lie buried beneath the coverlet of this pastoral haven. These delicate flowers, these fruitful orchards, were they all the more beautiful and bountiful for their native soil being awash in blood? History, it seems, would chide us that man's glory is bred of bloodshed. It is a disquieting thought to ponder on.

My pranams to Mother and Father, my love to all the sisters.

Affly yours, Dada

CHAPTER SIXTEEN

War And The Home Front

We are no other than a moving row
Of magic Shadow Shapes that come and go
Round with the Sun-illumin'd Lantern held
In midnight by the Master of the Show.

– Omar Khayyam, *Rubaiyat of Omar Khayyam*

FAR AWAY, IN THE Western Desert, the siege of Tobruk remained at a stalemate. The Desert Fox had, so far, been unable to breach the henhouse where the Allies (the Australian 9th Division, 18 Brigade of the Australian 7th Division, four regiments of British artillery and some Indian troops) were desperately holding him at bay. Their front line of defence was a perimeter of ditches and dugouts, built nine miles out in the desert and left behind by the Italians when they had been routed earlier that year. Now, mined and fortified by the Allies, these proved a most effective deterrent against Rommel's attacks.

Holed up for months in this deep-water port so crucial to the shipment of their supplies and troops, the stubborn defenders of Tobruk earned the nickname "The Desert Rats." And, finally, when the Desert Fox suggested they should surrender with honour, the Australian Commander of Tobruk, General Leslie James Morshead, promptly returned this short reply: *Due to prevailing dust and the need to ration water, no white handkerchiefs are available.*

And so it went, month after month. Both besiegers and besieged, suffering the same desert privations, faced each other across the mines and barbed wire of no-man's land in what, some believe, was the last war to be fought with any sense of honour and mutual respect.

One incident that might well exemplify this occurred when the Australians sent some stretcher bearers, under a white flag of truce, to collect their wounded and dead from no-man's land. According to record, this mission received a warning from the Germans as they approached a minefield. Going one step further, a German Lieutenant, accompanied by a doctor and several men, came out with a metal detector to facilitate the Australians safe loading of their wounded and dead onto lorries. Upon completing this shared mission of mercy, the two sides saluted each other respectfully – the military salute, not the Nazi one – and returned to their respective camps, and to war.

The physical war in North Africa was contained in the desert mainly, and unlike that in Europe and elsewhere, it took place, for the most part, away from human habitation. As such, the terrible destruction to civilian life and property was avoided to a great extent, and the desert warrior, spared the guilt and remorse of this aspect of war, was able to maintain a certain civilized perspective and sense of honour. This might give hint to a certain phenomenon, in this time and place, during the eight-month siege of Tobruk, that transcended all barriers of language and nationality, making short shrift of the politics of war.

For lonely, battle-worn soldiers, far from home and loved ones, music was an opiate to soothe the soul. Aware of this, both the Allies and the Axis set up special radio stations to broadcast the latest popular wartime songs to their troops. There in the desert, weary from long months of hardship, and worn down by the monotony of their surroundings, the soldiers took comfort in these songs that spoke of love, of home, and pride of country. Aired daily, by the BBC Forces Programme on the one side, and by Soldatensender Belgrad (Soldier's Radio Belgrade) on the other, lilting sounds of music could be heard from both camps – soft in the stillness of the desert, wafting through the evening dusk, mingling the sentiments of the two enemies.

One August night, when Radio Belgrade signed off the air at precisely 2155 hours, a song was heard from the German camp. Soft as a sultry sigh and just as heart-rending, it filled the silence with nostalgia and longing:

"Vor der Kaserne vor dem grohen Tor,
Stand eine Lanterne und steht sie nach davor…"

Huddled in their trenches, the Allies heard it. To most, the words made no sense, but that melody and that melting voice were quite another matter. Listening raptly, someone called out, "Turn it up a smidge, would you! Louder, please, louder"…and all North Africa fell in love!

The voice of Bramerhaven singer, Lale Andersen, was later described by an Allied SAS Officer. Oxford-educated, he was eloquent in his rapture – "husky, sensuous, nostalgic…sugar-sweet…seeming to reach out across the desert"….A perfect soldiers' song, sad and tender, about a girl who was that enigmatic paradox, that irresistible something between faithful sweetheart and seductive camp follower. So universally appealing, the song crossed all boundaries, mine-fields, barbed wire and frontlines, to conquer both Axis and Allies alike. (John Bierman and Colin Smith: *War without Hate*)

Born German, the song would eventually be adapted into for-ty-eight languages. First adopted by the British, Australian, French, and Italian armies in the desert, each quickly turned it to their pur-pose. Till, finally, this song that was destined to become a legend among soldiers of all nations, "Lili Marleen", was officially rechris-tened "Lili Marlene" in English. It retained the sentiment with some deftly wrought changes to the wording and was first sung for the Allies by Anne Shelton.

> *Underneath the lantern, by the barrack gate,*
> *Darling I remember the way you used to wait*
> *'Twas there that you whispered, tenderly…*

It was, however, most famously sung by Vera Lynn, the WWII soldiers' sweetheart.

> *Resting in our billets just behind the lines,*
> *Even though we're parted your lips are close to mine.*
> *You wait where that lantern softly gleams…*

The North African desert warrior's anthem would take the war-wea-ry world by storm. The why and wherefore of it were without answer, and therefore inconsequential. Put simply, in Lale Andersen's own succinct words, "Can the wind explain why it became a storm?"

To THE EAST OF TOBRUK, some four hundred and fifty-two miles, Cai-ro lay asleep, dreaming fitfully along the Nile. The city of a thousand minarets, wrapped in moonlight and night shadows, rested from the toils of the day. A clear sky, heavy with stars, hung over the desert, casting timeless shadows around the Great Pyramids and the silent Sphinx, secured against war-time damage with sandbags and stones.

East of Cairo, approximately one hundred and twenty miles across the dark Arabian Desert, the Suez Canal journeyed from the Medi-terranean Sea in the north to the Red Sea in the south. To the west of the old city, lay the first silver stretches of Egypt's Western Des-ert. Here, due northwest, about one hundred and twenty miles, the Mediterranean seaside resort of Alexandria huddled, under cover of darkness, dodging the moonbeams that spilt across its roofs and splattered its shores – for despite the tranquillity of the star-studded heavens, danger lurked in the moon-washed skies overhead.

Founded by Alexander the Great in 332 BC, Alexandria became the capital of Egypt during the reign of the Ptolomies, thriving as a port and a centre for trade, and rivalling the culture and learning of Rome and Constantinople. It was witness to Cleopatra's glory and demise, and to the invading armies of Rome, Byzantium, the Muslim Arabs, the French and, finally, the British. Slowly, however, over the centuries, Alexandria's glory faded.

Its two famous libraries were destroyed by the armies of Julius Caesar and Theodosius I, and eventually, when the Arabs moved the capital to Cairo, the port fell into decline. The famous Lighthouse of Pharos, once among the seven wonders of the ancient world, slipped beneath the waves and disappeared forever. And rumour had it, that somewhere below the silver-tipped waves now lapping the harbour, the lighthouse still guarded the sleeping ruins of a forgotten city and a sunken palace that had, long ago, been the royal abode of Egypt's most celebrated Queen…Queen Cleopatra.

Life, however, is an eternal cycle, and once again the port had come into its own. Present day Alexandria was not only a seaside resort of silver sands and sapphire seas, beautiful enough to have been elected 'The Pearl of the Mediterranean', it was an important port of call for maritime travel as well. Now, more so than ever. With the war raging in North Africa, its strategically positioned harbour was of paramount interest to Allied shipping. Consequently, Alexandria, home to the British Mediterranean Fleet, and the Suez Canal, gateway to British India and the Orient, both became prime targets for Axis aerial bombardment. And Cairo lay squarely between these two targets.

Usually, the planes came at night, and moonlit nights were the most fraught with danger. To minimize this, it was concluded, after some consideration, that a little good old-fashioned magic was in order. Subsequently, with the help of a magician from London, named Jasper Maskelyne, the British decided to use smoke and mirrors to 'hide' both Alexandria and the Suez Canal.

Earlier in the year, Italian aircraft had managed to put the Canal out of commission by mining it. As a result, hundreds of Allied ships sat, useless and vulnerable, out in the Red Sea, their silhouettes etched darkly against the skyline as they waited to dispatch their much-needed cargo. To avoid another such fiasco, it was given to Maskelyne and his crew, The Magic Gang, to preserve the integrity of the one-hundred-and-three-mile-long Canal, and its much-need-ed docks.

They came up with the ingenious idea of installing twenty-one immensely powerful search lights along the Canal, each intensified with a cleverly constructed cone of twenty-four mirrors. At night, these were pointed skyward, and then spun to create a dazzling strobe-light effect that blinded oncoming aircraft and disoriented their pilots. It proved a great success.

In the case of Alexandria, the opposite was done, to create the illusion of disappearance. At the first threat of enemy aircraft, the city of Alexandria doused its lights and vanished into the night. Three miles away, in a small, deserted bay, lights suddenly appeared on a set built to closely emulate Alexandria, complete with its harbour and lighthouse. This decoy deluded the bombers, leading them away from the actual target to waste their deadly cargo, bombing an area of barren desert and an empty harbour.

It was not unusual, on a clear moonlit night, such as the one in early September, for Cairo to be woken to the wail of the air raid siren. Given her proximity to both the Suez Canal on her east, and Alexandria on her west, the danger of being caught in the bombing was ever present. Sometime or the other, it seemed inevitable.

It was late at night, and Hedeya had stayed up to finish Miriam Beshay's bridal peignoir. The girl was getting married the following day, and this was the last piece of her elaborate trousseau to be completed. The household, like most of the city, was asleep. In the bedroom, Bajo had been dreaming fitfully of a train journey, with young Hedeya by her side. They had boarded the train right from their very own kitchen, and much to her consternation, it was carrying them at breakneck speed to…some unknown…somewhere back…back…back to…to…NO!

She woke with a start to realise that the sound of the train was, in reality, the trundle of Hedeya's sewing machine in the drawing room. That sound had filled the house all evening, as her daughter had pushed down hard on the foot peddle of her machine and spun its hand wheel. And now, even at this late hour, the girl was still up working! Bajo slipped out of bed without disturbing Violette and made for the drawing room.

"*Lao, lao*, have you seen the time? When will you go to bed?" She came up beside her daughter's chair and rested a hand on her shoulder. "You should give your eyes a rest. You will ruin them if you go on like this."

"*Al-hamdulillah,* it's finished!" Hedeya pushed her chair back and stretched, as she thanked God in the universal Arabic fashion. "To-morrow morning Miriam's driver will come to collect these."

She folded the peignoir neatly, adding it to the small pile of ex-quisitely embroidered silk-and-lace chemises and night garments ly-ing on the table beside the machine. "I have written her a note to tell her the pink satin bed-jacket with the ecru lace is a gift from us." She glanced at the clock. "*Wakh lao!* I hadn't realised how late it is. Why aren't you asleep, Bajo?"

"Old age. I spend half the night trying to get to sleep, and in the morning, I find I am exhausted. So, now, I don't try. I am too old to chase anything – even sleep. I let it come and find me."

"So that's it! I always wondered why the English say 'going to catch forty winks'. It seems to be – how do they say it – 'a very slippery cus-tomer,'" Hedeya teased.

"Never mind the English and their sayings. I suppose if you look hard enough, you will find some wisdom everywhere – even in that language!" She patted her daughter's shoulder. "You know, I could hear the sound of your machine in my dream. I thought I was on a train, taking us back…" She stopped in mid-sentence. "It does not matter, thank God. And now that it has stopped, let us both go to bed and dream in peace."

———◆———

WITH ITS INHABITANTS AT last abed, silence reigned, and before long the house was stilled in sleep. Hedeya lay, listening to the small sounds of the family at rest; the occasional movements of her two sons dreaming soundly in their room, her daughter curled into a soft bundle between her and Bajo, in their big brass bed. She stared at the shifting shadows, thrown onto the ceiling by the streetlight outside, as it filtered in through the curtains with every breath of air. Just beyond those curtains, hidden within the dark folds of night, was a slumbering world that would turn to turmoil with the coming of day – turmoil she had to contend with, day after day. It was a heavy burden to carry all on her own, and she often felt out of her depth.

It had been different when Baba Taht was alive. No matter how bad things got, he had been her source of strength, her anchor. No matter he had grown old and weak, he had held her world together. Then, suddenly he was gone, and there was no one to turn to. And though she had married, she was separated, with three children of her own, and quite unprepared for the kind of responsibilities that had fallen on her shoulders when he died – running his small shoe store and keeping an eye on his share of the trucking company – and eventually she lost them both. She was forced to sell the store for next to nothing and, worse still, when Baba Taht's partners in his trucking business informed her that business had gone belly up, there was no recourse but to accept their word for it.

What did she know of business? She was twenty-eight years old then, and his death from pneumonia pulled the rug out from under her feet. It left her shaken, and with a sense of such utter helplessness, she was almost overcome by it. Yet, she came to realise, although she missed her father everyday, she couldn't allow the family to see just how much; or how afraid she felt of being unable to cope with the responsibility of three children and an old mother who, more and more often these days, seemed to take refuge in the past. Bajo's flights of fancy were getting ever more frequent, almost as though she, too, were looking to the past for the security she lost with the passing of her husband. Poor Bajo, sometimes the past and the present were so intertwined in her head, she had a hard time sorting out where one ended and the other began.

Then, there was the matter of the childrens' education. If only she hadn't been forced to broach the subject with Mahran! But she was so hard-pressed to make ends meet, somehow, she'd swallowed her pride and reminded him of his responsibility to help pay for their schooling. And in doing so she played right into his hands.

"I warned you how it would be," he lorded it over her, adding foxily, "but you know how you can solve the problem. You can always come back."

"That will never happen, and you know it." She had stood up and walked away, putting as much distance between them as she could. "We tried that once and it was the same story as before. It was over even before we..." she shook her head angrily. "Ahh! Why do you waste your time and mine..."

"There you go again, hot-headed as ever. Too proud to give in, no matter what. Sit down, sit down." Mahran had laughed. "You're the devil to deal with, but I must say, anger becomes you."

Unwilling to be drawn in or to indulge his banter, Hedeya remained standing. After a moment, he got up and walked over to her. "I'll take the boys. You manage the girl. There's my offer. It's the only one I'll make, and it's in everyone's best interests – unless, of course, you change your mind and decide, maybe..." he had raised a quizzical eyebrow, but beaten a hasty retreat at the thunderous look on her face.

"Never!"

Nonetheless, she had wrestled with the problem ever since. She guessed why he was agreeable now to taking the boys. They were growing up, and he realised their potential for adding to the household income – he realised, as well, that she hadn't the means to hold out till that time came. All along he had been angling to get her back, and to that end, perhaps as punishment even, he made it as hard for her as he could by reneging on his end and withholding his support.

Oh, she knew only too well how his mind worked! Before too long the boys would finish school and have the capability of earning; Victor would soon be there, and Louis was not that far behind – and before that time should come, he was 'offering to take them off her hands'. All in all, at this stage the boys would be less of a liability for him, while she, he guessed rightly, would still need some support to clothe, feed, and especially to educate Violette. Even without the boys, she would be hard put to providing for a family of three – and he was not about to make it easy for her!

His motives were selfish, but she knew, in his own peculiar way, he cared for the boys as much as he could care for anyone; and they would, at least, be looked after materially. He would do his best, and whatever that was, it would be better than she could manage. Guiltily, she thought of the two occasions when she had added water to their milk so it would be sufficient to fill all three small bellies. She knew he could give them the food, clothing and education she could not manage on her own. A woman did not have the same opportunities a man had; neither was her work valued in the same way.

She was aware, under the circumstances, what the most practical decision should be. But no matter how sensible an argument she put forward, the thought of giving him her sons brought a tightness to her throat and chest so that she could hardly breathe. Sooner or later, she would have to decide, and the knowledge of what that decision would have to be haunted her dreams.

Of course, there was always Sallah. He had asked her, repeatedly, to marry him. He was a good man, there was none better, and he got on well with the children. But…he was Muslim! And so, what if he was, she chided herself. She had learnt to deal with it on every level, so why not this one?

Because, after the horrors they had suffered at the hands of Muslims, this acceptance of a Muslim as head of her household, and protector of her family, required the faith and trust that could come only with complete forgiveness. And, although the body had healed, no matter how hard she tried, she could not forgive or forget the desecration of her mind, or the deep, dark bruises to her soul. She could not bear anyone to see them, could not allow anyone to touch them; the memories made her feel a shame which, sometimes, amounted almost to revulsion. And what of Bajo? Had she and Baba Taht gone through all that grief and loss, determined to preserve their identity, only to have her lose it now by handing it to a Muslim?

My God, she thought, what kind of mess have we created in your name! How did love for you turn to such hate between your children? For, mingled in with all the raw emotions, she felt keenly the guilt of her prejudice. There were so many decent people, friends, who were Muslim. She reasoned with herself, it was ungenerous to continue feeling this awful sense of fear and mistrust. In fact, if it hadn't been for the Muslim family in Diyarbekar who had hidden them, none of them would be alive today. She fell into a fitful sleep plagued with uneasy dreams.

———•◆•———

THE SPIRALLING WHINE OF the siren began as a moan that grew into an insistent wailing. It woke Hedeya immediately. She was out of bed in a trice, even before it reached its ear-splitting crescendo. The awful sound, fraught with such terrible urgency, had been unnerving when first heard over the city. But, by now, response to it had become second nature, and Hedeya was already shaking Violette awake while grabbing their coats and shoes. Bajo hadn't stirred. She was sleeping on her left side, her good ear pressed into her pillow. As her right ear was almost completely deaf from a slap dealt her by an angry Turkish soldier in that terrible time long ago, she hadn't heard the siren at all. Not that it mattered, because she refused to go to the air raid shelter anyway.

"What for?" she had demanded. "You think God has nothing better to do than to leave everyone and drop the bomb on Bajo's head? And even if He does, it will be because He has decided it is my time. Who am I to try to hide from Him! I've lived my life. I would rather go in my bed than buried like a rat underground. You go with the children, leave me here, I'm too old to run about the streets in the middle of the night." And that was that, nothing would budge her.

So, Hedeya left her sleeping, but before leaving the house, she always turned the main electric switch off, a precaution, in case the old lady woke up and, unaware of the blackout in force, turned the light on by mistake. At the very least the penalty was a large fine, at worst it was a beacon inviting misfortune and disaster from the skies.

"Ta'al heyna. Yalla!" Hedeya hurried the boys, half-asleep, out of their room and down the stairs, trying to get their jackets on over their pyjamas as they went. She herded the three children across the street, making sure they held hands tightly as they mingled with the orderly crowd hurrying in the same direction. The policeman on night watch was a familiar and reassuring figure. He greeted Hedeya and the children as he moved everyone along, towards the underground shelter where sandbags had been piled high on either side of the entrance.

"Mama, look!" Violette stopped and pointed eastward. "Look, how pretty! There are four moons in the sky." Sure enough, large, bright lights hung suspended in the eastern sky, like four glowing moons.

"The planes have parachuted lights over the city!" someone in the crowd shouted. An uneasy murmur rippled through the crowd.

"They are trying to light up the city!" another voice cried out. "*Allah!* The planes are going to bomb us!" The ripple of unease billowed into fear.

From a nearby mosque, the siren at the top of the muezzin's turret was still going full blast when Cairo's anti-aircraft guns opened fire. Far in the east, towards Abbassia, the first dull thud of falling bombs could be heard. Frightened screams rent the air, and the crowd broke in panic, pushing its way frantically towards the entrance of the shelter, like a gigantic, undulating wave, thrusting forward blindly, sweeping everyone in its path.

Hedeya and the children were pushed along by the sheer force of seventy or eighty bodies compacted into one solid mass. She shouted to all three to stay together, to hold on tight as they entered the shelter. She had managed to push a little to the side, away from the centre of the heaving crowd when, suddenly, she heard a small, high-pitched scream next to her rise above the pandemonium of the crowd. And, at that moment, she felt Violette's hand slip from hers.

Hedeya turned back, grabbing frantically at the empty space where her daughter had been. She saw the girl, an arms-length away, beside a man. Both her hands balled into two small fists, she was pounding on his belly while he tried to fend her off.

"He hurt me, he hurt me", she shrieked over and over again.

In an instant, both Victor and Louis threw themselves upon the offender, fists and feet flying, kicking and pummelling him anywhere and everywhere they could.

"You don't touch my sister," Victor was shouting. "You leave her alone."

Eyes blazing with fury, Hedeya turned on the man, *"Kelb ibn kelb,* do you have no shame?"

The man threw up his hands in bewilderment. "Madam, please, I have done nothing, I swear to you. It is I who am being hurt. She has gone quite mad and is beating me for no reason at all. The more I try to get away from her, the more violently she beats me, I swear it!"

Hedeya looked into the man's eyes and saw that he was speaking the truth. By now, they had all been propelled into the shelter and had washed up on the edge of the crowd. Violette was still pounding the man's belly with one fist, while her other hand had grabbed onto his jacket and was pulling him along. Man and girl seemed to be attached to each other in some odd way and, all at once, Hedeya realised why.

Unknown to them both, Violette's curls had become entangled in the unfortunate man's jacket button, and each push and pull of the crowd tugged hard on the little girl's hair. Furious at the pain this caused her, she attacked the only source she was able to associate with her misery. Her innocent victim, confounded by the ferocity of his little assailant, tried his utmost to get away, but the harder he tried, the more frenzied the attack upon him became.

At last, matters were put to right and apologies made to the battered and bruised gentleman, who beat a hasty retreat to the far end of the shelter, keeping, Hedeya noted ruefully, the entire length of the shelter between them.

Above ground, the dull pounding of the AcAc guns could still be heard. A woman next to them started wailing loudly. *"Khalas, khalas,* we're finished. Surely now we're going to die." A titter of hysteria began to swell through the crowd again.

"Abadan. No, those are our guns," Louis called out above the din. "They are shooting at the planes to keep them away. As long as they are firing, they'll keep us safe."

"Listen to my brother," Victor said proudly. "He knows what he is saying."

When the all-clear sounded, the little group returned home to find Bajo standing at the French windows. She had opened the *sheesh* and was looking towards the east, where the sky was lit up, bright red and orange. Parts of the city were on fire.

"No matter where you run, the killing follows you," she said, sadly. "Is nowhere safe from human folly? Loss of material possessions is a discomfort that fades, but loss of loved ones is an ache to be carried always. Ah! What we were once and what we have come to! Our family, how close we all were! Now, we are scattered, like sand, driven by the winds of fear and hatred."

Her voice, no more than a murmur, was soft with memories.

"Families build communities and communities build nations. Our nation is an ancient one…they tried to wipe us out…but, are we too not God's children?" She turned to Hedeya. "I must see Shamun. I must go to Qamishli and see my brother before I die."

Next morning, the newspapers carried the headlines:

7th September 1941. Cairo bombed. Thirty-nine dead, ninety wounded. Last night bombs fell in the north-eastern district of Abbassia where British camps and the aerodrome…Britain threatens to bomb Rome in retaliation…

CHAPTER SEVENTEEN

The Unlikely Mascot

*And strange to tell, among that Earthern Lot
Some could articulate, while others not;
And suddenly one more impatient cried...
Who is the Potter, pray, and who the Pot?*

– Omar Khayyam, *Rubaiyat of Omar Khayyam*

IT WAS THE SEASON of holy festivals once again in India. In Bengal and Nepal, the first Goddess to be honoured is *Durga*. Amid great joy and splendour, attired in all her finery and adorned with jewels, she arrives to spend a ten-day visit on earth. She brings a bounty of blessings to the faithful, and the faithful thank her, each in their own way. Thus, depending largely on the region, both time and manner of the festivities may vary.

One might draw a paralell in the Christian world where most observe Christmas on December 25th, except for the early Christians – the Copts and the Armenians – and those who belong to the Eastern Orthodox churches of Europe and Africa, who observe it, some on the 6th, others on the 7th of January. And they celebrate, each according to their customs.

Similarly, the festival of *Dashera* is celebrated in Bengal on the tenth and final day of *Durga Pujo*, while the Nepalese and Gurkhas observe it on the eighth day. In Bengal, the age-old custom of sacrificing a buffalo on that day, to symbolise *Durga's* victory over the buffalo-demon, *Mahisasura*, has been replaced with offerings of vegetables, fruits and sweets to celebrate her triumph of good over evil. (Santi recalled that Grandfather had instituted the 'sacrifice' of a pumpkin in place of a buffalo.) The Gurkhas, however, still maintained the old ways. It was tradition, nay, indeed, it was believed to be auspicious for the general good fortune and well-being of all concerned – including, of course, that of the animal – that the beheading be completed with a single, swift stroke of the *kukri*.

As there was no buffalo to be had on this occasion, a billy goat was procured instead from a nearby village, and since it was, by comparison, a small substitute for the usual sacrifice, the 'fattening of the calf' began in earnest.

A few errors occurred along the way – the first one being, the animal, at some point, was given a name. Santi's young medical orderly, Hirasing Limbu, astute as ever, pointed out that their new goat with his long, tufted beard looked remarkably like a venerable old *mullah*. Everyone agreed, the name took, and the grave little goat was so christened. He grazed the lush pastures, sniffed out his surroundings, and roamed the camp at will. His diet was supplemented with the best scraps and leftovers from the Officers' Mess and the men's langar. And so, he grew in size, in strength and, amazingly, in wisdom too, for it wasn't long before Mullah knew the ins and outs and whereabouts of the whole camp, with all its comings and goings.

He seemed to understand instinctively that he had Hirasing Limbu to thank for his new name, and the two could often be found in each other's company. Mullah's day would begin early each morning with Reveille, when he would be seen on the parade ground, standing to attention beside his young Gurkha – who happened to be the battalion bugler as well – as he bugled the hoisting of the Union Jack. In the evening, at Last Post, there he was once again, solemnly assisting with the lowering of the flag.

Santi, Iran, 1941..

Mullah took to joining the Battalion on parade as well, inclining his head smartly to the right in response to the order for the march-past. He even accompanied them on a route march once, but that single experience was enough to dampen his enthusiasm for any further such unnecessary physical endeavour. From that day forward, he would follow the men to the perimeter of the camp where he would see them off, and when the last soldier had disappeared over the ridge, he would contentedly stroll back to the tent he shared with Hirasing, to wait there in comfort for his return.

One day Santi heard voices outside his tent. Glancing through the tent flap, he saw Hirasing in earnest conversation with Dilbahadur. Hirasing looked and sounded anxious. Wondering only briefly as to what was transpiring, Santi returned to the book he was reading.

After a while there was silence, and a moment or so later Dilbahadur quietly entered the tent.

"*Sahib?*" The orderly shuffled his feet, speaking softly. He hesitated slightly. "*Sahib*, Hirasing..."

Santi looked up from his book. "*Ule ke bhandaichha?*" he prompted, gently.

It turned out that Hirasing had come to seek *Daktar Sahib's* advice regarding Mullah's state of health. The animal seemed, inexplicably, to have become somewhat indisposed; he had gone off his food and just lay in the tent, moaning softly. Was it possible for *Daktar Sahib* to examine him and find out what was wrong?

Santi explained that he was not sure he would be able to help since he was not an animal doctor, but he agreed to take a look. Putting his book aside, he rose, and was about to duck through the tent opening when Dilbahadur stopped him: *Sahib* had forgotten his *daftar* bag, the soldier reminded him mildly, handing him the small satchel in which Santi kept his stethoscope and other medical essentials. Keeping a straight face, Santi solemnly thanked his batman and then accompanied Hirasing back to his tent and his protégé.

Sure enough, as he raised the tent flap and entered, the sound of Mullah's moans could be heard. Beside him lay a bowl of uneaten vegetable peels and some bruised fruit. Santi examined him with his stethoscope. He tapped Mullah's chest and tummy and drew a blank. He recommended plenty of rest and fluids.

Walking back to his tent, Santi was struck by a thought. After some consideration, it prompted a visit to the village where Mullah had been born.

The next day, Santi visited Mullah again. He noted the bowl of old vegetable peels and leftover fruit had been replaced with a new one, much the same as its predecessor. This too lay untouched beside Mullah. Had the *jantu's* appetite not returned?

"*Hunna, Sahib,*" Hirasing shook his head, glumly. "*Kaile, kaile aunchha, kaile, kaile aundaina.*" No, *Sahib*. Sometimes it does, sometimes it doesn't.

Santi examined Mullah once again with the same result – nothing. He pushed aside the bowl of vegetable peels and replaced it with an offering he had brought of fresh, leafy green vegetables and fruit; apples and oranges, raisins and flax seed. The new meal was a result of research he had done among the locals in Mullah's village, and he now placed it close to the ailing goat. Then he stepped back, and they waited.

After a minute, Mullah's nose began to twitch. He raised his drooping eyelids, and looked around. Santi pushed the dish a little closer. As though with great effort, Mullah lifted his head and sniffed. Slowly at first, and then with increasing pleasure, he began to munch on the delectable victuals before him. Santi and Hirasing looked on in amazement.

Mullah, it would seem, had lodged a complaint about the quality of his rations, and now appeared to be tolerably well pleased with the resolution and its resultant outcome.

Unit mascot, Mullah, Iran, 1941.

The following day Santi went once more to see his patient. As he approached Mullah's tent, all was quiet within. He came around softly to the entrance and lifted its flap. The minute Mullah saw him he set up a gentle moaning sound. Apparently, his hunger strike had produced such gratifying results, he knew a good thing when he found it. His food had improved ten-fold, and he now had his own personal physician who made house calls! Why then, he seemed to figure, should he take half a loaf when he might have a full one by milking this opportunity commensurate with his abilities? Why indeed, Santi thought, amused. The wily little goat could teach the best of us a lesson or two!

As a result of further homework Santi had done with the village folk nearby, he now presented Mullah with some grain – oats, barley and rye – sprinkled with a mineral supplement the villagers had given him. These were placed beside his fresh veggies and fruit. Now, Mullah had achieved paradise! He had fresh green pastures he could graze at will, and his own personal, hand-delivered service of fresh fruits and vegetables. Surely this was goat heaven!

Santi spent some time petting him, then he went outside and listened. The little moans of complaint had ceased. All was quiet within the tent, except for the contented sounds of munching, as the happy goat dug in. Santi smiled and assured Hirasing there was nothing to worry about – his friend was definitely on the mend.

The following day Mullah was up and about his duties, heartier than ever before. He added one more task to his daily routine. Each morning he faithfully accompanied Dilbahadur when the orderly took Santi's tea to him. First, he made sure all was as it should be – had his doctor slept well? Had his tea been served piping hot?

Then, he would share a friendly biscuit with Santi, after which he would go about his business of the day. If he was anything, he was certainly mindful of favours rendered!

As *Dashera* approached, Mullah busied himself with his chores and his daily perambulations in the usual manner – but a pall of unease hung over the rest of the camp. Hirasing's face settled into lugubrious lines, and every mind was occupied with a problem no one quite dared formulate into words. The festival arrived, and it became apparent its usual unalloyed enthusiasm was tainted with a sense of foreboding. The only one unaffected was Mullah, who was revelling in the amount of attention and consideration he was receiving from everyone in camp. On the sixth day of the festival, the Quartermaster went to see the Adjutant in his office, and a short while later the Adjutant went to see the Colonel in his office.

"*Colonel Sahib daftar ma chha?*" Masters asked the office orderly. Is the Colonel in his office?

"*Hunchha, sahib.*" The Colonel was in.

Masters obtained permission and entered the tent. Once there, he hesitated a moment, then cleared his throat.

"Well, out with it, Jack," Willie looked up, frowning.

"Right, sir," Masters said, although he still looked doubtful. No use dithering. It was probably best if he went straight for it, he decided – even if it meant a carpeting. "I'm afraid it's about day after tomorrow's ceremony, sir. The men feel it's inauspicious not to have it, but I can't find anyone who is willing to…er…well…" – Masters couldn't bring himself to utter the actual word, the thought was unpleasant enough – "to…perform the deed. You see, Mullah…he isn't just any…I mean, everyone has grown very fond…well, you know how it is, sir!"

"Dash it all, Jack," Colonel Weallens snapped, "just sort it out will you! Surely there must be…why don't you ask the QM to round up a whole mess of chickens instead. I certainly wouldn't be able to sit down to a meal...I mean one can't eat...for heaven's sake, just get some ruddy chickens and be done with it!" Willy finished hurriedly.

"Right you are, sir," Masters agreed, much relieved. "Capital idea! I'll get on it straight away."

On the eighth day of *Dashera* there was a *barakhana* and everyone feasted on chicken curry, *rukshi* (rum) and whiskey. Mullah celebrated with the rest of them. They sang and danced...

> *"Dasarat raja ko tinota rani, kanchhi Kiake ko barasti bhayo*
> *Rama Lachhmi bani bani basa likhio, barasti chhatru ko rajai..."*

and made merry late into the night with the usual skits...

> *"Kaan pakr kanchhi malai rukshi khandi na...*
> *I hold my ears and swear, my lass, I have not touched a drink..."*

And when it was over, Mullah was officially designated Battalion Mascot.

———••———

TOWARDS THE MIDDLE OF October, the idyll came to an end. They were ordered back into Iraq, to a place called Hindiya, there to await further instructions.

"Couldn't last forever, I suppose," Temple lamented. "Probably thought we were getting too cushy, so some old goat decided...oh, I say! No offence, old chap," he apologised hurriedly to Mullah who was reclining close by, watching the last of the evening light as it faded over the mountains.

Except for a flick of his tail in Temple's direction, Mullah remained stoically indifferent to both gaffe and apology. He was not one to feel slighted by a passing remark, no matter how injudicious. The tranquility of his surroundings, as day slipped peacefully into slumber beneath a coverlet of nightshadows, was not to be disturbed by mere human indelicacy. He raised his head and sniffed the twilight contentedly. No, he had no complaints. From where he sat the world looked pretty good to him. Soon, the moon would awake, and accompanied by her starry handmaidens she would climb the heavens, her silver shod feet leaving gleaming footsteps on the snowy peaks. Long ago she had seduced a lovelorn poet... *"But see! Yon Moon of Heav'n again...How oft hereafter will she wax and wane; How oft hereafter look for us...Through this same garden...or for one, in vain!"*

Yes, Mullah decided, it certainly felt good to be alive.

THE BRIGADE BROKE CAMP, packed up, and descended, down through the mountains, back to the desert once more. Mullah, of course, went with them. With Hirasing responsible for the comforts of his journey, it was required only that he bid his birth country goodbye and look forward to the great adventure ahead. Summer uniforms were brought out for daytime use, but the nights were still cold; and before much longer winter would be along, bringing the weather close to freezing in the desert.

They headed south, and on the way, approximately fifty-four miles past Baghdad, they came upon the remains of ancient Babylon. This once glorious capital of ten Mesopotamian dynasties had flourished here before the advent of Christianity. The great basalt Lion of Babylon had stood through the ages, a proud symbol of the goddess Ishtar. And built into the thick masonry wall, guarding the once renowned city with its temples, palaces and gardens, was Bab Ishtar Babylon, the Door of Babylon, named in honour of the goddess. Through this entryway had run the Street of Processions. King Hammurabi had held court here in the first dynasty. The silent stones stood witness to the greatness of that old monarch who, in his wisdom, had laid the foundations, all those centuries ago, for what evolved into the civilisation of today.

And there lay the vestiges of the once grand Summer and Winter Palaces of King Nebuchadnezzar who had ruled during the last great dynasty five hundred years before the birth of Christ. His was a story of a love so great, it inspired one of the seven wonders of the ancient world. His beloved wife, the beautiful Mede princess Amytos, pined so for her mountain home, the King built her the extravagant Hanging Gardens of Babylon. But when the Mongol hordes, and later the Ottoman invasion, brought the once glorious city to its knees, sadly, it all sank into obscurity, overtaken by the desert and the inevitable sands of time.

When they arrived at Hindiya, it was found to be a river town which lay on the Euphrates somewhere between Babylon and Karbala. Santi sent the Rubaiyat and the letter he had written in Chashmeh Shah to his sister. He wondered if much would remain intact after censorship.

The Brigade was set to work on one of the many fortifications being built across the country in the event of a German invasion. Winter set in, and the weather turned remarkably cold. Everything froze over, car engines, water, even one's extremities. Winter uniforms came out once again and everyone wrapped themselves in their great coats, or *brandikots* as the Gurkhas called them.

At this time, Jack Masters was transferred out of the Battalion. His place as Adjutant was filled by Ben 'Quinine' Browne. It meant a parting of ways for old friends who had shared much together. Over the years, bonds had been built through mutual experiences, and now their paths needs must diverge. By comparison, Santi had known him only a few months, but he too was sorry to see Jack go. They had rubbed along well together. Years would pass and, writing his book "The Road Past Mandalay," Jack would recall sharing his first impression of Santi – "he's a good egg, sir" – with Colonel Weallens. As for Santi, the feeling was mutual. Although they would brush past each other later in the Burma campaign, they would never actually meet again. Jack would end up with the famous Chindits in Burma, while Santi's destiny – and the Battalion's – lay elsewhere, in a very different arena indeed.

On 15 November Santi received a summons from Colonel Weallens. He arrived just as Willie was finishing with Naule Thapa. "Carry on, Subedar Major," Willie said. "I'll be by later to see how work is progressing." The Subedar Major saluted and left, and the Colonel turned to Santi.

"There you are, Doc! Well, I have news for you; good news I'm glad to say. Your promotion has come through. Just received the signal. You've made captain. You had better get your new pips and make the necessary alterations to your uniform – Captain Dutt."

On 18 November, news filtered through official channels that the British offensive in North Africa – Operation Crusader – had begun in Libya. What did it mean for the 2/4? Did their future, by some chance, lie in that direction?

December 7 brought stunning news! In response to a coded Japanese radio message – "Climb Mount Nikita" – Japanese planes had bombed Pearl Harbor, with devastating results. Incensed, President Roosevelt declared it a date which would live in infamy. No longer protected by her oceans, and with the flames of conflagration now licking her shores, America suddenly found herself at war! In one fell swoop Japan had managed to accomplish what Churchill, with years of persuasion and pleading, had failed to do. And, if that were not enough, adding their insult to the injury already visited upon the waking giant, Germany and Italy declared war on America.

At last! Britain no longer had to go it alone!

This tempering relief, however, was cut short by dismay when further news was received, three days later – on 10 December, off the coast of Malaya, Japanese aircraft had sunk the battle cruiser "Repulse," as well as the Battalion's namesake, the battleship "Prince of Wales."

The whole absurd, unholy mess was now complete. By 11 December 1941, the entire world was truly at war. 'Lord Haw Haw,' the American-born British citizen, William Joyce, so strongly anti-semetic and anti-communist that he turned traitor, broadcast his propaganda from Germany. He warned of the imminent loss of India and ushered the year out with further taunts of Allied losses: *"This is Germany calling, Germany calling… The Royal Airforce is too weak. The Royal Navy is too weak. And as yet, the common sense of the British people is too weak to perceive the catastrophic nature of the plight into which they have allowed Churchill to lead them…"*

———— ♦ ————

To MILLIONS, CHRISTMAS THAT year was a sad reminder of home, of loneliness and loss. The world, devoid of peace and goodwill, was incinerating itself in a maelstrom of pain and hatred. The destruction knew no bounds, and man seemed to have lost all capability for mercy. Which side's suffering was the greater? It was impossible to tell. In any event, it made no difference, since neither side seemed able any longer to halt the insanity.

On Christmas Day, most everyone's thoughts turned homeward. Someone had received a couple of the latest records. Strains of "The White Cliffs of Dover" added to the nostalgia and longing.

"There'll be bluebirds over the white cliffs of Dover
Tomorrow, just you wait and see.
There'll be love and laughter and peace ever after
Tomorrow, when the world is free."

Col. Weallens' wife, Biddy, had sent him an extra-large Christmas cake, knowing full well that the confection would be passed round; and so it was, on Christmas Eve, much appreciated and accompanied by generous amounts of hot rum-toddy. The soldiers, too, got an extra ration of rum.

It was decided that in memory of better times – when peace had been the order of the day – they would attempt to recreate a semblance of 'guest night' as it was celebrated in the Regimental Head Quarters Mess, back in Bakloh, India. Makeshift though it might be here, a sharing of the familiar past would bring a sense of comfort and home and serve as a reminder that one day their world would return to normal; one day all would be as it should. For Santi, this ceremonial dinner was a brand-new experience.

That night, when the bugle sounded First Mess Call, the officers of the 2/4 answered. Sans the usual paraphernalia and accoutrements, they gathered, awaiting the Duty Piper sounding his summons to the officers of other Battalions, and those from Brigade. This was followed shortly with the arrival of Colonel Weallens, accompanied by his fellow Commanding Officers. As they passed, the Brigadier, being senior-most, greeted the junior officers.

"Good evening, gentlemen."

And received their unanimous reply, "Good evening, sir."

Now, Second Mess Call was given, and a scant two minutes later the sounding of the gong alerted them to dinner. As they all trooped into the tented structure that served as a 'Mess Hall', the band struck up *The Roast Beef of Old England*. Presently, when all were seated at table, drinks of choice were served – alas, not the usual array of port, madeira and sherry, but the more readily available whiskey and rum, elevated somewhat by a supply of wine brought down from Persia. The pipes picked up once more as the company tucked into their Christmas fare of roast wild duck, tinned steak and kidney pie, rounded off with Crosse & Blackwell's Christmas Pudding and lashings of custard.

In the men's langar the duck was curried and served with whole wheat chappatis, and when all had eaten their fill, the feast was finally finished off with generous servings of rice pudding and more than generous amounts of rum.

Back at the Officers' Mess, the meal was brought to its end with a toast to the King-Emperor, followed by sundry other toasts given and taken with equal vim and vigour. At this point, the Pipe-Master and Mess Pipers entered playing *Wi' a Hundred Pipers an' a'*, which changed anon to a strathspey, quickly followed by a reel.

In appreciation of his music, the Pipe-Master was invited to partake of a drink. Adhering to custom, he responded with the salutation, "*Thagra raho huzur,* be of strong health, respected sir." Then, tossing back the whiskey, he kissed the bottom of the empty glass in a show of reciprocal appreciation. Formalities almost at an end, the Pipers made their exit to the squirl of *Scotland the Brave*, and the ceremony was brought to completion with more song, whiskey, and rum.

From the mens' langar came the gentle nostalgic strains of a *jaunri,* the folk music of the hill tribes: *"Nainitalo, Nainitalo, ghumi ayo rela, ghumi ayo rela…"*

And from the Officers' Mess, the sound of men's voices raised in holy song, pleasantly discordant, filtered into the night air…*Hark the Herald Angels Sing, Good King Wenceslas* and *Silent Night*…. In the end, this served to make the slightly maudlin carollers more homesick than ever and encouraged them to drown their sorrows in a few additional, generously oversized pegs of liquid refreshment. Eventually, adequately sozzled and bleary-eyed, one and all stumbled to bed.

The next day, Boxing Day, a whispered rumour filtered down through the official grapevine. A rumour, unhappily, that proved to be true. Hong Kong had surrendered to the Japanese on Christmas Day, but for reasons of morale, the news was temporarily being kept under wraps. Joy to the world!

Before the year was out there was one more departure from their midst – Alistair 'Shirley' Temple transferred on to Brigade. Not long after, in the early part of January 1942, the Battalion was returned to its old haunt, Habbaniya, for a few weeks of rigorous training in desert warfare. To what end, they could only guess, but everyone had heard Rommel was gaining ground in North Africa – El Agheila, Benghazi – and Allied reinforcements would soon be gathering in a desperate attempt to stop his advance towards Cairo.

Meanwhile, further east, across vast continents and oceans, the Japanese had advanced into the Malaya peninsula. When Kuala Lumpur was taken and Malaya surrendered, 50,000 Allied troops were captured; but most inglorious of all was the fall of Singapore on 15 February, when a further 80,000 British, Australian and Indian soldiers were marched into captivity as POWs. In Churchill's words, it was the worst disaster and largest capitulation in British history.

Then, without let or pause, the triumphant Japanese marched into Burma. Capturing Rangoon on 8 March, pushing towards Mandalay, they seemed unstoppable as they headed inexorably for Britain's jewel in the crown: India!

It seemed the war was going quite nicely for the Axis, thank you very much!

CHAPTER EIGHTEEN

The Winds Of Change

For this is Wisdom; to love, to live,
To take what Fate, or the Gods, may give,
And speed Life's ebb as you greet its flow…
To have…to hold…and…in time…let go!

– Violet Nicolson, *The Garden of Kama*, "The Teak Forest"

IT HAS BEEN CLAIMED, with the many comings and goings throughout history, if any one sect could defend its claim to being the actual descendants of the great Pharaohs of Egypt, it would be the old Egyptian Christians known as the Copts. Among these people of ancient ancestry, these heirs of old Egypt who continued to live among the varied populace, some of the most prominent names were Ghali, Wahba, Boutross, Wissa and Khayyatt. (Artemis Cooper's *Cairo in the War*). It would seem, therefore, from Hedeya Khayat's family name – which literally, and in her case rather appropriately, translated to 'tailor' – that somewhere through the ages and meanderings of the peoples inhabiting this great biblical region, there came about a union between some branch of the Coptic family of Khayyatt with that of a family of Armenian descent. To this, Bajo brought the Greek lineage of her Kiriakos family.

Likewise, the reign of the Pharaohs was followed, though never eclipsed, by that of others who came and went and mingled through the ages, culminating with Ottoman rule. The present royal family was descended from Muhammed Ali, the Turkish commander of the old Ottoman Empire's Albanian forces in Egypt. But a crown never sat easy on any head, and although the only immediate contender for his throne was his uncle, nevertheless King Farouk had various factions in his own government all vying with each other for power. The Wafd was a democratic nationalist party that tended to walk a more moderate line than the Muslim Brotherhood, or the extreme nationalists fuelled by the likes of Sheikh el Maraghi.

The Prime Minister of Egypt, at the time, was Hussein Sirry who was somewhat amenable to the British. His opponent was Ali Maher, the King's advisor, who was openly anti-British, and not averse to siding with the Germans in the hope it would lead to consolidating power in his own hands. In early 1942, with the help of Sheikh el

Maraghi, he managed to stir up sufficient trouble among students, and fuel rioting among extreme nationalists, just enough to bring Hussein Sirry's government to its knees in chaos. It forced the resignation of the Prime Minister.

The British felt that the Wafd, though nationalist, was the only foil for Ali Maher's political scheming, and the one party capable of providing a moderate, stable government for the country. They told the King he should form a government with Nahas Pasha, the leader of the Wafd. When Farouk, egged on by Ali Maher, refused to comply, Sir Miles Lampson, the British Ambassador, issued an ultimatum: cooperate or else…

Tension mounted. On Wednesday, 4 February, all Cairo held its breath and gathered around the radio in anticipation of what would happen next. The 5pm deadline came and went. Around 9pm Abdin Palace was surrounded by General Stone's armoured cars and some six hundred British soldiers. Sir Miles Lampson's entourage drove through the palace gates with a document demanding the abdication of King Farouk on grounds he had breached the agreement between Egypt and Britain, cooperated with the enemy, and endangered the welfare of his country. The King had little choice.

With pen poised ready to sign, the abdication was stayed at the very last moment only by a hurriedly negotiated agreement for mutual cooperation: the King would form a government with Nahas Pasha, and the demand for his abdication would be withdrawn. It was a close call. He had, for the time being, weathered the winds that had swept chaos through his government. Unavoidably, however, the event, seen as unforgivable highhandedness, put a permanent dent in relations between the Egyptians and the British.

That Wednesday evening, Sallah had been visiting as usual. Louis was at a neighbour's in the next building where he had gone to play the one-legged game of catch known as *gendarme*, while Bajo had taken Violette to the miller's store to buy *amh*. Some of the grain would be purchased whole to boil with milk and sugar for the children's breakfast *billeela*, the rest would be cracked into *burghul* to be mixed with minced meat, parsley and onions for *kubeba*.

Grandmother and granddaughter had departed, trundling the children's old baby carriage which, having served its original purpose, was once more being put to good use carrying the wheat grain from store to house. On several occasions, passers-by had smiled down at the well-bundled 'baby' in the carriage and nodded at the kindly old lady and child wheeling it; and Bajo had responded in like manner, seeing no need to explain her true errand which would take too long and – whose business was it anyway! Besides, it was nice sharing smiles with strangers, no matter the reason.

The radio in the sitting room was turned on for the news. In front of it, on Samuél Khayat's old carpet, Victor was lying on his stomach ostensibly doing his homework. He was, in actual fact, more involved in demolishing the *kortas* of *sudanee* Sallah had brought, aided most willingly by Bagha, the cat who belonged to Majhda Khomsi, the lady doctor who lived on the ground floor. It was obvious not much was being accomplished in the way of homework since Bagha was squatting, in perfect feline fashion, on top of Victor's open book, keenly observing the boy's consumption of fast dwindling peanuts. And much to Victor's delight, as soon as he reached for a *sudanee*, Bagha would demand a fair share. If this was not forthcoming, the cat would insist. Nudging the boy's hand aside with his head, the canny feline would clear the way to dip one expert paw into the *kortas*, the paper cone, and adroitly fish out a nut. Next, with a dexterity that comes with practice, he would crack the shell with his teeth, and consume the nut with the utmost relish.

Sallah, who was watching from a nearby chair, laughed out loud. "That cat is human," he declared.

In the corner of the room, Hedeya looked up from her sewing machine and smiled. She stopped her work, and taking her foot off the pedal, pushed her chair back to rest a while.

"That cat," she nodded, indicating the little animal that presently had eyes for no one but Victor, "is smarter than many human beings I have met. He knows exactly what he wants and how to get it. See how shamelessly he is playing up to Victor? The little beggar has no conscience!"

"I have never seen a cat eat *sudanee* before. Look how cleverly he shells each nut!"

"Believe me this animal can smell freshly roasted nuts a mile away! If I bring some home, he is certain to appear on the doorstep; and the moment I open the door, he will run ahead of me to the table, jump up, and demand a share in a voice you cannot ignore. Clever! You should see just how clever he is! I put the *sudanee* in my pocket and stand up against the table, and the smart little creature will hook his paw into my pocket and actually pull the nuts out, one by one!"

Hedeya was still regaling Sallah with stories of the smart feline when the radio announced the long-awaited news broadcast. At the same instant there was an imperative knock on the front door.

Victor had just risen to discard his empty shells. "I'll go," he called. But before he could reach the door, it burst open, almost knocking him over, and Mahran stood in the doorway, flanked by two police constables.

"Oh! Hello Baba," Victor greeted his father in surprise, stepping aside to let him in.

Mahran ignored the greeting. "You see," he declared, triumphantly, pushing his way in, followed by the policemen. "What did I tell you? You see how she is entertaining this man alone in the house, in this unseemly manner?"

Taken aback by the sudden intrusion, both Hedeya and Sallah sat, momentarily speechless. Then, Hedeya experienced a small explosion at the base of her skull that seemed to spread upward, so that it felt as though her face and head were on fire. The voices around her became garbled, the sounds swimming in and out, growing muffled as her sight blurred. It seemed a long while before her head began to clear so she could think once again, one small thought at a time, and she realised she had neither spoken nor moved a muscle.

How long she had sat there she could not tell, but everyone in the room was staring at her, and it took a great deal of will power to force herself to move. Her body felt stiff as she tried to get out of her chair, and her face muscles were so tight, she found it hard to speak. She heard the policeman say something about going to the police station, and after a moment she heard a voice reply. It was only when she found herself standing did she realise that the voice had been hers, saying something to the effect that she needed to collect her handbag and coat from the bedroom. She did not dare look at Mahran for fear she would fly at him and scratch out his eyes. Her anger was so great, she could barely keep it under control. She could taste its bitterness, like venom, in the back of her mouth and throat, and the taste was nauseating.

She went into the bathroom to wash the acrid taste from her mouth, after which she went to her bedroom to collect her things. She found Victor standing in the doorway, clenched fists hanging by his side, a look of bewildered dismay on his face.

"Mama, what is happening? Why do you have to…" The boy's confusion was painful to see. He looked close to tears as he blurted, "I want to come with you."

"Shhh, it is nothing," she tried to console him. "I'll take care of everything and be back in no time. I'm leaving you in charge meanwhile, Victor. You are the oldest, and I need you to look after things till I get home. Make sure Bajo doesn't worry. Will you do that for me?"

The boy nodded dumbly. She kissed him and, quickly picking up her bag and coat, she returned to the living room. On her way to the door, Hedeya discreetly took Salah's ring off the mantelpiece and slipped it onto her finger. Before stepping out of the house, she made a request of the policemen that she be allowed to follow in a taxi rather than be driven in a police car.

"You understand, I have a reputation to maintain in this neighbourhood. Gossip is like the stench of garbage. Once you fall into it, the smell sticks to you, no matter whether you fell in yourself or," her voice shook, "someone else pushed you." The constables understood completely.

At the station there had been a change of Duty Officers. The new officer in charge held up his hand to quiet the chaos of everyone talking at once. "Silence!" he bellowed, at last. "Now, who is complaining about whom, and what is the complaint about?"

"This *effendi* claims there has been some impropriety between his wife and this man…"

Hedeya's face burned with shame and anger as she listened to the accusation being levelled against her in the presence of these strangers. She had not believed that Mahran would go to this length to make life difficult for her. How *dare* he make a public spectacle of their lives and bring this kind of disgrace on them all! If he imagined it would make her give up and return to him, then he certainly had misjudged her mettle. But the one thing he did know was that he could get to her through the children. She thought of Victor witnessing the scene back at the house and wished with all her heart that she could have spared him.

The officer turned to Hedeya who had remained silent till now. "Madam, what do you have to say to this accusation that your husband has made?" His voice was stern.

Hedeya tried to keep her voice steady. "This man is not my husband," her voice came out low and hard. "I am legally divorced from Mahran Merzian according to the Muslim law of *talaq*. He has no business entering my house without my permission, or interfering in my affairs. In any case, his accusations are groundless and without merit." She turned to the two policemen who had brought them. "I would like the two constables who came to my home – unannounced – to tell you exactly what they saw when they entered."

The two men stared at Hedeya, a little surprised by her request. "Please, just tell your Captain what you saw. Where was I when you came in?"

"Sitting at a sewing machine," the younger of the two replied.

"And where was this gentleman, whom you found in my house?"

"He was sitting on a chair by the radio," replied the other policeman.

"And was there anyone else with us when you entered the room?" Hedeya prompted him.

"The young boy. Your son."

"My fourteen-year-old son. And the front door was unlocked because my younger son was playing outside, and I was expecting my mother and my daughter back at any moment. You know this to be true because you opened the door and walked into my house without waiting to be let in. So, tell me, what kind of impropriety do you think could possibly have taken place between me and my fiancé," she pointed to Sallah while indicating her ring, "in a situation such as the one you and I just described?"

"I know what this man…" Mahran began, but he was abruptly cut short.

"Is this true that this lady is no longer your wife?" The Police Officer demanded, angrily.

"It is true that she divorced me in court by…by Muslim law, but my family honour…"

"Have you taken leave of your senses?" The officer shouted. "With all that is going on in our country right now, have you nothing better to do than waste the time of government officials in your private affairs with silly trumped up charges such as this? If anyone's behaviour has been questionable it has been yours, and if anyone has sullied your family's honour, you have done so by subjecting it to these disgraceful public accusations."

That night, Hedeya thought long and hard about her situation. Today had made her realise that Mahran, for whatever reason, apparently would not leave her in peace – unless, somehow, she put herself beyond his reach. That, of course, was easier said than done. How was she to sever all bonds with her present life? She could hardly abandon her responsibilities and the duties that bound her to the city – her work, the children's schools. Where would she go, and if she did leave, how would she support the five of them? It was hard enough even in her present circumstances. How in the world would she manage in unfamiliar surroundings, among strangers?

All at once she was gripped by fear. Lying in the dark, she felt alone and helpless, overwhelmed by her circumstances. What had she done! Legally declaring herself a Muslim had solved one problem, only to create another. It had given her a way out of her marriage, but she was bound now by the laws of that religion in all things public. Privately, and among close friends, she was still Christian. However, she could not openly declare herself as such, and in a new place, among strangers, she would have to pretend to be what she wasn't. Oh, why did Mahran have to create such difficulties for her? He had made her situation an impossible one!

Filled with despair, she spent long, fretful hours, tossing and turning…wondering…worrying. Finally, afraid she would wake Bajo, she chided herself: *You're being muddle-headed when you need to be strong and clear minded to solve the problem. Pull yourself together,* she told herself, sternly.

It was then a sudden thought struck her. What if she moved to another address without actually leaving the city? She could let it be *known* she had left. Mahran did not know which school she taught at, so there was no problem continuing on there. She would have to stop giving injections to Dikran's patients, more's the pity, but that couldn't be helped. However, most of the customers for whom she sewed, they at least were unknown to Mahran, so she could carry on with her dressmaking and embroidery, thank goodness.

But how would she manage with the children? Unreliable as it was, even the meagre help she coerced from Mahran once in a great while would no longer be available because, of course, the whole point was he should not know where she was. And then, without the income from Dikran's patients as well, it would be impossible to make ends meet. She would be unable to sustain the family, she realised, despairingly. Dear God! What was she to do?

Whatever it took! Because there was one thing she swore she would avoid at all costs – she would *never* allow the children to go hungry.

She remembered what it had been like for her. She was seven years old when her world crashed about her. Till then she had been sheltered, protected and pampered, even a little spoilt perhaps. They had lived in comparative luxury in their large, two-storied house, with the servants' quarters above the stables where her beloved cow, Mankara, lived with the horse, Zaino.

Oh, those summers, spent in the village, with its acres of orchards and vineyards, the nuts and fruit ripe for the picking, and pigeon kebabs from the crowded pigeon houses theirs for the asking! Then, for the long, cold winter months in the city, those nuts and fruits were dried and stored, as were the potato-shaped truffles, *kamà*, that pop-popped out from beneath the desert sands after the rains hit. Preserves were made from apricots, and *bastarma* from flanks of lean meat cured in spices, then hung in rows to dry in the sun; all stored for those times when snow barricaded the doors almost lintel high.

To keep warm during those winter months, a fire would be lit in the clay *tonir* in the main room where they all sat and ate, family and visitors, spreading a large quilt so it covered their legs and kept the heat from the *tonir* circulating around the feet. There had always been plenty to eat, no dearth of the very best of everything. Even in boarding school, she had the two older orphan girls from Karabash, Shamuné and Baizar, to take care of her; and in return, Baba Taht had paid for their education.

Then, suddenly, it all changed. Baba Taht had been taken away. Bajo and she had gone into hiding, like thieves slipping from one place to another. They had nothing, except the bag of gold coins Bajo had tied around her waist so that it dangled between her legs. It hurt when she walked, but if she complained, Bajo would say "Hush! This is our payment to the person who will show us the way to heaven. Remember, there is a price to everything, and we must always pay our way."

So she kept quiet and bore the pain. And always there was the hunger, gnawing like a small rat inside her stomach; and sometimes the rat seemed to grow really big, and the gnawing hurt so much, it made her cry. She was unable to comprehend what had gone wrong. Why, Bajo? Why can't we go home? They had hidden in the Syrian churchyard, amid the gravestones and the underbrush, with other women and children. She remembered the big pot of soup a kind Christian man had brought, all he could carry, to feed as many as he could. How good it had tasted! She made a silent promise then that she would never ever again make a fuss about food. The man with the soup had seen Bajo. He knew her. He put the soup pot down, held his head in his hands and wept.

"You! God have mercy that you should have come to this!"

No, she would never let her children go hungry; even if that meant having to give them up! She had known all along this time would come, when she could no longer put off making her decision. But now that it was upon her, she couldn't help shrinking from it. Maybe she should just remain here and deal with Mahran. And yet, when she remembered the look on Victor's face earlier that evening, she realised that allowing any of her children to be put through that kind of torment and shame again was not an option. She knew she had no choice.

From those days, far back in her childhood, she had fought to survive – and she was fighting still, not just for herself, but for her children as well. Whatever it took to ensure their safety, their survival, she would do it, even if it meant having to break up her small family. But then, there would be no one to mother her sons! Lying there, she felt the pain well up from deep within her heart and fill her eyes, scalding her face as it ran down her temples and soaked into her hair. He has won, she thought, bitterly; he has taken my sons from me!

She found it hard to breathe. She sat up, trying to swallow the hurt that was swelling inside her, choking her throat. Blindly, she got up and made her way to the boys' bedroom. She knelt between their beds. She would never share these moments with them again. She touched their faces, the rumpled hair, and listened to their soft breathing. She had always made sure they wouldn't see her fear, or how much she hurt. Close to them, fast asleep like this, she could let it all out. Tomorrow, she would be strong again. She would brace herself and face the winds of change that were blowing her family apart; but just for now...

After a while, she touched her lips to their foreheads: Louis, cool, serene, and Victor, warm and slightly damp. She got up and went back to her room. Slowly, she lay down on the bed, making sure both Bajo and Violette were asleep. Her mother, hadn't she always told her, face the world with a smile, even though your eyes are filled with a thousand tears? Time enough for that, for now she could hide her tears in the dark. Turning over, she buried her face and sobbed quietly into her pillow.

⸻ ◆ ⸻

THEY MOVED HOUSE IN the first week of March. It was generally put about that they were leaving Cairo for a small village in the Assiut area; no more, no less. Asis Habib had helped them find their new place, and Sallah helped them move. It was a small two-bedroom flat, No.65 Rod el Farag, a name which should, said Asis Habib, be taken as a good omen since it meant Garden of Hope. More important to Hedeya was its proximity to the boys' new school for, although this was to be kept from them, she had insisted on it as a requirement when they moved.

It had not been easy. Hedeya had done her best to explain the necessity of the move to the boys, without vilifying their father too much and, at the same time, while trying to assure them of her love.

There had been some tears, but then the change began to pique the boys' interest, especially when their father hinted, he might take them shopping in preparation for coming to live with him.

Bajo, too, had been distraught, which did not make matters any easier. Although her head understood the reasons for the painful decision, her heart refused to do so. She realised, of course, that her daughter was caught on the horns of a cruel dilemma, but surely there must be some other way? She went from consoling Hedeya to chastising her, and back again. Eventually, she did take consolation from the knowledge that almost everyday the boys would be so close, she could actually look from her balcony, across the road, straight into Louis's classroom and see him sitting at his desk.

Of course, under these circumstances, it was against all odds that the secret of their whereabouts would remain a secret for long. Despite being cautioned several times, Bajo's vigils from the balcony inevitably led to discovery. It happened one afternoon, standing there, so intent on gazing adoringly upon her grandson, she forgot to duck out of sight when he raised his head from the book on his desk.

Whether it was the pull of Bajo's love, or pure coincidence, Louis found himself staring straight into his grandmother's eyes. His mouth had fallen open in utter disbelief. He shut his eyes and squeezed hard to make sure he was not dreaming, but when he opened them again the incredible picture of his grandmother was still there. And then, the picture moved.

When Bajo realised she had given the game away, her first instinct was to raise her hand to her lips in consternation. However, as there was no undoing what had been done, and the cat was out of the bag so to speak, she turned the gesture into a tentative wave, wiggling her fingers at the dumbfounded boy still gaping at her with his mouth open.

With a yell, Louis flew out of his seat, past his startled classmates, and to the window. The next thing Bajo witnessed was an angry teacher grabbing him by the ear and marching him off, presumably to the headmaster's office.

"Now, Lord," Bajo muttered reproachfully, "was it necessary to make me an instrument of trouble for the child?"

That afternoon, when school was over, she was waiting outside for Louis, and when he emerged, she embraced him with all the pent-up love reserved for one who had been lost and was found again. And only when the boy began to demur at his grandmother's overabundance of hugs and kisses in full view of his friends did she restrain herself long enough to take his hand and lead him to the new house.

When Hedeya returned home a short while later, the aroma of *bastarma wu beyda* caught her at the door and led her to the kitchen, where she was stunned to find her daughter and her younger son seated comfortably at her kitchen table, enjoying a plateful of the preserved spiced meat and eggs.

"*Wakhfal-babkin!* Where did...how did...Bajo?" She dropped her bag, staring at the grinning boy. Then, all at once, he was in her open arms, and the why and the wherefore didn't matter, at least for that moment.

When, finally, they had all collected themselves and wiped away the last tear, and after the day's story had been recounted several times over, Hedeya began to worry that all the effort put towards staging their disappearance had come to naught. It was not so much Louis that she worried about, for he was a practical boy with enough foresight to keep his own counsel when required to do so. Victor, on the other hand, though older by two years, was an exuberant, outgoing young fellow, an open book without a secret thought or a hidden emotion to be found in either his head or his heart. Victor was sure to...by the way, where *was* Victor? How was it, Hedeya wanted to know, she had not caught even a glimpse of him these past few weeks?

"That's because he doesn't come to school anymore," Louis announced, matter of factly. "He's working with Baba at the garage."

For one long moment Hedeya stood very still.

"Why?" She burst out at last, turning to her mother. Her voice rose in anger. "*Ya msebty!* Was it so hard to wait till the boy finished school?"

"But he wanted to work," Louis explained, answering her question. "Baba asked both of us, and I said I wanted to go to school, but Victor wanted to work."

"How does the foolish boy know what he wants? He has always thought with his heart instead of his head!" She was filled with exasperation. "After everything it took to keep him in school, now it's all wasted. One of the main reasons I allowed their father to take them was because he promised to provide for their education."

"He promised, but do you expect a sieve to hold water?" Bajo asked quietly. She understood her daughter's anger over her son's aborted education. She, herself, had been one of the first girls to attend the American Missionary School in Merdin where her daughter later followed in her footsteps. "You knew he intended the boys should work in his garage."

"Of course I knew that," Hedeya replied, angrily. "Over the week-ends, or in their spare time, yes; but not full time instead of school. You tell your brother," she addressed herself to Louis, adding quickly, "without letting him know we met, mind you, tell him I will be very angry if I find out he's left school."

"But, Mama, how will I tell him that if I'm not to tell him that I have seen you?"

Irritated because she had no answer to her son's valid question, Hedeya threw up her hands and snapped, "So, I suppose that is that!"

Louis hesitated – then, hoping to somewhat better the situation he had so unwittingly created, he added, "Baba says it is for Victor's good. Bringing money in for the family will teach him to be self-sufficient and not depend for support on others."

A sound much like a snort came from Bajo. "Huh! Not depend for support on others, indeed! He said that, did he? Should the garlic be telling the onion 'you smell'? I think not!"

Powerless to change the course of Victor's life, Hedeya concentrated on her younger son. Every day thereafter, when school gave over, Louis would go over to the house next door where his grandmother would feed him and fuss over him, while his mother supervised his homework. The boy kept these trysts secret, just as he had been instructed to, explaining at home only that he was studying at a 'friend's' house – a story that stretched the truth somewhat, but did not stray too uncomfortably far from it.

And so it went till Victor's birthday, when Hedeya baked a birthday cake that Louis was to take home and share with his brother. Victor was to be told that Asis Habib had gone on a trip, during which he had visited Hedeya, and she had sent the cake to be given to him on his birthday. Things, however, did not go quite as planned.

Victor had not yet returned from work when Louis got home; but the boys' father had. Overriding his younger son's protests, he took the cake with him to a friend's place, where every last crumb was consumed. When Victor returned and heard what had happened, being quick of temper, he left the house in a fury, swearing never to return.

Seeing how upset his brother was, Louis followed, attempting to console him. "Don't be upset, Victor. Mama will make you another cake, you'll see."

"And how will she do that? Do you suggest that she post it to me? She isn't here to make one, is she? Foolish fellow!"

"Yes, she is!" Louis blurted, impetuously. In a single unguarded moment, the secret was out, the three little words tumbling off his tongue before he could curb it. Too late, he realised what he had done, but

Victor's remark had stung, getting his dander up so that he added defiantly, "And I'm *not* foolish!"

Victor stopped dead in his tracks and glared at his younger brother. "What are you talking about? Have you gone mad?" He noticed Louis's face had turned a particularly alarming shade of red.

"I have not!" Louis shot back, indignantly. Well, there was no going back now, was there; he had spilt the beans and he was in for it, so he might as well stand his ground. Tell it all. "I'll show you. I'll take you to her."

"Do you mean right now? Is she here? Is Bajo here? And Bebe? Loza! What do you mean?"

"Just follow me," Louis threw over his shoulder as he started to run.

When Bajo opened the door and saw both her grandsons standing there, she cried out with joy. The next thing she knew, Victor had grabbed her, and with a loud shout, he danced her to the middle of the room. Hearing the commotion, Hedeya and Violette rushed in only to be swept up in the whirlwind that was Victor, and amidst much squealing and crying and talking all at the same time, the family was once more united.

When a modicum of calm was finally restored, Victor was sworn to secrecy. He willingly crossed his heart and promised, most solemnly, to keep their whereabouts secret since it was, he said happily, the best birthday present he had ever been given.

CHAPTER NINETEEN

For Whom The Bell Tolls

Ah, make the most of what we yet may spend,
Before we too into the dust descend;
Dust into dust, and under dust to lie,
Sans wine, sans song, sans singer and…sans end!

– Omar Khayyam, *Rubaiyat of Omar Khayyam*

In March, news arrived from home. The letter had taken nearly a month to get to Santi.

Sudha Dutt
c/o Dr. J.P. Dutt, (Capt.) M.B., M.R.C.O.G.
36, Chowringhee Road, Flat No. 3A/3B
Calcutta, West Bengal
India   *6 February 1942*

My dear Dada,

We received your letter, number 14, yesterday. It arrived by the afternoon post and Father read it to us at teatime, when we got back from school and college. So far, all your letters have reached us, although they take a long time coming. And when they do, quite often parts have been censored. But I suppose, with everything that is going on in the world at present, we should be glad they get here at all.

The big news is Father has been transferred to Hooghly, as Civil Surgeon of that district. We will probably make the move at the end of April or beginning of May. Dr. Sengupta is going to take Father's place at Campbell as Head of Gynae and Prof. of Midwifery. Sadly, it means we will have to give up our two flats here at 36 Chowringhee.

I will probably have to transfer out of Bethune College after my intermediary, and Kamala and Lebu will leave Loreto House Convent for a school near Hooghly. Kamala's teacher, Mrs. Debenham, who lives in Flat 2C, says she is sorry to see us go. She is going to have a baby, you know. The frocks she wears are always so beautiful, even her maternity clothes are quite lovely. I remember you telling us we should always be demure and ladylike. Well, you should see the fashions these days! Last week I admired Mrs. Debenham's nail varnish, and when she came to Father for a check up yesterday (he told her she was doing fine), she brought the bottle and told me I could have it – such a pretty pink colour made by Tangee! Mother says, from the way she is carrying, she is bound to have a girl, but Father says that's just an old wives' tale and 'complete nonsense'. I don't think she cares one way or the other, girl or boy. We often hear her playing the piano, and judging by it, she's obviously happy just having a baby.

We are going to miss our neighbours – and Park Street, with all its shops and restaurants. And, of course, our lovely evening walks in the maidan, around Victoria Memorial. In fact, day before yesterday, Kamala, Lebu and I had gone for our evening stroll with Father and Mother, after the heat of the day had cooled down a bit, and we ran into Mrs. Cartwright from Flat 2D, downstairs. She was walking her three Scottish Terriers, which, as you know, she breeds, and she told us she has four new puppies. She's already found homes for them.

I wish we could have a dog again, but Father still hasn't got over the loss of Jimmy. He was such a clever dog – somehow, he always knew when we were dressing to go out and he'd go into hiding, and then, wily fellow that he was, he would try to follow us. Although, he learnt his lesson, I think, that time he followed us to the zoo. Remember? He jumped down into the rhinocerus's enclosure, and when the rhino started lumbering towards him, and he realised he couldn't get out, he began whimpering. We were all screaming for help, and you jumped over the railing, into the pit, and grabbed him and handed him up to us. I'll never forget how scared we all were, but you managed to climb back up, just in time! I'm sure Jimmy didn't forget either.

Mezda and his friend, Debnath Sen, are home on a few days' leave. His 'daak naam' is Chokon and they are training together on the 'Dufferin'. They treated us to the flicks – with Ma as chaperone, of course. The Lighthouse was showing "The Great Dictator", Charlie Chaplin's parody of Hitler. It was hilarious. You should have seen Mezda parading around in his navy uniform to impress the girls! I must say, though, he and Chokon look quite dashing, and don't they know it!

There is this very pretty Anglo-Indian girl who works in Lloyd's Bank next door, and Mezda has had his eye on her for some time. He always swore, somehow, he would get this girl to go out with him, and now he's in uniform, he fancies himself irresistible. So, under pretext of opening an account at the bank, he made friends with her, AND he's taking her to the pictures tonight. Maybe we should warn her – he can be a bit of a rotter after all!

He has 'borrowed' all the pocket money we three sisters saved, with the hollow promise of returning it soon. Of course, we'll never lay eyes on our money again! As usual, he will probably creep in very late tonight, in spite of being bawled out by Father for staying out late every night last week. When you were here, he could use you as an alibi, or scapegoat, now, of course, there is no one he can fob blame onto. Lucky for him, Father feels he is too old to have his ear pulled any longer, so whenever he has been particularly vexing, poor Father, all he can do is grumble to Mother, "Your son, Kanti, he's good for nothing but trouble…"

Dada, we all miss you and pray that you remain safe. As long as we receive your letters regularly, it helps Mother and Father cope with your absence. Please take care.

Affectionately, your (favourite) sister, Sudha

———

THE BATTALION BIDED ITS time, waiting for the finger of fate to point the way. Meanwhile, everyone gratefully enjoyed the basic amenities of life: good, hot, freshly cooked food, and – oh heaven! – freshly laundered sheets, clean baths and clean clothes! But then came an unwelcome piece of news – in the latter half of March the Japanese had landed on the Andaman Islands in the Bay of Bengal, and it stood to reason that the Nicobar Islands would be the next to fall. The enemy had actually invaded Indian territory and was now a stone's throw away from the eastern coast of mainland southern India!

Training continued, and their time off was well spent in the Club. They socialised with the RAF officers in station and their civilian guests, playing darts, draughts and attending picture shows. Hollywood had already jumped on the bandwagon and started making a slew of new war movies. The previous week they had seen Alfred Hitchcock's spy thriller "Foreign Correspondent", and the tragic romance "Waterloo Bridge", starring Robert Taylor and Vivien Leigh. The most recent had been "Sergeant York" with Gary Cooper playing a WWI hero.

Just outside the base, a large sign identified the station: 'Royal Air Force Habbaniya'. One day a new, rather wistful sign appeared beside it. Put up, no doubt, by some poor homesick blighter, it read: *'London 3287 miles – Baghdad 55 miles,'* and underscoring this message was the author's adornment of a melancholy, down-in-the-mouth face.

In April, that long-awaited appendage, the Finger of Fate, singled them out. Their time had come. Under orders from General Sir Claude Auchinlek, C-in-C Middle East Forces, the Prince of Wales's Own 2/4 Gurkha Rifles was slated for the Western Desert. Transferred out of 21st Brigade, they were to proceed immediately to North Africa to join their new brigade, the 10th Indian Infantry Brigade of the 5th Indian Division. There, they would prepare to go up against General Erwin Rommel and his Afrika Korps.

It was time for farewells all round their old Brigade. Captain MacPherson, the doctor of 157th Royal Artillery Field Regiment, an all-British outfit, came to say goodbye. He and Santi had spent the previous evening together at the Officers Club. They had got along pretty well together, exchanging professional points of view over a couple of drinks, and finally parting company in good cheer.

"Here you are, Dutt," MacPherson said, handing him a wrapped package. "I believe you will have need of these where you're going"

"What's this?" Santi asked, surprised. Undoing the parcel, he found eight Red Cross arm bands. During the course of their evening at the Club, he had mentioned to the British doctor how hard it had been to lay his hands on these elusive items. "I say Mac, this is awfully decent of you. You sure you can spare these?"

"I'll pull through. Had a couple going abegging, and I managed to scrounge the rest. You can't be racketing around at the front without these showstoppers, you know. Take them and use them in good health."

Preparations were well under way for their imminent departure when, early one morning, a truck pulled into camp and a tall lanky British officer stepped out, followed by forty-one Gurkha Other Ranks. Lt. Robert N.D. Williams was to be attached to H Coy as Intelligence Officer. He and the new contingent of forty-one GORs were newly arrived from the Mother House in Bakloh, India.

It was 11 April 1942. The 2/4 handed over their transport to the Duke of Cornwall's Light Infantry, and prepared to set off in a motley mix of civilian transport on a six-day trek across the desert. Unknown to them, in faraway Libya, another journey was being planned across another desert. Two German spies (one being the aforementioned Johann Eppler), along with their Hungarian guide, were soon to set out from Tripoli on their covert mission to Egypt. Their aim – to make life as difficult as possible for the Allies in the Western Desert.

As the convoy started up and the 2/4 began to pull out, a young officer from a British outfit was startled to spot a truck with what he perceived was…? Good Lord, could that really be…some sort of… animal … solemnly seated up front between the driver and a Gurkha medical orderly! Was that a…a…*goat?*

He immediately stopped the vehicle and demanded an explanation as to what the devil was going on. He was met with three blank stares; then, Hirasing shook his head and signed, feigning convenient ignorance of the English vernacular. The ploy bought him just enough time to think, and think fast, so when the indignant officer repeated his demand, he offered the first explanation that popped into his head.

"*Doodh*", he said, making milking motions with his hands. "Colonel Weallens *sahib*", and he gestured as though drinking.

Put on the back foot, the officer stopped to ponder the situation for a moment. He stared at Mullah and Mullah stared back, gravely. Something was not quite right here.

Taking quick advantage of the perplexed officer's hesitation, Hirasing saluted respectfully as he nudged the driver to get a move on. Before the lieutenant could gather his wits, the truck lurched forward and away.

Still flummoxed, the officer turned his attention to other pressing matters at hand. He was checking off the last truck on his list when, suddenly, he stopped dead in his tracks – that was it! He'd got it! He knew what had been wrong back there! Milk? Bleeding hell! That was no milking goat! He could swear that goat had been a bloody *billy* goat, for Christ sake!

They lumbered across the desert via Hit to Haditha, and from there, on to Landing Ground LG5 which they reached on 13 April. So far it had been half track and half road, which was bad enough, but then the road gave way completely and became all sandy track. The going got progressively worse, till they pitched up, on the 14th, at the oil pumping station, H3. Happily, the forty-mile journey after that, which took them forward to H4 on the 15th, was somewhat of an improvement. Still, it was a relief, finally, to stretch their stiff limbs at this last pumping station, and find the facility provided for a wash-up, albeit a rudimentary one, before they loaded in their trucks once again and staged across to Mafraq, ultimately reaching Haifa on 17 April.

The last leg of their convoy journey, rolling through Transjordan, the orange orchards and fertile olive groves of Palestine was pretty refreshing after the desert. At Haifa, they boarded a requisitioned train of the Egyptian State Railway and travelled in comparative comfort after the cramped quarters endured in the trucks. Santi watched the changing scenery and green hills flash by as they headed towards the Sinai and the Suez Canal till, finally, the sun sank below the horizon, and night shadows flooded the world with darkness. Someone turned the radio on; it was 2155 hrs and suddenly, German Forces Radio Belgrade came on the air. Sweet as honey, the strains of Lili Marlen, the desert warrior's anthem, filled the compartment:

> *"Vor der Kaserne vor dem grossen Tor,*
> *Stand eine lanterne und steht sie nach dvor."*

One by one they all joined in with their own unofficial 8th Army version:

> *"There was a song Eighth Army used to hear,*
> *In the lonely desert, lovely, sweet and clear.*
> *Over the ether came the strain,*
> *That soft refrain; each night again*
> *With you Lili Marlene, with you Lili Marlene."*

On to Egypt, to the Western Desert, and to war…and on to whatever destiny had in store for them.

CHAPTER TWENTY

The Fox And The Hound

Yesterday this day's madness did prepare
Tomorrow's Silence, Triumph or Despair:
Drink! For you know not whence you came, nor why;
Drink! For you know not why you go, nor where.

– Omar Khayyam, *Rubaiyat of Omar Khayyam*

I N ANOTHER ARENA, A different kind of war was being waged. It was the war of espionage and spies, the war of wits and wiles, fought in stealth and secrecy, its roots spreading far and wide from bordello to boardroom. Like a giant web, this intrigue was spun through the very fabric of the war. And relevant to this story, seemingly unrelated incidents that happened in far removed places were actually pieces of a giant jigsaw puzzle that, eventually, were to come together in Rommel's backyard.

Back in 1941, somewhere past the midnight hour on a dark September night in Rome, the shadows that cloaked the still neutral United States Embassy were disturbed by soft-footed, furtive movements. Under closer observation, the cause of this night interruption would prove to be a clandestine group consisting of two members from the *carabinieri*, the Italian police, plus two other Italians purportedly in the employ of the US Embassy – but actually in the pay of the Italian secret police.

Musssolini's Servizio Informazione Militari, i.e. SIM, possessed covertly duplicated keys to most of the foreign Missions in Rome. With a set of these keys, the group of four now gained access to the Embassy. Once in, the 'Embassy workers' unlocked the safe where the Americans kept their Black Code. This was the code used for the most secret transmissions to and from American Embassies and Military Attaches worldwide. That night, the code was whisked away and handed over to SIM who quickly photographed it, then immediately returned it to be locked away in the safe once more, thus leaving no one any the wiser.

The Americans never caught on that they had been 'burgled', nor that the enemy could now decipher their transmissions at will; and although in September 1941 America, ostensibly, was not yet an active participant in the war, Washington was keeping a careful finger on the pulse of world events, so there was much to be gleaned from its many messages back and forth. This act of espionage put forth roots which reached into many places where they grew and flourished; and, eventually, one such place where it bore abundant fruit was North Africa.

By 1942, Rommel's reputation was leaning towards legend. His expertise at tank warfare in the desert, and his uncanny ability to pre-empt his enemy's every move was eerily akin to mind reading. The Desert Fox, it seemed, was unbeatable, and he had the surprised British in full retreat. Imagine then, their astonishment, had they but known of the invaluable assistance he was receiving from a high-ranking source on their own side!

In Cairo, the American Military Attache was one Colonel Bonner Frank Fellers, from all accounts a decent and thoroughly amiable man dedicated to his work. In his official capacity, however, he held a rather dim view of Britain's ability to win the war. Unaware the code had been compromised, he transmitted his views to Washington, together with in-depth details of Allied troop movements and unit deployments, the strength and positions of their armoured cars, tanks and guns, the dates and strategies of their battle plans, and his take on both the capabilities and inabilities of their leaders. He was, if anything, diligent and thorough in his reports.

Unfortunately, he neglected to follow security protocol by varying the format of his transmissions which invariably began with, either, 'Milid Wash' (Military Intelligence Division, Washington), or 'Agwar Wash' (Adjutant General, War Department, Washington), and always ended with his signature. This made it sublimely simple for German interceptors to spot his missives, and with the help of the purloined Black Code, deciphering them was a walk in the park. Within hours of being transmitted, these messages would be snagged, decoded and delivered into Rommel's eager hands. So appreciative were the Germans for information thus gleaned, they dubbed him the 'Good Source'.

The Desert Fox, delighted with the intelligence he was receiving from Col. Fellers – straight from the horse's mouth so to speak – indulged himself in a little private humour by referring to them jocularly as his 'little fellers'. And he put these to very good use indeed, when he pushed the British back three hundred miles in seventeen days, and January saw his victorious take-over of El Agheila and Benghazi. (Will Deac: *World War II Magazine, Intercepted Communications for Field Marshal Erwin Rommel*).

The British eventually cottoned on to the security breach from the American Legation, but not before suffering its devastating outcome on large numbers of their troops in the desert. From late 1941 until June of 1942, Colonel Fellers kept his President and, unwittingly, his enemy apprised of current events on the Allied side: troop positions, armoured strengths, orders of battle. The consequence: it forever changed the fate of thousands of soldiers in the Western Desert, including The Prince of Wales's Own 2/4 Gurkha Rifles.

AROUND THE SAME TIME, a second tale of intrigue, codenamed Operation Kondor, was set in motion in Portugal. On 3 April, the wife of the Assistant Military Attache to the German Embassy in Lisbon took a casual drive down the Estoril coast. She stopped at a certain bookstore to make a rather unusual purchase: she required six copies of Daphne du Maurier's novel, 'Rebecca'. Returning to the Embassy with her acquisition, the six books were carefully packaged, and duly parcelled off to Abwehr headquarters in North Africa.

Meanwhile, in Libya, North Africa, in the same month of April, a few men were making their way to a gathering in the desert town of Tripoli. There they began to lay their plans for a fantastic cloak-and-dagger journey across the vast, treacherous Sand Sea to Egypt. Among these adventurers was the young German, Johann Eppler, recently returned from training in Germany; another, was a Hungarian desert explorer named Ladislaus Almaszy who had opted to fly for the Germans when war broke out. Long after his demise, this colourful character would be resurrected and thrust into Hollywood's limelight in a romantic, if rather inexact, film depiction of his love life.

Johann Eppler was born in Alexandria in 1914. His parents were German Roman Catholic, though not much is known of his father who disappeared, or died, when the boy was very young. Some time later, Johann's mother married an affluent Egyptian lawyer. Saleh Gaafer adopted the boy and raised him as a Moslem, consequent to which he was given the exemplary Moslem name of Hussein.

Gaafer became very fond of his stepson. He brought him up in the lap of luxury, sending him to the very best English schools in Heliopolis and Alexandria, so Hussein Gaafer grew up speaking German, English, French and Arabic. Typical of the indolent, aimless sons of wealthy parents, he spent his time in fashionable night clubs like the Kit Kat and Madam Badia's, at social haunts like Groppi's and the Lido, and in posh playgrounds like the Metropolitan's Dug Out bar, the Continental, Shepheard's terrace café, the Turf Club, and the race fields, golf courses and polo grounds at the Gezira Club.

Hussein continued to be comfortable in his identity as a privileged Egyptian until 1938. He was twenty-four years old, on vacation in Beirut, when he received a proposition from the Abwehr, delivered – if one can credit it – by a seductive Vietnamese prostitute named Su Yan. No matter the means, this offer would send his life careening in a wildly different direction.

The ardency with which Hussein rediscovered his Germanic roots during his two-year espionage training in that country rather took him by surprise. It is rumoured he might even have taken a Dutch wife and spent time in the Netherlands. Howbeit, somewhere along the way, at some point in his journey through the war-torn days and nights of WWII, Hussein Gaafer met and melded with his alter ego, Johann Eppler. In that union, from out the swirling mists of his combined heritage, there stepped a person the Germans believed would make the perfect spy. Primed thus for his new role, he was sent back to the Middle East where he went to bat for the Abwehr and Hitler's Nazi regime.

According to some, Eppler's first trial run had been his successful impersonation of Rashid Ali while abetting the escape of that Iraqi rebel in 1941. As mentioned previously, that ruse had enabled Ali to slip the net of the British and flee, through Turkey to Germany, with his enemies – including the 2/4 Gurkhas – hard on his heels. With that success to his credit, his next assignment would be far more important; and Hussein Gaafer, a.k.a Johann Eppler, was ready for this new role – codename, 'Kondor'.

'Operation Kondor' required a strategically placed mole to burrow deep into the heart of Cairo society, and a wealthy young man of dual lineage seemed tailor-made for the part of 'Kondor'. As a rich Egyptian playboy, he had the criteria to make all the right contacts.

Like many similar young men of his class, Hussein would often visit the Continental Hotel in Cairo. A frequent guest at its popular rooftop cabaret, he was already socially acquainted with the charms of the city's most famous belly dancer, Hekmat Fahmy. Soon, he would further his relationship with her, this time in the murky world of espionage. It would be the seductive Hekmat who would give him access to a certain unwitting British Officer who, in the throes of amorous euphoria, and floundering perhaps in the clutches of liquor-induced stupor, would betray official secrets for the pleasure of the belly dancer's sexual favours. It has been said that she, or a contact, put him in touch with the young Egyptian Nationalist, Captain Anwar Sadat – who, personally, was not much enamoured with Hussein's decadent ways.

A second member of this nest of spies was a German radio operator named Hans-Gerd Sanstede who had flown in from Germany with Eppler. Posing as an American of Scandinavian descent, he went along in the guise of an oil rig worker named Peter Munkaster.

The third man was the actual leader of the group. Not much is known about the origins of Count Ladislaus Edouard de Almaszy except that he was a Hungarian, born in Austria in 1895. Educated in Eastbourne, England, Laszlo Almaszy trained as a pilot. He was, as well, an experienced and dedicated explorer of the Western Desert, that part of the Sahara which lies between Libya and Egypt. Although a colleague of the British before the war, when hostilities began, Almaszy decided, for personal reasons or otherwise, to befriend the enemy.

One unverified story suggests a possible romantic entanglement. Contrary to the fictional love story put out by Hollywood, the apparent discovery of certain letters has led to some speculation of an affair between Almaszy and a young German Wehrmacht officer who perished in the war. Additionally, the title of Count has been brought into question, since his family, though noble, was not a titled one.

Be that as it may, Laszlo Almaszy now offered his services as guide to the Desert Fox, promising to deliver Kondor to the Egyptian border in the Nile Valley. The undertaking, codenamed 'Operation Salam', would turn out to be a hazardous two-thousand-six-hundred-mile journey east, across the Sahara Desert.

These three men, plus a few companions, now made ready to embark on that journey which would demand both courage and endurance. The spies carried two suitcases, one containing two transceivers and a copy of *"Rebecca"*, while the other was packed with £3000 in various denominations, as well as some Egyptian money.

On 29 April, carrying Rommel's hopes and blessings, the men of Operation Salam set out in several captured British vehicles to begin their eastward trek to the Oasis of Gialo. At Gialo they double-checked their provisions, water and fuel, then set off southeast across the great sand deserts to Egypt. It did not go well. Bogged down by sinking sands, broken down vehicles, and plagued by sickness, there was no option but that the travellers should turn back to Gialo, regroup, and start all over again.

This time it was decided the two spies and their guide would take a smaller contingent and head for Kufra, skirting the Sand Sea as much as possible. Subsequently, on 12 May, they left Gialo going south. They made good headway that first day. Turning east on the second day, they entered the Sand Sea, stretching endlessly into the horizon.

The Sand Sea was just that, a vast ocean of undulating heat and sand through which they had to navigate their vehicles with only the stars as a sure guide. Spread around them were miles of monotonous sameness, the desert and the sky flowing into each other, no landmarks to manoeuvre by, each massive dune rising before them, much the same as the one they had left behind. Hills of soft gold dust at sunrise, turning to blinding, unbearable white at midday, then magically washed with every shade of indigo, rose and violet by the breathtaking artistry of Amon-Ra's sunset, until the cold, dark of the desert night swept his pageantry away.

And then there was that eerie sound which was said to be the call of the desert. It was difficult to describe with accuracy but, sometimes, when the winds blew across the dunes, the sands would begin to whisper; softly at first, no more than a rumour, and then louder, and still louder, till there was a pounding out there in the desert, as of a thousand drums pacing the marching feet of that long-lost ghost army of Cambyses. The sound, they say, is caused by the friction of sand as the wind sifts through; but those who know the desert believe it is a warning and respect it as such.

That warning should have been heeded. Thwarted by this impasse, their journey now had to be rerouted to the Gilf Kebir and Kharga. This not only lengthened it appreciably but increased the risk of running into British patrols as well. Over the next few days, the landscape changed from shifting sands and towering dunes to craggy outlying crops of scrub and boulder, and back again. The journey was hazardous, requiring changes to accommodate the treacherous terrain. Every so often, hidden caches of water and fuel were left for Almaszy's return journey. Always on the lookout for the enemy, it wasn't long before they did spot a British patrol of the Long Range Desert Group on foray. Keeping well out of sight, they proceeded cautiously past Kufra, and on 17 May they crossed through *Bab el Masr*, the Gate of Egypt, out of Libya and into Egypt.

By turn, they continued to battle soft, sinking sands and rough, rocky ground till, finally, they reached the Gilf Kebir. This Great Barrier plateau of limestone and sandstone, with its painted caves and hidden *wadis,* told a story of long-ago lakes and rivers serving verdant valleys and lost civilisations thousands of years old. Wadi Hamra (the Red Valley), spectacular with its red sand dunes against the black rock face; Wadi Abd el Malik (Valley of the Servant of the King); Wadi Talh (Valley of Acacia) – the three *wadis* believed to be the ancient site where the long-lost Oasis of Zerzura once lay, in a time when the area was lush and fertile with water, vegetation and life in abundance.

At Wadi Sora, Almaszy showed them the prehistoric paintings in the Cave of Swimmers that he and his colleagues had discovered in 1933. He spoke of the ancient rock paintings they had found at Ain Dua in the great granite rocks of Jebel 'Uwaynat. What had life here been like, in that time of legend?

Resuming their journey, they stumbled, by sheer luck, upon some British vehicles, fuelled and parked, awaiting the return of their drivers. Helping themselves to the enemy's petrol, they set off in search of Al Aqaba (The Gap) that would allow them passage through the Gilf Kebir. It was not easily found, but find it they did, and checking to ensure it had not been mined, they drove through and across the Gilf Kebir. Now, in the desert region patrolled constantly by the British, Almaszy cautioned them to stay alert.

At dawn on 23 May, they reached the outpost of Kharga where, sure enough, they were accosted by two *ghaffirs.* Bluffing their way past this pair of Egyptian sentries, they sped through, passing the ancient temple of Ibis and the old Christian necropolis of Bagawat. A few hours after leaving the Kharga Oasis they reached the edge of the great Egyptian plateau from where they could see, spread below, the great river Nile flowing through its lush valley and the bright, white city of Assiut, basking in the afternoon sunlight.

Almaszy's task was done – with their arrival at the Nile Valley 'Operation Salam' had been successfully accomplished. He and his remaining contingent could now turn back with their vehicles and retrace their footsteps to Rommel's headquarters. There, the grateful General would award him the Iron Cross.

Perhaps, noteworthy of mention here is the final discrepancy between fact and fiction in Almaszy's life. Unlike the romantic Hollywood character who perished so tragically questing to save his lady love, the real protagonist would succumb to amoebic dysentery on one of his forays into the Sand Sea. Five and a half years after the war, at age fifty-five, he would die in a hospital in Innsbruck, Austria. It could be argued, however, that since the desert was so beloved of

Laszlo Almaszy, he did, after all, relinquish his life in pursuit of this one true and enduring love.

Eppler and Munkaster spent that last night in a *wadi*. At dawn, the two German spies researched the terrain and eventually found what they were looking for – a secluded spot where, beneath a boulder, they stashed one of the transceivers, along with £100 to be used for their return journey. (As things turned out, there is every reason to believe that 'pot of gold' lies hidden still in the desert to this day.) Then, attired in the get-up of businessmen – with Eppler posing as an Anglo-Egyptian merchant and Munkaster, as a Scandinavian-American oil rig worker – the men turned towards Assiut, three hundred miles south of Cairo.

Almost immediately their disguise was put to the test when they were accosted by an officer from a British camp that lay squarely in their path. Somehow their luck held. They managed to allay his suspicions, all through a pleasant afternoon, enjoying his invitation to drinks and luncheon. Afterwards, they triumphantly boarded the evening train to Cairo. They were unaware, however, that as a matter of routine the officer would dispatch a message informing Cairo of two new arrivals in the area.

It was May 1942, and all hell was about to break loose in the desert. In Cairo 'Operation Kondor' had been activated, and the 'Kondor' was poised for flight.

THE MONTH OF APRIL had been exceptionally busy at GHQ (Middle East Forces). Its offices, in the commandeered buildings in Garden City, were fairly jumping with activity, for this was where it was all being put together – the strategies and deployment of the British and Commonwealth troops that were gathering for battle in the desert. GHQ (MEF), under command of General Sir Claude Auchinleck, was responsible for, and in charge of, the Allied armies facing the Germans and Italians in the desert. It was distinct from BTE (British Troops in Egypt), which had been stationed in the region prior to the war and was responsible for the security of the entire area, from the Western Desert all the way to the Suez Canal.

Embedded in this latter branch of the forces, as Head of Field Defense Security, was Major Alfred William Sansom, a spruce, neatly groomed officer who somehow managed to wear his uniform with the aplomb of one sporting a modish ensemble of the latest fashion.

Topped with a swanky switch-cane tucked beneath his arm, he appeared to be the very epitome of what the frontline troops derisively referred to as 'the gabardine swine' – those who spent the war in comparative safety behind a desk, pushing pen instead of rifle, and enjoying the social and sensual pleasures the city had to offer, secure from the hardships and privations the desert troops had to endure. A paean composed to this indolent lot went like this:

> *We never went west of Gezira,*
> *We never went north of the Nile,*
> *We never went past the pyramids,*
> *Out of sight of the Sphinx's smile.*
> *We fought the war in Shepheard's,*
> *And the Continental Bar,*
> *We reserved our punch for the Turf Club Lunch*
> *And they gave us the Africa Star!!*

Notwithstanding this ditty – no book should be judged too hastily by its cover – Major Sansom was far from a passive, pencil-pushing desk jockey. Born and reared in Cairo, he had a natural flair for languages, and could speak several dialects of Arabic, plus French, Italian and Greek like a native. He was a razor-sharp Intelligence Officer with eyes that verily could see through walls, an ear fine-tuned to the barest whisper of intrigue, and a nose that could sniff a master spy out of his closest lair. Sansom was a master of disguise as well, with the instinct of a bloodhound.

Now, he had caught a whiff of something in the air, and his instinct twitched at news of the two newcomers who had just entered Cairo. He knew a leak of vital information was being passed on to the enemy, and he was positive he had picked up the scent of a trail that would lead him to the Desert Fox's spies.

It was the third week of a sweltering April, but the weather was not the only thing heating up. Out there in the Western Desert, both sides were gearing up for confrontation, and affairs were rapidly coming to a head.

ON 18 APRIL 1942, the 2/4 Gurkhas arrived by train at Qassasin. They had come via el Kantara and crossed the Suez Canal by way of a makeshift pontoon bridge. The camp at Qassasin was simply a large area occupied by rows of tents, but it provided fairly comfortable straw palliasses, showers and even cinema shows.

Vendors came by selling souvenirs, fresh eggs, local fruits and dates (whether the pitting customs here were any more hygienic or modern, one wondered!). And overriding everything were the swarms of flies you could never get away from. Seeking moisture, like every other living creature in the desert, they were partial to the eyes, the mouth and any other damp area on a generally sweaty body. Flies and heat made for a murderous combination, and it was a blessing when night brought a respite from the plague; however, night brought a pestilence of its own with clouds of ravenous mosquitoes exploiting cooler temperatures. It was difficult to pick which of the two afflictions was the worse.

The Battalion spent a week here, refitting and re-equipping to meet MEF requirements. Santi checked and rechecked his medical supplies and equipment, foraging for whatever extras he could lay his hands on.

Late afternoon of 22 April, a few twenty-four-hour passes were issued for a quick '*shufti*' around Cairo. Ben Browne sauntered over to where Santi was supervising the loading of his supplies. He had slipped into John Masters shoes and taken over the responsibilities of Battalion Adjutant with barely a hiccup.

"You done yet, Doc?"

"That's the last of it, although I could do with a couple more stretchers."

"Might as well ask for the moon," Ben snorted. "Everyone's scrambling for last-minute supplies, and our new Quartermaster, Middleton, is hideously out of sorts, drowning in requisitions. The queue outside the QM's runs from here to Cairo! Speaking of which, we've managed to wangle a few passes, and we're going into town tonight. Overnighting it. Willie's letting us off-leash for a spot of R&R, and Roger's got transport laid on. Wondered if you might like to tag along. We should be pushing off in an hour or so; I'm on my way now to pick up the passes from the Duty Officer."

"If you have a pass and room to spare, I'd be glad to go along," Santi thanked him, adding rather enigmatically, "I have a promise to keep."

"Come again?" Ben cocked his head to one side, his interest piqued; and when Santi explained to him the promise he had made to Samira in Iraq, and the message he was carrying for her cousin in Cairo, the Adjutant nodded. "Well, here's your chance to make good, Doc. A promise made should be a promise kept, eh? Shall we say an hour, then?"

"An hour it is," Santi replied as he watched the Adjutant walk away.

What an unexpected piece of luck! He hadn't believed he would get a chance to visit the old city or discharge his promise quite so soon. He was pleased Ben had thought to invite him along. He wasn't quite 'one of the lads' yet, but neither did he feel as much of a square peg in a round hole as he had at the start. And by the look of things, the feeling might actually be mutual. A year together seemed to have sorted out at least some of their differences!

Santi finished giving his trucks the once-over to make sure everything was well secured, then hurried to his tent to throw a few things together for Dilbahadur to pack. He would just about have time for a quick shower – that is, if he could find one free, of course. And he'd better not forget the cousin's address. What was her name? Ah yes, Hedeya Khayat! The address – where the heck was that address!

He asked Dilbahadur if he had found a piece of paper with an address in any of his pockets. No, the batman shook his head; if he had he would have returned it to *Daktar sahib*. Of that Santi had no doubt since he knew how meticulous his orderly was. But he, himself, usually so careful about things, how could he have lost the information after he'd given his word to Samira! Well, he'd have to think of something! As Ben had said, a promise was a promise, and he would have to do whatever it took to keep it.

Thank goodness, he at least remembered the cousin's name; and he was sure, if he thought a little harder, he would be able to recall the area where she lived. He remembered it as an odd sounding word…yet, strangely familiar…somewhat like the Bengali word for a morning greeting – *Shooprobhat.* Yes…Shoopra something…Shoobra? *Choubra!* That was it! Hedeya Khayat lived somewhere in Choubra, and although he hadn't the faintest idea how he would go about it, he had to think of a way to find her.

BY THE TIME THEY GOT to Cairo, the heat of the day had abated. The streets were coming alive as the city, having shaken off the drowsy afternoon, began to awaken for the night. The houses threw back their shutters, the shops flung open their doors, and the night spots began to shimmy with lights and music. Evening's soft shadows smoothed the wrinkles from the care-worn face of the daytime city. The dirt and poverty were painted over with twilight's gently luminous palette. All that was tawdry was made sumptuous beneath the shadowy veils of dusk and, although by day one could perceive her full-blown features, by night Cairo beckoned like a seductress.

Shepheard's Hotel. The very name had come to epitomize all that was glamorous about wartime Cairo. Originally a boarding house built on Opera Square by Sam Shepheard, a Victorian businessman, the hotel had, in the words of the British writer Desmond Stewart, evolved into "an island of English Imperial living." Long after the war, and its subsequent demise by fire in 1952, the name and reputation of that most famous of all Cairo's establishments would live on, evoking memories of sweet nostalgia in those who had experienced its luxuries, and a romantic longing in those who never had that chance.

Now, at the entrance to that grand edifice, a Nubian *bawaeb* in a long *galabeya* bowed them through doors he dutifully held open. Like some genie out of the Arabian Nights, he invited them to enter…to step in…and be swept into the glittering world of Cairo's social elite.

"Now this," declared Roger Werner, tipping his cap back so he could gaze all the way up at the lofty ceilings soaring above their heads, "this is what I call living!"

The room they stood in radiated luxury with its shimmering lights and ample furnishings that echoed the soft, muted shades of the desert and the distant past. The ceiling was held aloft by lotus-crowned pillars in the age-old Egyptian style. They rose from gleaming stone floors hand-polished to a mirror-like shine. Graceful potted palms stood between pieces of furniture inlaid with mother-of-pearl. And everywhere could be seen throngs of uniformed officers with, here and there, the elegantly attired men and women of Cairo's upper crust.

At the reception desk, they enquired about accommodation. The Swiss concierge levelled them with a frigid stare, all down the length of his imposing nose. *Rooms?* He retorted, icily. *Without reservations?* Oh, these ignorant army types! The breadth and depth of his scorn was apparent. *Gentlemen, this is Shepheard's!* His voice practically shook with mounting indignation. *Please, it is completely out of the question!*

Unprepared for this reaction, and somewhat daunted by the setback, the men decided there was nothing for it but to grab a drink at the bar while mulling over the problem of alternate accommodations.

Shepheard's famous Long Bar was packed with Eighth Army officers on leave from the front, intent on enjoying whatever short time had been allowed them in this city of sinful delights. Too soon they would have to return to the austerity of the desert and the hardships of war. There were GHQ types as well, and others from BTE, with the odd civilian surfacing every so often, like bits of flotsam, in that sea of uniforms.

A major from BTE made room for them at the bar. They thanked him and crowded in, only to find the bartender was busy at the other end. The major rapped the bar top with his swagger stick to draw the bartender's attention, then turned to them with a smile.

"Well boys, what's your poison?" He spoke loudly over the din of conversation that filled the bar. "Our friend Joe here is a master of his craft."

When it was his turn Santi ordered a scotch and soda, a luxurious change from the rum and occasional beer they were rationed – if they were lucky. The major gave their order, and his, to the bartender in flawless Arabic, then signed for the drinks.

"No, no," he insisted, when they demurred. "Allow me to put this round on my chitty. I have a running tab here."

While they were being served, he introduced himself as Major Sansom and struck up a conversation. Was this their first time at Shepheard's? Ah, first visit to Cairo! Just in from Persia and Iraq. Then they must join him on the hotel's famous terrace overlooking Opera Square. It was a window on the world that was Cairo.

"Thank you, sir. We would be glad to," Ben accepted for them. "And maybe you could point us in the direction of some decent accommodation. We were hoping to avail of the facilities here, but we've just been given to understand by the…the…"

"Pompous prig!" Roger Werner interjected, helpfully.

"…er…the person at the concierge desk that one cannot presume just to walk into Shepheard's and expect a room. We, apparently, ought to have known better. Sadly for us, we did not. Practically turfed us out on our ears!"

Major Sansom chuckled. "Gave you the treatment, did he? Hallowed ground and all that good stuff! Phillipe tends to take himself, and his job, somewhat seriously. If he considers anyone guilty of stepping out of line, breaking protocol so to speak, he rather enjoys giving the unfortunate transgressor the bum's rush. He's quite harmless, really. Hold on a tick, let me see if I can't wangle something."

A short while later the Major returned, smiling. "You're all set. Just required a bit of old-fashioned 'negotiation' is all. Here you go – three keys to three rooms; two of you will have to double up, I'm afraid. Best I could do. But come back after you've seen to your luggage and join me on the terrace."

And he refused to hear anything about any sort of repayment, pooh poohing it as too minor to bother about.

The concierge, despite having had his palm generously – albeit very discreetly – greased, still managed to maintain his air of supercilious dignity. He snapped his fingers for a *suffragi* who appeared instantly to lead them down marbled corridors to their sumptuously appointed rooms. They had drawn straws to determine who would share and, by dint of good fortune, Santi and Ben had won the single rooms.

Stepping through the door, Santi found himself in a large room. An intricately wrought brass bed draped with a mosquito net took centre stage. But no less impressive were the oversized, overstuffed chair and ottoman, and the gleaming granite counters holding polished brass artifacts and an elaborate alabaster vessel abundantly arrayed with fresh figs, dates and grapes. All in all, the room was an oasis of cool, relaxed opulence. Since it was too late to begin his search for Hedeya Khayat, Santi stowed away his meagre belongings and, after a quick freshening up, made his way downstairs to meet the others for a leisurely drink.

Out on the terrace, cooled by a soft evening breeze, Major Sansom had found a table adequate to their number where they could enjoy the view below.

A melange of humanity coursed through Ibrahim Pasha Street. The omnigenous Cairenes were a colourful mix of Egyptian Muslims, Copts and Jews, as well as Greeks, Levantines and Maltese; and then there were the far-flung foreigners who had added to their numbers, French, British, Italians, and other expatriates, many of them refugees who had fled the Nazis, including a few members from the various royal families of Europe.

Mingling with the dense crowds of Cairo's residents going about their business, dodging the hawkers, vendors and street urchins, were the soldiers of the Eighth Army; an army of diverse customs, creeds, religions and lifestyles; an army that spoke over forty different languages and had been culled from across the world: the Anzacs of Australia and New Zealand, the soldiers of Greece, Poland, South Africa, India, Free France and, of course, Britain. And threading their way between them all were the ever present, ever audible, cars, carriages and carts.

As they relaxed over drinks and small drifts of inconsequential chatter, Major Sansom gently probed them for information. So, they were with the 2/4 Gurkhas. Refitting at Qassassin, were they? Bound for the Western Desert? Did they know exactly where they were headed? He marvelled at how easy it was to glean information in a bar. It was like taking candy from a baby! Not that this lot had much to give away. He hadn't thought they had, but sheer force of habit had prompted him to sniff around. Besides, it was always good to keep one's hand in, you could never tell but one thing might lead to another.

This was the way he worked. Every so often, he'd do the rounds of the most popular night clubs and bars and, while seeming to enjoy a casually social evening, he would actually have his nose to the wind and his ear to the ground, sifting and sorting through tidbits of information he picked up. It was amazing how much he did pick up – quite often, all it took was a few drinks in a relaxed, friendly atmosphere to loosen the tongues and soften the minds of men otherwise tightly wound up with the tension and strain of war.

Well, he was done here, and it was time to move on to his next hunting ground. He was still running with a hunch that he had picked up the scent of one of Rommel's spies, and he wasn't about to let it go cold.

He got up to take his leave of them. "Well, I must be off. I hope you chaps enjoy the rest of your stay in Cairo. Just remember to steer clear of the dodgy areas where you're likely to get gypped. I always warn the inexperienced who arrive in town, bright-eyed and bushy-tailed, to beware the tout who promises delights beyond their dreams. A famous one you're likely to come across is '*my cousin as beautiful as Cleopatra*', or the other good one, '*my sister, so white, like Queen Victoria*'. All it takes is one drink too many for a chap to be press-ganged and dragged off to The Berka – that's Wagh el Birket street – where he's bound to get more than he bargained for; regrettably, most of it rather unpleasant I'm afraid!"

Amid laughter they assured him they would beware such chicanery.

"No, no, I'm serious, they are a wily lot." Major Sansom turned to Santi. "Doc, you're a man of medicine, and you will appreciate the problem we face. I tell you, in spite of regular 'short arm inspections' and the efforts of our Medical Corps who have tried to monitor the brothels in that bloody place – we have inoculation stations right at their doors for heaven's sake – venereal disease among the men has caused us almost as much grief as the enemy has."

"I believe you, sir. I myself have seen several cases among the men these past few months. We certainly intend to stay well clear of the place." Santi shook the major's hand goodbye. "Maybe you could give us some further advice. If you had just one evening in Cairo, sir, what would be your choice of venue?"

Major Sansom considered the eager faces turned to him, waiting for an answer. The trail he was following led to the Kit Kat Club where one of Cairo's most sought-after belly dancers, Hekmat Fahmy, performed. And she was, by any standards, certainly worth a visit. He attended the nightclub every so often and would watch her performance – not that anyone would have known, since he usually went in disguise, sometimes as a garrulous Greek war profiteer, at other times as a well-to-do Lebanese businessman, and once even as a slightly sozzled American civilian in transit. This time, however, as he was in uniform and not in mufti, this group of young officers looking for a good time could provide the perfect smoke screen for him to operate behind. It might work better were he to blend in as part of this innocuous group, rather than walk in conspicuously all on his own. The more he thought about the idea, the better he liked it.

And so, it was decided.

THE KIT KAT CLUB on the Nile was a popular night spot. The place was packed with British officers, wealthy Egyptians, Greeks and Copts who were aficionados of the belly dance, both as a true art form as well as a titillation of the senses.

It wasn't easy finding a table to accommodate their number, so they sat instead at the bar and ordered a round of drinks. A variety of acts came and went. Finally, the room tensed to the imperious clicking of castanets accompanied by the first tantalising strains of the belly dancer's sensual music.

All went quiet in anticipation as Hekmat Fahmy appeared on stage. She kept her movements to a minimum, but made each movement count; the rippling undulations of her body, the small flip and flick of each intriguing muscle, the beckoning of every voluptuous curve; the insinuation of each ebb and flow that teased and swelled into promise, every supple gyration a personal message that electrified the air with desire. And finally, when her pulsating body crescendoed and quivered to a shuddering stop, an audible sigh went up in the room – and she bowed to receive her due applause from the delighted audience.

Roger was the first to verbalise his appreciation. "By gad, what a fizzer! That's *some* muscle control, the lady has! That body would undo a saint!" There was hearty concurrence all round.

"It's awfully good of you to have brought us, sir," Santi thanked Sansom. "I must say, I haven't seen anything quite like it before." He was amazed to find how intensely his body had responded to the dancer's every intricate move. He lit a cigarette and allowed himself to relax slowly, one taut muscle at a time, as he took a sip of his drink.

"That goes for us all, I daresay," Robert Williams admitted. "Our first Egyptian belly dancer, and she certainly put on quite a show." He turned to Major Sansom. "I say, sir, speaking of shows, you couldn't tell us how far the pyramids are from here, could you? We haven't much time, but if it's at all possible to pack the visit into a day trip, that's something we shouldn't want to pass up."

"Easily done m'boy, one day is plenty," Sansom replied. "Tell the hotel concierge tonight when you get back; mention my name, and he'll make arrangements for your trip tomorrow. Have lunch at Mena House, right by the pyramids. They have a slap-up buffet; the pickings run from the everyday to the exotic. You might even get to sample one of their great delicacies – camel's testicles."

There was a strangled sound from Roger Werner whose memory of a not-too-distant encounter with a somewhat similar dish was reflected in the pained expression on his face. He bore his companions' laughter with rueful good humour as they recounted his Persian experience to the Major.

"It's an acquired taste, I give you that," Major Sansom admitted when he had stopped laughing. "But not half bad, actually, once you get over the squeamishness of what it is you're eating. Of course," he turned back to Robert Williams, "if you are not quite up to the adventure of it, they do serve more mundane fare, still excellent and well worth a try. Give it a go, you won't regret it, I assure you."

"We will, sir. Frightfully good of you, thank you very much."

While speaking to Williams, Sansom had been paying close attention to Hekmat Fahmy who was doing the rounds now, slipping from table to table. Having served up her dance routine as the first delectable dish of that evening's repast, she was now offering her guests dessert, pouring on her charm, like thick cream, and basking in their approbation. From the generous manner in which she gave of herself, it was to be assumed that she was an ardent admirer of the

British, and an avid supporter of their cause. As to her true leanings, well that was anyone's guess.

A slightly inebriated Major from GHQ, seated at a small table nearby, was vying for her attention. On the floor was an official bag which he kept tucked securely between his feet, and on the table, beneath his right hand, there lay a small object that looked like a jewelry box.

Without seeming to notice it, Hekmat circled the tables around him with slow deliberation, drawing ever closer, but remaining just out of reach. Eventually, when she felt her Circean web had been spun tight enough, and the Major had been worked into a sufficient state of floundering helplessness, Hekmat slithered onto his knee. She ran her fingers through his hair, down the length of his nose, till they came to rest on his lips.

With one eye on the trinket box lying on the table, she drew closer to him and, in order to do so, she attempted to dislodge the bag between his feet. The Major immediately grabbed the bag and held on to it with an urgency that was not lost on the dancer.

Her attention now turned away from the trinket box on the table to the bag on the floor. Without even looking at the box when he pressed it into her hand, she leaned into him and, while nibbling the tip of his ear, she whispered a few quiet words to which he nodded eagerly, a gratified smile on his lips.

The small vignette immediately piqued the interest of Major Sansom. This was just the sort of thing he was on the lookout for. A few minutes after Hekmat departed, he seemed to spot an acquaintance across the room. He waved; then, excusing himself, he retrieved his drink and got up to cross over to his invisible friend. As he passed the Major's table he tripped, spilling his drink on that officer's trousers and the bag on the floor, and making the man leap to his feet with a perfunctory curse.

"Blast!"

Profusely apologetic, Sansom grabbed a serviette off the table and picked up the bag to wipe it down, only to have it unceremoniously snatched back, out of his hands.

"I was merely trying to make up for my clumsiness," Sansom said, reproachfully.

"Forgive me." The Major from GHQ said, recognising Sansom's uniform and rank. "Didn't mean to be rude, but I'm not to let this bag out of sight. It'd be the devil if anything were to happen to it, I can tell you."

"You sound as though you were carrying the King's own orders."

"Just so," replied the Major. "From GHQ to General Ritchie. I'm headed for the desert right this minute…well, er…not precisely…I mean in just a…"

Listening to him, Sansom had raised an eyebrow. Now, he looked him squarely in the eye. "Major, I think you're quite right to leave at once. I wouldn't hang about this joint either if I were you. It's just the sort of place something untoward could happen to your bag, and one would have the dickens of a time explaining oneself, don't you agree?"

"As I was saying," conceded the Major, lamely. "Er…maybe a quick round…?" He looked about him for some support and got none. Looking a mite crestfallen, he announced, "I'd best be on my way, gentlemen, so I'll take your leave. Good evening."

Sansom watched as the reluctant man headed out the door. *Something of a rum customer that,* he thought. *I have a twitch about him. He could spell trouble when he's in his cups, and a strong hunch tells me he's going to merit watching.*

CHAPTER TWENTY-ONE

A Search Through Cairo

If in thy heart a seed of love is plac'd,
No day of all thy life can run to waste;
Whether for God's approval thou dost strive,
Or on the joys of Earth hast set thy taste.

– Omar Khayyam, *Rubaiyat of Omar Khayyam*

SANTI EMERGED FROM THE cool depths of Shepheard's Hotel into the already intense glare of the mid-morning sun. After the previous night's entertainment, he had slept like a log in the most luxurious surroundings one could ever have wished for. And, since first impressions were important, this morning he had dressed carefully in full uniform, despite the expected heat.

The blazing desert light bleached his surroundings of colour, and the city, through its pall of omnipresent desert dust, seemed to take on a pale, sand-washed hue. The *bawaeb* who had ushered him out through the great doors hailed a taxi for him and, holding the car door open, politely enquired after his destination.

"Choubra," Santi replied, getting into the taxi. The Nubian nodded, smiled, and waited patiently for the rest of the address. "Just… Choubra," Santi repeated, a little louder than before, trying to convey a firmness of purpose he was not altogether sure he felt. Then, leaning forward he addressed the driver; speaking slowly and carefully enunciating his words, he said "Take me to Choubra."

Looking puzzled, the driver turned to the doorman and an altercation ensued punctuated with much flailing of hands on the driver's part and shrugging of shoulders from the Nubian. Eventually, muttering under his breath, the driver took off at a speed that was meant to indicate his deep disapproval of the haphazard way in which his passenger was conducting his affairs.

Slung from side to side in the back seat every time the vehicle hurtled around a corner, Santi was beginning to seriously question the wisdom of his undertaking, when the taxi screeched to a sudden halt. The driver turned to Santi and, with the gesture of a magician pulling a rabbit out of a hat, announced "This Choubra." He then sat back and watched in his rear-view mirror to see what this strange passenger of his would do.

And indeed, now that he had arrived, Santi was at somewhat of a loss to know how he should proceed. The only details he could recollect from Samira's lost note was that Hedeya Khayat lived in Choubra; she lived here with her mother and still used her maiden name; she was Armenian, which meant, of course, she must be Christian; and that being the case, it was more than likely she attended church somewhere in the area. Yes, that would be his best bet. He peered out the window and spied a street sign which read Sharah el Tir'a el Bulaqiya.

"You know any churches here?" Santi asked the driver. He made the sign of the cross, folding his hands as if in prayer. "You know? Christian. Church."

"Church? *Ayiz aih*? What you want church?"

"We," Santi pointed to the driver and then to himself, "go to every church." He flung his arms wide in an all-encompassing gesture. "Find all the churches. Yes?"

"No! No, no," wailed the driver, slapping his forehead with the palm of his hand. He got out of the taxi and stood on the pavement. "*La', la'. Inta magnoon, wéiy!*

From a doorway one building down, a middle-aged gentleman of affable demeanour stepped out of his favourite *mata'am* where he had just enjoyed a good dish of *kosharee*. As usual, the rice, black lentils and small macaroni had been cooked to perfection, and the sweet taste of crisp fried onions still lingered on his tongue. Contentedly replete, he stopped for a moment to put away his wallet when he caught sight of the halted taxi. He waved to the driver: was he free to take another passenger?

Alas, that proved a mistake! The driver's response was alarmingly unexpected. The stunned gentleman found himself grabbed by the arm and propelled, despite loud protest, towards the taxi. Flabbergasted at this untoward turn of events, and intent only on breaking free of his captor – *what was this, was he being abducted!* – the distraught man could make neither head nor tail of the barrage assailing his ears. Like bees swarming about a hive, the words buzzed around his head, and he managed to catch just the odd one or two as they flew by. *Altercation? Well, that was between them, what had it to do with him, a stranger! Intervene? No, no, he certainly would not be willing. Whatever it was, he wanted no part of this madness…he was a passerby with his own business to attend…*

By this time, Santi had exited the taxi and was standing on the pavement by the open door. The stranger assessed the tall, swarthy, young man in uniform who seemed to be the cause of all the commotion. *This one, at least, looked to be reasonably sane…*

And, as common sense finally returned, he had to admit his interest was piqued. Concluding by now that he was intended no bodily harm, and that the path of least resistance was probably his quickest way out of this predicament that had so precipitously engulfed him, the gentleman sighed and gave in. *Yes, he would listen to his captor's woes…mediate even…if* – he made this request with wry humour – *if the taxi driver would kindly keep in mind it was that time of day when one's stomach was apt to work better than one's brain; as such, should he insist on unburdening his troubles, would he do so gently upon a body that was, at present, far too sated to be wise.*

The driver was in no mood for levity. He delivered a long string of indignant complaints and when, at last, he was done, he glared at Santi and grunted, "*Humph! Huwa magnoon awi!*"

There was a short silence during which the gentleman considered Santi thoughtfully. Eventually, he said as politely as he could, "This man thinks you are completely mad."

Santi nodded; in truth, he was fast reaching the same conclusion himself. What a blithering fool he had been to think he could find anyone in this manner. It was like looking for the proverbial needle in a haystack! How had he landed himself in this quandary, anyhow? But…here he was, for better or worse, so he might as well give it his all.

"I see his point of view," Santi admitted, "but can you see mine?" He tried to explain his predicament to the now openly curious gentleman. "I gave the lady my word, you see, so I must make every attempt to keep it."

The stranger eyed him sympathetically. "Ah, I do see! A gentleman's word given has left you honour bound, and now you have a big problem, my young friend. I am afraid I do not hold much hope for this undertaking of yours. Nevertheless, we must all do what we can to aid such a worthy mission. *Taht amrak,* I am at your command; and, as it happens, I do know of one church not very far from here – *Keneesa Rasuleya,* the Orthodox Church of the Apostle. It is as good a place to start as any; and, as I am going that way myself, let me start you on your quest by taking you to it. Maybe the priest there can guide you further down the road you have so gallantly chosen to travel."

The gentleman, who introduced himself as Ibrahim Sabit, then explained the problem to the taxi driver. Once that man was made privy to the whole story, he immediately converted to a willing champion of the cause. "*Itfadal, itfadal,*" he smiled widely, holding open the car door and bowing to Santi.

Relieved at his sudden change in demeanour, Santi thanked both men profusely and they all got in. At the crossroads of Sharah el Tir'a el Bulaqiya, Ard el Taweel and Sharah Ghattas, the taxi pulled up in front of an old building with a cross on its roof.

"Go", Ibrahim Sabit said, encouragingly. "Go, try your luck. We will wait."

WHEN THE HEAVY DOORS closed behind him, Santi found he had stepped into a large room filled with wooden pews and a deep, dim silence. He looked around; it was empty. Soft, multi-coloured light filtered in through two stained glass windows, and beyond the muted shadows, at the far end, he spied a door which he guessed must lead to a vestry of sorts. Moving as quietly as he could, since the ringing echo of his army officer's boots sounded almost sacrilegious in the hush of those godly surroundings, he made his way to the door and knocked gently – once. After a moment he knocked again.

The door swung open and an elderly priest appeared in the doorway. "*Aiwa?*" he enquired, quite obviously taken aback at the unexpected sight of a tall, young Army officer standing before him.

In his experience these foreign soldiers were usually accompanied by some sort of trouble. Just recently there had been a hue and cry in the city over an unfortunate incident that had taken place in a cinema house. It had resulted in an irate complaint from the incensed Egyptian Court to the British High Commissioner, Sir Miles Lampson.

Apparently, some rapscallions from the British Army Other Ranks – Australians, it was said – had risen with the audience, after a picture show, to stand for the Egyptian national anthem. Which was all very well; except that much to the indignation and affront of the Egyptian audience, they had then waxed poetic, belting out their own raucous version which went something like this: "*King Farouk, King Farouk, hang your bollocks on a hook…*" (John Bierman & Colin Smith: *War without Hate*).

Asis Habib tried to push the insulting incident from his thoughts and focus on the present. He examined this young officer carefully. He had to grant he seemed of a different ilk. Undoubtedly a British Army uniform, but obviously not British; not from that down-under place either, that Australia, thank goodness! Still, be that as it may, his presence was baffling, and the priest was not at all sure what to expect. So, he cocked his head to one side, and waited for an explanation.

"Good morning Father. I am Captain Santi Dutt. I'm looking for a Christian lady named Hedeya Khayat. Do you happen to know any-one by that name?"

There was an astonished silence. Santi interpreted it as disapprov-al. Too late he realised the inappropriate picture he must present – foreigner, soldier, enquiring after a lady's home address! Add to that the bluntness of his approach and, well, it could not but serve to cause deep disquiet in the old priest.

Actually, at that moment, what Asis Habib was feeling was not so much disquiet as being abruptly set back on his heels. In truth, he was left momentarily speechless by the bizarre unlikelihood of what he'd just heard!

Why was this young man looking for Hedeya, of all people? And how had he found his way here? The impropriety of a foreign soldier, albeit an officer, asking after a young lady so brazenly was enough to raise concern in any man of the cloth. Fortunately, Asis Habib was not merely a man of the cloth, he was a man of the world as well, and astute enough to guess that in this instance there was probably more to the story than had, as yet, been divulged! It kindled his curiosity sufficiently to pull himself together that he might consider how best to dig for further clarification.

He contemplated the face of his unusual visitor, and found his scrutiny returned with equal frankness as the young officer looked him straight in the eye. In certain instances that might have led an individual hastier than himself to arrive at a conclusion of boldness. Always mindful of the good rather than the bad, however, Asis Habib took close note of the steady, serious gaze and saw it for what it was – a forthrightness that spoke to an open, honest nature, free from prevarication. Indeed, the man before him seemed to have a refined, well-bred manner and looked to be sincere. It eased his mind some-what. Slowly, he cleared his throat – to give himself time to ponder his next move – and decided his best course was to come straight to the point.

"Why are you looking for this lady?" he enquired, at last.

"Do you mean you know her?" It was Santi's turn to be astounded. Could he have been so lucky as to hit pay dirt on his very first try?!

"Did I say that? What do you want her for?"

"I'm sorry. I thought you meant…I have a message for this lady, Father, from her cousin in Iraq. While I was there with my unit that lady was kind enough to allow me the use of her school building as a medical facility. When I was leaving, she entrusted me with a message for Hedeya Khayat. I would like to repay the favour she did me by keeping my promise to deliver that message."

Santi paused, wondering if he was going too fast. Maybe he ought to slow down a bit. He took a deep breath and continued. "Unhappily, I have lost the address I was given; but I know she lives in Choubra, and she is Christian – Armenian Christian – and the only possibility of finding her, I decided, was to visit every church in Choubra to seek her information." He paused. "Your church, Father, is the first one a kind gentleman led me to."

Happenstance? Now, what were the chances of such a thing! Asis Habib sighed. It was not that he didn't believe the story. Who in his right mind would concoct such a one as this! The thing of it was, it left him in a quandary. It appeared, despite the uncanniest of odds, this young man had managed to find his way to this very door. But in doing so, he had created a situation Asis Habib was not at all sure how he should handle. Yes, he knew Hedeya and where she lived. He also knew she had taken great pains to keep her whereabouts private from all but a very few; that was the reason she had changed her address. Was he now to divulge her secret to this stranger?

The old priest raised his eyes towards heaven in gentle reproach. In his dealings with God these many years, he had come to realise that the Almighty often moved in strange, unfathomable ways. And if this uniformed apparition standing in his church was meant to be a test of some sort – of his judgement, his discretion perhaps, or the discernment of his duty even – then he had to admit, it certainly had him confounded on all three counts!

Should he give this young man the information he was seeking? And, if he did, what would Hedeya say to a complete stranger landing up at her house? A soldier no less! And without any forewarning at that! Knowing her as he did, he could imagine her displeasure. No, it did not bear thinking!

On the other hand, what were the chances that this person – not merely a soldier, but a doctor as well from what he just heard – a foreigner to the city, would have walked into his church, the very first church in his quest, if he had not been led there by Divine Intervention? The Lord did appear to be sending him some sort of message. What it was, he couldn't for the life of him fathom.

Asis Habib shook his head, perplexed. Only the Lord would have thought to devise such a predicament to drop him in, and then require his unquestioning faith to perceive the right path. Privately he had to admit, sometimes his Master betrayed a quirky sense of humour!

Ah well, who was he, humble servant that he was, to question the ways of the Lord, curious as they may be? And so, he delivered himself into the hands of the Almighty, permitting himself a single heartfelt sigh as muttered under his breath, "Putting me to the test yet again, Lord?"

"I beg your pardon, Father?" Santi strained to catch the old priest's mumblings.

Aloud, Asis Habib said, "What a story! The very first church, you say! Well, it seems to be the will of God, my son, for you have indeed come to the right church. I am Asis Habib, and I know the lady you are enquiring about; I have known the family a long time. However, you must understand that it is not seemly I should give you her address."

He held up a hand before Santi could protest. "But, if you bear with me while I take my next service, I will accompany you there myself."

Much relieved, Santi thanked him and went outside to inform his two companions who had so generously embarked with him on his quest that it had met with unbelievable success. Impossible as it seemed at the outset, Ibrahim Sabit had, against all odds, brought him to the one church in all Choubra that Santi had been looking for.

"This church? The first one!" Ibrahim Sabit stared at the edifice before him in awe. He shook his head in wonder. "Fate seems to have taken you by the hand, my friend. It has a purpose, no doubt about it. Pay heed to where it leads you." Santi laughed and assured him he would keep a close eye on the mysterious minx.

Ibrahim took his hand in farewell. "*Forsa Saeeda* – Happy Opportunity. I am glad we met. I wish you good fortune, and I hope you find what you seek. *Allah ya sallimak.* May God protect you."

Even the taxi driver shook his hand, pumping it up and down enthusiastically. Santi paid him well for his trouble, and when his offer of the same was unequivocally declined by Ibrahim, he thanked both men for their kind help and waved them goodbye. He watched the taxi drive out of sight, then went inside the church once more to wait.

A few people had gathered within, and a few more were slowly filtering in. Santi found himself a seat in the last pew and sat down to watch the proceedings. A small family had congregated near the chancel for the baptism of a baby girl. There was much low whispering as they arranged themselves in order of their relationship to the child, and then settled down to wait. Fifteen minutes passed before Asis Habib appeared and, after greetings all round, the ceremony began.

Santi had never attended a baptism before, and he watched the proceedings with interest. Between the figures of the participants standing around the font, he caught glimpses of water being poured on the child's head which elicited a small wail of protest from the bundle of white satin and lace. The prayers, the anointing of the head, the blessings brought smiles of pride and joy from the adoring group.

The ceremony continued through the hour and into the next, and Santi became aware that a few of the family members had begun to fidget and exchange surreptitious glances. But Asis Habib, it seems, was by no means done. A further twenty minutes saw him still going strong, despite the shifting and shuffling among his perplexed flock.

Was it their imagination or was the old priest repeating himself? Maybe he meant to emphasise the important texts for their benefit, but this was certainly the most protracted baptism any of them had ever attended!

Fifteen minutes more, and Asis Habib could no longer ignore the worried looks being thrown his way: *what was wrong with the poor old man,* they seemed to ask, *had he forgotten he'd just completed that part? And that! Was all well with him?*

The fact was, their priest was fully aware of the consternation he was causing his small congregation; the problem was, he was having grave misgivings about his earlier decision. The closer he came to taking that eager young stranger – no, worse yet, that unknown Tommy, as the British Army soldiery were generally called – to Hedeya's house without her prior permission, the more fervently he doubted the wisdom of his actions. He knew how private she was, and how particular she could be about such matters.

The more he mulled over it, the more concerned he became as to the prudence of what he had undertaken. And so, he decided to put the young man's mettle to the test. Perhaps if he prolonged the baptismal ceremony as much as possible, either, the soldier would run out of patience and leave, or he himself would be given a sign that somehow would lead him out of his predicament. After all, what the Lord maketh, surely the Lord might unmake as well!

Surreptitiously, the priest glanced towards the back of his church. Yes, he was still there, sitting, seemingly quite comfortable, with not the vestige of a sign he had any intention of leaving! One had to marvel at such patience – one might say almost the patience of Job – in one so young!

The priest sighed softly and decided it was time to accept defeat. He could prolong the ceremony no longer without seeming to have taken complete leave of his faculties. And so, to the relief of all concerned, he brought the proceedings to an abrupt close.

After the family had thanked him and left, he made his way to where Santi stood waiting, seemingly unaware of how he had turned the old man's perfectly good day on its head by impaling him on the horns of such a thoroughly disconcerting dilemma.

CHAPTER TWENTY-TWO

Fate Plays A Hand

Heav'n but the Vision of fufill'd Desire,
And Hell the Shadow of a Soul on fire......
Whether my destin'd Fate shall be to dwell
Midst Heavens joys or in the fires of Hell
I know not...yet my heart says, 'All is well'!

– Omar Khayyam, *Rubaiyat of Omar Khayyam*

THE TAXI RIDE TO Rod el Farag did not take long. After Santi paid the driver and alighted, he found himself standing in front of a sand-stone coloured, four-storied building. The sun was beating down hard, its heat reflecting off the buildings in a shimmering haze that pooled on the road surface. He followed the priest through the entrance before them and up the stairs to the third floor, where they rang the bell to the door on the left side of the landing. Voices could be heard from within, then a short squeal, followed by a soft peal of laughter, and the sound of approaching footsteps.

The door opened, and against the backdrop of filtered daylight that seeped through partially shuttered windows illuminating the room beyond, a figure stood silhouetted in the doorway. Caught in an errant sunbeam that had stolen past the lowered shades, red-gold glints danced through dark-auburn hair, the sunlight forming something almost akin to a halo around the head. Santi could not quite make out the features, or the expression on the face, but he could tell by the outline that the figure belonged to a young lady. He could sense as well that the lady was taken aback at the sight of them.

Once more, he felt the disadvantage of his position, not merely as a stranger, but very possibly an unwelcome one – one of that non grata 'mob' of foreign soldiers who had overrun the city.

Standing on this respectable lady's doorstep, he became acutely mindful again that he was, to the people of this country, what the British were in his – a trespasser and intruder. Suddenly, he was unsure of himself. Embarrassed, and not a little discomfited, he decided, he would quickly discharge his undertaking of passing on Samira's message, and leave as soon as courtesy allowed.

"Asis Habib?" Her voice had a liquid quality, but surprised disapproval was evident in its tone.

"Yes, yes, my dear," Asis Habib answered by way of both apology and explanation. He continued in Arabic. "Forgive this intrusion. I hope it is not a mistake. Do you know who this person is?"

"*Abadan*, I do not!" Santi did not understand the language, but the words sounded clipped and cold. She threw a glance at the tall young man in uniform, standing beside the priest. "You know I have nothing to do with any of these foreign soldiers, and I certainly have never met this one before."

"He claims to have come from your family in Basra. You have a cousin, Samira?"

"Aahh!" The reserve melted in an instant. "*Aiwa*! Of course!" Warmly, Hedeya welcomed them in. "Please," she spoke in English, "please, come in."

She had a marked accent when she spoke in English, a way of softening some of the consonants in her words that was oddly pleasing; and as she led them inside, he noticed a quiet confidence in the way she moved.

Santi took off his cap and slipped it under his arm. The room he entered was a simple yet pleasant one. He found himself standing on the edge of what looked like a Turkish carpet, dark maroon in colour, the body woven throughout with octagonal motifs of brown, ochre and black held within a double border. Santi hoped he had wiped his boots sufficiently on the doormat outside before entering.

Directly in front of him, in the centre of the carpet, stood a long, low table draped with a crochet lace runner. On his left a door led out, presumably to a balcony. It was flanked on either side by two sleepy looking windows whose half-closed slats were no match for the insistent sunbeams that nosed and pushed their way into the room.

Dark maroon curtains had been pulled halfway in an effort to fend off some of the growing heat outside, without imposing complete darkness inside. A couple of armchairs took up the area in front of the windows, together with a cushioned rocking chair which was occupied by an elderly lady. Before her, taking pride of place, a radio stood in a large, polished wood cabinet that sat approximately four feet high on the floor. Beyond that an open arch gave way to a dining area.

On the right side of the room a comfortable looking sofa with two end tables stood against the wall. A mantelpiece spanning a small fireplace held an ornate gilt alabaster clock flanked by a pair of intricately worked metal vases above which hung a portrait of angels. Sofa, armchairs and rocking chair all boasted antimacassars of delicately crocheted lace. And in the furthest corner stood a Singer sewing machine with a treadle, and a chair.

The old lady in the rocking chair looked up at the visitors. Her face was an older, somewhat crumpled version of the younger lady's. She had long hair that she had obviously washed recently and left loose to dry; and though there were just a few strands of silver gleaming through the faded tresses that must once have been a rich, vibrant auburn like her daughter's, Santi could tell from her careworn face that she was probably somewhere in her eighties. She appeared to have been listening to the news on the radio, and on the floor next to her sat a little girl who immediately jumped to her feet and ran over to the priest.

"Asis Habib! Oh, guess what! We just played a trick on Bajo!" The girl spoke in Arabic and was so eager to tell her story that she did not, at first, pay heed to the stranger standing beside the priest. "She asked Mama to turn on the radio for the news, but instead of doing as she was told, Mama hid behind the radio and pretended to read the news, like this: 'This is Radio Cairo calling Bajo. Bajo Saidé.'" She burst into gales of laughter.

"So, it was you we heard laughing, was it? And what did Bajo have to say?"

"She believed it," Violette giggled, gleefully. "She said, '*Wakhfal Babki*! They know my name! Did you hear that? Bajo Saidé, they're calling me.'"

"Shshsh, Violette, don't be such a chatterbox. Can't you see we have a guest?" Hedeya admonished in Arabic, but her tone belied the reprimand. It served, however, to draw the child's attention to the uniformed figure next to Asis Habib, and she peeked up at him, suddenly shy.

"Who is this?" she asked, retreating behind the old lady's chair.

"He has come from our family in Iraq," Hedeya explained to the girl. Then, leaning towards her mother, she raised her voice slightly. "He has brought news from Samira and Habib."

Hedeya turned and smiled at Santi – and he felt his heart tilt.

He was staring into a face like no other he had seen before! In that single moment he was aware of nothing else. He saw an aquiline nose, high cheekbones and a firm, almost stubborn mouth. He could not be sure whether it was a trick of the filtered light, or the diffused reflection thrown by the rich, dark-auburn hair framing her face that gave her skin the creamy, translucent hue of smooth sun-kissed Egyptian alabaster.

Above all else, Santi was transfixed by those eyes that were looking straight into his; soft brown and fathomless beneath perfectly arched brows, they were filled with an inscrutable emotion he found hard to define. Later, as he came to know her better, he would constantly be startled to catch, within those dark depths, conflicting glimpses of trust mingled with doubt, softness that lay alongside a steely strength, humour penned in by the rigours of hardship and responsibility... and memories...memories of laughter dimmed with tears, of love scoured by pain. It was, altogether, a strong yet sad face etched with a haunting poignancy he found indescribably beautiful. And he was quite unprepared for the effect it had on him.

So, this was Hedeya! She took his breath away! A sensation he had never experienced before ran through his body. It set his heart pounding, in his chest, in his ears. He tried to catch her words.

"This," she was saying, indicating the child, "is my daughter, Violette. And that is my mother, Saidé. We call her Bajo." She lowered her voice slightly. "You will have to speak a little loud to her because she is a bit deaf."

"Humph! My ears hear what they need to hear. What use do they have for the rest?" Bajo extended both gnarled hands towards Santi. "*Itfadal!* Come. Come close, let me see you." Her voice was warm. She peered at this bearer of tidings from afar, eager for his news. "Sit and tell me everything. It has been so many years since we met them. How are they? Tell me how they look."

With an effort, Santi turned his attention away from Hedeya towards her mother. Till now, he had been only vaguely aware of the rest of his surroundings, but ever respectful of his elders, he now tried to focus on what Bajo was saying. It was no good. He could not take his mind off the extraordinary young lady standing beside him; her physical presence was so strong, he could feel the pull from where he stood. And the response it awoke in him left him shaken.

Her short-sleeved, lace-collared frock revealed a slim neck and slender arms, the pale-green material softly skimmed the lines of her firm body. A hint of her perfume wafted across the room to him, stirring something from the past. A memory: the *pukur* opposite Grandfather's house, its summer waters smothered with the pale, glowing blossoms of the lotus, the monsoon air gently spiced with their perfume as the first raindrops touched the unfurled petals.

"Hedeya, turn off the radio," Bajo said in Arabic. "The news this young man brings is far more important than that nonsense on the radio." In English she said, again, "Come, sit and give us all their news."

Santi tore his eyes away from Hedeya with difficulty. Back home, his five sisters often brought their girlfriends to the house, but none he met had ever affected him quite like she did. With his family background, with the prospects his education had to offer, and his physical assets, he had been considered eligible by many a girl's parents who would have welcomed him into their family as a son-in-law; but not a single one of their daughters had aroused these feelings. He actually found it hard to breathe! The sound of his heart was so loud, he was sure it could be heard across the room.

"Would you like some coffee or tea? Maybe something cold?" Hedeya's voice cut through his tumultuous thoughts.

Almost afraid to speak lest his voice betray him, Santi shook his head. He was disconcerted by a strange quivering sensation that had begun in his chest and was spreading rapidly through his body and down to his knees. Unable to trust his legs, he quickly sat down, grateful for the chair Bajo had indicated.

Realising that Hedeya was still waiting for an answer, he cleared his throat. "No, thank you," he said at last – and was surprised his voice sounded as steady and normal as it did. "Please, don't put yourself out. Really, I'm…I'm fine."

*But I'm **not**, his inner voice contradicted. I have this indescribable need to reach out and touch her, and I don't know what to do about it. If only we'd shaken hands when I came in, I could have held her hand in mine – if only for a moment. Maybe just a touch would have been sufficient to quell this feeling...* He hoped his face did not give his thoughts away.

"But tell me," Hedeya's voice sounded perplexed, "how did you find us? We just moved from our old place, and no one knows this address in Rod el Farag." A frown creased her brow. "I have not yet written to Samira with our new address, so it is impossible that she could have given it to you."

"Well, in that case, it must be providential that I mislaid the old address your cousin gave me. You see, when I realised I had lost it somehow, I knew I could not just give up. I could not allow my own carelessness to prevent me keeping the promise I'd made to a great lady like Samira. It would be most irresponsible – especially after the consideration she had shown me and my men. Luckily, I did remember that '*Choubra*' was part of the address, so I determined to do whatever it took to fulfill the request she had entrusted to me; even if it meant a visit to every church in the area to find you. Incredibly, I was saved that effort. As it turned out, Asis Habib's church happened to be the very first one I visited and…well…as you see, he was kind enough to bring me here."

There was an astonished silence in the room. After a long moment, Bajo put her hand on Santi's arm. "Thank you. You are a good man. Your footsteps must have been guided by Someone who knew the way, and we are grateful to Him, and to you."

Asis Habib was relieved. All had turned out well. Yes, mulling over it, he too concluded that such a set of occurrences could be nothing other than a Divine Nudge, a Definite Push actually, into carrying out the Lord's bidding. Now, with Bajo's words, he felt vindicated.

Hedeya stared long and hard at the man sitting in her living room chair. What she saw made an agreeable impression on her. She quickly looked away. Her initial surprise had made her withdraw when first she set eyes on him standing in her doorway; now she felt something else stir within her. It was a feeling that had lain dormant so long she didn't recognise it at first. She knew only that something inexplicable about this man made her acutely aware of his physical presence in her home.

Maybe it was his long, lean physique, his athletic gait and ease of carriage when he moved; it spoke to a kind of quiet, inner strength. She took in his dark, refined features, the sensitive well-defined mouth, strong jawline and straight nose. His dark wavy hair was swept back except where his cap had dislodged a small rebellious curl that fell across his high forehead. Yes, just observing him sent a warm rush through her.

She caught him staring at her, his look so intense he seemed to have read her thoughts. She felt the heat rise to her cheeks. Suddenly aware of her rather crumpled house frock, she put a self-conscious hand up to straighten her hair where it might have strayed out of place. Excusing herself, she went to quickly freshen up.

When she returned, she was astonished to find Violette, normally quite reticent with strangers, perched comfortably on Santi's right knee.

Painfully shy at first, the child had eyed him from a safe distance behind her Grandmother's chair. Who was this man in the soldier's dress? The little girl had never spoken to anyone like him before. Mama had told her always to stay away from the soldiers, but this one seemed to be a friend. He had put his hand on her head when Mama had told him her name, and she had liked how that felt. She could feel the warmth of it even now, and she wondered what it would be like to hold that hand.

Slowly she had emerged from her hiding place and, ducking behind Asis Habib so no one would notice, she had stared long and hard at this unusual visitor, watching his every move as he spoke with Mama and Bajo. He looked like a nice man, she decided, and she really would like to talk to him too. But she was too shy to step out of the shadows and draw attention to herself, even though she longed for it. Wistfully, she had stood there, half-hidden, hoping she would be noticed, and then again, hoping that she would not.

After what seemed like the longest time, her curiosity got the better of her. The nice man in the smart uniform with its row of multicoloured ribbons and brightly polished buttons eventually proved irresistible. She had begun to inch forward, slowly – like she did in the game of 'Statues' they played in school, where a chosen 'den person' would have to close her eyes and loudly spell out L-O-N-D-O-N, LONDON, while the others quickly, very quietly moved forward. And when the den opened her eyes and whipped around, they would all have to stand perfectly still, like statues, because anyone caught moving would be out of the game.

She was good at Statues; it was a favourite game, and she played it now till she was quite close to the man. Slowly she had sidled up to Santi, and when he smiled down at her she had tentatively accepted an invitation to climb into his lap; and there she was now, seemingly quite at ease as she examined his uniform with its shiny brass buttons and insignia. Since she spoke only a few words of English, and he spoke none of the Arabic or French that she knew, the communication between man and child consisted of a few odd words strung together with some well-chosen signs.

Her face rather doubtful, the little girl pointed to herself. "Missy no English." She shook her head, seriously.

Equally serious, Santi pointed to her and replied, "Missy learn English, yes?"

A smile broke across the small face and lit her eyes as Violette pointed to Santi again, "Missy learn you." She settled comfortably into the crook of his arm.

Hedeya felt a deep appreciation for Santi's kindness. Violette was born three months after Hedeya walked away from her husband and, unlike the boys who experienced some sort of father-son relationship, between the girl and her father there was no bond. Nothing. He didn't seem to care much one way or the other. Hedeya knew her daughter missed the affection of a paternal parent and, consequently, she was a diffident little thing who was not sure of herself around too many people. There is much we have to answer for the consequences of our actions, Hedeya thought sadly as she watched her daughter relax comfortably in the arms of a stranger, if only we could foresee where those actions would lead.

Santi and Asis Habib were persuaded to stay for tea.

"Yes, yes, thank you. I am quite parched after that particularly long service this morning," Asis Habib admitted. As for Santi, anything that gave him a reason to remain in Hedeya's company, to watch the way she moved, the way her expressions changed when she spoke…

Afterwards, when it came time to take their leave, he searched frantically for an excuse, any excuse to see her again. Without allowing himself much time to think in case he got cold feet, he blurted out the first thing that came to mind. Could he invite her to the pictures? He saw the look on her face and hurried on. He could get four tickets for the afternoon show at the cinema house he had seen down the road, and they could all go.

Hedeya hesitated a moment, and then shook her head. Violette hadn't been too well, which was why she was home that day, and she was expecting her son Louis who would be walking in any time now with his homework.

The disappointment in her visitor's face was evident and, feeling somewhat guilty, Hedeya tried to soften her refusal a little…maybe they could do it some other time?

But I don't know if there will be another time, Santi thought, hopelessly; and though he hadn't uttered the words, she saw them in his eyes.

Bajo saw them too. "You go," she said to Hedeya in Arabic. "Poor man has probably spent half his leave trying to find us, and after all the trouble he has taken it would be ungrateful not to repay his kindness. He knows no one else in the city. I'm here to take care of Bébé and Louis. There is no reason why you should not go."

"Bajo! What are you saying! How will it look? He is a soldier, a stranger. I know, he has been very kind, but you have always said…"

"Yes, yes, under the sheikh's hat sometimes there is a monkey." She glanced over at Santi. "But, does the Bible not tell us also to be kind to strangers? Remember, one might just turn out to be an angel. And this one is not a stranger; he is a family friend. One can tell he is well brought up, decent, and he has Asis Habib's blessing otherwise he would not be here. Go. God knows, it will do you good too," Bajo ended firmly.

And so, it was decided; that afternoon Santi would take Hedeya to the pictures. He left, feeling elated.

Until now he had not given much credence to the English expression of 'walking on air'. It had made no sense before. What a fool he'd been! It made perfect sense now.

You know you're grinning like a jackass. It was that persistently oracular voice somewhere inside, always willing to air an opinion and pull him up short. But Santi would have none of it. *And what the heck is wrong with that?* was his response, as he strode down the street, much pleased with the outcome of the day.

There was no argument, it felt extremely good to be alive. Who would have guessed that out of the blue, a chance meeting would have spun his whole world around! The feeling was euphoric. He hadn't a thought beyond the present, or a care whether he stood on his head or his heels. Now if that wasn't worth grinning about then, really, he had no idea what was!

Anyway, hadn't Father often advocated that standing on one's head did a man a power of good? *Now you are being silly!* Oh, I know, I know, Father was referring to his daily yoga, of course, not this 'devil may care' feeling that had swept all before it except the one thought: Hedeya! She made him, Santi, believe in Fate, in Lady Luck, in the Impossible, in – dare he say it – in Miracles!

Yes, he was head over heels and revelling in it! Good old Father, he was right, it did do a man a power of good to turn the world upside down now and then! A sudden picture popped into his mind's eye, stopping him in his tracks. Clear as you please, he saw Father, solemn as ever, regular as clockwork, in a perfect yogic headstand as was his wont every morning.

Santi's grin widened. "And, if it's good enough for Father, it's darn well good enough for me!" he declared. And he laughed out loud at the absurd trend his thoughts had taken.

"Effendi?" A passer-by addressed him, uncertainly. He had been observing the tall young man in uniform, as he approached. He seemed to be in very good spirits, smiling and striding along – which no one should fault him for, certainly. But then the foreigner had come up to him and laughed. *What could be so amusing,* the man wondered nervously, looking down to examine his attire. *No, nothing wrong there. What then? Could there be something on his tarboosh?* He put up a hesitant hand to check his hat; *all was well there too.* Then, there could be only one other explanation! *Surely the soldier was not...he did not seem to be drunk...although it had looked, just now, as if...*

Keeping his distance, the man enquired a trifle dubiously, "You… you are well, yes?"

"What? Oh yes, I am very well. Very well *indeed*." Santi smiled happily. He drew a deep breath, filling his lungs with air as though he were drinking in the elixir of life. Yes, it *was* good to be alive! Alive, and young…and full of hope. In fact, he couldn't remember when he had felt more stout of heart or confident of mind. And it filled him with a warm cordiality towards the whole world which, at that moment, seemed manifest in the kind, decent, perplexed little man standing beside him.

"Believe me, I've never been better!" Santi approached the fellow and shook him vigorously by the hand. "You are a good man, sir, and today is a good day. Thank you. I am glad we met."

"Met? But…we have not…I don't…" the astonished man called after the receding figure, his outstretched hand still lingering in midair where Santi had left it. After a moment he shook his head, shrugged, and continued on his way. Certainly, there had been some very peculiar goings on ever since these foreign soldiers had blown into town with all their drinking and roistering. To be fair, this one had not seemed the drinking or roistering sort; nevertheless, he *had* been walking down the street, *alone*, and one could have *sworn* he seemed to be talking to himself. And *laughing*! So how else could one describe such behaviour but strange? Very strange indeed! It was getting so, one hardly recognised one's own city anymore! Ah well, the man sighed, *Inshallah*, God willing, this war would be over soon, and all would return to business as usual once again.

CHAPTER TWENTY-THREE

The Spell Of Hathor

Give me a scroll of verse, a little wine,
With half a loaf to fill thy needs and mine;
And with the desert sand our resting place,
For ne'er a Sultan's kingdom would we pine.

– Omar Khayyam, *Rubaiyat of Omar Khayyam*

STEPPING OUT OF THE taxi, the tall, dark young man dressed in a Captain's uniform of the British Indian Army held open the door for his companion. The lady in the silk dress got out and stood beside him. Her dress of dark silk was patterned all over with tiny sprigs of orange and cream flowers. It was one of her own creations and draped elegantly along the lines and curves of her body. A necklace, alternating mother of pearl and multicoloured mosaic beads fashioned from opaque Venetian glass, graduated around her neck, and she carried a tawny two-tone handbag that matched her shoes. The palette of colours caught the autumn shades in her hair and did wondrous things for her complexion and eyes. They made a striking couple as they entered the foyer of the Cinema Dolly, chosen not so much as a venue for seeing "The Thief of Baghdad", as for its convenient proximity to the lady's house.

Hedeya was not altogether pleased at the number of curious heads that turned to stare at them. This was a middle-class neighbourhood where a woman seen out with a foreign soldier might well give rise to certain rumours regarding her character. Of course, her escort was no ordinary 'johnny' – a disparaging name reserved for the rank and file soldiery of the British Army, who regularly queued up in The Berka for a quick encounter with those Handmaids of Hathor (a snide reference to the goddess of love). No, it was plain to see – as plain as the nose on any busy-body's face! – here was an officer and a gentleman. And surely *her* proper demeanor must be apparent to every pair of inquisitive eyes!

Be that as it may, her visitor had piqued the curiosity of her neighbours when he arrived to fetch her that afternoon. He was wearing the uniform of the occupying forces, and that in itself was sufficient to cast doubt on a lady's reputation. The last thing she needed, she thought with exasperation, was to complicate her life by exciting silly gossip!

Well, civility demanded a show of gratitude for the trouble he had taken to find them and deliver Samira's message as promised. After this, should he ask her out again, she would not be remiss in tactfully refusing; and hopefully he would show good breeding by understanding her situation. That, then, would be the end of that.

Inside, the hall was filled with shadows and the almost inaudible, somnolent whirr of numerous *marwaha*. Unlike the Metro on Sharah Suleman Pasha – the only cinema house in the city with air conditioning – here at the Dolly these fans still circulated the air made fragrant with a hint of rose water intermittently sprayed to relieve the rather stuffy atmosphere. Cinema Dolly had another advantage: between shows its innovative ceiling could open to the heavens to allow in sunlight, or starlight, to refresh the hall.

Now, the cool shadows in the auditorium brought a modicum of relief from the outside heat and hustle of the city. In the dimness, Santi held Hedeya's elbow lightly, guiding her to their seats. Aware of his proximity and the firm, faintly proprietary feel of his hand on her arm, she was somewhat flustered to find it both pleasing and disquieting at the same time.

As it happened, "The Thief of Baghdad" proved fitting to the occasion in that the film married the charm of India to the romance of the Middle East. The star of this magical Technicolour fantasy was Selar Shaik Sabu, a young boy from India recently discovered by Hollywood.

"In real life," Santi informed her, "he used to be the Maharaja of Mysore's *mahout*, a keeper of the royal elephants."

"Elephants are bigger than camels, yes?" Hedeya was curious. "And this Maharaja, does he ride them? Is he the ruler of your country under the British King – like King Farouk, here, in Egypt?"

"Yes," Santi replied, with a laugh, "elephants are bigger, and heavier. But in my country, we have many small kingdoms, or states, each ruled by its own maharaja or *nawab*. The British King is known as the Emperor of India, and under him each maharaja, each nawab, rules his own state and subjects. They live in palaces and, yes, they keep elephants used for ceremonial rides, like other kings keep horses. So, you see, the headkeeper of the elephants is of some importance, as was Sabu, working with him and the royal elephants."

It all fit; Hedeya recalled that not so long ago she and Bajo had taken the children to see the film, 'Sabu, the Elephant Boy' – a Rudyard Kipling story in which young Sabu had seemed a natural with the elephants. The picture had been much enjoyed, and the whole family had been thoroughly charmed by the lively actor.

Now, once again, Sabu was endearing as the wily orphan Abu who eked out his living as a thief in Baghdad – as had his father, his grandfather, and his great- grandfather before him. Brimful with characters essential to a fantastic magical extravaganza – a beautiful princess and her prince, a villainous vizier, a genie, a flying carpet and, last but not least, a mysterious goddess with an 'All Seeing Eye' hidden away on a mountain top that reached the sky – the fairytale was brought to a romantically fitting end:

> *"Where have you come from?" the princess asked the prince.*
> *"From the other side of time," he replied.*
> *"How long have you been searching?" she wanted to know.*
> *"Since time began," he answered.*
> *"How long will you stay?" she wondered.*
> *"Till the end of time," he promised.*

And so, as it should, good triumphed over evil, the prince married the princess, and everyone received their just deserts. It was all fun and fancy – just the thing, Hedeya decided, the children would enjoy. Even she had found the light-hearted tale a pleasant interlude from the responsibilities that weighed so heavily on her these days; they seemed to have shifted somehow, leaving her almost uplifted. A temporary reprieve brought on, no doubt, by the frivolity of the movie with its happy-ever-after ending. It did not occur to her that her companion, in fact, might have more to do with her feelings than she was willing to acknowledge.

Later, at home, while recounting the story to Bajo and Violette, Hedeya had admitted with a somewhat self-conscious laugh that something about Sabu's adventures had put her in mind of her escort. The moment the remark escaped her lips, she had been embarrassed. It was not like her to indulge in such imaginative nonsense, and she hurried to explain it had nothing whatsoever to do with any similarity of feature – other than a swarthy complexion perhaps. Of course, the other thing in common was their country of birth. And then, there was that youthful determination with which both men seemed set to best life's problems no matter the odds. (After all, most anyone having lost her address would have given up their quest, would they not!)

Yes, indeed, the comparison may well have been prompted by the rather quixotic farings of these two men, venturing forth to fulfill promises with the unshakeable belief and optimism of youth, while mayhem and peril abounded in the world around them. Of course, Santi's twenty-seven years could hardly be considered all that young! It just seemed so from her perspective of being older.

Their six-year disparity in age had come to light whilst exchanging small pleasantries during intermission; inconsequential little nothings Hedeya believed would safely skim the surface without causing too many ripples. But words sometimes have an unpredictable way of prying open a small chink, like a chink in a window. And such a window might eventually allow for a surprise intrusion as easily as any unlatched door. All it would take is a single unguarded moment, and before you knew quite how or when, someone will have breached the bolts and walked right into your life; and without so much as a by-your-leave, you find they have pulled up a seat and made themselves comfortable in that innermost place of sanctity where you hide your private feelings and thoughts. Suddenly you have an uninvited squatter! Oh yes, Hedeya knew full well, squatters of that kind meant grief and were to be avoided at all costs!

Over time, experience had taught her to exercise care and a certain proficiency in barricading intruders from trespassing into the private places in her life. And so, she had tried to fill the space between Santi and herself with polite tidbits of conversation when, without warning, the 'age thing' popped out of nowhere. Unaccountably, it pried open that tiny chink in her guard. Hedeya had been unaware of this at the time, and it would lead to her undoing.

Why, he was younger than she had believed! His uniform and his serious, rather formal demeanour made him seem older than his years. But, really, there was nothing of concern here! He was young, somewhat adrift and lonely. Away from home and surrounded by strangers he was merely looking for some pleasant company. Young, adrift and lonely – the dangerous appeal of such a combination eluded her even as it spoke to that nurturing feminine instinct usual to women. A small red flag went unnoticed; that was her first mistake.

Slightly less guarded now, she had allowed herself to relax a little. As discreetly as possible, she studied him. She had to admit his courteous manners were pleasing; and by every indication he was, as Bajo had observed, well-bred, a person of honourable character. All things considered, she decided, he was a casual visitor who would hardly pose any real threat to the order of her life. With that she began to feel more at ease. Her head start in years gave Hedeya the misconceived notion her experience would chart a safe path through the afternoon. She had made her second mistake.

She continued her observation quietly. There was no denying he was a fine example of young manhood – good strong physique and sensitive, well-defined features. There was a pronounced air of dependability and purpose as well, unusual in a person of his years. His face reflected a virtuousness of mind and heart – she guessed he was still pristine, untrammelled. Had he known many women? Any women? She decided he was probably without much experience. The notion was strangely intriguing. And the more she considered it, the more unaccountably diverting she found it to be.

Prudently, she had pulled her thoughts quickly back to safety. There was no need to go wandering down *that* path she told herself sternly. After all, it was up to her to set the guidelines of propriety. Yes, and then she would make sure their association proceeded to a sensible and timely conclusion.

Her additional years instilled a sense of security she really should have questioned. If she had, she might have realised the contrariness of her thoughts was bound to end in a muddle: after all, how did one steer a steady course when every so often one's thoughts veered, unbidden, into something much like quicksand? It was here she made her third mistake, resulting in the unfounded belief she had control of the situation. In actual fact, all the while the situation was inexorably changing her destiny. Persuading herself she was perfectly capable of handling things, she ignored the warning tug of restless stirrings that should have made her aware the 'chink' in her window was about to open onto dangerously uncharted territory where, suddenly, the whole balance of their relationship would shift.

***

WHEN THE PICTURE ENDED, they emerged from the dim recesses of the cinema house. Despite the day having shrugged off the heavy heat of afternoon, its swirling remnants crept beneath their clothes and seeped up against their skin. But the blessed cool of evening wouldn't be long in coming now; and already the shuttered city was stirring in anticipation.

A slight breeze had picked up, heralding that welcome respite from the day's heat. Standing beside her, Santi saw it gently blow through Hedeya's hair, lifting it to reveal the strong profile of her face. It caught her frock, rippling it softly against the curves of her body, the length of her legs. The sight mesmerised him. She was beautiful! He couldn't take his eyes off her, and he knew he had to think quickly of some way to stop her walking out of his life!

He turned, impetuously, "Would you care to have dinner with me? I would very much like us to spend the evening together."

Hedeya hesitated. This was not something she had foreseen; his previous invitation had not included dinner, and her initial response was to decline. But how did one decline such a civil request without sounding ungracious? And, anyway, did she actually want to refuse dinner with him?

"Well, I..."

Sensing her ambivalence, he forestalled her. "Maybe you could suggest a place? I leave the choice to you. This is your city, and I'm entirely in your hands."

She glanced up at him, still hesitating. He was watching her intently. She realised he had just confirmed her earlier thoughts – he was at a loss in this unknown place. Bajo had said that he quite likely had foregone the company of his associates in order to deliver Samira's message to them. And now, he was at a loose end. He probably had a few short hours before he returned to the desert – and he found himself among strangers with nowhere to spend the rest of his evening.

She felt she bore some responsibility for his predicament. Besides which, his eagerness made it difficult to dash his hopes! What's more, she had enjoyed his company so far, hadn't she? And dinner with him did sound rather nice. Surely there could be no harm in it! Moreover, what had Bajo said about strangers turning out to be angels? She pondered his request for a moment, and then it came to her. Of course! She knew the perfect place!

"Your friends, you said they went to the Pyramids this morning, but you did not go because you came to find me. *W'Allah*! That should not be. Let me make up for it. You cannot come to Cairo and leave without seeing the Pyramids and the Sphinx!"

Santi breathed a sigh of relief. A pleased grin lit his face. "I would like that, if you would," he said, hailing a passing taxi. "Is there a restaurant in the area we might go to?"

"The Mena House. I think you will enjoy it very much."

Of course! Major Sansom had recommended the very place the night before. Really, things couldn't have worked out better if he had planned it, Santi thought, gratified. He helped Hedeya into the taxi, her hand soft and pliant in his, and got in after her. He listened to her give the driver directions in Arabic, her voice lending the language a lilting quality, and then they settled back for the nine-to-ten-mile drive through the early evening traffic. Anticipation of the evening ahead in Hedeya's company brought a warm rush of pleasure he was content to sit back and enjoy.

Approaching the Khedive Ismail Bridge, they passed the two majestic stone lions that flanked it on either side. The bridge took them partway over the Nile to the eastern side of Gezira Island.

"This bridge," Hedeya explained, "is named after the royal house of Khedive Abbas Hilmi II. Once upon a time, many years ago, they owned all this area. Now it has become the residence of many foreign families, as well as some well-to-do Egyptians."

As they drove across the island Santi saw large, elegant mansions set amidst well manicured, flower-filled gardens. Gezira was a halcyon retreat from the chaotic hustle and bustle of the city. Reaching the western side of the island, they once again crossed the Nile via another bridge.

"The Pont des Anglais," Hedeya informed him. "This bridge will take us to the Pyramids Road. It has many eucalyptus trees and leads to Giza which is known as the Gateway to the Western Desert.

"Kobri Badia," the taxi driver threw over his shoulder, and rattled off something at top speed in Arabic.

"Yes, of course," Hedeya laughed and translated for Santi. "He is reminding me that locals have a different name for the Pont des Anglaise. Because of a nightclub nearby owned by Madam Badia – very popular for belly dancers – the people of Cairo, they re-named the bridge Kobri Badia. And also, the Khedive Ismail Bridge, that first bridge we crossed, it has become known as Kobri Abbas. It is a joke, two bridges like two lovers – one of royal blood and the other a dance girl – always a sad story. *Anta betefham?* You understand?"

Santi chuckled. "Yes, I do – the romantic fairytale of the Prince and the Performer, the King and the Commoner. Star-crossed lovers usually make for stories with tragic endings."

———•◦•———

TUCKED INTO THE EDGE of the desert, almost at the feet of the three Great Pyramids of Giza, and guarded by the enigmatic Sphinx itself, was the establishment known as Mena House. Once the hunting lodge of Khedive Ismail, it was named after Menes, first king of Egypt, as inscribed in the famous Temple of Abydos, a place dedicated to the worship of Osiris, god of the netherworld.

Over the years Mena House had passed through various hands,

English and Australian, as evidenced by the Victorian embellishments that had been added to the original Moorish décor. With its well-appointed reading rooms and fireplaces, its verandahs and terraces all gazing out towards the Great Pyramids, Mena House lay with gracious elegance in its five-thousand-year-old setting. Now, surrounded by beautiful gardens, tennis courts and croquet lawns, and complemented by a large swimming pool and golf course, it was a beckoning oasis of luxury.

The hotel orchestra was playing the latest popular dance music as they entered the Al Rubaiyat, a sumptuous, domed dining room with pearl arabesques and *mashrabiyas*. A fair-haired English rose was crooning a pretty little love song about partings, rememberings and longings, while a few couples circled the dimly lit dance floor. Santi noted several uniforms. He looked them over but could make out none from his contingent.

Settling them at a table in the corner, the maitre d' took their order for drinks – a tall cool lemonade for Hedeya, and for Santi an ice-cold Stella, the local beer.

"Are you sure?" Santi pressed. "Wouldn't you prefer something else, something a little stronger?"

Hedeya shook her head. "I don't drink. Thank you."

The band struck up a waltz. Santi stood up and extended a hand to her. "May I have the pleasure of this dance?" His voice was gentle. His eyes, resting on her face, were soft.

Looking up into that eager young face, that steady, intent gaze holding her own, a faint alarm bell went off somewhere inside Hedeya's head, and she held back – for a single, brief moment.

As she laid her hand in his and felt his fingers close firmly over her own, a small shiver ran up her arm and through her body. She rose slowly, and held by his gaze, she allowed him to lead her to the dance floor. *He is pleasantly tall,* she observed incidentally, as she slipped into his arms and her feet fell in step with his. He danced surprisingly well, his guidance easy to follow.

Gliding across the softly lit floor in the arms of this man she had met only a few short hours before, Hedeya was aware of a stirring somewhere deep within her…new yet integrally familiar. She felt her heart quicken, felt her blood respond, sending a warm flush spreading through her body, reaching every part of her, pouring through like liquid honey…unsettling, uplifting, spinning her head and her heart, whirling away all thought, all rationale, making her almost dizzy. The music was soft, the words of the song floated about her.

Tell me I may always dance
The Anniversary Waltz with you.
Tell me this is real romance,
An anniversary dream come true.

She stumbled, and immediately his arm tightened protectively about her.

"Steady," he murmured softly into her hair.

She laid her face briefly against his shoulder as she balanced herself. It felt good to hear his heartbeat, strong and hard in his chest – almost as though it were beating deep within her body, indiscernible from her own heart. Her body moved easily with his. She leaned in towards him, just a little, her forehead resting against the small, insistent pulse-throb in his throat.

Her feelings were in discord, her thoughts in disarray. He was younger than she, and still much of a stranger, yet he made her feel safe, the way her father had so long ago. She believed herself settled in the life she'd made, but now, the comforting strength of his arms as he held her close, his firm body, reminded her how alone she had been these past years. She knew this would be the first and last time she would see him…and yet…

With a wisp of a sigh, hardly more than a breath, she allowed herself to settle a little closer within the circle of his arms. Surrounded by the warm, vibrant feel of him, she gave in to the moment, to the pleasure flowing through her as the music swirled about them…

Let this be the anthem to our future years,
Through millions of smiles and a few little tears…

———•◆•———

A HALF MOON HUNG over the Western Desert like the silver eye of Thoth, that wise Scribe of the Gods who was Lord of the Moon and Master of Time. Renowned no less as the Spinner of Magic, he rode across the ebony sky he shared with Hathor, Lady of the Stars, Goddess of Love. Together they kept silent vigil above the dark silhouette of the pyramids. This was their world, this chiaroscuro expanse of night shadows and moonlight, mystical in its sense of eternal timelessness, sacred in its obeisance to the dead.

After dinner Santi hired a couple of horses, and they rode through the moonlit night scented with the perfume of jasmine from the hotel gardens. The vast desert sands had turned to shimmering quicksilver, enchanted under the spell of the Moon God's eye. And above them, Hathor's glittering night sky danced, her dusk laden veils woven finely with moonbeams, and sequined with a million twinkling stars.

The music from Mena House began to fade into the distance, and with it, all vestige of that world; and though it was but a short ride to the ancient monuments, it was a timeless passage from new to old, from present to past, and soon all sound was stilled in the deep, plush silence of the desert, broken only by the jingle of harness and horse bell.

And then, there they stood, the mighty pyramids of Khufu, Khefhre and Menkauré. Looming shadows at first, towering into the giant gatekeepers of heaven. Planted firmly in the unmeasured sands of the desert, reaching from this mortal world of ours to that of the gods, beyond the starry firmament which bears their feet and bowers our heads. Far in the distance could be seen the glittering carpet of lights that was Cairo.

Despite the sandbags and stones protecting the Sphinx from an itinerant bomb – an uneasy reminder of their war-torn present – there was a haunting, boundless sense of the infinity out here that was beyond the scope of words; it could only be felt, within and without. Like a rip in the fabric of time, the world around them had dissolved and slipped away as they seemed to step back through centuries. Standing in the presence of this kind of history was like balancing at the very edge of time, staring into that immeasurable expanse, that great void, the face of eternity.

Hedeya spoke softly. "It is said here in Egypt, 'Time laughs at all things, but the Pyramids laugh at Time.' This," she gestured towards the largest of the pyramids, "is the pyramid of Khufu, one of the seven wonders of the ancient world…the oldest, they say. The others, all, are lost – the Hanging Gardens of Babylon, the Pharos lighthouse of Alexandria. But this one, it remains, it stands through time."

Santi stared in awed silence. The enormity of achievement quite beggared belief, even by modern-day standards. Yet, there it rose, overpowering and irrefutable, the majesty of this colossus towering above them, proclaiming itself to the heavens. And it had been built by man, not machine, thousands of years ago. *How* had it been done?

In silent reverence, he paid homage to the souls upon whose ground he stood. *I stand in the presence of Eternity, and though it speaks to my soul I am overwhelmed, for it is beyond all comprehension.*

Hedeya watched him, a tall lean figure beside her, his face soft with shadow-thoughts of…what, she wondered. He was so close she could feel the warmth of his body in the cool night. His physical presence was palpable, its pull on her so strong, if she moved an inch, took a deep breath even, their bodies would find each other in the darkness.

"Such majesty to commemorate death," he muttered softly, at last breaking the silence.

"No," Hedeya replied. "No, not death, but life. It is to…how do you say it…to commemorate life. Death is only a door through which you pass into the next life. That is what this pyramid is, a door through which the Pharaoh passed from this mortal world to the immortal."

Santi nodded. Of course! It made perfect sense. The pyramids were a portal to that other world beyond and, as such, they were a declaration of life, not death. These gigantic monuments were symbolic, not of an end, but of a beginning. The living had it all wrong!

"So, those ancients did not build these architectural goliaths as tombs for their dead at all. They built them as resting places to prepare for the long journey into the afterlife; as lych gates for their spirits to pass through on the road towards a different dimension."

He was struck by the similarity between the beliefs of the ancient Egyptians and those of his own country – the belief in reincarnation. And yet, there was an inherent difference. Old Egyptians believed they would be reincarnated as immortals among the gods, whereas Hindus believed they would be reincarnated into the mortal world, time after time, till they achieved the purity of soul that would allow them passage to, and union with, the Divine Spirit. A Hindu believed he must strive for immortality, and a single lifetime was insufficient to earn such a reward. Santi thought of another monument built to proclaim the eternal, a pathway from the mortal to the immortal.

He spoke aloud. "In a time long ago, in my country, there was a Moghul Emperor, Shah Jehan, and his beautiful Empress, Noor Jehan. When she died, the bereaved Emperor was stricken with a grief beyond words, so he carved his love in marble, an indelible message, dedicated forever to his beloved queen. He built the Taj Mahal , and on its arched gateway he welcomed their re-union, '*Enter thou my Paradise*', proclaiming his undying devotion for all eternity. The white marble walls were carved like fine lace, with gems of agate and carnelian and jade, even precious ruby, emerald and sapphire. So poignantly was his passion captured, even when he was old and blind, they continued to shine like the lovelight that once had filled his eyes when they looked upon his Queen. Even now, with the precious gems gone, like the eyes of the blind Emperor, the pure white marble still glows, undimmed by years, especially on a moonlit night like this!"

"How very beautiful!" Hedeya had seen a picture of the Taj Mahal once, in a magazine. At the time it had been just that, a picture of a grand old building. Now, as she listened raptly to its history, his heritage, it came to life for her. "Such a great love, so much sadness too. It is good that a thing of beauty should speak its message through time so that it is not forgotten."

Santi nodded. "People think of it as a mausoleum but, like the pyramids, it is so much more than that. I believe they are both symbols of hope – the one of abiding love and the other of everlasting life. Each in its own way transcends the boundaries of mortality with a promise of eternity."

Santi paused for a moment, his expression pensive, before continuing softly. "These grand edifices that have defied time are the long-ago language spoken by kings and queens; and we hear them, even today, reminding us of those great personages who once lived and dreamed, who people our history books today." He looked up at the silent, star-studded heavens. "But what of the humble builder, or the soldier upon whose sacrifice the glory of those kings and commanders is built, the widow who has given her mite, the farmer who grew their food...should they remain voiceless? They lay the foundation for the mighty ones, these unknown people with their unremarkable lives and unacknowledged deaths...how many, I wonder, lie buried here...forgotten."

The impending battle in all its uncertainty was on his mind. He looked down at her, his face wistful, and wondered what the future had in store for him. When he spoke again, his voice was reflective.

"What of lesser mortals such as you and me? What of our dreams and hopes? Do you not reach for the stars? Will my love not measure as great, as boundless as theirs? Who will speak of our legacy, I wonder?"

He fell into quiet contemplation, remembering sadly those of his countrymen recently buried with so little ceremony, so far from home. They might not be the Pharaohs of Egypt or the Moghuls of India, but they did deserve better. There was no voice for the toiling masses. History, it would seem, needs must be left to the illustrious few. And they, he thought a tinge bitterly, have neither heart nor voice enough to reach the little places, to speak for those who cannot be heard.

He felt a shiver run through Hedeya. The moonwashed world around them had long given up the heat of day, and a chill had set in as was usual at night in the desert. Santi quickly unbuckled the leather belt of his Sam Brown and removed the jacket of his Service Dress. Beneath this he wore a light cotton shirt. Leaning over her, he draped his jacket carefully across her shoulders. He could smell the perfume from her hair and skin. He breathed deeply, and felt a sudden, impetuous desire to hold her in his arms, to pull her close. Taken unawares, the urgency of his feelings left him weak and unsteady. He pulled away, bewildered by the demands of these new emotions coursing through him.

Hedeya was grateful for his consideration. She had not dressed for an evening in the desert and was unprepared for the cold night air. As she brought the garment close, feeling the weight of the brightly polished insignia and buttons, she became aware that Santi's arm had lingered momentarily while settling the jacket about her shoulders; and out there in the clear, clean desert air, the faint masculine smell of his body mingling with that of brasso, starched drill and polished leather was as pleasurable as the warmth from his jacket against her skin.

Her cheek brushed the rough cotton of his shirt and she paused; then, without further thought, she drew a little closer, resting her face for a short impulsive moment against the protective curve of his shoulder. A tingle, like a tiny electric shock ran through her, making her catch her breath. It was then, in that restful little niche, that she acknowledged for the first time the sound of that faint alarm she thought she had imagined earlier. Barely audible, it was like the slow, rusty creak of a long unused door, opening. And if it was, she was in trouble!

She drew back, flustered! She had, unwittingly it seemed, allowed a small crack in a window that now threatened to swing perilously wide upon its casement; a window, she began to perceive, that was starting to appear, more and more like that door she had shut so firmly, so long ago…a door about to permit entry to the knock of peril sounding in her head. She felt a stir in the air about her. Was it imagined, or was it a warning…that soft touch, light as a breath… could it be the treacherous breath of Hathor she had just felt?

CHAPTER TWENTY-FOUR
On The Threshold

Ah, fill the Cup...what boots it to repeat
How Time is slipping underneath our feet:
Unborn Tomorrow, and dead Yesterday,
Why fret about them if Today be sweet!

– Omar Khayyam, *Rubaiyat of Omar Khayyam*

APRIL 25 SAW THE Battalion prepare to entrain for Mersa Matruh, a small white seaside village some three hundred miles into the desert northwest of Cairo. Subadar Khagu Pun, Jemadar Shibjang and Jemadar Manbahadur remained behind with eighty other ranks from where reinforcements would later be pulled as and when it became necessary.

With them, Mullah was to remain behind while Hirasing Limbu was to proceed to war with the Battalion. The parting, which was deemed necessary under the circumstances, was done with a heavy heart on both sides; but Hirasing Limbu took comfort in the knowledge that his four-legged friend would be far safer behind the lines in the company of Jemadar Shibjang, who swore on all he held holy that he would tend to the goat's needs and care for him as though he were his own son.

Santi too came to say farewell, and the communion between doctor and one-time patient was an emotional one. The man petted the animal fondly – *stay well, old friend, may the grass be green wherever you roam, and your beard grow long and free of tangles* – and Mullah nuzzled the gentle, familiar hand with reciprocal affection – *may the benison of those you have served keep you safe from harm, my benefactor, may each kind word to those you have helped return to you as a blessing.* Words were not necessary, and when they took leave of each other Santi was grateful for the silent blessing he knew he had received.

The train took the Battalion as far as Musheifa. The single-track railway ran, for the most part, parallel to the Via Balbia, the coastal road presently bustling with unending convoys of transport carrying fuel, water, and food, running nose to nose with supply lorries, ammunition trucks, tanks, anti-aircraft and anti-tank guns.

The sight of this massive movement thrusting and grinding towards the frontlines engendered simultaneous feelings, both of power and impuissance. The colossal size, the overpowering noise, and the overwhelming might of this monster, growling and churning its way through the desert filled one with a sense of invincibility as well as the feeling of being swept up inexorably, and propelled towards an inevitable fate beyond one's control.

This was an army gathering for war, no doubt a mirror-image of the one preparing itself on the other side of the barbed wire on No Man's Land that separated them. As enemy fought enemy, these twin forces seemed to have taken on a life of their own, growing into a defiant, bloated menace, insatiably devouring all in its path. And now, everyone and everything was grist for its mill, fuel that was required in ever larger quantities to stoke its restive fires – war.

At Musheifa they loaded up and trucked south to Hamra, not far from Fort Maddalena on the Libyan border. The Fort had been captured from the Italians some time before. From here, their eventual destination was a defended area called the Kennels. There they were to join their new brigade, 10 Indian Infantry Brigade of the 5th Indian Division, under command of Brigadier C.H. Boucher and Major-General H.R. Briggs, respectively. Upon arrival they found their brother battalions in the new brigade were to be the 2nd Highland Light Infantry (HLI) and the 4/10 Baluch Regiment; and their new brigade belonged to XXX Corps which, together with XIII Corps, would collectively come to be known as the British Eighth Army.

Auchinlek, preparing for the impending battle against Rommel in the Western Desert, had dispatched Lieutenant General Neil Ritchie from HQ in Cairo to take command of Eighth Army. Ritchie was headquartered at Gambut in Libya, a sandy airstrip a little south of the coast, approximately three hundred some miles west of Cairo.

Away from the amenities and comforts of their homeland, the British, as is their wont, did what they could to make their alien surroundings more familiar. Well-known names such as Picadilly, Charing Cross, Knightsbridge and Hyde Park lent a touch of home to their temporary abode. Meanwhile, further west, beyond these places with nostalgic-sounding names, the battle line at Gazala was being drawn.

Warfare in the desert was usually fluid by nature. It took on the drifting quality of the desert sands. Its frontlines, mercurial as quicksilver, shifted, stretched, fragmented and flowed as changing tactics dictated. This time, however, the Allied frontline defence was an immutable forty-mile swath of land-mines laced with barbed wire that stretched across the Western Desert, from the coastal town of Gazala in the north to Bir Hacheim, the Well of the Wise, in the south. Bounded by the Mediterranean at its northern end and the intractable Sand Sea to the south, the Gazala Line was guarded at various points by keeps that came to be known as 'boxes'.

Each 'box' housed a brigade and was a mile or two square in size. Encircled first with barbed wire, and then with mines, it was fortified with guns bristling out in all four directions much like the quills of a vigilant porcupine. A pathway through the mines allowed for entrance and exit by day. At stand to, by dawn light every morning, mines were meticulously cleared to ensure paths of safe passage for the occupants of the box and their allies; at nightfall the mines were laid once again, with equal diligence, sealing the paths against possible marauding enemy patrols. Keeping vigil in the areas between these 'boxes' were the tanks and guns of the armoured brigades. Beyond, to the west of this forty-mile-long fortification, Rommel's armies were preparing for battle as well.

This, then, was the final line drawn in the sand between these two combatants who were readying themselves for a conflict that would decide the fate, not only of North Africa, but of the rest of the war. Quite simply, if the Allies lost Egypt and the Suez Canal, then India and the Far East would be in jeopardy, as would the oil from the Middle East. The loss of its eastern colonies would pose a severe blow and, worse still, without oil the Allies would not have the wherewithal to continue fighting.

The Brigade's sojourn at the Kennels was a time of intense training. They had eighteen days to become proficient in the handling and laying of mines, the use of the sun-compass for desert navigation, and in the formation of Jock Columns (devised by the late Lieutenant Jock Lewes) to facilitate the hit-and-run desert warfare waged so successfully by the SAS units; they had to become familiar with the new, much heavier 30-ton lorries and, above all, learn tank warfare which was pivotal to fighting in the desert. They had no experience whatsoever in these fields. There were unfamiliar map codes and wireless systems to be mastered, flag signals for communication between vehicles on the run, and training on the new 2-pounder anti-tank guns recently issued.

There was hardly time to breathe with all the exercises and training to get through, but despite the exhausting regimen, Santi found his mind preoccupied with thoughts of a very different nature.

Fate had thrown him a curveball, so unexpected, the emotional upheaval had sent him reeling. Completely unprepared for the strength and impact of the feelings Hedeya had aroused in him, he had hoped a little time and space would help put things into perspective. He had spent the past few days trying his darndest to regain some semblance of emotional and mental equilibrium. But, no matter how hard he tried, during the day, his thoughts kept skipping back to that day in Cairo, to his companion with the unfathomable brown eyes; and neither was there let-up at night when he slipped in and out of a fitful sleep, his dreams haunted by the soft perfume from her auburn hair.

Then, out of the blue, a week after their arrival at the Kennels, fate intervened once more. Santi discovered some of his supplies had gone astray leaving him decidedly short on morphine. Cursing under his breath at this last-minute hitch he set off to find the Adjutant.

"Confound it, Doc," Ben grumbled, "you're the second irate customer I've had this morning. I've just done dealing with Willie and now this!"

"Oh? What's up with him?"

"Well, the long and the short of it is we've lost our 2nd in Command *and* had our personal luggage mishandled."

"Don't tell me they've lost the whole jingbang?"

"Not lost exactly, just re-routed, which is bloody bad enough! To begin with the old man was not the jolliest after receiving Fullerton's transfer orders back to India. He's been up in arms, quite fraught that he's lost a first-class 2-IC. Granted, he knows Strickland will make a damned efficient 2nd in Command, but that ain't the point. It means having to shake up the ranks just as the show's about to start. Then, to top it all, we discovered this other bloody snafu with our luggage, and – Christ, did he cut up rough!"

"I can imagine! How the hell did they manage to bungle the job! Have they located our stuff yet?" Surely, if misplaced, there was still a chance their luggage might be retrieved, wasn't there?

Ben shook his head in disgust. "It's been located right enough! The whole damn lot's *here* instead of in storage! You'll recall, all officers were required to pack their surplus *jithi* before leaving Qassasin and the ruddy truck was meant to take our belongings to a Cox & Kings godown in Cairo till after the battle. Well, somehow it was diverted *here*, with *us* – trunks, suitcases, portmanteaux, the whole dashed lot! God alone knows how it happened but, as you can imagine, it's put Willie in one heck of a black mood – fit to be tied! And yours truly got the brunt of it, wouldn't you know! Made it my personal responsibility to escort our stuff back to the city and safely into storage where, drat it all, it should have gone in the first bloody place!"

"I'm sorry to add my problem to the mess," Santi felt genuine regret at compounding the poor man's woes. "I realise this is a nuisance, but it's absolutely essential I replace my missing supplies. It would be nothing short of a disaster being sent to the front without them."

"Hmmm," Ben looked thoughtful for a moment. "Well, let's see what tricks our Quartermaster might have up his sleeve."

They finally ran the QM to ground in the Duty Officer's tent, but when he was apprised of the problem, Middleton shrugged ruefully.

"Sorry Doc, can't help, I'm afraid. Haven't the foggiest where one might lay one's hands on extra meds out here. The supply trucks certainly haven't any, and I can't imagine anyone would be willing to share their quota." He scratched his head. "Wonder which bounder nicked our stuff. I'd like to lay my hands on the sneaky sod! Of course, that being unlikely, I'm afraid there's nothing for it, Doc, Cairo's your best bet I should think."

"You can hop a ride with me on the baggage transport, Doc," Ben offered. "I'm going in tonight, and I'm sure I can squeeze you in. That is if Willie okays it."

Cairo! Santi felt a sudden knot of excitement in the pit of his stomach. This *was* a lucky break! Suddenly, his annoying problem had given him a legitimate reason to visit the city, to see Hedeya again. It had to be Fate! But, would he have time enough to meet her? There was no question, somehow, he had to make the time!

Eagerly he followed the Adjutant to the CO's tent, wondering how he might possibly wangle a couple of extra hours in the city. The thought of seeing Hedeya one more time effectively pushed wisdom and perspective to the furthest recesses of his mind.

"Blast it!" Willie swore when he was informed of the situation. "I'd give my eye teeth to know which blighter's made off with our stuff. It can't have vanished into thin air. Some tosser's deliberately snagged it, I'll wager."

"I rather think that might be the case, sir," Browne ventured. "Another hash up, I'm afraid. And even if it weren't deliberate, it is highly unlikely whoever has it will give it up if they haven't reported it by now."

"The problem is, I do have to replenish my stock, sir," Santi pointed out, "and Middleton has assured me there's none to be had out here."

"You know I can't spare you chaps for long," Willie replied, frowning. "This really is a bloody nuisance. Damned unfortunate!"

There was a moment's silence while he sat, pulling on his chin thoughtfully. "Mmmm...on the other hand...we do have that new arrival coming in. Chap by the name of...er...what was the name... ah yes, Grose. Yes, Lt. M.A.S. Grose. Arriving from India sometime tomorrow afternoon, I believe. Someone would have to run him out to us, except...well, if you'll actually be in Cairo, Browne, you might contact GHQ and arrange to pick him up yourself. Save him time and trouble coming in by convoy, going through the sorting process at this end and finding his way to us. No one ought to have any objection, I shouldn't think, since you will in fact be taking him off their hands. But make sure you get those wretched medical supplies first, Doc; then locate Grose and you three get back here on the double. Right away, mind you."

Santi's heart sank. By the sound of things, there seemed little chance he would have time to meet with Hedeya. This trip to Cairo had dropped out of the blue, surely it wouldn't be a wasted visit!

——————•◆•——————

THEY ARRIVED IN CAIRO early the following morning. After securing their wayward luggage in its rightful place and chasing down the equivalent amount of Santi's missing morphine as speedily as red tape would allow, they made their way over to Garden City.

GHQ Middle East Forces was housed in a building known as Grey Pillars, off Sharah Kasr el Aini. A warren of offices stretched as far as the eye could see, and they were standing at the entrance considering which corridor they ought to chance tackling, when they bumped into an officer emerging from the labyrinthine depths of the building. By fortuitous circumstance, it turned out to be none other than Major Smith whom they had met at the Kit Kat Club a short while ago.

Clutching his inevitable briefcase, it took Smith a moment or two to part the curtains of alcoholic fog that somewhat shrouded that evening. When he did manage vaguely to recollect their previous encounter, he was good natured enough to feign immediate recognition.

"Ah, quite, quite! How are you chaps?" He enthusiastically pumped each one by the hand. "Fancy bumping into you like this. What brings you to my neck of the woods?"

Once they had explained their errand, he whisked them through a maze of passages honey-combed with doors till they reached the required department buried deep within the hive of office rooms. There he handed them over to a Lt. St. Claire who, after checking his paperwork, informed them they were quite right, Lt. M.A.S. Grose was due to arrive at the Kasr el Nil barracks that day, ETA 1600 hours.

This was good news, indeed, since it gave both Santi and Ben a chance to pursue their individual interests in the city. Santi was elated! With any luck, he would get to see Hedeya once more.

Before long they had made the necessary arrangements to meet the newcomer when he arrived, and found their way out once again into the burgeoning noon heat – Ben to head off to the Lido terrace at the Gezira Club to meet with a friend from GHQ, and Santi to hail a taxi for Choubra.

"Well, I'm off for a spot of slap-up *tiffin*," Ben smiled happily. "Make a damn pleasant change from the dodgy fare they've been feeding us. We'll meet back here at 1530 hours. Now, Doc, mind how you go. For Pete's sake," he added with a wink, "you won't go raring off and get yourself rumbled in some back alley souk, will you!"

Assuring him he had no such errant pastime in mind, Santi hailed a taxi. He had barely got in and shut the door when it took off, horn blasting an unmindful pedestrian, making him leap clear across the road; a discourtesy that earned them a scathing glance, an angry shake of the fist and what sounded like a flood of vitriolic abuse Santi was grateful he did not understand. Did every Cairo taxi race around like a bat out of hell!

Trying to settle down, Santi glanced out the window. Though Cairo's motley inhabitants still thronged the streets, he observed a subtle difference. There was the usual hubbub of noise everywhere; and yet, the city had an unusual feel about it. Somehow, the face of the crowds milling about had changed.

At first Santi couldn't quite put his finger on why the pulse of the city seemed to be beating to a different tempo. He gazed out the taxi window at the city's denizens dealing with life in their usual manner. The everyday patrons at open air cafes sipping their fragrant, sweet, black *shai,* or the even sweeter, thick, black Arabic coffee; the *effendi,* his upper half buried behind a newspaper, having his shoes shined while he caught up on the day's news; there, in front of a tea house, men sat playing backgammon, solemnly smoking their *sheeshas,* the hubble-bubbles gurgling with each pull on the pipe.

Santi smiled; the scene put him in mind of Alice's Adventures in Wonderland with the hookah-smoking Caterpillar, and that odd little character's gravely delivered declaration: '*It is wrong, from beginning to end.*"

And so it seemed with the city! Well, maybe not wrong exactly, but decidedly different – in spite of the familiar clang of a passing tram, vendors calling out their wares of sugar cane and the ever-popular *sherbuli sherbet*, and donkey carts trotting by piled to capacity; in spite of the cacophony of horns vying with the steady clip clop of horse's hooves that heralded a passing *arabiya hantur* which, when the carriage swayed into view, revealed two grinning urchins clinging to the back, enjoying a purloined ride. Other street urchins loitered about, searching the ground in hopes of reaping a rich harvest of discarded cigarette butts that littered the streets. These they would later empty, re-roll and sell for a hundred percent profit, a particularly lucrative and competitive business ever since the foreign armies had swollen the ranks of the city.

And, all at once, it came to him. Of course, that was it! The troops were gone. It was the absence of uniforms that gave the place that peculiar half-deserted feeling. There was still the odd khaki here and there, mostly officers and personnel from GHQ, but the thousands of ordinary soldiers had vanished into the desert; and the city, emptied of them, seemed to be waiting with bated breath for the storm to break. Which way would it blow? What would it bring in its wake? An uncanny air of expectancy hung over the city, similar yet different to that building up in the desert.

The city clung tenuously to a semblance of normalcy, yet its uneasy sense of anticipation lent an undeniable edge of anxiety and excitement that tittered through the thinned out cafes, night clubs, cinemas and social parties: storm clouds were gathering out there, just beyond its fringes, and although the city consoled itself that it was removed from the eye of the storm, it could feel the rumblings at its edges, and everyone knew no matter which way the tide turned, it was only a matter of time before they would be caught in the backlash. Try as they might to root themselves in the present, the universal question was – what would the morrow bring? What did the future hold for this much-used city?

In the desert, on the other hand, one could not distance oneself from reality by taking comfort behind the veneer of 'out there' or 'beyond the fringes', for there was no mistaking the here and now: it was here in their midst, and it was now in the present, the unmistakable signs of a massive battle gathering all about them. It felt as though the desert stillness trembled with this knowledge, and its dire circumstance loomed so large and threatening that it crowded out all else with its presence and obliterated the future. *Carpe diem quam minimum credula postero. Seize the day and trust as little as possible in the morrow.*

For those in the desert this was the only certainty, this present, this time, this day, as they prepared to face a change so great, they knew better than to lay odds on how – indeed, more to the point, if – tomorrow would play out.

GROPPI'S ON ADLEY PASHA was not as crowded as usual. Passing through the elaborate mosaic entrance into the elegant interior, Santi and Hedeya were ushered to a side table in the famous tea house.

Santi ordered ice cream – a Péche Melba for Hedeya and a Maruska for himself – and from a large glass display case that groaned beneath the weight of its delectable burden, they chose some petit suisse and crème cakes. They were served by a red-fezzed *sufragi* attired in a white uniform held at the waist with a matching red cummerbund – much the same colours as a bearer's uniform at home, Santi noted. Their table looked out onto a garden where jazz bands entertained of an evening. After sundown myriads of coloured lights would lend magic to the cool night air perfumed with the scent of flowers. Right now, it sat vacant, despite the large, multi-coloured umbrellas shading a few tables, nothing other than the heat stirring the air outside.

He didn't have much time – an hour at most, if that – before he would have to see her home and head back to GHQ himself. It had played out that way, although he had wasted no time in getting to her house. Eagerly, he had knocked on her front door, and Bajo had answered: Ah! But Hedeya hadn't returned from her school yet – however, she was expected back presently, not long now. He was disappointed, resenting every minute that was lost.

"Come inside. Come, sit and wait," the old lady invited him.

But he declined, with the promise he would be back soon. There was something he needed to do.

On his way to the house, he had noticed a music shop to which he now returned. Did they have a gramophone record with the song, The Anniversary Waltz? By Bing Crosby! Yes, thank you. He bought a copy of the 78-rpm vinyl record. When he fetched her, Hedeya noticed the package he was carrying in the taxi, but he kept silent about it all through the ride; till now.

"I have something for you." He took the record out of the package and laid it on the table before her. "I would like to thank you for the other day. I hope this small token will remind you of the evening we spent together." He continued, his voice serious. "It meant a great deal to me."

Caught somewhere between the whisperings of nascent emotions and a pragmatic warning somewhere inside her head, Hedeya sat silent, staring at the object lying on the table between them – an innocuous gift conveying a simple thank you. What reason, then, for the peculiar flutter in her stomach? Surprise, she assured herself, it was only because the unexpected gesture had taken her by surprise.

Oh, who was she fooling! It was more than that! She knew it, and she believed he did too. This was definitely getting complicated. The gift, the words, this young man's company filled her with something beyond simple appreciation. It was a deep, warm sort of pleasure that set her atingle; the sort of pleasure, she told herself nervously, that presaged a problem.

Hedeya touched the record in front of her. It lay there, seemingly harmless enough; but it was not. It was a small but certain step beyond the safety of simple friendship. Whether either of them admitted it or not, it had strings attached, and invisible though they were she could feel their tug. Even more disturbing was her desire to follow where they led, despite knowing no good could possibly come of going down that road. She had better tread with caution before it was too late; before these uncalled-for feelings landed her in a tangle too hard to untie. *Be careful!* Bajo often said. *Make sure you do not open a door you will be unable to close.*

Well, then, she had better find a way to decline his gift, to swiftly cut those invisible strings, without seeming churlish or rude – above all, without hurting his feelings. That, he did not deserve; he had been respectful, a gentleman from the start. He might be the cause of her predicament, unwittingly so, but she had walked into this with her eyes wide open. She could hardly blame him for her turbulent thoughts, or the sudden disarray of her emotions, could she?

She had almost refused his invitation this afternoon for fear of where it might take her, but she succumbed eventually, against her better judgement, and only because – so she told herself – Bajo had reproached her for being ungenerous and unkind. Generosity had nothing to do with it, she wanted to tell her mother, nor had kindness; it was simply a matter of self preservation that concerned her here.

A few short days ago this complete stranger had walked into her life, unexpectedly, out of nowhere, and absurdly, since then, she had been unable to put him out of her mind. And here she was now, her mind and her heart locked in a tussle she could feel bringing down the walls she so painstakingly had built around herself. The sudden onslaught of emotions he unlocked within her had taken her un-awares. Really, she chided herself, it wasn't at all like her to be acting so giddy. What *was* the matter with her! She was no adolescent fool! This was only their second meeting, surely she knew better! She, of all people, ought to have learnt from the bitter disappointment she had suffered with Mahran.

She knew nothing of this man! A foreigner. A soldier, for good-ness sake! One of thousands who had flooded the country, and whom – need she remind herself – all well bred young ladies knew to avoid. Granted, her association with this soldier had not been of her doing. Blame it on fate in the guise of Cousin Samira who sent him! And his obligation to Samira, his sense of duty, had brought him in search of her – which she then felt obligated to repay. Thus far it was all perfectly proper, and the matter should have ended right there.

But it hadn't, had it! They had gone on to spend an evening to-gether, and it had sparked something between them; she was aware he had felt it too. That 'something' brought his return today, so here they were once again, within touching distance of each other; and because it made her almost heady with pleasure, she knew the situa-tion was perilous.

No fault of his, of course. His intentions seemed beyond reproach. Here he was, on his own in Cairo, and it was only reasonable he might wish to enjoy some casual company. A lady's company, understand-ably. After all, he was a young man, far from friends and family, and in the middle of a war. And yet, those very three reasons might well prompt him towards impetuous decisions. Well, then, surely that was reason enough *she* should keep a sensible head on her shoulders to avoid the abyss she now found herself edging towards.

So, why in the world was she wavering? What about her respon-sibilities? She was older, divorced, and with three children. Grant-ed, her two sons now lived with their father, but she still had her daughter and mother to care for. All things considered, *he* might be excused his lack of judgement, but not she. Remember that. She glanced at the earnest young face before her – fine-looking, so appealingly intense and hopeful…

Yes, yes, but what has that to do with anything? She thought, agitated. *Have you taken leave of your senses! Oh, there was that ridiculous little flutter again!*

She studied the thin gold rim of her coffee cup, hoping he would not read her thoughts. Really, she *had* to pull herself together, keep a clear perspective. Circumstance had brought this person into their lives. She knew next to nothing about him, and it wasn't her business anyway. He was simply passing through – here today, he would most certainly be gone tomorrow. Someone she would never see again. After all, with the war on, these were the times they lived in. She would remember him as a pleasant visitor, engagingly so. Rather serious for one so young…but too young to be taken seriously…

This had to stop! She was doing it again! Thoughts that were absurd, and risky, and spelt nothing but trouble! She *must* remain focused, sensible. She lifted her gaze from the coffee cup. It came to rest on his face where it happened to catch a small smile that lingered on his lips, turning up the corners of his mouth. It was a captivating smile that had a way of drawing one close. *There! There was that silly little tug in the pit of her stomach again!* She tried to ignore it so she could think clearly. Rationally.

She saw the smile travel from his lips to his eyes and she tried to look away. *Careful! This path is a treacherous one.* She felt flustered. *You know there is no sense encouraging or prolonging this.* Instinct warned her it would mean only heartache in the end. *Run. Get up now…leave. Go home to safety!*

Hedeya closed her eyes for a moment. She was sitting in Groppi's opposite someone she hardly knew, and because of him she was having the oddest conversations in her head; nothing seemed to make sense anymore, and she was starting to feel frighteningly out of her depth. She felt his eyes touch her lips, felt them brush her cheeks, feather-light they traced the length of her neck, she felt their warmth search the hollow of her throat, linger a moment, move past, down, coming to rest…she opened her eyes, flushing at her thoughts, and his.

Santi watched keenly the flitting shadows that filled and darkened his companion's eyes and sat in little creases on her brow. One could lose oneself in those eyes, those deep pools flecked with hidden memories that seemed beyond reach. Somewhere in there, if he found the entrance, was a stairway to her soul, and from there a road that led to her heart – and straight back to his own. Though she was older than he, and had experienced life in ways he hadn't, and though it had made her fiercely independent, there was a vulnerability about her that awakened in him a fierce desire to protect her, to shield her from care. He realised, with a sudden flash of insight, that she had no idea how to handle him, caught as she was between his youth and manhood.

He saw her lower her eyes, closing herself in from the world. When she lifted them again, he observed the changing expressions chase each other across her face, doubts that clouded, then cleared, and clouded her features once more. He smiled at the transparency of each nascent thought before it went into hiding, and he lost it somewhere in the depths of those fathomless eyes. And he fell in love all over again.

He fell in love when she met his smile, and he saw it reflected, hesitantly at first, then slowly growing, till its warmth reached across and closed the space between them so the space was no more, till it bound them, one to the other, in a fleeting moment of intimacy that held them both; one long, exuberant moment, in a private world all their own where no one and nothing else mattered.

The sudden intensity of that moment was heart-stopping; and the world beyond that moment was stilled, silent, seeming to fall away, soundless and shadowy, like the fabric of a dream. And when, after what seemed an age, it took shape again, when sound and sight returned, they discovered nothing in the room had actually changed. They had felt their world shift, yet they were sitting just as before, while around them all was as it had been. The world was going about its business just as it should. No one in that tearoom noticed the extraordinary union of two people at a small side table, who, for one perfect, unforgettable moment, had found each other – two lives that had touched and held together, in a compelling fate-altering moment of shared desire that would be their last before he was claimed by the desert and the war.

CHAPTER TWENTY-FIVE

News From Far and Near

Whether at Naishapur or Babylon,
Whether the cup with sweet or bitter run,
The Wine of Life keeps oozing, drop by drop,
The Leaves of Life keep falling one by one.

– Omar Khayyam, *Rubaiyat of Omar Khayyam*

MAY 15: NEWS ARRIVED from two quarters. The first, from the home front, came in the form of a letter from Lebu. The second, from the powers that be, would move them ever closer to the front.

His little sister Lebu was a gamine creature. Her pretty features, forever framed by free flying curls that bounced and blew in all directions in perfect mimicry of her unfettered spirit, she was supremely uninterested in her appearance and undaunted by most things; if she believed there was a wrong to be righted, you could bet you would find her in the thick of it.

Young, idealistic, pure of heart, the family's Joan of Arc. What had she been up to? He and Bela were constantly worrying she would forge ahead, fearlessly flying the flag of faith, and plunge herself into some sort of hot water or other, her unfailing companion, Kamala, induced by fair means or foul into following close in her footsteps. Of one thing he could be sure – his youngest sister's letters could never be boring! He opened this one eagerly, yet not without a little trepidation, and was surprised to find it had taken a mere twenty days for the letter to reach him; as such, it made a pleasant change in that the news it brought was fairly up to date.

Shoba Dutt,
c/o Dr. J.P. Dutt, (Capt.), M.B., M.R.C.O.G.
36, Chowringhee Road, Flat No. 3A/3B
Calcutta, West Bengal, India   *25 April 1942*

Dear Dada,

I am sorry I have not written for some time, but I'm sure Didi has kept you abreast of our news here. I know she has apprised you fairly regularly of the political rallies and meetings that have taken place in Calcutta and, yes, feelings have been running high, especially after the failure of the Cripp's

Mission this month. Most people saw it as a feeble, empty gesture that didn't amount to a hill of beans! A poorly disguised, worthless attempt at appeasement to gain our cooperation in the war! It has served no purpose other than to rile all factions and set the cat among the pigeons, so to speak.

I know you are anxious about our safety, and fear that our actions might compromise Father's position; but you needn't worry, I promise not to take any undue risks. However, I do believe one has a patriotic duty, and so I have joined the National Indian Ambulance Corp. Kamala is training in first aid as well so she too can do her bit, helping with injuries that sometimes occur during anti-British rallies and protests. So, you see, you may rest assured we have our priorities right – though we will fiercely protest British rule, we won't be involved in anything that might compromise the war effort. In fact, here is something I heard at a meeting the other day: 'Confusing and contradictory as it may seem, my enemy's enemy is not always my friend; it depends on which is the greater evil.' So, Dada, you need have no anxiety on our account, and I hope you won't be too put out by my news. In fact, we are all proud of what you are doing and what it stands for. There, I've said it!

And now for other goings-on even closer to home. The household has been taken apart and packed into boxes in preparation for our move to Hooghly. We are all rather sad at having to depart our Chowringhee Road home. The suburbs will probably be horribly boring. We are leaving here on the 27th, two days from today. Everyone in the building now knows of Father's transfer, and knowledge of our departure led to an incident that caused a proper commotion night before last. It makes for quite a story.

It was an exceptionally hot night, so hot and humid that even though the fans were going full pelt, they merely circulated the steamy air. To somewhat relieve the stifling heat, we had opened the windows and french doors before going to bed. Father was asleep in his bedroom as usual; but Mother, unable to stand the heat, had taken her pillow and chador and spread them on the floor in front of the French doors in the dining room, hoping the cool stone, and a little outside breeze, would bring some relief.

That afternoon, Mezdi had come home for the weekend, and so the four of us – Mezdi, Kuti, Kamala and I – were in our bedroom. It was almost like old times, even though Didi, of course, was missing. Of late, with Didi and Mezdi both away, the two joined beds we sisters have always shared seemed, somehow, over-large with only three of us in them. Those two wedding beds, you'll remember, are really massive – one was Father's and Mother's, and the other, I think, belonged to Jattha and Jatthi.

Anyhow, after we had nattered and caught up on our news, we were ready to drop off to sleep – all except Mezdi that is. Every time a slight breeze would blow in the trees outside, or the curtains would move against the windowpane, she would prod us awake and insist a thief was breaking in. Eventually, when she found that prodding no longer worked, she proceeded to twist our toes, which made Kuti yelp loudly and prompted Father to yell, "Bina, Sudha, stop that hulla and let us all sleep." Finally, we threatened to throw Mezdi out of bed and make her sleep alone on the floor – you know what a scaredy cat she is – and that did the trick; finally, there was peace and quiet.

Then, in the very early hours of the morning, Mother was disturbed by a strange sound. She half opened her eyes and, at first, all she saw were shadows. Suddenly, outside the French doors, one of the shadows moved, and she made out a figure standing on the narrow parapet that runs around the outside of the building. Whoever it was must have climbed up the servants back stairs and over the stair rail onto the parapet. As you know, the distance between the staircase and the French window is about six feet. The figure had crossed that distance, and before Mother could bring herself to do anything, it began to climb in through the French door, almost falling over her.

She said later, she could hardly think above the hammering of her heart – 'buk dhor-phor kortè laglo'. She just lay there, every muscle frozen, as the intruder gingerly stepped over her and crept towards the drawing room. It was then Mother opened her mouth to scream. At first, nothing came out. She tried again, and this time she found her voice, but it came out in a strangled gurgle, low at first, slowly increasing in volume. It stopped the figure dead in its tracks, and I really wonder who was more terrified, Mother or the thief!

Father meanwhile had woken up. He heard this eerie sound, he told us later, and thought Mother was having a nightmare. As he got up to go over to her, he saw the intruder through the doorway of his bedroom. He shouted at the top of his voice, and, having nothing else at hand he grabbed his pillow and threw it at him. The man fled. He leapt over Mother, out the French window and was gone in a trice. Father picked up his weapon – the pillow – and gave chase.

By now we had woken, and Mezdi added to the pandemonium, wailing loudly that she'd told us there was a thief, no one had listened to her and now we were all going to be murdered in our beds. We were cowering under the sheets, when we saw a figure rushing towards us with what looked like a big white sack. We could just see the very worst of Mezdi's predictions come true, so we covered our heads and our whimpering and crying turned into loud bawling.

Of course, it was only Father! When he realised that the thief had vanished, he rushed into our bedroom – still clutching his pillow – to make sure we were safe. We thought he was the thief running towards us, carrying his sack of stolen goods, or with some diabolic intention of taking a hostage…well, it was enough to make anyone panic! Especially with Mezdi screeching on about murder, and Father standing there waving his arms to quiet us, which only served to make matters worse since it looked like he was about to attack us!

Finally, when Father realised we were neither listening nor looking at him, and he was making no headway over our caterwauling, he thundered "Choop koro! Stop that infernal squealing. Look, you silly things, it's only me."

That got through. We sheepishly emerged from under the sheets to see Father glaring at us. "Hrrrmph!" he snorted to Mother, in disgust. "Grown girls, indeed! They sound like hysterical mice."

By the end of it all we were wide awake and too excited to sleep. So, we got up and, after Father alerted the old chowkidar downstairs (who must have been fast asleep instead of keeping watch), we closed and locked the French doors despite the heat, and we all had a cup of tea. It was a good hour before any of us could even consider going to bed and, this time, when Mezdi began her whimpering about strange noises, we put a pillow over her and sat on her till she promised to shut up.

The thief got away, of course, but the incident caused quite some excitement in the building the following morning. Oh, speaking of excitement, there have been rumours that the Japanese bombed a couple of coastal towns not far from here, and on the 6th of April they sank a ship in the Bay of Bengal, a few miles from Puri. That means blackouts are going to be enforced in Calcutta. In Hooghly too, of course, and the next time we write to you we will probably have a great deal to tell you about the new place. Meanwhile, don't worry about us, we are all doing well and praying that this war will be over soon. Just take care of yourself and come home safe.

Affly, your sister, Lebu

PS. If it is allowed, Dada, could you please send us your photo from wherever you are. It would do us all, especially Ma and Baba, a power of good to see that you are well.

THE SECOND PIECE OF news arrived that same day as well, and it came from Eighth Army Headquarters: 10th Infantry Brigade would be moving forward to Gambut, to protect the airfields surrounding General Ritchie's Headquarters. They were leaving the Kennels to move up, finally, inexorably, towards the front. Rumours had begun to fly fast and furious of a sudden increase in supplies and troop movements on the German side. Air reconnaissance indicated the 15th and 21st Panzer Divisions were being deployed forward. The time had come, it would seem, when their woefully short training in desert warfare was to be put to the test against the fabled Desert Fox

and his well-seasoned Afrika Korps. How they would fare, remained
to be seen.

Western Desert, 8th Army troop train & convoy, June '42.

Meanwhile, a few of the much-needed stretchers and elusive Red
Cross armbands Santi had requested finally arrived. After he had
taken delivery of them, he made his way to his tent, lost in thought.

Ever since his departure from Cairo his mind had been stumbling
around in circles, trying to regain some rationality, warily sidestepping the confused emotions that had tied his thoughts into knots,
each one at variance with the other; one minute he was ready to
throw all caution to the winds, the next he was brought down by
doubts. His spirits rose and sank on the ebb and flow of these tides,
lifting him with elation one minute and sweeping him into a trough
of despondency the next. He was aware that this was dangerous. It
was neither the time nor place to take on any kind of distraction;
certainly not one of such personal magnitude. He would need all his
wits about him, every iota of concentration he could muster to get
through what lay ahead. People's lives, and his own, depended on it.

I know that, blast it! Of course I bloody know that!

He shook his head impatiently, trying to clear away the muddle
in which all good sense and reason seemed to have become lost. But
there were those confounded memories; beautiful, insidious, they
jolted his heart, took his breath away, and sent sound rationale careening out the window. When he was with her nothing else seemed
to matter, and when they were apart, he could not stop thinking of
the all too brief time they'd spent together; just a few short hours,
but like some crazy carousel he had inadvertently climbed onto, unable to step off he was spun around, his direction changed entirely.

And then he would think of his life back home, of her family here

– and it would pull him up short. It was utter foolishness! Wasn't he being irresponsible and immature? After all, they had met twice, just twice, and…think about the problems!

Ah! But remember Groppi's? He had never been more certain, never wanted anything more in all his life! Even now, the memory swept through him, the longing so strong it left him weak-kneed. Surely, she had felt that way too, hadn't she? It hadn't been his imagination, had it?

Hold your horses! **You** *fell, head over heels, like a schoolboy. And you don't seem to know your own mind anymore! Then, how could you possibly know hers? So, she spent a few hours with you, out of courtesy for delivering Samira's message. And then…when she realised how you had begun to feel… think back…think clearly…had she actually encouraged you, or had it been wishful thinking on your part? Maybe she'd been too polite to rebuff you out of hand!*

Santi stopped in his tracks, embarrassed and exasperated with himself in equal measure. *Look at you! The lady shows you a kindness and it's enough to make you believe you've lost your heart when all you've really done is lost your mind!*

It was true, the relationship was an implausible one – and, in hindsight, quite likely one-sided. Whatever the case, she was probably too sensible to allow for anything so impractical. Normally, he too could be depended on to deal with life's matters in a responsible manner, and his behaviour in this instance was uncomfortably out of character. What in the world was he contemplating? He certainly could not go into battle in this state of mind. He had to find some resolution to his dilemma. In fact, hard as it might be to face, there could be only one resolution; and if only he could quell these feelings that were running riot within him in the most unreasonable fashion, he knew his mind would tell him he had to be pragmatic. His emotions were confounded and made no sense at all, and the sooner he faced reality the better for all concerned!

Once again, his thoughts skipped back to his family, his home, Calcutta, and the outcome if he should throw good sense and caution out the window…. It wouldn't do. Quickly, he reverted to the present, accelerating away from the inevitable fiasco he knew would result if ever such an alliance should come about.

There could be no doubt it would be fraught with obstacles; impossible, seemingly insurmountable obstacles. He had his responsibilities in India, she had hers here in Cairo. He must stop sidestepping these issues and come to grips with the truth: his feelings were not the only consideration here. The repercussions of his decision would affect far too many people adversely, so the sooner he put an end to the matter, the better.

Of course, that was easier said than done, but at least he had taken the first step to acknowledge, what he believed, was the only responsible, the only rational thing to do. Best for all concerned. The next step of how to actually close the chapter, how to put the subject entirely out of mind – that, he knew, would be much harder.

"Penny for 'em, Doc"

"Huh…? Oh, hello Williams; sorry, I didn't see you."

"Almost ploughed right through me there! You seem to have a great deal on your mind."

"Don't we all," Santi smiled, ruefully. He examined Robert Williams with mild interest. "And from your get-up you look like you're off to parts more civilised."

"Cairo," Williams declared. "I have a pick-up at MEF Headquarters. Would you believe, the boys at BTE Intelligence have an inkling they've stumbled onto something not quite pukka! They're pretty sure there's a leak somewhere along the pipeline, so they're playing it safe, avoiding the official runner and going instead with someone outside MEF, HQ – your's truly. In fact, to make doubly sure, they've requested not one, but two couriers for the job – keep an eye on each other, don't you know!"

Santi stared at Williams in disbelief. Listening to him, a thought had jostled its way past all his recent doubts and arguments, to lodge itself firmly in his head. A trip to Cairo! This was more than a coincidence, wasn't it? Here was his chance to meet with her one last time, to say goodbye. Who knew where they might push off to after the battle! Now, if he could somehow work it so he could go along...

"And, as Battalion Intelligence Officer, you got picked for the job?"

"As I.O. it seems I was the obvious choice – along with none other than our own Roger Werner."

"Werner too?" Santi exclaimed. "I say, what a lucky break – even if it is just an official run there and back. All that cloak and dagger stuff at BTE makes it rather exciting, don't you think? By the way, that Major we ran into in Shepheard's, the one who took us to see the belly dancer, he's with BTE, isn't he? What was his name? Sansom, wasn't it?"

"Oh, right you are, Doc, so he was. Those fortunate punters headquarter at the Semiramis Hotel, would you believe! Now that's what I call a cushy job! Anyway, it wasn't all a question of chance they picked Roger and me, you know. Since our Brigade is due to move up shortly to Eighth Army's Advance HQ at Gambut, apparently that clinched the deal. We're to dispatch certain 'urgent documents' from Cairo to General Ritchie at Gambut – more than likely our battle orders if you ask me – so it's a quick jaunt there and back without much chance for any recreational delights, worse luck. Beastly unfair, but there you have it. Bad timing for a romp through the old city, I'm afraid!" Williams laughed, ruefully.

"I say, Williams, if I clear it with the C.O. would you mind if I tagged along?"

He could say farewell in person, like a gentleman. He couldn't leave the relationship with Hedeya – they shared a friendship at least – without some sort of closure. It would rankle like an exposed nerve. It wouldn't do to just vanish into the war without so much as a single word. If it had to be goodbye, hard as it was, it would be better this way; it was necessary for his peace of mind, as well as being the courteous thing to do. Moreover, the gods certainly seemed to be in agreement, why else would they have dropped this opportunity so unexpectedly into his lap!

Robert Williams eyed Santi with interest. "You're welcome to cadge a lift, Doc. Be glad of the company…" His words trailed off as Santi thanked him hurriedly and rushed off in the direction of Colonel Weallan's tent.

Something's afoot here, the Intelligence Officer decided with a mental tap to the side of his nose. He watched the doctor's figure stop in front of Willie's tent, announce himself briefly, then duck in.

Colonel Weallens looked up from the map spread out on his table. "Cairo? Again! You have a special interest in Cairo, Doc?" The CO demanded a mite irascibly.

"I do, sir."

There was a short silence. "Something important?"

"I believe so, sir."

Willie studied him quizzically for a moment. "You're a dark horse, Doc," he declared, finally. "Very well, whatever it is, if it is that urgent a matter you might as well get it out of your system. Go if you must, but you won't have much time, mind you. A couple of hours, three or four at most. As long as that's understood, and you have everything in order before you leave, ready to shove off, you have my permission to go."

CHAPTER TWENTY-SIX

A Priest For Proxy

Ah Love! Could you and I with Fate conspire
To grasp this sorry scheme of things entire,
Would not we shatter it to bits....and then
Re-mold it nearer to the heart's desire!

– Omar Khayyam, *Rubaiyat of Omar Khayyam*

"COME, SIT. I WILL make some Turkish coffee – good, strong coffee. We will drink together, and we will wait for Hedeya. Soon she will come home, it is almost time." Bajo saw Santi settle down on the sofa, and then went into the kitchen.

He looked around him. The room was as he remembered it, bright, homey and peaceful. At any other time, it would have worked like a salve after the harshness and rigours of the desert, but he was on tenterhooks today, and he brought a certain restlessness to the halcyon setting. He didn't have much time. He hadn't stopped to think she might not be there. He should have, of course, considering the last time. But then, she had turned up eventually, hadn't she!

What if she didn't this time? What if this was all for nothing and he missed her? He couldn't allow himself to think that way. She must, and she would, walk in that door! And what would he say to her when she did? Well, he would tell her…he would explain.

Dash it! He hadn't prepared himself at all! Well, he would just have to take it a step at a time. First, he had to see her, after that…

He shut his eyes and tried to relax. He saw her in his mind's eye as she got off the tram; he saw her walk down the street, enter the building; he heard her footsteps on the stairs, the key in the lock; he held his breath and waited, willing her to walk through the door.

After a moment, he jumped up, strode over to the door and opened it, listening. There was nothing. He closed the door and glanced impatiently at his watch. He had half an hour, no more, and he cursed his luck that it should be wasted, waiting like this.

Bajo returned with the coffee and some *kehkè*. "Take my biscuits. Fresh from this morning. Eat, it is good with coffee."

Santi didn't feel much like eating, but out of courtesy he helped himself, thanked her and bit into the plaited savoury sprinkled with black onion seeds. Nigella. It was used extensively in Bengali cooking and known as *kala jira*. The slightly pungent taste was pleasingly familiar.

"This is very good," he said. Trying hard to mask his increasing anxiety with each passing minute, he made an attempt at polite conversation. "Back home we too use this to flavour our food, especially when we cook vegetables and lentils."

Bajo could sense the tension in her visitor. She caught the quick glances at his watch, saw him press his lips together, tightly. She had become a little concerned about the way things were going between him and her daughter. She liked this young man; he was well-mannered and seemed of good character. But exactly what was it he was looking for regarding Hedeya, she wondered. Of course, she never would dream of insulting him with questions as to his intent since he was, after all, a guest. Nevertheless, the situation worried her.

Hedeya had not volunteered anything as to the exact nature of the relationship, but it was this very silence that had begun to unsettle Bajo. Surely these two young people realised the danger of stepping beyond the bounds of friendship? She knew Hedeya, and she knew her feelings had been stirred; knew too the deep hurt she hid beneath a show of strength and determination. *Bimbashi*, Bajo would sometimes call her daughter, teasingly: *Commander of a Thousand.*

But she knew the show of strength hid a soft underbelly. She doesn't deserve to be hurt again, Bajo thought. She has endured enough of that. Did she not, then, see the danger of opening her heart like this? What could he possibly offer her in his circumstances? The outcome could not be a good one. Surely, surely, they realise this cannot be.

Maybe she had been wrong to encourage Hedeya into accepting his invitation that first day. She wished now she could find some way of averting the disaster she foresaw for them. Maybe, after all, it would be for the best if they didn't see each other today. She saw him look at his watch once again. The action was one of controlled desperation, she could tell.

"Don't worry, I will give her your message," she said softly, feeling sorry for him, yet hoping he would take the hint of her offer and leave before her daughter returned.

"I'll wait just a while longer," Santi replied, his voice hollow with strain. "I can manage a few minutes more before I must leave."

"Then drink the coffee and give me your cup. I will tell your future," Bajo said making a kindly attempt to distract him from his thoughts.

"You can do that?"

"Maybe, maybe not. We shall see."

He drank the thick, sweet concoction she had made for him, sipping it slowly, trying not to think of the seconds ticking by. When he finished, she instructed him to swirl the dregs around the bottom of his cup, then cover its mouth with the saucer and quickly invert it so the contents from the cup would drain into his saucer. A couple of minutes later she picked up the cup and examined it. Frowning slightly, she pondered the patterns left on the bottom and sides.

"*W'Allah*! I see many journeys in your life. Yes. Many countries too."

That wasn't too difficult a guess, Santi thought, faintly amused. It would be plain enough to 'see' that this past year had been chock full of 'journeys' across the Middle East. Nevertheless, he appreciated the old lady's efforts to keep him occupied, so he nodded and tried to look as though he were paying serious heed to her words.

"But darkness is coming, very near now. And where life started will not be the place of its end," Bajo continued. "There is much distance between the two."

Santi squirmed uneasily, in spite of himself. That doesn't bode too well, he mused wryly. He wasn't superstitious, but the impending battle loomed large in his mind. Let us hope the end isn't here and now. There is certainly 'much distance' between this place and where I was born.

Bajo's next pronouncement eased his mind a little. "But your life is solid." She saw the question in his eyes. "*Yanè*…you know…steady life. Look. See here?" She pointed to two smudges. "You will have two children. Boy? Girl? It is not yet seen. The first will marry, there are children. The last…ah! I see you will be blessed…the last will stay with you always, always." She offered him another biscuit. "Please, eat."

Somewhat reassured he had a future after all, Santi smiled. "No, thank you," he shook his head. Then, quickly glancing at his watch once again, his expression changed. His face set, he got to his feet reluctantly. "I am afraid I really must leave now. I am late as it is."

There was nothing for it; he would have to leave without seeing Hedeya. He felt bitter disappointment, almost to the point of despair, at the wasted opportunity. He had come so close, only to miss her in the end. But it couldn't be helped; he had no choice, he had finally run out of time.

Where *could* she be? What if she arrived mere moments after he left? He clenched his fists. It would be too bad if he missed her by a matter of minutes. Of course, it hardly made a difference whether it was by minutes or hours; the point was he had dragged out his stay to the very last second, unwilling to believe that opportunity had brought him thus far only to have his hopes dashed. What absolutely rotten luck!

He tried to focus on the kind old lady who had shown him such hospitality. He was grateful, and he made an attempt to pull himself together to thank her as politely as he could. It wasn't the end of the world, he reasoned with himself, surely there would be an opportunity some other time. But the thought afforded him little consolation; his future was so uncertain, he was not at all convinced there would be another time.

Again and again he had imagined, so vividly, her footsteps on the stairs outside, so intensely the sound as she opened the door, that he was taken aback when he turned to go and found her actually standing there.

Overwhelming relief surged through him, a sudden rush which left him, for a split second, feeling light-headed as though his blood had drained away. He had come so close to walking away without seeing her, and now it was all he could do to contain himself, to stop from striding over and taking hold of her, to make sure she was real.

All good sense flew right out of his head – and in that moment he knew he could not bring himself to say goodbye. That was not the real reason he had come. His true reason for being there could no longer be denied – she was standing right before his eyes, and there was no way he could let her go.

From the look on Hedeya's face it was obvious she was quite as taken aback at the unexpected sight of Santi as he was at her sudden appearance. She had been thinking of him as she climbed the stairs, thoughts that came unbidden to her mind more and more often these days – unreasoning, disruptive thoughts. And when she opened the door, it was as if those thoughts had materialised, uncannily, into his physical presence before her very eyes. The sudden leap of joy she felt startled her into dropping her handbag. In spite of herself, the sight of him standing there filled her heart and washed warmly through her entire being, flushing her face, rooting her in the doorway where she stood.

Bajo, still seated in her rocking chair, looked up when her daughter entered. What she saw made her heart sink. Dear God! It was too late!

Santi was the first to recover. He was at her side in two quick strides. He picked the handbag off the floor and placed it on the small side-table nearby. Silently he thanked fortune, fate, the gods!

Filled with a heartfelt gratitude for this chance, last minute though it was, of a few moments with her, he knew he had to tell her how he felt. It was imperative she know. There was no time to think, but he had to explain, to make sure she understood…somehow.

His thoughts and words jostled each other so, his mind was plunged into sudden chaos and he found it hard to think straight. He heard himself speak: *he had just dropped in on the off chance she would be home, and he had very nearly missed her; he was sorry he had to leave right away, he was running awfully late already; but he wanted to tell her how grateful he was for the time she had spent…for the kindness shown him* …He stopped, dumbfounded.

What was he saying? His words had tumbled out in a jumbled mess of inconsequential trivialities that conveyed nothing of what he had actually wanted to say, nothing of the thoughts, the feelings she had woken in him: the confusion, the despair of just a moment ago when he believed he would have to leave without seeing her, the realisation at last of how he truly felt about her and, yes, the problems they would have to face if they…damn it! There was so much he needed her to understand, but with no time left, and no experience to draw from, he found himself unable to express any of it without sounding commonplace or trite.

He was acutely aware of Bajo's presence in the room. He couldn't just blurt it all out! He was trying to sort through words that kept skipping around in his head, to find the right ones to explain himself without making a fool – no, without sounding completely insane!

After all, they'd had – what was it – just a few short hours in each other's company? How could she take him seriously? He was unknown to her, a foreigner, a soldier going off to war. He hadn't the faintest idea what lay in store for him; he could make no promise that he would return; and if he did, there was no guarantee it would be as he was now. With all that for her to consider, what had he hoped for? A commitment to…what….to wait for him? What right did he have to expect that or anything else from her? What had he to offer her in return? The more he considered it, the more preposterous the whole thing became, even to him.

Hedeya had stepped into the room. Dimly, through the rush of noise in her ears and the loud beating of her heart, she managed to grasp something of what Santi was saying, and his words felt like a slap in the face. She tried to speak, to keep her voice steady.

"You are leaving…now? You came to say goodbye!" She drew a deep breath. Well! What *had* she expected?

"No! Yes! I must get back. I cannot miss my ride. I came to tell you that I don't know when…if…I'll be seeing you again…"

He couldn't tell her, or anyone else, that they were about to go into battle. Regardless of anything, that information was top-secret.

Something in her expression seemed to shut down, and he saw her withdraw into herself. It was almost physical. She had not moved, and yet it felt as though she had backed away from him. He watched, dismayed, as her face set into an expressionless mask.

He tried desperately to reach past it. "I want you to know that being with y…you…the time I've spent with you has meant a great deal to me." Each word was like a stone, building a wall between them.

Somehow this was not coming out the way it was meant. His words made no sense, not even to him, they told her nothing of how he felt. But, how in the world did you tell a woman you had just met that you were desperately in love with her and couldn't think of life without her! That kind of thing only happened in romance novellas or in the cinema. And if that wasn't difficult enough, how the ruddy *dickens* did you tell her something like that when you had all of thirty seconds before you rushed off to war! Sensible people didn't behave that way. He certainly didn't! What was happening to him?

Her face was blank, frozen. When she spoke, her tone was clipped, her words sparse and emotionless. "We are happy that you came. Thank you for bringing Samira's message. We wish you good luck."

Santi was stunned. Although she stood as still and stiff as a statue, she had managed to put a great distance between herself and him; she had slipped beyond his reach. "Hedeya…" He stopped, at an awful loss for words.

He saw her try to smile, a small tight smile that did not move beyond her lips. It did not reach her eyes which remained shuttered and cold. "Excuse me, please, I too am late. I must change. I have a student coming for her embroidery class. Goodbye." She turned away from him and disappeared into the bedroom.

For a long moment Santi was unable to move. When he managed to get his legs to work, he found his way to the door. He had mishandled it all somehow. The opportunity had seemed like a godsend, but it had gone hideously wrong in some uncontrollable way. He managed to say goodbye to Bajo, who patted his hand and told him to go with God's blessing.

"My daughter is right, your news brought us happiness. You will be in our prayers always. *Ma'a salama*, be safe"

Santi fumbled down the stairs. He felt a sense of tremendous loss, the greatest in his life, almost as though he had just had part of his insides gutted and left them lying in the room behind him. As a doctor he understood physical distress, but this unfamiliar pain he was feeling somewhere in his chest, so intense it was almost palpable, actually made him double up. He tried to breathe past it, to collect his shattered thoughts as he stepped out into the open, and…blinded by the sunlight…ran headlong into a man who had just turned the corner. Gasping, he started to apologise, when he recognised the familiar figure. Asis Habib.

The winded priest was still trying to catch his breath as he peered up, teary-eyed, and recognised his assailant.

"Ah, it is you!" he managed between painful gasps and was about to attempt a humorous response to their precipitous encounter, when he noticed there was something very much amiss with the young man who had instigated it.

"Are you all right, my son?" the priest asked, forgetting his own discomfort, concerned only with the distress that was obvious in Santi's face. "Are you hurt?"

"Father," Santi appealed to him, "please, help me!"

"But of course!" The priest put a reassuring hand on Santi's arm. A second glance told him the pain he observed was not of the physical type. The tall, straight-shouldered soldier standing before him suddenly looked very young and vulnerable. "What is your trouble…"

"I don't know who…I'm not sure but…I think I may have offended Hedeya, and that was the last thing I intended. I have the greatest respect…I mean, I realise things are so uncertain right now…maybe I don't have the right to ask…but, Father…I…"

At last, in sheer desperation, Santi threw his cap over the windmill, and abandoning all caution, he blurted impetuously, "Father, I have very little time but…would you ask Hedeya Khayat…if I should make it back…would she…would she marry me!"

Asis Habib's mouth fell open. It was uncanny how this young man, whose existence he had been unaware of till just a few days ago, had a dismaying propensity for landing him in the most confounding situations. It seemed to be a habit!

This was the second time they had met and, as though the first time had not been discomposing enough, on this occasion he succeeded not merely in physically knocking the wind out of the old priest's sails, he verily set him back on his heels! Asis Habib would have liked to sit down for a moment, just long enough for his head to stop spinning so he could make some sense of what he thought he had just heard.

He tried to speak, but nothing happened. He seemed to have lost his voice along with his faculties. Santi's words were swimming in and out of his head like so many inconsiderate fish.

"You see, Father, in my country it is customary to approach the man of the house regarding matters such as marriage, but in this case, there is no one except…well, except maybe you. And here you are! I could not explain myself up there just now…how I felt…I know it sounds impossible, but…you could speak for me…ask her for me. Please, Father. I really do have to leave this very minute. I don't have time to explain further, but somehow – I don't know how – I will get in touch with you. I hope you will have her answer for me."

While he was speaking, Santi had managed to hail a passing taxi. He was going to be awfully late. He was *already* awfully late. He opened the door to get in. Williams would be wondering where the devil he had got to. "Father, I need to know, I must know, will you do this for me? Please!"

Asis Habib tried to think of something appropriate to say to this person who, one day not so long ago, had suddenly appeared in his church like a bolt out of the blue. From that moment on he had, it seemed, proceeded to set all their lives at sixes and sevens, and was now proposing to vanish into the desert, leaving behind a situation that he, Asis Habib, had not the slightest idea – or inclination – how to handle.

"Asis Habib, *please…*" Santi's voice sounded strangled.

With some effort Asis Habib pulled himself together. Somehow, he had to make it clear, as gently as possible, that this absurd request was…well…was inconceivable! Searching for suitable words, calming words, he began to shake his head when, quite of its own volition, he felt his head begin to nod instead. Stop, this was madness! What was he doing? It was a mistake…he must explain that it was impossible, preposterous!

At last, he found his voice and started rather shakily, "Y..y..you see, my son," his voice was not in very good working order.

Santi had jumped into the taxi and was looking up at him, beseechingly.

Quick, Asis Habib thought, explain before it was too late! "It…it is not a simple…I don't…don't worry…" He was horrified to hear himself say, "I will take your message to her. Yes, yes, go on, don't worry, and may God protect you…" Asis Habib paused, "…and me!" he added lamely as Santi shook his hand gratefully, thanked him profusely and sped away.

No! No, wait! It was not he who had spoken just then, surely! Of course it wasn't. He knew exactly what he had been about to say; but Someone, he looked up accusingly at the heavens, had twisted his tongue so that it changed the words as they came out of his mouth.

"Why do You put your old servant through this, oh Lord!" he lamented out loud. "At my age, after all my years of devoted service, do I not deserve a little peace and quiet?" He looked around to make sure no one had observed him talking to himself, shook his head in exasperation, and muttered, "Well, since You got me into this predicament, I hope, at least, You will help to get me out of it!"

Glumly, he watched the taxi disappear and then, very slowly, he made his way up the stairs. Bajo opened the door for him. He asked for Hedeya and was told she was in her bedroom. Asis Habib recounted, as best he could, the happenings of a few minutes ago and was surprised to find that it did not much disturb the old lady's equanimity. She nodded when she heard his story, then went into the bedroom to call her daughter. Far be it from her to meddle with fate; such things were best left in the hands of He who was much wiser than she.

When Hedeya came into the room, Asis Habib noticed she looked rather drawn. She greeted him, and he watched her closely as he said, "I met your young man downstairs. He was leaving as I was coming in"

Hedeya's face became quite flushed. "He is not 'my young man'," she retorted in a cold voice.

"You surprise me," the priest replied. "Indeed, you surprise me a great deal since he has just asked me to let you know that he would very much like you to marry him."

There was a sharp intake of breath. Her cheeks bright red, Hedeya snapped back angrily. "Why don't you give him one of your daughters to marry?"

"Because he has not asked to marry one of my daughters, Hedeya. It is you he wishes to marry," Asis Habib replied softly. "From what I could tell, he seems to be very much in love with you, and he was greatly agitated because he had been unable to express his feelings or explain himself to you just now. He was afraid he might have caused you some pain, and he hoped you would forgive him, and give him a favourable answer"

"This whole thing is foolishness! There is no reason why he should think he could hurt me. We hardly know each other, and nothing happened that…that…" Her voice caught in her throat.

Then, as if she were trying with all her might to hold something within, Hedeya pressed her lips together till the corners of her mouth turned white. Suddenly, with a loud sob, she sat down on the sofa and covered her face with her hands as though desperate to shield herself from the world outside.

CHAPTER TWENTY-SEVEN

The Drums Of War

Tis all a Chequerboard of Nights and Days
Where Destiny with Men for Pieces plays:
Hither and thither moves and mates and slays
And one by one back in the Closet lays.

– Omar Khayyam, *Rubaiyat of Omar Khayyam*

MAY 18, 1942: 10TH Indian Infantry Brigade pulled out of the Kennels and headed towards Eighth Army's Advance Headquarters at Gambut. The 2/4 Gurkhas, together with their brother battalions the 4/10 Baluchis and the 2nd Highland Light Infantry, travelled in desert formation up the Trigh Capuzzo, a road that bisected the unfriendly desert approximately halfway between the Mediterranean coastline to the north and Bir Hacheim, the Well of the Wise, in the south.

The journey was made even more wretched when they ran afoul of a sandstorm that blew them northward at sixty to eighty miles an hour. It transformed everyone into featureless, unrecognisable, grey blurs, swallowing all in its path, obliterating their world in a formless reddish-brown swirl that was a gritty, searing nightmare. The velocity of wind and sand whipping against open skin acted like sandpaper, chafing it raw. Even those parts that were covered suffered painful abrasion from the insidious grit that burrowed into and under one's closest layers of clothing. The fine powder rode the wind like an avenging demon that blew into mouth, nose, eyes and ears, rasping them sore and making life indescribably miserable.

Mouths became parched, tongues swollen, throats dry and choked shut; nostrils burnt and it almost hurt the lungs to breathe in the searing, sand-laced air; eyes smarted and teared from the painful onslaught of sand, while ears were deafened with the incessant shrieking of the wind. It was like being chased by the very devil as he tried to climb inside you. And, when at last it had reached a point almost beyond that of human endurance, that desert-devil crept back into its lair and the ordeal came to an end – till the next time.

The local Arabs were well acquainted with the violence and anger of this rampaging *afriti* and did their best not to cross its path.

The following day they camped gratefully in a pleasant green valley, but the respite was short-lived. Twenty-four hours later, the 2/4 received orders to proceed on to El Arid and the defence of its aerodrome. There was nothing to be said for the place – the name said it all – and no one was sorry to leave it behind when, two days later, on 22 May, they pushed on to Bir Arca to defend Gambut Satellites One and Two.

In a landscape that was rough and scrubby, Gambut straddled the road that led to Tobruk, El Mrassus and Gazala. General Ritchie's HQ bordered one side of this road where it hummed with the business of war: messengers, couriers and officers of various ranks swept in like the wind and out again, nipped at the heels by the sharp teeth of expediency; convoys of supplies, armaments and troop transports roared in on clouds of dust, unloaded their cargo and lumbered out again for a repeat performance.

On the other side of the road, two makeshift airfields stretched over flat, barely cleared land, home to the Desert Air Force and Air Vice-Marshal Coningham's HQ. Here air traffic was constant with the comings and goings of supply planes, training flights, bombing runs, and fighter escorts, and their swaggering pilots who flew hard, played hard and drank hard. And everywhere the journalists, press photographers, and army publicity corps men nosed around the action, drawn to the scene like bees buzzing a honey pot. History was in the making.

With the spectre of battle drawing ever closer, the air crackled with urgency. By day the troops were kept busy: the QMs laying their stores and obtaining necessary supplies; the signallers installing telephone wires and communication outposts; the sappers laying mines to defend their positions; the graders constructing pipelines for precious water, as well as roads to aid the newly laid rail lines in the massive transportation of men and materiel; and the motor transport boys camouflaging, repairing and servicing the vehicles that would carry them all down those roads into battle.

At night too there was no let up. Enemy aircraft came over on bombing runs, regular as clockwork, and the night-sky lit up by default with the brilliant and belligerent reply of the Allied ack-ack guns' vociferous response.

"Predictable devils, aren't they? One can practically set one's watch by them!" Robert Williams remarked caustically as he and Santi watched the display of pyrotechnics from their slit trench. "I wonder they don't think to vary their routine. Surely the bloody fools must realise their wretched night runs serve no purpose apart from being a damned bother. What the hell are they about? Some sort of postprandial romp?"

The enemy aircrafts' staunch adherence to a daily schedule was truly inexplicable. Without the element of surprise, their target was always well prepared in advance and no one really got hurt – unless, of course, one took into account the time a stray bomb very nearly landed between Slogger Marten and Subedar Sukdeo, as they huddled in their trench. It practically blew off their outer garments and rendered them quite deaf for a couple of days; and deuced annoying it was too, trying to hold any kind of conversation with either one until the malady had worn off!

So it was, despite his personal dilemma, both day and night being fully occupied with the business of war, there was hardly time for Santi to think of much else. Sometimes at night, just before he fell asleep, his mind would touch on that last day in Cairo; it hung in his mind, unresolved, open-ended, like an unfinished pipeline carrying his emotions…nowhere…always nowhere. Inevitably his mental grapplings would be overtaken by exhaustion and he would slip into oblivion, taking his unsettled thoughts with him into a dream. Had Asis Habib spoken to Hedeya? And if so, Santi wondered, what had been her answer? How was he supposed to find out? Maybe if he wrote…?

He realised with a sudden jolt of dismay that he had neglected to get a full postal address! He knew the street, the cross street, so that he could get there by taxi; in his mind's eye he could see the building itself, but he had failed to get the name or number of the building, or the apartment.

What had he been thinking! But that was just it – that last day he hadn't been able to think at all! Now there was no way for him to get in touch with her until all this was over and he could, somehow, find a way to return to Cairo once more. God alone knew how long that would be, he thought, dispairingly. He could have kicked himself for being such an idiot!

———————

THE BLEAK, BROWN MONOTONY of the desert stretched unbroken for miles, a harsh, barren landscape as far as the eye could see. By contrast, the startling appearance of the Mediterranean Sea was akin to stumbling upon a glittering jewel.

Edged with silver sands, those dark sapphire waters sparkled beneath the dancing feet of soft sea breezes with the iridescence of a dragonfly's wings. Just a few short minutes away, in the cruel desert, the merciless sun would fry a person's brain as easily as it would fry an egg on the roof of a tank; but here, mellowed by the tender touch of cupid-like breezes, it kissed the spangled waters and, like two lovers joined together, light and water burst into myriads of golden stars that soothed sunburnt bodies and salved heat-scorched minds.

On those rare occasions when time and circumstance permitted, small groups of men would get down to the beach for a much sought-after palliative swim in the balmy waters. All one had to do was follow the sign some hopeful had posted: "*This way to BRIGHTON BEACH. Ladies welcome.*" Wishful thinking!

And it was probably the same nostalgic author whose wit had embellished the bivouacked area with this wry declaration: "*BUCKIN'M PALACE. Good 'nuf fer royalty, good 'nuf fer me.*"

Humour, it had been discovered, could provide the wings for flight however frail or fleeting, and well-wrought humour leavened, albeit momentarily, the harsh reality of the impending battle.

However, with each passing day, attempts at these light-hearted pastimes grew more infrequent as preparations became ever more hurried and harried. A palpable sense of the inevitable began to spread among the troops. The wait was finally over.

No more the tedium bred of long marches as they leaguered across the desert beating back the heat, the sand, and the rampant fleas and flies that were a blight by day; or the long, restless nights fending off the cold and hordes of mosquitoes that attacked by dark; no more the monotonous stretches of camp life with its daily drudgery of mundane, everyday chores, or the boredom they attempted to while away in any manner one could devise, from card playing to lounging, letter writing and sleeping.

Those past adversities now dwindled before the enormity of the conflict that loomed over them. They were surrounded by the trappings of war. Tanks, gun carriers, machine guns and men had been amassed on a heretofore unseen scale. This was what they had been preparing for these many weeks and months past – this terrible reality of the killing fields.

There could be no doubt in anyone's mind, the battle ahead of them, the culmination of this journey through the desert, would be a milestone like no other in each man's life. It created a feeling of charged anticipation that swung between exhilaration and apprehension. The first was openly voiced, the second was deeply personal; and regardless of rank or creed, both emotions, whether shared or sequestered, were common to one and all.

There in the open desert, on both sides of the man-made line that separated them, men who had been displaced from homes in the four corners of the earth faced each other; and behind the casual stance so often and so carefully adopted, under a fragile veneer of studiously achieved nonchalance that disguised nerves taut as stretched wire, they waited, uneasy in the knowledge that no man there captained his life. They were but cogs in a giant wheel poised for a sudden massive push by the all-powerful, invisible arm of High Command that would sweep them, in a lightning lunge, to achieve that initial surprise attack so crucial to the success of the coming conflict.

British Grant tanks ready for battle, 31 May '42.

A foreboding lay thick and oppressive in the air. So tangible, it was like a physical taste in one's mouth, a smell in one's nostrils, the tension building to collision force as these two armies braced for a face-off. Though it remained unspoken, they knew that many of their number would not come through the days that lay ahead; those lives could be counted in hours now. Who would they be? Who among them would be chosen for life, and who for death?

Fortune's wheel would soon be spun, remorseless and blind-eyed, and all a man could do was try his damndest to keep from dwelling on the outcome; that, or try to seek refuge in quiet, fervent prayer, praying like never before to be spared the mischance of being in the wrong place at the wrong time. There was nothing else a body could do. The thought that one might drown in fear, that terrifying, powerless feeling that could so easily freeze mind and body, twist one's guts into knots so one could hardly breathe – no one could afford that sort of panic!

No! Life, that fragile, precious commodity, needs must be dealt with one day at a time. Today was real, one could count on it, savour it, fill it with all the memories of their yesterdays. There was no place in their uncertain world for tomorrows, nebulous and overcast by the shadow of death. Why waste precious time on something that might never be? Besides, it was dangerous to believe in tomorrow, rather like tempting fate, asking for it as it were. And so, every man settled his affairs privately, each in his own way, each within his own personal world, each between himself and his own God.

———•◦•———

ELSEWHERE, BEHIND THE SCENES, other wheels were turning in the world of politics and spies. Unknown to the men at the front, the outcome of these events would greatly impact the lives of those who were fighting in the desert.

Adhering to strict instructions, Robert Williams and Roger Werner had hastened to hand-deliver the top-secret packet they'd brought from Cairo to General Ritchie's HQ in Gambut. There they bumped into none other than the seemingly ubiquitous Major Smith himself. Smith was, apparently, on one of his regular 'top secret' runs between MEF, HQ in Cairo and the General's Advance HQ at Gambut, and the two covert couriers were careful not to divulge that the true nature of their mission was to circumvent possible leaks along just such normal channels as his.

They exchanged a few pleasantries after which Major Smith bent their ear with details of the languorous hours he had recently enjoyed in the delectable arms of the enchanting Hekmat Fahmy. Since it seemed expected, the duo applauded the Major on his enviable good fortune, and then quickly took their leave of him; but they made sure, later, to pass the conversation along to the appropriate authority – just on the off chance it might prove to be of some importance.

It was a good job they did, for at that moment, far out in the desert, Operation Salam was progressing well, bringing Kondor and his radio operator to the heart of Egypt – and soon their path would cross with that of Major Smith.

In no small part, it was just such tidbits of information that eventually would help Major Sansom of British Intelligence to capture Kondor and his companion before much damage could be done. Upon interrogation, those two spies would turn into songbirds and confess all to save their skins. Both men would then be interned as POWs for the duration of the war.

As for Major Smith, when finally hauled up for his indiscretions, he would make a last-ditch effort at reparation. A red herring, he would willingly run his vehicle into an enemy minefield from whence the Germans could retrieve his official valise and papers – sadly, so reported, at the cost of his life. Thus, his final legacy was that last seemingly vital but false information to the enemy – a piece of expertly crafted misinformation to bait a carefully laid Allied trap.

However, the security leak that would most directly impact the 2/4 Gurkhas and their brother battalions at the front actually sprang from that previously mentioned source, the American Legation in Cairo.

The US Military Attache in Cairo, Colonel Frank Bonner Fellers, had been transmitting messages to Washington with the regularity and diligence his job called for. His one mistake? With similar regularity he stuck to the exact same format for all his transmissions.

And, far out in the desert, the German outposts were keeping an eager ear to the ground by scanning the airwaves.

With the aid of the Black Code previously pilfered from the American Embassy in Rome, it was now comparatively easy for them to identify and decipher the American's messages.

A security breach compounded by an intelligence leak made it possible for Rommel to be in possession of the Allies' battle plans almost immediately upon dispatch. Thanks to what he fondly dubbed 'his little fellers' he had precise details of troop deployments, unit locations and armoured strength, the defences of the Gazala Line, and the mined areas running along it, start to finish.

There was one other piece of crucial information Colonel Fellers unwittingly gave the Germans for which they were immensely grateful.

The little island of Malta lay along the path of Rommel's supply route from Sicily to North Africa. A base for the RAF and Royal Navy, both of which had played havoc with German supply convoys, the island had long been a thorn in the German General's side. Finally, Hitler ordered the island pulverized.

Throughout 1940 and 1941 Malta was bombed, and the intensity of that bombing was stepped up in early 1942. By late April more bombs were dropped on that island than on London during the Blitz. As a result, by May 1942, Malta lay practically in ruins, and enough German shipping was making it through to ensure Rommel's armies in Libya were well supplied and adequately equipped for the Battle of Gazala.

To prevent further damage to the island, it became obvious the German bombers had to be stopped before they took off from their desert bases. Consequently, a top-secret Allied plan was devised to attack and destroy certain strategic Axis airfields by dint of covert air and commando raids.

In June, while Allied and Axis armies were battling in the Western Desert, Colonel Fellers sent a message to Washington with precise details of the intended attack: *Nights of June 12th June 13th British sabotage units plan simultaneous sticker bomb attacks against aircraft on 9 Axis aerodromes. Plans to reach objectives by parachute and long-range desert patrol. This method of attack offers tremendous possibility for destruction, risk is slight compared with possible gains.*

Of course, this message was intercepted – the enemy was waiting, and the operation ended in disaster. (Tim Clayton and Phil Craig: *End of the Beginning*)

As the 2/4 went into battle with the rest of XXX Corps and XIII Corps, little did they know that Rommel was confidently following their every step. So sure was the Desert Fox of victory that Lt. Anwar Sadat of the Egyptian Army was making simultaneous preparations for the German General's triumphal march into Cairo. In anticipation of that event, he even found and reserved a grand mansion on the Rue des Pyramides, not far from Mena House Hotel, to serve as the conquering hero's residence cum headquarters.

As for Colonel Bonner Fellers, when the British finally did trace the leak to him, they found themselves in something of a quandary. They were, at the time, in desperate need of American goodwill. This fact, together with the rueful recognition that the damage was already done, prompted diplomacy rather than denouncement – to cry harrow on the Colonel at this stage would be of little gain and serve only to muddy the waters of alliance. Consequently, the matter was swiftly dealt with by Feller's discreet removal from Office in Cairo. Transferred back to the United States, he remained tucked away for a while in the Office of Strategic Services, where his unwitting contribution towards the enemy's successes that June of 1942 was never brought up for scrutiny.

But herein lies a great irony, for two-faced history has often proved much like the veritable double-sided coin: It is believed in certain quarters that information gleaned from one or more of Colonel Fellers's final messages led to a German air ambush on 7 August: the target was a certain Bristol Bombay aircraft. This resulted in the death of Lt. General 'Strafer' Gott, the Commander slated to take over the Allied forces in the upcoming attack against Rommel. A veteran of WWI, Gott was a proven leader, well respected and well liked. The outcome of the desert conflict under that leadership will never be known.

Be that as it may, the Allies quickly turned this loss to gain. And here it may be argued, Colonel Fellers became an instrument of fate that led to ultimate success for the Allies when, subsequent to the loss of General Gott, his replacement, General Bernard Law Montgomery, would lead the Allied forces in their first turnaround victory of WWII.

A newcomer to North Africa and the Western Desert, Montgomery would head the Eighth Army and win a resounding victory in the small, till then insignificant, railway stop of El Alamein, just a few miles distant from the Cauldron. That pivotal victory would catapult him to fame as 1st Viscount Montgomery of Alamein. It should be added here, his success was aided in part by espionage not dissimilar to that which previously helped his rival Rommel.

On an old 581-acre country estate in the county of Buckinghamshire in England, there stood a large Victorian-Gothic mansion. Bletchley Park was a sprawling red-brick building, and it housed Winston Churchill's most closely guarded secret. The hub of secret intelligence, such as MI-6, it was home to a large and varied body of decryptors gathered for the sole purpose of breaking enemy codes and ciphers. It was here that Colossus, the world's first electronic programmable computer, was invented. Bletchley Park was the nerve centre of Britain's most secret and high-level intelligence – code named Ultra.

In April 1940-41 the German Enigma code had been partially cracked at Bletchley Park. Nevertheless, successful deciphering was minimal as Enigma machine settings changed every day, producing a variety of ciphers which the Germans regularly switched around in order to confound an enemy eavesdropper.

Eventually, however, persistence paid off; in the latter half of 1942 and first half of 1943, the British achieved greater success, thanks to the increasing carelessness of the Germans. Instead of configuring fresh, random settings for Enigma to formulate new ciphers, they resorted to using old key sheets. Further compounding this error, a large number of consistently repetitive messages, sent at frequent and regular intervals, facilitated comparison to codes already deciphered by the British – with admirable results.

Gordon Welchman, a Cambridge mathematics lecturer working on Enigma at Bletchley Park, was one of a team of four known as The Wicked Uncles. He vouched: *We developed a very friendly feeling for a German officer who sat in the Qattara Depression in North Africa for quite a long time reporting every day, with the utmost regularity, that he had nothing to report.* (Williamson Murray: *The Quarterly Journal of Military History, Spring 2002*).

Consequently, as a result of Ultra, Montgomery was privy to many of Rommel's plans and strategies. On one occasion he was able to access a dispatch from Hitler even before Rommel did. And he laid his plans accordingly, refusing to be hurried by Churchill. In fact, much to the PM's annoyance, it took Montgomery five months before he felt sufficiently prepared to avenge the debacle of the Cauldron and achieve final victory over the wily Desert Fox.

Regarding Col. Fellers, despite the part he played that June of 1942, high praise was bestowed on him for 'his profound knowledge of matters in the Middle East'. It was even suggested, 'brilliant and thoroughly informed' as he was, he might do well as C-in-C, Commander-in-Chief, Egypt! And a few months later, in appreciation of 'the clarity and accuracy' of his work, he was awarded the Distinguished Service Medal.

By all accounts the Germans were in perfect agreement with these lavish accolades, a fact made apparent by a memo that came to light later in Berlin. Dated 29 June 1942 it lamented the passing of those good times: '*we will not be able to count on these intercepts for a long time to come, which is unfortunate as they told us all we needed to know, immediately, about virtually every enemy action*'. (Tim Clayton & Phil Craig: *End of the Beginning*)

---

26 MAY: THE DESERT sunset had been especially beautiful that evening. Robed in indigo and purple and crimson-pink, it wrapped the horizon in a shawl of shimmering light that was like tissue of gold. Each perfect moment lingered, preening itself as though loath to

abandon its fleeting mirror-image in the sea below. But at last twilight had descended on the desert, soft as thistledown, melting away the heat and the last vestiges of day; and with it came the dewfall, and night settled in, all dark shadows and glittering stars. Huddled in their trenches like the jerboa rats of the desert, the Allies waited for the usual nightly strafing of enemy planes. For once it did not come. Instead, somewhere out there, floating on the night air, could be heard the strains of that song about their Lili of the lamplight, *Lili Marlen*. It was 9.55 pm exactly. Someone had caught Radio Belgrade.

> *Vor der kaserne vor dem grohen tor*
> *Stand eine lanterne und steht sie nach davor…*

Across no man's land an answering voice picked up the refrain in English…

> *Time would come for roll call, time for us to part,*
> *Darling I caress you and press you to my heart…*

With the darkling hours the desert chill had set in, and shortly the still of night would deepen over their world. Sound travelled far in the desert, but in that moment, out there in that vast expanse, nothing disturbed the peace across those silent, silver sands. Nothing, except the small sounds of the camp settling down as weary men spent a few final moments with their thoughts; scattered thoughts that drifted, carrying them towards the edge of sleep. And, as he followed suit, Santi's drowsy mind wandered…fitful, hovering…back to Cairo…his last visit…such a muddle. The memory was like an ache. He'd left matters painfully uncertain…unresolved…and now…there was no way of finding out…

CHAPTER TWENTY-EIGHT

Into The Fray

I have got my leave. Bid me farewell, my brothers!
I bow to you all and take my departure.
Here, I give back the keys of my door…
And I give up all claims to my house…
The lamp that lit my dark corner is out.
A summons has come, and I am ready for my journey.

– Rabindranath Tagore, *Gitanjali*

MAY 27: DAWN BROKE in the eastern sky. Pearly and luminous, it gently lifted the dark muslin veils of night, and as that mistress of shadows slipped away, and the soft nacre of first-light melted in the golden crucible of the rising sun, the day began its usual mastery of the desert. And yet, beyond the way it began, there was nothing usual or ordinary about that day in May.

The two opposing commanders, General Auchinlek and General Rommel, had been attempting to outguess each other with mental manoeuverings. The former believed, and correctly so, that the latter would mount a feigned attack in one direction while actually attacking from another; unfortunately, his field commanders misjudged which was which.

When the enemy was first sighted in and around Segnali in the afternoon of 26 May, a *khamsin* was blowing. The blinding dust made it difficult to gauge the strength of the enemy's forces, and it reinforced the belief that the real attack would come in the centre of the Gazala Line. However, during that night Rommel began to move southeastward. By light of moon, he stole through the night shadows, and although some of his movements were reported to the powers that be, they were deemed just part of the ruse.

It was nearly 0630 hours on the morning of the 27th when 3rd Motor Brigade sent out an urgent SOS: they were being engaged by *"a whole bloody German armoured division!"*

In point of fact, the attacking force was the Italian Ariete armoured division; and only now, finally, was it realised that Rommel had pre-empted them with an attack southeast of Bir Hacheim. (Michael Carver: *Dilemmas of the Desert War*). He had hooked under the southernmost defences of the Gazala Line, thus bypassing it, then swerved up again, pushing north to emerge among the Allied forces like a fox among the chickens.

All that day and into the next, the dust of battle could be seen for miles around as the two armies clashed. They quickstepped back and forth across a stretch of desert, thirty miles wide, that extended all the way up to the Knightsbridge Box and eastward across the El Duda ridge to Bel Hamed. A steady stream of casualties began to flow through to the rear; and at Gambut disquieting rumours began to filter back from the frontlines. The balloon had gone up, and it wasn't going the way it was supposed to.

A ragtag stream of vehicles brought the wounded from the front, and Santi had been busy all morning tending to injuries the like of which he had never seen before. In response to a summons, he had just entered Colonel Weallens tent to acquaint him with the condition and number of incoming casualties, when Ben Browne poked his head in through the half open flap of the entrance.

"May I come in, sir?"

"Indeed you may, Browne. Come on in."

"They seem to be kicking off in earnest at the front, sir. Another truckload of wounded just pulled in. Chap from 7th Armoured Division says they were overrun shortly after 1000 hours this morning, following 3rd Motor Brigade who went down just before 0830. Jumpy as the dickens, poor fellow; claims it was arse over tip in the south when he left – er, sorry sir, his words not mine," Ben added hurriedly. "Something else he's prattling on about, though; says General Messervy was captured, but canteen gossip has it that soon after being gaffed he made a getaway. Any truth there, sir?"

Santi nodded; he had heard a similar rumour. "The story making the rounds is that he managed to pass himself off as an ordinary soldier by discarding his pips, then somehow gave them the slip under cover of an artillery attack, courtesy our side."

"There have been various accounts of an escape, no official confirmation yet," Willie said, rubbing his chin. "But, knowing the old man, if indeed he was scooped up, I would be willing to believe there's a good deal of truth to what we're hearing."

When the facts of Major-General Francis Messervy's escapade eventually came to light, they did not fall short of his reputation. It turned out the minute he was captured he had indeed, with great presence of mind, discarded all insignia and badges of rank. He then attempted to present himself as the officers' mess cook. However, his advanced age caught the attention of an observant German officer.

Eyeing him suspiciously, the officer decided to accost him.

"Aren't you a bit old for a private?" the German demanded, looking the old codger up and down.

British Matilda tank passing Knightsbridge Junction, Cauldron, Battle of Gazala, June '42.

"You're right," agreed Messervy, feigning disgust. "It's a bloody disgrace they've called me up at my age!" (John Bierman and Colin Smith: *War Without Hate*)

Despite facing gallant opposition, Rommel's thrust into British defences was achieved so speedily, its very success now landed him on somewhat of a slippery slope. His supply lines were stretched thin and he found himself caught between the minefields and fortified Boxes of the Gazala Line on his western flank, and to his east, the tanks of the armoured brigades and divisions around Knightsbridge and El Adem. This area would later come to be known as the Cauldron. Now, Rommel's predicament here was compounded by heavy bombardment from the RAF's Kittyhawks and Hurricanes which made regular forays from the Gambut airfields in a desperate attempt to stall his advance.

The fighting continued thus until nightfall. Slowly, the tide of battle seemed to turn in favour of the Allies, and Rommel withdrew, falling back into the British-laid minefields in an apparent state of confusion.

"He's scarpered!" A jubilant cry went up among the rank and file. "Rommel's done a runner, he has!"

"'E's bleedin' done a bunk that's wot!"

"Right 'n' all. We'll send 'im skedaddlin' right orf back ter that little feller 'Itler, see if we don't!"

When news of Rommel's retreat reached the 2/4, it was met with mixed reactions.

"By Jove, I think we have him!" Robert Williams exclaimed to Santi.

"By all accounts it would seem so," Santi agreed. "I hear he retreated in complete disorder and is stranded in our minefields. But, I wonder, do you think he's actually done for?"

"It would be a mistake to underestimate the chap. He's certainly taught us a thing or two these many months past; but I think he's finally got his come-uppance."

"Well, there's a fine how d'ya do!" Roger Werner sounded disgruntled. "We haven't had a bash at the Germans yet, and already they're legging it back to Libya. All this way, and we didn't get so much as a whiff of the old Fox! Dashed rotten luck, if you ask me! What I call a jolly poor show."

"Careful what you wish for, Roger me old blood!" Ben warned with a laugh. "You know what they say about wishes. Some have the darndest way of coming true."

By the following day the feeling of astonished euphoria had spread to Advance HQ in Gambut where it was believed a victory was, indeed, at hand. When news reached England, a congratulatory signal arrived at MEF Headquarters in Cairo, egging Auchinlek on to greater glory: The missive, duly signed by Churchill, bore the sign-off: *KBO – Keep Buggering On.*

And well it might have gone the desired way for the Allies had the opportune moment been used to advantage, and British armoured brigades been properly organised alongside the infantry for immediate, simultaneous attacks on Rommel's forces. Forces that were, by then, subsisting on a half cup of water per man per day, and very little food, petrol and ammunition to boot. Better than anyone else, the Desert Fox realised his dire situation. If the British were to go on the offensive right now, he would, more than likely, have to surrender. In fact, he had felt honour-bound eventually to release a few hundred Allied prisoners of war for lack of food and water – especially water – to sustain them.

But inexplicably, no effort was made to exploit Rommel's position of weakness and confusion following his retreat. For the Germans, this omission was a turn-up for the books. For the Allies, this omission by their proven commanders might lead one to wonder if there could indeed be some truth to the local belief that the desert was apt to play tricks on the soundest of minds. Howbeit, differing opinions among the three Allied commanders resulted in misinterpretation of the enemy's actions. This led to a somewhat optimistic complacency, culminating in delays and missed opportunities.

While Ritchie and his two most senior Commanders, General William 'Strafer' Gott and General Willoughby Norrie, were attempting to reach a meeting of the minds, the window for a swift attack on the exhausted enemy trapped in the minefields was allowed to slip by. Under the assumption that he had not only been beaten back, but most effectively foiled as well, plans were being hammered out at Ritchie's HQ for Operation Aberdeen, an Allied mop-up of the defeated enemy. This oversight gave Rommel the time he so desperately needed to change the course of events. Indeed, while the British were commending themselves, still perceiving the mirage of victory, the Desert Fox was pulling his own rabbit out of a hat.

Late on 30 May, Commanding Officers of 10th Brigade were informed they would leaguer the following day at El Mrassas, fifteen miles west of Tobruk. Acting on orders that this was more of a clean-up operation, they were unprepared for what actually lay ahead.

Rommel had already begun regrouping and refitting. Now, under cover of a convenient dust storm, he managed to clear two pathways through the minefields of the Gazala Line, one at Bir et Tamar on the Trigh Capuzzo, and the other about ten miles south of the first. In so doing he managed to isolate 150 Brigade Box at Got el Ualeb, which now lay between the two newly created pathways; and with this success all thought of retreat vanished from his mind.

Banking on the continued dalliance and overly cautious mindset of the British Commanders, Rommel now prepared for an about-face to make his stand. To this end he set to bringing in his much-needed supplies and petrol from the west. By 31 May, the wily Desert Fox had dug his way out of a predicament and into a position to be reckoned with. Once again, the pendulum was about to swing away from the Allies in favour of the Axis.

⸻ ◆ ⸻

Captain SP Dutt
c/o Middle East Forces
Letter No.21   *30 May 1942*

Shree-Charaneshu Baba aar Ma (Revered Father and Mother whose feet I touch),

We have received news that seems to indicate we will soon be going into battle, probably to mop up after Rommel. There is not much worry there, since he is on the run. We are told he is desperately fleeing through our minefields, leaving behind all personal possessions – kambal and lota, blanket and mug

— while the RAF is making chhatu, pulverising his tanks. If our advance helps destroy his remaining tanks, this chapter of the war at least will be brought to a close. The sooner this human debacle is over the better.

Life here is a strange, almost indescribable experience, indeed. We spend much of it quartered in the earth just like our companions, the jerboas, little desert rats that live here in holes. By comparison, the odd cave we occasionally come upon is a luxury. Every time we move, we dig ourselves dozens of fresh slit trenches. In many areas, the ground is stony and ungiving, making the going harder than when it is soft and sandy. At surface level, all along the length of these trenches, we pile sandbags and drape grey-brown camouflage netting overhead the openings — and this is where we conduct our lives.

These slit trenches serve as sleeping quarters, eating quarters, even latrines — separate, of course — but whatever manner of trench, it is essential to survival since there is so little natural cover in the desert. It is 10° cooler below ground as well, a real blessing during the blistering heat of day.

Of course, as it is for us, so it is for our enemy. We suffer the same heat and privations, so when we are not battling one another, we are battling our common adversities — the desert with its scourge of heat, flies and mosquitoes. At times this is exploited by both sides, at other times it creates an uncanny sort of empathy and respect between us that is difficult to explain. On both sides, men and machines — tanks and vehicles — are carefully camouflaged with tans and browns and covered with burlap so they disappear, chameleon- like, into the endless brown and grey sandscape.

Mostly, this is a world without colour or contour; but at night, lying under the vast desert night sky, as the warm sand beneath you begins to cool with the touch of dew-fall from a heaven thick with stars…one is filled with an immeasurable sense of freedom. How should one describe this place, strangely beautiful sometimes, despite the havoc we are wreaking? Somehow, at night, when man's turmoil is stilled and Nature spreads her quiet, you are reminded of a Great Force out there — and, without a doubt, you can feel the presence of God…

10TH INDIAN INFANTRY BRIGADE left for El Mrassas on the morning of 31 May. Travelling westward along the asphalt coastal road they soon began to see, all around them, devastating evidence of this desert war. They had believed themselves prepared, yet, the extent of the violence took them aback. On both sides the road was littered with the debris of battle: bombed-out, broken-down vehicles, burnt-out tanks, some of which were still smouldering, and the smashed, skeletal remains of downed aircraft. The enormity of the destruction was dismaying.

Even more disquieting was the human element of this atrocity that lay littered, like trash discarded across the sands. Sad and sorry, without regard or respect for what once they had been: the now useless belongings of some brave fallen warrior, private possessions that had at one time been prized enough to fetch a smile, a tear, raise a hope in someone's heart; things, once dear, their worth not bound to size or cost, but measured by the comfort wrought to body and mind, to heart and soul. And now…mere trivia, abandoned, good for naught, exposed to the ignorance of passing strangers and the destructive forces of the callous elements. Santi was deeply moved. The fleeting value and transience of all material possessions could not but leave a profound impression and change one's entire perspective of life.

Most horrifying of all were the bodies; crushed, twisted, charred. Even before they saw them, they smelt them – the strange, sickly-sweet smell of decay and, from time to time, of burnt flesh. Although the men tried to remain stoic, the stench assailed their nostrils with such force, it made them gag. Someone in Santi's lorry threw up. The human remains were shocking, some even beyond recognition as anything human; and startlingly, a few seemed to move – till you got up close.

"*Sahib,*" Dilbahadur whispered in horror. "*Kiraharu chaldai chha!*" The bodies were not moving, it was the squirming maggots and the buzzing flies that infested them!

"*Ho,* Dilbahadur," Santi replied, his voice low, shaken by the sight of this corruption that once had been wholesome, breathing, living men. "*Yo manchhe thiyo!*"

The men looked on in stricken silence. Just a short while ago these…putrid objects…this terrible mess lying there…had been someone's comrade in arms, with brown eyes or blue perhaps, light hair or dark; no matter that his features might have been comely or homely, what counted were his feelings and dreams, the sound of his voice, the fullness of his laughter, his life – its promise that lay so grievously spilt upon the desert sands. Whichever side he had belonged to was inconsequential; he deserved better. This ghastly waste of humanity was devoid of all dignity and belied all reason.

"For God's sake, do not write about honour and glory…war is a stinking, ugly, horrible business."

A weary WWI combatant had pleaded with the world, twenty years before the outbreak of this war. Had no one heard him, had the world been deaf? How could humanity have forgotten its suffering in so short a time? It seemed nothing had changed as they went headlong into a repeat of that 'stinking, ugly, horrible business', intent on outdoing themselves. In the face of such egregious error how could one possibly believe in the sanity, responsibility or future of mankind?

We are the echoes of our ancestors, the sum total of their experiences, born in the light of their achievements and in the shadow of their mistakes; we are the better for lessons that have been learnt, and doomed to repeat those that have not.

And as the living drove past the dead, their silence was filled with pain for those unknown soldiers, the lost fathers, husbands, brothers and sons, whose fate it was to remain here, forever strangers in a strange land, far from home and those who would mourn them.

"Dear God!" someone muttered, softly. "Poor devils."

After that no one spoke for a long time. Carnage on this scale was a shocking new experience.

Travelling by both main and side roads, the Brigade passed through Tobruk and continued westward for a further fifteen miles till they reached El Mrassas at 2100 hours. Their arrival had been noted and, as they were preparing to bivouac on the outskirts of the town, they were met with a short but fierce bombardment from enemy aircraft. Fortunately, however, there was not much damage. An hour later, they had just set up camp and begun to disperse for the night, when Lt. Peter O'Bree, the Battalion's Liaison Officer with Brigade, arrived – he had news.

"Word's just in; we've received our Uncle Charlie. Orders are we're to be on the ready…" He was cut short by a chorus of groans and weary protest.

"Oh topper! Wouldn't you bloody know it! Would someone please turf this maggot out!"

"Drat! Something told me I should have kept my ruddy boots on!"

'Blast you, Peter, you have rotten timing! I'm so tuckered out, I could sleep standing up."

O'Bree grimaced. "Sorry chaps! Take heart, it isn't quite as bad as all that, you know. We've been put on one hour's alert for deployment to the front, but at least we're not having to pull out immediately. We'll have to remain in full gear, of course, but there's nothing else for it I'm afraid." Hoping to lighten the mood, he added, "the Colonel's gone ahead for a *dekho;* meeting with Brigadier Boucher outside Tobruk at a place known as – wait for it chaps – Mussolini's Arse."

This irreverence was met with shouts of laughter.

"Mussolini's *what*!"

"I say, jolly good show! Can't think of a more appropriate description for this infernal hell hole."

"Oh, well done! That should put the wind up His Italian Majesty's whoopsy daisy!"

O'Bree grinned. "I would wager that was the precise intention of the genius who thought it up. Actually, if you must have it, it's Mussolini's Arch; but that ain't nearly as appealing now is it?"

"What gives, Peter? What's afoot? Any word from the top brass at Brigade HQ?"

"Not so much as a whisper, I'm afraid – just this order, prepare to shove off at short notice. Suppose we'll know more of what's in the works when Col. Weallens returns. Meanwhile," O'Bree turned to leave, "we might as well grab forty winks, or whatever we can under the circumstances."

"Lord knows we need it," Santi muttered, worn out by the trek across the desert as well as the ravages they had witnessed along the way.

As it happened, Colonel Weallens did not return that night, and fortunately for the exhausted men, the order to stand-to did not carry through either. Enemy planes did visit, however, a thorough nuisance that managed to create quite a to-do for a while; but as soon as they left, those desert warriors, in full gear as they were, slept the good sleep of the weary.

CHAPTER TWENTY-NINE
A Close Call

*Would some wingéd Angel ere too late
Arrest the yet unfolded Roll of Fate,
And make the stern Recorder otherwise
Enregister, or quite obliterate!*

– Omar Khayyam, *Rubaiyat of Omar Khayyam*

JUNE 1ST: A DAY of much needed rest and recreation. Once they had replenished their water supply at the water point guarded by a South African unit, the men spent the day taking turns visiting the beach. Fresh and relaxed after enjoying a long, languid swim, Santi sat down to finish the letter he had started two days earlier. He made no mention of the disturbing sights and the devastation of war so recently witnessed:

May is over and it is now June. I was unable to finish this letter the other day, but I will make sure it catches today's outgoing post. Yesterday, I received Kamala's letter together with the photo I had requested of you both. I will be writing to her myself soon but, meanwhile, please thank her for sending it to me so promptly. I feel it is auspicious that your photo arrived when it did. I shall carry it, and your blessings, with me through the days ahead.

This morning I managed a quick trip to the seashore. It isn't often we enjoy this proximity to the sea, and as you approach it from the desert you can almost taste the salt air. What a relief! We make up bathing parties and, armed with grenades in case a shark turns unfriendly, we take every advantage of our short-lived luck.

After days in the hot, arid desert, its sand and grit embedded in every pore, the simple pleasure of once again being able to immerse your whole body in warm, fresh, sparklingly clean water is beyond anything you can imagine! It is a heavenly luxury one would not trade for a kingdom! I do not believe any of us will ever take the basic commodity of water for granted after this.

It was my turn early this morning, and believe me when I say, the joy of washing off days of encrusted sweat and sand, of reverting from a filthy, weary wreck to some semblance of a human being once again, cannot be conveyed in words; it has to be experienced to be understood!

On my way back I happened upon a Senussi Beduin selling fresh eggs. He was not interested in our money, of which he seemed to have wads, but he was willing to trade for items such as tea, sugar, cigarettes. So we bartered, and for three packets of cigarettes I was able to procure six wonderfully fresh eggs. I am almost certain the Senussi would have agreed to two packets of cigarettes, but since I believed I was getting the better end of the bargain anyway, I was filled with such gratitude and goodwill, I gave him the third packet willingly. We parted company, both pleased with the outcome of our negotiations.

Later, I shared my good fortune with my batman – of course, slim pickings as it was, he received two eggs only while I retained four. From those four, he was good enough to prepare two perfect fried eggs for my breakfast while the other two went into an egg curry I relished with much enthusiasm for my lunch. What a feast! So you see, all in all, I have done very well for myself of late.

I will write again, as soon as I have more time, regarding a certain matter of recent occurrence. Though it could wait, since it is early days yet, I believe it to be my duty that you, as my parents, should be informed of any important decisions I take in my life.

I realise, now, how much concern I must have caused you by joining the army in the manner I did, and I am truly sorry for the anxiety I put you through. Rest assured I am taking every precaution, so there is no need to worry unduly. Keep in mind, as a doctor I am well away from the fighting, and safe from harm. And, God willing, this will end soon so we can all return to our homes once again. I have come to realise that nationalities and sides do not matter; we all have families who miss us, and homes we long to get back to. Somehow, it must, it will, all work out in the end.

I ask for your blessings and I pray for your good health. My pranams, my deepest respect and love to you both.

Your son, Santi

After he finished the letter and folded it, Santi pulled a curious looking object from his pocket. At best it could be described as having a somewhat squarish body from which dangled five flaccid tentacles. From this 'tentacled object' he carefully removed his wallet, and immediately the strange article reverted to the recognizable form of a surgical glove. (Since the old plastic wrap used these many months past to keep his wallet safe from sun, sand and sweat had recently disintegrated, expediency prompted ingenuity, and one made do with whatever replacement came to hand.)

Inside his wallet – well-worn despite its meticulous wrapping – was an old family photo he had carried since leaving home. It had become rather the worse for wear, faded and dog-eared. He laid the photo aside while he retrieved a small wooden box from his luggage. He opened it, revealing a stack of letters within. He withdrew the topmost letter, Kamala's letter, and from its envelope he removed the recently received photo of his parents. He turned it over and read once again their message to him on the back. It was in Bengali:

With each passing day we give thanks you have been kept safe from harm, and we pray each tomorrow will continue to bless you with well-being and life.

Carefully he placed the new photo, along with the old one, in his wallet, tucked the wallet safely back into its protective glove and, once more, returned the all-important packet to his pocket.

1500 HOURS THAT AFTERNOON finally brought the order for their immediate departure. O'Bree was the bearer of tidings once again. They were to rendezvous that night at a place in the desert known simply as Point 169, ten miles east of Knightsbridge, where further orders would be given for their advance to the front. The urgency of the message did not bode well.

"What's going on?" Santi asked O'Bree. "I thought Jerry was making a run for it through our minefields – lock, stock and barrel, so we were told."

"Duff gen, apparently. Seems we misjudged the old Fox. While we were thinking victory, he was refuelling and refitting. We gave him the chance, and now he's done an about face. Putting on quite a show for those poor devils at the front!"

"Well, we're in for it, then. Looks like Werner's about to get his 'bash' at the enemy. He was somewhat miffed when he thought he'd missed out on the 'fox' hunt."

"Far from it! I'll lay you a wager, six to one, this ain't over by a long shot. We're bound to be in the thick of it before too long."

The bad news in the desert was tempered by some 'heartening' news from England – that is, if the devastation of cities, enemy or otherwise, could be considered as such.

In 1940 Germany had bombed the English city of Coventry, and in 1941 large areas of London were devastated by the Blitz. By the time it was over, forty thousand people had been killed. In retaliation for the bombing of London, the RAF bombed the German cities of Essen, Hamburg, Dortmund, Bremen, Stuttgart, and the medieval cities of Rostock and Lubeck. In response, Hitler chose England's ancient and beautiful cities of Exeter, Norwich, Canterbury, Bath and York as targets. An eye for an eye and one better!

Now, on the night of 30 May 1942, in an all-out attempt to demoralize the enemy's civilian population, the RAF sent 1,047 aircraft on a massive bombing raid to Cologne. In the largest raid to date, two thousand tons of incendiaries were dropped, spreading devastation over hundreds of acres across the city. This remorseless annihilation of life and property was deemed necessary to break the spirit of the German nation; and the triumph at its success spoke to the nature of the times and the madness that had gripped both sides in this terrible war.

Sadly, this retaliatory madness would only escalate, till, in the last months of the war, a combined RAF and US Air Force bombing of Dresden would create a firestorm that obliterated that ancient German city. (Tim Clayton & Phil Craig: *End of the Beginning*)

WWII was truly humanity's sad fall from grace.

British 25 pounder gun, night action, Battle of Gazala, June 1942.

THE TREK UP TO and through Acroma was without mishap; but soon after, as night overtook the convoy, the sands began to stir as though awakened. The wind picked up, and the desert – quick to anger and ever ready to assert its mastery – whipped into a furious sandstorm that swept all before it. With no control posts to guide them, the Brigade became badly scattered. Somewhere ahead the bark of gunfire and the thunder of cannon shot could be heard. A massive tank battle was underway, and the appearance of wreckage about them made it clear it could hardly be far. Blinded, however, by swirling dust and darkness that played havoc with the senses, the actual location or distance was hard to tell.

Burning tanks and trucks loomed out of the dark like ghostly spectres, and in the all-round confusion it was impossible to make out friend from foe. The convoy had disintegrated into small, disoriented groups of vehicles. Many found they had been driving around in circles, and some lorries, unwittingly, had come dangerously close to running into the enemy. In fact, there were several instances when the foe was, indeed, mistaken for friend, very nearly resulting in capture.

Allies capture German PanzerIII tank, 1942.

At one point, the lorry carrying Santi and his stretcher bearers seemed so irretrievably lost he ordered Lal Bahadur, his driver, to halt so they might get their bearings. Sitting up front, he would not, he knew, get a correct reading from his compass inside or close to the truck. He cracked his side door open a couple of inches, then shut it again in a hurry as the storm pounced on him with the whiplash of a frenzied banshee.

If I go out there, I'll run the risk of getting lost in that orange hell, he thought, peering with misgiving at the howling wind-driven sand outside. *It would be the easiest thing to become completely disoriented merely by stepping away from the truck. Yet, if I don't…*

He mulled over the situation a moment longer before making up his mind – it had to be done. There was nothing for it. He would have to get out and walk a few feet away, at least, to get a reliable reading. He would have to take every precaution, keep his wits about him. Hopefully, there would be no need to go too far for a correct reading.

Raising his voice above the rush of wind and the rumble of their lorry, Santi instructed Lal Bahadur to turn off his engine. He tried hard to listen for a sound, any sound, but it was difficult to hear anything above the wailing of the wind and that eerie drumming of the desert. Donning his goggles, he wrapped his kerchief over his mouth and nose in order to minimise the sand he knew he would ingest with every breath. Then, cautiously, he alighted into the clutch of the devil's own hellion.

It was, of course, a vain attempt to thwart the sand, invasive and searing like the breath of hell. Even inside the vehicle it filtered through every chink and cranny, and it seeped through each pore and crevice of the body, coating both inside and out with a suffocatingly fine, beige powder that transformed everyone into replica figures of indistinguishable grey. Now, outside, Santi felt the full strength and fury of the whirling dervish.

Lowering his head against the lashing of wind and sand, he held onto the vehicle as he made his way carefully to the rear of the lorry. He undid a corner of the canvas flap that secured the back of the vehicle and peered inside; several Gurkha faces peered back at him. He recalled previously seeing a rope in the truck, he explained; could someone have a look and pass it to him?

When it was found and handed to him, he secured one end to the steel frame of the vehicle and fastened the other end with his lanyard to the belt around his waist; then, using it as a lead, he stepped into what seemed the very heart of the shrieking storm.

Gingerly, he took one step into the swirling void, followed by another, and then another, counting as he went. He halted and shone a torch on his compass to get a reading. He wiped his goggles and blinked hard to focus. He could just make out, his compass indicated he was facing south-west. Good.

About to return to the truck, he became aware of a familiar sound mingling with, and barely audible above, the shrill whistle of the wind and the distant, dull thud and roll of gunfire. Lal Bahadur had obeyed the order to cut his engine, and yet Santi could hear a sound much like the throaty rumble of one or more heavy vehicles. He listened intently; yes, there it was, cutting in and out with the wind. There had to be another vehicle, somewhere, very nearby.

Hoping to link up with the convoy, or at least with one of its number, Santi decided to investigate. He concentrated, listening as best he could for the direction of the sound; it wasn't easy since the wind whipped sight, sound and all other senses into a whirl of confusion. When he thought he had it, he moved. Head low, butting hard against the full force of the wind, he fought his way towards it.

He had covered no more than a few steps when he made out the vague outline of a vehicle directly ahead of him, perhaps some twelve to fifteen feet away. It had loomed up so suddenly, and so close, he had almost run into it.

With a surge of relief, his first instinct was to call out. It was quickly followed by the realisation it was nigh impossible he would be heard from where he stood; no sooner would the words reach his lips than the *khamsin's* greedy, thieving fingers would reach in to snatch them right out of his mouth, and toss them contemptuously to the howling gale. He needed to get closer, he thought. But hardly had he put thought to action, than he felt a tautening of his rope, indicating his safety line was about to run out. He certainly couldn't risk that. It was his lifeline, the only way he had of getting back and finding his own truck.

He halted. Cautiously he tugged and managed to close some little distance between himself and the unknown vehicle – he seemed almost within touching distance. Mingled with the throb of the engine that carried towards him in the storm, he could just make out ragged snatches of wind-torn conversation. Thank goodness! If he could hear them, then he was probably close enough to be heard as well. And not a moment too soon, as the unyielding tension on his rope told him it was stretched to its limit. He was, quite literally, at the end of his tether.

Straining into the night, he was about to shout out, when that small voice inside his head advocated caution. And it served him well. Listening intently a moment or two longer, he became aware from the flotsam of conversation blowing his way, the voices were speaking German. The realisation halted him dead in his tracks.

As quietly and as quickly as he could, hand over hand on his lifeline, Santi beat a hasty retreat. When he arrived at his lorry, he uttered a single word – *dushman*, enemy – and gestured a quick command for silence. It was speedily obeyed. Everyone was acutely aware, but for the wall of opaque dust which hid them, they were practically sitting on top of the Germans! There could not have been more than a few scant metres separating them from the enemy!

Headlights were doused, and no one moved a muscle as they waited in pin-drop silence. The next few minutes seemed to stretch into an eternity while Santi considered his options. There was no knowing if the vehicle he had come across was a lone wolf, or whether more were scattered around. They might very well be surrounded! If he chose to move while the storm was still raging, they could well blunder headlong into the enemy. However, if he decided to remain, to wait out the storm, it was possible the Germans, equally befuddled, might opt to do the same. In that case, his truck would be spotted immediately.

A regular Morton's Fork, if ever there was one, Santi thought wryly. Damned either way! Nonetheless, choose he must. And so, he took the plunge and decided his best bet was to chance moving away as quickly and as quietly as possible. Praying there were no more enemy vehicles in their path, he gave the order, and as everyone held their breath, Lal Bahadur turned on the engine. The minute it growled to life, they slipped quickly into the arms of the storm, heading downwind to the best of their ability, hoping the *khamsin* would swallow their sound and carry it away from the Germans.

Their luck held. The decision to make a break for it proved to be the right one.

"*Kali Ma ki jai!*" Softly muttered praise for Mother Kali's beneficence went up from the Gurkhas. It was surely her divine protection that had safeguarded them from disaster! They were fortunate indeed, the sound of their engine had been drowned out, both, by the enemy vehicle and by the storm, allowing them to slip away undetected; but it had been a call too close for comfort!

After that narrow squeak with fate, they continued cautiously, edging their way in the dark as best they could. It was completely by chance they almost ran into the Jamedar Major's car, with three more carriers in tow. Much relieved at having strengthened their numbers, Santi determined not to run the risk of separation again. In order to prevent any further straying, he once again hauled out the sturdy rope he had used earlier as a lifeline.

Lal Bahadur looked on doubtfully. "*Sahib, rassi tyo lorry samma pugdaina.*"

Assuring the driver he had worked out a plan to ensure the rope would have sufficient reach, Santi set about securing his lorry to the one in front, tying the rope to the cords of both vehicles' camouflage.

The Gurkhas, watching with interest, quickly caught on. Directed by Santi to forage for more rope in the other vehicles, they made short shrift of securing every vehicle to the one preceding it.

Ready to move on, Santi consulted his compass to confirm their direction, and they proceeded in convoy, the storm keeping them at no more than a Canterbury pace. Once more, as much by chance as by calculation, the small entourage fell in with Armoured Brigade Headquarters. Here, at long last, they were able to obtain directions to their own Battalion HQ and, after a fifteen minute, much appreciated rest-up, they prepared to tackle the final leg of their trek.

They ventured into the storm again, past the wrecks of broken, burning tanks and trucks, all the while blown mercilessly ragged by the wind; and when nature's fury finally had been exhausted, enemy aircraft took the advantage, buzzing overhead, dipping low and dogging them with bombs all the way to their destination.

"And where the flaming hell was our RAF?" Roger Werner demanded indignantly, when they met up later. "Not a single bloody crate showed up to take on those beggars. The cheeky sods dropped their damnable payload on us, easy as you please, and not a flyboy in sight!"

Santi nodded wearily. "They had a field day with us as well! Damn things came in so low, when they opened their bomb-bays you actually got to see into their bellies. Bloody lucky no one bought it!

Werner snorted in disgust. "I'll say! Bad enough trying to herd our lot while being blown all about the desert in that beastly awful sandstorm, then the Luftwaffe gets into the act – and not so much as a pip or squeak from our lot! So much for the RAF! The whole thing was a right-royal shambles, I tell you! A proper fiasco!"

In the end, it was rendered impossible for the Brigade to reach its destination by nightfall; but gradually, individually and in groups, the fragmented convoy rallied at Point 169. Santi's small company reached it at 2200 hrs, followed soon after by Ronnie Smith and his contingent. As it turned out, by the time the last stragglers had found their way to Point 169, shepherded in willy nilly by Peter OBrie liaising all night long, it was the early hours of 2 June; the storm eventually had abated, and the moon had rallied bravely in the sky.

CHAPTER THIRTY

Angel Of The Full Moon

Hey diddle diddle, a Girl with a Riddle
Was born on the Night of the Moon.
A little Cat prowled and had such fun
Till the night she was smacked with a Spoon.

– Adapted from a Nursery Rhyme

HEDEYA WAS IN A hurry – already three minutes late, and if she did not leave the house in the next seven minutes, she would miss her tram. That would never do. She was a punctual person by habit, and always at work on time. This morning, however, after spending another restless night trying to banish fruitless conjecture, and the memory of a face that persisted in haunting her in the most unsettling way, to add to that inconsideration, Bebé had delayed her with uncommon foolishness.

The morning started out quite as usual with Bajo getting the child ready for school; but for some reason, the normally sedate little girl played up. In spite of being chided, she insisted on repeatedly jumping off the bed to see just how much further she could manage with each leap. Having driven her Grandmother to distraction, and having thoroughly exasperated her Mother, the inevitable happened – Bebé fell and split open her right knee.

Of course, soothing the child – and scolding her at the same time – whilst washing the cut and bandaging it required the attention of both women; and by the time the tearful girl was patched up and packed off to school, Hedeya herself was running late. So, when Bajo entered the bedroom, she hesitated, watching silently for a moment as Hedeya hurried about trying to make up for lost time.

"We will need some milk for tomorrow," Bajo spoke softly as though that would make the interruption less intrusive.

"There's some money on the dressing table. It should be enough…" Hedeya broke off, frowning momentarily before adding. "I thought we had enough to last for two days more?"

"The cat," Bajo said casually.

"What cat?"

"You know, that cat, Hoory. The one Fatma Halabi told us about."

Hedeya stopped brushing her hair, and turned. "You saw her?"

"I didn't actually see her, but this morning I found the milk jug overturned and small milky paw-prints leading to the window. Who else could it be?"

"So, you really believe her story about the black cat then!" Hedeya laughed, putting the brush down on the dressing table and hastily applying a dab of lipstick to her lips.

"Whether I believe it or I don't does not make it true or false. Laugh if you must, but one thing I do know – there are things in this world, and beyond it, that are hidden from the eyes on our face. It is with the eyes of the soul that we must learn to see. Sometimes strange happenings take place around us that cannot be explained. One day you will understand."

"Yes, Bajo." Looking appropriately serious, Hedeya kissed her mother goodbye, grabbed her handbag and ran down the stairs. She had almost forgotten the strange incident that occurred two days after they first arrived in Rod el Farag.

It had been midmorning, and Hedeya and Bajo were still settling into the new place when they received their first visitor. She introduced herself as Fatma Halabi, a resident from three doors down, across the street, and she bade them welcome to the neighbourhood. Hedeya invited her in for a cup of coffee and left her to chat with Bajo in the drawing room while she went into the kitchen to put the *kanaka* on.

Fatma Halabi seemed like any ordinary, friendly person and Hedeya was grateful she had taken the trouble to pay them a visit. It was a kind, neighbourly thing to do. However, about fifteen minutes into the visit, when Fatma made her strange request, she was not so sure.

"If you see a black cat, please, don't hurt her."

Hedeya had smiled reassuringly. "Of course not! You don't need to worry. We would never hurt your cat. We are all fond of cats here. What is its name?"

"We call her Hoori for short, but the name she was given at birth was Hooriyah al Badra – Angel of the Full Moon."

"What a beautiful name! She must be a very special cat with a name like that. You must love her a great deal"

"I do, and…she *is* special. She is very…precious to me. You see, she…" the woman's words had faltered for a moment "…she is my daughter. But sometimes…" once more she'd hesitated, "sometimes she does things she should not do. It is not because she is bad. It is just that she is very young, and she doesn't realise…she means no harm…" Her voice, strangely pained, broke a little, and she stopped as though she were not sure how to continue.

"How long have you had her?" Hedeya asked, gently.

"My daughter is five years old."

A strange sensation ran down Hedeya's spine. Her visitor's answers were perplexingly odd. She could appreciate a cherished pet being a member of one's family, lovingly referred to as a son or a daughter; but the way this woman insisted that her cat *was* her daughter was, well, rather peculiar – as though they were one and the same, as though she could not separate the two. In fact, there was something truly unsettling, almost eerie about her manner.

Hedeya had stolen a quick look across at Bajo, wondering what she thought of this extraordinary affair, but her mother's face had been expressionless. *Maybe*, she thought, *I have just misunderstood what the woman is saying.*

"Is Hoory your daughter's cat?" she ventured at last, politely

Fatma had stared silently at Hedeya for a moment; then, getting up, she had walked to the window. "Come, let me show you."

When Hedeya followed to stand beside her, she pointed across the street to a small green patch – it was too small to be called a park – where two children were playing. "Do you see that little girl, the one with the dark hair, in the pink and white frock?" Curious to see what was going on, Bajo too had ambled up to the window. "That is my daughter."

"*Zayy il ful!* You have a very beautiful daughter, Fatma, like a jasmine flower. *Mabrouk.*"

"She is a beautiful child, is she not? Like an angel!"

"Yes, she is just like a little angel." For a few moments Hedeya had gazed at the two children playing together. What she saw looked quite ordinary. More puzzled than ever, she turned back to the mother and added with a small laugh, "But that lovely child doesn't look anything like a black cat."

Fatma's voice, when she answered, was softly reflective. "When I got engaged to be married, my mother wanted to make sure it would be a good marriage, so she took me to see Khaireya Badawi, the soothsayer. We had been told, not only could she tell someone's fortune but, in some instances, she could fix it as well." She paused before continuing.

"She took some time looking into my future, and then she left the room. When she returned, she told me I had nothing to worry about in my marriage, all would be well; and she gave me this small amulet to wear."

Fatma pulled out something small hanging on a chain inside her blouse. Both Hedeya and Bajo leaned forward to see a tiny, finely carved figurine of Bastet, Cat Goddess of the Moon, symbol of motherhood and protector of women.

"I was told to wear this always if I wanted to have a child." Fatma had turned from the window with a sigh. Returning to the chair she had vacated, she sat down. "I never took it off, and yet, it was seven years before I became pregnant. My husband and I had almost given up hope, so you can imagine – we were ecstatic. And…somehow…I knew we were going to have a little girl."

When she spoke again, Fatma's voice was soft, almost as though she were talking to herself. "The night she was born there was a full moon. I had been taking a bath that night, and the moonlight was pouring in through my window; it was so lovely and bright, I remember thinking it was like magic, and I did not switch on the lights. The water was washed silver, it was almost like bathing in moonlight, and I did not want to spoil the feeling."

With her eyes closed, Fatma continued. "I touched the amulet at my throat, and I told myself, if she should be born that night – I was already a week late you see – it would be with the blessing of Bastet's moon, and I would call her Badra, Full Moon. So, when it happened, and she was born three hours later... so beautiful…so small and soft, and moist… almost glowing ... I called her Hooriyah al Badra because she really was like the Angel of the Full Moon."

She stopped then, and in the short silence Hedeya glimpsed the shadow of sadness darken the face of her strange visitor. When she spoke again, her voice held a note of anguish.

"Maybe we should have called her something else. Maybe without realising… You see, it happens only on full moon nights."

What? What was supposed to happen on full moon nights? Was this some sort of joke played on newcomers to the area? The woman sounded sincere, but her story made no sense at all. Unless…

Poor thing! She must be quite mad, Hedeya thought, pityingly.

Almost as though Hedeya had spoken her thoughts out loud, Fatma shook her head. "I know what you are thinking. But I am not mad. Do not ask me to explain it. I cannot. No one can, but as Allah is my witness, I am telling you the truth. I am standing here before you, telling you that this…this terrible change afflicts my daughter; that beautiful child out there…that little girl…so normal in every way…turns into a black cat."

Hedeya gasped in disbelief as Fatma continued.

"Do you think this is an easy thing for a mother to do? Everytime someone new moves into the neighbourhood I have to make sure they know, so no harm comes to her by mistake. And every time, I see the same look I see on your face right now. They think I am mad. But what else can I do? It is the only way I can protect her. You must believe me and promise me you will not beat her if she steals from your kitchen. Sometimes she is naughty that way."

"But Fatma, things like this don't happen in real life! What makes you think your daughter changes into a cat?"

"We found out two years ago. Till then we had not paid much attention to the little stories she sometimes told of her nightly escapades – we thought they were just her imagination, or dreams. Then, one evening my husband took Hoory with him to work, to the small restaurant he owns two blocks from here. After a while she grew tired, but he could not leave to bring her home since it was a very busy night, so he put her to sleep in a small room in the back. Some time later, he was in the kitchen serving some *mukh wa kebda* onto a plate for a customer, when a small black cat jumped up onto the counter and tried to steal some of the food from the plate in front of him. Startled, he gave a shout and made to hit it with the spoon he was holding. The cat ran away, and it was then that he heard Hoory crying in the back room.

When he went to see what was wrong, she complained that he had scolded her and attempted to hit her. My husband tried to soothe her, telling her she had just had a bad dream and that he would never raise a hand to hit her.

'Not your hand, your spoon!' she cried.

"As you can imagine, my husband was taken aback and told her she was mistaken, but Hoory shook her head and said, 'I only wanted a small piece of *mukh*, Baba, and you beat me and chased me away.'"

Fatma's voice, slightly unsteady, died away leaving an astounded silence in the room. A cold prickling on the back of Hedeya's neck made her shiver. She shook her head, unable to accept what she had just heard. Surely there had to be some rational explanation to this bizarre story!

"It could be a mistake," she offered at last, rather lamely.

"No. After that we started keeping a close watch on her and we found, sometimes, on the morning after a full moon night, she would tell us that she had visited such and such neighbour and she had eaten so and so from their kitchen. We would check with the neighbours and it would turn out to be true. Sometimes they would even see the black cat. It was a shock, but eventually we had to believe what was true. One time our next-door neighbour threw a *taasé* at her, and we found a large bruise on her small shoulder next morning. After that we decided we could keep it a secret no longer, so we told all our neighbours and requested them not to harm her in any way. They have all been most understanding and kind."

Weeks had passed after that curious visit and, after a while, memory of it faded and was almost forgotten. Now and then, Hedeya would see Fatma or little Hoory and she would wave in passing. But she never did see the black cat. Now, according to Bajo, it had paid them a visit! Of course, it was quite absurd, but she knew better than to try to convince her mother.

Then, one night, not long after, it happened. Hedeya had stayed up late to put the finishing touches to a chemise she was sewing for a customer. After a while, feeling thirsty, she had gone to the kitchen for a glass of water.

Moonlight poured in through the window, and a full moon hung large and low in the night sky; and there, on the windowsill, sat a small black cat comfortably washing its face, and behind its ears. Hedeya stood stock still and stared at it. It looked quite ordinary, its black coat shining like satin where the moonlight reflected off it.

"*Ahlan,*" she greeted it, softly. "Is that you, Hoory?"

The cat turned and stared at her with the most incredible green eyes; they glowed, the colour of water-emeralds. Slowly, Hedeya took a few steps towards it.

"I don't suppose you can tell me your name, can you? It wouldn't happen to be Hoory?"

The cat mewed softly, and Hedeya had given a low, self conscious laugh that she should be conversing with the little creature and actually expecting it to answer back! *I must be quite as mad as Fatma!* She had brought a small saucer of milk with a little bread and placed it on the sill. Immediately, the tiny animal started lapping it up, purring loudly. Gently, Hedeya stroked the soft silky coat, and the cat had purred even louder.

It was a week later, while returning home, that she saw Fatma and her daughter across the street. They waved and hurried over. Hedeya had never seen the little girl at close quarters and, as they approached her, she was struck once again by the child's radiant beauty.

"Hoory wanted to thank you. She told me you were very kind to her when she visited you." Fatma turned to her daughter. "Hoory, remember what you told me?"

"I like Tanté Hedeya," the little girl said sweetly, looking up at Hedeya. "She's nice. She gave me cold milk with bread to drink, and she patted my head."

Hedeya was stunned. The words she had just heard left her speechless. She stared blankly at the strange child before her. It was not possible! It had to be some sort of trick! And yet, how could it be? No one other than she – and the cat, of course – had been privy to that night. Trying to get a hold of her thoughts, she looked searchingly into the pretty little face…and was transfixed! She found herself staring into the most incredible green eyes, the colour of water-emeralds!

CHAPTER THIRTY-ONE

The Devil's Cauldron

The fires that burn like glowing hills, light up the landscape grey,
The arid desert land bestills the fervours of the day.
The clear white moon sails through the skies and silvers all the night,
As if those eerie, ghostly flames had need of other light.
The death sighs of a thousand flowers the wretched day has slain
Are wafted through the star-filled hours, and whisper -
'Oh, for shame'!

– Violet Nicolson, *The Garden of Kama*, "Khan Zada's Song" (adapted)

WHILE 10 BRIGADE WAS roaming around lost in the sand-storm, Rommel remained undeterred by weather conditions. In fact, he turned them to his advantage. Having taken good measure of his enemy, and correctly assessing the mindset of British leadership, he decided to do the unexpected – he made a quick about-face. Taking full advantage of the two gaps he had cleared earlier through the Gazala Line, he launched a surprise attack on 150 Brigade Box at Got el Ualeb near Sidi Muftah.

The Yorkshire Territorials of 150 Brigade, already isolated between these two gaps, now caught the head-on impact of Rommel's onslaught. They put up a strong resistance that actually surprised the Germans; yet, as bravely as they fought, in the end they were unable to withstand the superior armour of the enemy. After enduring a severe pounding from his ground and air forces, they were finally overcome.

By midday on that first day of June, it was all over for 150 Brigade. The Allies suffered an embarrassing reversal that saw 3000 prisoners taken, and the Commanding Officer, Brigadier Clive Haydon, killed. It was an unforeseen disaster that called for quick, decisive containment.

Subsequently, at 1600 hours that same day – expecting 10 Brigade already to have rallied at Point 169 – Brigadier C.H. Boucher issued orders for 2/4 Gurkhas to advance two companies to Bir et Tamar, which lay on the Trigh Capuzzo. The advance was to start on the Dahar el Aslagh ridge at a reference point known as Barrel 180. This was but one of a series of 'barrels' painted with numbers that acted as survey points, thirty miles apart, and used as coordinates in a desert otherwise devoid of any reference points.

From Barrel 180 the Battalion was to then proceed three miles west to Bir et Tamar, located near the northern gap in the minefields. This was not far from where 150 Brigade had been vanquished. With the advance scheduled for 2200 hours that night, Colonel Weallens proceeded ahead to see to arrangements and mark the area with a heap of jerry cans. However, by 2100 hours the Battalion had failed to arrive at Point 169 as planned; along with the rest of 10 Brigade, it was still struggling in the desert, battling its way through the dust storm. As a result, the order for advance to Bir et Tamar was postponed to the following day – unfortunately so, as each hour's delay proved detrimental to the Allies and, conversely, of much advantage to the enemy.

2 JUNE: EVENTUALLY, AFTER its previous day-long joust with the dust storm, the weary Brigade came in from its wanderings in the desert. In the very early hours of the morning, in bedraggled dribs and drabs, the men drifted into Point 169, where they dug the essential slit trenches and fell into them to snatch a few short, but very grateful, hours of kip.

Short indeed, for not long past dawn Santi was awakened by Dilbahadur bearing a steaming mug of tea. The preparation of this beverage, commonly referred to as a 'brew-up' in the British Army, was prepared with some ingenuity by troops on the move. Typically, in the desert, a petrol can was filled with kerosene-soaked sand and set alight. On top of this, a second improvised petrol can was placed in which the tea was 'brewed'. While the brackish water thus boiled was barely improved by the addition of tea leaves and condensed milk, nevertheless, it was hot, it was sweet, and the concoction, though rampant with the flavour and smell of kerosene, was always most welcome. Indeed, it was a well-known fact that a 'cuppa cha' – frequently abbreviated further to a succinct 'cuppa' – had become the standard brew the British Army marched on.

By early light the men of the 2/4 gathered their belongings and made ready to pursue the previous day's flouted plans. But the new day was to prove worse than the one previous when a second, even more violent sandstorm blew up. They hit the desert in the middle of that raging storm. With the fierceness of a dragon's breath, it transformed their world into an orange, burning haze of flying sand, scorching the air as it melted the will of man and bent it to that of nature. How, one wondered, did the insects and animals of the desert survive this ferocity!

Once again, Santi used the camouflage cords to tie his vehicle to the one in front, keeping as short a gap between the two as was safe. But in the end, nature won the day. This was, after all, the realm of the desert, and it demanded an obeisance that would not be denied. It was wont to teach any who dared intrude upon its sands – be it lone traveller or great army – the futility of pitting oneself against its eternal might. Consequently, after a quick briefing, it was determined that the original destination of Bir et Tamar be aborted, and the Battalion should head south instead, towards Hyde Park Corner and Bir el Harmat.

It wasn't until 1700 hours that the scourge of wind and sand abated, and they were allowed passage through a now quiescent desert. Grateful for the reprieve, the Battalion trekked its weary way south and stumbled into Bir el Harmat. Here they dossed down for the night in their usual manner, on the desert floor, in freshly dug slit trenches, canopied overhead by heaven's vaulted expanse of wide starry skies.

---

3 JUNE: MORNING BROUGHT an onslaught of enemy artillery fire. It was returned with interest and, despite heavy enemy shelling, the various patrols held through the scuffle, managing to dig in and hold their ground. Fortunately, reinforcement by the remainder of the Brigade arrived in the nick of time, and the enemy finally was pushed back.

The British, with wry humour, had promptly named the two gaps that comprised Rommel's southern clearing through their minefields. Perched as they were along the Allied barbed-wire minefield, the gaps were duly christened Peter and Paul, after those two dickie birds known to every child who had sung the nursery rhyme.

Now it was decided the 2/4 would position on the left, around Bir el Harmat, to guard Peter and Paul and the southern clearing in the minefield, while the 4/10 Baluchis would occupy the area in the centre around Barrel 231. This would leave the 2nd Highland Light Infantry to hold Barrel 230 towards the rear right. And none too soon, for these three Battalions had barely taken position when, once again, they encountered the enemy who had infiltrated the minefield.

Santi had set up the RAP at Battalion HQ to ensure easy access for the wounded. Immediately, it began filling with the first casualties of the day. After one severe bombing attack at midday, Strickland limped in with a knee injury which effectively put him out of commission. Another notable among that day's wounded happened to be mess orderly Manbahadur Nandu. Much to that senior Gurkha's chagrin – and the high amusement of the young Gurkhas he was wont to keep in strict order – an errant bullet, aiming straight and true, had chosen to lodge itself with neat precision in that grizzled warrior's left buttock.

And so it went, a constant stream of the wounded kept coming, men from the Baluch patrol and several Gurkhas from Marten's platoon. As he administered to these hardy mountain men, Santi's respect for the Gurkhas' stoic, uncomplaining character reached ever greater heights.

All throughout that day, columns of enemy vehicles could be seen heading towards, and around, the southern end of the minefields. Keeping them under close surveillance was a patrol under command of 2nd Lt. Peter McDowall. Thanks to information thus obtained and relayed back, Allied artillery was able to pepper these enemy vehicles with pretty effective fire. This, inevitably, attracted retaliation from the enemy, and as the continuous rain of shells intensified, it began wreaking havoc around the RAP. When the shells reached the wounded, Santi decided he was situated in a less than desirable area. He went to see Colonel Weallens about it.

"Request permission to move the RAP, sir. We're set up near the carpool area which seems to be a prime target for the enemy. It's receiving rather heavy artillery fire, and we're coming in for quite a clobbering in the bargain. My wounded are lying exposed, getting the worst of it, I'm afraid."

"What do you suggest, Doc?"

"I would like to move a few yards north of our present position, if I may, sir. It would avoid further unnecessary injury to my casualties."

With Willie's blessing, the RAP had just been established in its new position when a very young 'tommie', probably no more than eighteen years old, was brought in. He was heavily splattered with blood, and some sort of gore that looked suspiciously like human brain. The boy, upon examination, did not appear to have a single scratch anywhere on him. His body, however, was wracked as if by the ague. Quite apart from the trembling of his body, his head and hands shook uncontrollably and, inexplicably, he seemed to have lost his ability to see.

Studying the young man's stricken face and unseeing eyes, Santi realised he was dealing with his first case of severe shell shock. He had heard of shock-induced blindness, deafness, muteness, even paralysis; and careful examination now convinced him this was not a physical injury but a mental one that had produced physical symptoms. Using a voice that was softly reassuring, Santi spoke to the boy – he really was hardly more than that – What was his name? Was he feeling any pain? Did he know where he was?

The young lad's mouth worked soundlessly as his face spasmed and his body jerked. The soldier who brought him in volunteered the information that he had been found holding part of a head, staring vacantly at it, as he rocked back and forth.

"Seems 'twer a friend of 'is, sir," the volunteer said, shaking his head pityingly. "One minute they was talkin' to each other and the next… Look at 'im, poor sod, 'e's a bloomin' basket case if ever I saw one!"

Silently, Santi had to agree. Every time there was a loud noise or report of any kind, the lad would practically jump out of his skin. He would cower, pulling his body inward almost into a foetal position. From the look of him, it was obvious he would require complete rest and quiet for some time. He would need careful handling if his condition was not to become a long-term one.

For now, a few comforting words of reassurance, a warm blanket and a few spoonfuls of hot sweet tea would have to suffice till he could be evacuated to the Field Ambulance's Advance Dressing Station. From there he would be sent down to Division's Main Dressing Station before being passed to the CCS, the Casualty Clearing Station at the rear. Santi hoped he would be sent to a hospital, somewhere far from this fracas, to give him ample time to heal. It would be a long time – if ever – before he'd be ready to return to the front lines. Often this kind of injury buried itself deep in the mind, remaining hidden and unrecognised, causing permanent damage, both mental and emotional.

It was at this point Roger Werner rushed in looking for Santi. "I say, Doc, you couldn't spare a few minutes, could you!" he burst out breathlessly. "There's a chappie on the front lines with a chest injury and he's in pretty bad shape – rather a mess, actually. Unable to breathe, poor blighter, and we daren't move him."

Santi looked around at the large number of wounded lying about him. They *all* desperately needed attention; more were arriving every minute, many too critical to be left without a doctor for long. He hesitated as he carefully considered the situation.

Havildar Birbahadur Pun, the Battalion stretcher bearer, had gone with the ambulance to help bring back a soldier with a serious stomach injury. If Santi left before his return, it would leave Havildar Puransingh Thapa to manage on his own. He was a good man, loaned to him from 'A' Coy. Nevertheless, it would be impossible for him to handle this many wounded alone. Damn and blast! What wouldn't he give for a medical assistant right now!

"Just how far away is he?" Santi asked finally.

"I can get you there, and back, in a jiffy. But I must warn you, we'll be running the gamut of some pretty bothersome artillery. They're creating merry hell out there."

Santi frowned slightly. What the deuce was he supposed to do after such a warning! If he refused now, Roger just might decide he was a coward.

Well, so be it! All things considered, his priority was for the greater good. He was needed here. Maybe he could send Puransingh and hope for the best.

At that moment, the ambulance rolled up with Havildar Birbahadur Pun, who began unloading the latest batch of wounded. Santi immediately sought out the stomach injury, which proved not quite as bad as he had feared. He gave the rest of the newcomers a quick once-over. Assured they could be managed in his short absence, Santi reversed his decision, and resolved to go. He would leave Birbahadur Pun and Puransingh Thapa in charge of the RAP. Chenchum Ale, the young medical orderly who had been assisting him, could help with the newly arrived wounded. If it would take no more than a 'jiffy', as promised, they would hold the fort till he got back.

Wasting no further time, Santi jumped into Roger's transport. They drove as fast as they could, all the while dodging bullets and shell splinters that flew past in every direction.

Hells bells, Roger certainly wasn't exaggerating, Santi thought, ducking some shrapnel as it whizzed by, singeing his hair and the tip of his left ear. *Too close for comfort, that one!*

The pneumothorax case turned out to be a 2nd Lt. from the H.L.I. who had been shot in the chest. Santi found the bullet had left a good-sized hole on the right side, penetrating both the chest muscle and parietal pleura. Every time the chap drew breath, in an effort to fill his lungs, it proved futile. Instead, air would get sucked in through the hole in his chest filling the pleural cavity, putting pressure on the outside of the lungs so that, in effect, they collapsed. As a result, it left no room inside the lungs to fill and expand with air.

The patient was making desperate wheezing sounds and, with each rasping gasp for air, blood would ooze and bubble out of his chest wound.

Very quickly Santi applied the sulpha powder M&B to the wound, then covered and bound it tightly to prevent penetration of air into the pleural cavity. It provided some temporary relief, enough to get him safely back to the RAP where Santi was able to stitch and close the wound sufficiently to tide him over till he reached the ADS. The effect was dramatic; the wounded man's distress was immediately alleviated, and he began to breathe with some degree of normalcy as he awaited transportation to the rear.

4 JUNE: SO FAR Rommel had taken the offensive while the Allies had been hedged into defensive positions. This was about to change.

At General Ritchie's HQ there had been ongoing confusion and indecision stemming from too many 'cooks', too many 'broths' and, finally, the succession of desert storms which had scattered armies so that front lines dissolved like spilt quicksilver. The front-line troops had gallantly held on in spite of inferior guns and tanks, while arguments bounced back and forth in favour of, and against, various strategies…Operation Limerick or Operation Aberdeen…

Still believing in the enemy's retreat, a decision was finally reached in favour of Operation Aberdeen. It was time to rally the troops!

On the morning of 4 June, the order for an attack was passed along the lines. Major General Harold R. Briggs, GOC 5th Division, arrived at Brigade. He impressed upon them that this was to be the most crucial battle of the campaign, one on which rested the future of the British in North Africa – nay, even India and the Far East. Let there be no doubt as to the importance of this impending battle – the welfare of the entire British Empire rested on their shoulders!

The attack would commence just prior to 0300 hours on the morning of 5 June. The Start Line was to be Trigh Bir Hacheim. XXX Corps would capture, destroy and re-occupy Sidi Muftah, Got el Scerab and Dahar el Aslagh. Within this framework, 10th Indian Infantry Brigade would attack and capture certain objectives so 7th Armoured Division could then clean out the Cauldron. This would enable 9th Infantry Brigade to pass through and occupy the area all the way up to, and including, Rommel's northern gap in the minefield west of Bir et Tamar. Further north, 32 Army Tank

Brigade and 69th Infantry Brigade of XIII Corps would co-ordinate with the attack.

This was the final plan, the order of battle with which Ritchie's Eighth Army was to go to war. This was Operation Aberdeen, and it was on a strictly need-to-know-basis. Or so it was presumed.

No one was aware that on both 1 June and 4 June the Germans had again intercepted messages from the American Legation in Cairo. Colonel Bonner Fellers faithfully informed Washington of the latest strengths, weaknesses and deployments of Allied troops and artillery; the state of their ordnance and supplies; his rather unfavourable take on British training, competency and morale; and, finally, the Allies' assessment of their enemy's positions and intentions. (Tim Clayton and Phil Craig: *The End of the Beginning.*)

The intercepted information was of immense benefit to Rommel in his plans for the upcoming battle and lent itself greatly to the myth of his uncanny ability to mind-read his enemy.

And it did much to seal the fate of the Allied troops fighting at that time in the desert.

THE PRINCE OF WALES'S Own 2/4 Gurkha Rifles began preparations for a night departure: ETD 2000 hours. Its companies would be trucked in a formation of columns that would proceed under cover of darkness to Barrel 230. The going would be tricky, with all the usual hazards entailed in a night-time desert manoeuver. And the enemy, of course, could be depended upon to do everything possible to add to their hardships.

Santi had been working non-stop with the aid of three helpers, gathering supplies to load into their truck preparatory to departure, when a wounded sepoy stumbled in. He had made it, but there was an injured sapper out there who couldn't manage the walk. Following the sepoy's directions, Santi drove to where he found the man lying in a nearby *bir* with his left foot blown away, very probably by a landmine.

It was too late. Like an injured animal, he had crawled to shelter where he had lain, hidden and alone, long enough that he had bled to death. This was a life he could have saved, there was no reason this man should have died from his wound. The poor blighter had made a bid for safety and, believing he had found it, the choice had sealed his destiny. It was ironic, Santi thought bitterly, was this the insouciance of fate, or the long arm of karma?

Hindus believed karma was the only baggage a soul arrived and left this world with. And although it is said one's fate is preordained, the firm belief is that it is tempered by one's choice of action, the reasons for that choice and its repercussions – all tipping the scales of karma. Set upon its voyage towards Nirvana, a soul travels through numerous lives. Blest with a certain freedom of choice, each chosen action is laid as a steppingstone that paves the path the soul builds to carry it on its journey of transformation – each life a credit or a debit that earns the soul its karma.

Santi said a silent prayer to speed this soul on its way. Then, checking the man's ID, he carried the body to his truck to be sent back, if possible, to the correct unit for proper burial. That done, he headed back to Battalion HQ to find out the latest about movement orders and times of departure.

The camp had been in full spate all day, with much scurrying from pillar to post as everyone made their arrangements to get under way. After handing over the dead sapper, all Santi could glean at HQ was that departure – delayed again – was now scheduled for somewhere around 2400 hours. He'd better get back to the RAP right away.

Evening was setting in, and it had become strangely quiet. A few people here and there were still completing their final checks when, close to 1730 hours, twenty-four enemy Junkers – JU 88s – flew in from the south to pay them a visit.

Heading north, at first Santi heard nothing above the noise of his truck – that is, until the aircraft swept in, almost directly overhead, as they strafed the Field Battery, Battalion Headquarters and the Brigade watering point. Too late! With bombs exploding all around him, he realised the vehicle made him a prime target! He leapt out and, finding no slit trench, did the only thing he could do – he threw himself flat on the ground and rolled away.

The aircraft passed over him, touching him with their shadow of death. He closed his eyes tight as bombs thundered all around him, sending twenty-foot geysers of sand into the air and bomb splinters whistling past mere inches from where he lay. He pushed his body hard against the ground as though he would, by dint of his very weight, burrow right into it. He had not had time enough to put a safe distance between himself and his truck and, exposed as he was, he realised he presented a target they were hardly likely to miss. Best to draw as little attention as possible, he decided. There was nothing for it but to lie there clutching at the earth, trying to blend into it, all the while expecting each second to be his last, and most fervently willing it not to be so.

A distinctly insistent whistling sound caught his attention. It seemed to be hurtling towards him, getting louder and shriller by the second. Suddenly, the sound stopped. The ominous whistling was replaced by silence, that eerie silence when everything seems to go into slow motion in the last few seconds before a bomb hits – and it told him he had been targeted.

No matter to what depths one's faith might be shaken, or how much one might rant against the Almighty for the hideous carnage of war, they do say that on the front lines there are no unbelievers. And so, Santi found himself praying. Instinctively, he called upon his God, beseeching her protection. He did so with a fervour far greater than the matter-of-course prayers he had offered in her temple at the outset of this soul-searing journey; at that time, he had been in all innocence of the terrors of warfare.

Ohm! Shyama! Koral Bodoni...Moha Kali, ahsroy dao!
Ohm! Dark Mother! Fierce of feature...Great Kali, give me shelter!

The bomb landed directly behind his truck, heaving the ground beneath him and rocking the vehicle so violently, it tilted to one side.

A close call! Santi shook his head to stop the ringing in his ears. When he opened his eyes, he was dismayed to see the bomb had put paid to his transport. But at least, he thought gratefully, it had passed him over.

As the barrage continued, he pressed his face against the ground, and dug his fingers into the hard-packed sand; and he waited helplessly, praying harder than ever that the next bomb, and the next, should not find him.

Wrong place, wrong time. He gritted his teeth and cursed his confounded bad luck that he should have been caught short like this. *Damn! Damn! Damn!*

He pictured his parents, clear as day, and felt the enormity of their grief at the news they would receive; so too with the girls, his sisters, of whom he had always been so protective. Protective enough? Overprotective, perhaps? He wondered wryly, had he done well by them all – the very best he could? And then there was that beautiful face framed with auburn hair that filled him with such a burning desire to live! He felt a sudden, deep ache of loss, an overwhelming regret for what might have been – for moments lost, and dreams unlived, for desires that would remain unfulfilled, hopes stillborn...

Oh God! There was so much promise yet to life! Feelings to be explored, laughter to be shared, tears to shed! There hadn't been time enough to give, to take, to touch and taste, to keep faith, to nurture… grow memories he could pass down…He felt a mind-numbing disbelief that it should all end as pointlessly as this, without achievement or fulfilment, an utterly senseless, awful waste.

A sudden, unexpected flash of defiance shot through him. *No!* He refused to accept it. He was not ready to relinquish any of it – neither his future, nor his place in this mad, chaotic, imperfect world; this was *his* life and too much had gone into the making of it. His life had been all preparation till now; he had not yet made his mark on the blueprint handed down to him: *we are the echoes of our ancestors, the sum total of their experiences, born in the light of their achievements and in the shadow of their mistakes.*

And what of his achievements and mistakes? His time had been too short to make any of sufficient consequence to add to that ledger of legacy. It could not, must not end here! He carried not only his own dreams and hopes within him, but those of all who had gone before. He would not allow anyone or anything to cheat him of his time, to spill his life's blood in this barren waste of sand. Not now. He had too much to live for. Hadn't Bajo foretold his future from his coffee cup?

Whether by dint of will, prayer or luck – or possibly a combination of all three – the Fates seemed persuaded. They were, apparently, not quite done with him; for, against all odds, the rain of bombs did miss him. Perhaps the number of trucks parked all around helped to draw the attention of the planes, and thus save the day for him. No matter the reason, after they had wreaked their damage, the aircraft roared on towards Hyde Park Corner and 'D' Company, spreading their mayhem in that direction and sending everyone on the way madly dashing for cover.

Santi got to his feet. For a split second his legs felt like jelly. But – he was alive! He had beaten them! This was the second time they had come close to pinning his hide, yet, damn the lot of them, he had *survived!*

He began running, and soon he was sprinting the remaining distance towards the RAP. With each stride, he exulted in the strength of his legs, the wholeness of his unimpaired body, the vitality of life coursing through his young heart with its every beat. Somehow there was a new dimension to his surroundings, a clarity, a resolve greater than there had been before. He had nearly lost it all in a single flash! They had tried to take all this from him, but without success. As he ran, he felt like shouting: *I'm alive; my God, I'm alive!*

Life was to be lived; not a minute of it wasted. And that was just what he would do. The first chance he got. When this was over – tomorrow, the day after, next week – somehow, he would return to Cairo…

How could he have known, fate would decree otherwise!

———————

LOCATING THE RAP WAS no easy feat; men and machines were on the move, and the scene was one of chaos and confusion. When he did eventually come upon it, he found his medical orderly and two stretcher bearers had completed loading the last of the supplies and baggage onto the three-ton truck; and much to his relief, both men and truck were unharmed.

Together they returned to where he had left his damaged vehicle and, after attaching it to the three-tonner with a towing chain, they hauled it back to Battalion HQ. There it was left in the care of their Motor Transport Officer, Roger Werner, who was frantically rounding up all damaged vehicles. The harried MTO could be heard venting a stream of profanity, so imaginatively descriptive, repeating it would put the most hard-bitten of men to the blush.

Santi's tin trunk, bedding and gear had already been packed and stashed by Dilbahadur. Personal baggage and kit were always the last to be put on board. Knowing his batman's diligence, Santi was confident all was in good order, with no detail overlooked; there was no need for a follow up. He was, therefore, never able to explain, then or thereafter, on what whim he picked up his pannier to check its contents. But pick it up he did, mere moments before he heard the planes return for a second, vicious swipe over the camp. This time they were greeted by anti-aircraft guns spitting vehemently into action.

Damn the bastards, Santi thought, thoroughly exasperated by the persistence of the enemy. *Don't they ever bloody give up!*

Aware that his entire stock of medical supplies was now loaded on the truck, his one thought was for its safety. At any moment it might all be blown to kingdom come – and he'd be right royally sunk! Distracted with the thought of such a calamity, he held to his place, pannier still in hand, scanning the skies for the intruders.

Wisdom should have prompted that luck having brought him through twice before, chancing it to hold a third time was pure folly. Alas, in that moment Santi recognised neither wisdom nor folly, only the consequences of his loss should his truck be hit. And so, he remained rooted to the spot, standing futile guard over his precious supplies.

He could hear the roar of the planes, their thunder increasing as they approached, as they swung into alignment with their target and dove in to release their cargo. He watched with frustration as the bombs began to fall to earth, coming ever nearer, almost in slow motion, the scream of the aircraft deafening him as they swooped overhead. It all played out in a matter of seconds. Finally, as the violent explosions shook the ground and swayed the truck, sight and sound jerked him back to reality and galvanised him into action.

"Take cover", he yelled to the Gurkhas.

And none too soon. As all four men flung themselves towards the nearest slit trench, pursued by the all too familiar whistle of approaching bombs, there was a devil of an explosion fifteen yards in front of them – and then another, even closer. The ground seemed to erupt from below, the force practically lifting them right off their feet and flinging them pell mell on top of each other amid a shower of flying debris and sand.

Santi felt something slam hard into his left side, throwing him backward against someone's boot. The impact sent an electric shock coursing along his spine, and for one blinding moment the pain disoriented him. Dazed and bruised, he lay still, allowing the pain to gradually subside. When he could at last draw breath without wincing, he moved his body slightly, carefully. Then, spitting what felt like half the desert he seemed to have ingested, he managed to gingerly extricate himself from the tangle of arms and legs. He rolled over slowly and was surprised to find he was able to pick himself up, dust himself off and get back, albeit rather shakily, to his feet.

His back was painfully sore, and the pain in his side seemed to suggest a fractured rib. A rudimentary check revealed some rather bad bruising, and if there was a hairline fracture, at least nothing vital was visibly broken. It was then he noticed the blood on his uniform, and it surprised him. He knew he had not sustained that severe an injury to either back or side, and he felt no pain elsewhere. Perplexed, he proceeded to examine himself more closely – and discovered the laceration to the back of his left hand. It looked quite bad, but oddly, the wound hurt not at all. Doubtless, that would come later, and could be dealt with then, he decided. Right now, his concern was whether it might hamper his work. Still, all things considered, he was, thank God, as far as he could tell, all in one piece.

But what of his stretcher bearers?

Santi noticed Havildar Puransingh Thapa wobbling to his feet. Trying hard to remain upright, the Gurkha's two legs were planted wide to maintain his balance. In the manner of some reveller who had imbibed far more than he should, he rocked back and forth, each sway putting him in imminent danger of toppling over. Remarkably, however, the staunch soldier held his ground; and luckily, apart from this peculiar condition, he looked to be without injury.

Havildar Birbahadur Pun, meanwhile, still remained on the ground. From his trance-like expression, it seemed obvious any movement, however uncomplicated, would very likely prove unmanageable for the moment. A quick examination found him to be winded, but otherwise unharmed, barring a minor gash to his left palm.

The third body lying on the ground, face down, was Hirasing Limbu. Santi was struck by the young stretcher bearer's unnatural stillness. Pushing aside the awful thought that sprang to mind, Santi hurried over hoping to detect some sign, any sign, of life in the prone figure.

"Hirasing? *Aré,* Hirasing!" Although the ringing in his ears had subsided somewhat, Santi's voice echoed oddly inside his head, and he shook it impatiently.

"*Uslai kya bhayo, sahib?*" Puransingh stumbled precariously over to find out what had happened.

"*Koni,* Puransingh, *pichhai bas.*" I don't know, Puransingh, stay back.

Holding his left hand with his right, whilst pressing down hard to stem the messy bleeding, Santi anxiously leant over the medical orderly. He winced at the stab of pain that shot through his ribs.

After what seemed like an excessively long pause, there came this muffled reply, "I am here, *sahib.*"

Thank goodness, at least the man was alive! "Are you all right? Are you hurt?"

By way of response, Hirasing moved his arms and legs ever so slightly. After a moment, Santi received confirmation. "Everything seems to be in working order, *sahib.*"

Much relieved, Santi quickly examined the young Gurkha to make sure he was, indeed, 'in working order.' Finally, having ascertained all was well with his men, he turned his attention to what other destruction the bomb might have caused.

His supplies, he discovered, had been spared, but not so the truck itself; the front had sustained extensive damage. Santi realised that but for the truck acting as a buffer, one or more of them probably would have lost their lives. Though he was, once again, without transport, under the circumstances, he was grateful to pay the small price.

An object lying on the ground nearby caught Santi's eye. On closer inspection, it turned out to be his pannier – or, more correctly, what once had been his pannier. It now lay, ripped open by shrapnel, seemingly beyond rescue. Santi remembered with an ugly jolt that he had been holding it when the bomb fell.

He was standing there, alive, because his pannier, quite miraculously, had intercepted the bomb splinter that otherwise would most certainly have ripped open his side. In its final hour, the bag had shielded him, allowing him to escape practically unscathed. It had saved his life!

His spectacles, he discovered ruefully, pulling them from his pocket, had not fared quite so well. Quick examination revealed a cracked frame but lenses still intact, so all was not lost perhaps – battle-worn they might be, but a quick patch-up of sorts could save them yet.

Grateful to the gods that he had scraped through with no more than a possible fractured rib, some rather bad bruising to his back, and a comparatively minor injury to his hand, Santi applied sulpha powder to the wound, bandaged it lightly so as not to hinder movement too much, and then looked to the business at hand.

Elsewhere around the camp several other vehicles and carriers had taken direct hits, and there was a mad scramble to put out the fires. All loaded up and ready to move out, they had made a perfect target for a very timely air raid.

It was Roger Werner, surveying the various damages done to his transport, who so aptly gave expression to the general feeling running through the camp. Shaking a furious fist, he yelled after the departing perpetrators, "Infernal scummy scoundrels! You damn flying buzzards! You'll get your come-uppance, you poxy bloody bastards, see if you don't!"

"Poor old Roger," Ben pulled a wry face as he walked up to where Santi and his orderlies were tending to the wounded. "He certainly received the heavy end of that walloping; enough to give anyone the pip, I should think!"

Santi nodded. "It is rather uncanny, don't you think, how those planes seem able to pinpoint us so precisely?" His damaged three-tonner, now partially unloaded, stood nearby where it had been abandoned when the casualties had begun to come in.

Ben was thoughtful for a moment. "The thought has presented itself; I must say their timing and objective could hardly have been more bang on." He grimaced at the sight of the wreckage. "What a frightful hash! It's deuced shoddy luck. One might almost suppose they'd been privy to some sort of tip off, mightn't one!"

They were unaware how close to the mark their instincts were. For, indeed, their misfortunes had more to do with espionage than with the long arm of Fate.

A MESSENGER DASHED IN with urgent word from 'D' Company, deployed at Hyde Park Corner: it was mayhem over there! They had come dangerously close to being completely cut off by the enemy. Everyone, it seemed, was scattered everywhere, and everything was all over the bloody place!

As for McDowall's 'C' Company, it found itself precipitated into the minefield as it tangled with enemy lorries. After a hairy tussle, one vehicle was put out of action and two frightened Italians spilt out. They were promptly collared by Robert Williams and frog-marched off to Brigade HQ for interrogation.

Despite the ongoing trials and tribulations, departure for the frontline was somehow executed by midnight when the Battalion eventually began a piecemeal move. With so many vehicles out of commission, transport was short and space at a premium. As a result, an order was given: Take only the absolutely necessary, leave all the rest behind.

When all Santi's casualties had been evacuated to the rear of the Battalion, only Subedar Sukhdeo remained with 'B' Company. Santi was still waiting for his ambulance to return from its last run when Dilbahadur returned with news – the vehicle had caught a flying splinter and suffered a burst radiator, causing all water and petrol to spill out. *Blast!* Cursing his misfortune, Santi caught timely sight of Roger come to shepherd the last of the Battalion on its way.

"I say, Roger, I'm in a bit of a spot! My three-tonner was done for in the bombing, and now I hear my ambulance has had it as well. How the devil do I get my wounded from the front to the MDS without any transport?"

"Believe me, Doc," came the frazzled reply, "you're not alone. It's all gone to hell in a handcart out there. Those bounders wreaked havoc on my motor pool – lost a dozen vehicles in one fell swoop.

Y'know, either they have the devil's own luck in reading our minds or – and I'm almost ready to take an oath on it – someone's been tipping them the wink!"

"Strange you should say that," Santi replied, frowning. "Ben said much the same thing not a moment ago. If true, it's a disturbing thought; all the more reason to worry about the wounded, don't you think?"

"Let me put it this way, Doc – I'd be bloody grateful for a good, old-fashioned donkey cart right now!" Roger shook his head glumly. "I don't know what to tell you. Maybe…now, I don't hold much hope, mind…but, let me see what I can come up with."

Eventually, before pushing off with 'B' Coy, the beleaguered MTO managed to procure a half-maunder for the stranded medical team. With Dilbahadur's assistance, Santi salvaged what he could from his personal belongings in the damaged three-tonner. According to orders, it could not be much – his bedding, a small suitcase and his haversack – the rest would remain behind to become a dismal part of that discarded flotsam of war they had witnessed, littered across the sands when first they entered this desert. Was it a mere four…five… days ago? It felt like a lifetime!

<hr>

MANOEUVERING THROUGH THE DESERT at night was, at best, confusing; and oftentimes, during those hours of pitch darkness, the never-ending mile after mile of featureless sands could make a journey downright treacherous. It was easy to become disoriented and end up chasing around in circles or, worse still, blundering into the enemy.

Happily, it was not the enemy but Subedar Balbir Pun's 'D' Company, adrift in the darkness, which Santi and his orderlies ran headlong into. It was hail-fellow-well-met all round, after which, their numbers reinforced, Santi took quick charge and the company proceeded to forge its way through the pitch-black night.

Not too far along, however, they were brought up short by an unmistakable grinding, growling sound they immediately recognized; it was the ominous noise of multiple tanks, and the particular pitch indicated they were, in all probability, enemy tanks. Fearing they might be surrounded, Santi advocated lying low in complete silence. He hoped fervently that the sound of their lorry had been drowned out by the heavier noise of the tanks which seemed wary of lighting up and giving away their position in case any Allied tanks might happen by.

A very tense half hour crept by with everyone on tenterhooks. All it would take to spell disaster was a single tank altering course in their direction; they appeared to be in such close proximity, there was a good chance it would run straight into them. With the strain mounting in that close, silent darkness, Santi couldn't help but muse wryly, *we've landed ourselves in something of a cat and mouse situation – with us being much the hapless mouse in this quandary.*

Fortune, however, favoured them with a reprieve, and the tanks finally rumbled away without an untoward incident. A few cautious minutes later, 'D' Coy gently revved its engines and continued on its way, thankfully melting into those darkest of dark early morning hours. And just a short while later it managed, without further mishap, to locate Battalion H.Q. Fretful with mounting concern, Colonel Weallens greeted them with visible relief.

"Dashed glad to see you made it through, Doc. The show's about to go on the road but we still have a few stragglers out there. Stay put, will you, till all the company commanders have pulled their outfits in. If we manage to stick to our scheduled departure of 0200 hours, give or take a few minutes, I believe we might yet arrive at our AP in good order."

And come in they did. One by one, lost and found, the various groups stumbled in, and much to Old Willie's gratification, right on the hour, the Battalion sallied forth. Depite all difficulties, the assembly point at B.230 was reached in good time, and with the arrival of the two sister Battalions as well, Ten Brigade was rendered complete and ready for deployment.

Under command of Lt. Col. William Weallens, 2/4 took up a position of reserve behind a squadron of Valentine tanks of the 4th Royal Tank Regiment. It was to remain on guard at the gaps in the minefields till it was relieved – as once before in Iraq – by its old friend, the Duke of Cornwall's Light Infantry. Meanwhile, Lt. Col. Douglas Thorburn with his 2nd H.L.I., decked in their Seaforth MacKenzie tartan, marched forward to Bir et Tamar, while 4/10 Baluch led by Lt. Col. Sundius-Smith proceeded to B.178. Each Battalion had under its command a squadron of 4th R.T.R. Valentines, and each in its appointed place stood ready for the fray.

IN THE CHILLY EARLY-morning hours the desert lay steeped in an unbroken silence. At 0230 hours, in the deep, dark quiet, sentries woke those hardy souls who had managed to fall asleep. Men and machines manned their positions. Final checks were made – supplies, fill-ups, tightenings and tensions; defences were beefed up, inter-unit and company responsibilities co-ordinated, covering fire arranged and patrol tasks detailed. Ten Brigade stood poised, ready for orders. Then, they waited. And knowing what lay ahead, the waiting was hardest of all.

Those last moments were the worst. The nerve-wracking apprehension played havoc with one's mental and bodily functions, and every man fought his demons, each in his own way: there were the fidgeters whose jangled nerves would hardly allow them to keep still; there were those who took a stab at irony, attempting to make light of their fears through ridicule.

"Wot's the matter Binky? You scared or somefin'? If yer shake any 'arder them Jerries'r liable to 'ear yer bones rattle clear 'cross the desert, an' then we'll all be bloomin' done fer."

"Aw, give orf, Dusty!" came the quick reply. "Its yer own knees knockin' like a flamenco dancer's castanets that'll give us away; so there's no use pretendin' yer don't give a monkey's arse!"

"Stop yer jawin', will yer! This aint some flippin' lark!" An irritable growl from some tetchy soul put an end to that exchange.

And then, there were those who sought the solace of silence, who withdrew into a deep quietness within themselves till the command for attack came to jolt them back to the present. But no matter how he dealt with those final moments, each man was aware they might very well be his last. No matter their differences, they all waited as one. And at the back of every mind there lurked that fear, that unmentionable fear of cowardice: *Please, God, let me not be found wanting; let me measure up in the eyes of those around me; please, let it not be me who....* The last refuge was prayer.

Dry-mouthed, stomachs heaving with an awful nausea, each man silently battled to stay in control, his heart pounding so hard it muffled all other sound and made breathing difficult; shivering from the cold, and their own thoughts, they hunkered down. Ten Brigade steeled itself and waited for the order, "*Take Post.*"

By now the skies had cleared. The moon had appeared, and the night of 5 June 1942 was deceptively calm. The desert was awash with moonlight, its sands seeming to ripple like liquid silver. The ancient land lay silent and serene, wrapped in its own secrets; high above, the pre-dawn canopy of dark blue velvet was hung with a zillion icy bright stars that glittered, diamonding the darkness in a way that was unique to the desert. There was a great stillness out there, a silent imminence that grew with every waiting minute. And they all knew, for them it was the quiet before the great storm.

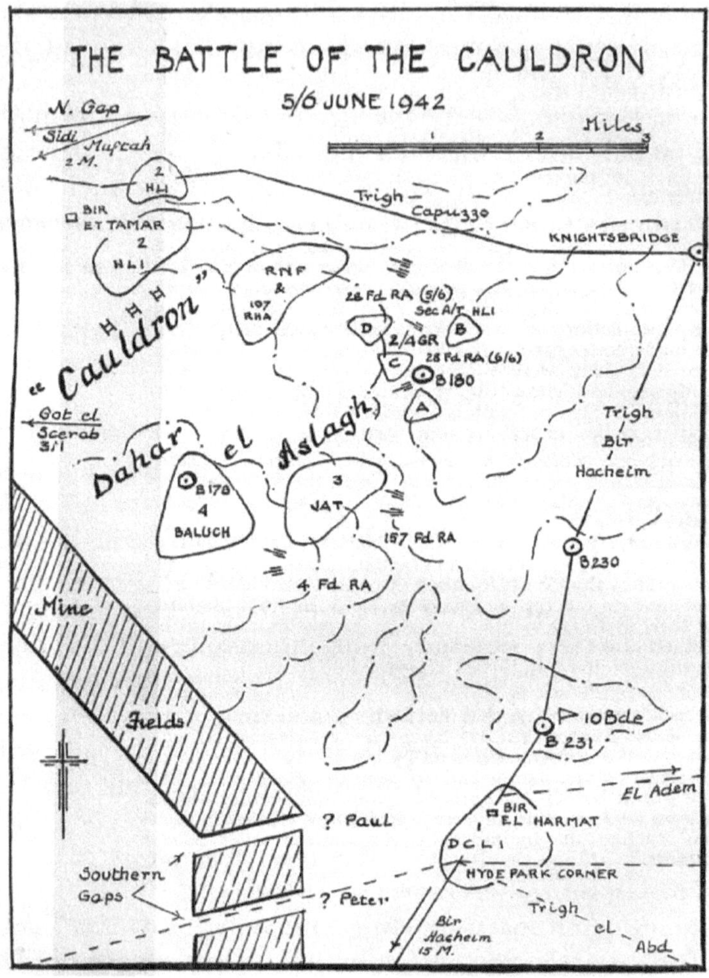

HLI=Highland Light Infantry / RNF=Royal Northumberland Fusiliers / 2/4GR=2/4 Gurkha Rifles / DCLI=Duke of Cornwall's Light Infantry / 10Bde=10 Brigade / Fd RA=Field Regiment (Credit: A History of the 4th Prince of Wales's Own Gurkha Rifles:Vol III, by Col. J. N. Mackay, D.S.O.)

CHAPTER THIRTY-TWO

The Wrath Of Set

And Caesar's spirit, ranging for revenge,
With Ate by his side come hot from hell,
Shall in these confines with a monarch's voice
Cry 'Havoc' and let slip the dogs of war
That this foul deed shall smell above the earth
With carrion men groaning for burial.

– William Shakespeare, *Julius Caesar*

JUNE 5: AT 0250 hours exactly, Operation Aberdeen commenced. *Fire!* And the heavens were rent as the earth split asunder, spewing forth the wrath of hell. The night erupted with savage violence into a fiery, thunder-ridden inferno. One hundred guns boomed in ferocious unison, firing four rounds per gun per minute as they opened up from three regiments of Field Artillery and one of Horse Artillery. The volley of sound was so intense, some of the gunners' ears bled.

As hundreds of red tracers from the tank squadrons arced overhead with splendid grace in the paled moonlight, the fierce blaze from the guns roared into battle and lit up the night with a brilliance that fairly dazzled the vision as their ear-splitting din rolled and bounced across the open expanse of desert.

Boom…boom…baboom…baboom…baboom. It was the flash of gunfire one saw first, then came the shrill scream of the approaching shell riding a shockwave from the blast that slammed into a body like a giant wave. And when that shell hit the ground, it shattered the darkness, exploding with a burst of furious sound that ricocheted through the smoky sand-filled air: *Vrrrrumphh!*

The noise was astounding, the sight spellbinding; and for the moment, sound and sight masked the hideous face of death. There was, in fact, an awful, stunning beauty to it, and the display of sheer power sent a thrill of exhilaration coursing through the veins chasing away all else. The bombardment continued ceaselessly for thirty minutes, peal after peal that shook the desert and made the night shudder with its ferocity.

For the 2/4, as for so many others who had but recently arrived in the Western Desert, this tank battle was a first experience; and as the machines engaged, guns and cannons spitting, Santi watched the bullets and shells zinging through the night, following each other as though attached, blazing a trail in waves of continuous lines, looking for all the world like a flying sheet of light; a mesmerizing phenomenon that brought a startling, incongruent image to Santi's mind – a *sari,* that graceful, feminine Indian garment, billowing and flapping on a washer woman's clothes line.

The illusion was jarring! The peaceful home-scene amid all the frenzied clamour of war was a complete anomaly; so incredibly dissonant in the present circumstances, it was disorienting. Santi felt a strange sense of weightlessness; somehow his feet could not feel the ground, as though he were floating about an inch above it. Reality and imagination, life and death, peace and violence fused together into an experience somewhere beyond the realm of space and time. He watched, fascinated, as every now and then a bullet or shell would ping against a tank, or ricochet off a stone, bouncing out of line in an abrupt change of direction, followed similarly by others sliding through the dark like silver snakes.

He felt lightheaded, his ears peculiarly muffled as though the blood had drained out of him. This was not fear, for at that moment he knew no fear at all, nor was this any of the preceding anxiety of anticipation. It was exhilaration, like a river rushing through him; a heart-pounding excitement at sight and sound of the devastating, colossal might that had been unleashed – and it sent the adrenaline surging through his body!

Thus it went, platoon against platoon, company against company, in a macabre dance of death. Finally, at 0320 hours, the barrage ceased, leaving the night air choked with thick smoke carrying the stench of acrid cordite, spent petrol fumes and burnt oil. It stung the eyes, the throat and the lungs. But the fever pitch of the chase was on, now that they believed they had their enemy on the canvas.

"Look, sir, it's green. Over to your left, they're signalling success" the squadron leader of 4th R.T.R in reserve indicated to Santi, peering through the pall of smoke. "Our tanks are giving us the thumbs up." As a tank rolled up out of the smoke and dust, heading back for maintenance, he called out to it. "Splendid show, lads! You seem to be having a ruddy great knees up! But you'll let us have a crack at the bastards as well, now won't you!"

The RAF too had been busy. Roger Werner and his orderly had lent the bombers an enthusiastic hand, building a large fiery V- sign on the ground indicating the direction of the enemy. Using petrol-soaked sand in kerosene tins, they set the sign alight, despite vigilant, accurate enemy gunfire – a feat calling for some remarkable spryness. Indeed, egged on by loud cheers from their friends, and a stream of bullets from their foes, both men exhibited an exceptional fleetness of foot any Olympian would have hailed as none too shabby!

Amid the ensuing applause, Ben Browne trundled up with further good news. "Thought you chaps might like to know the H.L.I. and the Baluchis have reached their objectives. Looks like the Fox is going to ground."

But their euphoria was short-lived once the casualties began coming in. The wounded and near-dead were brought to the Regimental Aid Post, and among the former lay Hirasing Limbu. The medical orderly's left arm had been shattered by a shell splinter when he had gone to the aid of an injured gunner. Santi examined him carefully and concluded he would have to amputate two of his fingers. It was unfortunate, but at least there was a fair to middling chance the rest of his hand and arm could be saved. The young Gurkha's fighting days were definitely over, however. He would have to be sent home. Which, in a way, made him one of the lucky ones since he was, at least, going home alive.

Santi patched Hirasing as best he could and had him laid alongside the others waiting to be transported to the ADS at the rear. "You will be all right now," Santi reassured the rifleman. "They will take care of you."

"*Sahib,*" Hirasing's eyes were full of gratitude. "You have saved my arm. How can I thank you?" He tried to raise his good arm to touch his forehead in a salute of respect.

Santi stopped him. Instead, he took his hand gently and shook it. "*Timro bhagya ramro chha, timi ghar jandaicha.* You are fortunate, you are going home." He spoke, softly. "Your friend, Mullah, is waiting for you. Go and live long and well together. Live for those who will not be so fortunate. Live for us all."

The young man nodded and, very softly, he spoke the age-old Gurkha blessing customarily reserved for the Commanding Officer on Regimental Mess Night: "*Thagra raho huzur.* Remain strong and in good health, respected sir."

THE LIGHT OF DAWN began to wash out the last lingering shadows of night, filling the desert sky with exquisite colour. It filtered through the dust clouds of battle, now seen boiling like a thunderhead on the horizon, gilding them a pale, translucent gold that disguised the obscenity of war behind a veil of shimmering beauty. A mirage that vanished so swiftly with the strengthening light, it was a memory almost as soon as it was perceived. Like the click of a camera shutter, daylight now brought the debris of war sharply back into focus; and it became apparent from the disarray of vehicles making a pell mell return from the front, all was not quite as it should be.

The two forward battalions, staunchly advancing into battle to the tune of *'Highland Laddie'*, had indeed reached their objectives successfully. Each piper, his finger firmly on the chanter of his bagpipe, had sounded the brave clarion call to herald his battalion's attack on Bir et Tamar; but there the sound of bagpipes had been drowned out by the din of battle as 2nd H.L.I. had run into trouble.

Their 2-pounders had been no match for the much superior German 88s that had decimated the Royal Tank Regiment's Valentines. Consequently, it was no surprise when Brigade Liaison Officer Peter O'Bree brought the order from HQ that 2/4 Gurkha Rifles would go to their immediate aid, moving forward in the direction of Knightsbridge; first to B180, the reference point at Dahar el Aslagh, northwest of their present position, and then forward to take up position with the 2nd H.L.I. at the front.

Under constant shelling from the enemy, the Battalion arrived at B180, the designated barrel, only to find 2nd H.L.I. had been overrun. With neither artillery nor tank support, its position had become impossible to sustain. The Grant tanks of the Royal Northumberland Fusiliers of 22 Armoured Brigade stood to their rear, but they failed to go to the aid of those beleaguered troops.

Whether miscommunication or tactical reasoning was the cause – might a gap left unguarded have given access to the enemy? – the H.L.I. was badly cut down. The seriously wounded, and there were many, were taken to the RAP in carriers, when available; those that remained, and were able enough, attempted escape; most found themselves trapped. One such was Private Campbell; with a last valiant cry of "*withdrawal impossible!*" he charged a German tank firing his Bren gun at point blank range. (Antony Brett-James: *Ball of Fire, The Fifth Indian Division in the Second World War*) Valour and tragedy went hand in hand on countless occasions that day.

At 1500 hrs Brigadier C.H. Boucher himself arrived to inspect the frontlines and determine how matters stood. Having confirmed that 2nd H.L.I.'s position had indeed become untenable some two hours previous, he gave the order: at all costs 2/4 was to hold fast at B180, thereby allowing the tattered remnants of 2nd H.L.I. a chance to limp back to Brigade HQ at B231. Col. Weallens assured him they would stand firm, at the same time requesting 28 Field Regiment be deployed in support of his Battalion's position at B180. The Brigadier, happy to comply, came back with a final hitch.

"'Fraid we have a slight problem here, Weallens. General Briggs has just informed Colonel Needham that he lost his doctor this morning. Chappie fainted – sheer exhaustion. Your doctor, Captain Dutt, will have to carry the extra load of wounded. I've heard he's a top-drawer sort of fellow. You think he's up to snuff? His RAP will have to double up, so to speak. I can have the other outfit's senior medical orderly, and some of its supplies transferred over to assist him."

"Not to worry, sir. I have every confidence in Captain Dutt; first-class officer and a bloody good doctor in a crisis. I assure you, there isn't a better man, or one more capable of handling the situation."

General Briggs nodded. "Glad to hear it, Willie; that's high praise, indeed, coming from you. I'd like to meet your good doctor when all this is over. He certainly sounds like a top-notch officer."

And with that settled the Brigadier took his leave of them; it was 1700 hrs when he headed back to Brigade HQ. Unknown to him or anyone else at the time, Brigade HQ was about to be taken, and Brigadier Boucher himself was headed for disaster.

— ·◆· —

Foxy Jones, the medical orderly from 28 Field Regiment, was a Barrow Boy from the East End. Taller than most, he was crowned with a mop of wiry, red hair beneath which his sunburnt face was smothered in a startling array of freckles that marched impudently across his forehead, nose and cheeks. Blessed with a sense of humour to match, and an accent that flummoxed most people, sometimes even his own, he turned out to be an experienced medical orderly and – when he could be understood – just the asset Santi had been praying for.

"Cor blimey, sir, if this don't taik all! Oi swears on me Muvver, Oi 'aven't seen the laikes o' this b'fer now, Oi 'aven't!"

"Your muvver?"

"Ah beggin' yer pardon, sir, Oi knows Oi shouldn' be swearin' on me Muvver. She'd be maikin' me wash me mouf out, she would, if she'd 'ave 'eard me. Good ol' Mum!"

Ah, Mum! There was a familiar word! It cast some light on the content, if not the language – that had sounded completely alien to Santi's ear. *It's his mother he's speaking of,* he realised with a sense of relief that was halfway between amusement and irritation.

They were tending to a young two-striped bombardier named Kempton, whose mangled left arm had been blown away by a German 88. The arm was beyond saving, and Jones was administering chloroform to the soldier so Santi could amputate the limb ("I'm glad it isn't my right, sir" was all the boy said before he went under), and Santi had to admit, in a way, Foxy Jones' prattle lightened the gruesome task at hand.

Aloud he said, "This is a bit of a shambles, isn't it!"

He stopped short. *Good grief! These Englishmen were rubbing off on him! He was beginning to sound increasingly like them,* he realised, ruefully. He'd better be careful the osmosis didn't extend to his Cockney companion's strange lingo! He smiled inwardly at the thought. *His own muvver wouldn't recognise 'im then, fer sure!*

"It's that 'n' all, sir, it's that 'n' all," Foxy Jones continued, unabated. "Them murderin' bastards wot 'ave done this 'ave a lot t' answer fer. An' just t'other daiy, that there damn Axis Sally, God rot 'er soul, was spreadin' 'er bloomin' porkies, smarmy as you please!"

Santi had a bewildering vision of little pigs running amok. "You've lost me, Jones. Spreading what porkies?"

"Oh, aye sir," Jones chuckled, "and 'eres me rabbitin' on, fergettin' yer a furriner – er, no offense intended, sir" he added hastily. "It's just a waiy we 'ave of saiyin' fings where Oi comes from; yer know – pork pies, lies – a kind uv 'ome grown 'abit we 'ave uv sorta rhymin' fings togever like. Well, as Oi wus saiyin', that Axis Sally she's a liar that one she is..."

(Mildred Gillars, aka Axis Sally, was an American who broadcast Nazi propaganda from Radio Berlin. Her most infamous broadcast – for which she would be convicted after the war on grounds of treason – would be put out on May 11, 1944, the eve of DDay. Called *Vision of Invasion,* it would be a chillingly realistic enactment of an American mother dreaming of her GI son dying on a burning ship in the English Channel. The terrifying background sounds of the screams and moans of wounded and dying soldiers being raked by gunfire were especially harrowing. Ironically, after serving her sentence, Mildred Gillars would retire to a convent, remaining there as a teacher until her death in 1988.)

———•·•———

THE GERMAN 88s, MORE powerful than anything the Allies had, were inflicting terrible damage to both man and machine. Bringing them forward, their gunners ranged their shots for precise measurement of distance – first in front of their target, then behind, pinpointing the rest to land with devastating accuracy. The incoming sibilant hiss and heavy, violent *whhumpp* was the sound of death. The Allies' guns, mostly 2-pounders, and a few 6-pounders, had neither range nor power to return much damage to the enemy's tanks, and were no match for the German 88s which sliced clean through the armour plate of the Allied tanks like a hot knife through butter.

Santi was tending to an H.L.I. gunner whose eyelids and upper face were embedded with needle sharp splinters from a stone that had shattered when a shell hit the ground. The shards had spread through the air with a force not unlike the released quills from a porcupine, but with much deadlier effect. Fortunately, the gunner had been quick enough to shut his eyes just as they struck, and it was hoped his quick reflexes had saved him from permanent blindness.

To that end, removing each razor-sharp sliver lodged in the flesh of his eyelids and face was a painstaking endeavour that required the utmost care. It was going well so far, and Santi was hopeful there would be no long-term damage to the man's sight.

He was just done bandaging the gunner when Robert Williams rushed up looking for help. A few short yards away a tank commander had been hit and killed as he'd stood up to better survey the battle.

"His head's been blown clean away, Doc, but the rest of his body is slumped over the opening of the turret blocking any means of escape for the lads trapped inside. It's a gory mess. What's worse, the tank's treads are on fire and there is imminent danger of it spreading. I need to get those men out before they…well, before it's too late. Gave it a bash, but no room for more than one, and the body is so contorted I couldn't get it to budge. I'm stumped. The whole bloody thing's turning hot as hell, liable to go up any minute. You got any ideas?"

This was what tank crews dreaded above all else: being trapped and burnt to a crisp inside their own machine was a most fearful way to meet one's end. In an effort to make small of this fear, the men often drew on black satirical humour, referring to it as a 'brew-up' – a macabre comparison to the brewing of tea in the desert.

At the scene, Santi quickly sized up the situation and concurred

– it was dire indeed for the men inside. Their desperate shouts and screams were terrible to hear. It would be getting unbearably hot in there, and if they were to be saved there was no time to lose. The dead gunner, a sergeant, was well and truly wedged, and once more proved too cumbersome for him and Williams to shift on their own. Searching desperately for a solution, a sudden idea struck Santi. Maybe, just maybe if they used their webbing belts…

Acting quickly, he removed his belt and told Williams to do the same. Desperately working against time, they fastened the belts to the dead man's torso to form a sort of harness. Calling for additional help, they set to hauling the body out of the way. The task was most unpleasant and certainly not an easy one.

What remained of the gunner was an awful mess, and a dead weight that seemed to be stuck fast. Santi remained on the tank to push on the body while the rest pulled with the help of the lanyards. His feet could feel the heat from the metal tank begin to scorch through his boots. He realised it would soon be impossible to bear, but those awful screams from the men inside egged him on.

It took the combined efforts of four men in a frantic tug of war to finally budge the body and enable those trapped inside to escape. And not a moment too soon! Seconds later, the tank was too hot to allow for any proximity and, not long after, all that remained was a blackened, charred shell.

After quickly administering to the burns and blisters of the tank crew, Santi hurried back to his patients, arriving just as Tularam Bura and Narbahadur Rana carried in a prone figure on a stretcher. The head was swathed in blood-soaked bandages.

"*Sahib*, this one very bad," Narbahadur Rana said.

Santi lifted the rudimentary dressing covering the head. He heard Narbahadur's sharp intake of breath, and his heart sank at sight of the dreadful mess that lay exposed. The top of the man's skull had been blown away leaving his brain partially exposed; the gray matter was clearly visible at the top of the bony cavity.

The injured man was a young British tank commander who most probably had been shot in much the same way as the poor bloke Santi had just helped haul out of his tank. So many of these men suffered a similar fate when they stood up in the turrets of their tanks, risking their lives in order to gain a wider view of the battlefield. They did so in spite of being warned of the danger, because vision from inside the tank, through their periscopes, was so frustratingly restricted. Santi examined the wounded man carefully and found he had stopped breathing. It seemed nothing more could be done for him; he was obviously beyond help. There were others, however, to be saved and no time to lose.

Nevertheless, Santi hesitated. The poor man's colour was horribly pallid, his young face, so defenceless, looked as though he were asleep. Somehow, he deserved better than to be left in that condition. Coming to a quick decision, Santi attempted to cover the exposed brain with a dressing. As he put gentle pressure on the soft grey mass, he received a shock. The man, who previously had shown no sign of life whatsoever, began to breathe. Taken aback, Santi involuntarily removed his hand. Believing he must have made a mistake, he re-examined the patient. No, the man definitely was not breathing. Tentatively he applied gentle pressure to the brain once more and…there it was! Shallow, uneven – but without a doubt he was breathing! This man was actually, miraculously, alive!

Santi was stunned. It was impossible! He was a man of medicine, and everything he had been taught told him this could not be possible. Who would believe him if he lived to tell such a tale! He could hardly believe it himself! And certainly, in these wretched circumstances, in this place of horrors, no one could be expected to believe in miracles. How could such a thing happen!

He felt a sudden, unexpected flash of anger. What sort of cruel joke was this? Against all odds, after all that had been done to him, this young soldier was fighting to live. But he didn't stand a ruddy chance, did he? Out here in the middle of the desert, the unsterile surroundings, the dust and sand, the less than rudimentary care available, what hope was there for him? Wasn't the outcome a foregone conclusion? What bloody-minded God would prolong his agony like this? And to what end? For shame! Did any God, no matter what His name, have the right to play ducks and drakes with men in this manner?

Suddenly it was all too much for him – the terrible waste, the desecration of these young lives, the enduring courage and sacrifice that was heartbreaking to witness, and the unremitting pain of it all – it was hard to believe that this killing made any kind of sense anymore. Nothing could be worth the dehumanisation of ordinary, decent men, or justify their descent into this sort of barbarism. My God! What had they all become!

The monstrosity of it all hit him with a violence that was so physical he gasped as though in pain and, try as he might, he found it difficult to draw air into his lungs. He felt something close to panic begin to surge inside him, almost like a wave, drowning him. What could possibly be expected of him in the midst of such madness! He had never done anything like this before. Nothing he had been taught, nothing he had experienced had prepared him for this ordeal, for mental and physical anguish on this scale. How could anyone ever have imagined this purgatory of suffering!

The responsibility of all these men around him, their living and dying, had been thrust upon him. He held hundreds of lives in his hands and – dear God, he was afraid! Afraid he was not up to it! How was he supposed to live up to all their expectations! Something that felt like bile rose into his throat, making him feel like throwing up. He closed his eyes, willing himself to contain it.

Desperately fighting back a sense of hopeless inadequacy, he forced himself to focus on the injured soldier. *For heaven's sake pull yourself together*, he told himself severely. *You can't afford a single moment wasted on personal feelings or doubts at a time like this. No matter what, you're a doctor; you are all they've got. But you're no damn use to anyone in this state.*

Slowly, very deliberately, he took a first shaky breath; then a second deeper one. Holding it inside him, he forced a stillness to settle in his chest, allowed it to swirl up into his head so it cleared the fog in his brain and the haze before his eyes. Finally, when his heart had stopped pounding, and his eyesight was no longer impaired, he went back to work. With great deliberation, and compassion, Santi bandaged the wounded soldier's head. The pressure on it had to be just right; firm enough to keep the man breathing, without being too tight. It was all he could do. The rest was up to a God who seemed to have abandoned them all.

***

DUSK HAD BEGUN TO fall at last, but the fighting had not abated one whit. Now the twilight was punctuated with bright flashes from the guns, while streamers of light from tracers pierced the gathering shadows festooned with those multi-coloured Very lights, yellow and green, sent up by both sides.

To minimise the danger of being overrun by the enemy and 'put out of business,' Santi had requested and received permission, towards evening, to move the RAP to a more central position within the Battalion's triangular formation. This made it more accessible to the wounded as well, who were coming in from the various Companies on all sides, far and near. To accommodate the ever-increasing numbers pouring in, he quickly had new slit trenches dug. It hadn't been easy, the ground around here being as hard and stony as it was. And now those trenches were almost full to capacity, and more would have to be dug.

Before long the Regimental Aid Post was inundated with casualties of every sort. They were coming in faster than Santi could get them patched up and rolled out: the miner with his foot blown clean away when he stepped on an anti-personnel blast mine, the sapper whose buttocks had been blown away by a bounding mine aptly nicknamed 'Bouncing Betty' because, when stepped on, it bounded or bounced up off the ground to explode three to four feet in the air. It was especially nasty as it released fragments that sprayed the surrounding area.

Soldiers arrived without arms, others without legs, some were brought in with limbs so badly mangled they needed to be amputated right then and there; there were those with holes where their stomachs should have been, gunners with their head injuries and chest injuries, tank crews with their burns, three of them so bad their skin had crisped as though they had been barbequed; the crippled, the dying, the dead. Santi did what he could for them. Tragically, quite often, it wasn't enough.

A young lad from the H.L.I., who was hardly more than eighteen or nineteen, was rushed in tightly clutching his bandaged right hand with his left. It looked badly mangled and when Santi loosened the boy's grip and the dressing to take a look, the injured hand fell away, almost completely severed at the wrist. Seeing his hand lying there, separated, as though it were no longer a part of him, the boy's face froze in shocked disbelief. The disbelief turned to fear and, unable to control himself, he retched violently. Then his body started to tremble, and he began to weep.

Speaking calmly all the while, Santi quickly saw to the wound and then, making sure enough morphine had been administered, he bandaged the hand back into place, duly marked him and rushed him to the rear. In all probability the hand could not be saved. But then again – Santi recalled the soldier with the exposed brain – one never knew. And with the lad going into shock the way he was, it was better for him to believe…

He was attending to Aimansing Rai, a Gurkha rifleman whose thumb had been blown away, when a sapper was brought in screaming with pain. The poor chap had been unfortunate enough to step on a bounding mine that had mangled his left thigh and his testicles. As the stretcher bearers laid him down, Aimansing said softly, "Don't worry about me, *Sahib*. His need, God help him, is far greater than mine."

Here was another casualty of the infamous 'Bouncing Betty'! Santi quickly administered a good dose of morphine to minimise his pain and then proceeded to tend his wounds. Patching up his thigh was fairly straightforward, but his testicles had been practically torn away by fragments from the bounding mine. There was not much that could be saved there. Doing the best he could, given the circumstances, he marked him with an M for morphine and sent him to the MDS with instructions that he be transferred right away to the Casualty Clearing Station.

Earlier that afternoon Lt. Col. Douglas Thorburn had been brought in with a head injury. Standing on a tank, vehemently exhorting a nearby tank commander into battle in support of his beleaguered troops, he had been hit by a fragment of flying shrapnel. He had pushed himself to carry on until the injury, finally, had proved serious enough to merit a forced departure from the battlefield.

"Patch me up, Doc, would you. I've left a flaming great mess back there that's threatening to turn into complete catastrophe. I need to return ASAP."

"I wouldn't advise it, sir. Your injury needs more than a patch-up job. It requires proper treatment that I can't give you here."

"Oh codswallop! It's a bloody fiasco out there, and my laddies are right in the middle of it all. I can't just drop 'em in it and go haring off, now can I? Afraid you'll have to do the best you can, and it will damn well have to serve for now."

Santi hesitated. He sympathised with the Colonel's dilemma; he would probably have done much the same in his shoes. Point was, he was not in his shoes, he was his doctor; and it was his job to caution him against any fool-hardy action that might put his health at risk. "Sir, the consequences could be…"

"The devil take the consequences, Doc, and I'll deal with him later on that one. It's the devil out there giving my boys a pasting that I'm concerned with right now."

"But, sir, you do understand the seriousness of the wound you've sustained…!"

"Point taken, Doc, but there's nothing for it I'm afraid," the Colonel's voice made it clear he would brook no further argument. "Dash it man, I'm not laid up yet, am I? Just give it your best shot and let me out of here, there's a good chap."

And with that Santi had to be satisfied. Lt. Col. Douglas Thorburn rushed off to the front where he valiantly continued to do battle. Eventually, however, his wound took its toll and Santi evacuated him by ambulance to the ADS. (Timely intervention and his own strength of will saw the Colonel through the day, and the grace of God bought him a whole year. Sadly, his luck ran out when he was killed during the Allied invasion of Sicily the following year.)

Allies storming through fog of war, 1942.

CASUALTIES KEPT COMING IN from the various companies. Out there in the dark, multi-coloured Very lights from the German side could be seen illuminating the night skies, and there was a very real suspicion their Battalion was slowly but surely being surrounded. What had become of the rest of their Brigade was anyone's guess, and the fate of the H.L.I. and Baluchis could only be gauged by their tattered numbers as they arrived at the RAP throughout the night.

Santi was numb with fatigue. Amid so much pain and suffering, ministering to men physically and mentally stretched beyond all reasonable endurance, left no time for any consideration other than the pitiable human crises at hand. Food, a bath, a change of clothes, sleep, these were impossible even to think about. But when Col. Weallens staggered in, exhausted and almost dead on his feet, Santi took one look at him and realised it was imperative the man take a break. Knowing the sort of resistance he was likely to face, he decided to muster as much authority and firmness as he could in order to successfully stable the old war horse.

"You look completely knackered, sir. You really must get a couple of hours' kip."

"Out of the question, Doc," Willie declared, firmly. "I'm here merely because I gave that Baluchi Havildar Major a lift. Chap was making his way over to you with a shattered collarbone and I happened to be passing."

"May I ask, sir, when you last had any sleep? Forty-eight hours? Seventy-two?"

"Sleep! For Christ sake, Doc, there's the devil to pay out there, don't you know! When did *you* last catch forty winks?" Willie shot back, frowning.

Ignoring both question and frown, Santi stood his ground. "Sir, Narbahadur will fetch you a mug of tea. The hot, sweet drink will do you good, and a short rest will have you back on your feet as good as new. Believe me, I would not insist if it were not absolutely essential. We need you at full capacity, sir, you know that. I'll have word sent to Browne that you can be reached here should it become necessary."

All at once Willie seemed to give in. Bone-weary and overcome by fatigue, the thought of an hour or two of blissful oblivion was hard to resist. A half smile softened the tired lines of his face.

"I see the whelp has developed a bark," he muttered, softly.

Armed with a blanket personally loaned him by Santi – since his own bedding had gone astray – the Colonel took his doctor's advice and succumbed to the demands of his tired mind and body.

Outside, just beyond the threshold of merciful slumber, the war continued to rage, unrelenting; and with no time yet to spare for regret, human folly blundered on. It seemed as though the vengeful fury of Set, lord of the desert, god of disorder and violence, had been unleashed amid the outlanders who dared invade his domain; and now, nothing would contain his wrath.

5 June would later be described most aptly by a borrowed quote from A.E. Houseman: "*the day when heaven was falling, the hour when earth's foundations fled.*" (Antony Brett-James: *Ball of Fire, Fifth Indian Division in the Second World War*)

CHAPTER THIRTY-THREE

The Miracle Of The Seventh Day

– Author

AWARE OF THE BATTLE that was raging in the desert mere miles to the west, Cairo was tense with anticipation. There were rumours that sometimes favoured one side, sometimes the other, but no one knew for sure where the fickle finger of fortune would eventually come to rest.

Although everyday businesses had fallen off, the clubs and cafes were crowded and rampant with gossip; people seemed to take comfort in the proximity of large numbers and shared conjecture: how dire *were* the imminent changes looming over their city? And if not in so public a venue, then behind tightly shut front doors, in private, the social stalwarts threw themselves into round after round of inner-set parties in a determined effort to bury their misgivings. If one held at bay these uncertain times, this unpredictable future about to breach their lives, maybe, somehow…

And yet, at all times of the day, and late into the night, radios could be heard, mostly in Arabic, at times in English, as people tuned in to the news hoping to gain some insight into what the coming days held. Far away to the west the faint growl and rumble of battle could sometimes be heard, and Cairo waited with bated breath to see which way the tide would turn.

———◆———

IT WAS A SUNDAY morning. It is said in the Bible, on this seventh day, God rested from the labours of creation; it followed, therefore, to be the day of rest for Christians of the city. Muslims had been ordained to rest on Friday, and their Jewish half-brothers to maintain their Sabbath on Saturday. And so it stood to reason, Sunday being the third and ultimate day of God's ordinance to these not so disparate sons of Abraham, it would prove to be a good day for miracles as well.

It happened, on this holy day, there were no sewing or embroidery classes to be taught in Hedeya's Muslim school. In the morning Bajo, Bebé and she had gone to church as usual, where Asis Habib had requested the congregation say a special prayer for the men fighting in the desert, and for a return to peace and sanity in the world. When they were leaving, he had pulled her aside to ask if she had had any news. She had feigned nonchalance, and answered that she had not, and did not expect to hear any. Asis Habib was much too astute to be fooled by this pretended disinterest. He shook his head sadly and, clucking like an expectant hen about to drop an egg, he rolled his eyes heavenward.

"My poor child!" He emitted a few more clucks. "We must pray for his safekeeping. Such a good man. A man of his word. We all must agree, from his promise to your cousin in Iraq one whole year ago, to his determination in finding you, he is a man of commitment – don't you think?" Asis Habib paused, then let out a heartfelt sigh. "In this day and age that is hard to come by, eh?" He stole a quick look at Hedeya to gauge her reaction.

"I'm sure you are right, Asis Habib. I haven't had much time to think about anything but work lately. In fact," Hedeya kept her voice as casual as she could while she sought a means of escape, "I have to get back as quickly as possible to finish stitching Nafeesa Asfour's jacket today."

Back in the house, Hedeya changed Violette out of her Sunday frock, and then changed into some comfortable work clothes herself. As she entered the drawing room, she heard the vegetable vendor's cry from the street below.

"Tama'a-tim wu bamyaaaa."

Calling to alert Bajo, who might have missed him due to her impaired hearing, she went out to the balcony and hailed the seller. "How much? No, no, the *bamya* – is it fresh? How much?"

"Get some tomatoes too, if they're good," Bajo said, poking her head out onto the balcony. "We have none. Get enough of both so I can cook for tonight and tomorrow; Loza can have some after school." Hedeya nodded; they both knew Loza was partial to okra cooked with tomatoes.

Very few residential buildings had lifts, so in order to save running up and down long flights of stairs, shopping from street vendors was conducted via a simple, home-made pulley system. On the balcony of each flat was kept a basket on a rope, oftentimes attached to the end of a short wooden pole so the basket could be held away from any architectural impediments on the way down.

When one had haggled one's way to a deal, the basket would be lowered to the vendor in the street; he would put the purchases into it to be hauled up for scrutiny. If satisfied, the customer would empty its contents, place payment for the goods in the basket and lower it down once again to the vendor. Such transactions were a daily occurrence throughout the city and served to develop a relationship of mutual trust between customer and vendor as they gradually came to know each other thus.

Bajo joined Hedeya as she lowered their basket over the right side of the balcony. As a courtesy, baskets were usually hung to the right or left of a balcony whenever possible so transactions conducted would not impede the flow of pedestrian traffic on the pavement below.

As mother and daughter both peered over their third-floor balcony, keenly watching their vegetables being weighed, Fawzia, the second-floor maid, strolled out onto the balcony directly below them. In her arms she carried Mahmud Abou Talib's baby daughter, A'idah. Fawzia, who had just turned sixteen, had been with Abou Talib's family from the day his wife became pregnant, and she had cared for little A'idah from the very first day she was born. Consequently, the two were practically inseparable.

Now, the young girl leaned against the balcony railing, crooning to the child and swinging her gently in her arms as she showed her the goings on and the traffic in the street below. Hearing Hedeya's voice, she looked up and smiled. Her arm still circled about A'idah, she rested both against the balustrade and pointed upward, trying to make the baby look up so the two ladies on the floor above might admire her. At that precise moment there was a loud report from the street below. It set off a chain of events that made time stand still for those horrified spectators who witnessed it.

The sudden noise caused the startled Fawzia to jump and, as she did so, her grip on A'idah faltered. She was never able to explain how it happened, but the child seemed to fly out of the astonished girl's arm — and plummet downward. From the balcony above Hedeya and Bajo watched, horror-struck, as she fell towards the street. The descent seemed to happen in slow motion and the helpless onlookers, rooted in place, were powerless to prevent it.

Why the unknown French architect, so many years previous, should have built the first-floor balcony deeper and wider, so it jutted out further than those above it, was anyone's guess. Whether for the sake of aesthetic appeal or by some fortuitous whim, it was impossible to surmise. Be that as it may, the child, by some astounding chance – nay a miracle – landed on the wide balustrade of that lower balcony and, somehow, against the wildest odds, remained perched there in a sitting position. And then disaster struck.

Nadia Gaber had been sitting on that first-floor balcony painting her fingernails bright red, while she drank Arabic coffee and listened to the lovelorn voice of Oum Kalsoum. A flash of movement caught her eye, and when she looked up, she couldn't believe what she saw! There, in front of her, was a small human child sitting on the balustrade of her balcony!

Only a minute prior, the afternoon had been perfectly ordinary, and everything around her quite normal, just as it should be. Then, all at once, without rhyme or reason, without any warning whatsoever, she seemed to have wandered into the middle of what could only be one of those peculiar dreams there was no accounting for; and the subject of this dream, having appeared out of nowhere, just sat there looking at her as placid as you please.

Nadia shrieked, and rose halfway out of her chair. Whereupon, the apparition wobbled slightly, rocked back and forth a couple of times, then somersaulted and disappeared over the balcony. Nadia's shriek turned into a strangled gurgle in her throat as she froze, in mid-upright position. Then she began to wail.

"Ya dahwety, ya dahwetyyyyy!"

It was several moments before she was able to rally her wits enough to rush over to the railing. Wringing her hands, and terrified of what she might see, she forced herself to look over – and there lay A'idah in a basket of tomatoes and okra, its thunderstruck owner squatting by her side, staring at his unexpected visitor in speechless amazement.

When Fawzia rushed down to the street, she was sobbing hysterically. Hardly able to see for the tears that blinded her, she found little A'idah mushy with vegetables and a mite slimy all over; but the child was gurgling and smiling as though nothing untoward had occurred and, unlike the thoroughly shaken adults around her, really none the worse for wear.

In the days that followed, when Fawzia was called upon to recount the story, her telling of it never wavered. She bore unfaltering witness to having seen a pair of outspread wings – she swore they were immense, white wings – appear out of nowhere to gather up the child, breaking her fall, and gently, miraculously, deliver her to safety.

CHAPTER THIRTY-FOUR

The Killing Fields

The thundering line of battle stands,
And in the air Death moans and sings;
But Day shall clasp him with strong hands,
And Night shall fold him in soft wings.

Julian Grenfell, *April 1915, Flanders,* "Into Battle"

J UNE 6: WITH DAYBREAK, German shelling and machine gunning resumed with a vengeance. At first, they had been shelled from the northeast, then from the south, and now it seemed to be coming in from all directions. There could be no mistake – 10 Brigade was completely surrounded by the enemy. Out in the desert three dismayed onlookers were reluctantly coming to the same unhappy conclusion.

After his conversation with Colonel Weallens the previous afternoon, and seeing to the rearrangements for Santi's RAP, Brigadier Boucher left the front lines to make his way back to HQ – and he ran smack into the enemy at every turn. Taking unforeseen fire from several German and Italian tanks and columns, he became separated from his escort, his carrier took a hit, disabling it and killing one from his contingent. Despite the onslaught, there was nothing for it but to set out on foot.

Eventually, coming upon a bombed out three-tonner, the Brigadier and his two remaining Baluchis gratefully went into hiding. There they spent an uneventful, if rather fitful night, listening to the traffic of war trundle by, unable to discern whether the columns of tanks growling past in the dark were those of friend or foe.

At dawn the two sepoys cautiously emerged to answer the call of nature. Looking for some privacy, they ventured off aways, quite unaware they had attracted the attention of two groups of tanks leaguered close by, one German and the other British, one to the west of them and the other not far to the east.

Having located what they considered a convenient spot, the two sepoys had just eased themselves into comfortable positions for their commune with nature when, all at once, they were interrupted by a devil of a ruckus as shells and bullets thudded and pinged all about them.

Both the British and German tanks, spotting the two men, had opened fire simultaneously – and surprised each other into the bargain. Immediately changing focus, the two sides went for each other, opening up with all barrels – and the hapless duo found themselves caught in their crossfire. Startled out of their wits, the two sepoys hurriedly pulled up their pants and scuttled back into hiding. Only after the British tanks were beaten back and the firing had abated, did the three fugitives hightail it across the sands as fast as their legs could carry them.

It was at this point in their flight they came upon the scene of battle where 10 Brigade was fighting for its life. From a distance they could both see and hear the 4/10 Baluch under attack. Hurrying towards the battle, they drew sudden fire from some German guns close by, forcing them to seek shelter in an abandoned trench.

They managed to cover themselves quickly with sand and twigs, and all might have gone well had a German soldier seeking shelter from enemy artillery not chanced upon the same trench. The man jumped in, headlong, right on top of the Brigadier. Even then all might not have been lost if it hadn't been for the Brigadier's boot.

British infantry advance behind knocked-out Panzer tank.

Tempted by the sight of a good boot peeping out of the sand, and the further promise of its pair hidden somewhere beside it, the German yanked at the boot. Having taken the owner of the boot to be a corpse buried in the sand, imagine his amazement when out popped a Brigadier! The ensuing commotion brought the two sepoys as well out of hiding, straight into the arms of the Germans. Making sure the desert had no more hidden surprises to yield, all three fugitives were marched off by their captors to become prisoners of war. (Antony Brett-James: *Ball of Fire, The Fifth Indian Division in the Second World War*)

———•◆•———

THE ALLIES' GUNS FINALLY fell silent. Their supply of shells almost exhausted, the order had been given that no one was to fire until enemy tanks were well within range and one could veritably 'see the whites of their eyes'. But the Germans kept their tanks comfortably out of reach. Since the German 88s could easily out-range any fire power the Allies had, they were able to keep a safe distance as they picked off their enemy's sadly inadequate 2-pounders and 6-pounders which sat, silent and useless, while the Allies fumed.

Unable to retaliate, the Allies were caught in an incessant barrage of Axis anti-tank shells pouring down in a heavy, solid rain of iron. A single strike and you were done for, no question. And adding to the mayhem of widespread injury and death were the range-finding shells constantly bursting overhead, creating a pall of heavy black smoke through which they released a deadly deluge of shrapnel, the flying splinters spraying large areas with lethal effect.

This continuous scourge of cannon and mortar shells, combined with incessant machine gun fire raking the entire area, decimated the exhausted front-line troops.

Since morning an ever-increasing number of casualties had been streaming into the RAP with practically no let-up. The injured, both walking and carried, were arriving in droves, the latter in every serviceable vehicle that had space to spare. A replacement three-tonner and ambulance had been provided, the former running the injured from the front lines to the RAP while the latter evacuated the more serious cases to the ADS at Brigade HQ.

And where the hell was that ambulance, anyway?

All night long it had evacuated large numbers of wounded to the ADS, but the last time it took off with a full load, it failed to return. In the confusion, no one seemed to have the slightest inkling as to the whereabouts of the missing vehicle. With so many wounded being brought in by the stretcher bearers' three-tonner, the overcrowding was fast becoming critical. *Something* had to be done!

Santi sent Birbahadur in search of the ambulance, but the Gurkha, having dodged a hail of flying bullets, returned without news of the transport. Santi fumed, where the *ruddy* hell could the dratted ambulance have got to?

Peter O'Brie had the misfortune to turn up just then and – who better than the Brigade Liaison Officer! – Santi collared him, somewhat irately demanding an answer: for heaven's sake what had become of his ambulance?

"Terribly sorry, Doc, but it's bloody murder at the ADS! The place is inundated with casualties and every vehicle that could be spared has been pressed into service transporting wounded to the MDS and onto the CCS. It's a devilish business, I know, but I'm afraid your ambulance has probably been dragooned and is on its way to Tobruk, worse luck!"

"That's all very well," Santi snapped, thoroughly vexed. "But what the dickens am I to do with my lot meantime? Look at them! They're stacking up here as well. I have nowhere left to put them."

As he parted company from Peter he was thinking hard – somehow, he had to transport his wounded to the rear. He had to find the means, improvise if need be. He was still pondering the matter when two lorries rolled up to the RAP and began unloading casualties from the front lines. Well, wherever or whoever they belonged to, they would have to answer! If only as a temporary measure...at least one quick run...

Without further ado, Santi commandeered both vehicles with the order they be packed to capacity with the most serious cases for the ADS. It was, of course, a mere stopgap, not a solution, since those vehicles returned to the front immediately after. His slit trenches fast began to fill to overflowing again, so much so, there was no option but the injured be left lying on open ground, unprotected under heavy bombardment. Santi decided he had no choice but to chance sending out a second envoy.

This time Havildar Puransing Thapa would carry the message to Ben: *it was imperative a telephone call be made to Brigade HQ urgently requesting an ambulance.* Once more this proved to be a fool's errand, and very nearly cost the stretcher bearer his life.

Matters took a further turn for the worse when the stretcher bearers' replacement three-tonner stopped a shell, leaving them without any means of transport, either incoming or outgoing. The situation had now escalated from critical to dire.

The bombardment was growing heavier by the minute. Santi felt he could no longer ask his men repeatedly to risk their lives – and thus far to no avail. If a risk was to be taken, it should be his. He would go himself. He would have to entrust the RAP to their care once more, and with any luck he would return soon.

When told of his decision, there was strong protest from his men, but Santi's mind was made up; it was important they know he would never expect more from them than he was prepared to give. Last-ditch effort though it might be, he determined to give it a shot.

Gurkhas leaping into battle.

On this side, both Ronnie Smith's machine gunners and Grose's A Coy were putting a shoulder to the British Gunners' 25-Pounders. And not to be outdone, young Peter MacDowall could be seen dashing from trench to trench shouting "To it, Gurkhas!" urging his men against the enemy, "do your damndest and show the *dushman* a bloody thing or two."

In the rear, Slogger Marten's B Coy fiercely fought off an attack, while Ewen Kerr's 2-Pounders – hardly more effective than peashooters against the German guns – kept bashing on regardless, in a valiant if futile attempt to give the enemy some sort of push back.

And through the din of battle the blood-curdling cries of "*Aayo Gorkhali!*" could be heard from Subedar Balbir's D Coy and Subedar Gumparsad's Carriers as they threw themselves into the fray. Later, Robert Williams, with a burst of pride, would declare it "a true show of that old cavalry fashion, '*Charge and be Blowed!*'"

Santi paused, his heart pounding. For one swiftly fleeting instant an anachronic thought flashed in and out of his mind. School. Professor Tuheen Mukherjee's English Lit class. The frenzied scene around him was surreal enough that he might very well have stepped straight into the world of Tennyson's *Charge of the Light Brigade*! Substitute tanks and vehicles for horses and riders, and you have it: *Half a league, half a league, Half a league onward, All in the valley of Death Rode the six hundred.*

No wonder his orderlies had been unable to make it through! Any attempt to continue would be nothing but foolhardy. His chances of survival wouldn't be worth a tinker's damn. The only sensible thing would be to turn back.

But then, close on the heels of self-doubt came the thought of his wounded, of their plight. How could he go back without giving it his all! He *had* to try! He shut his eyes and drew a deep breath. And then he made a dash for it.

The adrenalin kicked in. Santi sprinted through the chaotic inferno, diving for cover from flying shrapnel, machine gun bullets and shells. Deafened by the sounds around him and the roar of blood in his ears, his ragged breath torn in painful gasps from his heaving chest, he prayed his luck would hold. Don't think…don't think…

Canon to right of them, Canon to left of them, Canon in front of them Volley'd and thunder'd…just a little further…duck left…NO, right…close call…

That he got through at all was more by dint of luck and prayer than anything else; so much so, when he eventually ran the harried Adjutant to ground, Ben was amazed he had made it. The news, however, was not good.

"Sorry Doc," Ben half raised his hands in resigned disgust, "I don't know how in hell you made it through, but I'm afraid I've nothing for you; telephone lines seem to be down, all communications are gone, and we're up the sodding creek out here. We've lost contact with Brigade; can't raise a soul. An absolute lash up! And if you ask me, it looks like we've been pretty well hobbled."

"You believe we're actually surrounded, and it's over?"

"Haven't the foggiest. Certainly seems that way. All I know is, it's a bloody mess and no one's been able to get through. Every time I've sent someone, he ruddy well hasn't returned! Middleton's sloped off with his supply truck, so we're out a Quartermaster. No MTO either – last I saw of Roger he was rounding up all vehicles, except the most essential, to evacuate them to the rear; haven't laid eyes on him since. As for Robert and our Intelligence Havildar, Narain Singh, the pair took off last night with the cooks' convoy. They were to fetch our nosh from the rear echelon. Well, wouldn't you know it, the whole blasted lot, to the last man and meal, seems to have vanished down a rabbit hole! Dashed inconvenient and a *bugger* of a nuisance."

"I ran into Williams last night as well." Santi remembered seeing Robert Williams briefly, presumably before he had done the 'white rabbit' act Ben had just complained of. "He told me the upshot of all this is we're ordered to hold our ground, to the 'last man, last round' apparently."

"Well, there you have it, Doc. One doesn't *want* to believe we're done for, but it doesn't auger well, so we had best be prepared I'd say. All signals have gone unanswered – not a peep out of Brigade or Div.HQ. We seem to be well and truly cut off, completely on our own in the midst of this merry hell."

"Sounds like they might have gone down too, then."

"Your guess is as good as mine, Doc. Let's just say I wouldn't wager a brass farthing for our chances now. The whole thing's a fearful hash and…well, I'm afraid we're for it."

Santi pursed his lips in vexation. So much for procuring an ambulance! Everything was at sixes and sevens, and it was obvious there was absolutely no transport of any kind to be had; there was nothing for it but to manage without. How the fighting would eventually pan out was a question to be left for later. Now, his primary concern was to get back to look to the welfare of his wounded as best he could. The furore out there on the frontlines meant soon his RAP would be overwhelmed past the point of mayhem.

Well, if that was the way of it, if they were to hold ground and make a stand to the very end, then so be it; if he was to go down, then his place was at the RAP, with the wounded, and he'd better return as soon as possible. That crazy dash through hell and high water had been for nothing; and now, somehow, he would have to run the gamut all over again!

———— • ————

ON THE WAY BACK the artillery barrage was ferocious. A stygian pall of dust and smoke, mixed with a thick stench of burning oil, flying debris, exploding shells and shattered pebbles, made vision difficult and the going treacherous. Tripping over camelthorn and saltbush, the acrid smell of cordite burning his eyes and throat, Santi made his way through the noise and confusion, dodging machine gun fire, mortars and anti tank-shells that zinged and exploded about him in a blaze of deadly pyrotechny.

Never again would he enjoy *Diwali* fireworks with the innocent abandon of his boyhood! Gone forever the pleasure of *morché* fire-crackers which henceforth would remind him always of anti-tank shells whizzing past, much too close for comfort! The infernal things came without let-up, bursting every few seconds around him; and those that landed on the ground nearby seemed to leap-frog, so, no matter how many he managed to sidestep, there was always the threat of another that followed.

Besting the mayhem one way was surely an act of Providence; surviving it again on the way back to the RAP, was without doubt an absolute miracle! And when he arrived there, Santi found the place under continuous heavy bombardment, with the injured piling up faster than ever in the open. To avoid the tragic furthering of injury and death, it was imperative some plan be devised at once. Somehow, the casualties had to be moved immediately they were stabilised. Stop the bleeding, dress the wounds, administer morphine if required, then promptly dispatch them back to the trenches by whatever means – the same transport they had arrived in, and if transport was unavailable, they would have to be carried on foot. Far from adequate of course, but given the circumstances, it was all that could be done.

Throughout the morning as the battle raged, the wounded continued to arrive, and the injuries grew ever more horrific. Santi was heartsick. To witness such awful human suffering, such wanton destruction of the body, mind and spirit was enough to shake any man to the very depths of his being. The killing was shocking, the pain endless.

But the day wore on, relentless. There was no time to think or feel for, as always, the first hour was critical to a man's survival.

That afternoon, under perilous fire, with no available vehicle, Santi was helping transport one of the many serious stretcher cases to the trenches. With Narbahadur Rana holding up the rear of the stretcher and Birbahadur Pun manning the front, Santi was walking in the middle, supporting the injured man's head.

As they reached the trench, suddenly, Narbahadur seemed to trip. Santi turned to find a look of stunned surprise on the stretcher bearer's face. He saw the young Gurkha look down at his body, saw his eyes fill with terror as he clutched his midsection…as he gradually folded…and crumpled in on himself.

Following his glance, Santi realised a piece of shrapnel had struck him, breaking his arm and ripping open his stomach. As though it were happening in slow motion, he saw, to his horror, the man's guts begin to spill out. Shouting to Birbahadur to look to the stretcher, Santi leapt to Narbahadur's side and, without a moment's hesitation, attempted to catch the spillage as best he could. Without any coherent thought beyond that dreadful moment, he began pushing the stomach contents, slipping and sliding, back into the injured man's body.

When Dilbahadur got news of his brother, he rushed to the RAP. Santi had just begun to operate on Narbahadur. The patient had been laid carefully across the knees of three soldiers in the trench, and Dilbahadur immediately took his place at his brother's head.

"How is he, *sahib?*" The look in Dilbahadur's eyes told Santi he knew how serious his brother's injuries were, yet refused to believe the worst. "Please, *sahib*, do whatever you have to. I know you will save my brother. If anyone can save him," the older brother pleaded desperately for his younger brother's life, "I know you can."

Santi felt the burden of the man's pain and trust placed squarely on his shoulders. He concentrated with all his might, taking the utmost care to put everything back in its proper place as best he could; and then, carefully, meticulously, he began to stitch the stomach wound.

Please, please, please, the word kept repeating inside his head. Santi realised he was pleading for a miracle, praying frantically…to whom? *Not God, surely*, he thought, bitterly. *He did not seem to be listening any longer.* His shoulders felt stiff with tension, the back of his neck ached, and his temples felt as though they were in a vice. He could hear Dilbahadur praying softly. Birbahadur had already put a splint on Narbahadur's broken arm. *Please, please.* With every stitch he was willing life into the figure lying prone beneath his hands.

He was halfway through closing the stomach wound when they heard the high-pitched whine of an approaching shell. There was that eerie something about the sound which made it stand out from the others. It started a long way off and seemed almost to go on forever; and the longer it went on the louder and more insistent it became. It was a dreadfully familiar sound.

When the explosion came, it was deafening, and they ducked instinctively as the splinters whistled past their heads. The shell burst so close, the eruption of sand felt like a ton landing on them, burying nearly everything.

For a split second no one moved. Both Santi and Dilbahadur had tried instinctively to shield Narbahadur with their bodies; but when they pushed the sand away and shook themselves clear of it, they found that almost half a *seer* (approximately one pound) of sand had fallen inside the patient's stomach. Santi knew then, with certain and utter despair, that it was hopeless. There was nothing more to be done. He looked across at Dilbahadur's stricken face, and what he saw made him close his eyes, to shut out, for a moment at least, that terrible look of agony.

A feeling of bone-weary helplessness overcame him. Once again, he felt that awful inadequacy in the face of this unbridled, this insane destruction of human life.

They were blowing each other to bits faster than he could possibly put them back together again. His mind jerked spasmodically as though pulled this way and that on a string. What good did it do to repair the damage? Of what use was the care and effort, the time spent in trying to heal them? The men he saved today would in all probability be dead a few days, maybe even a few hours, from now.

It was as though there were thousands of madmen out there who had turned into monstrous killing machines, and only one of him in here. They had turned into the servants of Death, doing his bidding in a frenzied rampage of barbaric savagery; and only when they were brought in here with their mangled, broken bodies did these dealers of death take pitiable human form once more.

And this young man lying here had risked his life, time and time again, eventually surrendering it in the service of saving them. Outraged and sick to his stomach with revulsion, Santi felt like throwing down his instruments. He was fighting a losing battle! What the blasted hell was he supposed to do with the odds stacked against him like this? He felt a sudden, throbbing anger surge, uncontrolled, through his chest and explode in his head.

Stop! He felt like shouting. *God damn you all, stop this obscenity!* But the words stuck in his throat, choking him.

Removing his battered glasses, he wiped a bloodied sleeve across his face. He realised his hands were shaking. He had to get a hold of himself; he could not allow the men to see him lose control and go to pieces like this. He gritted his teeth, forcing himself to calm down before anyone noticed. Slowly, deliberately, he coaxed his muscles to relax; his fingers, his arms, his shoulders and chest; and then he forced himself to carry on, gently, almost tenderly, wiping Narbahadur's pallid face and torn body.

And when he could, Santi spoke, softly, his voice still slightly unsteady with emotion. "*Ki kornu*, Dilbahadur!"

Tears ran unchecked down the hardy little Gurkha's face. "*Sahib, ki kornu!*" What can be done!

Santi could find neither word nor reason adequate to the situation. Together, they cleared away as much of the sand as possible and then, carefully, silently, Santi finished stitching the wound. After administering double the usual amount of morphine, he left the wounded man in his brother's care. When he checked back an hour later, he found Narbahadur still groaning with pain. Santi quickly eased him with another large dose of morphine, and a few hours later, as evening approached, mercifully, so too did death. His release came finally towards close of day when, just before nightfall, the young Gurkha passed peacefully beyond the realm of human suffering.

Advance Dressing Station, wounded being tended & hydrated, 1942.

CHAPTER THIRTY-FIVE
And Into The Bag

Full many a flower is born to blush unseen,
And waste its sweetness on the desert air…
For them no more the blazing hearth shall burn,
Or busy housewife ply her evening care:
No children run to lisp their sire's return,
Or climb his knees the envied kiss to share.

– Thomas Gray, "Elegy Written in a Country Churchyard"

GERMAN TANKS CONTINUED TO destroy one Allied canon after another. For accuracy of distance, a first shell would be lobbed to land in front of a cannon, followed by a second one behind it. Measured thus, the third could be delivered spot on, blowing both the cannon and its gunner to bits. The force of the explosion flung pieces of twisted metal and human parts skyward to land, far and wide, wherever they might fall. Santi watched in dismay as four cannons were destroyed in this manner while they sat, powerless and silent against the enemy's more powerful 88s.

And there, in the very midst of this devilish shootout, Colonel Weallens met with Lieutenant Colonel DesGras, C.O. of the Royal Northumberland Fusiliers. As described later, "with all the dirt in Africa flying about their heads," the two Commanding Officers shook hands, displaying the same courtesy normally reserved for the best drawing rooms. With a splendid nonchalance, almost amounting to a thumbing of the nose at their enemy, they set about exchanging information:

Earlier in the day the Baluchis were overpowered and so, apparently, were the Jats.

Bad business about Colonel Marshall of 157 Field Regiment. Splendid fellow; afraid he bought it today.

And now it seems Battalion HQ's gone west, and HQ 28 Field Ambulance has been overrun.

They discussed strategy:

Any anti tank guns to spare?

Sorry, clean out of those; only two 6-pounders and a few, a very few 2-pounders still operational; we're batting on a sticky wicket, I'd say.

Well, there's nothing for it but to go the distance. Good luck!

Their luck held. In robust health, and in their own good time, they saluted and coolly took their leave of each other.

On his way back to his HQ, Col. DesGras came across a 2-pounder gun position being attacked by an enemy tank. One of the gunners had been killed. Observing the lone remaining gunner's harried efforts, Col. DesGras promptly went to his aid. Later that day news reached Col. Weallens: the enemy tank had opened fire on the gun position at close range, and Lt. Col. DesGras had been killed on the spot.

Oh, the irony of it all! So went the war, minute to minute. (*History of the 4th Prince of Wales's Own Gurkha Rifles, Volume III, Col. J.N. Mackay*)

With all their guns in ruins, defeat could no longer be gainsaid. Completely surrounded, and without the support of artillery, it was impossible for their infantry to continue its fight against the enemy tanks. And ultimately, when the German tanks rolled in, the stark choice became one of survival or annihilation. One by one, the enemy tanks positioned themselves directly over the trenches and ordered everyone out at point blank range. The barrel of a gun at such close quarters presented an argument that was hard to ignore.

Yet, the choice was far from simple. The ignominy of defeat was hard to contemplate – more so when remembering the many who had fallen in the fight to avoid it. Still, by 1830 hours a sense of the impending end began to trickle through to the men in the trenches. It spread slowly among the ranks till, eventually, a few Tommies were seen stepping forward, shame-faced and reluctant, hands in the air. Some in the trenches, still unwilling to face the humiliation of surrender, began to swear at them.

Among these was Premsing Thapa, Jemadar Adjutant's driver. Livid at the *goras*, he cursed the 'white men' for cowards, practically wringing his hands in an agony of shame.

"*Herai, sahib! Tyo sala haru mancche lai herchha?* Look, sahib! Do you see those dastardly good-for-nothings? Shaming themselves and us by surrendering to the *dushman*! With what face do we stand before the enemy now? *Hai Ram!* Surely they will think we have livers filled with ditch water instead of blood!"

"*Hoina* Premsing. *Dushman charai tira hunchha.* We are surrounded," Santi told the unhappy Gurkha. "Dying uselessly now is unwise. It is better to live so one can fight another day, is it not"?

No longer hindered by Allied cannons now completely silent, German tanks approached the RAP. They were met with some sporadic fire from pockets of infantry who refused to give up, determined to keep up the fight to the bitter end. But as comrades fell in ever increasing numbers, the futility of their sacrifice and the hopelessness of their situation became painfully apparent; and, ultimately, common sense prevailed. One by one, all around, men hesitantly, grudgingly, put up their hands and stepped forward to give themselves up.

"*Sahib*, what should we do?" Birbahadur asked Santi, nodding towards the enemy. "Do we also have to surrender like that with the others?"

"There is no need," Santi said firmly. "Leave them to go about their business and let us go about ours. Their battle might be done, but our fight still goes on here. Look around, our enemy now is a different one. We are fighting death and it is going to be a long, hard fight to save lives from such a greedy enemy. We have plenty of wounded to tend, and no time to waste with surrender or putting our hands in the air. Let us put them to good use instead."

Santi had barely finished speaking when he noticed the advance of two German tanks towards them. They appeared to be making a bee line for the RAP. He could see German infantry soldiers toting Tommy guns following close behind. As the tanks rolled forward, he steeled himself for the confrontation to come.

Approximately 20 feet from where he stood, they came to a halt and surveyed the area. For what seemed an ominously long time – though probably no more than a minute or so – the outcome hung in the balance. Finally, having apparently concluded this was, indeed, nothing other than a medical facility for the wounded, they moved away. As the tanks started to head away from them, however, Santi noticed out of the corner of his eye, two German infantry soldiers approach the RAP.

"*Sahib*," Birbahadur's voice was low and anxious, "these two look suspicious. *Malai tyo dui jana ko alik shak lagyo.* They have something on their minds and, from the look of them I don't think it is at all good."

The soldiers came up to where Santi and Birbahadur were working on a head wound, and signed that everyone should raise their hands and follow them. Santi stepped forward so he stood between the soldiers and his men. Once again, the Germans indicated that he should surrender. Aware he was being looked to for direction, Santi stood his ground, and with a firmness he was far from feeling, he faced them squarely and uttered one of the few German words he knew.

"*Nein.*"

He pointed to his insignia of rank, and in a voice he hoped resounded with authority, he addressed the Germans. "Captain Dutt. I am a Doctor." He indicated the medical aid area, crowded with the injured, and spoke precisely and clearly. "Hospital. These are wounded men…my patients. They need care…medical care"

There was a long, tense silence; then one of the soldiers swung his rifle and pointed it. Santi could actually hear his heart pounding in his chest but, refusing to budge, he remained facing the Germans, maintaining a stolid front, his face rigid and carefully emotionless. The second soldier quickly searched and confiscated the few weapons in the area. When he was done, he aimed one of the captured rifles at the ground and discharged all the bullets; then he swung the rifle up, and holding the barrel, he brought it down hard, in one swift movement, burying the bayonet firmly in the sand. Having thus marked the area as searched and safe, both soldiers saluted Santi briefly and left.

Santi slowly let out his breath; he felt almost squiffy with relief and not a little weak at the knees! With not much chance yet to gauge the Germans in their role as victors, for one awful moment there he had thought…

Foxy Jones gave a soft whistle under his breath. "God luv yer, sir! That were enuf to bleedin' scare one 'alf to deff!'"

Santi nodded. It had been a close call. Even more so because only he was privy to the knowledge that he had not complied with the order to surrender all weapons. The soldiers had missed his revolver which was lying beneath some medical supplies along with his bedding. If they had found it, they would have construed, quite rightly, that he had concealed it, and the situation could very well have turned ugly. He was lucky in that, till now, there had been no call to use the weapon. He had kept it close at hand, always at the ready should he be forced to defend himself or his men; but so far, he had not, thank God, had cause to kill or harm anyone with it. That burden, at least, he had been spared.

"We need to put up some sort of sign to avoid another such encounter. I'm afraid the marker I had has been destroyed"

"Ah, 'ang on, sir! Oi fink Oi 'ave just the ticket; 'old on 'alf a tick and oi'l ave a butcher's," Jones offered, going into his kit bag.

"Jones?" Santi was thoroughly flummoxed, and not a little irritated with the man. His strange expressions had absolutely nothing to do with the English language as he knew it. Butchers! What in heaven's name did a butcher have to do with anything in their present circumstances? He made no sense whatsoever!

Jones turned to Santi, looking a mite sheepish. "Sorry, sir, oi keep fergettin' yer unfamiliar wiv our language. Oi meant to say oi'd ave a look, which rhymes wiv butcher's 'ook, see? H-o-o-k is 'ook, 'butcher's 'ook' and 'look'. It's that rhymin' fing-ama-jig agaiyn."

He had continued to delve in his bag as he was speaking and now, much like a magician pulling a rabbit from a hat, he produced an Aid Station Marker, a large Red Cross flag. With a triumphant "There you go!" he waved it at Santi who immediately forgave him his oddities.

It was planted without delay beside the upended bayonet in the sand, and like a beacon it brought in the wounded, ally and enemy alike; those who could walk did so, those who could not were brought in by the Germans in lorry loads. In no time at all casualties were spread out over the entire area, lying cheek by jowl, with more coming in every minute.

***

TOWARDS EVENING THE BATTLE began to abate, and as darkness gathered out in the desert, groups of Italian soldiers swooped in and began looting. Like packs of jackals, they fought among themselves. Some even attacked the RAP, taking all they could find: blankets, foodstuff, even tea reserved for the wounded was not spared. Santi protested furiously, but he did so in vain; and when the scavengers pinched his binoculars, he determined, on no account would they get their hands on his pistol which the German soldiers' earlier search had missed. To that end, he quickly buried the weapon in the sand; better to let the desert have it than allow it to be filched by these marauders.

As usual, many of the casualties were sappers, miners and gunners. Among the more serious cases were two, who, sadly, had no chance of survival. Santi administered a large dose of morphine to each, to ease his pain and passage. He remembered how, at the very start, he had hesitated to give more than the prescribed dosage; but that had changed quickly. Watching a dying man's agony had posed a very strong moral dilemma for him. What rules applied in this hell of horrors? How did one judge when the need for mercy outweighed all else? Making such a judgement call had caused him profound mental agitation, but soon he had come to realise these were extraordinary circumstances.

Regimental Aid Post, wounded awaiting treatment & surgery, June 1942.

In these abnormal times, in this infernal abyss of perdition, when there was nothing left that could possibly be done to save a man, the kindest thing he could do, the only moral thing to do, God help him, was to ease the man's terrible suffering as best he could, and to allow him, at the very least, some sort of dignity in death. It still weighed heavily on him, and each time he called upon the Almighty to lighten the burden of such an awful responsibility. Then, when the screaming stopped, and he saw the relief and the gratitude in a dying soldier's eyes, he knew that his prayer had been answered. In spite of this, it never did get any easier.

With his back aching from interminable hours of bending over the wounded, his body almost numb with fatigue, Santi pushed himself to keep going. His injured hand throbbed, his fractured rib cage hurt like hell with movement, and his feet felt like lead; he could hardly stand any longer, yet the wounded kept coming without let-up. It was hard to recall when last he had slept, what day it was, or night. And, finally, around 2300 hours, Dilbahadur insisted he take a break.

Almost asleep on his feet, he realised, indeed, if he was to be of any use to anyone, it was imperative he catch a quick couple of hours' kip. More tired than he had ever been in his life, his eyes gritty and sore, his lids so heavy he could no longer keep them open, he gave slurred instructions that he be woken in an hour, sooner in case of an emergency; then he wrapped himself in the same blanket he had lent his Colonel the previous day, and gratefully found himself a spot to lie down.

Slowly, as the horrors of the last few days released their grip, his taut mind began to relax and let go. Edges started to blur and fade, and he felt himself slip gratefully into the soft mists of oblivion. For the first time in what seemed like an age, he thought of home. War and chaos dissolved as his ravaged mind took refuge in a time when the comfort of ordinary, everyday peace had been taken for granted; before ever he had heard the dreadful sounds of bombs and guns, or witnessed their hideous outcome – the horrifying screams and agonised cries of the injured and the dying, the moans that searched desperately through so much pain, reaching for the comfort of a loved one, a wife, a sweetheart; the pitiful childlike sobs of grown men as they called out for their mothers – *Mum! Oh God...Mama, Mama!...Mutter, hilf mir!...* And everywhere the appalling, the grotesque sound, sight and smell of death.

As his exhausted mind began to shut down, he sank into slumber through a haze of images: clean, wholesome days...the spun-gold silences of early mornings filling slowly with the warble and gossip of waking birds; sultry afternoons heavy with the smell of ripening fruit, the still heat broken only by the merciful whisper of a vagrant breeze; and long, quiet evenings, dew-cooled and redolent with *rajani gandha*, the jasmine-scented twilights slowly melting into ebony nights. Ah, those soft, dark nights that folded you in silken shadows while, high above, a great golden moon-ship navigated through velvet skies luminous with a million starpoints. The quiet order of his past felt unreal, dream-like; it belonged somewhere so far removed from this hell hole, it almost felt imagined.

Real or imagined, these floating fragments of memory soothed and comforted his bedevilled mind. And then, just before he fell into a fitful, disturbed sleep, he saw...Grandfather's banyan tree, its branches spread wide, their dense shade all about him as he lay between the pillars of its aerial roots...peaceful, protected...he could even smell the fragrance that would sometimes waft up from the lotus blossom when the first drizzle of raindrops danced upon the *pukur* by Dadu's house...that fragrance, slight and sensuous...stirred another, more recent memory...a soft, haunting perfume...and his very last thought, set apart from all the rest...that lovely face...that auburn hair...those deep dark eyes...and skin like alabaster...

CHAPTER THIRTY-SIX

Chinsurah

There was a little girl who had a little curl
Right in the middle of her forehead.
When she was good she was very, very good,
And when she was naughty she was horrid!

– Nursery Rhyme

IT WAS THE END of May, the air heavy with heat and the breathless expectancy of the approaching monsoon. The family had settled quite well into their new Chinsurah residence. Built by the Dutch who had occupied the area in days gone by, it was a two-storied lineal building surrounded by well-maintained gardens. From the road at the front, a massive iron gate gave onto a driveway that swept up one side of the compound, following the curve of the gardens around to the other side and out again. At back, the property looked onto the Hooghly River – the name given to the Ganges where it passed through the outskirts of Calcutta. Here, broad stone steps led down to the muddy waters churned even muddier during the monsoons.

The building itself consisted of six flats, three on the ground floor and three on the first floor above. Along the front, both upper and lower floors boasted wide stone-flagged verandahs with colonnaded archways that ran their length from end to end where they wrapped around and continued, albeit with less grandeur, along the back. The ground floor verandah, unfettered by rail or baluster, opened freely onto the gardens, while the upper first floor was adorned with a fine decorative wooden balustrade.

In front, on the left, the right and the centre, three stone stairways ascended from the lower verandah, leading occupants and guests to the three upper flats where massive doors opened from each room onto the balcony to encourage the free passage of air and light. To further aid in the fight against Calcutta's heat and humidity, the enormous rooms were interconnected, and large fans whirled from the high ceilings overhead while, underfoot, the intricately laid mosaic-stone floors were pleasantly cool to the touch when barefoot. Servants and service personnel used the three wrought-iron spiral staircases at back that led directly to the kitchens.

The Civil Surgeon's flat was on the upper floor to the right of the building. The ground floor flat beneath the Civil Surgeon's was occupied by a Miss Babaneaux, daughter of the late padre of the neighbourhood Church of England. After the padre's demise, in acknowledgement of services rendered to the care and spiritual fostering of the subjects of the Raj, a courtesy had been extended to his daughter that granted her permission to remain in the residence she had shared with her late father. The remaining four flats were occupied by high-ranking government officers and their families, including the District Inspector General and the Superintendent of Police.

Captain J.P. Dutt and his family were the sole Indian residents in this otherwise British-occupied building, and his daughters, curious about their new surroundings, lost no time assessing their neighbours.

The most interesting – and friendliest by far – was Miss Babaneaux. A lady of fashion, despite the austerity of her upbringing, her collection of the latest foreign haute couture magazines – *Vogue, The Queen, Ladies Home Journal, Women's Journal* and even a copy of the French *Tailleur Luxe* – was enough to endear her to any modern young girl.

None more so than Sudha, who spent many a blissful hour poring over the fairly recent issues, her interest in clothes and make-up made all the more avid by a new relationship in her life. This attachment had quietly blossomed between her and Chokon Sen, ever since Kanti had brought the dashing young naval cadet to their Chowringhee flat.

Inevitably, Usha Moyee would discover her daughter ferreted away in some secluded corner, crouched on elbows and knees in a bottoms-up position, chin cupped in hands as she perused the latest fashions with a diligence that should have been, but alas was not, reserved for her studies. Mother described it as her '*olla*' position since it reminded her of that particular type of large black ant endowed with a rather prominently upturned protuberance for a rear end.

In addition to her treasure trove of magazines, Miss Babaneaux's large library of books and novels proved to be a source of pure delight for Kamala and Lebu. Both voracious readers, they were often to be found, hour after fascinated hour, buried within the pages of a Jane Austen, a Bronte, or a Dickens – even, perhaps, a Georgette Heyer, for the light-hearted wit and dash of a Regency romance.

So taken were the girls with these charming pastimes, so caught up in their dreams of fashion and fantasy, they often lost all track of time. This was bound to have consequences. Eventually, it came to Father's attention that his daughters habitually were not to be found when *master moshai* arrived for their math, physics and chemistry tutorials.

Bibhuti Bhusan Bhar, a scholar and a Hindu gentleman in every aspect, was himself much too kind to lodge a complaint of any sort. The erudite teacher, humble in spite of his double Phd, had been tutoring the Dutt girls in various subjects, as needed, for some years now; and he had agreed to continue, despite the distance in travel, when the family moved to Hooghly, and thence to Chinsurah. In fact, having grown genuinely fond of his charges, on special occasions such as a birthday, he would break journey along his way at Dilkhush, a shop in North Calcutta famous for its *aloo chops.* Knowing them to be a favourite with the girls, he would purchase a half dozen of the delectable potato chops with their savoury filling of minced lamb and boiled egg coddled in the centre, and he would arrive bearing this gift for his students.

Impeccably attired in his pristine, well-starched *dhuti panjabi,* topped off with a black jacket and cap, the *master moshai* was a man of habit, punctual to the minute. Arriving on the dot of 6pm, he would stash the big black umbrella he carried regardless of weather, hang up his hat and coat, and take his usual seat on the verandah. Then, regular as clockwork he would produce a snuff box and help himself to a swift snort of its contents, ostensibly as a cure to a mysterious allergy of sorts. This would cause him to sneeze twice, a malaise that would plague him throughout the evening at evenly spaced intervals.

Those first sneezes would indicate to Mother that *master moshai* had arrived and was ready to be served with a cup of hot tea, one freshly made *shingara* and a *sandesh,* those everyday savouries and sweets common to Bengali households.

Preparing to demolish this repast, he would settle himself comfortably in his usual manner, elevating his right foot by bringing it up and over to rest across his left knee. This stance would trigger a reaction, much like a twitch, that would begin as a gentle tremor of the left leg. The movement would soon gather momentum and spread to the right leg, as a result of which, before long, Bibhuti Bhusan Bhar's entire lower body would be on the move.

The most fascinating, nay hypnotising, aspect of this feat was its wayward movement; for, as the left leg swung from side to side, the right proceeded up and down. In a country where leg shaking could almost be considered a national pastime, this phenomenon, to the best of anyone's knowledge, was never to be duplicated by another living soul!

It was in this trance-like state that Father, upon his return home one day, came upon *master moshai*, patiently awaiting his pupils.

He immediately went in search of his wife and found her in the kitchen with Shonkar, the cook, overseeing the menu for the next day. "Where are they?" he demanded angrily.

"Who?" his wife parried, feigning innocence.

"Who? Who, do you think? Your daughters, of course! Why do I bother wasting money on their education when they behave like vagabonds. Worse than vagabonds!"

"They will be here. You know your daughters are responsible. And they are young ladies, not vagabonds. *Master moshai* arrived only a few minutes ago; he has just now finished his tea."

"Hrrrumph! This man is too easy on them. What is the use of being brilliant if he is incapable of controlling them? At this rate they will remain clods! Duffers! Do you know what Bina did to him back in Chowringhee? The minx quietly stuck a 'For Rent' sign on the man's back as he was leaving the flat. There he was, standing at the bus stop, the butt of everyone's laughter while your four daughters were on the balcony tittering and waving – and what's more, the poor fool was smiling and waving back at them with his silly umbrella, fondly imagining it was an exhibition of their affection for him! What do you think of that for being responsible and ladylike, eh?"

Usha Moyee quickly put her hand to her mouth so her husband wouldn't see the smile that threatened to break through. In his present mood levity most certainly was not the response he was looking for. Nevertheless, she couldn't help the small giggle that escaped her as she pictured the dignified little man and his umbrella, basking in the attention he was receiving, blissfully unaware he was being advertised for rent to the world at large. It really was too naughty of the girls! Tsk! And Bina studying to be a teacher herself! Still, she could see just how hilarious it must have been at the time.

"That's right, laugh! You are the one who spoils them," her husband scolded, though he turned away to hide the small twitch of a smile at the corner of his own mouth.

The memory of that incident was one he was not likely to forget any time soon. He had been delayed more than usual at work that day and had ordered the office clerk, eventually, to pack his pending paperwork to finish at home. By the time the office *chaprasi* had stashed his bulging briefcase in the car and Balaram, his driver, had battled through the writhing traffic of cars, buses, rickshaws, cows, pi-dogs and humans, he had arrived home quite a bit later than was normal.

As the car approached the house he had, he recalled, first been amazed and then, grasping the situation, hard put to it not to burst out laughing. There was Bibhuti Bhushan, innocent of the prank played on him, graciously bowing and acknowledging the smiles of those around him at the bus stop. And up there, on their veranda, J.P. Dutt just caught his daughters as they bobbed out of sight post-haste.

Quickly stemming all outward signs of amusement – since it certainly would not do to let the pranksters see him condone their behaviour by displaying mirth of any kind – he went to the rescue of the kindly old pedagogue.

J.P. Dutt knew his daughters well and, as he ran his mind's eye over them, he had a pretty good idea as to the instigator of this waggish deed. His oldest daughter Bela, a year and a half younger to Santi, would be beyond reproach as her influence on her sisters had always been a steadying one. However, with her away at Medical College, his four younger daughters, he was ruefully forced to admit, were apt to cut some surprising capers. He considered them carefully, one by one, starting from the bottom up.

He knew that Lebu, his youngest, was a creature of strong convictions and lofty principles, and no matter her tiny stature, she was a giant in whatever cause she chose to champion. Kamala, on the other hand, (his little *matu,* his favourite, though he never would admit it to anyone) was the most diffident and timid of the bunch. Yet, even she quite often had proved willing to be coerced into misadventure by her closest and much bolder younger sibling. In this instance, however, neither Lebu nor Kamala quite seemed to fit the bill.

As for Sudha, if she set her mind to something, she could be pretty wilfull in her own right, but her interests were usually focused on girlish matters such as fashion, make-up and the like. With a little luck, marriage would take care of that one.

And so, finally, his thoughts came to rest on Bina, oldest of the four girls remaining at home and well-known for her penchant for mischief. It was this daughter, he determined, who had to be the architect of this most recent frolic, just as she had been of so many others in the past – including those perpetrated on Lokhi, the long-suffering *ayah* the girls had when they were younger. All things considered, he was fairly certain he had the chief culprit to hand!

To this day poor Bibhuti Bhushan was innocent of the joke played on him, no small thanks to J.P. Dutt's quick reaction. Having astutely gauged the situation, he had ordered Balaram to immediately stop the car. Alighting from the Austin, he had thrown a single thunderous look in the direction of the gleeful mischief-makers on the balcony above who disappeared into the house like vapour. Walking up to the tutor, seemingly to enquire into the progress of his daughters' studies, he laid a casual hand on that gentleman's back as though to draw him aside in private conversation. In so doing, he managed to remove the offending sign without causing further embarrassment to the good man.

The girls, he noticed, were nowhere to be seen; they had vanished as magically as freshly fallen snowflakes caught in the sun. Not, he thought sternly, that this would save them from the rollicking he was about to visit upon their heads when he did catch up with them!

Shaking this memory and harking back to the present, he left his wife with a parting shot for his truant daughters: On his way back home, he informed her, he had made a special stop at Jalajog, their favourite sweetmeat shop, where he had purchased a box of sweets the whole family was partial to – *amriti, shon papri*, even some *payodhi*. Armed with his purchases, he had returned home looking forward to sharing them with the family after dinner.

Now, he waved this bag of delights under his wife's nose.

"I have a good mind," J.P. Dutt threatened, "to make them forego the *mishti* I purchased for them. Since they haven't learnt what it means to behave like adults, then they should be treated accordingly; if they will act like unruly children, they should most certainly be punished as such."

Usha Moyee was not unduly perturbed by her husband's tirade. She had been given in marriage to this man before she had turned quite fifteen and he had barely reached his nineteenth year. Since then, their years together had taught her to discern when he was in no mood to brook an argument. At such times – and this was one of them – it was best to hold her own counsel and let matters lie. For, while he was ever the strict disciplinarian with his sons, when it came to his daughters, her husband's bark was far worse than his bite.

And later that evening, she was proved right. After dinner, the sweetmeats were brought to the table, where the girls sat looking as guileless as lambs. And right under Father's nose, they made short shrift of the sweets while no further mention was made of mischief or misdeeds, of pranks or punishments.

CHAPTER THIRTY-SEVEN

The Wounds Of War

The stars are not wanted now: put out every one;
Pack up the moon and dismantle the sun;
Pour away the ocean and sweep up the wood,
For nothing now can ever come to any good.

– W.H. Auden, "Funeral Blues"

JUNE 7: WITH THE dawn came the grim but not surprising discovery that a number of the more serious casualties had not made it through the night. With no means of transport, or provision for further care, the outcome was inevitable. Santi asked Foxy Jones to arrange for the burial of the dead while he tended to the living; in the dark and desperately urgent turmoil of the night before, the bandaging and dressing of wounds had, of necessity, been a rushed job, much of which now needed to be addressed.

German and British wounded had been brought in and placed willy-nilly wherever space allowed, and all morning Santi and his orderlies had tended the casualties of both sides. Now, as he made his way among them, he saw a wounded Allied soldier lying side-by-side with a young German who seemed to have passed out. The German's head had tilted sideways to his right, as though the two had been communing, and his right arm had fallen, almost intimately, against the Tommy's left side; the inadvertent effect of companionship made for an aberrant sight, indeed.

To think only a short while ago these two soldiers would have fought each other, bitter enemies to the death; yet, here they were, after all the havoc they had wreaked, their enmity for each other dissipated, trivial in the face of a common enemy, the real enemy – that insidious victor whose name was Death.

Santi stopped to examine them both. The Tommy had suffered a bullet wound that had mangled his shoulder and incapacitated his right side but, for the present, the wound had been sufficiently well tended to tide him over till he reached the ADS. The German had recently been brought in and was the more serious of the two. He was so very young.

As he knelt beside him, Santi was moved by the boy's unfledged appearance; and, when the covering was removed from his wound, the horrific extent of his injuries became apparent. Most of his left leg had been blown away, the ragged ends of tendon and muscle dangling from the raw, still throbbing stump. He had lost a fatal amount of blood, and when Santi touched him, he moaned. He opened his eyes and they were full of pleading as he looked up at the figure leaning over him. Without taking his eyes off Santi's face, he half raised his right hand. It was a feeble gesture, seeming to draw attention to something he clutched in his fist. Santi took the proffered hand and, holding it gently in his own, he carefully pried loose the lax fingers. In the palm lay a small mangled photograph of a young girl, blonde, smiling, shiningly innocent.

Here was the face of the enemy! This boy, for that was all he was, no different from any of their own who were grist for the terrible, indiscriminate mill of war. A short while ago he had been a youthful Adonis, beautifully whole and complete in form, beloved of this enchantingly fair creature in the ragged picture. A very short while ago they had shared hopes and dreams, believed in a life together, a family, growing old.

Santi bit his lip as he turned away from the crippled body to hide his dismay. He allowed himself a quick moment to regain some composure. Would there never come a time when he might manage to steel himself against this abhorrence? Would it never get easier?

No! God forbid that it should!

Once again, he experienced a flash of searing anger at the colossal waste of such vital youth, such promising life.

Dear God! What were they doing here! Theirs had been the cause of the just, hadn't it? The good fight to ensure the salvation of mankind! But somehow, somewhere, they must have lost their way, for surely they had travelled down the road of insanity and passed through the doors of bedlam to descend into this perdition – perdition they had created with such unmitigated savagery, there was no longer any clarity between right and wrong. After the atrocities that had been committed, neither side could lay claim to being on the side of the angels.

How would these men ever be able to atone or forgive one another for today's ravages? At what point would the horror start to fade so one might try to forgive and, somehow, begin to forget? Could there be enough forgiveness in this world to surmount the iniquity they had so shockingly perpetrated on each other this day? It is impossible to hold onto one's faith or beliefs in the midst of this bloodbath, he thought bitterly. All sanity is drowned in the abomination of this hell! Here they were all lost souls, for where can you find redemption when you are in the very pit of hell?

Forward Field Station, Overcrowded wounded awaiting evacuation, 1942.

In that split second, he knew, with a certainty beyond all doubt, he would never be free of these sights and sounds; they were indelible. He would carry the memories of this infernal place, seared into him, forever. Like a curse of the gods, the malignancy would stay with him all his life; through the years, burrowed in his soul, haunting his dreams, growing old along with him, changing him forever; never leaving, never fading into merciful oblivion. He would need all the blessings of Kali to protect him from the demons unleashed this terrible day.

And he was not far wrong. It would be well over two decades before his fervent prayers for redemption were answered, and he no longer woke suffocating on the screams of his grotesque nightmares. When they did eventually start to dim a little, to fade somewhat around the edges, they merely crept into the dark recessed abode of the subconscious where unwelcome memories are exiled. And there they dwelt for all time, threatening shadows that loomed, at times taking over his body and his mind in the night; and those painful visitations, though mercifully dulled in some measure with the passing years, never quite left him, nor allowed him to put to rest, to forget, the evils of this time and place. They remained with him, intermittent resurrections, unholy hauntings that plagued him till the day he died.

But right now, at this moment, he could not allow the dark despair of his thoughts to take over. Trying to reflect a reassurance he was nowhere near feeling, Santi attempted to comfort the young soldier. Carefully, he folded the boy's limp fingers over his prized photo. He did not have long to go. The wounds being as extensive as they were, there was not much could be done for him; moreover, the shock of transporting him – if transport there had been just then – would only hasten his end. His only friend under these circumstances was a good dose of morphine.

Santi quickly administered this to make him as comfortable as possible, and to ease him through the short while he had left on this earth that he might make his peace with a God who, in bitter regret, had surely turned away from the human race.

Rommel's staff car pulled up some distance from the RAP. The General scanned the area through his field glasses, pausing briefly at the scene of the young Indian doctor ministering to the injured and the dying. He was impressed by the manner in which both friend and foe were tended. It spoke to an integrity and devotion to his medical duty. Here was a man of honour. He turned to his driver, a soldier named Helmut, and tapped him on the shoulder. *What was the young doctor's name? Find out,* the General instructed. *Find out and let me know.*

Santi had moved down the line a couple of paces to attend another casualty when he heard the British soldier's soft voice crooning behind him.

"There, there lad. No need to worry. You'll be home soon, and right as rain."

He stopped and turned in surprise. The German was no longer moaning. His hand was resting in his enemy's lap, but his open eyes had glazed over, and he was very still. Santi went to him, bending over the quiet form for a quick examination.

"Is he dead, sir?" The weary voice was tinged with pity, a sad resignation at the inevitable.

Gently Santi shut the young panzer's eyes. "I'm afraid so; he was badly wounded and had lost a great deal of blood. At least he isn't suffering anymore."

"I told him there was no need to worry," the Tommy said. He closed his eyes and continued. "He's home now, right as rain, just like I said."

Santi found it hard to qualify the sudden emotion that welled up inside him. It filled his chest and throat, and he felt it sting his eyes. Maybe it was pity...surprise...or some sort of gratitude? Perhaps all three combined in the resurrected hope that, unbelievably, they might yet achieve salvation after all! Apparently, he had underestimated the fortitude of the human spirit and its capacity for forgiveness.

In the midst of this abyss of death, like a phoenix rising from the ashes of this terrible destruction surrounding them, the human spirit had not only survived, it was alive and well and, evidently, stumbling along the road to recovery. Could it be that in spite of its errors, humankind still had the ability for greatness? Maybe they had not been completely forsaken, after all!

Now, a British Brigade had advanced and begun to bombard the Germans. By afternoon, unaware of the exact position and circumstances of their captured brethren behind enemy lines, their shells began to fall indiscriminately on both enemy and POWs alike.

The RAP was in the direct line of fire. During the mad scramble for cover, everyone who was able, pitched in to get the casualties out of harm's way. After a while, mercifully, there was a short break in the bombing. Taking quick stock of the damage, Santi decided to send Dilbahadur in search of a spot that might afford the injured a little more protection.

Meanwhile, cut off from the rest, Roger Werner, the missing Motor Transport Officer, found himself trapped on the far side of the minefield, well behind enemy lines. Having ducked into a slit trench, he could see the battle still raging around him as dozens of enemy tanks approached, followed by tracked vehicles carrying guns together with the men who manned them. An account of his predicament, later related during "one of those unguarded moments when the reunion of companions, long parted, unseals a man's lips," was subsequently and faithfully set forth in *The History of the 4ᵗʰ Prince of Wales's Own Gurkha Rifles, Volume III.* It went as follows.

Having endured fire from his own Allied artillery, heavy and accurate enough to fill him with a pride that almost allowed him to forget his own plight, Roger felt it was his patriotic duty to complement their efforts with some of his own.

Still in possession of his trusty rifle, he decided to put it to good use. Forthwith, he set about taking pot shots at the enemy, no matter they were too far to incur any actual damage, for the effort had a distinctly heartening effect on the shooter himself. In fact, so wholeheartedly intent was he with the business of decimating the enemy, he failed to notice a tank approach from behind, until it came to a halt practically atop him. Its black shadow lying like a heavy thunder-cloud about him, Roger turned to find he was being observed, very seriously, by a head sticking out of the turret.

Caught red-handed, like a schoolboy at a prank, he sheepishly tried to conceal the evidence of his handiwork; but even as he attempted to smuggle the rifle out of sight, a gruff command of "*Raus, Raus*" stopped him in his tracks.

Finding an automatic pointed unwaveringly at him, Roger speedily chose wisdom over valour and dropped his weapon, raising his hands to acknowledge capture. And then, rather optimistically, he ventured to intimate he would like to retrieve his greatcoat; after all, the night *was* ruddy cold!

A threatening wave of his captor's levelled weapon swiftly telegraphed refusal. Undaunted, Roger decided to push his luck just a fraction further in a last-ditch effort to recover his coat, for surely no one could get shot for such a thing! He soon discovered his mistake. As he reached for it, a bullet zinged past, almost taking his fingers, convincing him in no uncertain terms, it was far healthier to brave the cold than risk the displeasure of his captors.

———◆————

TOWARDS EVENING ON THAT fateful day, Ben Browne was roaming the throngs of weary, disconsolate and injured POWs. Amidst the devastation on the battlefield, and the confusion that followed their capture, it was near impossible to tell just who had been bagged and who had managed to slip the net; equally hard to ascertain was the precise number that had been nabbed, or where the dickens they all were!

As Battalion Adjutant he was trying to identify, shepherd and reassure those of the 2/4 taken captive, when suddenly, out of the fog of smoke and darkness, an enemy tank materialised and advanced towards them. He recalled later how it rolled right up and stopped, ominously, not ten feet from where he was standing. The turret hatch clanged open and a head popped out. Curiously, it peered around at the crowd of woebegone prisoners and, after a moment, was followed by the rest of its body. And then it spoke.

"I say," a voice called in impeccable English. "Any of you chaps here from Mill Hill?"

There was a moment's astounded silence before a hesitant voice from the crowd replied, "I am."

A pleased grin broke across the German officer's face. "Good show! So am I. Anyone for some hot coffee?"

———◆———

LATER THAT SAME EVENING Dilbahadur's search proved fruitful when he came across a *bir* not far from B180. It would serve very nicely indeed as the relocation spot for the RAP. The *bir* had already been claimed by a Captain Norman, but that British medical officer was perfectly agreeable to sharing the dry watering-well since it was large enough to accommodate both his wounded and Santi's as well.

With still enough daylight to effect the transfer, this was painstakingly undertaken, one casualty at a time, till the entire RAP had been relocated. Hopefully, here they would be out of direct range of the guns. To make doubly sure, Foxy Jones displayed the large Red Cross flag as a clear indication that this was a medical facility.

No sooner had he done so than two German soldiers drove up demanding immediate attention for three of their wounded. After a quick examination revealed none of the three wounded Germans was in serious condition, Santi indicated they would have to wait their turn to be treated.

The soldiers' response turned aggressive with renewed demands; and when one, more belligerent than the rest, decided to remove the RAP's Red Cross flag to set up their observation post in its stead, Santi decided he'd had enough. He made a firm stand on both counts: No! This was a medical aid post, not a combat zone, and the flag would remain as a clear indication of that. Moreover, in this place there was neither victor nor vanquished. Here, all had been equalised by their suffering, and no preference would be given to any man other than that dictated by the severity of his wounds.

The ensuing altercation grew so heated it eventually attracted the attention of a German officer. The young captain demanded to know what all the commotion was about. Apprised of the cause, he spoke to the soldiers in a firm tone of voice, and although neither Santi nor Jones understood German, the name 'Rommel' was easily understood when mentioned twice. Finally, the Captain turned and addressed himself to Santi.

"Der has bin a misunderstanding, doctor. Ve haf orders, you vill not be disturbed. Please, feel free to carry on vit your vork." He saluted smartly and walked away, followed by the soldiers.

"Cor blimey! Rommel, eh?" Foxy Jones puffed out his chest, visibly crowing with triumph. Reining himself in, he muttered after the retreating figures, "That'l teach yer ter mess wiv us, yer daffy twerps!" And with that he took himself off to procure water and whatever blankets the Italians might have missed or discarded.

Dusk descended on the RAP. The wounded lay everywhere – some had managed to make it in on their own steam, others were carried in; men with broken bodies and, following capture, broken spirits too, having suffered hardship and trauma beyond the bounds of all human endurance. And still, all around them, the awful, unrelenting din of battle continued without let-up.

As night shadows began to lengthen and darken the *bir*, an urgent search went out for some sort of light. Eventually, someone produced a half-used three-inch candle and a box of matches.

That night the two doctors worked by the light of that single precious candle – staunch the bleeding, splint the breaks, amputate when necessary, bandage, morphine and mark, treat for shock, on… and on…and on…

Years later newcomers to the Battalion would be told how the wounded were tended by candlelight that, against all odds, endured far into that night giving aid in the fight that saved the lives of so many; for such is the stuff that legends are made of.

There was the very young bombardier whose head was cradled on the lap of a kind Samaritan while Santi amputated his arm and Captain Norman carefully doled out the anaesthesia. A sapper had caught the blast from an exploding shell case on the right side of his face and neck; it had partially dissolved the eye, and what was left was hanging out of the empty socket. A young British officer, a Lieutenant, from the 4/10 Baluch was brought in with a bullet wound to his stomach and another to his head. The head injury was not too serious since the bullet had grazed his skull and, fortunately, not touched his brain. The injury to the stomach, however, was another matter. Despite this, he was one who had some chance of survival if proper, timely treatment was received. Santi fixed him up, gave him some morphine, marked him accordingly, and hoped to God there would be some sort of transport soon to dispatch all these casualties to a German or Italian hospital.

Stomach wounds, chest wounds, head wounds. The smell of blood and the sounds of pain mixed in with the clamour and confusion of battle. But no matter how bad the injury or how high the price paid, there was not a single complaint to be heard, and these men who had sacrificed so much, somehow, still had a joke to spare:

"Cheer up, Andy me old cock!" a Tommy who'd lost a leg called out to a friend. "Think uv all them pretty young nurses who'll soon be fussin' over us, tuckin' us up in clean white sheets. I tell yer, it's the cushy life fer yer an' me as I'm thinkin' of all them soft, sweet hands we'll get ter hold. Just yer watch, matey, I'm aimin' ter have m'self a fair bit uv the old slap and tickle when I get home! 'Course, you don't have me good looks, worse luck…"

"Ah, shut yer gob Davy and be done with yer badgerin'! Me face is me fortune and I've still one good arm ter hold a pretty lass with. When wuz the last time yer took a look at yer mug in the mirror, then, yer dozy beggar? 'Tis a sight'll frighten the devil himself and send him scamperin' back ta hell!"

In another area, a soldier with bandaged eyes turned towards the sound of soft groaning coming from a figure one down to his left. "That you, Pete? I lost you out there in that bedlam. Glad to know you made it, mate."

"Don't think I will, Harry. I feel awful queer," came the shaky reply. "I think maybe I'm done for."

"Blimey! I never did hear such a load of old cobblers! You give over with that daft talk for I'll not be having you welch on me now, laddie. You owe me five quid from our last wager, and I don't aim to let you off that easy. So you'd best buck up, you hear, and don't you so much as think of going west." There was a short pause. "Tell you what, boy-o, I'll even give you a chance to win your money back, fair and square; I'll wager you a quid we'll be having a right old chinwag, you and me, bending the old elbow down Whitechapel way, quicker than you can say Jack Robinson, how's that then!"

By late night on the 7th, notwithstanding the overcrowding and the severely depleted medical supplies, most of the wounded had been cared for as well as could be expected; and now there was nothing to be done except wait. Although, both a German and an Italian doctor had come by earlier with promises of an ambulance, so far nothing had materialised. Continuously through the night, German soldiers pressed past the *bir* in their advance forward, towards the re-treating British front, leaving the RAP now well behind enemy lines. To compound this situation, somewhere close to midnight, the RAF retaliated with a bombing run, effectively strafing their area as well.

Captain Norman, unfortunate enough to sustain an injury to his right foot caused by a flying splinter, was prompted to vent the general feeling of those caught in the quandary: "The devil of it is one is hard put to decide whether to cheer the Air Boys with a resounding tally ho for some bloody decent target shooting, or curse one's ruddy luck for being at the receiving end of it!"

Fairly quickly, however, it dawned that this latest tribulation might just be turned to the good. With the scream of aircraft overhead, the pounding of anti-aircraft guns following the stream of tracers hunting across the night sky, and bombs crashing all around them, the ensuing chaos handed the able-bodied a good chance to make a dash for it – and Santi's immediate instinct prompted that he avail himself of the unexpected opportunity. He had lost count of the many moments of sheer terror and unending hours of mind-numbing exhaustion he had forced himself to keep going, to carry on – and now, all at once, a possibility of escape had presented itself.

The surge of adrenaline lasted but a brief moment before reality asserted itself. He realised, with growing dismay, without him many of his casualties would almost certainly die. It was a fact he had to face – the choice between saving his own life or the lives of the helpless wounded he had fought so hard to save all night long.

There really was nothing for it, there was but one decision to be made – as desperately as his instincts urged him to grab his chance and make for safety, his sense of duty told him the injured needed him here, and he could not desert them. He had to stay.

Without further thought, Santi abandoned his idea of escape, but determined that his three remaining Gurkha orderlies and Foxy Jones should make a bid for freedom. He encouraged Captain Norman to accompany them as well; with the injury to his foot, it made sense he should avoid internment as a POW – especially as Foxy Jones' offer to help increased his chances of success.

And so it was decided, he would remain to hold the fort so they could make a break for it.

With a hurried handshake, Captain Norman and Foxy Jones used the ongoing air raid to make their escape. However, when it came turn for the three Gurkha orderlies, Dilbahadur refused to go. No matter what argument Santi made, the loyal batman insisted he would remain behind with *Daktar Sahib* and, since precious moments were awasting, Santi eventually gave in. That left the two stretcher bearers, Havildar Puran Sing Thapa and Havildar Birbahadur Pun, who said their farewells and, with Santi's blessings, made a run for it.

Now, left on their own, Santi was grateful for Dilbahadur's company. He turned to the faithful orderly and, laying a hand on his shoulder, he said softly, "*Shabash*, well done, Dilbahadur."

As luck would have it, Captain Norman and Foxy Jones were apprehended almost as soon as they set out. Fortunately, it was without mishap and they were returned later to the RAP, disappointed but unharmed.

And what of Havildar Puran Sing Thapa and Havildar Birbahadur Pun? The two NCOs slipped into the shadows, wrapped in Santi's maroon blanket to help blend into the dark night. Many a time narrowly escaping capture, they made their way with stealth towards the British lines. At one point they came dangerously close to a column of enemy tanks resting silently, nose to tail. Careful to avoid any sentries who might be posted, they manoeuvred around the halted column. The stentorian snoring from within the parked vehicles assured the two men, here at least, the exhausted enemy was fast asleep. They crept past with the utmost caution, then fled into the desert where they spent the entire night trudging through the sands, finally reaching 7th Armoured Division the next morning.

There they related the story of that last night in battle; how the Battalion, steadfast to the end, holding to the order of 'last man, last bullet', had finally been overrun by the enemy, and almost everyone who had not been killed had been taken prisoner. The two men were quickly dispatched to rejoin the small contingent that remained of the 2/4 Gurkhas. And once again, Havildar Puransing Thapa (No. 7071) and Havildar Birbahadur Pun (No. 7727), sole witnesses of those last fateful hours, recounted to their dismayed unit the story and circumstances of the Battle of the Cauldron where, at the end, practically their whole Battalion, tattered and defeated, had been marched off into captivity, or killed.

CHAPTER THIRTY-EIGHT

Fair Is Foul And Foul Is Fair

Perhaps 'tis pretty to force together
Thoughts so all unlike each other;
To mutter and mock a broken charm,
To dally with wrong that does no harm.

– Samuél Taylor Coleridge, "Christabel"

IT WAS UNUSUAL FOR Hedeya to be home on a Monday. Then again, it had to be said, there was not much could be considered usual about that particular Monday. She had left for school all right, but then, after the 'incident', she had been brought back to the house where she was put to bed and told to rest.

The morning started out well enough considering the rising panic that had begun to grip the city. There was no specific news from the front, at least nothing definite one could depend on, but the air was rife with rumour – all of it not good.

As in every other household, they had their radio on at every opportunity, though Hedeya could hardly bear to listen to it; and yet, she couldn't bear not to. Going about the normal routine of getting ready for school, she could hear Bajo fiddling with the radio in the drawing room, trying to capture some station, any station that would give them news as to what was afoot. God alone knew what the morrow would bring! The one thing that seemed imminent – the Germans were coming!

That, however, was a problem for tomorrow. Today, Hedeya was plagued with other fears; they intruded on her dreams at night and, try as she would to not think overmuch, they made her head ache during the day. It irked her that it should be so. This was so unlike her. Thoughts of Santi were like a physical presence in her life. How could this man leave her with so many memories in such a short time! And, no matter how hard she tried, she could not rid herself of the awful foreboding of loss, the near overwhelming dread that dogged her. She was unable to explain the depth of it, and was dismayed at how far within her it reached, almost as powerful as the pain of bereavement. She admonished herself, impatiently trying to shake loose the feeling.

Have you lost all commonsense? You don't know anything about this man, where he is from or where he is going. You spent a few hours in his company, and now you spend all day and all night thinking of him. He's gone. He came, and now he's gone. He passed through your life, brought by the war like a wind that seems to have scattered all good sense and stirred the impossible. What is the matter with you! These are unsettled times, confused and uncertain. Caught in their throes, alone, was it any wonder a young man, prompted by a friendly face, a few kind words, might imagine himself in love! You cannot take such declarations seriously, or believe in the soundness of such a proposal. You know better than to let yourself be swayed by his emotions of the moment!

She pressed her fingers to her temples and tried to massage away the tension. She must make a concentrated effort to take her mind off these disruptive thoughts that were throwing her life into turmoil; they served only to make her miserable. Maybe it would lift her spirits if she wore the new outfit she had finished yesterday.

She pulled out the slimline dress and jacket of soft beige silk with dark brown piping, buttons and epaulettes. The brown silk was a small discarded remnant from a customer's dress that perfectly matched the beige silk Hedeya had found on sale a while ago. Together with the buttons that had come off an old dress too drab for longer use, she had put together a smart outfit that looked as though it had been tailored from an haute couture pattern. She made practically all their clothes – her's and Bajo's, and the children's – by mixing and matching bits and pieces no longer required with remnants procured on sale.

Donning the outfit, Hedeya looked at herself in the mirror. Yes, it fit well, she was pleased with the way it had turned out. As she left the building and crossed the street to the tram stop, her neighbour, Nadia Gaber, had called to her from her first-floor balcony.

"*Sabah alkhair*, Hedeya. Good morning"

"Ah, Nadia! *Sabah alnur.*"

"*Kaif halik?* How are you?"

"*Masha'Allah, ana bekhair.* God's will, I am very well."

And all was well till Nadia's next remark. "What a beautiful dress! Is it new?"

The moment the words passed her lips, Nadia's hand had flown to her mouth as though she would press them back. Hedeya winced ever so slightly as she made a deprecating gesture at her frock and replied, as casually as she could.

"This old thing? Oh, it's something I put together from a few forgotten rags. Nothing much at all."

Hedeya was not superstitious, but the whole neighbourhood knew to beware of Nadia's *aino*. The good-hearted lady was believed to have the curse of an 'evil eye'; her remarks, well-meaning though they were, seemed to work in reverse. Poor Nadia knew it herself, and she tried hard to refrain from complimenting her friends or neighbours, for every time she did so, some sort of mishap seemed to befall the recipient. She made every effort to curb her tongue but sometimes, as now, despite her efforts she would blurt out something, with regrettable consequences. It was a bane she, and those around her, had to endure.

Now Nadia quickly tried to make restitution. "Yes, yes, I see now, it is an old dress. I don't know what I was thinking. It must have been the sun in my eyes. *Ma'a salama*, Hedeya, go with God."

Shortly after, as Hedeya was changing trams, a car veered out of control and hit her. The uncanny thing was, when they brought her home, except for some minor cuts and bruises, Hedeya was strangely unharmed. The dress was another matter – quite destroyed, not so much as a fragment was left that could be put to any use whatsoever.

FOR A COUPLE OF days after the accident, Hedeya's entire body was stiff and painful; it felt as though every bone in her body had been broken. By midweek, however, her recovery was almost complete.

She insisted on attending school Thursday afternoon, and it probably stood her in good stead, for when she awoke on Friday morning, though the bruises were still visible, hardly a vestige of the pain remained. Her strong, young body seemed to have healed itself quite dramatically, so much so she was fully prepared for the visit she had planned with her friend Elsie for later that same afternoon.

Elsie was the beautiful, vivacious daughter of Bajo's old friend, Araxes Deuvletian. The girl, some years younger to Hedeya, had recently created quite a stir among friends and family by impetuously marrying a young Royal Navy seaman named Joseph David Arathoon. The thing of it was, by pure coincidence – or perhaps by the direct hand of insouciant Fate – Joe Arathoon happened to be an Armenian from Calcutta, so Hedeya was more than a little eager to find out what Elsie had learnt about the place. As it turned out, it wasn't much; there simply had been no time. Being in love was a full-time affair, so Elsie blithely dispensed with such mundane matters as questions about her future home; nothing mattered beyond the handsome sailor she had set her heart on.

The chain of events began when Elsie's brother, Haik, met and befriended Joe in the Muski. It happened on a day when Haik, after enjoying his customary cup of good, strong *ahwa* in the company of friends, had departed the El Fishawi Cafe, a well-known haunt of local artists and authors. Threading his way through the narrow, labyrinthine alleyways to Khan el Khalili, he had come upon the young seaman bargaining for a *galabiya,* a local male robe. Amused at first by the foreigner's futile efforts at besting the wily shopkeeper, he was moved finally to help him; then, discovering in him a fellow Armenian, he immediately invited him home for a meal.

When Joe met Elsie, it was love at first sight; a feeling that was returned in no half measure. The smitten couple got married first, and told everyone later. Elsie confided to Hedeya she had dreamt of a ship the day before she met Joe; and since it could only be a good omen, proof positive that destiny had called, what else could she do but answer, and that was that. When Joe shipped out Elsie cried for two whole days, and then set about shopping, preparatory to following him.

Hedeya made her some beautiful clothes as part of her trousseau, and when Elsie's friend, Aghavni Hovartian, had seen Hedeya's work she asked Elsie for an introduction. Aghavni was collecting her trousseau as well. Her wedding was a mere month away, but being struck by an inopportune illness, she was nowhere near ready for that day. Would Hedeya be able to salvage the situation? With Aghavni still under the weather, it would require a visit to the house for there was not a moment to spare. She would, of course, pay handsomely if Hedeya could prepare her in time for the wedding.

Since such an offer could hardly be passed up, Hedeya had agreed to the visit – even if she had to work around the clock to complete that trousseau, then that is just what she would do. She needed the money. And so, that Friday afternoon, Elsie came to take Hedeya to Aghavni's house, just a few short blocks away.

It was a pleasant day, and the two friends enjoyed the walk. They chatted as they threaded their way between passers-by when, all at once, Elsie came to an abrupt halt. She grabbed Hedeya's arm and let out a strangled shriek. The shrill sound startled Hedeya, making her jump, and it turned every other head on the street.

"*Y'Allah,* Elsie! What is it?" Hedeya turned to her companion and noticed, with alarm, that Elsie's face had turned a peculiar shade of mottled red. She laid a concerned hand over her friend's, whose grip was proving quite painful. "*Maalak?* What is the matter? Are you ill?"

Standing rigid as though she were unable to move, Elsie tried to speak. Her fingers were still digging into Hedeya's arm while her other hand had flown to her lips as though to stifle, too late, the scream that had made its involuntary escape. Hedeya had to lean close in an effort to catch her friend's mumbled words.

"Hide me," Elsie whispered at last in a muffled voice.

"Hide you?" Hedeya repeated, perplexed, looking around for any source of potential danger. There was nothing unusual to be seen – that is, until she noticed the stunned looks on some of the faces around them, and the inexplicable look of amusement on others. "What are you talking about? From what?"

Elsie rolled her eyes downward. "That! There"

"That...!" Hedeya took an involuntary step backward and looked down where Elsie's eyes seemed to indicate – and there, around her ankles, in plain sight, lay Elsie's pretty, white, lace-trimmed knickers!

Hedeya gasped in horror. The elastic that secured it at the waist had given way somehow and the garment, unhindered by clasp or fastening of any kind, had fluttered into a soft white puddle on the ground. Painfully aware of the titters and glances being cast their way, Hedeya could feel the heat rise to her own face and knew that its colour probably rivalled Elsie's. At that moment she would have been grateful if the ground had opened and swallowed them both!

Quickly pulling herself together, she shielded her unfortunate companion as best she could. "*Ya kharabi*! For goodness sake," she snapped in a low voice. "Did you have to scream and draw every-one's attention? Just step out of the stupid thing and put it in your handbag."

The sharpness in Hedeya's voice penetrated Elsie's frozen mind. She dropped her bag and, bending as though to retrieve it, she stepped out of the embarrassing undergarment, and in a single swift movement whipped it into her bag. As soon as she clicked her bag shut, Hedeya jerked her upright.

"Walk!" Realising her friend still hadn't quite gathered her wits, Hedeya gave her a sharp nudge. "Don't look around, just walk." Holding Elsie's elbow, she propelled her forward, and the two ladies, standing as tall as they could, continued down the street as though nothing untoward had occurred.

By the time they arrived at Aghavni's house, away from inquisitive eyes, they had gone from a stance of forced composure to an attack of helpless giggles. Quite breathless, they stood outside her front door, trying hard not to dissolve into hysterics yet again at the memory of their discomfiture over the horrid incident of a moment ago.

Inside, after greetings had been dispensed with, the story told and laughed over, Elsie begged the loan of a safety pin and disappeared into the bedroom to put things to right. Hedeya settled down with Aghavni to the business of discussing her trousseau, while sipping *ahwa* from delicate blue and gold demitasse cups and nibbling on sticky, sweet *zulabya* freshly prepared by her mother. When Elsie returned, Mrs. Hovartian clucked and fussed about her daughter's visitors much like a plump little hen around her brood.

"Come, Elsie, tell us your news," Mrs. Hovartian patted the sofa beside her, inviting her guest to sit. "Are you really going to *Hindiya?* It is so far away. Are you not afraid?"

Elsie laughed. "Why should I be afraid?"

"She's in love and it makes her brave, you see." Aghavni interjected.

"But what do you know of the country? Just think how different everything will be, the customs, the language, the food; how do you know you will like it?"

"Of course she will like it. She's in love, I tell you," Aghavni insisted.

"Look," her mother picked up a copy of the weekly magazine, *Akher Sa'a*, and pointed to a picture of a bony old man, completely naked except for a white cloth tied loosely around his loins, brown leather sandals and a walking stick. "See? Last Wednesday's issue. This man is their leader. Half-naked. If their leader looks like this, what about the rest of them? They must be very backward."

"That is Gandhi. Have you not read about him?" Hedeya asked. "I've heard he is not an ordinary leader; he is half holy-man, half political-leader who guides his country along a spiritual path to its political destiny. He does not believe in material things, he is concerned with the soul of his nation; that is why he dresses in that manner."

"How do you know all this?" Mrs. Hovartian asked.

"I have been reading about him. In his country, they too are struggling for freedom from the British."

"Are you sure of this?" The old lady looked doubtful. She hesitated for a moment, then, quavering nervously, blurted out, "I have heard they eat white people there. Maybe they will eat the British."

"Eat the...wherever did you hear such a thing! Have you not met Indian people who live here? People like Mr. Bhamun and Mr. Hassaram? Real gentlemen, and quite civilised." Hedeya laughed. "No, no. It's complete nonsense. If they ate white people in India, the British would have disappeared from there a long time ago!"

"*W'Allah,* Mama! You pick up the strangest gossip! *Da kalaam ayy kalaam!* Such utter nonsense!" Aghavni threw the old lady a baleful look. Imagine repeating something like that to Elsie! She turned to her friend. "But I do think it takes courage to leave everyone and everything you know for the man you love. I'm glad my Kachik lives right here in Cairo. As much as I love him, I don't know that I would have wanted to marry him if I had to move to some other country, not even to one as close as Lebanon."

"Well," Elsie piped up cheerfully, "*I'm* not afraid of change and adventure."

To prove her point, she covered the mouth of her coffee cup with its saucer and swirled the dregs of coffee around in the bottom of the cup; then, in one smooth flip, she turned both cup and saucer upside down and set them on the table.

"Let us see what life has in store for me," she challenged, laughingly. "Hedeya will read our coffee cups."

"*Abadan!*" Hedeya objected, immediately. "No, please! I know nothing about reading coffee cups."

"Nonsense!" Elsie exclaimed. "You've done it before. Oh come, just for the fun of it. Please? See, Aghavni has her cup ready as well. And since I'm already married, while she is still a bride-to-be and her romance is yet to blossom, I say her fortune should be told first."

In the end, persuaded much against her will, Hedeya gave in. As the three women gathered around, she turned Aghavni's inverted cup over to peer studiously inside. The dregs of sediment from the coffee had emptied into the saucer, leaving an intricate pattern on the bottom and all down one side of the cup. Hedeya frowned, concentrating hard on the dark brown squiggles and streaks in an effort to conjure images she might use as symbols for her 'fortune telling'. She cudgelled her memory, trying to haul up any tidbit she had been told about Aghavni. Ah, yes! Her illness!

"Oh, my," she muttered at last, her voice low and serious. "Look, here in this corner. Can you see the star? It is above these dark patches that look like clouds – some sort of difficulty, I think. See this big one? It is almost touching the star. But over there, beyond all this darkness, there is a door, and it is open. It is a way out of the dark area and the star seems to be guiding you towards it."

"*Ya salaam!* She is right! You see, Aghavni, it is the bad time of your illness, but soon you will be married, and it will be like a door into a better time." Mrs. Hovartian patted Hedeya's arm. "Go on, go on; tell us more."

More? Hedeya wracked her brains; what more was there to tell?

Nothing came to mind...except.... Suddenly she recalled Aghavni's firm declaration that she would never want to move away from Cairo, not even to nearby Lebanon. In that case, maybe...

"Your family ties will be strong, three generations strong." It was safe to surmise the family would remain close, at least in the near future, and when Aghavni had children, there would be three generations looking out for each other – mother, daughter and grandchildren – all together in Cairo.

"Can you see how many children I will have?"

Aghavni's query remained unanswered, for it was at this point the interruption occurred; and though it saved Hedeya from having to spin any further credible sounding yarns, it snared her in a web she had quite inadvertently woven. Her unfortunate 'prediction' of a looming difficulty seemed, somehow, to materialise into reality when Aghavni's younger sister, Anahid, burst through the front door, frantic with the news that Kachik had met with an accident.

Thereafter the afternoon dissolved into chaos. Mrs. Hovartian would have it that the 'dark cloud' Hedeya had pointed out in her daughter's coffee cup, the one reaching for the star, had manifested itself in this dreadful mishap which had befallen her future son-in-law.

Despite Hedeya's earnest protestations that it was pure coincidence, and had nothing whatsoever to do with clairvoyance, psychic powers or the ability to see into the future, Mrs. Hovartian would have none of it. She believed what she believed and would not be moved; once Hedeya had shown them the cloud about to overtake the star, why, she had seen it as plain as the nose on her own face! Could anyone doubt it had been there? Of course not! Therefore, any attempt to refute Hedeya's gift for prediction was pointless, even her own. Mrs. Hovartian had experienced its power first-hand, and there was no more to be said about it! *Finis*!

After all the tears and hysterics had been spent, it was discovered, much to everyone's relief, Kachik was alive and well. He had, indeed, slipped and fallen down the stairs of his building, but apart from a dislocated shoulder and a few minor scrapes and bruises, he had suffered no long-term injury. The wedding – thank that lucky star! – could go ahead as planned.

For Hedeya, however, it was a lesson learnt. She knew full well her predictions had come out of nowhere, arbitrarily plucked from thin air. It was meant to have been an amusing pastime, instead it had turned into an emotional mess, and she swore never to let anyone talk her into such a lamentably awkward situation ever again.

CHAPTER THIRTY-NINE

Aftermath

Out of the night that covers me
Black as the pit from pole to pole,
I thank whatever gods may be
For my unconquerable soul.

– William Ernest Henley - "Invicta", 1857

JUNE 8: AT LONG last Santi's casualties were being evacuated. Starting that morning they were taken, a few at a time, to an Italian ADS in the rear. By now, no small thanks to the Italian scavengers, neither food nor water remained. Nothing was safe from that lot, not even a chap's undergarments! The previous night, before snatching an hour of much needed rest, Santi had put his *ganji* out to air dry, but when Dilbahadur had gone to fetch the under-vest in the morning it was nowhere to be found. Some light-fingered prowler had filched the darn thing and made off with it during the night!

Now, under close guard, and surrounded by the Germans and Italians on all sides, any attempt at escape was futile. And this time the Germans removed the Red Cross Marker. Their appreciation for services rendered seemed to have run dry, Santi thought wryly. In its place they built two gun positions close by and a mortar position behind the *bir*.

Towards afternoon MacFarlan, a gunner doctor, joined Santi and Norman. All his casualties had been evacuated by the Italians; and now, while Santi oversaw the transportation of his wounded, the three medical men exchanged news and found time at last to tend to themselves.

"There you go, old chap," MacFarlan finished cleaning and disinfecting Norman's wound sustained in the previous day's bombing. "We have that last piece of the splinter out. You shan't be able to rhumba for a while, I'm afraid, but what say you we get this foot properly bandaged so you can do a slow hobble at least." He threw a quick glance Santi's way. "Oh my! You two *have* been put through the wringer, haven't you! I think I'd better have a look at that hand as well, don't you think? I must say, it doesn't look too good."

There was not much to be done about Santi's injured rib cage, but the wound to his left hand did require attention. The deep gash, caused initially by shrapnel, had sustained further injury and contamination from the fatal explosion and flying sand that killed Narbahadur. With the maimed and dying all around him, Santi had failed to adequately bandage the reopened wound, and some of that sand was still embedded in it. Fearing it would hamper his work, he had made do with a perfunctory sprinkling of sulpha powder and a light wrap of gauze. That neglect, seemingly, had allowed all the blood, dirt and sands of Africa to contaminate it and, Santi thought ruefully, chances were infection would probably set in.

He looked at his hands; they were filthy, just like the rest of him, and under his fingernails, dried blood had crusted. He took a packet of cigarettes out of his pocket and, trying to light one, realised his hands were shaking – from exhaustion? Shock? Or a delayed reaction to the fear that had heaved his guts from time to time? It was, quite possibly, an amalgam of all three…

These last few days had changed him immeasurably. He had felt the touch of Death, its hand on his shoulder, its breath in his face. He had fought it on every level – with a visceral fear when it had come for him; with despair and futility as he had battled it for the lives of the young men in his care; even in anger each time he lost that battle and felt he had betrayed their trust.

But with mounting awareness he had come to the eventual realisation these emotions were a fruitless distraction that inevitably played into the hands of one's opponent; and with Death on the prowl, that wiliest of all opponents, monstrous, rapacious, victoriously rampant all about him, he needed all his wits and a steady nerve. He had no time to waste on thoughts that weakened his resolve.

He was thankful he had managed to send home those last two letters before being swept up in this whirlwind of unspeakable horror. Somehow he had felt it – they all had – that this time around would be different; this time the battle that loomed ahead seemed to blot out the future. It had brought the smell of death to each man's nostrils. He wondered if those two letters would be the pallbearers of his final thoughts and feelings or, indeed, if they would reach their intended destination at all.

Nevertheless, regardless of what fate decreed, he had felt the need to reach beyond the uncertainty around him for the comfort, the stability, the calm of the familiar. And so, it was to his mother he had turned…*Shree-Charaneshu Ma…Revered Mother, whose feet I touch….* And to his sister, strong and steady Bela…*My Dear Bulu…I pray you are all safe and well at home…*

He had tried to convey some deeply personal part of himself to them. He had had to employ caution so as not to allow the turmoil of his emotions to spill onto the pages in his writing. Thus, he had spoken to them, stilted, yet as best he could, across the miles and circumstances that separated them, harnessing his words and curbing his feelings carefully. To his mother he sent his gratitude and his love. To his sister he imparted his aspirations and his dreams. It was important those flimsy, crumpled scribbles should, somehow, express to his loved ones, those things about himself he had, till now, left unspoken. Had they succeeded? Had the letters even been received?

The chasm between their world and his seemed unbreachable. He was a different person to the son, the brother they had known. He understood now what his father had known all along; the terrible experience of war would wreak havoc, it would shake his beliefs to their very foundation, it would change him profoundly. Such an experience – unique to each blighted soul – the unutterable anguish of it, the feelings of horror and fear and despair it had wrung from him, the scars that would blemish his subconscious mind as long as he lived, these were things he could never speak of to those who had not shared them with him. They were beyond the comprehension of anyone innocent of the experience. And he would wish, pray, they may forever remain so.

In rare moments of fleeting privacy, he had reached for Hedeya as well; in the safekeeping of his heart, he held onto growing thoughts of her, nurturing the passion of his unfulfilled desires. He might never get another chance, a real chance…

All at once a longing so intense overcame him, it set his whole body trembling. He had held her in his arms, felt her body against his; he remembered the movement, the warmth, the fragrance of her, but he realised with deep regret he did not even know what it felt like to kiss her! If only he had her address! What would he have told her? What *could* he have told her?

No, as things stood, he simply had nothing to offer. His unaccountably precipitous feelings, the uncertainty of hers, the chaotic, hellfire future he faced – it would be too shabby, dishonourable even, to burden her with the whole unreliable mess. No, he could not, should not have bared his heart to her…not yet.

He had hardly slept for four days – an hour at most last night while he kept vigil over the wounded, less than that the night before, and only in intermittent snatches during the forty-eight hours prior.

But, in spite of being dog-tired, he was afraid of falling asleep, afraid of the dreams that would crawl out of his head, like maggots gorging on the horrors of the past few days. The last time he had dozed off, just for a few minutes mind you, he woke up screaming from a nightmare. Starting up, he had been mortified at having made a spectacle of himself. But then, much to his relief, he realised the scream was inside his head, contained within him; it had remained hidden, heard only by him, safe from everyone else on the outside. Nevertheless, it was a close call. Next time, he was afraid, he might not be so lucky.

9 JUNE: AT 0830 hours the last casualties were readied for transportation to the Italian ADS, seventy or eighty miles away; and after they had been thoroughly searched, all three doctors, together with Dilbahadur and Foxy Jones, prepared to accompany them. No one could remember when last they had eaten. Even prior to the pilfering of their rations, there had been neither time nor mind paid to food. Now, while they waited, Jones managed to rustle up a concoction he aptly called 'burgoo' – a decidedly revolting looking mess that looked lethal and could, at best, only be described as 'goop'.

"What is it?" Santi looked askance at the offering, while Dilbahadur examined it with an air of deep distrust.

"Desert Porridge, sir"

"Is it actually edible?"

"It oin't 'alf bad, sir. There's me ration uv oatmeal bickies, and a tin uv condensed milk Oi ferreted away in me Medical Bag, all mulled in loik wiv a good snatch uv cocoa and a last bit uv marmalade left. There oin't much, but we can all 'ave a go, sir, its good stuff an' all. I make the best bloomin' burgoo this side uv Alex, even if I sez so m'self!"

Realising he was, in actual fact, quite hungry, Santi decided to take his life in his hands and ''ave a go'; and when he did, he was surprised to find that Foxy Jones had not been bragging in vain after all! Gratefully, he tucked in. Whatever it was, it would at least provide strength for the journey ahead.

THE JOURNEY WAS A cruel one for the wounded who were bumped and bounced the entire way. The Italian lorry drivers did not spare them much thought or consideration. It would seem, for some reason entirely unknown to any but themselves, that vying for first place in some strange and perverse race through the desert was, somehow, a matter of life and death.

The convoy drove along the rough desert road, nosing its way through thick brown clouds of dust churned up by its wheels. On either side of the road, the once pristine desert sands were marred by the grotesque misfortunes of war: charred, bloated bodies of men; skeletal remains of burnt-out trucks; bombed guns and tanks, all frozen in an accusing arabesque of death. A whole generation of young men sacrificed to a war that had taken unto itself the best part of them, leaving only their pitiful remains strewn across this bloodied wasteland.

These lives cut short so unseasonably, so violently, these sad ghosts, would their recriminations not haunt the world forever? Surely their ultimate sacrifice would not be in vain? They deserved to live! Perhaps, as long as they were remembered, sheltered within the hearts and minds of those who cared, they would remain alive. But then, slowly, gently, down the years they would be laid to rest in the graves of long bereft fathers and mothers; gradually, inevitably they would be interred along with the aged memories of grieving widows and siblings. And what of the children, the pain of their loss, their deprivation of loved ones? After the children, who would remember these men and their sacrifice as they slipped into the anonymity of history?

It would take generations to mitigate the mistrust and the anger, who knew how long before wounds this grievous could heal? The devastation was terrible to behold, a most bitter lesson for mankind, and Santi hoped to God it would never be repeated.

When they arrived, the Italian ADS was a mess. The wounded, brought in and dumped regardless of their condition, lay everywhere unattended. The three doctors got to work immediately, making do as best they could with what medical supplies remained.

The young bombardier whose arm Santi had amputated earlier in the *bir* lay in a gun pit in the blazing sun. In acute distress, he had been calling for a drink of water for hours.

"*Aqua...aqua...*" His hoarse voice was barely a whisper.

Santi quickly gave him the last few sips left in his own water canteen, and after examining his arm to make sure it had not become infected, he adjusted the dressing to ease the man's distress and make him as comfortable as possible. This one would live if he did not become completely dehydrated, and if proper, timely care was received.

Continuing to make his way among the casualties, checking each one quickly down the line, Santi was interrupted by a *sepoy* gunner from 4/10 Baluch who ran up to him with an urgent request.

"*Sahib*, kindly come, please. My Battalion's Lieutenant *Sahib*, his condition is very bad and he is asking for someone from our Battalion. I cannot find one single Officer *Sahib* from 4/10 Baluch. Please, you see him before it is too late."

"*Naam kya hai tumhara?* What is your name?" Santi asked the sepoy

"*Sahib, naam hai mera Nadim Shah.*"

"*Accha, Nadim Shah, chalo.* Good, Nadim Shah, let's go."

Santi hurried after the Moslem gunner who complained bitterly about the convoy that had brought them to the ADS. He cursed the Italian drivers and the way they had driven, with no regard for the wounded thrown and bounced about in the backs of the trucks. It was no wonder, declared Nadim Shah angrily, that his Lt. *Sahib* and the others were in such a bad way!

When they arrived at their destination, Santi saw that the sepoy's complaints were fully justified. There, to his dismay, he found the young Lieutenant from the 4/10 Baluch whose stomach and head injuries he had treated two days ago. He was lying on the ground partly delirious and, examining him, Santi discovered his stomach wound had reopened. He had lost a great deal of blood. This poor man who could have been saved was, indeed, in bad shape, and the inconsequence of his plight to his captors was infuriating!

At Santi's touch, the injured man half opened his eyes. "Please… help me…"

"Lt. Farnsworth, is it not? Don't worry, I'll have you feeling better in no time. Do you remember me? Captain Dutt. I'm the doctor who patched you up a couple of days ago, and I know just what you need. Now, relax, lie back. Good! That's it." Santi kept up the chatter as he injected morphine into the dying man.

"No, please…" the wounded man made a feeble attempt to hand him a letter, slightly blood stained, together with a ring. "My mother…tell her…it was in battle…not this…ugly last memory. Better to believe…" as the medication began to take effect, his words started to slur slightly, "you know…'God for…Harry, England and St. George'…all that…old bosh." He tried to smile, but it turned into a painful grimace on his pale lips. "Return ring to Amelia…my love, and…remember her always…so sorry…" He died a very short while later with his hand in Santi's.

Late that evening they were packed into lorries and moved once more. They hadn't travelled far, however, when their transport met up with a large convoy halted on the road. The reason for the delay was unknown, but as the shadows of night gathered and descended about them, it was obvious that nothing was moving, and this was where they would spend the night.

10 June: Morning saw all the POWs searched once again and finally, at long last, the convoy moved on. After a while they met up with, and passed, other convoys, some large, some small, each with an ambulance at its head conspicuously flying a Red Cross flag as its pennant.

At 1430 hours they reached the Italian hospital in Tmimi, where they were subjected to yet another search. Whatever little they had was now taken from them; Santi had to give up his field medical bag with the very last of his supplies, and the last two blankets he had managed to save for the wounded. His haversack and bedding were taken as well, exchanged for a mosquito net and one thin, cheap blanket that didn't amount to much. It was during the confusion of being stripped of their belongings that, unknown to Santi, Norman and MacFarlan were taken away.

Shortly thereafter, Santi, Dilbahadur, and Foxy Jones, together with four casualties, were evacuated to Derna. Being Indian, and a Captain to boot, was still something of a rarity to the Italians. As a result, throughout the journey, Santi stuck out like a sore thumb – a rather unfortunate circumstance since the treatment meted out by their captors was atrocious, and attracting any attention was unpleasant to say the least.

When they arrived at Derna the casualties were dropped off at the hospital there, after which Santi and his two medical orderlies were taken to prison, where they were finally separated. As they parted company and said their goodbyes, the two soldiers saluted him. Santi shook them both by the hand and thanked them for their help; it was the last he saw or heard of Foxy Jones.

At Derna prison Santi caught up with Robert Williams. Two other British Officers, Major Barbar and Captain Porter, had been brought in as well; they had been captured when their unit was overrun on 5 June. Major Barbar being the senior most officer present, Santi handed over the letter and ring Lt. Farnsworth had entrusted to him in the hope the Major would, somehow, at sometime, find a way to get it to the man's family.

And there was Mac! Good old MacPherson – the doctor from 21 Indian Infantry Brigade, the 2/4's previous home; Mac who had so kindly given Santi the Red Cross arm brassards prior to his departure from Iraq – he too had been bagged when 157 Field Regiment had gone down. God! What a bloody shambles!

That evening as they were swapping stories – each filling in for the others his details of the fiasco they had just come through – a young 2nd Lieutenant arrived, and the instant he was brought in everyone gagged from the smell.

"What the…?"

"Hell's bells! What a pong!"

"Good grief! Where the blazes have you been mucking about?" Major Barbar gasped."

"Sorry, sir," the newcomer apologised, looking sorely embarrassed. "I've just run the gamut of a pelting with some pretty nasty stuff – the worst of which, I'm afraid, was…er…nightsoil. Left me a mite fragrant as you can no doubt tell, sir."

"This is no time for modesty, old son," Major Barbar retorted, trying to hold his breath and failing. "You're way past fragrant, you're past bloody overripe!" He was subjected to an extra potent whiff as the newcomer tried to remove the offending outer garment. "Dash it man, don't thrash about so, what the deuce are you thinking! Oh for God's sake, someone get the lad some water to wash himself off before we all pass out here!"

11 June: In the afternoon a very young German sergeant appeared with some food for the prisoners – one thick slab of bread each and a small half pound tin of meat. It would turn out to be the only meal of the day, which was probably just as well since toilet facilities and sanitation were hellish. Notwithstanding these drawbacks, Santi was able to borrow a razor Captain Porter had somehow managed to hang on to and, taking great care not to get caught, he gave himself a quick shave of sorts. The whole surreptitious exercise, from start to finish, was an achievement that left him feeling oddly victorious on two counts: first, having a stab at a clean up, however rudimentary, allowed him to feel somewhat human once more which, in turn, gave him back a modicum of dignity; and second, that minor act of flouting his captors, no matter how inconsequential, returned to him a small sense of control. In the greater scheme of things it didn't amount to much, but asserting himself, however he could, was a very personal, albeit slight victory.

Later that evening Santi was allowed to visit the dispensary where his hand, red and swollen with infection, was treated and freshly bandaged. He was pleased to meet up with Dilbahadur once again and a few other soldiers from the Battalion. Relieved to see him, his batman immediately appealed for help with a dilemma he and his companions were facing.

"*Sahib*, the men refuse to eat," Dilbahadur informed Santi. "Someone said the tinned meat the enemy is feeding us is beef. Is this true? You know our religion does not permit the eating of beef."

This, Santi thought in dismay, had the potential for disaster. Religion was important to these men, but if they did not eat the already miniscule amount of food being given, they would starve. Somehow that had to be avoided at any cost. He silently asked forgiveness for what he was about to do and launched into a prevarication, not exactly a lie, hoping for the understanding of the ever wise and all-seeing deity whose priests' arbitrary demands required such obeisance.

"Don't worry, I too am Hindu, but you see, I am eating it. Don't you know the Italians eat horsemeat? I know it tastes strange, but remember, it is our duty as soldiers to keep up our strength."

Whether they actually believed this or not, the Gurkhas were a practical lot and, above all, dedicated to their duty as soldiers; that meant trusting their officers and obeying orders. Reinforced by hunger as well as character, they were soon eating willingly what food was given them, secure in the conviction that the responsibility for any sin, if there be one, was no longer theirs but lay squarely with the good *Daktar Sahib*.

12 June: Major Barbar was the first to be taken away. A short while after the day's only meal which had left them still ravenously hungry – once again, a single slab of bread accompanied by a half pound tin of meat – the rest of them were herded into trucks, much like cattle. Inexplicably, Santi found himself bundled into a lorry with Robert and 15 Tommies, while the remaining prisoners – most of whom were Indian and Gurkha soldiers from various units – were accompanied by the other three British officers. The reason for such an arrangement was hard to surmise, but they were on the move once again, bound for a destination yet unknown.

The convoy passed through a part of Libya that had long been an Italian stronghold, a stunningly green oasis in the otherwise starkly arid desert. All along the way a few small towns, neat little Italian settlements, dotted the countryside.

Now, as they drove through, the inhabitants lined both sides of the street and hurled insults at the prisoners. That was not all they hurled. Their angry gestures and ugly grimaces were accompanied by garbage they threw at the POWs – in a couple of instances, a suspiciously foul-smelling liquid that brought to mind the pelting endured by the unhappy young Lieutenant who had joined them in Derna. At that time, the sympathy of his audience had been marred somewhat by the pungent smell his presence had forced upon them. Now, subjected to the same indignity, Santi felt true empathy for the young man riding in the truck behind his – suffering this sort of vile experience once was bad enough, but twice in as many days was too bad by far!

Additionally, their captors were not averse to enjoying the POWs' discomfiture. Having endured the humiliation of previous defeat at the hands of the Allies, that rancour was bolstered by a growing suspicion of their own government and a war they were no longer sure they believed in. Consequently, the Italians' pent-up frustration now took its full measure in the gruff treatment meted out to their British captives.

Soon, however, a change in scenery proved a welcome distraction as they began the climb through the Jebel Akhdar Mountains which were truly as green as their name promised. In this biblical land, Arab tribesmen lived in caves and grazed their goats and sheep in the age-old way of a hundred, nay, hundreds of years. Some held out eggs to the convoy, hoping to barter for commodities such as sugar and tea. Sadly, for the hungry POWs, there were none to be had.

At 1830 hours their convoy passed through Fort Madalena and on through the surrounding countryside of cultivated farmland, well kept and carefully tended by Italian settlers. Not long thereafter they arrived at a prison compound just outside Barce where they found themselves in the despondent company of 150 other officers from various units that had become casualties of the desert war.

Upon disembarking, Santi and Robert were ushered to a hut where they discovered, with mixed emotions, seven brother officers from the 2/4 – Ben Browne, Ewen Kerr, Roger Werner, Ronnie Smith, Peter McDowall, Middleton and Grose had all been gaffed!

"Marten's been nabbed as well," Ben informed them, "just been carted off to hospital." He grimaced. "Poor old Slogger, felled by a thundering bout of desert dysentery. I know what that feels like! Quite knocked me for a six, didn't it Doc?"

"It does tend to do that," Santi agreed, recalling Ben's introduction to the Battalion. It seemed a lifetime ago! "Anyone know the whereabouts of Colonel Weallens?"

"Willie and O'Bree were brought here earlier," Werner volunteered. "Apparently those two are already en route for Italy."

Although it was dismaying to find such a large number had been taken prisoner, it was good to know they were at least still alive. Moreover, after the confusion and uncertainty they had just been through, there was a certain comfort to be had in the company of one's familiars.

It turned out most of the G.O.R.s (Gurkha Other Ranks) and all the G.O.s (Gurkha Officers) were there as well, except for Mangal Singh, who had managed to slip away, and Subedar Prem Sing who, sadly, had been killed.

All new arrivals were given an advance of 50 lire each. It seemed a hopeful sign that the Geneva Convention would be respected. They were given a piece of cloth as well for use as a towel, 2 packs of Italian cigarettes, a single sparse blanket and a few lozenges. A loan of a billycan for 'personal' use was also made. For these amenities their captors deducted 15 lire!

13 June: That morning, trucked in convoy once more, the road ran alongside the Mediterranean as they headed to the town of Benghazi. At the Benina airstrip several aircraft stood at the ready to fly them, in groups, to Italy. Though unaware at the time, they were among the lucky few who escaped the perils faced by later POWs shipped across in dark, dank holds in the most hideously crammed and unsanitary conditions. Bad enough as that was, those poor blighters often fell prey to the bombs and torpedoes of their own RAF planes and Royal Navy submarines.

Boarding the Savoia Marchetti aircraft for the next leg of their journey, Santi's batch realised each plane had only a few Italian guards armed with long rifles, an unwieldy choice of weapon in a confined space. A wild plan for escape began to hatch among the POWs. One officer claimed to have some experience flying a seaplane, and enthusiastically offered to have a stab at piloting.

Robert Williams later related: *"The plot was to dish guards and crew, take over the plane, turn it eastwards and hope to land somewhere near the Allies. British fighters and, of course, landing the plane presented the main difficulties. Someone had a jack-knife, others had various weapons, and I still had my tin hat, the edge of which could deal a nasty blow.... It was, perhaps, a hair-brained scheme and might never have worked, but even an attempt was kyboshed by three Colonels who ordered us not to be such blithering young idiots – 'you bloody fools, shots fired inside the plane could quite possibly result in a wrecked aircraft and a long swim in the brine, don't you know'."*

And so, the idea, hair-brained or not, was scuppered.

Thus ended Operation Aberdeen and the Battle of the Cauldron. The Allies had suffered an inglorious thrashing. In the early morning following the battle, it rained heavily. An officer from the Highland Light Infantry remarked wearily, "A good thing; it washed the blood off our vehicles." (Antony Brett-James: *Ball of Fire, The Fifth Indian Division in the Second World War*)

And what remained of the Prince of Wales's Own 2/4 Gurkhas? Just eight days previous, that Battalion had rallied to arms. When the thunder of battle was stilled and the fog of war had cleared, a final count found those taken captive were 11 British Officers, 1 Indian Officer, 17 G.O.s, 613 G.O.R.s and 30 non combatants. And of that stout-hearted Battalion, those tattered few who remained were just 1 officer and 156 men who stepped out of the debacle that would come to be known as the Battle of the Cauldron.

Why had it gone so terribly wrong? In some quarters it has been said that the leadership was ill chosen, while others would have it that undue political pressure was brought to bear, making for a situation that was, at best, one of confusion and frustration.

Certainly, no doubt could be cast on the overall fortitude and courage of the troops in the field; but one irrefutable truth was the inexperience in desert warfare of the infantry battalions sent to the front, some having arrived just two weeks prior to the battle, others a mere twenty four hours before. Compared to the enemy they were inadequately equipped and, due to insufficient recce, incorrectly informed as to the enemy and the terrain. Tank crews and infantry were untrained to coordinate tactical planning, and the 'boxes' set up for the defence of the Gazala Line were static in a desert war that was as fluid as a war at sea. This limited the mobility of the infantry. Consequently, when Allied tanks and guns were destroyed by the enemy's superior 88mm guns, and all remaining vehicles were evacuated to the rear to avoid destruction or capture, the infantry found itself stranded.

Last but not least, the breach of security and the leak of detailed top-secret information to the enemy put the Allies at an enormous disadvantage as well. Bitter lessons had been learnt, however, that would stand in good stead for the future.

All told and well summed up in the graphic words of one frustrated officer, *"they bloody well dropped us in it and left us hanging bare-arsed in the wind."*

CHAPTER FORTY

Journey Into Captivity

And that inverted Bowl they call the Sky,
Whereunder crawling, coop'd we live and die,
Lift not your hands to It for help...for It
As impotently moves as you or I.

– Omar Khayyam, *Rubaiyat of Omar Khayyam*

T HE FOUR-HOUR FLIGHT across the Mediterranean was without mishap; that is until they reached the heel of Italy's boot where strong winds caught and buffeted their plane, turning the ride unpleasantly bumpy. The pitching and shuddering resulted in a good deal of physical discomfort and some upchucking. Besides, the sight of the machine's wings wildly undulating in the wind like some great bird flapping in distress did little to lessen the considerable unease suffered by the passengers.

For such 'old hands' as Santi and the other 2/4 officers, broken in somewhat by the experience of their one and only flight from Basra to Habbaniya, it was not quite as daunting as it was for those who had never flown before. Of course, that had been a mere overland hop compared to this journey crossing the sea; but, counting one's blessings, at least this time they suffered no encounters with enemy aircraft of any kind.

Late that afternoon of 13 June they landed at a place called Lecce, in southern Italy. Driven through streets lined with townsfolk, it became apparent the Italian authorities were parading the POWs in a show to boost their nation's flagging morale. Young and old, shook their fists and pitched insults. Mercifully, however, there was no hurling of refuse, and for that the POWs were silently thankful.

They eventually arrived at their destination, tired, hungry and dispirited, to be herded into what turned out to be a tobacco factory. There, among other groups of earlier POWs, they spent an uncomfortable night with no proper arrangements for sleeping. Looking a sorry lot the next morning, they were taken to the train station. There, they were summarily divided into groups once again, and it became obvious that their company was to be parted. The time had come, it seemed, to bid goodbye to Ben 'Quinine' Browne, Ewen Kerr, Peter McDowall and Slogger Marten.

"Well, chaps, looks like it's cheerio for now. Let's hope our next *bustee* is a tad more comfortable than the last one."

"No matter, old son, won't be long before we make a break for it. I'll wager we'll be out of here in a jiff. We still have a war to win, you know!"

"Right you are. We'll catch up as soon as we get out of this ruddy awful mess, eh?"

"Make sure you take care of that malaria, now."

"Will do, Doc. You keep up the good work. And thanks for everything"

The group of four, it was later learnt, were among those taken to Chieti, a POW camp half-way up the east coast of Italy. As they marched off to board their train, someone began whistling 'The Bonnie Banks O' Loch Lomond' – and one by one the others picked up the tune. For Santi, the silent words of farewell to that whistled refrain would prove prescient, as he would never meet with any of them again.

From that group, some would attempt daring escapes after the Italian armistice. All, but one, would eventually make it back to England. Young Peter McDowall would succeed in reaching Switzerland where, sadly, he would succumb to the rigours of his escape and perish.

***

THOSE POWs REMAINING, ALL gathered their meagre belongings, and were prodded along by their Italian guards to where another train waited. Unceremoniously bundled into two reserved carriages, with the doors securely locked down, the train began its journey up the eastern coast of Italy, heading north, and then cross-country, heading west. In the cramped quarters of those small compartments, two benches faced each other, providing just enough room for the crowded occupants to sit.

They sped past villages and through towns where no one got on or off. Except for necessary stops made for refuelling and replenishing, the train chugged right through all stations. In any case, with the carriage curtains drawn, the passing countryside was not visible, and random chatter was discouraged. Undeterred by this, in Santi's carriage various ideas for escape cautiously made the rounds; but all were discarded with no solution for dealing with the two armed guards who remained on constant vigil at either end of each compartment.

Finally, a chance did present itself, however. The two guards in Santi's bogey, having rather unwisely enjoyed a substantial meal washed down by more than the usual amount of wine, began to dose off. By dint of stealthy signs silently exchanged, a decision was reached to jump the somnambulant pair and overpower them. Santi, Robert, Ronnie and another young lieutenant had half risen from their seats when, most inopportunely, at that precise moment, the train rattled through a large station and the change in its tempo and sound alerted the drowsy guards. Immediately, the four would-be assailants found themselves staring down the barrels of two menacingly persuasive rifles

The rather lame offering that they had merely been attempting to rotate seats was scoffed at. Shoved rudely back to their places, they were left in no doubt as to the consequences they would suffer should they be the cause of any further disturbance. Santi, however, managed to use the short-lived commotion to some advantage. As the train trundled through that station, he was able to push a tiny chink through the curtain and, flashing by, he read a name on a signpost – *Napoli*.

They all settled down once more in crestfallen silence. The journey thereafter was short and uneventful, for just under forty-three kilometres north of Naples the train stopped at a place called Capua. They had, it seemed, reached their destination. Roughly, the guards made them disembark – they were not about to take any unnecessary chances with this scurvy lot of POWs – and marched them some distance to a transit camp emblazoned with the sign *Prigionieri di Guerra Campo 66, Capua, 3400* – Prisoner of War Camp 66, Capua, Military Area 3400.

It was 16 June 1942. They were far from family, friends and all the familiar things of home. They were prisoners of war in Italy… *Yet stands the church clock at ten to three? And is there honey still for tea?* (Rupert Brooke)

---

26 JUNE '42: IT was a strange month for Usha Moyee. Three weeks ago, the monsoons had broken – at last. The first soft murmur of rain quickened into a squall, and then into a pageant of lightning and thunder. But even after that first long-awaited storm, the rains were unable to quench the heat. It seemed unusually oppressive, and although she did not understand the why or wherefore of it, an

odd sensation in the region just below her breastbone – maybe what was termed the pit of one's stomach – boded there was something amiss; in fact, she was positive something was wrong.

She had woken one morning towards the beginning of the month with the terrible feeling that she had had a nightmare, but she could not for the life of her remember anything about it. Nevertheless, it had left her with a restlessness she had been unable to shed; and something else – a sense of anxiety that niggled at her all through the day, and disturbed her sleep all through the night, so that she woke up each morning feeling worse than ever and uncharacteristically despondent. Most unsettling of all was her inability to make head or tail of what it was she was feeling so awful about. And this state of incertitude had persisted, had dogged her, all through the month.

She had just gone to lie down for a few minutes, with a wet towel pressed to her forehead, when the loud ringing of the front-door bell made her jump. Her husband had left for work, but she knew the girls were still home, just about finished with breakfast. She hoped one of them would get the door because, for some strange reason, her body felt as though it weighed a ton, and no matter how hard she tried she found it impossible to move a muscle, leave alone raise herself from the bed.

"I'll go, Ma," she heard Lebu call out.

She heard a low murmur of voices. A short silence followed, a sort of heavy stillness that suddenly turned her body ice cold, weightless; and, light as a feather, she felt herself floating, unable to control what was happening around her. She tried to call out to Lebu, to warn her – *stay away, don't go to the door* – but, somehow, she seemed to have lost her voice as well. She could feel the presence of something that frightened her, a premonition of some awful calamity. And then it came back to her in a rush – her nightmare! She recollected it, the dream she could not for the life of her remember when she woke up; the one where she would hear someone at the door, but when she went to open it the figure standing there was faceless!

Panic galvanised her as she forced herself to sit up. She had to stop Lebu! The room blurred, it was hard to focus, and when at last she dragged herself to her feet, Lebu was standing in the bedroom doorway; she was holding something in her hand, and she looked as white as a sheet. A telegram! Usha Moyee felt her life drain away, from her head, from her heart, down through her body as stiff and heavy as a log of wood; and as it ebbed and pooled at her feet, without a sound, she lost consciousness and fell to the floor.

JUNE HAD BEEN A MONTH of near pandemonium in Cairo. It started with an air of uncertainty, but as the month progressed that grew into a spreading hysteria, fuelled by whispers and rumours filtering back through cracks in the censorship from sources both reliable and unreliable.

At first they hung in the air, hovering like dust motes caught on a sunbeam; and then like the sand that blew in on the desert wind, those whispers and rumours pervaded the city, laying an ever increasing film of unease over everyone and everything in it. It was hard to know what to believe, hard to make out what was garbled and what was not, to sift the grains of truth from the chaff of gossip and propaganda.

However that may be, one thing became clear, the Allies were taking one hell of a drubbing out there in the desert, and the thunder of retreat could now be felt in the tremors that reached and shook the foundations of the old city. It seemed the Germans really were at its doors.

Newspapers, radios and newsreels blazoned their stories in the city's streets, parlours and theatres; everyone had a take on the subject, and it culminated in what the British themselves wryly dubbed 'The Flap'.

After the Battle of the Cauldron, the Allies had made a desperate bid to halt the onslaught of Rommel's Panzerarmee. It had proved in vain. Unit after unit went down in domino fashion and were taken, or inexorably pushed back; and in the helter skelter retreat, it often happened both armies ran neck and neck, on occasion even overtaking one another so that there were times when no one knew quite which was which or who was where.

All through the month of June the desperate race was on till, finally, the Allies were backed up to the border with Egypt. Tobruk, which had held out through months of hell and high water, capitulated at last on 21 June. On 29 and 30 June the Royal Navy evacuated Alexandria. Then, in July, Rommel finally crossed the border into Egyptian territory, and both sides faced each other at a small railway station called El Alamein, seventy miles outside Alexandria.

In Cairo it was common knowledge, both in army and civilian circles, at a mere 136 miles from Cairo, Rommel was but a step from the Capitol; and depending on one's allegiance and point of view, anticipation of his arrival was fraught with dread or eagerness.

For Egyptian nationalists such as Anwar Sadat and Gamal Abdel Nasser, working towards ousting the British from their country, it was a time of hope and preparation. For the palpably beaten British and their allies, even for much of Cairo's high society intuitively wary in the face of invading forces, the time was one of anxiety and retreat.

Consequently, banks were overwhelmed with city-block long queues of panicked customers demanding their money; the airport, train stations and streets were jammed with people attempting to flee and finding no means of doing so; and GHQ literally seemed to be going up in smoke. Dark grey columns of smoke from hurriedly lit bonfires made of files, plans, reports, maps, signals and messages rose up and spread like a pall, aided by the wind which scattered the crematory ashes of the British Occupation of Egypt over her capitol city. In Cairo that desperate Wednesday of 30 June 1942 became known, rather aptly, as Ash Wednesday.

When Hedeya opened the morning edition of the *Egyptian Gazette*, the headlines blazoned across the front page hit her with a force that shook her. The words dissolved, seeming to melt into each other as they swam in and out of focus. She had been haunted by an inordinate anxiety ever since news of the battle had reached the city; nevertheless, she was unprepared for the intensity of this moment's reaction, for the sudden surge of fear that now made her almost nauseous. It filled her heart and lungs and seemed to squeeze out all the air so that she found it hard to breathe. And, incomprehensibly, it stirred a memory – the memory of being left suddenly unsheltered and adrift, after her father's death, in a world that had bewildered and frightened her.

The association was baffling. That had been years ago, why remember it now? Why that same feeling of abandonment now? She closed her eyes and tried to take a long, deep breath. Maybe, she told herself after a moment's thought, maybe because for a short while, a very short while, she had been reminded what safety in the strength of a good man felt like. And these were frightening times. War and its attendant horrors made for bad news that was bound to affect everyone; in her case it went even further, reaching into her terrified childhood. Black memories of past killings and death came flooding back, unbidden, and she hurriedly folded the newspaper and jerked her mind away from the abominations.

It was no secret that British losses had been great. Reports said the dead and wounded from both sides were lying out there; so many missing – nameless, faceless. And their loved ones had no way of finding out! One could not help but feel dismay at such a terrible waste of life; more so because it stirred up the painful past.

In her heart, however, Hedeya knew she was praying for one man in particular. Santi. He put a face, gave a name to the horror out there. He had been so young, his mind unscarred and clear, his body strong and perfect with the promise of life. And now? What had become of all that unblemished youth and strength? Was it lying broken, bleeding? Was he somewhere, wounded and helpless? God have pity! Was he dead or alive! She *had* to believe he was alive!

It had been a long time since a man had touched her feelings in this way; not since her husband had she allowed anyone to get close to her. But this young man had been special and, quite simply, he'd caught her unawares. She had lowered her guard. She chided herself repeatedly that she should have known better. She usually did have more sense than to allow for such imprudence. And, to compound her confusion, he had proposed in the most reckless manner – through Asis Habib, no less – then rushed off into the desert before she could catch her breath.

Such rashness, she determined, was not the proper basis for a lifetime's relationship; such impetuous emotions could amount to no more than a short-lived fancy that would undoubtedly wear off or lead to disaster. Of course, this outrageous nonsense was due to the times they lived in. So, better it should end before any real harm was done. She should consider herself lucky he had gone away...

And yet, here she was! In defiance of all good reasoning her mind kept slipping away from common sense to revisit those short, sweet memories of the times they had spent together. And each time it did so, she would pull back and tell herself firmly that getting involved with a man she knew almost nothing about, one who was going off to war, was unthinkable for someone in her situation. There couldn't possibly be a more ill-fated combination!

Why, at this moment he very well might be...she felt an icy cold sensation swirl in the pit of her stomach. It turned her legs to water, then climbed up through her body till it reached her head which began to throb again, so that a sudden spell of dizziness made her feel quite faint.

Seated alone at the kitchen table, she covered her face with her hands as she hurriedly shied away from the dreadful direction her thoughts kept taking her. No, no; as things stood, events would prove her right.

Of course they would! Who in their right mind would take the sort of risk such a relationship demanded? It was fortunate that time and opportunity had been too short for anything more than a fleeting acquaintance. It had been a pleasant interlude and his attentions had, no doubt, been flattering. For a moment in time, they both had taken leave of responsibility and cast it to the wind. But in the end good sense had to prevail; their worlds were much too far apart to allow for anything more substantial to grow between them. All said and done, it was for the best. Imagine her predicament now if she had allowed her heart...

Absolutely not! She was done with romantic dreams. She had learnt the hard way that the heart could not be trusted, that one had to be strong-minded and practical in life.

Why then, she thought dismally, did she feel this ache of loss if there had been nothing to lose in the first place? Why this empty, hollow feeling she could neither understand nor explain? She could not rid herself of a sense of regret that reached so deep, it seemed to have turned her inside out and, irrevocably, to have changed her life forever.

CHAPTER FORTY-ONE

Prigionieri Di Guerra Campo 66, Capua

In the fell clutch of circumstance,
I have not winced nor cried aloud:
Under the bludgeonings of chance
My head is bloody, but not bowed.

– William Ernest Henley, "Invicta," 1857

CAPUA WAS A LARGE prisoner of war camp meant to serve as a transit quarantine camp. However, most of the POWs would spend months here in deplorably overcrowded, insect-infested conditions without adequate sanitation and ablutionary facilities before finally being moved to other permanent camps in various parts of Italy and Germany.

The camp was built on flat, drab terrain and was sectioned off by barbed wire into several compounds. Accommodation was the most basic. Within the officers' enclosure that would become their residence, the newcomers were dispersed to long wooden hutments that stood in rows, each hut housing a number of primitive iron bedsteads laid with three wood slats, a straw palliasse and two blankets. One hutment was reserved for dining. The cook house and latrines were installed in wooden buildings to the north of the hutments, as were the showers which left much to be desired. Additionally, along the northside of this officers' compound was another larger compound of four sections that held all and sundry other ranks from British, Dominion and Commonwealth troops.

A shortage of water, soap and disinfectant meant that scheduled ten-day intervals between baths sometimes stretched to twenty-one days. Weather didn't help. Punishing circumstances like these could bring out the best and, sadly, the worst in human nature, as was soon discovered when soap, underwear and such began to disappear — and officers, no more or less than anyone else, were not above pilfering and deceit. A very miffed Roger Werner threw down the gauntlet one day.

"Very well then, which one of you poxy bastards has made off with my jocks! If I ever nab the cad who's nicked them, I'll have him singing soprano, I promise you that!"

By and large, however, they did their best to alleviate the misery of their circumstances and the depression that threatened by making light of them and trying to keep in good humour. It wasn't easy as conditions became increasingly worse with every shipload of prisoners that came in, mostly from North Africa.

Dirty, diseased and sick from being crammed into filthy, dark holds with hardly room to stand, and no provision whatsoever for sanitation, they had spent days at sea without food or water. Those who still wore a semblance of clothes were in tatters, others were wrapped only in a blanket. Most tried to put a brave face on things. Seeing their pitiful state, Santi realised the officers and men of the 2/4, being among the initial POWs bagged in the Cauldron, were fortunate to have been flown rather than shipped over.

Inundated with prisoners, the overwhelmed Italians were unable to segregate the various nationalities in accordance with the requirements of the Geneva Convention. So much so that British, Australian, South African, Rhodesian, a smattering of Free French and even some Sudanese, Cypriots and Serbians were all held in the same camp; and held together with the King's Commissioned Officers were some Indian Viceroy's Commissioned Officers from various units as well. Roman Catholic services and Sunday Mass were held in a building dedicated to that purpose. All others – Protestant, Hindu, Sikh, Moslem – were left to follow their religions, or not, as they saw fit.

The camp was under the command of Lt. Col. Guglielmo Nicoletti, and discipline was strict. The day began with a wake-up call at 0700, followed by an order to parade, and roll call at 0830 hours. Initially, this rarely went smoothly due to the Italians' inability to articulate certain names. Such a one was St. Leger (sel-injer), a name which unfailingly was malformed beyond all recognition. Here, one had to admit, the error was perhaps not quite without reason – but, inexcusably, even the simple name Dutt was unspared, being persistently distorted into a rough 'Doot'. By way of retaliation, a POW, when thus called, would feign ignorance and refuse to acknowledge the offensive misnomer, leading to all round confusion abundantly enjoyed by the prisoners and of considerable ire to the Italians.

However, since those with the upper hand invariably win the day, this was not allowed to continue for long. After repeated corrections from the POWs, which availed them naught but several punishments for breakdown in discipline, the injured parties were forced to accept defeat and suffer their indignity in silence.

Dawn parade and roll call were followed with breakfast, which meant a mug of ersatz coffee brewed from acorns. Midday brought a hunk of rather stale bread with a rock-hard lump of Parmesan cheese – this repast was aptly described as 'dog and maggot'.

To say merely that the food was meagre would be to describe insufficiently the plight of the POWs; in fact, their rations were hardly enough to sustain a grown man. And what little there was of it was almost inedible, except that hunger forces one to eat almost anything to assuage the pangs of a painfully empty stomach.

The one actual meal of the day consisted of another piece of bread accompanied by watery macaroni with a few pieces of floating vegetable. Sometimes it was an insipid cabbage or minestrone soup which, the recipients held, bore a disgustingly close semblance to their dish water. At other times the order of the day was a small piece of tinned meat or a piece of fish. It was a bad day when fish was served; a groan went up at sight of it for they were sure to remain hungrier than usual as the fish was often disgustingly close to rancid. Tea was brewed from lettuce leaves which produced an unappetising bitter liquor that was, for the seasoned Indian and British tea drinkers, pure punishment.

Of course, there was a marked difference in the quality of food on those days the camp was inspected by a representative of the International Red Cross; these inspections took place approximately every two months and were eagerly anticipated by the prisoners.

Sometimes, to augment their rations, the Italians would provide onions, enormous ones that the POWs could bake in the hot embers of whatever fuel might come to hand. However, when it came to light that wooden planks from the hutments were being pilfered for fuel, they were threatened with a loss of this privilege unless the culprit desisted immediately and owned up to the crime. No one ever did.

To the south and southeast of the camp where the Italian officers messed and quartered, vegetables and tomatoes had been planted, ostensibly for the entire camp, but none ever reached the POWs. With such scant rations, Santi worried about the Gurkhas refusing meat when it was served. He was relieved, therefore, to hear that Dilbahadur – who had been allowed to continue as his part-time batman – had done an excellent job of shoring up the belief it was 'horsemeat', alleviating the problem of the Gurkhas' rations.

Camp money was issued according to rank, but was barely enough to cover the essentials, such as maintenance and messing (eleven lire a day), let alone any pittance remaining for sweets from the canteen store.

Red Cross parcels – *when* distributed – were gratefully received as manna from heaven. They came from Canada and England with much appreciated goodies such as butter or margarine, jam or marmalade, egg flakes, powdered milk, rolled oats, and that good old staple, bully beef. Some even brought horlicks or ovaltine, Bovril, sardines, biscuits, chocolates, and cheese. Other eagerly awaited items were condensed milk and, oh joy, real tea and coffee! Occasionally, they brought prunes and raisins, and Ambrosia creamed rice. Even those long-anticipated tins of fifty Gold Flake cigarettes!

Physical activity was minimal. Weather permitting, a ball was sometimes made available to kick around and, now and then, under heavy guard, short walks were allowed beyond the camp's confines

"Imagine this, Doc," Robert Williams declared during one such sally into the countryside, "we are standing on the very spot where, it is said, centuries ago Hannibal's armies camped in the winter."

This tidbit of historical trivia was met with lukewarm interest; one could hardly give a tinker's damn for the history, lauded or not, of this drab little valley since it brought little comfort to their present situation. Conversely, no one could gainsay that these infrequent perambulations past cultivated fields and olive groves were a pleasant diversion from the monotony of incarceration. More significantly, they served to provide a first-hand idea of the general lay of the land, and many a mental note was made with escape in mind. When the rains arrived, however, the surrounding area turned muddy; outdoor activity ended abruptly, and being cooped inside, day after gloomy day, became close to unbearable.

Language classes were arranged, and Santi managed to pay a guard for a small English-to-Italian dictionary. Since there was a dearth of reading material to go around, card games became quite the thing. Santi learnt to play bridge; it helped somewhat to pass the time. In fact, with little else to do, the game became an annoying obsession for some. Sessions would start in the morning and continue through the day, hardly breaking for mealtimes. Then, too, plays were argued to death, and not even 'lights out' would abate the discussions. Frequently, they continued in bed, often loudly and heatedly, till the players, having exhausted themselves and everyone else within earshot, were finally bested by sleep. It reached a point of utter irritation for those uninterested in this pastime.

"Oh, for Pete's sake!" Robert Williams burst out late one night, having stuffed his ears with his blanket to no avail. "Belt up, will you! All this bloody natter about *bloody* bridge – the lot of you have turned into blithering idiots!" Completely brassed off with their mania for the game, he vehemently foreswore it for life. "When I get out of here, I never want to see, or hear, of the beastly game ever again!"

THE BOREDOM, OVERCROWDING, AND close quarters began to rankle with the best of them. However, being among one's own kith and kin eased these circumstances somewhat and, as a consequence, small racial cliques began to draw together for solace; the flip side of this coin, at times, was racial discord.

The Moslem custom of prayer, facing in the direction of Mecca, their holy city, takes place at four given times of the day. Among those taken captive were several Moslem Junior Commissioned Officers, or JCOs, who would gather at these ordained times to perform *namaaz*. Some officers from wholly British regiments were unacquainted with this practice; and a few, more intolerant in their ignorance than others, made sport of it, indulging in raucous laughter and howling to disrupt the prayers.

This show of disrespect infuriated the British Officers who had served in outfits such as the 2/4. They had lived and fought beside Hindus and Moslems in their regiments; they had shared in some of their festivals, taken steps to learn their languages and customs, come to appreciate their courage and loyalty and, ultimately, faced death together on the battlefield.

"Take no notice of their foolishness," Santi told the slighted JCOs in a voice just loud enough to carry over. "They shame themselves with their callow behaviour."

"They're a damn disgrace," Robert Williams snapped in disgust. "Their yobbish behavior reflects on us all. But no use getting your dander up, Doc, not with their sort. Insufferable pratts!"

"I say," one miscreant drawled back, "no need to get miffed, old chap. No harm done. Just a bit of a lark, is all."

"Well, there's the rub, old fellow!" Ronnie Smith threw back, emulating his casual insolence to perfection. "Seems we don't sing from the same hymn sheet, can't you tell – so naff off and play elsewhere, why don't you. Your sort is a right royal *pain in the arse!*"

Fortunately, this unequivocal disapproval from fellow British officers soon put a damper on the spread of such loutish behaviour.

On the other hand, there was one particularly dubious JCO whose frequent visits to the Commandant's Office irked one and all. These unexplained meetings with their captors roused a deal of conjecture, rife with rumours of collaboration and spying. So much so, when he suddenly disappeared one day, there was a general suspicion he had, in fact, joined the IRCM.

All Indian personnel in the camp – officers and men – had been subjected by their captors to a rousing speech on nationalism and loyalty to their Motherland; the aim was to garner volunteers for a recently formed unit of the Italian Army known as the Ragruppamento Centri Militari. This unit, like the Tiger Legion of the German Army, purported affiliation with the free Indian National Army (INA), or *Azad Hind Fauj,* headed by Subhash Chandra Bose.

Italian propaganda advocated, the patriotic duty of every upstanding Indian was to fight for his country's freedom by joining with them against the British. This did not go over too well with most of the POWs. The majority of Indian officers and men, despite a deep admiration for Bose and his fight for freedom, had already searched their souls and opted for what they believed to be the right course.

The soul search had not been easy, fraught as it was with divided loyalties and inequitable contradictions. But, after painful consideration, most had gone beyond the immediate benefit of self and country and weighed in on the side of universal morality and justice for mankind. Ultimately, of the thousands of Indian POWs, the Italians were able to turn a mere four hundred or so to their cause; and even they were not entirely convinced. Four months later, in November, many mutinied and were returned to their respective POW camps.

The Indian National Army was formed by Subhash Chandra Bose. Following his escape to Germany in 1941, he recruited as many as he could from the POWs taken in the Middle East to create the Tiger Legion in the German Army. However, after the fall of Malaya and Singapore in 1942, and the capture of thousands of Indian soldiers by the Japanese army, Bose believed he would do better recruiting for the INA in South-East Asia. In 1943, he journeyed to Japan where his efforts were met with greater success. Sadly, at the war's end, and his demise in a tragic plane crash over Burma, most who were recruited in the Far East would face trials for treason.

As for those unfortunate men who were finally convinced to prove their loyalty to their Mother Country by joining the ranks of the German Tiger Legion, their fate is unknown. With Germany's defeat at the end of the war, what became of those Indians who fought with the Axis in Europe remains a silent mystery. To this day the tragedy of their disappearance has never been resolved.

CHAPTER FORTY-TWO

The Aegis Of Kali

Mother, I shall weave a chain of pearls
For thy neck with my tears of sorrow…
Let me not forget for a moment,
Let me carry the pangs of this sorrow
In my dreams and in my wakeful hours.

– Rabindranath Tagore, "Gitanjali" (adapted)

JULY 10TH: KAMALA WATCHED as Father read the Army telegram for the umpteenth time.

Dr. (Capt.) J.P. Dutt, M.C.O.G, Civil Surgeon's Quarters, Senior Provisional Administrators Bungalow, Chinsurah, Hooghly, W Bengal
A.G.'s Br. (A.G.16a No.U/O. No. B/75856/III/AG16 of 23/6/42:
Regret to inform Capt. Santi Pada Dutt Missing in Action

She was worried. Father looked old and dazed sitting in his chair, and his hand shook visibly as he held the telegram. Two weeks had passed since it arrived on that awful afternoon in June, and he had carried it with him all this while. Now, his body was slumped in the chair before her, his eyes empty, as though he had vacated his corporeal shell; as though he were somewhere else, in some other place inhabited by the shadows of memories from the past. Just yesterday he had started up, rising halfway out of his chair and, staring at the doorway as though he could see what no one else could, he had called out to his son. Other than that, he had uttered not a single word since the telegram, not even to her, his favourite child; and it frightened her.

And today, like a ghost from the past, Dada's last letter had arrived. She had been shocked to find the familiar-looking missive lying there with the rest of the morning post. When it sank in that it was, in fact, a letter from him, her heart had leapt so high, it made her dizzy. *The telegram was a mistake. He was not missing after all! He was out there, somewhere, still fighting the war. Here was the proof. Someone had just made a horrible, horrible mistake.*

And then she'd noticed the date on the letter and realised it had been written before that momentous telegram. Her disappointment was bitter, and she just stood there, quietly crying. Sudha had found her that way. Without a word her sister put her arms around her and held her close. But then, she'd taken the letter, and as soon as she began to read it, she too burst into sobs, unable to control herself. They sat on the floor, the two of them, holding onto each other and crying. And eventually, when they calmed down somewhat, they had taken the letter to Ma and Baba.

Reading it had pried open their parents' wound and renewed the pain of their loss all over again. This letter from their son, this false resurrection that seemed to bring him back to life, in it he told them he was well; he spoke to them of his life in the desert, the things he was doing, the pleasures of enjoying fresh eggs, of bathing in a warm blue sea, even the company he was keeping. This person was alive! His day-to-day actions, thoughts, feelings, were of this world; so earthbound, surely, they must still be real! The letter negated any other truth but hope, a need to believe that they clung to because the other was unbearable.

Ever since that awful telegram Mother had been half mad with grief; she neither ate nor slept, and spent her time between weeping and praying, tending to the lamp that was kept burning all day and all night at the altar of the Goddess in her bedroom.

Father had put one in the front room window where it remained lit twenty-four hours. He had called everyone, anyone who might have news, and then he withdrew into a deep, dark silence, his shoulders stooped as though under a burden too heavy to carry. Both parents visibly aged overnight, looking suddenly old far beyond their years.

In desperation they enquired after two reputed astrologers in Bhatpara and Howrah, seeking some insight, some guidance in the search for their oldest child. They hung on every word of the daily radio bulletins aired by the Red Cross, listing the latest casualties and internments. Every evening, when it was time for the broadcast, they remained glued to the radio in hope of obtaining some news of their missing son. Pray God it was not bad news!

The agony of not knowing haunted them day and night; yet, they clung desperately to the belief that somewhere in their fearful limbo there remained, perhaps, a small glimmer of light. They had no knowledge of the fate of their beloved son beyond the news of grave danger. If captured...even wounded...maybe there could be...there had to be some hope.

The Red Cross often was the first to know. Being an impartial organisation, it was allowed to visit the hospitals and POW camps on both sides to oversee the welfare of casualties and prisoners, and to ensure the rules of the Geneva Convention were upheld. And so they prayed…and listened…and prayed even harder. But, still, there was nothing. Nothing at all. Perhaps, if their prayers were laid on Kali's doorstep… Ma and Baba were convinced it was time to make a personal offering in the house of the Goddess. After all, it was widely believed that miracles took place from time to time in the temple in Kalighat.

The Hindu pantheon of gods is headed by the *Trimurti* of Brahma, Vishnu and Shiva. Legend has it, Shiva's wife Dakshayani immolated herself in protest over an insult her father made to her husband. Informed of the tragedy, Shiva, known for his mighty rages, transformed himself into Rudra the Roarer, God of Storm and Wind. He retrieved the body of his deceased consort and, carrying her aloft, began the Rudra Tandava, the dance of creation and destruction.

Being in the destructive mode, he danced himself into a trance that annihilated all around him till, finally, Vishnu felt compelled to intervene before complete chaos overtook the world. He removed Dakshayani's body and delivered it to the wind which carried various parts to fifty-two different places across the country. It is believed the goddess' right foot fell near a small Kali temple. As a result, the small temple became a sacred place of divine feminine power, it grew in fame, and many came to pay homage.

Fortunately, the sad story of Dakshayani had a happy ending. As all things are possible in the realm of the gods, she was reincarnated as Parvati; and Shiva, as quick to forgive as he was to chastise, restituted and made good all he had destroyed.

Meanwhile, back in the world of mortals, where the small Kali temple once stood, a new larger temple was erected to the Mother Goddess. It was here Santi had prayed to Kali before going to war. And it was here that prayers would be offered now, supplicating for his return.

So, in the very early hours of the morning Ma awoke and prepared large quantities of food. While still dark, she and Baba carefully packed their offerings and set out for Kalighat. They arrived at the temple at 4 am that morning. The *purohit*, apprised of their special need, allowed them into the inner sanctum where they might offer their prayers in private to the Goddess while he performed his own first *pujo* of the day. Already, at 3.30 am, he had prepared the deity with her ritual bath of yogurt and Ganges water, followed by annointings with perfumed oils and vermillion powder. Finally, dressed in a fresh Benarasi silk sari, she was ready to receive her devotees.

The larger-than-life, black stone *murti* of Kali is of awesome proportions. Centred in her forehead she wears a third, all-seeing, ruby-red eye, and displays a protruding tongue forged in gold. Four sturdy arms are symbolic of her powers. One hand holds the sword of Divine Knowledge used to sever the head of Ego, held in her second hand. Her third hand wields the *Trishula* or trident. At her feet lies the vanquished demon, *Mahisasur*. Truly she is a warrior goddess! Yet, close beneath this fearsome outer aspect flows the gentle love of a mother, depicted by her fourth hand held up to bestow her blessings of guidance and protection to all her devotees who come to plead their cause and to worship.

Ma and Baba had brought offerings of fruits, sweetmeats and a coconut. They placed these before the great goddess as they knelt at her feet and beseeched her to intercede for their son, the first born she had blessed them with. *Protect him, oh Mother, shelter him from harm. In your divine mercy spare him and give him back to us. In return ask of us what you will; we surrender unto you.*

In addition to the abundance of sweets and fruits they also left large quantities of rice-pulao, fried *luchi*-bread and prepared fish, as well as milk to be offered up with further prayers the *purohit* promised to perform throughout the day; after which these blessed offerings would feed the poor.

Finally, they conferred with the temple astrologer who advised them, henceforth, to abstain from consuming any form of meat. Their food should consist only of rice and certain vegetables, boiled without the addition of salt or spice; they were to partake of a single meal daily, in the afternoon, and any remaining food was to be thrown into the river before sunset. This ritual was to continue every day until their prayers were answered one way or the other. Above all, they must place all their faith in the mercy of the Goddess.

Promising humble devotion, Jagadish Pada Dutt and Usha Moyee Dutt returned home to their vigil.

Bela was there to receive them. Being next in line after Santi, and the oldest child now remaining in the household, she accepted, unhesitatingly, the responsibility for the welfare of the family should rest on her shoulders. By nature, Bela was a practical, sensible girl, and an even more dutiful and caring daughter, and she now tried to spend as much time at home as her studies would allow. In the absence of both her brothers, she realised it fell to her to be the 'man' of the family and support her parents through this terrible time of loss and suffering. She understood quite clearly what was needed of her; what was unclear to her was whether she was strong enough to pull it off. Santi's shoes would be hard to fill.

Her own grief over the loss of her older brother ran very deep, at times it overwhelmed her. She felt unbalanced by his absence. It had been different when first he had gone to war. Then they believed his absence to be a temporary one, merely involving a certain length of time before he returned; that was all. They had all needed to believe that, and nothing beyond that. It was different now; they were forced to face the dreadful possibility that his absence was permanent, absolute, forever – and she was unable to accept that possibility.

She too had received his letter...*My dear Bulu, I pray you are all safe and well at home....* She realised instinctively that he had been reaching for the comfort and stability of home and family; at the very moment of danger, the thought of their well being would have been a source of solace and comfort to him. Strong, gentle, dependable – his love had been all these. She missed him terribly.

When she came home, there were times she almost expected to see him walk through the door, calling her name. She could understand Sudha's refusal to accept that anything 'dreadful' could really have happened to Dada. She realised, till now, none of them had used the actual word. It was too final and too awful. Thank goodness she had Bina staying with her in Medical College; it helped to have company – although, as company went, Bina's was hardly uplifting since she was constantly bursting into tears every time she thought of Dada.

"I didn't say goodbye properly," she had wailed when she heard the news. "And now...now..."

"*Choop koro!*" Bela rounded on her immediately. "Don't you dare say it! Dada is alive and well. Read the telegram; all it says is they don't know his whereabouts. But that doesn't matter because he *will* come back." Her voice shook slightly as she added softly, "He *must* come back."

It was Lebu who suddenly announced that, all things considered, Dada's letter having arrived the same afternoon of Ma and Baba's pilgrimage to the temple might well be taken as an omen, an auspicious sign, an answer even. The idea brought Lebu comfort; especially because ever since the arrival of that horrible telegram, she found her brother's face had become a blur – even when she closed her eyes and tried as hard as she could to concentrate on her memories, she could no longer see his face clearly. She was dismayed by this failure; it felt as though she had broken faith with him, and the feeling filled her with a sense of guilt she could share with no one.

Surprisingly, although her mind's eye could no longer trace the lines of his face, although his features remained stubbornly out of focus, she could recollect quite clearly the warm, damp, masculine smell of his quick hug when he thanked her for helping him slip past Father after a forbidden football game. The sweet memory of that impulsive brotherly gesture heightened her belief that her inability to remember his features was an act of disloyalty that had condemned him to oblivion, so that in some awful way she was partly responsible for his being taken from them. She must, she decided, do some sort of penance to make up for her betrayal.

When eventually she confided her thoughts to Kamala, her sister would have none of it. "Rubbish! You're talking nonsense," she chided Lebu. "The one has absolutely nothing to do with the other."

Nevertheless, knowing that once Lebu had latched onto an idea there was no prying it loose, Kamala agreed to go along with her sister's self-inflicted 'penance'. Thereafter, every night before they went to sleep, Lebu would stand on the bed and, as per instructions, Kamala would hold aloft, as high as she could, one end of their mosquito net. Sudha's part in this pantomime was to stand at a distance of six feet and one inch – the exact measurement of Dada's height – to act as both marker and safeguard lest there be a mishap; and finally, when both sisters were in place, Lebu would launch herself off the edge of the bed, in an attempt to cover, in one giant leap, the distance between the bed and Sudha.

Success meant all was well and Dada would return safe and sound. If she fell short, which was more often than not, considering her tiny stature, she would promptly make reparation by standing on one leg for six minutes and one second – Dada's height – without losing her balance or falling over. It was her personal way of bringing Dada home. And since she did not believe in doing things by half-measures, she determined as well to curtail a favourite pastime – reading.

Days passed, filled with hours of agonised listening, wondering, praying. The waiting – at times hopeful, at times tearful, always fearful – took its toll on everyone. Mother began blaming herself for persuading Father to give his consent for their son to join. She would sit by the trunk wherein she had put away her son's belongings, safe and ready for his return. Silently she would go through them, holding first one garment and then another against her face, remembering the little, everyday things about him: the young boy whose eyes shone with pleasure when she prepared his favourite sweet of *nolen gurer payesh* with *pathishapta*; the older brother loyally bearing the blame for Kanti's misdeeds; the schoolboy back from boarding whose tall, athletic body was fast maturing from puberty into manhood; and, in later years, the glorious young man, steadfast and sensitive, her eldest, the look of affection he threw her every so often in recognition of her support and love for them all. It was as though he understood the special bond between them, mother and first born.

She had been so young, merely fifteen, when he started to grow inside her. He was the first child she had held in her arms and, small and helpless as he was, he taught her the joys of motherhood; as she held him to her breast, he opened the floodgates of her love for them all. She had watched over him as he grew in stature and strength, that first small bundle that had fit so snugly, so miraculously against the curves of her body, and just as he'd turned into a man of promise and potential, just as he'd begun to watch over her, he was taken... Usha Moyee's agitation and despair were boundless as she prostrated herself before her household deity: *Great Mother of the Universe, show us mercy; and in your benevolence, I implore you, protect him...*

That single-line telegram telling them he was missing had changed their lives completely.

Then one night, towards the middle of September, Usha Moyee had a dream. She saw a large number of soldiers standing about. Frantically searching for her son in that milling crowd, she saw him at last as he turned and began walking towards her. In his uniform he was so real, so close, that she reached out to touch him.

She woke, crying out his name, to find her cheeks wet with tears and her arms outstretched in the darkness; but strangely enough, she was suffused with a sense of comfort.

Next morning, she recounted her dream to her husband. For a single long moment Jagadish Pada Dutt sat stock still in his chair; then he leaned back and said, quite simply, "There is no need to worry. He is alive."

On 13th November a telegram arrived at the Civil Surgeon's Bungalow in Chinsurah:

U.O. NO. Z-22404/DMS 1(a) dated 21/10/42 from AG 14(c) of 3/11/42 to Medical Directorate (DMSI (a)):
Confirm Capt. Santi Pada Dutt POW in Italy.

CHAPTER FORTY-THREE

The Ghosts Of War

Why don't you write, Young Fellow My Lad,
I watch for the post each day,
And I miss you so, and I'm awfully sad,
for it's months since you went away.
And I've had a lamp in the window lit,
and I'm keeping it burning bright
Till my boy comes home;
and here I sit into the quiet night.

– Robert Service, "Young Fellow My Lad" (adapted)

JUNE TURNED INTO July, and July into August. All the while Santi worried about home. The POWs had been given Red Cross cards to fill out – name and rank only – to send home, and Santi wondered what had become of his. Had the family received his news? Did they know he was alive? A prisoner of war? Were his parents grieving, believing he was dead? He felt deep regret for the pain he knew he was putting them through. He hoped they had been informed of his capture so they would not suffer unduly; and if they had not, he prayed they could feel his life force, his spirit, still sharing this world with them.

He contemplated his present circumstances ruefully; his world was so far removed from theirs, he wondered if any sort of communion were at all possible. His own memories, prior to those last days in the desert, often behaved much like a mirage; they were disconcertingly nebulous. Home and family had become a part of some distant world that was someone else's reality; an intimate from a time long ago whose normal routine life was so comfortingly familiar, he seemed to have borrowed those memories for his own. It was a peculiar sensation that left him feeling strangely unsettled and adrift with no point of reference.

Memories, even the recent ones of Cairo, of Hedeya, were out of focus. But through the haze, buried somewhere inside him, he could still feel the painful confusion of that last parting; the desperate urgency – time had been so short – trying to explain what he himself did not fully understand; the despair at his failure, and the ache of his loss. How could one feel the loss of something one never actually had? The urgency of that moment might have passed, yet, against all reason, the persistent ache lingered on.

But what had he expected? Now, in hindsight, he realised he had been unfair to her; he had acted on impulse, giving no thought to her circumstances, or his, or the dilemma he was putting her in. He had as much as asked her to give up everything she had known, to live her life with him when he didn't know if he would even have a life to offer her. What a muddle he had left there! Would he ever be able to return, to see her again? Would there be an answer waiting? Or had he missed his chance? Had there ever really been any chance? *Some*how he had to find out...maybe in time he could...

There had been a complete rout in North Africa with thousands of Allied soldiers taken prisoner. Trying to sort through the missing and the dead had been a nightmare, and in the ensuing pandemonium, all signal, telegraph and telephone lines became clogged, official dispatches and mail that should have taken one week were taking as much as five to six. Personal letters were taking even longer – and lucky at that to reach their destination.

A Papal Nuncio had paid the camp a visit the day prior and made a list of their names to send to the International Red Cross. Although an Attache from that organisation had previously done the same on an earlier visit and taken the information back with him to headquarters in Switzerland, the Pope's Emissary had gone one further and made a count as well of the next batch of POWs to be transferred, both to Germany and to other camps in Italy. Then, to the faithful, he handed out holy pictures and medals blessed by the Pope, and to the rest, gifts of table tennis, chess, harmonicas and stamp sets. Not being a Christian, Santi received a stamp album with Vatican stamp sets, starting with those issued in1929, the inaugral year of its independent Statehood.

The distraction had been a welcome one but, infrequent as such distractions were, it did little to alleviate the endless boredom or the frustration of incarceration. Although some were able to adapt better than others, it told on everyone and showed up in different ways with different people.

One officer, a young lieutenant from an artillery regiment, was so stricken by his circumstances he lay abed, depressed and listless. His ennui grew to the point where his friends, fearing for his life, called Santi in to take a look at him.

"Look here Phips," a friend tried to rouse the ailing man. "You have a visitor. Come now, snap out of it, there's a good lad."

"He's been this way, Doc, ever since he received news of his wife, poor beggar. Got it off one of the new arrivals who came in last week."

"What news is that?"

"Dashed rotten show! Hit him for six, I can tell you. Seems his wife was on a ship bound for England – didn't want to leave, met and married in Cairo, only six months, you see – but with it all going down the way it was those last few days, Phips urged her to return home along with other English families being evacuated. Thought he was sending her out of harm's way, back home to comparative safety, you see. Instead, he gets news that right about the time he was bagged, her ship had been torpedoed and had gone down with everyone on board. No survivors, wouldn't you know."

"Oh, good Lord!" Santi muttered, imagining the mental burden the poor chap was carrying.

"I'll say! His grief that fate should allow him to survive when his wife did not has been almost too much for him to bear. There's a tad bit of guilt there as well I suspect, which is a load of dosh of course, but we're afraid he's losing it; at this rate he's liable to end up a fruit-cake! *We* can't seem to get through to him, but you have a crack at it, would you Doc, see if you can't shake some life into him."

"I'll need your help. We must take his mind off his grief by keeping him busy any way we can. Get him involved in things; remind him of the rest of his family. Maybe even cook up an escape plan of some sort to get him thinking of those who love him, waiting for him at home. It's important that he get up and get some physical exercise as well. Start out slowly by helping him walk around the compound. And he must eat; he has to keep up his strength."

While imparting this advice, Santi had been carefully examining the young man and he noticed what looked like a rash all over his prone body. On taking a closer look the rash turned out to be hundreds of bites. Bed bugs!

When this malady was announced, one of the more senior officers took matters firmly in hand. "That's it! First order of the day, m' lad. Up you get so we can strip your bed and find out just what sort of rum customers you've been keeping company with!"

The offending bedboards were taken outside, and when a fire was lit under them, Robert Williams swore he counted well over three hundred bed bugs making a mad dash for cover. How he accomplished such a feat as they scattered was anyone's guess!

All the POWs suffered from bed bugs, fleas and lice, but an infestation this bad was enough to alarm even the prison authorities. A scare of diphtheria and typhus spread through the camp, and everyone was made to undergo a saliva test. Thirteen carriers of the former were discovered among the internees and, after they had been isolated, everyone was vaccinated against the disease by Captain Camillo, the camp Medical Officer. The procedure brought tears to grown men's eyes and left grave doubts as to the veracity of the MO's profession.

"I'll be blinkered! What in God's name is the old codger using?" Ronnie groaned, rubbing his arm as he joined Santi and Robert.

"A bayonet with a stirrup pump, I'd say! Damn sawbones!" Robert volunteered with a grimace, still smarting from the jab.

Santi laughed "Just make sure you stay fit. Imagine your plight if you happened to need an appendectomy!"

"Perish the thought, Doc!"

During the day most of the men managed to keep themselves fairly well occupied. Although they had no way of knowing whether their mail reached home, each man was allowed to send one weekly letter of twenty-four lines or less, and one postcard of not more than ten lines. Some kept busy fashioning makeshift mugs which they cut, hammered and shaped out of empty cans left over from Red Cross parcels. And, when all else failed, there was always the sport of resorting to crazy schoolboy antics just for the heck of thumbing a nose at their captors.

Such an opportunity sometimes presented itself at the raising and lowering of the camp flag every morning and evening respectively. On occasion the contraption would stick fast, and the flag would stubbornly refuse to budge past half mast. Invariably, it would require one of the more nimble guards to scramble up the flagpole to coax it into compliance, egged on with delighted hoots and howls from an enthusiastic audience of POWs – all of which detracted immeasurably from the dignity of the ceremony and added greatly to their captors' irritation.

Then, furthering their aggravation, the rabble-rousers would chose partners and waltz solemnly alongside the retreating guards as they marched off to the accompaniment of their trumpeter's fervent rendition of a tune unfamiliar to all except, of course, Robert Williams, who swore it was 'Aste Con Brio'. And try as they might, no one ever could discover his source for these sundry tidbits of local information!

There was another song, however, that had an entirely different effect on the POWs. By 1942 Lili Marlene had been translated into

Italian. Though the words were unfamiliar, there was no mistaking the haunting melody that would be heard, every so often, coming from the rooms of an officer or one of the guards. For the desert soldiers, especially, it evoked nostalgic memories of absent friends in a different time. Often, they would join in with their own version, but it didn't take long to pick up some of the Italian words.

> *Tutte le sere sotto quel fanal,*
> *Presso la caserma ti stavo ad aspettar...*
> *Con te Lili Marleen, con te Lili Marleen...*

And so they managed to pass the days. It was the still of night that was hardest of all to endure, the spectres that flooded back haunting the darkness. Past the barricade of tightly shut eyes, still they persisted, filling every crevice and cranny of the mind. That narrow margin, that floating step, that fragile bridge of passage twixt waking and sleeping; a portal of shadows and dreams barely slipped through, and then, so often, that precipice, tumbling into nightmares.

The inexplicable guilt of being alive when others had died so violently right beside you was a malaise that visited all of them at one time or another, pushing out the comforting thoughts of home, smothering the healing thoughts of loved ones. What right had one to comfort and healing when others had made the ultimate sacrifice and would never enjoy such things again!

Last night it had been Santi's turn. He had had that terrible, suffocating nightmare; they had come to him, those faces, torn, bloody, distorted with pain. He had looked down at himself to find he was covered in blood; the blood of all those men, on his hands, on his clothes, and he had woken up sweating, the taste of the desert like grit in his mouth. He was unable to breathe under the weight of his memories, the screams and moans mixed with the unforgettable din of battle still thundering in his ears.

Even awake he could not shut out the pitiable faces, or the stench of blood and fear still in his nostrils. All those men – he had watched over them, held them as the life-light dimmed and faded from their eyes, reassured them as he helped them to die. He had looked into their faces, seen their silent pleading, and been unable to aid them any longer. With neither medicine nor means left, he had failed them in their final moments of need. So many dead, so many unnecessary dead!

No man could forget those looks, those sights, those sounds, burnt into the fabric of his brain, branded forever into his soul. He had shared their confusion, their pain, those last private, precious seconds, indescribable at the end as life ebbed, and helpless, they had no choice but to trust him, stranger, doctor, friend. He had been their family, their father-confessor and, ultimately, their deliverer. For when they drew that final breath, his was the last face they saw, the last hand they held as he eased them towards their release; Hindu, Christian, Moslem, together at the last they knew that religion no longer mattered, all souls shared the same Great Spirit and all Gods became One.

Finally, his body had stopped shaking, and his breathing returned to normal. Slowly he became aware of his surroundings. He was not alone in his torment. He listened in the dark to the sounds around him; the disjointed mutterings, the moaning, the stifled cries, and the occasional suppressed scream, and he knew he did not lack for company in this place filled with tortured memories...

'*It's only at night when the ghosts awaken, And gibber and whisper horrible things...*'

The irony of it all! Those lines penned by Robert Service in that first Great War spoke to the same horrors and shared suffering. How long would it go on! God forgive them for what they had done to themselves and to each other.

Both perpetrator and victim, they had inflicted and suffered the most grievous harm, human beings no longer being human, so that they had forfeited all claim to a clear conscience; restless souls forever condemned to roam the purgatory of their deeds, however justified the cause, as they searched in vain for the way back to some place of peace, some signpost or landmark that would guide them back to the normal life they had lost.

Santi reached for the pack of Goldflake beside his pillow and pulled out the last fag. He lit it, striking the match as quietly as he could, and took a deep drag, filling his lungs with smoke. He felt comforted by it.

The Red Cross Food Parcels had better come soon, he thought, watching the end of his cigarette glow red in the dark. He was out of ciggies, and he had run out of camp money to boot.

CHAPTER FORTY-FOUR

A Bid For Freedom

Beyond this place of wrath and tears
Looms but the horror of the shade,
And yet the menace of the years
Finds, and shall find, me unafraid.
— William Ernest Henley, "Invicta", 1875

AUGUST 19: THE DAY was heavy with gloom, darkened by the incidents of the night before that hung like a pall over the camp. There was a sombre silence beneath which there stirred a nervous restlessness among the POWs, and it seemed dangerously close to exploding. They all knew a tragedy had occurred; but more than that, rumour had it that much of the tragedy ought to have been avoided, that what had gone down was, in fact, not only a tragedy, it was a war crime.

It was every POW's duty to try to escape and, as such, escape plans were continually being hatched throughout the camp. On the night of 18 August, the camp had retired at the usual time, and all was quiet throughout. Past the midnight hour, silence reigned over all as the camp slept. None seemed to be astir, except the guards on duty.

Sometime into the early-morning hours of 19 August, there had been movement in the shadows of the northeast hutment in the officers' compound. A low whisper from a concealed lookout signalled that the sentry at the east guard-post seemed to have nodded off, at which point three dimly outlined figures slipped out of their hutment and prepared to cross the compound to its east gate.

"Get a move on, will you!" the look-out hissed urgently. He raised a hand in brief salutation. "And – good luck. Give our regards to Blighty, boys."

As they passed through the gate – which remained unlocked so the sentries might patrol the area as duty demanded – very cautiously, first one figure, then a second, followed close by a third, began to steal up the east road towards the front of the camp, heading for the main road that ran along its south end. The time was 0245.

Lt. J. Reeves, Captain Spragg-Mitchell and Captain Gordon Clover had been planning their breakout for some time now, and they had enlisted the help of certain brother officers in their hut to act as lookouts. As the three men crept through the dark, a slight movement in the guard-box halted Gordon Clover bringing up the rear, warning him that the sentry possibly had been alerted.

Unable to caution his two companions who were already some distance ahead, he hesitated. Believing, if they had indeed been spotted, the chances of all three making it past the guard were less than slim, Captain Gordon Clover quickly stepped back into the shadows. Pressing himself into the darkness, he beat a hasty retreat back to his hut. And none too soon, as the crack of rifle shots shattered the night.

"What the ruddy hell is happening out there?" Captain Anthony Dunlop Steven, one of the lookouts, grabbed hold of Clover as he slipped in the door.

"They rumbled us – right from the get-go. Couldn't warn the others. Devil of it is, I could swear, somehow, they knew what was going down tonight. Walked right into it, I'm afraid."

"Bloody Jesus! A snitch? But who?"

"That damn chappie! What's his name – odd sort of bloke – tries to curry favour with the guards. You know, he's forever hobnobbing with the Italian interpreter. Yugoslavian or some such, no one really knows where he's from – changes allegiance like my sis changes beaus. I'll wager it's him; bent as a nine-bob note, that one."

"I know the one. Sullen sort of cove, hangs about just within earshot. Told him to shove off the other day."

"Bugger that for now! Quick! Stash your kit. Get the ruddy thing out of sight; they're bound to land on us like an act of God!"

"What the dickens happened to Reeves and Mitchell? They're in for it, I daresay."

"Gone over the top, I think," Clover said. "Can't see how they'll make it though, poor bastards. They were way out front when the flap began – there was no way of warning them. Just made it by a whisker m'self."

Lt. Reeves and Captain Spragg-Mitchell had, indeed, made a mad dash for the main road at the front of the camp. By then, however, the sentry in the southwest guard-box had opened fire as well. Somehow, with all the odds stacked against them, both men managed to get past the wire and into the field beyond. Sadly, their freedom was short-lived – and here they were brought down.

Sentries from the guardroom by the main gate ran up, and in spite of finding both men lying on the ground in obvious surrender, the Italians kicked the prone bodies and continued firing at point blank range. Captain Spragg-Mitchell received eighteen wounds to his head and chest. He died on the spot. Lt. Reeves, though partially protected by Mitchell's body, was wounded seventeen times. Amazingly, he remained alive.

By now the camp was agog with rumours. Peering out of his hutment window, Santi saw the guards carry two bodies, stretched out on ladders, to the MI Room in the far southeast corner of the camp. Before long, everyone was ordered to the dining hut where Lt. Col. Nicoletti took roll call; and when the identities of the two escapees were brought to light, the assembly was informed both men had been shot, regrettably resulting in the death of one of them. In the shocked, pindrop silence that followed this pronouncement, the Commandant further informed them that both, dead and wounded, now lay in the infirmary.

When they dispersed, Captain George Burnaby Drayson, then Senior British Officer in camp, approached Santi.

"Doc, while Nicoletti was giving his spiel, I managed a quick look-in at Mitchell and Reeves. What I saw was an absolute shocker, and I don't believe all that guff about 'regrettable'. Something doesn't smell quite right here. Their wounds are much too extensive to be explained away that simply. Seems to me, somebody's made a right balls-up of this entire affair, and now there's an attempt at a cover-up – and if there is, by Jove, there'll be the devil to pay, I promise you that!" He shook his head angrily. "Why in blazes should it have come to this? It's a rotten thing to have happened. There has got to be an investigation, and I won't accept the folderol they are trying to feed us. It won't do I say!"

Santi nodded. "I'd like to take a look at Reeves and Mitchell myself – at least to make sure Camillo, the MO, is doing everything possible for Reeves. Maybe I can assist Captain Camillo in taking care of him. If they've nothing to hide, he should be glad of the help. Besides, depending on Reeve's condition, he might be able to tell us first-hand what actually happened. It's our only chance of getting to the truth. And Mitchell's wounds should help fill in the rest."

"Certainly the information will be necessary for a proper investigation," Drayson agreed, thoughtfully. "But, we will need Nicoletti's permission, of course."

"As Senior Officer you have every right to ask it, don't you, sir? And in the capacity of British Medical Officer, I could request that I be allowed to accompany you."

When approached, Camp Commandant Lt. Col. Guglielmo Nicoletti, despite furious objections, refused to allow anyone access to the two men in the MI Room. For the three hours that Lt. Reeves remained in camp at Capua, not a single British officer or doctor was granted permission to attend him or, in any way, to see to his welfare.

Eventually, he was removed to the hospital at Caserta, and Captain Camillo and his staff retired for the night. Medical Orderly Corporal Mair, RAMC, a Scotsman, was left in charge of the MI Room, and it was only then that Santi and Captain Drayson were able to gain access to the body of Captain Spragg-Mitchell.

What they saw both horrified and angered them. The young man's body was riddled with bullets, sixteen in all, with a couple of bullet wounds to the head as well. His face looked like it had been kicked or bludgeoned with the butt of a rifle. It was not until a few days later that anyone would learn further details of what had occurred that night of 18-19 August, 1942.

———•◆•———

CAPTAIN SPRAGG-MITCHELL, CAPTAIN Gordon Clover, Lt. J.H. Reeves and Lt. John William Burman had been planning their escape for a while. But, before they could put their plan into action, Lt. John William Burman had the bad luck – or so he believed at the time – to be struck down by illness. The unhappy young man had contracted jaundice and, consequently, was removed to nearby Caserta Hospital. The three remaining protagonists decided to forge ahead with their plans, regardless.

On the morning of 19 August, Lt. Burman was still in Caserta Hospital, lying in bed, recovering from jaundice and unaware of the events that had taken place in camp the night before. But he did witness first-hand what occurred later, when Lt. Reeves was brought into the hospital. And, upon his recovery and return to camp, he was able to recount for the other POWs the details of that morning.

It was obvious Lt. Reeves had been shot several times – seventeen times Lt. Burman was to learn later – and before he was taken into surgery, in spite of his critical condition, he managed three words to Lt. Burman.

"They got Mitchell."

Later that same afternoon, when Reeves was brought out of surgery, he was put in a bed not far from Lt. Burman. The proximity was intentional, overseen by Lt. Col. M.R. Sinclair, the British Medical Officer at Caserta who had operated on him.

"How is he, sir," Burman asked.

"Still groggy," Sinclair replied. "A word to him now and then, if you would – might help to know he isn't alone."

"Of course, sir. Is he going to make it, you think?"

Sinclair was silent for a moment. When he spoke, his voice was low. "He's in bad shape, I'm afraid. Lost a great deal of blood due to the delay in bringing him here. He needs a blood transfusion if he's to have any sort of a fighting chance, but these tossers refuse to give him one. I tried insisting, but the Italian doctors will have none of it. Blackguards, the lot of 'em! I believe they feel it's a waste of resources."

He shook his head angrily as he leaned over the wounded man. Reeves hadn't stirred. Assuring himself, for the present, there was nothing more to be done, Sinclair departed with a promise to look in later.

"What became of Reeves?" Santi prompted.

"At first there was no way of communicating with him," Burman said. "After Col. Sinclair left, a group of Italian Officers gathered round his bed, and in spite of his condition, insisted on interrogating him – but Reeves refused to speak to them. Finally, when they left, we managed to exchange a few words. He hadn't much strength left, but seemed to want to talk."

Reeves was unusual in that he had not started out a subaltern. He was a 'squaddie', a tough young man of good, hardy British stock who had joined the 42nd Royal Tank Regiment as an enlisted man and worked his way up through the ranks. His enterprise had led to promotion, from sergeant to 2nd Lieutenant and the officer corps. Now, despite his weakness, he fought hard for his life, and even drummed up enough spirit to indulge in some slight banter.

"Good thing you were not there, eh John? Bleedin' cock-up, it was." He had smiled wanly. "Who'd've thought you'd be grateful for comin' down with the jaundice like you did?" He stopped as though he found it difficult to go on.

"Don't talk just yet, old chap" Burman had advised. "Time enough for that later. Save your strength for now, rest a while."

Reeves shook his head ever so slightly, and continued. "Must...tell someone. Mitchell and me...made it over the top, y'know; but they did us in the field." He paused, closing his eyes for a moment.

"Those few seconds...freedom...too few.... Damn good feeling though. Heard 'em behind as we legged it...the noise, shouting, shooting...giving chase...heard Mitchell cry out behind.... Tried to turn...got hit then. We tried to...to surrender, you know...but the... swine...gave us a real stuffing! Kept firing, kicking too...we were down, but.... Bastards...good as murdered poor old Mitchell."

He stopped, exhausted. Finally, he said very softly, "Too bad. We could've made it back, you know. But...John...I think my goose is cooked..."

As the day progressed, he became increasingly restless, and although he tried valiantly to fight for his life, by nightfall he had grown much weaker. As the night wore on, it became obvious he was losing the battle.

Burman called to him a few times to let him know he was not alone, but Reeves was unable to respond. The next morning, he lingered on the verge of delirium until sometime in the afternoon when he slipped over the edge into unconsciousness.

Lt. J.H. Reeves, thirty-two years of age, never regained consciousness. He finally, quietly, passed away on 20 August, 1942.

THE CAMP REMAINED UNDER a cloud of gloom, and in that dismal atmosphere their confinement irked the POWs even more than before.

On 27 August, a week after the killing of Reeves and Mitchell, Royal Artillery gunner Harris Stanley in the ORs compound was unable to bear incarceration a moment longer. Half crazed, he made a desperate bid for freedom by flinging himself on the barbed-wire fence in broad daylight. He was shot immediately. His twisted body hung on the wire, twitching, a ghastly spectacle for all to see, until a couple of guards removed him to the infirmary where he died.

Lt. Reeves's body had been removed from Caserta Hospital and buried in the cemetery in Caserta. Captain Spragg-Mitchell had been buried in the cemetery in Capua where Gunner Harris Stanley was now to be interred as well.

If not in life, at least in death their funerals were shown due respect by the Italians. All three men were buried with full funeral honours in accordance with the rights of the Anglican Church. Notification of both incidents was made – from the Italian standpoint – and was given by the Italian Foreign Office to the Red Cross in Bern.

After that the days passed in dreary succession, each one duller than the last. And, as the weather began to turn cold, life settled into a monotonous affair that continued until the advent of winter. Like most of his companions, Santi lost weight due to the quality and lack of food, and to sleep harrowed by nightmares. Slowly, they learnt to compensate for those things they did not have, and to make do with what they did have or could scrounge. The overcrowding was distressing, and it increased with each batch of new arrivals.

However, in November, all thought of discomfort was temporarily forgotten when a small group of prisoners arrived with news that lifted the spirits of the interned men. Bernard Montgomery had finally landed a defeat on Rommel at El Alamein, the Allies had recaptured Tobruk, and the enemy had been pushed back west, to Tunisia once more. At last!

Furthermore, on 8 November, an American convoy from the United States had landed in Morocco, French North-West Africa, fifteen miles north of Casablanca. There, the French, after some tepid resistance, had decided to join the Allies. More heartening still, came news that additional British and American forces from England had landed in Algeria.

Operation Torch was in full swing. The battle in the Western Desert was ongoing, but the Axis, squeezed between British and American forces, were being driven out of North Africa.

Finally, the gods seemed to have smiled on the Allies in Egypt! And, to the sound of church bells that had remained silent for three long, dark years, Churchill announced to the beleaguered English nation: *"We have a victory – a remarkable victory!...Now, this is not the end. It is not even the beginning of the end. But it is, perhaps, the end of the beginning."* (Lord Mayor's Luncheon, Mansion House, London, 10 November 1942)

The Battle of the Cauldron had been avenged, but the war wasn't over by a long shot.

<hr>

TOWARDS THE END OF November, orders came for the transfer of prisoners to permanent POW camps. Some were to go to Germany, while others were to be sent to various camps in Italy. The time had come to say goodbye.

Santi discovered, only after the fact, that Dilbahadur and the Gurkha Other Ranks had been taken from camp a day previously; their destination was unknown. He had been unable to properly thank the intrepid Gurkha who had taken him under his wing when they left their native shores together, who had stood by him and, without demur, served him so loyally as batman, medical orderly and noble friend. Santi hoped, wherever he was, he would, somehow, receive his silent messages of appreciation and gratitude.

He shook hands with Robert and Ronnie. As he took his leave of the two Englishmen, he realised that the initial reserve and awkwardness he had felt in their company had been replaced by a comradeship of sorts – an unspoken kinship of mutual respect, forged in fires that had changed and shaped each one, leaving hidden scars that could not be shared, or understood, by anyone who had not been there.

They thanked one another and parted company, going their separate ways. Robert and Ronnie were sent north to the POW camp at Fontanello, while Santi was transferred to Aversa, a POW camp for Indian officers, a little south of Capua. They were never to see each other again, but they carried memories that would last a lifetime. Memories Santi would lay to rest in a small box, carefully hidden away, until their discovery by his daughter nearly six decades later that would lead her to search and piece together, once more, the story of these old comrades-in-arms.

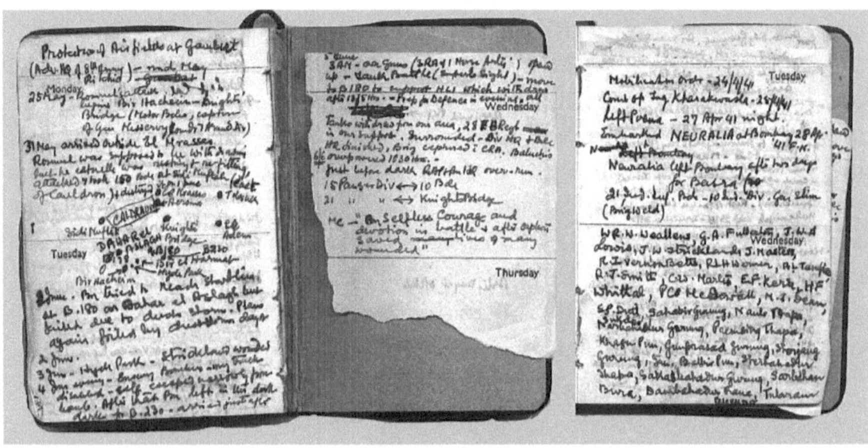

Santi's wartime diary.

CHAPTER FORTY-FIVE

The Viceroy's Tea Party

Hatter: Do you care for tea?
Alice: Why, yes, I'm very fond of tea.
Hatter: If you don't care for tea,
you could at least make polite conversation!
Alice: Of all the silly nonsense…well…!!

– Lewis Carroll, *Alice in Wonderland*

OVEMBER WAS THE HERALD of winter, and towards the end of that month the weather had turned pleasantly cool. The *pujos* were over – not that anyone had enjoyed them much, under the circumstances – but news had arrived finally that Santi was alive, a reprieve that lightened the atmosphere almost to the point of euphoria in J. P. Dutt's home in Chinsurah.

The fact he was a prisoner of war somewhere in Italy, perhaps even wounded, was still cause for concern; but at least now, God willing, there was a good chance that sometime, when the fighting was over, he would return home. For the present, that hope, compared to the utter despair of losing him forever, was more than sufficient reason to give thanks.

November, as usual, also saw the return of the Governor General of Bengal to Calcutta. Together with his entourage, the Governor and his family vacated their summer abode in Darjeeling to return to Government House in Calcutta, where they remained in residence until the commencement of next summer's heat.

Through the holiday season, and all through the winter months, Government House saw a flurry of dinner parties, balls, 'at homes' and levees thrown for select officials and very select members of the public. Accordingly, an invitation had been issued to Dr. J. P. Dutt, Civil Surgeon of Hooghly, to attend a garden party in honour of His Excellency the Viceroy, Lord Linlithgow. The gilt-edged card included an RSVP to be returned to the Governor General's Aide-de-Camp intimating the exact number of guests who would be attending.

J. P. Dutt felt it behooved his position to attend, but Usha Moyee, not bound by any such duty, immediately declined; until her son was safely home, she had no heart for social gatherings of any sort. As for the remaining family, the last time such an invitation was received, the older siblings had attended. This time, much to their delight, it was to be the younger girls, Sudha, Kamala and Lebu – and, in spite of their stalwart support of the freedom movement, young girls will be young girls, and this function, which promised to be no mean affair, was not something to be passed up lightly.

Eventually, the day dawned, and Government House was abustle with pomp and circumstance. J.P. Dutt arrived at 6pm with his daughters in tow. Visitors were still arriving in droves, under the watchful eye of two smartly uniformed sentries standing guard on either side of the imposing front gates, now thrown open to admit them.

Once inside, the high fashion ladies and gentlemen, clad in their finest, picked their way up the gravel path to mingle with, and swell the ranks of the elegant company already present in the garden. It was a bright, busy scene with the Viceroy's guests pooling into small groups that dotted the grounds; friends and acquaintances exchanging pleasantries, while others wended their way to small tables arranged for them on the immaculately manicured lawns.

To one side, at the ready, stood a band uniformed in red and gold. On the other side, a marquee had been erected beneath which long buffet tables were laden with a spread of pastries, petit fours, tartlets, and a choice of dainty tea sandwiches made with wafer thin slices of cucumber, egg salad with cress, and fine slivers of smoked salmon on cream cheese. Aromatic Darjeeling and Assam teas, and a choice of cold beverages were available to quench the thirsty.

Amid this very English repast, a single Bengali sweet, *ledikeni*, held pride of place on the table. It was, in a way, a byproduct of the Raj from it's nascent days when Lady Charlotte Canning was first Vice-rene of India. Having taken a fancy to the *pantua*, a humble Bengali dessert, that lady decided it should be served at a party on the occasion of her birthday. Renowned confectioner, Bhim Nag, was put to the task of making some slight modifications, and the result proved so outstanding, it became a custom perpetuated by the Vicerene's successors down the years. Subsequently, a colloquial corruption of 'Lady Canning' resulted in the dish being called '*ledikeni*', and it took its place among the vast array of Bengali sweets available to this day.

Now, to ensure the guests enjoyed this lavish spread, uniformed bearers with starched turbans and scarlet, gold-trimmed cummerbunds stood at the ready with replenishments so no plate, cup or glass should, at any time, remain empty.

Dr. J.P. Dutt and his three daughters joined the melee. Though she had deemed it inappropriate for herself, Usha Moyee had done her daughters proud for this occasion. Sudha's sari was a gorgeous *benarasi* of heavy purple silk, its border and *pallu* embroidered with gold, while Kamala shimmered in an elegant *mysore* silk of magenta and green, finely edged with gold. Both girls had their hair swept back into elegant *khopas* perfumed with jasmine flowers, the buns lying softly low at the nape, in true Bengali fashion. Even Lebu had been persuaded to bring her mop of unruly curls into a submission of sorts. She had been coaxed, cajoled and eventually threatened with being left behind unless she dressed and behaved like a young lady of standing. Now, wrapped in a soft bisque *tasore* silk elaborately embroidered throughout with birds and flowers in pale shades of pink, green and lemon, she passed muster very nicely indeed.

Bright and brilliant as the girls were, there was no concern of being overdressed. Their attire was perfectly in keeping with that opulent assembly which had turned out, as expected, in all its glory. His Excellency's visitors flitted about the gardens, looking for all the world like a collection of brilliant butterflies and cockatoos.

Across the spectrum could be seen Britishers and Indians, as well as an assortment of Anglo-Indians, Armenians, Parsees, Jews, and various other foreigners; the women in their fashionable hats and swirling dresses, their ornate sarees and jewels sparkling in the evening light; the men in their best suits, their national dress and, last but most certainly not least, to complete that gala crowd, the ever-present officers resplendent in their respective uniforms.

All at once the band struck up, and everyone stood for the arrival of Lord and Lady Linlithgow, Viceroy and Vicereine of India. Their Excellencies were followed closely by the Governor General Sir John Herbert and his wife, together with other members of their inner circle. After the formality of an opening speech from Lord Linlithgow, short enough to welcome the guests but not long enough to bore them, Sir John Herbert invited all and sundry to enjoy the evening's hospitality, a signal that they were free to mingle once more at will, and to partake of the repast laid out for their pleasure.

Picking their way through the array of refreshments, Sudha, Kamala and Lebu then went in search of a vacant table. One that held promise was occupied already by an elderly British Officer and a fractionally younger, very respectable looking Indian gentleman, both deep in conversation.

After introductions, it turned out by pure coincidence, that Major Billingsby-Smyth, now retired, had served several years with the 4th Gurkhas, and was but recently returned from a visit to his old

Regimental Headquarters in Bakloh. He was delighted to learn the young ladies had a brother, presently attached as doctor to the 2nd Battalion of his old Regiment. A well-renowned Battalion to be sure, the erstwhile soldier nodded, and what a pleasant circumstance they should meet like this! His companion, Prasanta Chatopadhay, was a Bengali doctor who, as the conversation progressed, was equally pleased to discover that he could, in fact, claim the acquaintance of their father. What a small world, indeed!

Seventy-eight-year-old Major Billingsby-Smyth averred, though he might be British by nationality, he could just as well lay claim to being Indian; not only by dint of his birthplace, but by a distant – albeit very distant – connection to Major-General Charles 'Hindoo' Stuart, that engaging officer of the British East India Company who had enjoyed life in Calcutta in the late 18th to early 19th century. Major Billingsby-Smyth proclaimed the relationship could be traced back, by a somewhat tenuous thread, to a shared ancestry that hailed from the town of Limerick in Ireland.

"But why '*Hindoo*'? Why was he known as '*Hindoo*' Stuart?" Sudha asked, her curiosity piqued.

"Ah, well! Therein lies a tale, m'dear. It seems my illustrious ancestor earned that unusual moniker due to his practice of certain customs and rituals that went with a Hindu way of life.

"Oh? Such as?"

"Well, contrary to social mores of the time, it seems he rather preferred certain Indian traditions to those brought over by the Europeans. He is said to have taken an Indian *bibi*, eschewing the usual European companion – which would, as his kin, ratify my claim to being Indian, would it not! To compound all, the hearty fellow, quite openly, would trot down to the Ganges every morning to join in the religious rites of the bathers in that holy river. Later, he would be seen, comfortable as you please, attired in Indian dress, enjoying his hookah while holding forth on the benefits of local customs."

The Major paused a moment before continuing. "Of course, he was by no means first to break ranks. Another such was Job Charnok, founder of this city, who not only donned Indian garb but went one further by marrying a young widowed Hindu lady he rescued from the fires of *suttee*. Quite a romantic story that – and quite a thriller too, for they say he managed, in the very nick of time, to pull her from the flames of her old husband's funeral pyre. Yes, yes indeed! Intermingling was not that uncommon in the days before the 'fishing fleet' arrived."

"What fishing fleet?" Lebu frowned. "Who were they, and why did their fishing change things?"

"Who were they, you ask!" Billingsby-Smyth gave a hoot of laughter. "Well, I'll tell you. They were young women out of England, dozens of them, who came here by the boatload in the hope they might catch and land themselves a husband. They were dubbed, appropriately if rather unkindly, the 'fishing fleet'. And with them came an unwelcome snobbery that ruined everything. Men still wielded the power of government, but women now dictated the class distinctions that would divide society.

"Before long there was no place for good men like Charles Stuart, willing to flout their petty discriminations. What a character! He would attend Hindu religious ceremonies in his Indian attire, sitting cross-legged on the floor among the locals, quite as much at ease as though he had been born to it. As a matter of fact, he had a vast and varied collection of *murtis* of the Indian gods and goddesses to whom he paid homage. Went native and gave the Christian missionaries quite a turn, so I'm told," the Major chuckled.

"He might actually have been a Hindu in some previous life, and the old customs might have come naturally to him," Kamala suggested, thoughtfully. "We do believe in reincarnation, you know."

"Or, perhaps," Lebu piped up, eyes dancing with mischief, "he might even have been Nawab Siraj-ud-Daulah, nemesis of the British! You remember him? Ruler of Bengal, fought the English, was said to have imprisoned one hundred and forty-three of them in the Black Hole at Fort William." She gave an exaggerated shiver. "And maybe, because of that wicked, wicked deed, it was his karma to be born an Englishman in his next life…"

"Really, Shoba!" Sudha rebuked her youngest sibling. "You've always said you don't believe in such things. And anyway, he was Muslim, not Hindu, so it doesn't fadge." She turned to the Major with an apologetic smile. "She has a wild imagination and comes out with the oddest things, as you can tell. But please go on; tell us about your ancestor. What became of him?"

"Became of him? Why, he is buried right here in Calcutta, in the South Park Street Cemetery – just as he should be, don't you think? And his grave is easily found. In the midst of all those very proper Christian mausoleums, it stands out as bold as you please – a remarkable black stone edifice built to resemble a Hindu Temple, wouldn't you know!" The Major gave a hearty guffaw. "He has the best of both worlds, you see, for he is interred in an Anglican cemetery while being surrounded by his favourite Hindu deities."

"What an interesting man he must have been," Lebu declared. "I should have liked to have met him. A most unusual Englishman who…"

"No, no! Dear me, not an Englishman! Let it never be said he was English! It was an Irishman he was, and very much so."

"Well, a Britisher then, who came to India and learnt to respect our customs instead of trying to make…ooomphh!" Lebu gasped, clutching her right side and glaring indignantly at Kamala.

Her sister had nudged a hard elbow into her ribs – a painful necessity, she explained later, to prevent her 'putting her foot in it as usual'; and while Lebu tried to catch her breath, Kamala deftly drew attention away from her sister's intemperate remark.

"We've often passed by that cemetery," she smiled, "but we've never been inside. Next time maybe we can stop and visit your ancestor; I would like to see Major-General Stuart's grave."

"Your's seems to be a long and illustrious history in this country, Major Billingsby-Smyth," Dr. Prasanta Chatopadhay interrupted. His English diction betrayed only a glimmer of the usual Bengali accent, but no hint of the history that had gone into acquiring it.

English delivered in a true-blue Bengali accent had certain inalienable idiosyncracies that were hard to miss. Typically, when a Bengali attempted the oral delivery of the delicate letter '*v*', it would almost invariably be usurped by its assertive relative in the alphabet, the stubborn letter '*b*'. Then again, the sounds of the letter '*s*' and the combined letters '*sh*' would oftentimes, quite without rhyme or reason, switch places. And the perfectly unobjectionable, everyday '*ah*' would more often than not find itself rolled into a softly rotund '*o*'. As for the unfortunate letter '*w*', in some instances it would be irretrievably lost, never making it beyond the lips no matter how earnestly they were puckered in anticipation of delivery.

These mispronunciations, however, were hardly discernible in the case of Dr. Chatopadhay, who had divested himself of them during his student years in England.

He had first arrived on the shores of that country at the tender age of nineteen, in the year 1897; it was the year of Queen Victoria's diamond jubilee, celebrating sixty years on the throne. Inexperienced and quite green, he had attended the festivities with a like friend who had managed, somehow, to find a place of some promise amid the crowds thronging the streets; it would, with any luck, afford them a good view of the royal procession as it passed by.

Come, come quickly, his friend had called loudly, beckoning him. *Thees 'ould be a bhery good place phor us. There ees nowhere to shit, but as se passes se bhill hear us eef we call out weeth gusto, 'God shave the Queen!'*

At the time they had been unable to fathom the strange looks thrown their way. But much had changed during his many years sojourn in England, and now the good doctor continued in near perfect Oxford diction. "And you say you were born here? In Calcutta?"

"Indeed, I was born on the 5th of October 1864, a good twenty-four hours later than I was expected," Billingsby-Smyth replied. "And I should be glad of the delay, so I am told; for heaven help me, I might never have arrived had I been punctual and kept to the time of the previous day the doctor had predicted. That, you see, was the day of the great cyclone of Calcutta which brought everything to a standstill. And although there have been one or two others in the years that followed, I have been given to understand that this city has witnessed nothing quite like that one before or, indeed, since."

"Why is that so? What happened?" Lebu wanted to know.

"Well you may ask, my dear, and I shall tell you too, just as it was told me. No one could come or go that day, and the violence of the winds was not to be withstood. It uprooted trees, toppled houses and blew ships moored in the Hooghly into a monstrous pile – as far inland, would you believe, as Howrah Railway Ghat.

"No! Could that actually happen?" Sudha asked, incredulous.

"Yes, yes, terrible." Dr. Chatopadhay concurred. "Heard it wreaked havoc in the city and its surroundings. Even though, as one can imagine, the populace was nowhere near as dense as it is now."

"But, I mean, did anyone actually see ships pile up like that?"

"Our old *khansama* swore he did," said the Major. "Chappie worked on a P&O boat before he came to us; and it was many a tale he told of an evening when the winds were high and stormy, and the air smelt of impending rain. The gusty weather always seemed to stir his memory of that terrible day.

"A giant wave, full thirty-four foot high, he said, rushed up the Hooghly from the Bay of Bengal at twenty miles an hour and smashed into Diamond Harbour. The boat he worked on was found near the Botanical Gardens. Another, a China steamer appropriately named *The Thunder*, was deposited onto the Strand, at the end of Hastings Street. And yet another vessel – now what was it called? Ah, yes! *The Earl of Clare* I think it was – well, she was discovered, if you please, near the Baranagore Jute Company!

"The city was in utter shambles, turned quite topsy turvy; and there were a number of deaths among the local citizenry. Most unfortunate. Nobody is quite sure how many perished. Alas, life among the poor is held cheap, don't you know. Nevertheless, it was a catastrophe that went down in the annals of this city's history which is, as one is well aware, known for its upheavals."

"Mmm, worst storm of all time." Dr. Chatopadhay chimed in. "Widespread disaster. Not as built-up as now, however."

"Ah, yes," concurred the Major, "quite different from the present. Very few multi-storieds in those days. It was all stately homes and bungalows with well-kept gardens, and a great deal of open space, as I remember. Quite outstanding!"

"Yes, yes, just so," the Doctor nodded agreement.

"Did you know," the Major turned to address the girls, "the site where our Grand Hotel now stands on Chowringhee was occupied by two small homes and a nice little boarding house run by an English lady, a widow named Mrs. Monk. I resided with her my first three months in this country, before I went on to a bachelor chummery. Those were good days, and I remember them fondly."

The Major leaned back. "No cars around then, just *palki-garries* and *ticca-garries,* manned by *coolie* and pulled by horse. And of course, the elegantly appointed private horse-drawn carriages used to be quite the thing. It was very fashionable to be seen in one, promenading of an evening along the waterfront of the Strand, or the Red Road beneath the *gulmohar* trees in full bloom, the ladies dressed in all their finery and the season's latest styles; very *beau monde,* indeed!"

"Similar to the *tongas* of today," Kamala offered.

"Certainly not! By no means can that fine mode of transport be compared to the mundane horse-drawn vehicle of today. Then, it had a certain refined presence about it that would disallow such comparison. I must say, those were splendid days, quite splendid!"

Billingsby-Smyth sighed, reminiscently. There was a long silence. The Major seemed lost in thoughts that took him meandering into half-forgotten, rambling byways of the past, and the girls waited patiently.

"Pomp and circumstance!" Dr. Chatopadhay piped up suddenly, breaking the silence.

The abrupt interruption startled his companions, and set Lebu giggling. The manner of it was so like that of the dormouse at Alice's tea party! She glanced over at her two siblings. If she remembered correctly, weren't there three sisters in that dozey little creature's story as well? *Once upon a time there were three little sisters…and they lived at the bottom of a well...a treacle well...*

Lebu giggled again as she looked around the table. What a curious company they made! Not as curious as Alice's tea party, of course; but then again, if Alice were present, might she not have insisted there was, indeed, *much of a muchness?* Lebu suppressed another giggle, and looking up, caught baleful glares from both her sisters.

Behave yourself! Sudha mouthed silently. *Or I will tell Father!* She was rescued from further reprimand by the Major, roused from his reverie.

"Quite so!" He took up where he had left off. "Yes, yes. Back then even our state occasions far outdid those of today, and an invitation to Government House promised an elaborately ceremonious affair. I must admit, the most memorable of all was the occasion of the Prince of Wales' visit to Calcutta. I was just a boy then. Perhaps it was the awe of a twelve-year old, but the gaiety and glamour dazzled my childish eyes and I remember it well – the winter of 1875. Calcutta was the capital of the British Raj then." The Major paused to help himself to a cucumber sandwich.

"Where there not two Princes of Wales who visited India?" Lebu interrupted.

"There were, indeed. But I refer to Queen Victoria's son, Prince Edward, later to become King Albert Edward VII. He had a great appreciation for India and her people, and was greatly appreciated in return; so much so, his visit to this country earned his mother her title, Empress of India."

"When he arrived here, what a to-do there was! We watched as His Royal Highness steamed up the Hooghly on the *HMS Serapis* to thunderous gun salutes from Fort William and three Royal Navy ships flying their colours. Flags flew and people cheered. A ceremonial *durbar* was held in the Prince's honour. Lord Northbrook, then Viceroy, resided here, at Government House, not Delhi as they do now. New Year's Day, the grandeur and pomp of the Chapter of the Order of the Star of India was quite the thing to see, let me assure you!"

"It must have been a very fashionable affair. Did you dress up to personally attend the ceremony?" Sudha leaned forward, agog with interest.

"Indeed I did. Of course, as children we were not to be seen or heard. We were allowed to watch the goings on from a discreet distance, under the chaperone of our *ayahs* and nannies. A magnificent marquee was erected, and leading up to it was a wide avenue hemmed on both sides with small tents for the convenience of those personages, both European and Indian, who were to be honoured that day. Dear me, what a splendid show it was, attended by Rajas and Ranis, Princes and Nawabs, even a couple of Begums in purdah! They were pointed out to us children, each ruler as he trod that path of honour, arrayed in magnificent robes bearing the Insignia of the Order of the Star of India. Each was attended by a retinue of servants carrying aloft their master's banner, flying it proudly high above his head. And throughout the ceremony the Royal Marine band played, till finally, all who were to be invested were seated on either side of the throne."

"And then? What happened next?"

"And then, finally, the Viceroy and the Prince of Wales arrived, escorted by a full bodyguard resplendent in brilliant scarlet tunics, flamboyant head-dress and gleaming Hessian boots. With their lances and their red and white pennants fluttering in the breeze as they went, I tell you, it was a sight to behold! Quite spectacular! The entire city was festive with buntings and flags – no decorative lights, of course, as we had no electricity then; it was candles and gas lights, and *punkah-wallahs* fanning us – all of which vanished with the turn of the century, like so much else…into the pages of history…"

Major Billingsby-Smyth paused on the edge of that youthful memory. He leaned back and sipped his tea. And, as his rapt listeners watched, he seemed to drift back once more into that long-lost world he had recalled, where he had taken them on a sprawling journey into a dim and distant past…through the looking glass and back again…

———•◆•———

THE OTHER SIDE OF the looking glass – outside the ornate gates of Government House, and in stark contrast to the goings on inside – in the outskirts of the great city of Calcutta, a very different sort of life prevailed; it was to have an impact that was already being felt in the bowels of the city.

Earlier that year, on 26 May, Burma had fallen to the Japanese. This had a two-fold impact on Bengal: the large imports of Burmese rice ceased, and an imminent Japanese invasion of India sent ripples of trepidation through the city. To impede the advance of the enemy, all boats were denied, and a 'scorched earth' order was executed in the Chittagong area bordering Burma. The disruption this caused to life in the area was compounded by thousands of refugees fleeing the war, crossing the border from Burma into India.

Furthermore, on 16 October the same year, a cyclone hit the east coast of Bengal and Orissa, flooding miles of rice fields and destroying the autumn crops. It caused such a shortage of food in the villages that the seed normally reserved for the winter planting had to be consumed for the villagers to sustain life.

What with continuous food supplies needed for frontline troops, and the hoarding of grain by nervous citizens and greedy black marketeers alike, the shortage of rice would soon spread to the city, and the resulting escalation in price would put what little remained beyond the means of the poor.

Sadly, with everything else going on in the world around them – the war, the struggle for freedom – these problems took a low priority. So much so, by the time the authorities did take heed, the crisis was full blown. It would culminate in a devastating famine starting in May 1943. The warning signs of this disaster could already be seen.

People had begun leaving the villages of Bengal, making their way to the mecca of the big city with its perceived promises of food and work. They came to Calcutta, on a journey made with faith and hope. A trickle at first, but before long they would be pouring in till they inundated the city, young and pitifully old, families squatting, living, dying on the streets of the heartless urban sprawl they had believed to be a beacon of salvation.

Men who could no longer raise their flagging hands, only their empty eyes, to beg; but mostly, the victims of this tragedy would be starving women and children. Women so emaciated and weak, they could hardly drag the shrivelled children who clung to them or bear the shrunken babies at their flaccid breasts, begging wherever they could, at shop entrances, in the doorways of private homes, for a little gruel, or even the starchy water discarded after rice is boiled:

"Ektu phan dao, Ma". Give me a little rice water, Mother.

This desperate plea for help would be burnt into the conscience of Bengal. The dreadful Bengal Famine of 1943-44 eventually would claim the lives of somewhere between two to three million of the poorest in the State and its surrounding areas. It was to become the swan song of the British Raj.

CHAPTER FORTY-SIX

Prigionieri Di Guerra Campo 63, Aversa

In the purple sky above me, showing dark against the twilight,
Long wav'ring flights of homeward birds fly low;
They cry one to the other, and their weird and wistful calling
Makes most melancholy music as they go.

– Violet Nicolson, *The Garden of Kama*, "Ojira"

SOME FOURTEEN MILES NORTH of Naples, within sight of old Mount Vesuvius, stands the medieval city of Aversa. It lies tucked away in the Campania region of Southern Italy, an agricultural area known for its wine and cheese, and especially for its buffalo mozzarella.

Of course, the inmates of the POW camp at Aversa enjoyed none of these amenities. The camp, reserved mainly for the internment of Indian Commissioned Officers, NCOs and VCOs of the British Indian Army, provided a near starvation diet of boiled macaroni and hard cheese, with the odd meal of rancid-smelling boiled fish and stale bread – hardly enough to keep body and soul together.

Santi, along with some of the VCOs from Capua, arrived at camp on a cold wintry afternoon. They took in the twelve-foot-high double surround of barbed wire that fenced almost forty muddy looking hutments, some larger than others. The larger ones were open dormitories that housed thirty beds each, with shared Indian-style lavatory facilities at one end; these buildings provided the accommodations for the VCOs. Separated by a shorter barbed wire fence and gate stood the smaller bungalows, each divided into six rooms, two beds to a room with private lavatories mid-building; these were the living quarters for the officers. Three bath houses, two mess halls – one for the officers and a separate one for the VCOs – a canteen and a recreation room completed the ensemble of buildings in use. There was a particular comfort to be had from being among one's own again.

The wood-framed prison barracks were constructed with a double layer of falsite and an outside covering of concrete camouflaged with variegated paint. This did little to keep out the cold, so in winter, as it was now, the barracks were freezing and dank. This misery was made worse still by the lack of warm clothing, and the only covering was two inadequately sparse blankets, issued to and paid for by each individual POW. Since layering was known to maximize the retention of body heat, these blankets were layered with their sheets not only as a covering for the night, but as a wrap for the day as well. Yet, nothing the POWs contrived could keep the bitter cold at bay.

Meals and amenities had to be paid for. A small stipend, in the form of coupons valued in lire, allowed the men to buy basic necessities at the canteen; at times, a few extras could be purchased as well, from an outside source, to augment their meagre diet.

This wretched state improved when Red Cross parcels began to arrive with warm clothes and packaged foods. Santi became the grateful owner of a pair of woollen gloves and a serge greatcoat. Later, when he acquired a pair of serge trousers as well, he felt himself to be in pretty good nick; he had decently warm clothes, his hand had healed well, as had his ribs, and he was fit, if a little thin. All in all, this was certainly better than Capua! On a whim, and to occupy himself, he even experimented growing his first moustache which, after some cultivation, reaped him a fairly decent reward.

Time did, indeed, lie heavy in the camp. There were books to read, cards and chess to play, and eventually the POWs were allowed to turn a large adjacent area into a playing field and basketball court, all of which helped to alleviate some of the boredom. For Santi and a few others who shared a similar bent of mind and body, basketball was a good way to sweat out the frustration of captivity.

Of course, nothing could compensate for the lack of freedom. Fortunately, one's mind retained the ability to escape the fetters of physical incarceration, remaining at liberty to fly above and beyond the confines of both barbed wire and armed guards. And these flights of fancy allowed the POWs to remain in touch with all they once had been – husbands and lovers, fathers, sons and brothers. However fleeting, this ability helped to maintain some sort of sanity. There were, as well, a few other doctors from Bengal, which allowed for some pleasant reminiscing of familiar haunts and customs of home. Among them was Satyen Basu, a few years senior to Santi. On many a boring evening, Lts. Basu and Sahabzada Yaqub, camp philosophers and poets both, could be counted on for some lively discourse on language, painting, music and dance.

Other times, when alone, Santi made the solitary journey back to happier realms, his thoughts winging their way free of his dismal surroundings, over treetops and mountain ridges, like a homing pigeon looking for a place to roost. Inevitably, on that homebound journey, a halfway resting place presented itself; a place of disconcerting memories and unanswered questions – a lovely face, a cloud of auburn hair, a tangle of emotions that sent a rush through him and made his heart swell so, he could feel it beat, hard, inside his chest, against his ribs and in his throat, almost as though it too were trying to break free.

POW Santi Dutt, 1943.

Cairo. Lying back on his bunk, his hands folded beneath his head, Santi wondered – what were winters like in Cairo? He imagined the desert would be bitterly cold this time of year. He remembered that cool summer evening when they had stood on those moonlit sands under the stars, the warmth of her body close against his; he recalled the fragrance of her in his arms when earlier, they had danced. The memory sent a shudder of desire through him. He felt his body tense, his muscles harden, and the intensity took him aback. He tried to picture Hedeya in the setting of her everyday life, and it irked him that she kept eluding his mind's eye. Did she think of him at all? And if she did, *what* did she think of him? What indeed! He had certainly set the cat among the pigeons at their last meeting and he hoped, rather ruefully, that she did not think him to be anywhere near as foolish as he felt.

And what of the others? What must *they* think of him; Bajo, politely putting up with his edginess as he waited, each passing minute pushing him closer to despair in the belief that he would have to leave for war without one final chance of seeing Hedeya, of telling her how he felt; the mind-numbing relief when she turned up at the last moment – he, so very nearly having missed her, already on his feet, ready to leave – and the consequent tongue-tied hash he had made of it after all that! And last, but certainly not least, the way his wild outburst had quite literally knocked the wind out of poor Asis Habib. He winced recalling it all, his behavior so surprisingly out of character, without deliberation jumping right in, impetuously following his heart, leaving his mind raising dire warning flags that went unheeded. Lord, what a chump he had made of himself!

His thoughts drifted homeward to find more solace there. Unlike memories of Cairo that caused him such mental and emotional turmoil, remembrance of home brought a sense of calm and comfort.

Calcutta winters were pleasantly cool, the evenings tinged with the promise of a gentle chill in the night air. By now the city would be welcoming its denizens returning from the hill stations as those closed for winter. And though the *pujos* would probably be over by now, at the first hint of cold weather, Calcutta would begin to prepare for the approaching Christmas season. The city would burgeon with holiday visitors come to enjoy the parties and merry-making, the decorations and lights that transformed it through the New Year.

And even after those revels were over, it was during the mid-winter months when the kitchens of Bengal would begin their preparations for *Poush Shankranti*. Sweet aromas of *puli pithey*, *pathishapta* and *malpua* would fill the air, fine confections of coconut cooked into a condensed cream laced with date-palm jaggery and spiced with cardamom, delicate crepes of rice flour and semolina steamed to perfection in sweet, thickened milk. God, he was hungry! Nostalgia filled Santi with a sudden wave of homesick longing.

Thus, evermore frequently in the days that followed, his thoughts would journey homeward, visiting loved ones and familiar places, building an album of carefully preserved memories. He learnt to use this avenue as a brief escape from the stark privation of the prison camp by blotting out his surroundings and turning his mind's eye inward, allowing it to wander through his stash of memories; to browse, to lift out this one, or that, to gently unfold it and slowly steep himself in the familiar warmth, wrapping it about him, savouring each sensation of pleasure, loss, amusement, nostalgia, that he might forget the present and immerse himself in the comfort of better times.

One cold winter afternoon, taking his regular walk, Santi strode along the cemented area between the rows of hutments, the pale sunshine pleasantly warm in his face and on his back. In the distance, the snow-clad summit of Mount Vesuvius belched smoke, a sleeping dragon wreathed in memories of a long-ago glory. On rare occasions, at night, the small flame-tipped tongue of this somnambulant giant could be seen flicking its lips in patient anticipation – *beware, be warned, for one day I shall awake!* An eerie yet magnificent sight to behold.

Today, however, the mountain dozed peacefully, and only the smallest puffs of dragon-breath hinted at its dreams, past and future. Santi's thoughts were far away. He was pulled back to the present by the sudden appearance of a prison guard on a bicycle who hove into sight around a corner. As the man peddled away, a second guard ran up, into the path of the oncoming cycle, frantically waving it to a halt.

A stream of Italian curses, vividly descriptive, filled the air as the cyclist tried, unsuccessfully, to comply. He landed instead in a heap at the feet of the culprit who attempted to sidestep this accident he had caused – not swiftly enough it would seem, for as the angry cyclist went down, his arms flailing wildly to save himself, he latched onto the one object left standing in his vicinity and took him down as well. The sight of the two men struggling in a tangled heap on the ground flipped Santi's mind back to a long-forgotten memory from his boarding school days; and as the amusing incident slipped into focus, it brought a smile to his lips that slowly widened into a grin.

He had learnt to cycle when he was just a hair shy of fifteen. That year, during the *pujo* season, Hare School's football team had been invited to play a match against a longtime outside rival team. After winning the game, instead of heading straight back to school with the other boarders – as he ought to have done – he decided to pay a visit to a nearby temple. It was neither the noble call of salvation nor the reverent need to worship that prompted this presumably pious act; if truth be told, it was the very earthly and rather base sin of gluttony that tempted the schoolboy, for it was common knowledge that a sumptuous vegetarian meal was always served upon completion of the *pujo* offered in honour of the deity being celebrated.

Santi had, by now, mastered the art of cycling, but had not yet endeavoured a lone journey of much length on the teeming streets of

Calcutta. However, he was trundling along very well indeed, concentrating hard on manoeuvring the pitfalls and potholes along the way, when a respectable looking Bengali gentleman attired in a bright white, beautifully laundered *dhuti panjabi* stepped off the kerb, almost immediately in front of the cycle.

Peering down the road faced away from the oncoming cycle, the dignified middle-aged gentleman was quite oblivious of the impending disaster behind him as he raised his umbrella to hail a passing taxi. Santi swerved, desperately trying to avoid the man, but the cycle wobbled so furiously it was all he could do to keep from falling off.

It was at this point the bicycle decided to assert itself. Uncannily, almost as though it had a will all its own, it carried Santi forward and, with the curiosity of a friendly dog, it nosed its way from behind and nudged itself between the unsuspecting man's legs. It scooped him up so swiftly, and with such perfect precision, the astounded man found himself lifted off the ground, into the air and deftly deposited astride the front wheel of the bicycle.

The next alarming instant, he was sailing along with his *dhuti* billowing out about him in glorious white clouds, like a parachute. For a few stunned seconds the dazed man sat dumbfounded, quite robbed of his wits – and then the full portent of his ignominy struck home. With a loud outraged yell, he went into attack mode. Facing away from Santi, all he could manage was a wild flailing of his umbrella as he attempted to shower blows on the miscreant behind him while he thundered insults in three languages.

"*Shala, shuwarer bacha! Haram zada!* Rapscallion! Bounder, Son of a Pig! Offspring of Iniquity!"

Desperately, Santi tried to ward off the blows, apologizing profusely all the while as he attempted to mollify his unwilling passenger, explaining that his hijacking had been completely unintentional. It was at that precise moment the school bus happened along on the scene, bringing loud hoots of laughter with much hilarious encouragement from its occupants. All of which only went to fuel the older gentleman's fury and the younger one's misery – misery not only inflicted by the renewed barrage of blows being rained upon him, but in the certain knowledge as well of the unmerciful ragging he would no doubt endure later.

The last scene witnessed by the gleeful school boys as their bus turned the corner was that of both cyclist and passenger tussling frantically on the ground with nine yards of *dhuti*, all tangled up in the still spinning wheels of the bicycle.

Sure enough, news of the escapade filtered back to school, and the next day, after tiffin, Santi received a summons from the Headmaster. Obeying, he dragged himself on feet of lead to Dr. Raisaheb Adyanath Roy's office, and with ever increasing trepidation he waited till, finally, he was bid enter that inner sanctum sanctorum.

"Mister Dutt."

"Sir." Trying hard not to squirm, he stood before the Headmaster's desk, and swallowed nervously. He had a fairly good idea what lay in store for him and strove, unsuccessfully, not to shuffle his feet.

Dr. Roy eyed the boy sternly. He knew him to be a good pupil and an excellent athlete, but rules were rules and not to be flouted. It would do no harm to let him sweat a few seconds longer. And so, after what seemed an age, the Headmaster barked a single sentence.

"Truancy and public misbehaviour, I believe."

Santi hung his head, forcing himself to stand straight, while wishing desperately he might disappear into the ground.

"As I see it," Dr. Roy continued, "you have a choice. Either I inform your father of the implausible prank you pulled yesterday, or I mete out your punishment myself, here and now. Which is it to be?"

Santi did not hesitate for an instant. Inform Father? Never!

"I'd rather go with the latter, Sir."

Dr. Roy nodded, picking up his cane. "Very well. Hold out your hands."

Two swift, sharp swats on each palm later, the Headmaster added, "You are too old to be sent to Coventry, though your behaviour certainly merits it. We do not tolerate hooligans here, Mister Dutt. This is an establishment for the education and nurture of young gentlemen. To that end we must impart discipline; it is the pillar, the struts and beams that support the vaulted ceiling of one's character, essential if such an edifice is to weather the storms of life. Please keep that in mind in the future."

Luckily the episode had ended there and, despite the welts on his smarting palms, Santi was grateful that Father never did find out. *That boy and his damn football again*, Father would have sworn – and his punishment, he was quite certain, would have been far more severe.

Those boyhood school days! How long ago it all seemed...

<hr>

"You seem to be a long way from here, Captain Dutt." A voice to Santi's left tugged him back to the present. He turned to find the senior officer in camp standing beside him. "Dashed good thing they can't incarcerate the mind, eh?"

Santi gave a short laugh. "Right you are, sir. Brings back memories of boyhood days."

He nodded towards the two guards who had, by now, picked themselves up off the ground, dusted themselves off and were involved in a graphic exchange of insults and gestures.

Major Paramasiva Prabhakar Kumaramangalam, a twenty-nine-year-old gunner officer from Tamil Nadu in South India, was the son of the Chief Minister of Madras Presidency. An Etonian who went on to graduate from the Royal Military Academy in Woolwich, he had been fighting with 2 Field Regiment when captured in the fracas in the Western Desert on 27 May, a scant nine days before the 2/4 had gone down in the Cauldron. This officer would later be awarded the DSO – Distinguished Service Order.

Aversa prisoner of war camp, Italy, 1943.

When first Santi had arrived in camp he had gone over and introduced himself to Major K as he was informally known. As Camp Senior Officer, the Major had given him the rules and regulations set by the camp authorities, as well as those set by the internees for themselves. A few days later, after a careful sounding out, he had taken Santi into his confidence and informed him of an ongoing plan for escape.

The plan was code-named 'Nargis', after the name of their homeland contact. Santi had been a willing recruit. The endeavour, regardless of outcome, broke the monotony and gave the participants a sense of purpose that helped to lift flagging spirits, and keep the doldrums at bay. The Major's next words immediately focused Santi's attention in the here and now.

"My last letter home was dated numerically rather than in the usual longhand – a pre-set code, as you know, indicating some of us are prepared to escape. I have just now received a coded reply from our contact, 'Nargis', which, I do believe, intimates that the next few parcels from the Red Cross should be of particular interest."

"Good to hear, sir! Any idea when we might expect them?"

"Fairly soon, I should hope. From what I gather the 'special' ones are collected from MI9 and, along with others from various collaborating sources, dispatched onward by the Red Cross. Only a select few officers are aware of this, so I have given instructions, upon arrival, I'm to be informed. The parcels are not to be disbursed till we've had a go at them first. Lts. Naravane and Tikka Khan, our Quarter Master, will see to that."

"Might I be of assistance as well, sir? Be happy to help if I can."

"I would like you to be present when the time comes. There will be the usual Italian officer overseeing each parcel and its contents. I'd like you to act as decoy. Distract him as best you can, but deftly, not to arouse suspicion. There is always the fear, of course, something unforeseen could raise a red flag, and he might tumble to what's afoot. Do what you can, bribe him if you must. I'm told those MI9 boys are up to snuff though, so we shall see what they manage. Meanwhile, have you met our Camp Adjutant, Lt. Yahya Khan? From 4/10 Baluch, your brigade, I believe."

"I haven't caught up with him yet, Sir. I look forward to it."

As it turned out, MI9 exceeded all expectations. Besides actual Red Cross packages, others were gathered from various foundations and organisations in England and Canada. Most were genuine charities, but some were carefully set-up fronts for MI9 to smuggle contraband escape items. Regardless, all packages were channelled and distributed through the Red Cross to POW camps in Germany and Italy, according to the number of internees in each camp.

Although there ought to have been one food package per POW per week, in actual fact, a substantial number quite often went to their captors instead, leaving the POWs to share the contents of a single package between five to eight men. Shared or otherwise, these food parcels were an invaluable lifesaver, received with much appreciation and gratitude by the homesick men.

On this occasion, Santi, Lt. Naravane and Lt. Tikka Khan took delivery of the packages. News spread quickly through the camp, drawing a large crowd of eager POWs to gather in anticipation of the goods being distributed. As expected, upon inspection it was apparent a fair amount of food stuff had been pilfered, but what remained was still a welcome bounty. Besides the usual bully beef (for the Muslims) and spam and bacon (for the Hindus), there were some very welcome tins of sardines; and in a nod to the ethnicity of this particular camp there were, would you believe, some parcels of rice, flour and *ghee* for a good old Indian cook-up, and – wonder of wonders – even a few well-assorted packets of spices to render the rather bland western victuals more acceptable to an Indian palate!

There was more: sugar, jam, margarine and Kraft cheese; dried egg flakes; Nestle's condensed milk, Allenbury's pre-digested milk, cereal and porridge. Satyen Basu edged into the inspection area, eyeing the Cadbury's chocolate, digestive biscuits and, oh joy, real tea and coffee! Even such luxuries as Ovaltine, Horlicks and Bovril had been included. A veritable feast! There was a large supply of vitamin tablets to keep everyone in good health. And, of course, those long-awaited cigarettes, Gold Flake packed in beautiful tins of 50.

The Red Cross kept all food packages perfectly above board and safe from compromise. Not so with every non-food package, where, here and there, prudently distributed among the contents, some articles were not at all what they purported to be. With every batch of parcels that came in, the POWs would search for these items till they had amassed all that was required to effect an escape.

To this end, it was essential that the Italian officer on duty be manoeuvred adroitly away from too close an inspection of the non-food parcels. It would require further sacrifice of some choice edible pickings, Santi realised, but well worth their loss if it prompted his quick departure. It did. The Italian hurried off to squirrel away his ill-gotten gains for later enjoyment – and, the way cleared, the packages of 'interest' were quickly removed to Major K's bunker.

With Satyen Basu posted as lookout to prevent any unwelcome intrusion, they fell to the task at hand. The third package Santi opened produced some boxes of matches and a few lighters. Upon closer scrutiny, however, something else was brought to light.

"Look here, sir," Santi exclaimed, "would you look at this! A small Minox camera! It's genius!" Encouraged by this first discovery, Santi pried open another parcel to reveal several uniforms.

"I say," he frowned, "I can't quite make it out…there seems to be something decidedly odd about these. Take a look, would you, Khan."

The two men examined the uniforms every which way. Only when turned inside out did Santi cotton on to their secret.

"This is incredible! If I'm not mistaken, these are designed to reverse into civies. What a damn ingenious idea!" Ingenious indeed; even more so when it turned out, one button on each jacket concealed a miniature compass!

"We've even been sent money. Probably fake, but it looks like the real thing." Lt. Khan shook out a shaving brush and two hair brushes that had been stuffed with Italian currency. "I almost missed these. Who would have imagined, the handles unscrew the wrong way!"

And so it went in the weeks and months that followed. Rooting through later arrivals of much appreciated home-knit sweaters, scarves and socks, a couple of boots produced two 'gigli' saws; the flexible wire instruments familiar to surgeons had been cleverly sewn into the laces. A few handkerchiefs were found to be mapped with invisible ink that, apparently, would turn visible when treated with one of the simplest, most easily available of all substances – urine!

"Well, well," Major K squinted through a small telescope, extracted from a cigarette holder. "This should come in very handy, I daresay."

Over a period, further consignments delivered still more seemingly innocuous everyday items, some of which, to those in the know, offered so much more. Pens held a special liquid dye in place of ink, playing cards and the odd gramophone record revealed maps pressed on very fine silk. A chess game yielded two subtly marked pieces concealing forged stamps for the preparation of false documents. A monopoly game, marked with a red dot, hid more Italian currency and maps inside the board. They had even thought to include concentrated food tablets concealed inside smokers' pipes!

Somehow these treasure troves passed inspection and, quite miraculously, came through completely undetected.

And then the final trophy arrived – a much sought-after crystal radio stowed inside an ordinary looking cribbage board. Manoeuvering the pieces on the board had revealed the secret compartment. However, after this initial delighted discovery, they were stumped.

"But how does it work?" Basu peered at the contraption. "What use is the bloody thing if we cannot use it!" He shook the offending object and dumped it back in its box, glaring at it.

"Well, it doesn't help to break it at the get-go, does it Basu?" The Major reprimanded him, mildly. "Patience, man, patience. It might require a little fiddling, but we'll have it going, I'm sure." He was interrupted by an excited exclamation.

"Hold on, I think I have it!" Santi had been twiddling the dial, tweaking it this way and that, when all at once the radio offered up a blip of life. "Listen! It seems to be doing something."

He had worked out that the key to the puzzle was the exact position of the dial at the precise time of broadcast on the right frequency. Simple! Still, another exasperating half-hour later, when every conceivable attempt had ended with much annoyed swearing, they were ready to give up. And then it happened.

"Eureka!" Santi's shout of triumph made everyone jump.

The radio sputtered, sank into sullen silence, hiccupped a crackle several times – and suddenly caught the wavelength the BBC used to broadcast on! Success, at last! And when the words "*This is London calling, with Alvar Liddel*" were heard, delighted whoops went up all round. Finally! Real news from the outside world at last!

Major Kumaramangalam was highly pleased. "Well, the MI9 boys have done good. Now it's our turn. With this lot added to our previous stash we should be all set. Let's get to it then." He rubbed his hands together in satisfaction.

The eager POWs lost no time putting their store of contraband items to use. Previously, tentative plans for escape had been discussed, and most had been discarded. Now they were threshed out once again, and a final plan was voted and agreed upon: a tunnel would be dug towards one of the two railway lines that ran outside the camp. It would reach a safe distance beyond the tracks so the escapees, when they did pop out of the ground at night, would be far enough from the camp not to be seen in the dark. What remained to be determined was exactly where the two railway lines led, and which would make the best destination.

Fraternising between guards and prisoners was frowned upon, but it had become obvious by now a little bribery with some of the more desirable contents of their Red Cross food parcels would go a long way towards loosening tongues and turning a blind eye. After all, goodies pilfered by the Italians were kept mainly among the higher echelons while the guards saw none of it – and most of them were, by now, fairly fed-up with the state of things.

It didn't take much to realise the Italians held a deep grudge against the Germans whom they found to be arrogant, high-handed and cold; a far cry from the highly emotional, gesticulating Italians who were naturally garrulous and lived life out loud. The Germans seemed to consider themselves masters and made no attempt to hide this belief; and the disgruntled Italians resented them, their deprecating attitude and this war they felt had been foisted on them for no bloody good reason at all. They had had enough, all they desired was to return to life as it had been before. Once they realised this, the POWs put the knowledge to good use.

It took some debate, but finally the unanimous choice for the escape tunnel was Hut 4, between beds 11 and 12. Lts. Mela Sing and Abhey Singh – who hailed from the princely state of Kotah – were the occupants. And Mela Singh was just the man for the occasion!

Lt. Mela Singh was a traditional Sikh officer who, as the custom of his religion dictated, was unshaven of face and head. His full beard, which had eschewed the ministrations of scissor and razor, was neatly netted and rolled-up to his face, while his long hair, worn tightly knotted atop his head, was wound over with a perfectly pleated turban. Happily, these genuine requirements of the Captain's religion were well-suited to the purposes of the would-be escapees. And so their work began.

Some time previous the internees had been allowed to build a stage. It had cost most of their pooled coupons to purchase the necessary tools, including an unused, ramshackle hut which had been dismantled to provide the material needed to construct their stage; but it had been worth it.

Various talents – thespian, song and dance, and comic – were discovered among the King's Commissioned Officers and the VCOs. These, combined with a surprisingly innovative genius for creating makeshift costumes, delivered a production that turned out a howling success. More so after a Papal visit, when a harmonium, promised by His Holiness, was delivered to the POWs. Many a skit entertained both captives and captors alike. It was the only time caricatures were permitted with impunity, even if the subjects were Italian, and the entertainment proved so popular, it became a fortnightly event.

Now, left-over scraps of wood from that endeavour proved most handy in building a wooden platform to hide the entrance to the tunnel, with the remaining wood slated to shore up the tunnel itself.

Placed over the intended entrance, the wooden platform was then covered with a threadbare prayer mat belonging to a brother Muslim officer. Upon this simple edifice was displayed, in harmonious array, religious pictures donated by all and sundry – Kali, protective mother and goddess of war, Ganesh the elephant god and remover of obstacles, Hanuman the monkey God of strength and courage, and Guru Nanak first prophet of the Sikhs.

It was hoped this ostensible arrangement for worship would discourage earthly interference and encourage heavenly intervention in the enterprise at hand – after all, the very survival of their artifacts through the travails of war and captivity could only be proof positive of the cumulative powers of these Almighty Beings! As for those who were Roman Catholic, Sunday mass was conducted by the resident padre, a benign officer who gave tentative consent for his flock to be represented in this makeshift place of worship by a wooden crucifix of Christ.

And so it was on this humble spot, in a prisoner of war camp far removed from the restrictions enforced by the usual priests, pandits and mullahs, all religions came together with equal respect for a common good. Would it were so in the rest of the world!

While work was in progress, lookouts were posted at strategic points, and upon any alert of impending danger – the approach of a guard and such like – all activity would cease, and the solemn figure of Mela Singh would be found, sitting cross-legged, surrounded by the pantheon of gods. He would remain thus in meditation, his back to the room, his face to the wall, emitting a low, humming sound; this would then build to a chanting that would increase in fervour till it crescendoed into what purported to be a trance-like state. The Italians were informed that in 'real life' he was a holy man renowned for the power of his dialogue with the Almighty, and since this was a ritual held most sacred by all Indians, he was not, in this ephemeral and highly fragile state, to be disturbed at any cost.

The ruse worked well enough; so well, in fact, that a couple of Italian guards even contributed the odd flower, surreptitiously delivered to the crucifix with a furtively uttered prayer for a personal request that needed fulfilling – and a quick sign of the cross to ensure the attention of the right God.

And so the tunnel began to take shape, notwithstanding a few hiccups. One such hiccup occurred when a young, newly arrived guard named Paolo first came upon Mela Singh in Hut 4.

On an errand that has remained forever clouded in mystery, Paolo entered the hut; and in passing the room that housed bed No.11 and No.12 his glance fell upon a sight that stopped him dead in his tracks. What he saw made him seriously doubt his own eyes.

Stunned by what he took to be a woman seated on the floor, wrapped in a white sheet-like cloth, long hair flowing down her back to spill luxuriantly about her waist, he thought for one very disturbed moment that he was suffering some sort of wild mental aberration. Hoping it would help, he closed his eyes; but when he opened them again the 'apparition' persisted.

Deciding then that the figure before him must in actual fact be real, Paolo felt called upon to investigate. How a woman could have been spirited into camp under the noses of the guards was a puzzle he could not fathom, but beyond a doubt it seemed to have been done, for there she sat, did she not, right before his very eyes! Well then, that being the case, and since it had fallen to his lot to have stumbled upon her, the young guard decided he would earn his first merit by taking her in. He was not to know that Mela Singh had been forewarned.

For, doing duty as look-out that day was a young Lieutenant by the name of Jog. This keen-eyed officer had signalled the guard's approach to Mela Singh who, in turn, had alerted the tunnel diggers. All work ceased immediately; underground, in the tunnel, the men sat as quiet as mice, while above ground Mela Singh arranged himself in a position of prayer.

Now, Paolo crept forward on silent feet till, at last, he stood right behind the seated figure; but then, he hesitated. The woman seemed to be humming – a strange one tonal sound he had never heard before. Being a full-blooded Italian with all the instincts of a young man in his prime, he was overcome with curiosity. Giving in to the ever-present male fascination for all things feminine, he was unable to prevent himself from reaching out and gingerly touching the silken tresses.

At that moment the humming rose and crescendoed into a long, reverberating '*ohhhmm*' as the figure turned, very slowly. To his horror, the young guard found himself staring into the accusing eyes of the most ferociously hirsute lady he had ever laid eyes on! Completely unnerved, he let out a strangled cry and, foregoing all further investigation, bolted from the hut just as fast as his feet would carry him – much to the delight of Lt. Jog who had been keeping a stealthy watch from the outside.

Naturally, the story did the rounds of the camp. Fanned by Jog's gleeful accounting of Paolo's discomfiture, it was fodder for much entertainment, and the unhappy young guard was teased mercilessly by his cohorts and the internees alike. Especially when his path happened to cross Mela Singh's, it made for an opportunity too good to be missed, and poor Paolo, much to his chagrin, was subjected to many a coy remark and romantic serenade.

Unhappily, this particular tunnel would eventually be discovered by the Italian ferrets, and the escape plan foiled; but that would be no deterrent. After all, it was common knowledge to captive and captor alike that every POW was duty-bound to attempt escape. If at first you don't succeed…well, bloody hell…have another bash at it… and another…till you damn well do!

And for some it would prove halfway successful. Lts. Hessem Effendi and Yahya Khan would walk their way to freedom. Major Kumaramangalam and Lts. Abhey Singh and Sahabzada Yaqub would be recaptured and sent to Germany, the Major to Stalag Luft III, made famous by the Hollywood movie, *The Great Escape.*

After the war, post Indian Independence and Partition, Tikka Khan would become Pakistan's Army Chief of Staff, Sahabzada Yaqub would become Foreign Minister and Yahya Khan would become that country's president.

Major Kumaramangalam would become India's 7th Army Chief of Staff. He and Santi would meet several times during their army careers.

⸻ ◆ ⸻

CHRISTMAS CAME AND WENT, and New Year's Day ushered in a dismal 1943. The weather grew colder, the days grew shorter, and everyone was grateful when hot water geysers at last replaced the smoky wood-stoves to provide for hot weekly showers. Showering was, perforce, a communal affair, and since nudity was not customary among Indians this took some getting used to.

New arrivals to the camp brought news from home: the Quit In-dia Movement was in full swing.

In the summer of 1942, when Mahatma Gandhi's exhortation to the British – '*Leave India to the Gods*' – went unheeded, the country rallied to his cry '*do or die*'. On 8th August, he called a meeting at Gowalia Tank Maidan in Bombay where he advocated a countrywide movement of nonviolent civil disobedience. Its aim was to get the British to leave India.

The new movement required a name to appropriately convey the nation's demand and determination. One enthusiastic, if rather brusque slogan – '*get out of India*' – was put forward, but quickly re-jected as unacceptably impolite. Ultimately, a simple yet eloquently civil rallying cry gained Gandhi's approval – and thus the 'Quit India' movement was born.

The British failed to appreciate the civility. Apprehensive of trouble brewing, they decided to nip it in the bud. The morning following the day of the rally, Karamchand Mohandas Gandhi, along with three other Indian leaders, Jawaharlal Nehru, Vallabhai Patel and Maulana Azad, were all arrested and thrown into jail, and the body of the Indian Congress was outlawed for good measure. So began *Bharat Chodo Andolan* – the Quit India Movement that would plague the British to the very end.

The recently arrived POWs brought one other snippet of news that was of interest, particularly to those who hailed from Bengal: On 24 December, at midnight that Christmas Eve, while people were praying for peace in their churches, the Japanese bombed Calcutta. The physical war had finally reached India.

In the third week of January, Santi received his first letter from home. Till recently mail from India had come through Turkey via Istanbul and Sofia, and quite often letters had taken as much as three to four months, if they arrived at all. Now with the facility of airmail, letters hopefully would be more regular, and Santi eagerly opened his.

Dr. J.P. Dutt, (Capt.), M.B., M.R.C.O.G.
Senior Provisional Administrators Bungalow
Civil Surgeon's Quarters, Chinsurah
Hooghly District, West Bengal, India   *November 29, 1942*

My dear Santi,

Your Mother and I were greatly relieved to learn, finally, that you are safe and well. When first we were informed you were missing in action, I tried every means at my disposal to obtain further details, but to no avail. We spent weeks and months without any news, till finally, 13 November brought the army telegram informing us of your capture. However, it was not until yesterday that we were able to ascertain where to address our correspondence to you.

I am sure you are aware how essential it is to keep your health up as best you can. Make the most of every opportunity for exercise, fresh air and nutrition that is available to you. Your Mother worries they are starving you. Now that she feels her prayers have been answered, she almost seems her old self once again and is busy preparing a parcel to send to you.

Your sisters are all doing well; Bela has made quite a name for herself in Medical College and Bina shares her residence in the hostel, except for the odd occasion when they both manage to visit home. Kanti has completed his training on the H.M.S. Dufferin, and is stationed in Bombay awaiting further orders. Sudha is doing fairly well in college. She would do better if she spent more time on her books and less on those fashion magazines she gets from our neighbour, Miss Babaneaux.

As for Lebu, I gather from a rather pointed remark recently directed at me by our other neighbour, the Police Commissioner's wife, that she has made herself quite prominent by initiating a 'Quit India' movement in her school and rallying her fellow students to Gandhiji's most recent call. As you can imagine, the authorities view such activities with a fairly jaundiced eye, but that is by no means a deterrent to your youngest sister! And, of course, where Lebu goes Kamala is never far behind! So you see, after all said and done, at this end we are getting on just as we should, each one much in his own fashion.

In the coming year I am to be transferred as Civil Surgeon to Burdwan District, just northwest of Hooghly. I will send you the new address as soon as I have it. If you are allowed to write, please send us news of yourself so that we may be assured you are well. Hearing from you will put your Mother's mind and heart at rest.

Both of us send our blessings to you, and we pray for your continued good health and well-being. Your sisters send their affection.

Affly, Father

CHAPTER FORTY-SEVEN

Eye Of Newt And Toe Of Frog

Double, double toil and trouble;
Fire burn and cauldron bubble...
By the pricking of my thumbs,
Something wicked this way comes.

– William Shakespeare, *Macbeth*

NOVEMBER WAS COLDER THAN usual that year. It rained heavily and there were a number of cases of influenza and typhus in the city. That November morning, however, as Hedeya sat at the table sipping her coffee, weak sunshine streamed into the kitchen, burnishing the autumn glints in her hair before settling in small, lukewarm puddles on the floor. The breakfast remains having been cleared away, she had pushed back her chair just far enough to accommodate the spread of her newspaper; she had spotted an article on King Farouk, and she settled down to read it.

His Majesty, apparently on one of his wild sprees the day before, had contrived to overtake a truck in the face of an oncoming car headed straight in his direction. Expecting nothing less than right of way for his Royal Personage, it seemed he had sped past the truck only to be forced to swerve, right in front of it. Naturally, this resulted in an all-round crash. HM was rushed off to the British military hospital in Qassassin where it was discovered he had suffered fractures to two royal ribs and his majesty's pelvis.

Of course, the incident and his injuries led to some wild speculation and rumours that made for particularly interesting reading, and Hedeya was immersed in this when Soraya Abdo's maid arrived with a message: her mistress was unwell and urgently requested a visit.

Hedeya went at once. Upon arrival she found her friend indeed laid up in bed, pale and fevered, her clothes in a state of disarray and her hair quite dishevelled, looking as though it had been pulled every which way.

"Soraya, you look terrible! Have you seen a doctor?" Unable to speak, Soraya shook her head, large tears rolling down her cheeks and off the tip of her nose, so that Hedeya went quickly to put an arm around the poor woman. "Oh, my dear, what is it? *Maalak,* whatever is the matter?"

Soraya let out a loud wail that dissolved into great gulping sobs and collapsed into her friend's embrace. Hedeya, really concerned by now, rocked her back and forth, murmuring platitudes that served no purpose whatsoever since she had not the faintest inkling as to the cause of the distress that was being so vehemently vented upon her shoulder. After what seemed like an age, when Soraya's violent blubbering scaled down to a spasm of hiccups, she managed a single, muffled utterance.

"Tewfiq." Unfortunately, this brought on a fresh bout of tears.

"Has something happened to him?" Hedeya spoke carefully for fear that a wrong word might reopen the flood gates with renewed force. "Where is he?"

"Gone!" Soraya moaned, pitifully. "He has gone."

"My God! So suddenly! When did this happen? How did this happen? *Ya kebdy zalek*, Soraya, I am so sorry. But why did you not let us know immediately that Tewfiq had passed away."

"Passed away!" Soraya sat up, indignantly. "He isn't dead! *Kelb ibn kelb*," she spat the angry words, "the son of a dog has run off after another woman!"

Hedeya leaned back against the bedpost, stunned. What, she wondered, does one say in a situation such as this? She floundered around, at a complete loss for words. "Are...are you...sure?" she asked at last, rather lamely.

"Sure? Of course I'm sure. I even know who it is; body like an ibis and as ugly as sin. Such an insult! The man has gone mad!"

"Hopefully just a temporary leave of his senses," Hedeya added for want of something better to say.

"Senses! What sense can a fool have? She has put a spell on him, I'm sure of it. Listen Hedeya, have you heard of Khaireya Badawi? She is a well-known psychic and soothsayer."

"I have heard the name," Hedeya admitted hesitantly, "but I don't believe in..."

"Never mind that." Soraya suddenly seemed fully recovered and filled with a sense of immediate purpose. "*I* believe if anyone can twist *that woman's* nose, she can. I must see her, Hedeya, and you must come with me."

"Don't be so silly!" Hedeya's voice was firm. "You don't really believe such nonsense? It's nothing but trickery and the selling of false hope. You will spend your money to hear someone tell you a whole lot of rubbish that will eventually disappoint you and hurt you; and I certainly want nothing to do with it."

"But you must." Soraya began to tear up again, her eyes welling and threatening to spill over. "I cannot do this alone. I need the support of a friend." She started to wring her hands. "Hedeya, please, just this once and I promise I will never ask you again!"

Backed thus into a corner by the woman's mounting hysteria and the prospect of having to stem another deluge of tears, Hedeya found she had no out but to give in.

———————

SORAYA AND HEDEYA SAT across a small round table from Khaireya Badawi. The soothsayer was difficult to describe; although small in stature, her presence loomed large in the room and gave an impression of strength and size. From a certain angle she looked old and wizened, from another her face looked remarkably smooth and quite free of lines. The duality was uncanny. Although the room was not overly dark, her eyes too seemed to change from deep to light while her hair was the one thing that remained constant; it was pure silvery white.

"Have you brought me something that belongs to your husband, something he keeps close at hand?" Her voice rustled like old silk.

Soraya handed over her husband's *masbaha,* the smooth alabaster worry beads cool to the touch. With her eyes closed the soothsayer held them for a long moment between clasped palms, as though communing with them. Finally, she opened her eyes and, reaching under the table, she brought forth a tray of objects which she set beside her. From among these, she chose a three-footed bowl wrought of copper and silver, and inscribed all over with odd looking sigils and hieroglyphs. Inside this she placed the *masbaha.*

Next, she took a piece of very fine, almost transparent parchment-like paper covered with strange writings and figures of the ancient Egyptian gods; Isis and Osiris to represent love, and Hekka the worker of magic spells. This she carefully laid as well inside the metal bowl and, picking up a sistrum, she waved the rattle three times over the surface of the bowl.

Hedeya and Soraya watched, fascinated, as the sistrum was exchanged for an ancient gold amulet inscribed on one side with an ankh, and on the other with the wedjat, the eye of Horus. From an aged, dark stone pitcher their host poured Nile water over the amulet into the bowl. Slowly, the writing on the parchment-like paper began to disappear, almost float away, into the water. When first the writing and then the paper had dissolved completely, the soothsayer peered intently into the water for a minute or so; she then closed her eyes and instructed Soraya to drink it.

Finally, Khaireya Badawi opened her eyes again and informed Soraya that a spell in the form of an 'egg' had been buried near the railway tracks. It was an 'egg' made of some substance much like plaster of paris. It would be found to contain three chicken bones, some eggshells, a piece of paper with old Coptic and hieroglyphic writing on it and, last of all, a small crudely formed clay figurine bound with string and pierced in various places by 13 copper needles. With the insertion of each needle the architect of the spell would have chanted '*as I pierce you here, you will think of no one but me*'.

It was imperative the 'egg' be dug up whole, and making sure not to break it, immersed carefully in boiling water. When completely dissolved, the entire thing, contents and water, were to be thrown into the Nile; within twenty-four hours the errant husband would return as though nothing had happened.

The location where the 'egg' had been buried turned out to be beside the railway line in Helwan; and since the exact spot was right behind the school where she taught, Hedeya bluntly informed Soraya that her part in the whole ridiculous affair had gone far enough. As a teacher she could hardly be expected to run the risk of being seen on such a fool's errand by someone from the school. And heaven forbid it should be one of her pupils who caught her in the unaccountable act of clandestinely digging up the railway line! Oh no, from here on her friend was most definitely on her own!

"Come with me," Soraya pleaded with Hedeya. "You know the area. Help me find this horrible thing and get rid of it."

"I will do nothing of the sort," Hedeya declared. "Do you realise what you are asking? Even if the silly thing is really buried where it is supposed to be – and let me tell you, I don't for one moment believe that it is – I can't take the chance that someone from my school might see me digging for...what? What do I tell them? That I am looking for magic spells buried in the ground behind the school? What do you think my students will say to that? They will be quite convinced I have gone completely mad, and I will never be able to convince them otherwise!"

This time Hedeya stood firm. No matter what Soraya said, she was adamant and would not be moved.

A week later, however, on her way back from school one day, she stopped by to find out how her friend had fared. Soraya greeted her with a big smile, looking very much, Hedeya thought, like the cat that got the cream.

"Well...?" Hedeya began, but Soraya quickly put her finger to her lips.

She pointed to the bedroom and whispered conspiratorially, "He's back."

"What happened?" Hedeya asked, astonished.

"Exactly what Khaireya Badawi said would happen. I found the 'egg' and did exactly as she asked and, believe it or not, no more than a day later he was back; without a single word, behaving as though he had just returned from the office!"

Alas! In spite of such a promising outcome, Soraya's story did not have a happy conclusion. In fact, if truth be told, it seemed without any conclusion whatsoever!

Just two weeks after his return, Soraya's husband absconded once again. A second frantic visit to the soothsayer unearthed a second 'egg'...and a third...a fourth...a fifth...

When she heard of these goings on, Bajo's warning '*a dog's tail, if curled, cannot be straightened*' went unheeded. And so, on down the years, the two women, wife and mistress, would doggedly continue to bury and dig up, bury and dig up – and with every 'egg' they buried and dug up, the unwitting man would shuttle back and forth between them like a wayward ping pong ball. It was exhausting work and, eventually, of the three, it was hard to tell which turned out the greater cuckold.

CHAPTER FORTY-EIGHT

Where Home Fires Burn

Far from the madding crowd's ignoble strife,
Their sober wishes never learn'd to stray;
Along the cool sequester'd vale of life
They kept the noiseless tenour of their way.

– Thomas Gray, "Elegy Written in a Country Churchyard"

I N THE DISTRICT OF Burdwan the Civil Surgeon's bungalow was a large two-storied building set amid massive grounds. Although there were other bungalows in the area, the distance between was so great, the privacy enjoyed was tantamount to a sense of isolation. The first residence along the road was the District Magistrate's, followed by that of the Inspector of Police. The Civil Surgeon's Bungalow came next, beyond which the road led to the Civil Engineer's residence and, finally, to a sumptuous guest house belonging to His Royal Highness, the Maharaja of Burdwan.

Settled comfortably in the very centre of this march of residences, the Civil Surgeon's Bungalow was fronted by a wide iron gate. It opened onto a circular driveway that bordered an expansive central lawn area. To the east and west of this, the compound disappeared into extensive groves of mango trees – *Langras* at the front of the house and *Phojlis* at the rear, both equally sweet and luscious, yet each with a distinct flavour and aroma that set it apart. The driveway curved past flower beds up to a huge covered portico supported by columns. Here, five wide stone steps brought one into a foyer.

A staircase with a polished wooden handrail wound up from the foyer to a spacious first-floor landing. From there one could step through large doors that opened onto a balustraded terrace which sat atop the roof of the portico, providing, on many a waning evening, the ideal place where one might sip tea and enjoy a full view of the manicured gardens.

There were four bedrooms upstairs, with two attendant bathrooms to their rear, each equipped with a walled off area for bathing, cold running water and two 'thunder boxes'. This last contraption, which served as a commode, was simply a lidded wooden seat with a hole cut out in the middle that supported an enamelled metal pan shaped like an inverted top hat. The metal receptacle would be removed by the sweeper every morning and evening for cleaning.

Behind the bungalow stood the servants' quarters where the *khansama* or houseboy, the cook, and the driver lived. And although he spent most of his days and nights in the gatehouse at the front, Bahadur, the Nepalese *chowkidar*, had a room here as well; beside this room stood a shelter where he safely tethered his milch cow at night. During the day, the animal was allowed to roam and graze freely under the mango trees, disturbed only by the cheeky, black-faced Hanuman monkeys that roamed their branches. The remaining servants – the gardener, sweeper, *tthika-jhi* who washed the kitchen utensils, and the *dhobi* who washed the family's clothes – all lived off-premises.

It was late one evening, and after tea on the portico terrace the family had lingered awhile, watching falling shadows steal out from beneath the mango trees and climb silently over the garden wall. In that gloaming hour, as nature called its daylight creatures to their rest, the monkeys too were bedding down for the night, their constant chatter subsiding into stillness. The air was faintly fragrant with the last of the mango blossoms, for the trees were already heavy with fruit, plentiful enough to content the tree dwellers who naturally had first bids on the harvest when it ripened; and after they had feasted, there would still be ample left for the consumption of whoever happened to occupy the house at the time.

The terrazzo flagstones, still warm from the afternoon sun, were spread with metal trays of raw mangoes drying, and bottles of mango *achars* and *chutneys* already prepared. Later, when the fruit had ripened on the trees, Mother and cook would squeeze the sweet mango pulp into large, flat metal trays to dry into sheets of *aamshoto*. The laden trays would be taken in every night and brought out again in the morning, a procedure that would be repeated until the *aamshoto* was properly preserved and ready to be stored for use after the mango season was over.

That evening the discussion had ranged from the girls' studies to Mother's impending visit to Calcutta to see Didima, Grandmother, who now lived with her youngest son, Bimal, and his wife, Dolly, in their Theatre Road flat. After Dadu's death, Didima, always sweet and gentle as a bird, had faded into a small, wispy breath of a woman who, despite her ailments, still had an inner strength that was pure steel. Her deep anxiety over Santi's safety, however, had taken its toll, and Mother felt that first-hand news of her first-born grandson would do much to restore her. And so, inevitably, the conversation had come to rest with Santi.

The news of his capture and the subsequent information of his whereabouts in Italy had been received amid tears and laughter. Yet, in spite of the family's overwhelming relief and joy, the uncertainty still persisted. What now? The war still raged on out there, and till he was home safe and sound, no longer on far-off shores or danger-ridden seas, the peril remained; and grateful as they were, it was unspoken but tacitly understood – until the day Santi walked through their front door, they would all continue to pray and hope with unabated fervour.

Finally, Father and Mother had gone into the house, but the girls remained, savouring the private moment broken only by their low voices, the occasional sound of their soft laughter and the jingle of gold bangles with every expressive gesture of their hands. In this far corner of the world peace reigned – and as night approached soft as thistledown on her ebony feet, gently whisking away the golden footprints of retreating day, it was hard to believe that chaos engulfed the rest of the world. The moment was as close to idyllic as one could get...if only Dada were home safe!

Soon, talk turned to personal chit chat and secrets shared between sisters. Sudha had received a letter from Chokon. He had, it seemed, taken to visiting Didi in Medical College and made her a confidant to his feelings and intention to marry Sudha. Mother had an inkling that something was afoot, but no one had dared yet broach the subject with Father.

The inevitable could not be put off much longer, however, as the girls were fast maturing into women, and the hint of romance here and there was adding a new dimension to their hitherto innocent young lives. In fact, Father had received a proposal for Bela as far back as her final year in school. It had come from the scion of an old, well-established, much respected family, the Chaudhuri family.

Mother's younger sister Chhaya Moyee, or Chordi (Little Sister) as she was familiarly known, was married to Charu Chanda Chaudhuri and they lived in Calcutta with their daughter, Krishna. As Father had been posted to Mymensingh in East Bengal during their school-going years, Santi, Kanti and Bela were put into boarding school in Calcutta where, sometimes, the shorter holidays would be spent with Chhaya *mashi* (aunt from mother's side) at her home in the city.

It was here that Charu Chanda's younger brother Nirad, a frequent visitor to the house, met Bela and was sufficiently taken with the young girl to contemplate marriage. Since Nirad was appreciably advanced in age compared to Bela, Father was not in favour of the union. Moreover, knowing his daughter wished to follow what was fast becoming a family tradition to study medicine, he felt marriage at her age, no matter how good, would shackle her ambitions. For a man who had endured much hardship in order to educate himself and his two brothers, the dignity imparted by learning and self reliance was of paramount importance, not to be hindered at any cost. Consequently, Bela continued her studies, became a doctor and achieved all that her father had hoped for her, while Nirad Chaudhuri married elsewhere and ventured on to become a famous writer.

With these reflections on the past, the girls were all of one mind – Sudha's chances of abandoning her studies to marry Chokon were pretty dismal. Father would *not* be pleased.

By now shadows had lengthened into pools of darkness in the hollows beyond the garden; it was time to go indoors. The girls watched in the fast-fading twilight as Bahadur left the gatehouse and walked past the flower beds into the mango trees to fetch his cow for the night. A moment later, a sudden, startled cry brought all three girls to their feet to see the dimly outlined figure of the watchman running towards the house. Leaning over the balustrade, they called out.

"*Kee holo*, Bahadur? What has happened?"

"*Akta shaap, khoob boro shaap*! A big snake!"

"*Shaap*! Where? What kind of snake?"

"A King Cobra; it is drinking the cow's milk!"

"*Oh Ma*! Is the cow dead?"

"No, no. No harm has befallen the cow, it is grazing peacefully. But I saw the snake coiled beneath it on the ground with its head raised up to the cow's belly; and when I cried out, it puffed its hood and began to dance."

"*Shorbonash*! Ma, Baba, come quick! Bahadur says there is a King Cobra in the garden."

Usha Moyee came out to see what the commotion was about and was met with a storm of babble from all three girls speaking at once; so much so, it took a few moments to untangle the jumble of words flying about her ears, and piece together what seemed to be the story.

"Bahadur, what are you going to do?" she asked. "What if the snake bites your cow?"

"*Na Ma*, it must be a good omen; Lord Shiva's snake has been sent with a message! I have heard that once his snake drinks milk from a cow, it receives Shiv-ji's blessing."

But Father, who by now had joined them, would have none of it! It was preposterous nonsense, a tall tale if ever he had heard one! Had Bahadur been drinking again? He marched off to see for himself and put to rest, once and for all, this fantastic story of Bahadur's milk thief. His family did notice, however, that he was armed with a good-sized stick in hand just in case it became necessary to do battle with the marauder.

Needless to say, when he arrived at the scene, save for Bahadur's cow still placidly chewing cud and observing the world with bucolic disinterest, there was no sign of a snake – drinking milk, dancing or otherwise. Whether Bahadur's intrusion had diverted its purpose, or it had, in fact, delivered its blessing and gone about its business, would now never be known.

Father, of course, was adamant the whole thing had been a figment of Bahadur's overwrought imagination. Given that it was common knowledge the old Gurkha sometimes enjoyed a tipple of an evening, he had a lingering suspicion that the night watchman – faithful and sincere as he was – had succumbed on this particular occasion to the temptation of a dash too much country liquor. It was, Father declared firmly, nothing more than a flight of fancy, an absurd tale conjured up in an alcoholic haze.

CHAPTER FORTY-NINE

Homeward Bound

What thoughts at heart have you and I
We cannot stop to tell;
But dead or living, drunk or dry,
Soldier, I wish you well.

– A. E. Houseman, "A Shropshire Lad" 1896

As WITH ALL MEN in all places, there are those who are honourable and those who are less so, those who are humane and those who are not; there are good men and bad among us all. And so it was in camp.

The camp 2IC – Second in Command – was a Major Alberici, a puffed up officer who never missed a chance to wield his authority over the POWs. Alberici was a martinet for discipline and dress. He took inordinate care of his own appearance and his uniform was better fitted, better pressed and better polished than any other officer's, including that of the Camp Commander, Colonel Vincenzo Cione. It stood to good reason therefore, he would earn the pillorying diminutive 'Popinjay' among the POWs.

Now, in February, Popinjay took malicious pleasure informing the POWs that their new ally, the Americans, had been unable to withstand the German war machine, and had suffered an ignominious defeat in the Kasserine Pass in Tunisia. It would seem, he snickered, despite their mighty new partner, the Allies were losing the war!

A month later, though, the prisoners more than got their own back, thanks to another more amiable gentleman officer. Lt. Gotze hailed from South Tyrol, a northern province of Italy that bordered Germany. He frequently fraternised with the POWs, enjoying the exchange of ideas on world affairs, during which his active dislike for the Germans became apparent. In one such discussion, while imbibing a bottle of wine he had very generously thought to share, he gave them the news that two thousand Italians had been taken prisoner outside El Hamma in the same region of the Allies' earlier defeat. This information did much to raise the general mood – finally the Allies seemed to be gaining ground in North Africa.

Spirits were raised even further when Allied bombers began flying overhead on their way to various targets. Naples, Rome, Bari,

Taranto and Milan were bombed, and so was the vicinity around the prison camp. It caused plenty of consternation among the guards and even a little among the POWs but, by Jove, it was worth it! Keep them coming, boys! The POWs lost no opportunity in flaunting their enthusiasm in the face of the disgruntled 2IC.

And then there was the incident with the eggs. One fine morning Jimmy Vakil of the Army Services Corps and A.S. Naravane, officers in charge of catering and distribution of Red Cross parcels, sat down to breakfast with a very large omelette. They announced, loud and clear, that one of the chickens purchased from an outside source had begun to lay eggs, and magnanimously offered to share this bounty with several friends. A couple of days later, a second good-sized omelette appeared and was once again consumed with much relish. After a third repetition, news of this reached the Italian 2IC. And it immediately piqued his interest.

That afternoon he sent for Jimmy Vakil, demanding the chicken be handed over. The eggs, he declared, were not Vakil's personal property to dispose of. Looking crestfallen, Jimmy meekly relinquished the fowl without argument – a fact that should have warned the 2IC there was more to the story than met the eye. On the contrary, believing his well-executed show of authority had won him a minor victory, he looked forward triumphantly to his personal stash of fresh eggs each morning.

They never came. Instead, with the dawn came the sound of loud crowing outside his window. Although an urbanite unfamiliar with fowl of any kind, it took little to put two and two together, and the bumptious Major soon learnt, much to his chagrin, that he had been the butt of a practical joke. He suffered gales of laughter and much 'crowing' from the POWs when Jimmy, camp prankster that he was, revealed the truth – the omelette had been prepared with egg flakes received in the newly arrived Red Cross parcels, and the chicken in question had never laid an egg in its life! It was, in actual fact, a very loud, proud old rooster!

TWICE A YEAR THE more seriously sick, wounded and maimed among the POWs were sent up for selection before the Mixed Medical Commission for the purpose of repatriation.

At the beginning of April 1943 just such a selection took place. As a result, 2,500 Allied POWs were to be exchanged in return for 12,000 Italian POWs. In Aversa, a number of doctors were selected to accompany the returning POWs who were gathered from various camps throughout Italy, and as luck would have it, Santi was among their number. So was Satyen Basu. They shook hands and congratulated each other. Liberation, at last!

It seemed too good to be true! Santi thanked the gods and dashed off a quick aerogram home with the news. (He was not to know this long-suffering missive, sent via Sofia and Istanbul, would endure numerous address changes and redirections in search of its destination, finally completing its seven-month journey well after its maker had returned home!)

On 6 April, the two doctors with their selected group travelled by train to Bari, in the south, where Italian hospital ships waited to be boarded. They were accompanied by Lt. Gotze who was kind enough to celebrate their release with a bottle of French champagne he had procured by means only he and the good Lord were privy to. They arrived at the Port of Bari on 8 April to join the growing numbers of POWs gathering there. Over the next two days these POWs were divided into groups, and after a doctor had been assigned to each group it was time to board. Bidding Lt. Gotze goodbye, Santi and Basu thanked him for his kindness, and wished one another God speed.

And so it was, that late afternoon of 10 April Santi and his contingent of 150 Allied POWs were shepherded aboard the Italian hospital ship '*Gradisca*'.

After conditions in camp, accommodations on the *Gradisca* were luxurious. Daily hot showers, clean clothes and fresh sheets belonged in some half-remembered heaven; and being allowed these simple amenities, these basic acts of personal hygiene, restored a sense of human dignity to the POWs. It was a first grateful step towards a renewal of self-esteem. With eager anticipation the men sat down to their first meal on board ship – until they saw the item of food served. It was met with universal dismay and protest.

"Oh Christ! Not ruddy macaroni *again*!"

"Have a heart! Don't the blighters eat anything else?"

"What were you expecting, lads, roast beef and Yorkshire pud? Just be glad this is the last time you'll have to face the blasted stuff."

The disheartened men reluctantly began their meal. It took no more than a couple of mouthfuls for disappointment to give way to surprise – this was a far cry from the slop they had been subjected to these many months in camp. By gad, *this* Italian cooking was *good*! And the accompanying red wine certainly helped things along! The sudden silence was broken only by the sounds of concentrated eating as hungry men delved heartily into a dish they previously had forsworn. And the speed with which all plates were emptied spoke to an apology for any previous, misconstrued blame – hell, it was not the dish, it was the bloody cook who ought to have been dumped with the garbage!

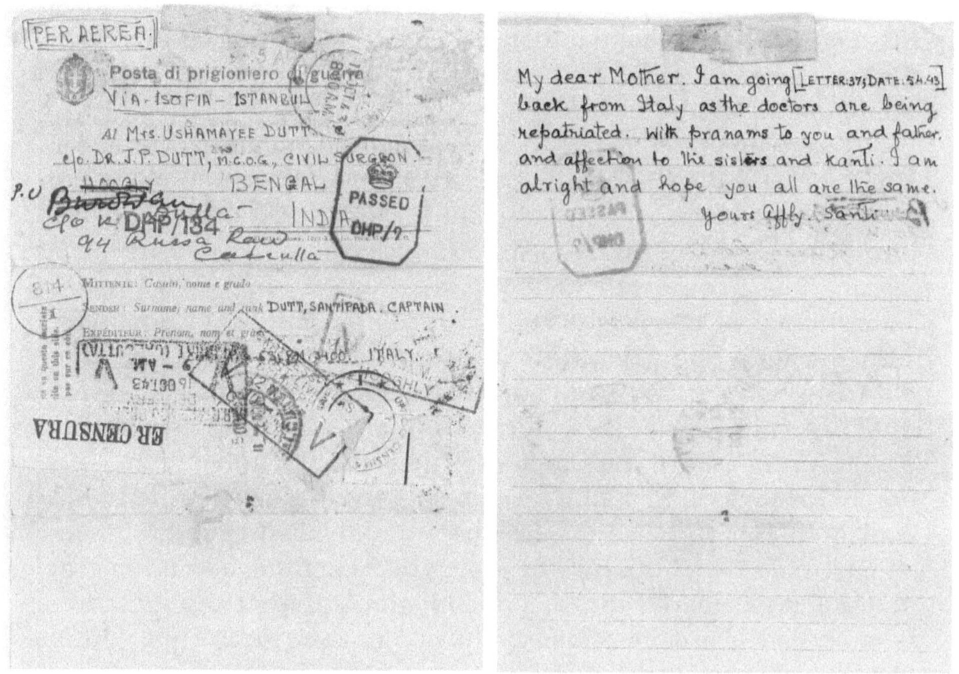

Letter from Capt. Dutt to Parents from POW camp, 1943.

That night there was jubilation on board as the concept of liberty began to transform into reality. It was reflected in the treatment they received from the Italian crew, the freedom to roam beyond their quarters without supervision, the bright green lights and bold Red Cross insignia blazoned on the ship as it forged its shining way through the night. There was no need to hide in the dark. This was a hospital ship. It was safe.

The second day out to sea Santi was on deck enjoying the sunshine, the fresh air and the taste of sea salt on his lips. It was the taste of Freedom! Of course, the war still raged on worldwide. Out there in the Libyan Desert the fight was ongoing. The previous November, when the Americans had landed in Northwest Africa, Montgomery's Eighth Army had driven Rommel's Afrika Korps fifteen hundred miles westward towards them. The fighting had continued through the winter; and now, the battle for Tunisia was in full swing.

Santi's thoughts, however, were elsewhere. His mind had crossed the waters and flown ahead of the ship, further eastward. He had worried and hoped these past months, agonised over how he would manage his return to Cairo, to Hedeya...and the whole situation had seemed quite impossible. Yet, against all the odds in the world, here he was. He wondered anxiously what lay ahead. Now that there was the possibility he might see her again, what should he say, and what would her answer be.

The very first time he had set eyes on her he had been, quite literally, knocked for six. He had surprised himself. It was out of character for him to give way to impulse like he had; he had swept aside all practicality, and without regard for any problems or consequences, his emotions had carried the day.

Examined in the bright light of common sense the difficulties seemed insurmountable – both from her side and from his. The age difference didn't matter; what did was that they both came from very different worlds. The ties to her world were numerous and strong; and as for him, Lord only knew how they would handle the news at home! He realised he hadn't even begun to consider how he would explain himself in Calcutta – how he would tell Father and Mother!

There was the child, the shy little girl. Something about her had plucked at his heart. But was that enough? And what about the two boys he had heard mentioned, but had not yet met? Their father had already parted them from their mother, so he gathered; but compounding the pain through further separation – was that right? Would she even consider it? And if not, would their father allow her to have them back to be raised so far away from him? Could he, Santi, be a proper father to all three children? Then there was Bajo, the kind old lady surely had a stake in all this, and therefore the right to have a say as to the final outcome!

There were altogether too many questions with too few answers and, unable to cope, he shut out the clamour. He would, he decided, cross those bridges when he came to them. All he knew for sure was that time had dimmed neither his desire nor his longing for Hedeya, and the thought of never seeing her again was unthinkable!

He was still lost in his thoughts when he was accosted by a young soldier who was missing an arm. He saluted Santi with his remaining arm.

"Captain Dutt, good afternoon, sir. I don't know whether you remember me, sir."

Santi returned the greeting. He stared at the man; no, he did not remember him, although his face was vaguely familiar.

The soldier indicated his missing arm. "You took it off, sir, after we were captured. And later, the Italians, they left me in the sun for hours with no water; and you came by, gave me the last of your water ration. I've never forgotten that. Don't you remember, sir? Bombardier Harry Brown. I've thought about you often these many months. You saved my life, sir. Thank you."

Of course! The young bombardier in the Italian ADS! Santi remembered him vividly now. He remembered the terrible state of his arm which had to be amputated after the RAP had been relocated to the *bir*; and how angry it had made him later to find the poor man lying in the sun pleading, '*aqua, aqua*'. Gratified to see he had survived, Santi took his good hand and shook it heartily.

"Glad you made it, Brown," he said, smiling broadly. "Sorry you had to lose your arm, but at least you're done with this mess now. And you're still young and strong, and you will be home soon."

"Yes, sir. God bless you, sir." Harry Brown returned Santi's smile and saluted him once more before walking away.

A thin, wiry British officer resting against the deckrail had been listening with interest to the conversation. Leaning heavily on a cane to support his injured right leg, he now approached Santi.

"Captain Dutt, isn't it?"

"It is, sir."

"2/4 Gurkhas?"

"Yes, sir."

"I was told you were on board. Been keeping an eye out for you. Glad to meet you."

"Thank you, sir," Santi replied, faintly perplexed as to who the officer was and why he should have sought him out. "I'm afraid..."

"Col. Llewelyn." The Colonel held out his hand and Santi shook it. "I was in camp with your CO, Col. Weallens. Spoke very highly of you, very highly indeed. You did some sterling work back there. I expect you know he's recommending you for an MC. Good show, young man."

For a moment Santi stared blankly, not sure he had heard quite right. Then he found his tongue, "What for?" he blurted before he could stop himself. "I mean...sorry, sir, I don't quite understand... huh...I think there's been a mistake..."

"No mistake, Doc. Weallens told us how you stayed the course, even when you knew it was all going down and you had the chance to make a run for it. Could have saved yourself, but you didn't...took on more than your share too. Courage and devotion above and beyond.... He was dashed proud, I can tell you. No. No mistake. He's putting in that recommendation and, from what I hear, you deserve it. Keep up the good work, Doc."

———•◦•———

ON 19 APRIL THE ship docked offshore in the harbour at Smyrna, in neutral Turkey. It was here the exchange took place – 1211 Italian POWs were transferred from a P&O ship to the '*Gradisca*' in return for 150 Allied POWs who were transferred to the British freighter '*Talmar*'. Two other British hospital ships anchored close by were taking on returning POWs being ferried to the waiting ships in boats manned by the Turkish Red Crescent.

The sight of the Union Jack clearly displayed on the British vessels' port and starboard sides, the blast of their horns hooting a welcome for the returning men, sent up a husky cheer and brought a lump to many a throat. The ordeal was over! They would soon be on the final leg of their journey to Port Said or Alexandria.

Who would have believed, Santi thought wryly, that he would be so heartened to see the British flag!

The returning POWs were plied with attention – good food, nourishing beverages, clean well-made beds; even sweets and toilet kits with basic necessities were supplied by the Red Cross and other concerned local organisations. It was difficult to imagine that out there, in the war-torn desert, Lt. General George Patton and Field Marshall Bernard Montgomery were continuing to make a final push for Tunisia.

The ordeal was not yet quite over.

CHAPTER FIFTY

Interlude In Cairo

They ask me where I've been, and what I've done and seen.
But what can I reply who knows it wasn't I,
But someone just like me, who went across the sea
And with my head and hands killed men in foreign lands....
Though I must bear the blame, because he bore my name.

– Wilfred Gibson, "Back"

A LIST OF RETURNING POWs was drawn up, names were sorted and confirmed, and telegrams sent out to their various kith and kin. One such telegram was on its way to India to be delivered to the Civil Surgeon's bungalow in Burdwan:

From: Adj. Gen.'s Branch [AG 16(a)] Battle Casualty Egypt.
U.O.No. B/75856/VI/AG 16(a) dated 30.4.43:
Information has been received that the following officers of IMS have been repatriated from Italy and disembarked Mideast on 22 April 1943: ...Capt. SP Dutt...

PORT SAID. SANTI WAS back in Egypt. His few remaining personal belongings were packed in a small, flimsy suitcase purchased from the Italian camp canteen. Now, he carried this beneath one arm as he stepped off the *"Talmar"* and onto British Occupied Territory once again.

Free! Actually free at last! The feeling was a heady one. After handing over the sick and wounded consigned to his care, he would be at leisure to go about his business. Santi felt strangely euphoric as he was trucked along with the wounded from the Port Said dock to camp on the outskirts of Cairo.

The war was still being fought in the desert, but from what he could gather, it seemed he and the other Indian doctors from Aversa were to be sent home where the Japanese were threatening an invasion of India. He had no idea how soon that would be, but he did know there was no time to lose – there was an unanswered question and matters to be settled in Cairo before he left.

8 Reinforcement Camp, Middle Eastern Forces: Far in the distance the desert loomed, inscrutable as ever, abode of the Great Pyr-

amids of Giza. Debriefing of all returned POWs took up most of the first two days. This included close interrogation of one's experiences, opinions and fealties, in case a year in enemy hands had altered previously held loyalties. During that time Santi wrote home to inform the family he was safe and sound. He still had no information as to the date of his return, but he promised they would know as soon as he did.

He saw to the wounded he had brought back and helped supervise their transportation to the various hospitals and rehabilitation centres. And finally, on the third day, issued with a new uniform, cap and boots, he got permission to visit Cairo. Not wanting to waste a single moment, he was at the Duty Officer's early that morning to pick up his pass, after which he managed to wangle a ride on one of the trucks going into town.

Impatiently, he endured the fifteen-mile drive which seemed endless; but he finally reached the city and caught a taxi. When it dropped him in front of the four-storied building on Rod el Farag, he bounded up the stairs, two at a time to the third floor, where he rang the doorbell on the left side of the landing.

He waited, his heart pounding. He closed his eyes and tried to breathe deeply as he heard soft footsteps approach the door. It opened, and Hedeya stood before him, outlined against the dim light of the shuttered room beyond, just as she had been the very first time he had seen her.

"Hello," Santi's voice was slightly husky. In that moment, that single word was all he could manage.

The sound of his voice sent a shudder through her, and she took an involuntary step backward, her eyes wide as though she had seen an apparition.

Dear God! Could it be? She felt the blood drain from her face. She had been so afraid she would never see him again! She had tried to imagine this moment so many times, and each time, at this very point, her mind had drawn a blank. Whether it was premonition or preservation she was unable to determine. She reminded herself that she didn't believe in bad omens; but in spite of being rooted in common sense it had perturbed her that she could not visualise his return, only their last parting on that day when he had walked into the desert and into that hellish battle which had gone so badly for the Allies.

For months she had been wracked by thoughts of…was he…had he been…? She would quickly pull back right there and tell herself not to be silly: the reason she could see nothing beyond that point was because there was nothing to see, because she realised there could be no future for them together. Sound reasoning and self-preservation, not premonition. And then she would begin to pray, trying to strike a bargain with God that she would accept never seeing him again just as long as she knew he was alive...

And here he was! She saw him smile, and a sensation like an electric current shot through her. Feelings of relief mingled with joy almost stopped her breath; she swayed slightly and looked as though she were about to faint so that he reached for her, strong hands on her shoulders, steadying her.

He gazed into her upturned face, studied those deep, fathomless eyes, her lips, the curve of her neck; they were exactly as he remembered, dreamt of these many months past – and now there was something else. He saw the unguarded play of emotions that softened those eyes, those lips, and what it told him made his heart leap with elation. The joy of it lit his face and his smile broadened.

So this was what a tug at the heart strings felt like!

That smile, the way he looked at her – all at once her knees buckled, compelling her to lean forward, to hold onto his shirtfront. She could feel the lean, hard muscle beneath the rough cloth of his uniform, feel too his grip tighten on her shoulders, holding her up; and without another thought, abandoning all argument with reason, she found herself stumbling into his arms.

He drew her in and held her close. For a brief moment he was stilled, both in mind and body, as though he were suspended in time; and then there was a rushing sound in his ears that seemed to start from the tumultuous sensation filling his chest; he could feel his heart pound hard against his ribs – or was it hers? He couldn't tell. Her sudden nearness, the joy of it, the relief from those interminable months of despair mixed with longing, filled the emptiness in him – it made his chest constrict and his stomach knot, draining the strength from him and leaving him almost weak.

She felt his body begin to tremble and, instinctively, reassuringly, she pressed against him, surprised at the sudden vulnerability she sensed in him. He was holding her tight, crushingly tight, and although she could hardly breathe, she didn't mind at all; it was good to feel his strength about her, filling her, so that she was able to return the gift when she felt his need for it.

"Marry me," he whispered into her hair, his voice gruff with desire.

Every instinct prompted Hedeya to give in, to allow herself to melt into the strength and safety of this man who had once more, against all odds, stepped back into her world. But those words of his, "*marry me*", pulled her up short. An almost forgotten thought pushed its way to the forefront, past the jumble of emotions jostling around inside her; a small memory that made her pull away, reluctantly, from his arms surrounding her.

Half-afraid, she remembered the bargain she had been willing to strike in exchange for his safety – she had prayed that no matter her feelings, she would forego being with him again as long as she knew he was alive. And here he was, alive and well, so what was she doing tempting fate this way? She stepped away from him.

She was not given to superstition, of course, but – now the implacable voice of reason intervened as well –there were other matters to be considered, other people to be taken into account. She had a family to think of, for goodness sake! And, as reality came flooding back, she felt a sudden wash of embarrassment for the intense intimacy they had just shared. She must be out of her mind! What was she thinking? Worse still, what was he thinking! He could not possibly have thought through all the consequences of his proposal – not for her, nor for himself.

"Do you know what you ask? It cannot be."

"Yes, it can," he insisted, fervently. "Marry me."

She shook her head as she led him to the sofa. "How?" She gestured to her surroundings. "This is my home, my family. You must understand. I have three children and my old mother. Yes, my two sons are with their father; and he has recently remarried, *al-hamdulillah*. She is a good woman, and that is a blessing. But *I* am still their mother. And my Bebe, and Bajo – I cannot leave and just go away. *Abadan*, never!"

She paused for a moment, searching his face. He looked older, thinner too than she remembered. This was not the diffident young man who had left to step into battle; this was a man in charge of himself and his surroundings. He had been gone close to a year, but the weariness chiselled into those youthful features added far more than a year to his face; there were fine lines newly etched at the corners of his eyes and mouth. She felt a strong urge to reach up and touch them, to wipe them away together with all the terrible experiences that must have put them there. She curbed the impulse quickly and, mustering what good sense she could, she continued to speak.

"And what about your family – have you thought what they will say when they hear I am older than you, that I am divorced, and I have three children? You see the problems – I cannot go and you...you cannot stay...can you?"

"You know that is not possible. I am still in the army and there is still a war on. But..." he took her hand and held it in both his, adding impetuously, "don't worry about my family; they will understand. Just say yes and I will take care of everything. I know it will take time, but I will make whatever arrangements are necessary to get permission for you *and* your family to come to my country. You will never have to worry again, I promise. Let me look after all of you."

She stared at him, amazed. "You would do that for me? Really?" She was deeply touched.

He gave a soft laugh. "You don't understand! *I* don't understand!" He shook his head, perplexed. "I have never felt this way before."

Pulling away, she began to reply; but he stopped her.

"I know what you are thinking. After all, how long have we known each other? A short while – and yet, these many months we've been apart, I have thought about you constantly, and I cannot imagine my life without you. All I know is that I love you. I cannot explain it, so don't look to me for answers; just say you will marry me. Allow me to love you."

He reached out and took her hand once more. "Do you know, it frightens me to think that we might never have met; one small misstep of fate, and we might have lived our separate lives, in our own separate worlds and never known one another." He gazed deep into her eyes, his look intense, his voice urgent. "I want to spend every day of the rest of my life with you. Please say you will marry me."

She saw his eyes searching her face, reaching for her thoughts, probing for the feelings that lay hidden beneath her heart. If only it were possible!

She raised her fingers and touched his lips, softly. "Can you make miracles happen? Bajo says I should believe in miracles. But I am afraid even to hope; I know how much pain it can bring." She gave her head an impatient shake as though to clear it and turned away from him slightly. "Oh, I cannot think! This is too much to think about."

"Of course, I understand," his voice was gentle. "There are many considerations, and you require time. The problem is I don't know if I have time. There's no telling how long before they ship me back to India; and there will be a great deal to arrange before I leave. I must inform my Commanding Officer. You will need to be cleared before we get permission from the Army to marry because I am in a foreign country. And though this is your country, as far as the Army is concerned, you are considered a foreigner. It sounds strange, but these are army regulations, and they have to be complied with. Then..."

"Wait, *wait*! You are going too fast. You see, already there are so many problems; and nothing is decided yet so, please, let us not speak of this anymore. We must be sensible. You have returned safe, *al-hamdulillah*! That is what is important – so for now let us give thanks just for that."

Santi paused, studying Hedeya's face for a moment. Finally, he drew a deep breath, and reluctantly conceded.

"Very well, for now we will leave it there, if we must. But look, since I am here in Cairo for the day, may we start by spending it together? The next convoy to India will be ready soon, and I will have to leave when it is; so, please, could we make the most of these few days we have together? May I see you when I'm able to visit the city? We could get to know each other better. I could tell you all about my family and my country; and later, when you have come to know me better, then you...just give us till then before you give me your answer."

———•◦•———

CAIRO'S FAMOUS EZBEKIYA GARDENS stood near the city centre, a stone's throw from the great Nile. There had been a lake once, but in 1870 at the behest of Khedive Ismail it had been filled in. As part of his dream to turn Cairo into Egypt's 'Paris on the Nile', he had contracted a Frenchman to design this tranquil spot and fill it with exotic trees and shrubs from all around the world. It boasted grottos and pergolas to provide shelter, a lake with bridges and paddle boats for pleasure, a theatre for amusement, and shops to suit a variety of tastes. European and Oriental tearooms and restaurants offered sundry repasts.

With such fashionable entertainment offered, there was something for everyone, and over the years Ezbekiya Gardens had become a much-favoured retreat where Cairenes could escape from the hubbub of their city. The gardens waxed particularly gay when, of an evening, military bands livened up the proceedings with their melodies and marches.

It was in these pleasant surroundings that Hedeya and Santi chose to spend their first afternoon together.

From a flower vendor at the entrance Santi purchased a garland of *ful* for Hedeya's neck, and the small, jasmine-like flowers filled the air with perfume wherever she moved. As they entered the gardens, strains of Lili Marlene wafted through the cool evening. They followed the music to the bandstand and a seating area where patrons were enjoying al fresco refreshments when Santi stopped abruptly, pulled up short by what he saw. Could it really be?

Yes, no doubt about it! There it stood, far from its native land, holding pride of place, gathering all that lay within the sheltering sweep of limb and leaf – a magnificent specimen of *ficus benghalensis* – a banyan tree. The bend of boughs and aerial roots reaching wide, into archways and hallways held aloft by stalwart trunks, separate, yet part of a whole. Grandfather's symbol of family!

Santi gave a soft laugh of pleasure at the familiar sight. It had to be an omen! A sign that the realm of a strong and loving family knew no bounds, either of ocean or land! Here was proof positive that he had Grandfather's blessing!

"What is it?" Hedeya asked, looking up at him.

When Santi explained how, from his youth, the grand old tree had remained Grandfather's symbol of the family, she did not speak. She had known neither grandfather nor grandmother on either side – they had been killed before her time – but a long-buried memory stirred and shifted, and the sudden movement caused her pain. Once, long ago, she had been part of a family of cousins, aunts, uncles, all decimated with such terrible brutality.

Quickly, she pushed away the memories, forcing herself back to the present – to the pleasant surroundings, to her companion. And as they walked under the trellised canopy of the banyan tree, a small yearning began within her, a wistful longing to share once again in the strength and comfort of a large, close-knit family the likes of which this man spoke of.

She believed him when he said he loved her, he would look after her. The thought filled her with a long-lost sense of comfort; and gratefully, for the moment, she wrapped herself in the warm pleasure of that feeling. She smiled at him with a newfound tenderness; it was good to be near him. Yes, her instinct had been right – he would be her safe haven if she allowed it.

Oh...if only it were that simple!

———◆———

WAITING FOR THEIR CONVOY to India, the other repatriated doctors from Aversa, unlike Santi, had time to kill; and so, they availed themselves of what entertainment they could. On occasion, on days Hedeya had to teach, Santi would join them.

The Femina Cinema House showed free pictures for the troops, and there was a most enjoyable trip up to the Nile Barrage, organised by the kind ladies of some philanthropic society. However, when the group decided to best use their time on a sight-seeing trip to Palestine and its surrounding areas, Santi declined Captain Basu's invitation. Though not privy to the details, his companions were aware of Santi's 'Cairo interest' and were unanimous in wishing him all success in his pursuit.

There was one invitation Santi did not decline. That Easter Sunday, a garden party was to be held at the British Residence in Garden City, home of the Ambassador, His Excellency the Honourable Sir Miles Lampson, and his wife, Lady Jaqueline Lampson. And the Indian doctors received a request to attend.

"I've heard tell," Satyen Basu volunteered to his companions, "the Ambassador's wife is the daughter of one Dr. Castellani, a well-known Italian authority on tropical medicine. She's quite some beauty by all accounts, and old man Lampson was smitten. Love marriage, it was."

"Odd! Did it not compromise Lampson, marrying an enemy alien? Set tongues wagging – you know, true loyalties and all that?"

"I do believe, at the height of the war she endured some unfortunate gossip; but tongues were stilled after her genuine concern for troops in the city could no longer be refuted. She did much for their comfort and entertainment, and all-round well-being, and is quite loved now"

Prior to the tea party, the invitees gathered at the new El Alamein Club where the Alamein Bell – the old station bell brought here from that now famous railway station – was rung in honour of that hard-won victory.

(After 1945, the bell together with a sum of £225,000 would be sent to the village of Enham, in England – a gift from Egypt in appreciation of the men who fought and died in the cause of her liberation. The money would go towards the Enham Village Charity for disabled veterans. In return, the village would acknowledge this generosity by changing its name to Enham Alamein where, to this day, the Alamein bell is rung every year to commemorate the anniversary of the Battle of El Alamein, Britain's first victory and a turning point in WWII.)

The afternoon event at the British Residence was a gala affair. Guests entered the building between two suitably imposing marble lions acquired by Lord Kitchner in 1913. Beautifully manicured gardens swept down to the Nile bank where the backdrop of the river, fronted with its palatial residences, was truly spectacular. A band played soft music in the background. The small group of Indian doctors, smartly turned out in their new uniforms, joined hundreds of guests milling about, enjoying all manner of delicacies that were laid on. Lady Jacqueline Lampson had gone all out to make her guests welcome.

The surprise highlight of the event, however, was a flying visit from the front lines by Field Marshal, the Viscount Montgomery of Alamein. On important business in Cairo, he managed to stop by. He congratulated the Indian doctors on their safe return, and promised them an outcome soon that would be suitable revenge for the Allies' earlier setbacks in the desert.

RATHER THAN CATCH THE tram, Santi soon discovered it was more expedient to hitch a lift in an army lorry, or even a passing civilian truck headed for the city. Lorry hopping on a civilian truck required the payment of one Egyptian pound to the driver; well worth it since it procured him a ride oftentimes to within walking distance of his destination.

His third visit to the house on Rod el Farag was a special occasion, and Santi arrived with a bounty of pastries and profiteroles from Groppis. He was to meet with Hedeya's sons. As he had done on his very first visit a year ago, he dressed in full uniform; first meetings were always important. The boys were hugely won over by the gifts, and even more by the uniform – shiny brass, polished leather and colourful ribbons – particularly Louis who was quite bowled over and took to calling him 'The Captain'. It had gone well!

He visited as often as he could wangle a pass, sometimes spending time at home with the family and, on a couple of occasions, taking them all to the pictures – these outings extremely popular with the children. Then there were those times, those special times, when Hedeya and Santi would go out on their own, just the two of them, getting to know each other slowly, visit by visit. It was a time of discovery.

On one such occasion, they took a taxi across the Tahrir Bridge to Zamalek Island. The Andalus Gardens in Gezira, with its promenade and its tall elegant palm trees, was a place of tranquil beauty where one could walk or sit and watch the *feluccas* on the Nile sail against a backdrop of the city skyline. The terraced areas provided secluded spots where people could picnic on refreshments brought from home, or purchased from vendors in *Geneyna Lemun*, the Garden of Lemons, just across the way.

Santi and Hedeya had done the latter. They bypassed the chorus from hawkers selling *beyd taza a'al*, eggs fresh and excellent, and *salata wu faseekh*, salad with pickled mullet fish – an Egyptian delicacy Hedeya was fairly sure would hold little appeal for Santi. Instead, she opted for freshly baked *sumeet wu gibna rumi*, sesame bread with white cheese; and, to spice their repast, she suggested some *dokka* for a dipping. To wash it all down, Santi armed himself with a couple of well-chilled bottles of Stella beer, while she decided on a bottle of *kazuza*, a lemony soft drink, purchased from a vendor carrying his wares in a pail of watery ice. By way of small eats with their drinks, they purchased some *termes* and *sudani*, lupin beans and peanuts, and made ready for their picnic.

They spent a short while looking for a suitable spot, roaming the Gardens with its three distinctly laid out areas, its beautifully patterned mosaic benches and steps, its colourful mosaic fountain and statues. When eventually they found a good spot, Santi spread his jacket on the grass for Hedeya to sit while he set out their picnic things. Then, with their drink of choice in hand, he sprawled out on the grass beside her and took a long sip of his beer. Life was good!

Propped to his right on one elbow, he lay facing her. He watched the sunlight dance through those auburn waves, outlining that face that had haunted him through so many dark nights and days. She sat upright, leaning on her left hand, knees bent to the left so her bare legs could be tucked close into her body on the right. The light filtered through the fine fabric of her summer frock, and as she raised her drink to her lips it caught the soft hollow at the base of her throat, touched the delicate shadow along her collar bone and came to rest on the gentle swell of her breasts. His breath caught in his throat!

He eased his long, lean body slightly the better to observe her, and as she lowered her drink from her lips, he noticed a small grimace screw down the corners of her mouth.

"What is it? What's wrong? Is something the matter with your drink?"

"This *kazuza*, it is not properly cold. It is, *yaané*…" she gestured with her hand, fingers outspread, a tipping movement from side to side.

"Tepid?"

She grimaced again and nodded.

"Here. Try some of mine, it's perfectly chilled. Have a small sip. I must say, it's not half bad, this Egyptian beer."

"I do not drink, remember?" she replied, declining his offer.

"Well then, how about a shandy? It can be quite refreshing on a hot day like this. Look, my beer is ice cold. May I mix some into your drink? I think you might find you enjoy it better that way. And, anyway, a little beer is good for you – doctor's orders. Trust me, I'm a doctor!"

Hedeya wavered; the look of that ice-cold beer was enticing in the heat. Just a small amount added to her *kazuza* might prove quite pleasant. A great many people seemed to enjoy the drink, so, really, there could hardly be any harm in trying it. The icy droplets condensing on the outside of Santi's beer bottle finally convinced her and, pushing hesitation aside, Hedeya decided to try something new.

It required a fair amount of beer, eventually, to improve the temperature of her drink, and the bitterness of the beverage, diluted though it was, made her wince. Nevertheless, the cold liquid sliding down her throat, through her chest and into her stomach felt quite pleasant, and Hedeya downed it quickly to avoid the taste as much as possible.

"Whoa! Slow it down there!" Santi exclaimed, laughing.

Too late the warning! Their outing ended somewhat abruptly with the discovery that beer had the untoward effect of making Hedeya drowsy; so drowsy, there was nothing for it but to pack up, hail a taxi, and head for home! It was a lesson learnt, a mistake never to be repeated, and therein the realisation that there remained, it seemed, a good deal yet to be discovered, each about the other!

CHAPTER FIFTY-ONE

The Anniversary Waltz

Ah my Beloved, fill the Cup that clears
Today of past Regrets and future Fears…
Tomorrow?…Why Tomorrow I may be
Myself with Yesterday's Sev'n Thousand Years.

– Omar Khayyam, *Rubaiyat of Omar Khayyam*

IN THE TIME THAT followed, Santi was careful to keep to his promise. He did not press his suit with Hedeya, although his manner made it clear that his intentions remained steadfast. Realising it was the only way, he was willing to curb his own urgency, however difficult, and give her time to sort her mind and arrive at a decision. He hoped, before long, she would of her own accord be ready to commit herself to him and come to terms with the inevitable changes that decision would bring to all their lives.

He was proved right for, as their association grew, so did her pleasure in his company. But unavoidably, never lagging far behind, that tiny serpent of guilt would rear itself, slithering through Hedeya's conscience so that her mind and heart remained in constant conflict, a painful tug of war that pulled her first one way and then the other.

She could no longer deny her feelings for this unusual young man. He had, in a most civil manner, appeared on her doorstep one day, duty bound to deliver his message whatever it might take; and in three short meetings he had managed, with the velocity of a whirlwind, to turn her world upside down by proposing, and then vanishing, so precipitously it had stunned her. The swiftness with which he had changed her life had made her head reel, and she had struggled, these many months past, with emotions that heaved her from zenith to nadir and zenith-ward again. Her efforts to forget him had been in vain; as for her efforts at being sensible, they had not fared much better either!

And now he was back – and, oh my, was she glad he was! Yet, that was the very problem; his return had thrown her into complete turmoil once again, calling for a decision that meant ultimate heartache, no matter which way it went. A decision that grew more complex the more time they spent together, so surely her wisest course, right now, right here, was to nip this relationship in the bud!

But then, she told herself dryly, who was she trying to fool? It was way past the bud stage, wasn't it! Wherever she turned, Hedeya found no resolution to her predicament, and so Santi remained without an answer. Till eventually, Bajo decided it was time to take the situation in hand.

It was the day Hedeya and Santi took a trip to Memphis and Saqqara. That morning, Santi hired a taxi, Hedeya packed a simple picnic lunch, and they set out some thirty kilometres south of Cairo, where, in the midst of the desert sands lay the ruins of Memphis.

Long ago, in the dim and distant past of the the First Dynasty, in the reign of King Mena, this once great city held sway as the ancient capital of Upper and Lower Egypt. Here, a giant thirty-two-foot statue of Ramses II still reclined, sans legs, guarded by a large alabaster sphinx, debated to be the likeness of either Ramses or King Tuthmoses. Whether fact or fiction, it is said that when the limestone statue was first discovered, it was completely crusted over with the petrified remains of thousands of scarab beetles.

In spite of a pleasant, light breeze, Santi and Hedeya soon found sightseeing to be rather hot, dusty work, and decided it was time to take a break. Their taxi driver, having studied his passengers with discreet interest, decided the tall, young foreign officer might benefit from a little man to man help from a local. Seemingly astute in matters of the heart, he approached the situation with delicacy. Pointing out the unsuitability of the tourist site for their picnic, he offered to take them to a more private spot, away from the hubbub.

"You come, *effendi.* I takes you good place. Alone place. Moustaffa show you. No much peoples to make nuisance noise. You see. Ok?"

Only too glad to get away from the clamour of persistent 'antique' vendors and urchins, Santi smiled at the man's eagerness. "Lead on, Moustaffa, we are in your hands."

Looking slightly perplexed as to what his hands had to do with anything, Moustaffa shook his head. "No, no hands. We go in taxi, not far. You come."

Curbing his amusement, Santi replied somberly, "Yes, we come. Thank you."

Since one good offer deserves another, they returned his kindness by sharing their lunch with him – fresh bread, mortadella, cheese and grapes. Moustaffa accepted graciously, but with admirable sensitivity, he insisted on leaving them undisturbed by eating in his car. When he gauged it to be appropriate, and no longer an intrusion, he produced a flask of hot, sweet, black tea from the car boot and suggested, after they had washed down their meal, that they drive the short distance to Saqqara.

"There many old, old tombs of great Pharaohs. Very many Kingses and Queenses buried also. And high-ups, like Wazir and Temple Man."

"I think he means priest," Hedeya whispered, smothering a giggle. "He will not speak to me in Arabic, to show you respect. He feels you are in charge, so you should decide."

"In charge, eh! Well then," Santi managed, straight-faced, "I had better play the part, hadn't I. After all, it wouldn't do to disappoint the good man!"

And so, after making a show of having given the matter due consideration, Santi informed the delighted driver that his idea was a sound one. Beaming widely, Moustaffa led the way back to the taxi, assuring them he would be more than happy to play tour guide.

A site that had served as the necropolis of the ages, Saqqara's tombs dated all the way back to the First Dynasty. But it was the Step Pyramid of Djoser, built in the Third Dynasty, that held sway over all others. Constructed by the legendary Imhotep in the time of the Old Kingdom, it was not as famous as its more illustrious companions at Giza, but it certainly outdid them in antiquity.

"Here is Step Pyramid," Moustaffa announced grandly, throwing his arms wide to encompass the entire structure. "It be built for King Djoser by great man Imhotep. Imhotep very good, not bad like in "Mummy" cinema." Moustaffa shook his head indignantly. "Big shame, make good man bad."

Believed to be the first architect of stone, and the true father of medicine, Imhotep had been Chancellor of Egypt, High Priest of Heliopolis, astronomer, engineer, scribe and grand magus. Deified by the Romans and Greeks for his healing and learning, he was unjustly resurrected in 1932 by Hollywood as a villainous high priest with frightening supernatural powers – undeserved for a man whose name, ironically, meant 'he who comes in peace'. It was an affront that, quite naturally, did not sit at all well with their Egyptian driver!

However, not being one to dwell on such wrongs, Moustaffa quickly forgave and forgot and moved on to more pleasant things. Pointing into the distance, he drew their attention to the shimmering outlines of some buildings. "See there? Dahshur and Red Pyramid. Building with red limestone. Red Pyramid be belonging to King Sneferu. Father of Pharaoh Khufu. Khufu very famous – he build Great Pyramid in Giza."

The architecture and history seemed as unending as the desert itself, and rumour had it that these sands had not yet yielded all their secrets. It was widely believed that lost pyramids of the First Dynasty still remained, buried here in the sands of time, and there was no telling what their number might be.

"Now we go under desert. See plenty more." Turning with a confidence born of purpose, Moustaffa signalled them to follow where tunnelled steps led to an entrance. Stepping through, they reached a subterranean labyrinth of catacombs and alcoves known as the Serapeum. Here, massive black granite sarcophagi carved with linear markings preserved the mummies of sacred Apis Bulls believed to be the reincarnation of the god Ptah, who was sometimes associated with Osiris. Rituals and ceremonies of bygone times had seeped into the walls and floor, binding past to present, and the place was steeped in the mysteries of resurrection, ascension and eternity.

But the afternoon was wearing on. It had been a pleasurable outing and, loath to end it, they had stretched it out as long as possible. Sadly, however, if they were to reach the city before dark, it was time to thank Moustaffa for his kind assistance, tip him generously, and head back for home.

The journey back seemed shorter, and it was still light when Santi saw Hedeya safely home. Putting things away in the kitchen, Bajo heard her daughter return with her companion, heard her soft peal of laughter, quickly hushed. She had not heard that sound in a long time. It was lighthearted, it had the ring of happiness to it; and when Hedeya entered the room alone a little later, her mother saw how, for the moment, that laughter had chased away the worry which seemed to bedevil her daughter's face these days.

Bajo felt something lurch inside her breast – it was love, the kind that exists somewhere between relief and pain. At last! Her daughter was a bird on the mend and had taken wing once more! She thanked God, prayed that her happiness would last and, to that end, decided their conversation could wait till morning.

Next morning while Bajo was chopping *kosa*, a kind of squash, to prepare for the day's meal, Hedeya walked into the kitchen to let her know she was leaving for school.

"I have only two classes today, embroidery and cutting, so I'll be home early. Do you need me to get anything on my way back?"

Bajo shook her head. "*Là*. I have everything I need for today. But," she sounded casual, "a funny thing; I dreamt of Shamun last night. We were sitting, talking – and yet we did not seem to be together, because he was telling me to come and visit him in Qamishli. Strange, isn't it? I have been thinking of my brother so often recently, it is almost as if he is sending me a message."

"Maybe you should write to him."

"How time flies!" Bajo continued reflectively, seeming not to have heard her daughter.

"Why don't you write him a letter today? I can post it tomorrow, on my way to school."

"No, that won't do; I wrote only a fortnight ago. No, no, too many years have passed since last I saw that brother of mine."

"Well, then, we will have to see what can be done about a visit sometime, won't we."

"Not sometime, Hedeya, I must go as soon as you can make the arrangements. I know it is time. I must see Shamun before it is too late."

Accustomed as she was to her mother's belief in signs and omens, nonetheless, this sudden insistence perplexed Hedeya; after all, arranging for such a trip required money, as her mother full well knew, and that was not easy.

"Bajo..."

"We were very close, Shamun and I," the old lady interrupted her, "and it has been too long we have been apart. I think I would like us to spend our last days together. But how can I leave you? You could not stay here on your own. Tell me, have you considered maybe it is time for you to decide what you are going to do?"

"Do? About what?"

"You know what I mean, Hedeya. How long are you going to carry on like this? Sooner or later, you will have to make up your mind. And for all our sakes it would be better sooner rather than later, or neighbours will start to talk. They know our guest was sent by our relative in Iraq, that he was brought to us by Asis Habib, but gossip spreads. As they say, allow the wind a chance to blow into your life and it will reveal all to the trees. You have come to a crossroads, choose your path. You of all people know that life must be lived with courage, and one cannot be afraid of change."

Hedeya remained silent, but the agony of indecision showed plainly on her face. So that was it! She realised, her mother had been leading up to this all along.

"Once in a great while," Bajo's voice was soft with love for her daughter, "fortune smiles, and one is given a glimpse of the heart's desire; often that is not so, for fortune is a fickle creature and she is not known for her generosity."

"I don't know what to do, Bajo."

"You have to make a choice. Nothing is given for free. There is always a price to pay."

Hedeya's voice sounded choked. "Don't I know it!"

"Do you love him?"

Slowly Hedeya nodded, her throat too tight to speak.

"Are you sure?"

Hedeya shut her eyes. Once, a long time ago, she had loved Mahran – or so she had thought – but it had never felt like this, as though her heart would burst! When she looked at her mother again, the answer in her eyes was plain to see.

"Then what are you waiting for?" Bajo's voice was gentle.

"What do you mean?" Hedeya stared at her mother in astonishment. "Bajo, you talk as if making a choice is simply a matter of throwing everything to the wind and following my heart wherever it leads!"

"Not throwing everything to the wind, but facing it. This is not a sandstorm you hide from in the hope that it will blow itself out. This is the wind of change sweeping away the past and clearing the path to your future. How long will you turn your back, hoping it might resolve itself so you do not have to weather it? Brace yourself, turn around and face it. If there is a journey to be made, then make it; brave it, one step at a time. Only you can decide if the journey is worth undertaking, no one else can do that for you. But you know you will never reach anywhere if all you do is stand still; that will bring nothing but regret later."

Hedeya's tightly clasped hands were pressed hard against her lips as though to keep the turmoil of her emotions contained. She stared at her mother with anguished eyes; then she walked over and, putting her arms around the old lady, she kissed her gently on the cheek.

"My life is here, but my heart..." She drew a deep, faltering breath and laid her cheek against her mother's. "You see, no matter what my choice, the price will be high; one way or the other my payment for it will be regret."

———•◆•———

SHE CONTINUED TO BE torn by indecision until one night in mid-May. News of a resounding Allied victory on 12 May had swept through the city in a tidal wave of jubilation. It was said that 275,000 enemy prisoners had been taken in Tunisia, resulting in the final and complete surrender of Axis troops in North Africa. The flotsam and jetsam from that final campaign for the Middle East had not yet reached the city to dampen celebratory spirits or mar the euphoria of that victorious May. The cost of that victory in human loss had not yet been counted.

Cairo was heady with triumph and relief, at least in the British and most of the elite quarters of the city. Santi and Hedeya stepped out into a beautiful mid-May night, awash with moonlight and overhung with clear, star-spun skies. Shepheard's Hotel was aglow, inside and out; the garden at the rear was drenched in stardust and moonbeams. Strings of low, softly twinkling lights chased the remaining errant shadows from the dance floor, and the air was heavy with the perfume of night flowers and music. Santi and Hedeya had just entered when, as if on cue, the band struck up a familiar melody – and as they were led to a table for two, the memorable strains of 'The Anniversary Waltz' filled the night.

"Remember?"

Santi held out his hand. The music lilted and shimmered, and without a word she walked into his arms, falling in step as he led her across the dance floor.

Yes, she remembered. That evening – how long ago it seemed – had opened doors to her heart she never imagined would lead to this moment. She remembered how smoothly he had partnered her, how strong and safe she had felt in his arms, then as now.

It was fairly crowded. Although the majority of troops were still out in the Libyan Desert cleaning up the debris of war, there was no dearth of uniforms among the guests on the floor and at the tables. Looking around, Hedeya could not but concede to a small thrill of gratification – her companion cut enough of a dashing figure to more than hold his own among those present.

She felt a warm rush of pleasure, heightened as he held her close and firm against him. The faintly familiar feel and smell of his uniform brought back vivid memories of that other evening when they had danced to the very same song – was it only a year ago? She smiled as she realised that this evening was, indeed, a first anniversary of sorts.

Surrounded by strangers though they were, her thoughts were like a secret bond bringing them together, spinning an intimacy, a magic caul about them that held the rest of the world at bay. The feeling quickened her senses, sending a flush of yearning through her for what could be, and she leaned into him, allowing herself to enjoy the sensuality of their closeness.

There was no need to speak, the words of the song seemed to say it all, as though specially chosen for the occasion. And then, as Santi swept her across the floor, she heard him murmur, his voice low but urgent.

"Say yes."

Hedeya raised her eyes to his. Though his face was still thin, his features still angular from the recent ordeals he had been through, it did not detract from his dark good looks. A sudden unbidden fire stirred deep within her. More than his outward appearance, it was something she read in his eyes, dark and steady, that spoke to her – the message burned strong and clear, a promise that, given the chance, he would always be there to love her, to care for her and keep her safe; it was a vow of lifelong devotion.

The depth of his feelings shook her, and it lit her love for him like a starburst. She could put her trust in him. She could, at last, unburden her fears. In that instant she realised, despite all the strings that bound her to her old life, she had come too far in this relationship, short as it was, and her love for this man reached too deep for her to turn back. The realisation was double-edged – as though her heart had taken flight like a bird freed of its cage, yet ambivalent in its liberty as it soared to incandescent new horizons, all the while suffering the tug of inalienable loves and lifelong attachments.

"Marry me." He had waited patiently, and long, allowing her time to find her way to him, but he could wait no longer. His words, his tone, told her so; now, he was pulling her in, he was claiming her answer.

Hedeya lifted a hand to Santi's face. She touched his lips as though she would catch the words he had just spoken. Very gently her fingers traced the curve of his mouth, perfect, sensual, the lean line of his jaw, down past the pulse point in his neck, bringing her hand to rest, once more, against his chest. She could feel his heart.

"When I think about it, my head tells me I am being a fool; but my heart, it seems, speaks louder than my head. *Ya rouhi*, yes, I will marry you."

It did not matter a jot that the literal meaning of the Arabic words she had just uttered was unknown to him. He had never heard the endearment before, but language proved to be no barrier, it needed no translation. He felt its meaning in the beat of his heart, the rush of his blood, the very depth of his soul. *Rouh*! Life Force! The essence of being that throbs in that small, secret hollow at the base of one's throat, that hidden place of deepest feelings where the breath of God is received and held, to blossom into the gift of life. The Soul.

Rouhi! He was her life, her breath, her soul! Santi's heart leapt with joy so that he was hard put not to shout his feelings out loud. He threw back his head with a soft, exultant laugh.

At last! He had finally won the day!

———————

THE FOLLOWING AFTERNOON, BROOKING no delay, he made enquiries for a reputable jeweller from where he purchased two gold wedding bands. On the insides he asked to have inscribed, simply, 'S.Dutt' for her and 'H.Khayat' for him; then, following the names on both bands, he immortalised the date she had promised to spend the rest of her life with him – May 16, '43. He held the two brand new wedding rings in his hand – he felt the weight and heft of them, solid, substantial; precious symbols, the bond of a lifetime. He closed his fingers over them. These small gold circlets in the palm of his hand would change his life's course forever.

CHAPTER FIFTY-TWO

Till We Meet Again

– A. E. Houseman, "Lancer"

IT NOW REMAINED FOR Hedeya to inform the family of her decision – and to return Sallah's ring.

Bajo received the news with a relief that was tinged with sadness; she was grateful her daughter and granddaughter would be in the safekeeping of a good man, and that far outweighed the sadness of their inevitable parting from her. She had prayed long and hard, and her prayers had been answered. For that there was no sacrifice too big to make. She thanked God and wrote to her brother, Shamun, preparing him, and herself, for the journey to Qamishli.

When Sallah visited next, Hedeya tentatively brought the conversation round to Santi.

"The soldier boy," Sallah laughed. "Is he still around? He seems to fancy he's in love with you."

Provoked by the flippancy of both his tone and his words, Hedeya replied tersely. "Maybe he is."

"Be careful, then, you don't break his heart. That would be a shame, wouldn't it?"

Trying hard to curb her growing irritation, Hedeya snapped, "And what if I told you he wanted to marry me?"

"Ah, a rival suitor!" he teased. "Does he love you so much? Well, I suppose if that is so, what could I do but selflessly agree to your choice of the better suitor!"

He chuckled, oblivious that he was treading dangerous ground.

Thoroughly irked by now at his casual dismissal of such a possibility, Hedeya stood up from the kitchen table. She stared at her companion in stony silence.

A moment later, her face set, she left the room to return shortly with his ring in her hand. It had remained on the mantelpiece where he had put it those many months ago. Now, she leaned over and placed it on the table in front of him.

"Well, then I think you better take this back."

Sallah looked as though a pail of water had been emptied over his head. It was obvious she had taken him completely by surprise. His smile faltered and, for a while, he just stared at the ring in front of him. Finally, he got to his feet and faced her.

"What is this, Hedeya? What are you doing? Surely you know I was teasing!"

"I don't think it is a teasing matter." Her voice was cold.

"I didn't think you were serious. How could it be possible? You don't know each other. Please, don't act in haste or in anger...." Too late, he realised he had misread her mood completely.

His bewilderment and dismay were genuine and quickly wiped away her annoyance of a moment ago.

Suddenly, Hedeya was contrite; here was an old friend who had been good to her, and he deserved better. The situation they found themselves in was not of his making. He was not to blame for the emotional wounds and scars of her childhood; it was not his fault that she had been unable to blot out those years of terror associated with Muslims.

All along her past had stood between them so that, despite her fondness for him, she had been unable to reciprocate his feelings sufficiently to bring herself to marry him. Yet, he had remained steadfastly patient in the hope that, one day, she would come to change her mind.

It had not happened, she had fallen in love with someone else; and instead of facing that truth, instead of breaking it to him gently, with consideration for his feelings, she was being oversensitive about her own. Was this her way of excusing herself for disappointing him? If so, it was unlike her and not at all well done.

"I'm sorry, Sallah, I cannot explain it..." She faltered, at a loss for words.

"You are serious about him!" he stared at her in amazement.

She nodded, dumbly. When she found her voice, it was low. "It is hard to believe, I know. I refused to believe it myself until I could no longer deny it."

"Do you know what you are doing? Have you thought...are you quite sure?"

She nodded once again. "I am now. My mind is made up. Forgive me, I didn't mean to hurt you, you know that. I thought I was sensible enough to control my feelings, but...how does one stop love?"

"How indeed!" Sallah spoke wryly. "And....what about the others...

Bajo, the children...?

The expression on Hedeya's face shifted slightly to one of uncertainty. She hesitated before answering.

"He is willing to take them as well – but Bajo says she is too old, she wants to go to her brother in Qamishli. And the boys...Mahran has already taken them from me, I don't know how...

"You know he will never give you the boys. Victor is already working and bringing in an income, and even Louis...did you know he has a little side business going with the American soldiers, bartering and selling cigarettes? I gather he is doing quite well in this trade."

"*Ya khaliq*!" Hedeya's expression was furious. "How can his father allow that? It is a disgrace! When they were with me, no matter how hard things became, I would not allow them to give up their schooling. He knew that. He knows how important their education is, and he knew I couldn't afford it without his help – he used that to make me agree to give them up. I thought he did it to punish me, but...I realise, now...oh, I don't know how he could do this!"

Hedeya shook her head angrily. "I heard Victor was working...but Loza!" She sighed. "You know, Mahran promised me – of course, I should never have believed him! I should never have given the boys to him!"

"There is no use upsetting yourself, he is their father and you cannot do anything about that. But I must say your soldier is a good man to offer..."

"Stop calling him 'my soldier'!" Still battling her fury at Mahran, Hedeya flung her words at Sallah. "His name is Santi Dutt – Captain Santi Dutt."

"Oh, I beg your pardon! Captain Dutt. Of course. Well, what I meant is your Captain...er, this Captain...he must love you very much; and I believe you must love him too if you are willing to undertake the risks of such a journey and such change."

He paused. "I wish you could have felt that way about me. But, if it cannot be what I'd hoped for, then I am glad that we can, at least, be friends." He shook his head as though to clear it. "And, you know, I must admit, I am glad the waiting is over."

"Thank you, Sallah, and forgive me." Hedeya's voice was soft with regret. "You have been a true friend, and always will be. I hold a fondness for you that will never be forgotten. You are a good man who deserves the love of a good woman. I know you will find her."

"From your lips to God. You are a brave woman, Hedeya, I have always known that, and I wish you success in your venture. I will do all

I can to help you. But remember, if for any reason it does not work out, if you are not happy, you must let me know. I will wait till then."

United Nations Parade of Nations, Cairo, June 14, 1943.

NOW THAT HE HAD received Hedeya's answer, Santi wasted no time in putting the rest of his plans into motion.

He informed his Camp Commander of his intention to marry, and that set the administrative ball rolling: a background check of the lady in question, and army clearance required for military personnel to marry in a foreign country; the request for her permission to travel to India made vide telegram from the British Consular Office in Cairo to the Office of Secretary of the India Government in Delhi; and lastly, the required provision for guarantee of support and payment of a return passage should it become necessary if things did not work out as planned. The person to stand guarantee would have to be Father, and so, of course, the person Santi appealed to was his mother.

Usha Moyee Dutt,   *Capt. S.P. Dutt*
c/o Dr. J.P. Dutt (Capt)   *8 Reinforcement Camp, MEF*
Civil Surgeon's Bungalow   *Letter No. 38*
District of Burdwan, West Bengal, India   *16 June '43*

Shree-Charaneshu Ma

I trust all is well with the family. Although I have been writing to you regularly, it has been some time since I had any news from home. At one point it seems there was some sort of muddle regarding my camp address; consequently, all letters must have been delivered to the wrong camp and have, apparently, gone astray. I trust there has not been a similar misdirection of my letters to you.

I have been here a while now and am well recuperated. Two days ago, on 14 June, a Military Parade of Nations was held. A colourful gala affair of five thousand marching troops, bands and flag bearers from the various member countries (including ours), tanks, armoured carriers and guns, and an RAF flypast. A grand show, this mighty arsenal of war, a gloss of glamour to hide the foulness of it all. A few decorations were given out as well.

I have been informed, off the record, that I am to be awarded the Military Cross, though I assure you I am much less deserving of it than so many of the men who fought and died beside me – good men whom I will remember all my life. Pray God this travesty may never be repeated.

The main purpose of my letter today is regarding another very special matter. I am acutely aware of the deep concern you have endured of late on my account, and I wish most sincerely that my news should not add to it. However, my decision has not been made lightly, or in haste, and now that I am certain, my respect and regard for you prompt me to confide it to you right away.

You see, I have met a lady here whom I would like to marry. She was married previously and is now divorced. She has three children, which makes her decision to leave her country very difficult indeed. The two boys live with their father while she takes care of her daughter and her elderly mother, as her father has passed away. Sadly, her fortunes changed after his passing, but she has breasted the course of hardships with strength and dignity.

Keep in mind the Army requires its own background checks be done before permission to marry is given in foreign lands. You will, no doubt, receive their intimation fairly soon.

Believe me, I have never met anyone like her before, nor have I ever felt this way before now. I have thought long and hard on it, and I am strongly convinced in both heart and mind that this was destined to be. I cannot explain it but, regardless of the many obstacles in our path, I know beyond all doubt, should I allow this relationship to slip away I would rue it the rest of my life.

Forgive me, Mother, if I have overstepped my bounds in expressing myself as I do, but I know of no other way to impress upon you how confident I am in this matter, and how earnestly I desire your consent and blessing. You must realise, of course, that I have addressed this letter to you alone in the hope that you will pave the way for me to broach the subject with Father! I am already indebted to you beyond measure and yet I am asking for your help once again, hoping that you, with all the understanding of a mother, will not fail to grant it. Despite the differences in our backgrounds, I assure you, you will not be

disappointed in your daughter-in-law when you meet her.
   Please accept my respectful regards.

   I remain, as always, your affectionate son, Santi

————•♦•————

WHILE WAITING FOR OFFICIAL clearance and permission, Santi busied himself with the many arrangements necessary for Hedeya's travel.

He made enquiries with Cairo Misr Travel & Shipping as to his options. They suggested the two most reliable companies – The Mogul Line Ltd. managed by Turner Morrison Co. Ltd., as well as Cox & Kings (Agents) Ltd., a Lloyds Bank company – both with addresses in Calcutta and Bombay. After some consideration, he decided on the latter. Conveniently located at 5 Bankshall Street in Calcutta, Cox & Kings would do very well indeed. Upon his return to India he could make all necessary arrangements once he was informed of Hedeya's final plans and date of departure.

Meanwhile, as per his paybook, and after necessary expenses, he would have approximately five hundred Egyptian pounds remaining from his army pay accumulated while he was a POW. This he would leave with Hedeya to use in any way she saw fit.

And so, as the days passed into weeks, and May turned into June, Santi felt the pull of a pilgrimage to be made. Before taking his final leave of the place that had written such an intensely memorable chapter into his life, and in order to find – if it were at all possible – some measure of closure to that chapter, a journey had to be undertaken; he hoped it might help to lay the past to rest in some small way.

He managed to cadge a lift off an American Army lorry driver on his way to a couple of outlying posts. The driver understood – *hell, yes, sir! He had been at Kasserine, hadn't he! And he'd sure be glad of the company.* Santi was told to hop right in, and off they headed into the desert.

The old desert road stretched long and empty into the horizon. Gone was the confusion of dusty convoys, tanks and troops on the march. Yet, the disquieting evidence remained – broken down lorries, blackened skeletons of tanks and guns, tangled barbed wire – abandoned by the roadside and scattered through the scrubby sands where ghost armies had fought and passed on. At least the bodies of the dead, bloated and decaying, no longer lay about! Mercifully, some good sense had prevailed to remove that indecency.

Their first stop was the old RAF Landing Ground – now American airfield – at El Amiriya where enemy equipment still lay heaped beside the road. One more stop further afield, and when that was done, they made a small detour to El Alamein (meaning 'the two flags'), that bleak railway station, undistinguished till the war came and swept it, unwilling and unwitting, into the pages of history.

Commemorated by a large cemetery that kept watch over the old desert battlefields, rank upon rank of rough white crosses, disciplined even in death, bore silent witness to the battles fought here and paid for with thousands of lives. These would be replaced later with permanent headstones.

There was a gentle quiet about the place, a listening silence as for lingering echoes; a haunting, otherworldly melancholy, as though all that had transpired here but a short while ago, the erstwhile armies that had marched and fought so recently, now laid to rest beneath the sands, had passed already into the realm of history. No longer part of the present, these poor felled souls belonged now to the past, interned forever in this place, first desecrated then sanctified by their presence.

> *There is on earth no worthier grave*
> *To hold the bodies of the brave*
> *Than this place of pain and pride*
> *Where they nobly fought and nobly died.*

In 1918, just before he died in the World War that had preceded this one – the war that was supposed to end all wars – Alfred Joyce Kilmer, a Sergeant in the Fighting 69th Infantry Regiment of the American Army, had paid tribute thus to the dead.

For Santi, standing there once again, the silence was in eerie contrast to the chaos and din of battle that he all too well remembered. Far away to the west, 2/4 Gurkhas and its companion battalions had fought, and died, and been captured. Where were their bodies? Had they been recovered for burial? And those who had required but not received the fires of cremation, had they been accorded the dignity of an honourable grave? How many of those good, loyal men were out there still, somewhere, lost to all but the desert, buried like his pistol, in the safekeeping of the sands. *And then you passed, and in your place stood Silence with her lifted face…*

The war had passed over this land, scarring it most horribly, leaving this memorial of destroyed hopes and wasted lives to bear witness to the tragedy of human error repeated. It was a sad mirror-image of the loss and despair that had clung to that earlier, decaying WWI graveyard the Battalion had passed through on its journey to Persia

– how long ago that seemed!

There had been another doctor in that war who stood before a wold of white crosses, just like this, stretching into the distance. As though aware he was soon to join their ranks, he had lamented the pain of those dead in a plea to the living. And his words, forever after, would render the red poppy the Flower of Remembrance:

> *In Flanders fields the poppies blow*
> *Between the crosses row on row...*
> *We are the Dead. Short days ago*
> *We lived, felt dawn, saw sunset glow,*
> *Loved and were loved, and now we lie*
> *In Flanders fields.*

It was thus, in 1915, that Lt. Col. John McCrae, MD, of the Canadian Army gave a voice to those who no longer had one with this simple reminder to make their sacrifice worthwhile:

> *To you from failing hands we throw*
> *The torch; be yours to hold it high.*
> *If ye break faith with us that die*
> *We shall not sleep, though poppies grow*
> *In Flanders fields.*

Nothing had changed; it never would until the real foe was identified and vanquished. The evil bred of greed and power. Can such a foe ever be vanquished?

Over 100,000 men had died in this desert war, most of them pitifully young, each one no doubt leaving behind loved ones. By all rights they ought to have lived their lives, chased their dreams, reared families and children, flourished and grown old fruitfully. But they had been called upon, yet again, to sacrifice it all; and, worthy men that they were, they had done just that – to save humanity, they were told. Was the human race worth it? This time would it remember, or even fully comprehend the enormous sacrifice made here in its name? The repetitive cost was heart-rending.

He had seen it, and he would never forget; known or unknown, these fallen soldiers were brothers-in-arms. Some had grown to be... friends? The word was inadequate. Facile. It held neither depth nor breadth enough to encompass relationships forged in an experience that would prove the most fearful of one's entire life. A heart-bursting, gut-wrenching experience that brands you – body, mind and soul – so you would be, forever, unable to speak of its horror to those who had not witnessed it. How could one find the words? Did such words even exist? They had stood shoulder to shoulder and faced death together. Men he had not known or seen before. He had held their guts, their brains, their lives in his hands; and sometimes he had held them as their lives slipped through his hands. He had prayed to the Almighty, and raged, and prayed again, and there had been no mercy. No. He would never forget.

As the sun went down over the western horizon in the sort of pageantry only a desert sunset could achieve, evening shadows began to lengthen across the sands. In that gathering darkness, just before night fell with its usual swiftness in the desert, he imagined he heard familiar voices.

"I say, Ben, have you heard the news...it's a bloody great knees-up out there...?"

"There you are, Doc! Williams was looking for you just then..."

"*Thagra raho huzur...*"

And then, across the moonlit sands, they would have heard that melting refrain wafting over from the German trenches at night... Radio Belgrade...2155 hrs...the voice of Lale Anderson...

> *"Vor der Kaserne vor dem grohen Tor,*
> *Stand eine Lanterne und steht sie nach davor..."*

And closer at hand, the lads of 8th Army picking it up in words someone had hastily slung together...their sentiments mingling with those of the enemy...

> *"There was a song 8th Army used to hear,*
> *In the lonely desert, lovely, sweet and clear;*
> *Over the ether came the strain,*
> *The soft refrain, each night again,*
> *With you Lili Marlene, with you Lili Marlene..."*
> *"Listen to the bugle hear its silv'ry call,*
> *Carried by the night and telling one and all..."*

He remembered words Bajo had once uttered as she mourned over a memory from the tragic times in Turkey. Her words had been stilted as she tried to translate from her own language into English. Then, he had caught their gist, but it was the intense experiences he had come through over this past year that had given him some understanding of the suffering that birthed her pain; her unforgettable words remained an echo in his head, growing within him these many months past, until, finally, they reached his heart: *Experience paints our lives in many colours. The pages of history cannot speak with the voice of those who have witnessed its passage; only those who have lived the time and survived its pain know its truth. The distant retelling of it is merely hollow interpretation, the rustle of dry words on paper, the empty echo of a storm that becomes merely a wind passing through time ...*

FINALLY, IN THE LAST week of June, army clearance and permission to marry were received; and none too soon since the convoy was almost ready for departure.

On 4 July, a telegram arrived from home. It pointed out with some concern, the risk of haste in a matter as important as the choice of a life-partner, and advocated that a little further time and thought were, perhaps, better suited to such a decision. Santi was relieved, under the circumstances, that the reply had not been a stronger objection; he would, he assured himself, be able to allay his parents' fears when he returned home. And, since he could not be more certain of his decision than he was at present, he had no qualms in soliciting Asis Habib's help one last time. Would the old priest further his success of Santi's initial proposal by proxy and ratify it now with the sanctity of marriage?

On 6 July 1943, Hedeya and Santi were married. They spent their one and only night together in Shepheard's Hotel, a single love-filled night of discovery, of rapture, making memories that would last a lifetime. He had waited so long for her, all his life it seemed; she realised, without knowing it, she too had been waiting for him, for this. They lingered over each other, drawing out each sweet moment, living it to the fullest, shutting out the world and the war as best they could. But when they rested in sleep, even as he surrendered his guard, the nightmares crept in, giving her a glimpse of the terrifying hell that tortured his soul. She wrapped her arms around him and soothed him till he returned to her again; and they clung to each precious passing hour with an urgency born of the knowledge that their ecstasy was all too fleeting, that time could not be halted, and morning would not be stayed.

And when it came all too soon, when the world could no longer be held at bay and the war came rushing in once more to part them, they knew, reluctantly, it was time to let go. Reality awaited and would not be denied. They held each other one long, final moment, drawing comfort from each other, reliving the taste, the scent, the feel of each other before they put away their dreams and shut the door on that small, fragile world they had made together.

Returning her again to her family, he thanked Bajo for her kindness, assuring the old lady she had no need to worry – he'd made sure Hedeya had all the necessary information, the right addresses and proper instructions. More than that, she had his solemn promise he would take good care of her daughter and granddaughter.

Their own goodbyes had been said in the privacy of their room and keepsake photos exchanged. Hedeya had slipped her's into Santi's breast pocket, pressing it close against his heart. But now, at the last minute, she insisted on accompanying him to the station; and though he protested mildly at first, in the end he was glad they had that little extra time to themselves.

He hailed a passing *arabiya hantur* and they drove together in the horse-drawn carriage, one final time, through the city streets lined with their beautiful buildings of French and Italian architecture. In these last shared minutes, there was so much that needed to be said and, yet, it was hard finding the words to say any of it. They held hands but could not hold back time. It flew by even though the drive took longer than expected, so that they arrived at the station with only minutes to spare before his train's departure.

On the platform, they tried to be circumspect in their goodbyes. Standing on the lower step of the doorway to his compartment, Santi held her hand tightly in his, assuring her all would be well. As the train began to move, Hedeya walked alongside it, keeping pace. She tried to smile, but her throat ached with the tears that were threatening to break through. She tried to swallow the lump in her throat. Santi noticed the small tremble at the lower left corner of her mouth, a tiny dimple that quivered into view on the edge of her lip and vanished almost before he caught it. He held her hand tight, so tight, it was almost painful. His jaw set as he fought to control the sudden, powerful emotions that welled up within him.

All at once he leant down, and, hooking an impetuous arm about Hedeya, he lifted her up onto the train step and kissed her, holding her hard against him as though he could not bear to let her go. That single kiss, as it surged through him with a hunger and fervour that parted her lips, told her of all the pent-up longing he would endure in the months of separation ahead.

"No matter what, remember I love you. I will always love you," he whispered against her lips.

The fierce urgency of his passion filled her, and she answered him from the depths of her being. For one brief moment, one last, long kiss compelling her to wrap her arms around his neck, they were lost in each other, oblivious to their surroundings. And then he put her down.

Unsteady with emotion, she stumbled, reaching for him. Flustered, tearful, she looked up. He was standing in the doorway, a crooked smile on his lips, waving farewell. That smile, that face, she tried to stamp every little line and curve in her mind's eye – oh, how *could* she do without him now! How could she surrender him to the war all over again! For a single night he had held her in his arms, and his love had set her heart alight and her body on fire. She had risen to meet his ecstasy, and it was like nothing she had ever known. For a few short hours he had lain in her arms, all hers, and she had tended his troubles and shared his contentment. Each moment had been measured with a heartbeat, each heartbeat an assurance of the love that bound them to each other. And now, all too soon, it was time to let him go.

Santi and Hedeya – Till We Meet Again –
Parting mementos exchanged, Cairo 1943.

The train picked up speed; his face blurred and swam through the mist in her eyes as it carried him away from her, further and further he receded, growing smaller; and then he was gone! All that remained was the distant whistle of the departing train, long and plaintive through a cloud of smoke, and she found herself standing on the platform, alone, among strangers.

Hedeya knew they had attracted curious, even some slightly reproving, stares; and she was surprised to find, for the first time, that she really didn't care at all. Let them look or think what they would. Did it really matter? Of course not! They didn't know her or anything about her. In fact, what was that funny saying of Bajo's? Oh yes, "*he who knows my father, let him go and tell him!*"

Still feeling the warm, demanding urgency of his lips on hers, she held her head high and, trying not to stumble through her tears, she walked defiantly out of the station. She would not allow the sadness of parting to mar the happiness of the last few days. They'd been given a mere handful of hours together, but they had woven a pledge for the future, hers to keep, no matter what. And as to the future – that last embrace and the sweet memories of the one night they had spent in each other's arms would have to suffice a long, long time, till destiny – and the war – allowed them to meet once again.

On 8 July, Santi, together with sixteen other officers and three VCOs, embarked on His Majesty's Hospital Ship, the *HMHS Karapara* waiting in convoy at the port of Suez. Three weeks later Hedeya received a telegram:

Disembarked Bombay 19 July. Two months repatriation leave: w.e.f. 20 July to 18 Sept. Two weeks war leave to follow: w.e.f. 19 Sep. Making all necessary arrangements for your travel. All my love. Santi

CHAPTER FIFTY-THREE

Burma: The Gateway To India

O, the road to Mandalay, where the flyin' fishes play,
An' the dawn comes up like thunder Outer China 'crost the bay…
For the wind is in the palm trees, and the temple bells they say:
"Come you back, you British soldier; come you back to Mandalay!"
An' I'm learnin' 'ere in London what the ten-year soldier tells:
"If you've 'eared the East a-callin', you won't ever need naught else"

– Rudyard Kipling, "Mandalay" (adapted)

WHILE THE DESERT WAR in the Middle East was progressing through its final year, on the eastern border of India the British Army suffered severe setbacks in the jungles of Burma. At one time integrated and governed as part of British India, Burma had become a separate British Province in 1937.

In the intervening weeks between the invasion of Malaya and the fall of Singapore, on 22 December '41, the Japanese invaded Burma. Looking to its oil, minerals, and large supplies of rice, they determined it would be their gateway to India as well. Of added importance to their war effort was the closure of the Burma Road, the route of communication and transport between the British and Chiang Kai-shek's Nationalist Chinese. In just over two and a half months, on 8 March '42, Rangoon fell to them, and by 26 May they managed to push the British into a full-on retreat, all the way back to Imphal in India. And there, finally, both sides were halted by the onset of the monsoon.

When the torrential rains at last gave over, the British, in an attempt to regain their ground lost in Burma, launched the Arakan Offensive. 14th Indian Division had some initial success but was, once again, beaten back. The battle for Burma waged on through 1942, into 1943; and in the early part of that year, under the codename 'Operation Longcloth', a push was made, approximately 3,000 men strong, from Imphal in India into Burma. Brigadier Orde Wingate and 77 Indian Infantry Brigade – which included the 3/2 Gurkha Rifles – gained renown as the Chindits (from the Burmese *Chinthe*, the mythical creatures that guard Burmese temples).

A number of these Chindit columns infiltrated deep behind enemy lines to create havoc with Japanese communications, and cause as much damage as possible to their supply and railway lines. Losses, however, were great – of the 3,000 men who went in, a third were killed, captured or succumbed to disease and starvation; in some cases, their plight was such, the desperate men were forced to eat their pack mules, those faithful companions who had laboured for them so hard and so far. As for those who did manage to return, many were much too debilitated for further active duty.

The Japanese now occupied much of Burma, and in August 1943 Japanese-occupied Burma proclaimed its independence from Britain.

Previously, in March of '42, the Andaman and Nicobar Islands had been occupied as well – the only Indian territory to fall to the enemy. And in April, eighteen Kawanishi H6K long-range flying boats – nicknamed 'Mavis' by the Allies – were stationed there, at Port Blair, within easy flying distance of Calcutta. This put the 250,000 tons of merchant shipping lying in Calcutta harbour at great risk. Moreover, on the weekend of 5/6 April, Ceylon's harbour and the cities of Kakinada and Vizagapatnam in South India were bombed by two carrier-based aircraft from a Japanese fleet positioned in the Indian Ocean; and fear that this fleet might any day steam into the Bay of Bengal and wreak havoc added to the furore in Calcutta.

In consequence of these events, on 14 April, two Lockheed Hudson bombers from 139 Squadron left Calcutta for Port Blair via a fuelling stop at Akyab. Skimming low over the water at 30 feet, they swooped in to destroy three aircraft and damage eleven more. A second raid on 18 April inflicted further damage and took out two additional aircraft. This time, however, there was a price paid with one Hudson shot down while the other limped home badly damaged. Even so, all in all, the RAF had succeeded – seventy merchant ships sailed safely from Calcutta harbour to scatter out of harm's way.

Still, rumours of invasion spread like wildfire and would not be doused. Additional squadrons of Hurricanes were hurriedly dispatched to defend the area, and new airfields mushroomed in and around the city. Most prominent in the city was the converted strip of Red Road, eleven hundred yards long, between the main thoroughfare of Chowringhee Road and the great, green expanse of the Maidan. Here, the sight of aircraft manoeuvring sharp turns over and around Firpo's fashionable tearoom, as they roared in to land, brought the war home to the general populace like nothing before.

Gradually, Calcutta absorbed these changes and life went on through the summer months. It was December that brought the first bombings. On 20 December eight Ki-21 Type 97 bombers ('Sally' to the Allies) of the Imperial Japanese Army Air Force hit the Budge Budge oil plant, south of the city. They landed a gaping hole as well outside the elegant Great Eastern Hotel, leaving its upper-crust clientele aghast and in total confusion. If that were not enough, they returned for good measure on 24 December to bomb the area of Chowringhee, Bentinck Street and Dalhousie Square, disrupting Christmas Eve and throwing the city into a state of unholy panic. Fortunately, the damage done was not great – though the statue of Sir Stuart Bailey in Dalhousie Square did suffer the indignity of some slight disfigurement – but the physicality of war now scarred the city, and thousands fled it, causing tremendous disruption along the Grand Trunk Road.

It became obvious there was an urgent need for defences to be strengthened. On 14 January 1943, RAF Squadron 176 was formed at Dum Dum airport. Reinforcing the city's Hurricanes, this Squadron's night fighter aircraft were the Bristol Beaufort torpedo bombers – the Beaufighters. Its motto was *Nocte Custodinus, We Keep the Night Watch*; its job was to protect the city of Calcutta. It became known as the Calcutta Squadron, and its baptism took place the day after its birth.

When the Japanese Sallys came over the city again on 15 January, it was a bright moonlit night and the Calcutta Squadron was ready for them. Three enemy aircraft were shot down by one of its aces, twenty-two-year-old Arthur Maurice Owers Pring. He had fought over the deserts of North Africa, he had defended Malta, now in 1943 his courage and daring would make him a hero Calcutta would take to her heart. And thus, under guard, the old city weathered winter into summer.

UPON HIS RETURN THAT summer of '43, Santi spent his first two days in Calcutta. He stayed with Kanti at his flat in Mohini Mansions, a pleasant, gated complex at 94 Russa Road, in South Calcutta. As usual, July in Calcutta was steamy hot, but he welcomed the uniquely familiar feel of his home-city as it wrapped itself about him.

Of course, there were differences. He was dismayed to see that the number of hungry poor on the streets had multiplied alarmingly. There were rumours of starvation in the villages, and the large multitudes of people sleeping and begging in the city streets seemed to bear them out. Human turmoil had taken over the world, and here its effect on the civilian population of his home-city was terrible to witness. How this tragedy would eventually be resolved hardly bore thinking!

Then, of course, the city's proximity to Burma, plus its standing as headquarters of the British war effort in India, left it teeming with military personnel; American personnel as well now, both army and air force. And the sight of Hurricanes landing on the makeshift airstrip on Red Road was an oddity indeed – albeit fitting, given the war footing of the city. Blackout restrictions were still enforced; Victoria Memorial wore a shroud, and the front faces of most official and large public buildings were barricaded behind sandbags and 'blast walls' built of brick. He had returned home from the front lines but, here too, his city wore those ugly stains of war. Despite it all, there was no denying, it was good to be back!

Since he had already reported for debriefing in Bombay, there was no reason for further delay in Calcutta. Moreover, there were matters to discuss with the family, urgent matters that would brook no delay. And so, accompanied by Bela and Bina, he travelled up to Burdwan where Father was still posted as Civil Surgeon. His homecoming was joyful, and he spent the initial half of his war leave resting, eating home-cooked meals, and trying to unwind while searching for an opportune moment and the appropriate words to broach the subject of his marriage and the official guarantee required for Hedeya.

He was surprised at how physically and mentally exhausted he was. The noisy, adrenaline-packed, horror-filled days, the sleepless, war-weary nights, the overcrowded, harrowing months in enemy hands, all had taken their toll. Now, secure in the quiet and comfort of home, trying to let go of those memories that dogged him, suddenly body and mind seemed to succumb to a weariness he had not expected. And he found, despite all efforts, there were walls with no way through. At first, this bewildered the family.

Eager to catch up on news, they gradually realised the one subject he was unable to talk about was the war. Previously, from that distant world of chaos, he had needed to convey some of his thoughts, share something of his feelings in his letters; now, they understood, the letters had merely skimmed the surface. And though it was done with, though he had returned, he seemed incapable of exposing or exorcising the demons that had followed him home; whatever they were, he found it necessary to bury them in a deeply excavated recess in some far corner of his mind.

The one person who could comprehend some of the camouflaged pain and horror was the father who had tried to shield him from them; you had to have been there to understand. He knew the son, the brother, who had left them two years before was not the same person who had returned. The rest of the family realised it too, but their only inkling of what he had endured was what they gleaned from the mutterings and thrashings to be witnessed while he slept. Then, when his guard was down and he lay helpless, those short, violent glimpses were disturbing; at times they were frightening.

In time, being home with family, back to his roots and in familiar surroundings, would begin to salve Santi's wracked mind and psyche. Each day the comfort of family life, of normal interaction, built his strength, and paved the road to recovery. But the memories of human suffering went too deep ever to leave him; those fiends of war would remain, lurking in dark corners within his soul till the day he died.

Santi eventually returned to Calcutta to arrange for Hedeya's travel permits. With Mother on his side, quietly batting for him, Father had agreed to stand guarantee as per army requirements. Accordingly, all the right forms and requests were obtained, filled out and submitted. Now, preparing for her arrival, he took a three-bedroom flat in Mohini Mansions, where Kanti resided, and furnished it from Whiteaways, Laidlaw & CO. on Chowringhee. And when he received Hedeya's final communication for a go-ahead, he went to the offices of Cox & Kings, where he arranged sea passage for one adult, with a child, to be purchased as soon as their travel permits came through.

The end of September, with his leave over, Santi reported to IMH Alipore, 352 Subarea, Calcutta. The last day of his leave, he and Kanti lunched at Firpo's, where they bumped into a group of pilots from The Calcutta Squadron; among them was Maurice Pring. During the course of the afternoon, Santi was to discover not only had the young pilot flown in North Africa, he had downed four enemy aircraft there and winged two more. Had their paths ever crossed, he wondered? The one on the ground, the other in the air? Could they have unknowingly been in the same place at the same time? But recalling memories of that time and place, even with someone who had shared them, soon proved disconcerting in a setting as opulent as Firpo's, and so Santi manoeuvred the conversation back to the present; it was safer ground.

Next day at work he found a steady stream of traffic passing through the hospital. He was kept busy with the usual injured and sick; the blessed difference being these facilities were far better, as was the sanitation. This was a proper hospital dispensing proper care – nothing like the appalling conditions in the desert!

At the racecourse the ladies of the Women's Voluntary Service had set up a makeshift hostel of sorts for soldiers coming and going: those on a few days much-needed furlough from the war, those on their way to join it, and those invalided and on their way out of it altogether. Facilities provided *charpoy* beds with clean sheets (though there was a running battle with bed bugs the men constantly brought in), hot meals, dances, and other entertainment when available. Additional services such as barbering, laundry, sewing and shoe repair were provided as well, plus help with the more personal needs of letter writing for the wounded who couldn't, and gift-shopping for those who didn't know how. A gift shop stocked the essentials, and even posted parcels home for the men.

From time to time, Santi was called in for an illness or injury, or to dispense vaccinations when the need arose. Through it all he continued to push through army red tape, trying to hasten Hedeya's travel permits; he was told it was a matter of waiting…and hoping.

At this time Allied Command in India had created SEAC – South East Asia Command – to oversee operations in Burma, India and the Indian Ocean. Field Marshal Archibald Percy Wavell (now Viscount Wavell of Cyrenaica and Winchester) was Viceroy of India, and General Claude Auchinlek had been appointed Commander in Chief of the Indian Army. In November Lord Louis Mountbatten took office as Supreme Allied Commander and, since there was by now a large American presence in India, United States Lt. General 'Vinegar Joe' Stilwell was made Deputy Allied Commander. Severally, and together, these men strategised the Burma campaign.

With the Burma Road closed by the Japanese, the only supply route between India and China was overland, across 500 miles of enemy occupied jungle and the treacherous Patkai, Kumon and Santsung mountains. US Air Transport Command nicknamed this eastern end of the Himalayas 'The Hump', and its pilots, flying their 'Gooney Birds' (C-47s) over ranges that rose precipitously up to 15,000 ft., managed, for the most part, to keep this lifeline open. Hundreds of thousands of tons of supplies, munitions, fuel, and men were airlifted, despite the uncharted routes and the unfamiliar weather with its hazards of thunderstorms, turbulence, and high-altitude icing.

However, with the Burma campaign ongoing, an overland route was deemed essential as well. The Allies under command of Lt. General Stilwell, and aided by Chiang Kai-shek's forces from Yunnan, undertook to build this road, the Ledo Road, and a railway link to the Burma Road. An engineering feat of no mean proportion, these would transport additional supplies and support troops across the mountains and rivers, deep into the jungles of Burma.

In December Santi was sent on loan from ADMS Fort William, Calcutta, to a Casualty Clearing Station at the Burma Front. Not completely recovered from the ordeal of war and malnutrition in captivity, Santi had suffered a bout of lobular pneumonia. Now, back on his feet, it was off to war once again. Just prior to leaving, however, he had his first encounter with Japanese planes. As in the previous year, December seemed their month of choice. It was Sunday morning, 5 December, a little before noon. A large formation of enemy aircraft flew well out over the Bay of Bengal to avoid detection, and then set course for Calcutta. Their targets were the Kidderpore docks and Howrah Bridge.

By now there were American and RAF bases at Alipore, Baigachi and Agartala. Incongruous as it was, even in Kumartuli where their images were crafted, the formidable Hindu goddesses, in respect of the times, deigned to share their domain with the strange modern warbirds of the sky. Calcutta Squadron was presently stationed at Baigachi. When the enemy was finally spotted, a warning was sent out to scramble. Despite being night fliers, four Beaufighter pilots from the Calcutta Squadron answered the call and took off instead in Hurricanes. Among these was Maurice Pring who was preparing to go on leave.

Miscommunication left the Hurricanes unprepared for the number and type of enemy aircraft they were up against. Three Hurricanes were shot down and the last, badly damaged, barely found its way home. Of the three downed pilots, only one made it back.

Beating all odds, the survivor walked, mile after mile for three days, until he reached Calcutta where he made a beeline for the Great Eastern Hotel. Unphased by his appearance, cool as a cucumber, he sauntered into Maxim's, bloody, muddy and thirsty from his adventures. Welcomed with much delighted backslapping from his chums, he planted himself at the bar and there proceeded to 'wet his parched throat and allay his appalling thirst'.

Fortune, alas, was not as kind to the other two pilots; one of whom was Maurice Pring. Forsaking his leave, the nightflying Beaufighter ace took to the day skies and lost his life flying a Hurricane. His loss was mourned city-wide where his body was laid to rest in the Commonwealth War Graves cemetery in Bhowanipore. (Joydeep Sircar: *In the Skies of Calcutta: A Tribute to Maurice Pring*)

SANTI WAS SECONDED FOR attachment as Medical Officer to an anti-aircraft unit. From time to time, dictated by necessity, he went up from the CCS to assist in the Main Dressing Station, and to help transport back the critically wounded. Casualties were heavy and there was little time for anything other than dealing with the men returning from the jungle – injured, exhausted, and sick with dysentery, malaria, scrub typhus and malnutrition. There were, as well, large numbers of men with jungle or Naga sores from infected insect and festering leech bites – the foot-long elephant leech being a particularly nasty offender. In between, one tried to grab a couple of hours kip, a bite to eat, and then one started all over again; but, never far from his thoughts, Santi waited eagerly for news of Hedeya's progress and date of departure. He hoped, the war permitting, he might wangle a week's leave when the time came.

British and American units were fighting alongside each other in this area of operations; and for Santi, the Americans were a new and very different experience. In February 1944 an American long-range penetration group arrived in Burma. This was Galahad Force. First formed in San Francisco, USA, it was made up of jungle-trained Guadalcanal veterans, American-Japanese Nisei troops, some Australians, Caledonians, and other US veterans, even some who volunteered their way out of various stockades. This mismatched unit landed in India, and after undergoing training in Deolali and Deogarh, it was put under command of US Brigadier General Frank Merrill and sent into the jungles of Burma to wage a war similar to that of the Chindits. Achieving fame as Merrill's Marauders, their success, like the Chindits, was gained at a heavy cost in human lives.

At the same time, Lt. General William Slim (the 2/4 Gurkhas old GOC in Iraq), now Commander British Fourteenth Army, together with US Airforce General George E. Stratemeyer of Eastern Command, issued a directive requiring reinforcements be flown into Burma. Three landing strips were cleared for this purpose: Piccadilly, Broadway and Chowringhee. Nine thousand men were flown in and, with the help of the Kachin, a tribe from the hills of northern Burma, they were to proceed to Indaw to help Stillwell and the Chinese forces clear the Japanese out of northern Burma.

In March further change took place. Brigadier Wingate, sadly, had perished in a plane crash. General Slim appointed another 4th

Gurkha officer, Brigadier Joe Lentaigne, in his place. From Santi's old 2/4 Gurkha Battalion, Robert Williams and John Masters, both, were somewhere out there too. In April, Masters, in command of 111 Brigade, pushed north through the sweltering jungles, hot, humid, and rife with sickness and disease. He was to establish Blackpool, a stronghold to block the road and railway at Hopin, thirty miles south of Mogaung. Santi learned later, he had withstood a first severe attack by the Japanese but, due to lack of support, the second attack had broken through his defences. There was nothing for it but that he evacuate Blackpool, and here he faced a terrible quandary – he was unable to move nineteen soldiers, so severely wounded they were beyond saving. They would have to be left to the mercy of the enemy.

Fully aware they would receive no quarter there, that their inevitable end would be gruesome if left to the Japanese, Masters acceded to their request for the dignity of a speedy end while among their own. Either way death stared them in the face, the only choice was whether it would be quick and merciful at the hands of friends or a tortured one in the hands of the enemy. It was a decision no civilised man should have to make, a memory no one should be required to live with. But make it he did. They were shot and their bodies were hidden in thickets of bamboo. He would write of it later, with great pain, in his book *The Road Past Mandalay*.

And so it went with these cobbled-together Allied forces. The fighting in Burma would continue with no let-up until 1945 when they would begin, inexorably, agonisingly, to regain the initiative. They would beat back the Japanese offensives at Imphal and Kohima till, finally, in March 1945, Mandalay would be retaken and Japan would, eventually, evacuate Rangoon and lose Burma. To honour their sacrifice and the loss of so many Allied lives in the jungles of Burma, a memorial was later placed on the north side of Victoria Embankment near the Ministry of Defence in London.

Despite their losses, Japan would continue to fight in the Pacific, even after Germany's surrender in May and the end of the war in Europe. Tragically, Japanese surrender would not come until August 1945. At that time, the Americans, on the horns of a dilemma whether to bomb Japan or invade it and suffer the loss of hundreds of thousands more men on both sides, opted to drop the newly developed atomic bomb on two Japanese cities, Hiroshima and Nagasaki. Thus, finally, the terrible conflict of WWII would be brought to its horrific end.

CHAPTER FIFTY-FOUR

A Parting Of Ways

Gone – flitted away,
Taken the stars from the night and the sun from the day!
Gone, and a cloud in my heart. and a storm in the air!
Flown to the east or the west, flitted I know not where!

– Alfred Lord Tennyson, "Gone"

IN CAIRO THERE WAS not much news to be had of the war in Burma; all Hedeya knew was, Santi was somewhere in that area. She worried constantly about him and the uncertainty of his whereabouts. Plus, what of his whereabouts when she landed in his country? Her travel permit having come through on 18th February, she had sent him a telegram. Wherever he was, all the necessary arrangements had somehow been made. And now, with their tickets booked, she was preparing to cross an ocean with her small daughter, to a place completely unfamiliar in every aspect – apart from what she had read recently. Little as that was, it was hardly enough to prepare her, and if it happened he was not there to receive them…! Her misgivings weighed heavy, but the memory of his love strengthened her resolve not to falter in her plans.

She would have to tackle Mahran sooner or later; she knew he could complicate matters, if he so desired, by refusing his consent for Violette to accompany her. However, since she was not one to procrastinate over anything, she decided to get the matter over and done with right away. She thought her strategy through carefully, and after she had decided on the best way to handle him, she sent a message through Loza requesting a meeting at her home.

When he arrived, she informed him of her plans, and told him it was now time for him to take on the responsibility of his daughter as well as his sons; now that he had remarried, she felt reassured the little girl would be properly cared for.

Mahran's comeback was unequivocal and exactly what she had anticipated. "When I took the boys, you tricked everyone into thinking you had left the city, and now that you are actually leaving you want me to make it easy for you by taking the girl too! Well, you know my mind on this matter – I have the boys, they are old enough to take care of themselves; the girl is another story. So what if I am married, you are her mother, her place is with you. I will no doubt have a family of my own soon to take care of."

Hedeya breathed a little easier – he had not called her bluff! She kept her voice soft, reasonable. "But I am leaving the country. I don't know what it will be like for her in India."

"That is your problem, not mine. You have always been bull-headed, Hedeya, so I realise once you have made a decision there is no turning you from it. You will do what you have set out to do no matter what anyone says. And, believe me, plenty will be said. People will say you have abandoned your children and run off with a soldier to some godforsaken place. Have you no shame?"

"Gossip that will be helped along by you, no doubt," Hedeya could not stop herself from snapping back. "But why should it bother me? I won't be here to listen to your stories, or theirs."

"Ah, that fiery temper never burns far from that cold surface does it!" Mahran gave a short laugh, wagging a finger at her.

"Well, what do you expect when you throw out accusations like that – and you know they are not true. I *could* have managed to keep them with me if you had given me a little help like you were supposed to. But you took the boys, and in spite of the promises you made, you have put them to work…"

"And what will I do with the girl? If you don't want her, leave her with your mother, don't foist her on me. You made your choices, you live with them. That's all I have to say."

The smug look he wore made Hedeya itch to slap his face – *how dare he!* Instead, she controlled the urge and attempted to pander to his sense of victory. She adopted a conciliatory manner, as though appealing to him. All said and done, he was Violette's father, and as long as she wasn't a burden to him, he must care in some way – especially if his reputation was on the line.

"What am I to do, Mahran? As you say, people will gossip. As far as I am concerned, there is no avoiding it, whether I take Bebe or leave her there will be talk. Of course, as I said, I won't be here to face it. But you will – and if I have to leave her with Bajo, can you imagine what they will say about you? That you are her father and you have abandoned your daughter to her destitute old grandmother who has no means of support – unless, of course," she stopped for a moment before adding, hopefully, "unless you intend to support them both."

The look of dawning consternation on Mahran's face pleased Hedeya. She was on the right track. She continued. "On the other hand, if I take her with me, you would no doubt tell everyone that I had kidnapped her. That would further ruin my reputation and poor Bajo would be left to deal with the malicious gossip. I cannot put her through that, so I think I will have to take your advice and leave her here with Bajo. It is the only choice that will work because public opinion will force you to take care of them."

Horrified by the prospect, Mahran stumbled over his words. "Hedeya, I swear I…I would never say such a thing. I promise…you can rest assured…" His voice faltered as Hedeya shook her head.

"I cannot trust you, Mahran. You never keep your word to me. You say one thing and you do another…" she broke off as though struck by a thought. "Well, maybe," she hesitated, looking doubtful, "if you wrote something for me…you know…that you agree I should take her…"

"Of course! I can do that right now," Mahran rushed to assure her – anything to rid himself of this sudden problem that had begun to loom uncomfortably large in his life! "Bring me pen and paper and I will give you my written consent. A girl's place is with her mother, no one can argue with that."

Hedeya pretended to look undecided. Curbing a desire to rush from the room, she rose at last and moving slowly, as though still unsure, she left the room. Returning a moment later, she handed him a sheet of paper and an ink pen, and when he had finished writing, she took them from him, careful to keep her face innocent of the relief she was feeling.

She saw him to the door and watched as he reached the lower landing of the stairs before she spoke. Maybe it was unworthy of her since she had achieved what she wanted, but she could not help herself.

"Mahran."

He turned towards her, half-expecting – what? Hedeya smiled; she chose her words carefully, savouring each one, aiming it with the precision of a dart. "I want you to know you have just given up one hundred *geneihs*. I was prepared to pay you for agreeing to let Bebe come with me – and she is not 'the girl', she is *your daughter.*"

It was small revenge for all he had put her through, but the stunned, then furious look on his face gave her some degree of satisfaction as she shut the door, once and for all, on her life with him.

AFTER PROMISING TO PERSONALLY ensure Bajo would reach the safekeeping of her brother in Qamishli, Sallah offered to accompany

Hedeya and Violette to the port of Suez.

Once reconciled to the path she had chosen, friend that he was, he felt he had no choice but to step up to the plate and facilitate her departure as best he could. Moreover, it behooved him to keep a door open to the future. For he harboured a hope still, albeit a faint one, that India might eventually prove too distant, its customs too alien, so that the consequent homesickness would prompt her to return to Cairo, and to him. And if, after all, that were not to be, then it was essential that these last few days be a fitting end to their relationship, that his final consideration remain a fond and lasting memory with her.

Officially, when she had made a show of changing her religion in order to get a divorce from Mahran, there in the court she had chosen her new name, Hoda, for her new Muslim identity. She had signed the necessary official papers with that name. Now, she realised, though the change of religion might have been a sham, the change of name was not; all her official documents, her travel documents, the laissez passer, bore that name – she still had a hard time actually saying it, owning it. Among so many other things, along with so much of her old life, she would have to leave Hedeya behind and go forth into the world as Hoda. It would take some getting accustomed to.

Finally, the time to bid farewell came. Although the boys had been prepared in advance, the goodbyes were painful. Hedeya and Bajo had explained the situation, and the boys were aware of the difficulties their mother faced, the responsibilities she had to contend with all on her own. Nevertheless, in the final hour, acceptance of her departure was not easy. Their home was with their father, separate from her, yet now the small feeling of abandonment edged with hurt could not be avoided. On Hedeya's part her sorrow, compounded by guilt over the separation her decision would bring, almost convinced her at the eleventh hour to change her mind about leaving. Her heart, literally, was torn in two.

"Mama!" She had not called Bajo that since she was a little girl. "I cannot do it." She sank to her knees, rocking back and forth, shutting her eyes to contain the pain that welled up and threatened to spill over. "Once before I had to give up my sons, I had no choice then. Now I am doing it all over again. No matter what, this is my home – here, with the boys, and with you."

She felt her mother's fingers touch her cheek softly; even more softly, she felt the old lady cup her chin in the palm of her gnarled, leathery hand to lift her daughter's face gently towards her own.

"My child, you must go with your destiny. *Il mattub ala gabeen; what is written on the forehead.* We each have been given a life to live, and the winds often do not blow in answer to a ship's wish. You and I, we have had our time together. And what a time it has been, eh? It has forged a bond between us that nothing can break. I thank God for you, for allowing you to survive, heart of my heart. All through those terrible years I managed to protect you. Till now." The old lady sighed.

"But now, my time is coming; I feel it in my bones. It will not be long before I am released so I may, at last, join your father. And what will you do then, *ya albi?* Sallah is a decent man, but – ahh! God have mercy on me for saying this! – after all that we have suffered at their hands, will you now become a Muslim? And your daughter too? Must all our efforts, your father's and mine, have been in vain? Never! Let me go in peace, knowing that now you both are safe.

"I have worried about you in silence and prayed, and I know my prayers have been answered. This man, this stranger who was brought to our house guided by a servant of God, he is a good man, and kind. Something about him speaks to my heart and puts it at ease. I know he will look after you. As for us, we will be all right. The boys have long been out of your hands, you know that. There is nothing more you can do for them. They are with their father, for better or for worse, and there isn't anything you can do to change that. But for Bebe now, you can make a good life for that little one. This man will be a good father to her, better than her own, may God forgive him! Have courage and do it for her sake."

Hedeya stilled herself and sat back on her heels. "Then come with me," she pleaded. "Help me! I can do it if you come with me, if we are together."

"Ahhhh!" the old woman's heartfelt sigh was filled with weariness. "This adventure is too big for such an old heart and body. I have stayed too long and seen too much of this world, and this is the wreckage that is left behind. I am done with all that. Now, I pray the few days left me will be days of quiet and rest. You know it has always been my wish, before I die, to spend time with my brother, Shamun, in Qamishli. Now is that time; allow me to have it. I have lived my life. Now, you must live yours. My heart is full, filled to overflowing with the love we have shared; there is no place left in it for more. But your heart, it still needs filling – and this is the man who will fill it. You have much to give and much to receive, and through it all he will be there to look after you. I look into his eyes and I see his soul, and I know if I leave you in his care he will remain at your side till the end."

"Oh, Bajo!" Hedeya laid her head in her mother's lap and her body was racked with sobs. "I cannot bear this! I don't know which way to go." Her voice broke with the weight of her grief.

Bajo laid her fingers against her daughter's lips. "Hush! Don't worry, *ya habibi*." She raised the face of her only remaining child and softly, lovingly, kissed her forehead. She rested her wrinkled cheek against the smooth one, feeling the dampness of its tears. "Wherever you go, I will be there with you. Neither time nor distance can separate our spirits. Courage, my little *Bimbashi*, courage!"

ON THE DAY OF departure Bajo handed Hedeya the eleventh-century family bible with the gold coin on the front cover. In Turkey she had almost paid with her life to save it, and now she handed it into her daughter's safekeeping. In a small packet she wrapped her blue enamel flower earrings with the rose cut diamonds, her ruby ring and the small ruby cross she wore, and the little gold heart she had made and lovingly inscribed with her daughter's name; they were not much but, other than her blessings, they were all she had left to give. And there were the memories. There would always be her gift of memories.

Finally, it was time; Hedeya and Violette took the morning boat train from Cairo. To spare Violette the undue grief of separation she was told they were going to visit 'The Captain' in his faraway country. The prospect of the adventure filled her with such excitement, she returned her grandmother's long, deep embrace, but could hardly contain herself.

The journey was a little over four hours. Accompanied by Sallah they travelled through this country Hedeya had adopted so long ago, and as she watched the changing landscape slip by, she had a clear precognition of the homesickness that would dog her in the months ahead. Her emotions were a painful mix of anticipation and trepidation, of joy and sadness, all tangles and knots.

For the second time in her life, she was leaving her homeland. The first time she had been a child, and the threat to their lives had left no choice; this time she was choosing to head blindly into a future that was so frighteningly far and unfamiliar, it was like stepping into a void. Her only beacon was the young soldier to whom she had given her heart. It was not like her at all, she thought with a sickening lurch of fear. But now there was no turning back – *too late, too late, too late*, the relentless wheels on the rails seemed to warn her.

They finally reached the Suez Canal, its water sparkling clear and blue as it ran between banks of fine sand. Inexorably, the train chugged onto the quay. Their luggage was offloaded – two trunks and a suitcase containing their clothes and personal effects. Additionally, three very large wooden crates with their household items, which included Hedeya's Singer sewing machine and Baba Taht's two carpets, had already been dispatched as unaccompanied luggage through Cox & Kings (Agents), Ltd. Since fares were appreciably lower on cargo ships than they were on passenger ships, their passages had been booked on a Greek cargo ship that was passing through, its hold laden with crates of oranges. Through Customs and Immigration, their documents were stamped, and luggage loaded onto the waiting ship.

A last goodbye with Sallah wishing her the best and telling her to write, assuring her of his help should she need it, and thus discreetly affirming once again that he would wait. She managed to thank him, to smile, despite the lump in her throat – and they set sail in convoy down through the Gulf of Suez. Through tears she no longer tried to hide, Hedeya watched the shoreline slip by as small rowboats of vendors touting leather, silver and silk goods scurried alongside the ships like shoals of importuning fish, loath to allow their departure; past Port Taufiq to the Red Sea, they left the free Port of Aden and finally sailed out, through the Canal, and into the Arabian Sea.

It was the 3rd of April 1944.

———•–•———

DAYS OF GOLDEN SUNLIGHT dancing on the water, magical nights when the ocean glowed green with phosphorus; and dolphins looking like enchanted creatures as they leapt and pranced around the ships as though guiding them through the ever-present danger of lurking enemy submarines. And so across the Indian Ocean without mishap till, at last, on the afternoon of Friday, April 14th, they came within sight of Bombay; and far in the distance, silhouetted against the skyline, barely visible, an immense stone edifice with four minarets – the Gateway of India.

Despite the blazing sun, Hedeya and Violette were topside, watching from the deck as the ship approached the shoreline. The heat in this part of the world was unlike the dry, parched heat of the desert. It was not yet the height of summer, nevertheless, the hot air was like a sponge, heavy with humidity so that clothes stuck to one's body, soaked with perspiration. To somewhat allay this discomfort, Violette was sucking on an orange one of the sailors had given her from the cargo in the hold.

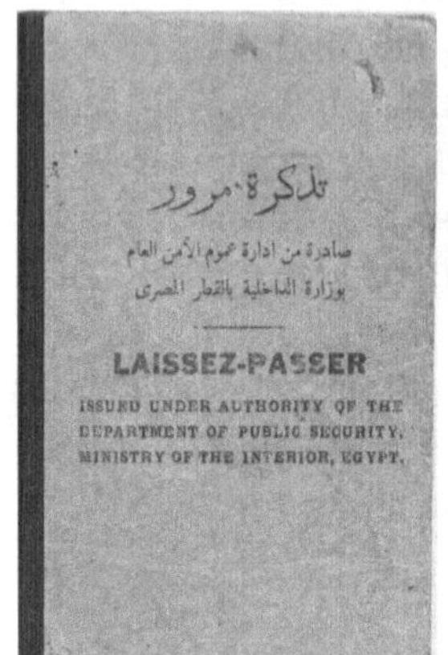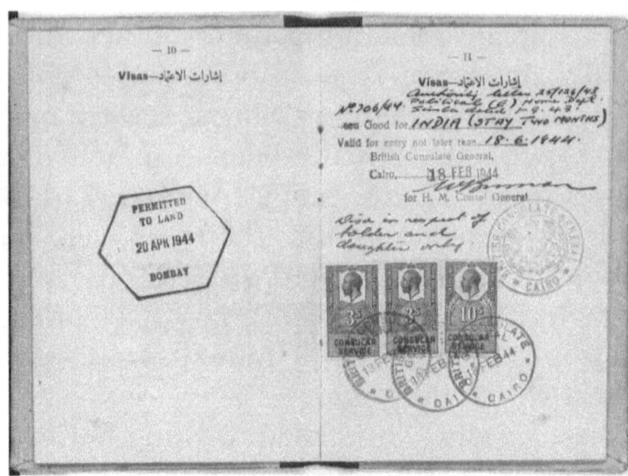

Travel documents for Hoda and Violette. 20 April, 1944, Bombay.

The time was approximately 3:45 pm, and though the ship was ready to slip into dock, they had been put on hold pending a clearance of some sort. In the distance, a thick cloud of dark smoke was the only clue, and there was much speculation among the crew as to its source. All at once, around 4:06 pm or thereabouts, a massive explosion rocked the area, followed some thirty minutes later by a second one. The force of the blasts made the ship shudder violently.

From her vantage point out at sea, Violette pointed delightedly. "Look, Mama, look – fireworks!" And indeed, the tremendous pops, bangs and whizzes resembled a magnificent display, prompting the child to jig up and down in glee. "Oooh! Such big ones! But, look Mama, that horrible smoke is spoiling all the fun!"

In actual fact, this was a disaster the likes of which had not been witnessed before in Bombay. Not only did the explosions shatter windows on shore over three miles away, the tremors were caught on a seismograph in the hill station of Simla more than 1000 miles distant.

Moored alongside eleven other ships that day, in Bombay's Prince's and Victoria Docks, was the *SS Fort Stikine*. One of the many Lend-Lease ships on charter from America to England, it had arrived from Karachi, its last port of call, carrying 8,700 bales of raw cotton in its lower hold. Above this was stashed a mixed cargo of fish manure, drums of lube oil, sulphur, timber, scrap iron, rice, resin and 1,395 tons of explosives which included shells, torpedoes, mine signal rockets, magnesium flares and incendiary bombs. It was a dangerous combination by any standard which, at the time of loading, had prompted a complaint from Captain Alexander James Naismith, the ship's commander.

Unfortunately, his objections had been impatiently brushed aside with a curt "doesn't he know there is a war on?" following which, Captain Naismith, believing he had no further recourse, conceded, albeit reluctantly. Unhappily, the mistake would cost him his life.

As it happened, that was not the only cargo the *Fort Stikine* was carrying. Known but to a select few, it had brought gold bullion in the form of ingots from the Bank of England to the Reserve Bank of India. Each ingot measured 15"x3"x1.5" and weighed twenty-eight pounds. All told, the bullion, estimated at somewhere between one to two million pounds sterling, was packed in thirty-one wooden crates, four to a crate. These were then welded inside a steel box.

The *SS Fort Stikine* made the journey in convoy from Karachi to Bombay without mishap; and on 14 April it lay in Number One berth in Victoria Dock, waiting to discharge its cargo. The actual cause of the initial conflagration of the *Fort Stikine's* highly combustible cargo was never determined, then or later, but the tremendous destruction caused to nearby ships, warehouses and docks took the lives of over eight hundred servicemen, firefighters, and civilians, with two thousand more injured.

The force of the first blast split the *Stikine* in half and blew its boiler a good half mile away, while part of its propeller travelled the distance of three miles to lodge itself in the grounds of St. Xavier's Boy's School. The blast created a tidal wave that broke the moorings of both the *SS Fort Crevier* and *El Hind,* which caught fire as they swept out and rolled in again, crushing those in the water. The second explosion sent debris flying almost three thousand feet into the air.

It also propelled Bombay's Fire Chief, Mr. Coombs, clear across the quay where, to his utter disbelief – and relief – he found himself to be still alive. However, to his dismay as well as his everlasting mortification, further examination of his situation revealed that his trousers were nowhere to be seen! That garment had blown clean off his body, but incredibly, nay miraculously, he had survived to tell the tale!

Not so Captain Naismith or his First Officer. Following the first blast those two courageous men returned to the ship to ensure no one was left on board – no one but the ship's cook, it turned out. Of those three, not a scrap of evidence remained to be found, then or in the days that followed.

The blast broke the back of the nearby *Jalapadma* as well, hurling its poop deck and 12-pound gun two hundred yards away, while the ship itself lay with its bow in the water and its stern sixty feet in the air atop a warehouse. The *SS Baroda* was thrown across the adjacent berth and, as the fire spread, ammunition on the neighbouring ships went up as well, adding to the mayhem. Shrapnel fell on the *Chantilly* in Alexander Dock, three quarters of a mile away. It had brought and landed a contingent of American troops and was in the process of conversion from troopship to hospital ship.

All in all, thirteen ships were destroyed – six British, three Dutch, two Panamanian, one Egyptian and one Norwegian; a surrounding area of approximately 300 acres had to be razed, and many nearby city buildings lay in ruin.

The cost in human lives and damage that day was tragic; and yet, for some, it brought unforeseen good fortune as gold bricks from the hold of the *Fort Stikine* were blown sky-high to rain down all over the city of Bombay. They came through people's roofs, landed in their gardens, and fell at their feet in the street. While a few were returned by scrupulously honest citizens to the appropriate authorities, most were not.

Of course, the sea laid claim to its share, and it guarded its treasure closely through the years, caressing it, sighing over it, wary of any who might wish to part it from so beautiful a plaything; but with the passage of time, occasionally…thirty years…sixty-seven years… whenever the mood would take it, the waters would relinquish an ingot or two as a reminder of the history that lies hidden within its depths, even to this day.

CHAPTER FIFTY-FIVE

New Beginnings

*The world is round and the place
Which may seem like the end
May also be the beginning.*

– Rebecca West, Quote

FOR FIVE DAYS THE harbours remained closed to all incoming and outgoing sea traffic. Ships stood out to sea, anchored in the Roads between the island of Bombay and the Mainland, waiting for alternate arrangements to be made. It was a slow process, but at long last, one by one, they were allowed to enter, nosing their way gingerly past the burnt wreckage of destroyed vessels.

Amidst all this chaos, Hedeya and Violette landed on the shores of India on 20th April 1944. And into something akin to bedlam. Destruction caused by the explosions was everywhere. The Customs Shed and Ballard Pier were jam-packed with passengers, coolies and officials, all tripping over one another. Makeshift arrangements had been thrown together, leaving people running helter-skelter, trying desperately to deal with the incoming flood of backed-up passengers and cargo. The result was pandemonium. It took hours to sort luggage, papers and forms. When finally they made it through, Hedeya was relieved and grateful to find Elsie Deuvletian – now Arathoon – waiting outside with a taxi.

"Hedeya! *Al-hamdulillah*! Five days I have been coming and going. What a time you chose to arrive, *ya habibi*!" Elsie embraced her friend and then threw her arms around Violette in a big hug. "Oh, but it is so good to see you. *Marhaba*, welcome to your new country. Some welcome, eh!" She laughed.

"*Wakh lao*, Elsie!" Hedeya examined her friend closely. "My goodness! Are you pregnant?"

Elsie giggled happily. "Why waste time? I told Joe that Khaireya Badawi said I would have two sons, and he said we might as well get on with it then. I have even chosen their names – this one will be Varouj, and the next one will be Levon."

"And what will you do if one or both turn out to be girls?"

Elsie gave a small smile as she patted her stomach. "Oh, I would like a little girl; a boy and a girl would be nice. But, somehow, I don't think so. Khaireya is usually right, you know. And it's strange," her voice was dreamy, "I can feel their presence already, my two beautiful sons. Already they are a part of my life." She laughed. "But come, come; we can talk in the taxi. I know you must be tired, so rest today, because tomorrow we have a lot to do if you are to leave for Calcutta the day after."

Since Joe and Elsie were in temporary quarters which they shared with another Royal Navy officer, Hedeya and Violette had been booked into a small boarding house on Marine Drive. It was run by an elderly Armenian gentleman. Manoeuvring through traffic, the ride to Petrosian's Boarding House took just under half an hour. When Elsie introduced them, it turned out that old Petros, too, was a survivor from Turkey – the only one of his family to have made it.

"Our tribe has suffered much" he said, shaking Hedeya's hand for a full minute. "My dear Hedeya, you must consider my home to be your home for as long as you wish."

Hedeya thanked him, and then explained to both him and Elsie, "I am no longer Hedeya, you know. According to my official papers I am now Hoda."

"That may be so," Elsie declared firmly, "but to me you will always be Hedeya."

The next few days went by in a whirlwind of money changing, train bookings, sending of telegrams – to Cairo confirming safe arrival, and to Calcutta intimating intended departure – so much so, by the time Hedeya bid Elsie goodbye at Victoria Terminus and found herself with Violette in a private first-class coupé on the Bombay Howrah Express train, she had hardly any recollection how they actually got there.

As the train chugged out of the station and Elsie's figure dwindled to a speck, Hedeya felt the last, tenuous tie to her old life vanish; and as the train gathered speed and cut across the flowing plains of this strange new country – its people, customs, and motley languages so different from everything she had known – the enormity of her undertaking hit home once again, and she was overcome with a sudden surge of loneliness.

By herself for the first time with a little girl of eleven, far from friends, from family and home, in a place unlike any she had experienced before, she was hurtling towards a future that was in the hands of a man she loved, but barely knew at all. She had felt great sadness leaving the country that had been her home; however, her love for the young stranger fate had brought into her life had given her a sense of purpose, of trust, that had tempered the sadness and lent eagerness to her journey. But now she was actually here, very much on her own for the first time, her surroundings vast and unfamiliar, fear began to sow the seeds of doubt again. What had she done! Had she made the right choice? Once again, the only answer was the unrelenting sound of the wheels as the train rushed on: *Too late, too late, too late.*

THE JOURNEY ACROSS INDIA took one and a half days and two nights. Hedeya and Violette kept to their coupé; they were exhausted and slept most of the way. They spoke to no one except the dining car bearer who spoke a strange sort of English but, after some difficulty, understood enough to fetch their food to the compartment. Here, too, they found themselves unaccustomed to local spices, and after one disastrous attempt, remained with more familiar western fare. So much that was so new!

To keep out the heat, which was stifling, the flies which were a pestilence, the mendicants and vendors who were persistent, Hedeya kept the doors and windows shut when the train pulled into a station. Although one dealt with similar problems in Cairo, here they seemed ten-fold, exacerbated by the unfamiliar humidity and heaviness of the approaching Indian summer, and the jumble of constantly changing languages with each station they passed through.

To let in a breath of air, hot as it was, Hedeya tried opening the shutters once the train pulled out again. But even then, on short hops between stations, there would be the curious eyes of the non-paying hangers-on clinging precariously to the sides and roof of the train like limpets, seemingly unphased by the velocity and jolting, quite as though this was their usual mode of travel. Eventually, sympathetic to her predicament, the bearer, a kindly man at heart, had taken it upon himself to haul in a couple of large blocks of ice which he positioned on the floor so they would catch and reflect back the air from the small, noisy fan that swirled overhead. The wet icemelt underfoot was a small price to pay for the cool comfort, and Hedeya showed her gratitude by way of a fat tip for the old man.

As the train sped from the west coast of India to the east coast, the countryside changed from arid desert to the lush green that was Bengal. It was early on the second morning when the train drew into what sounded like a very large, noisy station; and in comparison to the previous stops, this one seemed inordinately long. Hedeya ignored several knocks on the compartment door, believing them to be passengers attempting access to her private coupé which she had no intention of sharing; but after a while, she realised the bustle around the train had dwindled considerably, and still there was no sign of intended departure. She pushed open the shutters of one window and peered out.

The platform floor was littered with bodies, prostrate and curled, in various positions of repose. The train seemed to have emptied its passengers, and even the usual vendors and mendicants were fewer than usual. In fact, except for a couple of suspicious-looking characters in red shirts and black armbands with numbers on them – uncomfortably reminiscent of prison attire in Egypt – there was hardly anyone about. Perplexed, and growing increasingly anxious by the minute, Hedeya was wondering what to do, when an Indian gentleman in a suit passed by the window.

"Excuse me," quickly unlatching the door, she called out, "can you tell me what station this is?"

"This is Howrah, Madam."

"Oh. And does this train go to Calcutta?"

"This is Howrah, Madam."

"Yes, but I have to go to Calcutta."

The man looked infinitely perplexed. "Yes, yes, that is exactly why I am telling you, this is Howrah."

"I don't *want* Howrah," Hedeya said in loud exasperation. "I want to know if this train goes to Calcutta!"

"Madam," said the man, his bearing stiff with indignation. "This is Howrah; Howrah Station *is* Calcutta!"

Hedeya thanked him, feeling slightly foolish but increasingly more anxious. *Well…if this was Calcutta,* she wondered uneasily, *then where was Santi? She had sent him a telegram, so why was he not there to meet them?*

She had no time to dwell on the question, however. As she turned away, her eye caught sight of the three red-shirted men with black numbered armbands who, attracted by the interchange, had gathered by the door. They stared at her, talking loudly to each other in their language, and then, seemingly having reached a decision, two of them pushed their way into the compartment and advanced upon her. The third red shirt made as though to follow when, to Hedeya's utter horror, he turned his head and vented a long stream of blood red liquid.

The sight of men in red shirts, similar to prison uniforms in Cairo, advancing upon her as they spat out what seemed awfully much like blood, was, for one split second, enough to completely unnerve Hedeya. Uninitiated about *paan*, the betel leaf and araca nut commonly chewed by many Indians, or its red juice that requires expelling, and with Mrs. Hovartian's words ringing in her ears – *I have heard they eat white people there* – she panicked and jumped to the only conclusion her confounded thoughts would allow.

Oh, my dear God! It is true! Unbidden, and despite all good sense, reason went flying out the window.

Suppressing a scream, Hedeya waved her arms violently at the men. Terrified, she clutched Violette close and continued to flail her arms as hard as she could in an attempt to drive the men out.

Startled, the men backed away. *Ki holo re! Pagol na ki? Whatever has happened! Has she gone stark raving mad!*

The bewildered faces staring at her pulled Hedeya up short; and it began to dawn on her that they were quite as nervous of her as she was of them. This realisation prompted common sense to intervene. Gathering her wits as best she could, she managed to compose herself somewhat; and when her practical nature had re-established good sense once more, it took only a moment to register – *Of course! These men were attempting nothing more sinister than doing their job to earn a living! For goodness sake,* she chided herself, severely, *they were not quarrelling over who should eat them, but rather who should carry their luggage!*

Feeling quite ashamed of her foolishness, and more than a little apologetic for her rude behaviour, she attempted to make up for it by offering to hire all three *coolies*. The offer was too good to pass up. The men, still rather doubtful, and keeping a careful distance in case of another ranting fit, hoisted the three pieces of luggage, one to each head, and trotted down the platform, leading both lady and child out of the station.

Although accustomed to heat, this was heat like no other. Bombay had been hot and humid, but Calcutta heat slammed into one with the ferocity of a blast from an open furnace – it sapped one's energy and left one's clothes wringing wet in no time at all. Exhausted and limp, with her daughter weary and drooping at her side, Hedeya surveyed her surroundings.

She was standing in a large area where the choice of conveyance included a melee of horse-drawn carriages apparently known as *tongas*, and odd little two-wheeled hand carts pulled by men in loincloths. People hailing these handcarts called them *rickshaws*, and were actually climbing in to sit and be whisked away! On the far side, an array of conventional public buses and rows of taxis were visible as well.

Hedeya's heart fell; she had hoped against hope to find Santi waiting outside. Had he been ordered away at the last minute without a chance to make other arrangements? Taking stock of her situation, her feeling of unease grew. So far, her arrival had not gone at all well. They had narrowly escaped being blown up in Bombay, the train journey had felt like slow cooking in a *tanoor*, and her arrival at her destination had been, to say the very least, confusing and embarrassing. If this was anything to judge by…well…then, it seemed she had landed them in a real mess!

Whatever was she supposed to do now? She had his address, to be sure, and it seemed her only choice was to find her own way there. But…supposing she got there…and found…

Her thoughts were interrupted by a sudden onrush of taxi drivers and *tonga wallahs* who had spotted them as potential customers. At the sight of a foreign lady with a child, a squabble erupted among them as to who would win her fare. Not able to understand a word of the language, Hedeya nevertheless tried to make some sense of the argument in full spate about her. It seemed to be growing increasingly heated by the moment, until finally, with no end or help in sight, she decided some intervention was called for.

Having made up her mind, she stepped into the middle of the fracas waving her address book under the nose of a large, turbaned taxi driver, and in a voice she hoped would rise above the chaos surrounding her, she shouted, "Russa Road. RUSSA ROAD."

The driver, a burly Sikh with a fiercely bushy beard, swooped down on his newfound passengers. Pushing his vanquished contenders aside, he led them victoriously to where a rather worse-for-wear taxi stood.

Hedeya watched doubtfully as the *coolies* loaded their luggage – one trunk crammed into the boot of the car, the other along with the suitcase heaved precariously onto the roof luggage-rack – and as each piece was added, the sad old vehicle groaned in reproach and sank lower, as though too worn out and weary to bear such a burden. Finally, with a length of rope he fished out from somewhere, the driver bound the teetering tower of luggage to the roof carrier and triumphantly, with much gesturing, bid them enter the cabin. Hedeya paid the *coolies*, generously and without quibble, a gesture which earned her wide smiles and many *salaams* – positive assurance that all affront had been forgotten and forgiven.

Holding fast to Violette's hand, Hedeya stepped back. She surveyed the taxi driver's handiwork in dismay. *Would such a makeshift contraption actually hold up? What about the ancient taxi – would that hold out? Oh, where was Santi? He should have been here to take care of this!*

By now, what had started out as a niggling doubt had grown into real concern. Something had gone wrong. Why else would he not have been there to receive them – or, at least, made some alternate arrangement? He had to know how disconcerting her unfamiliar surroundings would be, how out of depth her arrival in a foreign country with its unknown customs would leave her. Her heart sank further. In her present frame of mind – tired, alone, and scared – she couldn't help thinking the worst!

No! She was not going to jump to any more conclusions! She had done enough of that today and very nearly made a fool of herself. She was here now, and she would just deal with the situation one step at a time. Stemming her anxiety, she looked around. She noticed other passengers with other similarly laden taxis and so, summing up what courage she could, she ushered Violette into the beat-up old back seat. Then, holding out Santi's address to the taxi driver, she repeated each word slowly and as clearly as she could – Mohini Mansions, Flat No.9, 94 Russa Road.

The man acknowledged her efforts with a big smile and a quick roll of his head, a strange circular motion somewhere between a nod and a shake that Hedeya took to be assent, since he slammed the pedal to the floor of the taxi and, heedless of the precarious pile of luggage swaying dangerously above their heads, catapulted the vehicle into traffic at what could only be described as death-defying speed. Across a long, heavily crowded bridge they shot, through city streets teeming with cars and buses, tongas, rickshaws, carts; and, everywhere, weaving through the stream of traffic, pedestrians dodged, dogs darted, and cows edged their way, regardless.

The drive was hair-raising, and Hedeya gratefully offered up a silent prayer when, approximately half an hour later, the taxi stopped. The driver indicated they had arrived at their destination. Her relief, however, was short-lived when she discovered they were in a narrow, dingy cul-de-sac; and it turned to pure dismay when she observed the dilapidated old building the taxi driver pointed out as the address she was looking for.

Hedeya stared at the dismal scene. Without warning she felt like bursting into tears. What had she done! She had taken this little girl away from her home, from everything she knew, and brought her to *this*. What *had* she been thinking! Certainly, this was not what she had expected, these awful, dirty surroundings she found herself in. She had travelled so far for – what? And he hadn't even been there to receive them!

Alone and unprepared for such an outcome, icy-cold apprehension filled her heart and ran through her body, from the top of her head down to her toes, so that she felt faint with a sudden panic that threatened to overwhelm her; she was overcome with fear, regret and mind-numbing despair.

It was a few seconds before she noticed the elderly man peering down at her from his first-floor balcony. Willing herself not to cry, she pulled herself together and called out.

"Excuse me, can you tell me if Captain Dutt lives here?"

The man cupped his right ear with his hand. "Eh?"

"Captain Dutt, does he live here?"

"Captain Dutt." The man thought for a moment then, slowly, he shook his head. "No. No Captain Dutt hee-ar."

"Are you sure?"

"Eh?"

"Are you sure Captain Dutt does not live here?"

"Madam, I am being more than absolutely su-ar – no Captain Dutt libs hee-ar."

Hedeya gave a heartfelt sigh of relief. "Thank you," she called up to the man, adding fervently under her breath, "and thank God!"

They set off once more, this time stopping on the way to ask directions of a well attired gentleman passer-by. The man studied the address closely and then gave the driver what sounded like a detailed and very long set of instructions that produced another roll of the head.

After he was done, the gentleman bent down and stuck his head in at the window. "Hab no phear Madam, rest assured you will now most certainly reach your required destination."

Unsure of anything anymore, Hedeya nevertheless thanked him for his kindness. Trying hard to curb her agitation, she set her mind to focus only on the road ahead. But as the taxi sped through crowded streets, every mile that took her further from the train station seemed a mile further from her home and her way of return.

At last, they pulled up in front of a set of stately wrought iron gates through which could be seen an expansive courtyard trimmed with neat hedges and some stone benches. The courtyard was flanked on either side by two long buildings of balconied flats that ran four floors high while, at the furthest end, there stood a smaller, two-storied building with a wide front portico. A uniformed *darwan* guarding the gate informed them they had, indeed, arrived at the right address. Flat No.9 was on the ground floor, second to last on the left.

Hedeya's spirits lifted just a little; this place, thank goodness, was nothing like the last one. She and Violette alighted, and while the gatekeeper summoned a couple of helpers to unload their luggage, she examined her surroundings. Russa Road was a fairly wide two-way street, and down its centre ran familiar looking tram lines. An oncoming tram packed with passengers spilling out the exits clanged loudly as it passed, and then disappeared beneath a stone bridge further down. Hedeya paid the taxi driver and followed the *darwan* and their luggage through the gate to Flat No.9.

A man servant answered their knock at the door and informed them in barely intelligible English, complemented with much gesturing, that no one was home. *Memsahib* could come in and wait. Hedeya and Violette entered a grille-enclosed verandah with three doors leading off it. They walked through the first door into the room beyond. After the blazing sunlight outside and the awful, sticky heat, it was dark with shadows and pleasantly cool from the breeze of a ceiling fan swishing giddily overhead. A dining table and chairs occupied one end of the room where a door opened onto what one took to be the kitchen, while a sofa and some easy chairs made for a sitting area at the other end. Two additional doors led off into what, apparently, were bedrooms.

With their luggage stashed neatly in a corner of the verandah, mother and daughter sat down on the sofa to wait; and it wasn't long before Violette had curled herself into a small bundle and fallen fast asleep, tuckered out by the rigours of the last few days. Hedeya watched her daughter's gentle breathing, the rise and fall of her small chest, and with every breath marking the passing minutes, the mother's tightly reined consternation grew.

Her decision to come had been a mistake. She could see that now. Santi's absence did not bode well. She had telegraphed from Bombay advising him of her arrival; either he had chosen to ignore it completely, or some misfortune had kept him. Both explanations filled her with alarm. Though not explicit, she had gathered from his letter received in Cairo that he had been sent to the Burma Front where the Japanese threat of invasion was imminent. But according to his letter he was to have returned by now; and if he had been kept from returning, would he not have made some arrangements for her

to be met? If she knew anything about him, she knew that he would
– that is if something had not happened to prevent him. She quickly
pushed that thought away.

On the other hand, they *had* been apart for nine months now,
so much longer than the short time they had spent together; and
though he had made a commitment by marrying her, what if, in
the ensuing months after he got home, his affections had gradually
changed?

In that case he should have informed her! Instead, his letters had
assured her he was waiting. Surely it was too late now for a change of
heart? But what if that were the case, and he hadn't known how to
tell her! The possibility filled her with misgiving; time and distance
often had a way of altering one's perception of things. And if she had
given up everything, come all this way for a man no longer sure of
his feelings, or his commitment – whatever would she do?

At that moment the front door opened, and a man entered. Hedeya's heart lurched before she realised the figure on the verandah
wore a white navy uniform and was shorter and rather more heavy-
set than the person she was expecting. The newcomer walked in,
took off his cap and called out to the kitchen.

"*Bishwonath, boro glash tthanda jol niyesho.*"

In the dimness she had the advantage, and could just make out
the man's dark, rather flamboyant good looks, the mole above the
right side of a full-lipped mouth. He seemed unaware of her presence, till his eyes slowly adjusted to the dark room when he suddenly
noticed her. For a brief moment he looked startled, but he quickly
regained his composure and, as he accepted the glass of cold water
the manservant Bishwonath brought him, he eyed her with some
interest. First, he examined her from head to foot; then he spoke.

"Good afternoon. May I help you?"

A lady's man this one, Hedeya thought. If this was the company
Santi kept, she dared not imagine what went on. Her throat felt dry,
and though she tried to answer as steadily as she could, her voice
sounded raspy. "Yes, you may. I am waiting for Captain Dutt."

The man's eyebrows rose in surprise. "Oh?" He threw her a quizzical look. "Are you, indeed!" He seemed to find it amusing. "Well,
Captain Dutt is not here I'm afraid. Meanwhile, I would be happy to
be of assistance in any way I can. I am his brother, Kanti Dutt."

"Thank you. I am Hedeya and..."

"You are...!" Kanti Dutt's eyes flew open, and for the first time he
noticed the small sleeping bundle on the sofa beside Hedeya. His

laconic manner changed to one of incredulity. "What are you doing here...he wasn't expecting you..."

What was she doing here? Hedeya could feel the heat of anger begin to rise within her. So, he was fine! No calamity had befallen him; he just hadn't been expecting her!

"It would seem so." Her words were clipped. "But unfortunately, as you can see, I *have* arrived. However, as soon as Captain Dutt can make arrangements for my return I will..."

"Excuse me," Kanti hurriedly cut her short. "I must see if I can find my brother." And without giving her a chance to finish, he grabbed his cap which he had laid on the dining table and dashed out the door.

Santi had returned from Burma just four days previous, but where was he at this precise moment? Kanti was hard put to hazard a guess. Damn it! From the look on Hedeya's face, he had no doubt there would be hell to pay!

Once again Hedeya was left alone with her thoughts which were, by now, in a state of furious turmoil. This was not how it was supposed to be; this was certainly not the sort of reception she had imagined, silly romantic that she was! It was obvious she had made a dreadful error by coming, and now she had to think how best to go back. How would she explain herself back home? Hurt, embarrassed, and angry both with herself and with Santi, she fought hard to hold back the tears.

Seething with conflicting thoughts and emotions, Hedeya was oblivious of the half hour that passed before the front door opened once more and a tall, uniformed figure she immediately recognised stood silhouetted against the glare of sunlight. The figure entered the room, cast a cursory glance in her direction, murmured a low "good afternoon" and quickly proceeded into an adjoining bedroom.

Hedeya was stunned. So, this was how it was! There was no doubt now where she stood. Her husband had barely acknowledged her! What an absolute fool she had been. Battling the onslaught of angry tears – this was no time to show weakness! – she stood up, trembling. She had no idea where she would go, or what she would do; all she knew was she had to get out of there as fast as possible. As she leaned over to wake Violette, she saw Santi back-step into the room.

He stared at her as though he couldn't believe his eyes. "It's you!" His voice reflected utter surprise as he squinted to adjust his eyes from the sunlight outside to the gloom inside. "You've arrived!"

"Unfortunately, I have – and now I am going back!"

"How did you come?" He seemed not to have heard her. "Why

didn't you inform me?"

"The telegram…" the words stuck in her throat.

"Telegram? What telegram? Dear God! I've been frantic with worry…"

He looked genuinely perplexed. For days he had been trying desperately for some news of her whereabouts, but he had been unable to get any information at all, he rushed on to tell her. It had been especially harrowing after news of the explosion in the Bombay docks. In fact, he had just returned from sending another signal to Bombay requesting that an enquiry and search be made for them in the hospitals. No, nobody had received any telegram. When had she sent it, and where…?

Santi stopped. Hedeya stood before him, perfectly still, as though she were made of stone. Her arms hung straight down at her sides, and though her head was held high and her chin thrust out, her eyes glistened with unshed tears. Her determined show of strength made her seem even more vulnerable. He saw the look of anguish on her face, and he felt a small explosion in his chest that made it hard to breathe.

Without another word he crossed the room in two swift strides and swept her into his arms. He held her to him with a fierceness that would not, could not be denied. After all they had been through, the war, separation, the whole world going to hell around them, she had made it! She had come to him. At last, she was his, to comfort and care for, to cherish and protect, to love as she had never been loved before. And he swore, silently, he would never let her go.

He felt her body, restrained at first, begin to soften against his. Suddenly, she made a small sound that could have been a half sob as her breath caught in her throat; she buried her face in his shoulder, the cloth of his uniform bush-shirt rough yet comforting against her cheek. Still holding her close with one arm, he gently raised her chin and found that she was crying. She could no longer keep back the tears.

He lowered his face to hers. He kissed her eyes and then her lips. Softly at first, then harder, his passion growing till she melted against him, rose to meet him, matching his command, strength for strength. He kissed her for a long time, drinking in the scent and taste of her. God! He had missed her! They had had one night together, and he had held the memory deep in his heart, re-living its passion, each tender minute, moment by moment. How he had wanted her! And at last she was here. He kissed her again, long and deep, and no words could have served better to tell her what was in his heart.

"Mama?"

Violette had woken up to a sitting position on the couch. Still holding Hedeya, Santi bent down and scooped up the child with one arm; and as he held both mother and child, Hedeya's thoughts tumbled through a cascade of emotions – relief, joy, gratitude – the happiness of that moment all the more poignant for the touch of sadness that lingered from the memory of all she had left behind, so much that was so dear to her.

The parting from family and home had been heart-breaking, a heartache she would carry deep within her to the very last; the distances she had travelled from that life to this were long and far; but here she stood with her daughter, within the arms of this man, this special man she had come to love so much, she had risked everything for him. It had required enormous trust and courage to undertake the journey to find him, to join him once again; and her mettle had been put to the test, time after time, along the way. But now that no longer mattered, now he had made it all worthwhile. At long last she was safe.

With her lips against the hollow of his throat she sighed, "*Ya hayati, ya rouhi,* my life, my soul."

She pressed closer to him; it was a small movement, a nestling sort of movement. And with that movement of surrender, with those words, Hedeya told Santi, finally, beyond all doubt, she had arrived where she belonged.

⸻◆⸻

TWO DAYS LATER A telegram was delivered to Captain Santi Pada Dutt at 94 Russa Road, Flat No.9, Calcutta:

Hedeya and Vio departing Bombay 4/22/44 stop Arriving Calcutta Bom/ How Express 4/24/44 stop Request please meet

⸻◆⸻

Where Destiny Commands, though it seem Earth's End,
There Fate stands, waiting, by road's curve and bend.

Santi and Hedeya, wedding celebration, Calcutta, 1944.

POSTSCRIPT

– Author

FINALLY, SHE HAD WRITTEN the last line, she had completed their story. It was done.

Reluctantly, she sat back and took a deep breath. Their life together had been their gift to her. Now they were gone, this re-counting of how and where it all began was her gift to them. Tender-ly, lovingly, she had laboured over it, and now that it was complete, she realised it had ended as it had begun.

Long ago, at the very start, a young woman had undertaken to leave her world behind and follow her heart. She had given it to a young man, a young stranger, who had walked into her life. Brought together by the war, then separated by it, nine months after his de-parture she had been compelled to follow in his footsteps, cross-ing oceans and continents, making the unknown journey from her home in Cairo to his in Calcutta. They had spent a lifetime together, two people who had loved so deeply, she had grown from their love. And now, at the end, he'd had to leave her once again to make his way from this world into the next; and just as she had done once be-fore, nine months after he had gone, one final time she had traced his footsteps into the unknown that they might be united once more, together for all time.

The daughter gazed at the mementos she had discovered among their things – the letters, the diary – intimate possessions that had told her their story; her photograph, a year-old child laughing in her father's arms, the eighteen-inch gold chain, his gift to her, reaching way down to her belly. Instinctively she reached up and touched the 22ct gold beads, now merely circling her neck. Her fingers found the small, distantly familiar indentations on their otherwise smooth surface, the long-ago legacy of her new front teeth pushing through as her body grew and developed. The imprint of her first year with them, preserved on this chain that had gathered her memories since then. She caressed the two wedding bands now held by it, and images flooded her mind. A young man and a young woman. Her life had begun with them, long before she had been aware of it.

She stared at the pages before her. Pages filled with long-buried memories that had shifted, broken cover and risen to the surface. Painful, precious memories, some tears, some smiles, those long-time companions she had sifted through and laid out like a jigsaw puzzle. Carefully, she had fitted the pieces together to tell a story wherein lay her own beginnings. She had held all of it – held them – close within for so long, now that it was finished, she felt emptied, poured out, as though she would collapse in on herself. It felt as though she had been deserted.

Through the quiet she heard them whisper...*It is time...time for us to go now.* She could feel their arms about her, the solace of their touch, on her face, stroking her hair. She closed her eyes and sat very still, listening. *It will be all right. Know we will be a part of you, as you will be a part of us, always. Go with our blessings...fulfill yourself...and live.*

Her beloved ghosts had not left her; they had found their rest deep within the very heart and soul of her, for she after all had grown out of theirs. They were her roots, she was a sapling of Great Grandfather's banyan tree that would spread its nurturing branches, so all who passed beneath might rest in its shade, to grow and to flourish. Through all time.

EPILOGUE

It matters not how strait the gate,
How charged with punishments the scroll,
I am the master of my fate;
I am the captain of my soul.

— "Invicta," William Ernest Henley, 1875

WHEN GERMANY FINALLY SURRENDERED to the Allies on 8th May 1945, it became known as VE Day, the day of victory that brought war in Europe to an end. Thousands of jubilant, cheering people thronged the streets of London and other liberated cities. Close beneath the elation and boundless relief, however, ran a deep sense of sadness in the awful knowledge of the calamity the human race had visited upon itself. Nations weighed down by six long years of suffering the destruction of their cities and lands, and thousands of loved ones lost, would find themselves in a vastly changed world. Those who had survived the turmoil and tragedy would face the bewildering task of trying to salvage what remained of their broken lives and, somehow, return to normal as best they could. It would take a further three long months before the horrific atomic bombings of Hiroshima and Nagasaki would lead to the surrender of Japan, and the final cessation of all hostilities in August 1945. Nevertheless, it was May 1945 that brought the first ray of hope and ushered in a time when a war-weary world could, at last, begin to look towards peace.

———•◆•———

THE END OF THE war, however, did not bring peace to India. It was a time that saw some old doors close and new ones open as she made a bid to throw off the yoke of imperialism she had borne for two hundred long years; a yoke imposed upon her by foreigners who first had landed as traders on her shores in the seventeenth century. Motherland to a diverse people of many languages, customs and religions who, despite minor squabbles, had managed for the most part to live side by side in relative peace, now her struggle for independence became tainted with the fears and prejudices of certain religious factions that spawned political unrest; and in spite of Gandhi's advocacy of *ahimsa* (nonviolence), in the moment of her rebirth, the unmitigated sword of religion cleaved the very heart of India and mortally divided that great nation forever.

For centuries India had been blessed and cursed with the caste system. Blessed because, in earlier times, it had founded and bolstered a way of life that worked; and cursed because, later, it bred oppression, and the lowest castes spent their lives under the heel of servitude. For them there was no escape from this abject state except through the hatchways of conversion. Thus, the Muslim invaders, and later the Christian missionaries, by dint of sword, seduction and sanguine promise, enjoyed much success. Yet, the main religion of the country remained Hindu. Besides the people of these three religions, there were others such as the Sikhs, Parsees, Buddhists, Jains, Jews, and Armenians who flourished throughout the country. And, in the matter of freedom, despite their many differences, these people of India were first and foremost Indian, and for independence.

Unhappily however, as the idea of independence swelled and suffused the country, with it, alas, spread a growing suspicion of political and religious inequity between Hindu and Muslim as nationalist and idealist struggled for power and a foothold in history. The British, severely weakened by the war and its ensuing problems at home, had neither will nor wherewithal to deal with the situation. Besides, the policy of 'divide and rule' had worked well enough for the East India Company to gain control in India over two hundred years before, and now the same might well allow its heirs to remain in India till such time as was expedient to their withdrawal.

Before long the misgivings on both religious sides turned to fear, and this lit a flame that seared India. From 1945 to 1947, amid the terrible chaos of pillage, burning and bloodshed, fourteen million people were uprooted and displaced as they fled their homes, and waves of terrified humanity desperately streamed across the breadth of India; it was the largest migration in history. Egged on by fear and divided by mistrust, neighbours and friends killed each other in the name of their God, families were torn asunder in the name of country as the opposing cries of Muslim and Hindu, 'Allahu Akbar' and 'Bandemataram,' rent the air. While May 1945 ushered in a time of peace, and the rest of the world looked to healing itself, India suffered two years of a most terrible bloodletting as her Muslim and Hindu sons slaughtered each other in the age-old conflict over their gods.

In that same month of May with its blessings and its bloodshed, in the old, care-worn city of Calcutta, a daughter was born to Santi and Hoda Dutt, sealing the love that had brought them together despite the travails and turmoils of war. Her birth came just as WWII came to an end; and like those many born after the war into a victorious new era with its own fledgling troubles, she embodied the triumph of life over the tragedy that was World War II.

In India this was the first generation born to a free country. It was this generation of Indians that would bridge the bygone India of the British Raj to the burgeoning new India of today. The independent India that Santi hoped would one day stand shoulder to shoulder with other free nations of the world, finally, had come to pass.

At the stroke of the midnight hour, when the world sleeps, India will awake to life and freedom. A moment comes, which comes but rarely in history, when we step out from the old to the new, when an age ends, and when the soul of a nation, long suppressed, finds utterance. ("Tryst with Destiny," Jawaharlal Nehru's speech to the Indian Constituent Assembly in The Indian Parliament, August 14, 1947).

Army Form. W. 3121

10 Ind. Inf. Brigade 5 Indian Division 30 Corps — Date Recommendation Passed forward

Schedule No. — Unit I.M.S. Attd. 2/4 G.R.

Army No. and Rank MZ.22404 — Captain

Name: Santa Pada Dutt, (M.B. Calcutta).

	Received	Passed
Brigade		
Division		
Corps		945
Army		

Action for which commended (Date and place of action must be stated)	Recommended by	Honour or Award	(To be left blank)
Defence of B.150 position, The Cauldron, near Bir Tamar, North Africa on 6th June, 1942. 2/4 G.R., with 28 Fd. Regt. R.A. in support, was occupying a hastily defended position, the only cover available being shallow slit trenches. From first light onwards the position was under continuous and heavy shell fire, and from 10.30 hours was completely surrounded by enemy armour, which closed in and subjected the garrison to heavy M.G. and tank gunfire from all directions; Casualties were heavy and could not be evacuated. Completely regardless of his own safety, Captain Dutt; M.O. of 2/4 G.R., worked incessantly at his exposed R.A.P. throughout the day on the many seriously wounded cases brought in to him. When the position was finally over-run he stuck by the wounded and persuaded the Germans to ameliorate their lot. /There	C.H.Boucher MC. Brig. Comd. 10 Ind. Inf. Bde. Lieut.-Colonel W. Weallens, Comdg. 2/4 G.R.	Military Cross	M.C 10.1.46

There is no doubt that, by his selfless devotion to duty and disregard of danger, Captain Dutt was instrumental in saving many lives.

W. Weallens Lt. Col

Comdg 2/4 G.R.

Prisoner of War – 6th June, 1942

General, Commander-in-Chief in India.

18. Nov. 45

Citation for Captain S.P. Dutt.

THE PILGRIM'S PATH

We've been glad because we knew
Time's too short and friends are few...
– Siegfried Sassoon, "A Letter Home"

BAJO REMAINED AT HER brother's house in Qamishli, Syria, where her instincts proved true. One day, a year after she had bidden her daughter and granddaughter goodbye, she bathed herself and retired to her bed. Her wish for their well-being now fulfilled, her body, mind and soul finally at rest, and grateful to have reached the end of a long and full life, she passed away peacefully in her sleep.

Sallah waited for Hoda till the day he received her letter informing him she had had a daughter. He then married Jamila Hussein, one of the Muslim teachers and a friend of Hoda's from her old school.

In 1955 Hoda and Violette, by then a lovely young lady, returned to Cairo for a visit. They were amazed to find the saga of Soraya's errant husband and the buried 'eggs' still ongoing. When Mahran learnt of Hoda's arrival, he paid her a visit, but did not meet with their daughter, Violette. Besides the three children from his first marriage, he would father four more in his second, and by all accounts they did well as a family. Many years later, as adults, the children from Cairo and from India would meet in the USA to mend fences and repair relationships, and to grow as one family.

In the years after their Mother's departure from Cairo, Louis and Victor both married. Victor opted to remain in Cairo where he passed away in 1990. He left two daughters and a son. While his son remained in Cairo, both daughters immigrated to California in the United States. Victor saw his mother one last time when he visited the U.S. just weeks before his passing. Louis emigrated from Egypt to the United States with his wife, his young son and baby daughter. He passed away in 2019 in Los Angeles where his children still live.

Violette married in Calcutta and had three daughters. She now lives with one daughter in Los Angeles. The youngest daughter lives in the Virgin Islands, the oldest in Calcutta, now known as Kolkata.

Of the seven Dutt siblings, none survive. Their various children live in San Francisco, Berkeley, and New York.

In 1956 the troubles that had been brewing in the Middle East since WWI and WWII boiled over into open conflict between Egypt and Israel. It was the precursor to a long, unending escalation of violence in the region that has touched the four corners of the earth and continues to plague the world to this day.

In a small village up in the Terai of Nepal, Hirasingh and Mullah lived long and well together, grateful for each other. Blessed by Santi's parting words, they never forgot those who had been less fortunate than they. Finally, in 1959, when it was time, Hirasingh chose a hillside facing his house where he laid his long-time companion to rest beneath a tree. And every morning, as long as he lived, the old Gurkha would pay the gravesite a visit; he would sit, smoking his *bidi* in the shadow of the peaceful Himalayas, two faithful friends sharing a companionable silence and the memories of a lifetime.

In 1966, twenty-one years after she was born in Calcutta, Santi and Hoda's daughter, Leila, visited Cairo. It was her first meeting with her half-brothers, Louis and Victor, and their families. Santi stayed on in the army till he retired as Lieutenant Colonel commanding Military Hospital Calcutta; his military career had come full circle, ending where it began. He and Hoda then turned the tables on the old British Raj and went to live in England where Santi held a General Practice for eighteen years. Finally retiring, they left England to join their daughter, Leila, and her husband, Ronjon, in the United States. They remained with them in San Francisco till their passing in 2001, thereby realising Bajo's dimly remembered foretelling of a daughter who would stay with them always…"*you will be blessed…*"

During the course of research for this book, it was discovered there remained two surviving members from that officer group who had shared in the WWII experiences of Santi Dutt. Tracing the whereabouts of Major Nigel Quentin Browne and Lt.Col. Robert N.D. Williams led to a memorable meeting in England when Leila and Ronjon were invited to attend the 2004 Remembrance Day reunion of her father's old regiment, the 4th Prince of Wales's Own Gurkha Rifles. The timing was fortuitous as, soon thereafter, both Major Browne and Lt. Col. Williams passed away.

'*A History of the 4th Prince of Wales's Own Gurkha Rifles, Volume III*' describes Captain Dutt's stint with the 2nd Battalion and his part in the Battle of the Cauldron: "*Our own Doctor, Captain Dutt, whose selfless courage and devotion in the battle, and after capture, saved the lives of many of our wounded…Captain Dutt was awarded the Military Cross.*" The name of Lt. Col. Santi Pada Dutt, M.C. is duly inscribed among those of his peers in the 4th Prince of Wales's Own Gurkha Rifles Memorial Garden in St. Giles Church at Stoke Poges, Buckinghamshire, England. There, in the churchyard, renowned English poet, Thomas Gray, penned his famous poem "Elegy Written in a Country Churchyard…*The curfew tolls the knell of passing day…*"

Captain S.P. Dutt's WWII Medals. (Retired Lt. Colonel)
MR-228 (AMC-REG), A/C No. 111/1/MED/2446:
Military Cross 1942, Battle of the Cauldron, Gazala North Africa,
1939-1945 Star, Africa Star, Burma Star, Defence Medal,
War Medal, 8th Army Clasp

4th Gurkha Memorial Garden and Plaque honouring Santi Dutt & Brother Officers, Stoke Poges, Buckinghamshire, England.

REFERENCES

- *A History of the 4th Prince of Wales's Own Gurkha Rifles: Vol III,* by Col. J. N. Mackay, D.S.O.
- *The Road Past Mandalay,* by John Masters
- *The Cat and the Mice,* by Leonard Mosley
- *Desert War,* by Alan Moorehead
- *War Without Hate,* by John Bierman & Colin Smith
- *Rommel's War in Africa,* by Wolf Heckmann
- *Intercepted Communications for Field Marshal Erwin Rommel,* by Will Deac
- *World War II,* by C.L. Sulzberger
- *The Tigris Expedition,* by Thor Heyerdahl
- *Cairo in the War 1939-1945,* by Artemis Cooper
- *The Levant Trilogy,* by Olivia Manning
- *Ball of Fire – The Fifth Indian Division in the Second World War,* by Anthony Brett-James
- *Dilemmas of the Desert War,* by Michael Carver
- *To War With Whitaker – Wartime Diaries, Countess of Ranfurly 1939-48*
- *End of the Beginning,* by Tim Clayton & Phil Craig
- *The Quarterly Journal of Military History,* by Williamson Murray
- *Gandhi & Churchill,* by Arthur Herman
- *Married to the Raj,* by Margaret Martyn
- *A Real History of WWII: A New Look at the Past,* by Alan Axelrod
- *Thy Hand Great Anarch!* by Nirad C. Chaudhuri
- *Bharat Rakshak: In the Skies of Calcutta,* by Joydeep Sircar
- *The Key to Rebecca,* by Ken Follett
- *Bodyguard of Lies,* by Anthony Cave Brown
- *Eagles of the Third Reich,* by Samuel W. Micham, Jr.
- *A Doctor in the Army,* by Satyen Basu
- Archives of the Imperial War Museum, London, UK
- The generous notes and anecdotes provided by Major Nigel Quentin Browne & Lt.Col. Robert N.D. Williams
- United Nations War Crimes Commission Sheets: Kind contribution of Debbie Burton, granddaughter of Lt. J.H. Reeves
- *Operation Salam,* by Kuno Gross, Michael Rolke & Andras Zboray
- *A Soldier's Life in War and Peace,* by A.S. Naravane
- *Unofficial History: Field Marshal, Sir William Slim,* by Cassell & Co.

Acknowledgements

My sincere thanks to friends and family for their unwavering support throughout the writing of this book. Most especially to Kabita Choudhuri and Tara Anderson for the infinite patience and diligence they brought to the many hours spent in editing; to Kamala Bhatt for her encouragement when the spirit was flagging; to my nephew, Karim Merzian (Louis/Loza's son), for the foresight of his recordings; to Nandini Pal who opened her heart and home, rallying me to brave my first public reading; to Sreela Sen, my sister-in-law, who, when required, has always had my back; to my dearest friend, Sanjay Bhatnagar, who, without quibble, has never failed to come through, no matter what. My deep gratitude to Derek Claudius, Ed Anderson, Michael Parker, and Mehul Dave for their advice and help in bringing this venture to fruition; to Jacqueline Gilman for her invaluable expertise, and her readiness to go the extra mile designing the book; to Donna Leppanen for her exceptional artwork and her immense generosity in sharing her talent with Jacqueline to create the cover that is such a perfect introduction to this story; to my ever-percipient cats for their company, and all the cuddles and purrs through the many solitary hours of writing; and, finally, most especially, to my husband, Ronjon, who somehow averted every disaster, and without whose staunch support and unfailing faith this book would not have been possible.

To my parents, my deepest love for all the memories, and for the wonderful family they brought me into.

ABOUT THE AUTHOR

LEILA SEN was born in Calcutta, India, at the end of WWII. They were the final days of the British Raj as India embarked on her fight for independence. She attended Loreto Convent School and College in Darjeeling and Calcutta, and received her education from the Irish nuns of that Order who encouraged her love of writing.

As a children's author, her storytelling has captivated children in local schools, Barnes and Noble, and the San Francisco Asian Art Museum. An award-winning poet, she won The Writer's Foundation America's Best in 1994 & 1995, as well as the Poets & Writers Nature Award. Her work has appeared in several anthologies, including *Waters Edge*, *Meditations*, and *Weber Studies*, and is much enjoyed by visitors to the Tourist Board of Wales' website of the Fairy Glen in the UK. *Canticles, A Collection of Poems*, was published in 2016. *Where Destiny Commands* is her first novel. Inspired by her parents, she undertook the writing of their story as a labour of love and has dedicated this book to them.

Leila Sen lives in San Francisco with her husband, Ronjon. For many years they enjoyed this beautiful city with several of the family members mentioned in this story. Now, they continue to live in the Victorian home they shared with her parents, and share still with their remaining family of rescued pets.